THE PRIVATE SPY

The *Ben Sign* Espionage Series
The First Four Stories

By

Matthew Dunn

FORMER *MI6 SPY* AND *BEST-SELLING* AUTHOR

CONTENTS

THE PRIVATE SPY enables readers to immerse themselves in the first four spy-crime stories containing British former MI6 officer Ben Sign. Books 1 to 4 in the series are presented sequentially. Three are novels. The fourth (The Kill House) is a novella. THE PRIVATE SPY contains the following stories:

THE SPY WHISPERER *(Book 1 in the Ben Sign series)*

THE FIFTH MAN *(Book 2 in the Ben Sign series)*

THE RUSSIAN DOLL *(Book 3 in the Ben Sign series)*

THE KILL HOUSE *(Book 4 in the Ben Sign series)*

ALSO BY MATTHEW DUNN

SPYCATCHER SERIES
Spycatcher
Sentinel
Slingshot
Dark Spies
The Spy House
Act Of Betrayal
A Soldier's Revenge
Spy Trade
Counterspy

BEN SIGN SERIES
The Spy Whisperer
The Fifth Man
The Russian Doll
The Kill House
The Spy Thief

PRAISE FOR MATTHEW DUNN

"Terse conversations infused with subtle power plays, brutal encounters among allies with competing agendas, and forays into hostile territory orchestrated for clockwork efficiency...." ----*Washington Post*

"Great talent, great imagination, and real been-there-done-that authenticity.... Highly recommended." ----Lee Child, author of the *Jack Reacher* series

"Dunn's descriptions of intelligence tradecraft bristle with authenticity.... Good thrillers have been thin on the ground of late. Mr. Dunn has redressed this balance." ----*The Economist*

"[Dunn] makes a strong argument that it takes a real spy to write a truly authentic espionage novel.... Dunn is a gifted storyteller." ----*Fort Worth Star-Telegram*

"Matthew Dunn is [a] very talented new author. I know of no other spy thriller that so successfully blends the fascinating nuances of the business of espionage and intelligence work with full-throttle suspense storytelling. ----Jeffery Deaver, author of *The Bone Collector*

"[Dunn has] a superlative talent for three-dimensional characterisation, gripping dialogue, and plots that featured gasp-inducing twists and betrayals." ----*The Examiner*

"A real spy proves he is a real writer. This is a stunning debut." ----Ted Bell, author of *Patriot*

"Not since Fleming charged Bond with the safety of the world has the international secret agent mystique been so anchored with an insider's reality." ----Noah Boyd, author of *The Bricklayer*

"Once in a while an espionage novelist comes along who has the smack of utter authenticity. Few are as daring as Matthew Dunn, fewer still as up to date.... Is there anyone writing today who knows more about the day-to-day operations of intelligence agencies in the field than Matthew Dunn?" ----John Lawton, author of *Then We Take Berlin*

THE SPY WHISPERER

A *Ben Sign* Espionage Story

By

Matthew Dunn

FORMER *MI6 SPY* AND *BEST-SELLING* AUTHOR

CHAPTER 1

No one at the Moscow dinner gathering knew their guest's real name was Ben Sign. And only one of the other eight Russian attendees knew the guest was a senior MI6 officer.

Today the forty nine year old British Intelligence officer called himself Tobias Harcourt. He'd chosen the nom-de-plume because it sounded posh and matched his fake backstory. He was posing as an aristocratic arms dealer; somebody who purportedly was looking to do an under-the-counter illegal weapons trade with Russian oligarchs. His real intention was to lure one of the men to Vienna, where that man would be snatched and interrogated by Austrian intelligence officers. Sign didn't care which of the men took the bait. His Russian agent at the table had set up the dinner. Both agent and Sign knew that all of their invitees were members of the FSB, the domestic successor to the KGB. With the help of the Austrians, Sign wanted to grab one of the FSB men and make him talk. Sign had advised his Russian agent that someone in MI6 was passing secrets to the Russians. Sign needed that name.

Some considered Sign to be too tall to be a spy. *We need grey men who don't stand out*, his MI6 recruiter had told him twenty seven years ago. Sign, back then a graduate student with a double first degree from Oxford University, had replied that in order to play the grey man one needed to stand out. His answer had made the recruiter smile. After extensive tests and interviews, his intelligence career began. Now, he was tipped to be the next chief of MI6. What he was doing in Moscow was his last official oversees assignment. After this, he'd be kept in London, ring fenced in order to protect him, so that in one year's time he could be interviewed for the post of one of the most prestigious roles in Western intelligence.

As he sat at the table, Sign thought of today as his last dash at the cut and thrust of the spying he so enjoyed. He was making the most of the job. Wearing a hand-tailored Gieves and Hawkes suit whose charcoal colouring matched his clipped hair, silk tie bound in a Windsor knot over a cut-away collar shirt from Saville Row, immaculately polished black Church's shoes, and a Rolex watch he'd borrowed from MI6's props department, he was ready to do business. Often Sign had to playact wholly different personas with very different attires. But today he was as close to his real image as possible.

And he kept the family backstory of Harcourt identical to his own. His parents were academics, but not eminent professors who could be easily traced. Plus, they were dead. He had no siblings. His wife was an NGO worker who'd been shot in El Salvador. They'd never had children. He was alone.

Sign opened his napkin and delicately placed it over his lap.

They were in the private dining room of the restaurant, sat around a solitary circular table that was adorned with a starched white cloth and accoutrements befitting of one of the city's finest eateries. The walls were draped with purple Mongolian sashes. The subtle glow from ceiling spotlights were enhanced by candles that were cleverly positioned around the room. Paintings were French and Dutch. And a small iron bowl of smouldering coals and rosemary was in the corner – there to produce an aroma that complimented the plat du jour of roast poussin, sautéed potatoes, winter vegetables, and Domaine aux Moines Savennieres wine from Roche aux Moines.

Sign's Russian agent, Peter, was a roguish businessman of many trades but with links to the FSB. Sign had been running him against the Russians for five years. Peter was ex-Spetsnaz, built like a prize fighter, a womanizer and heavy drinker, and had a permanent grin on his face. His attractive jet-black hair and green eyes were offset by his calloused and scarred hands. But like Sign, he was immaculately dressed. Sign had put him up for this job.

The MI6 officer had said, "Tell your FSB pals that there's a British arms dealer you know who wants to do business with Russia. Tell them the trade he's offering is worth billions. But also tell them that you can't verify if the weapons he's selling are of value to Mother Russia. Plant hope and doubt in their minds. Encourage them to meet me with suspicion in their minds."

Sign looked at Peter and the others. "Gentlemen: shall we begin." Sign's demeanour and tone of voice was as cool as cucumber. He spoke in English, even though he was a fluent Russian speaker.

Peter poured himself wine. Addressing the FSB men, he said, "I've known of Mr. Harcourt for years, but to my knowledge he rarely attends business meetings in person. In the past, I've spoken to him on the phone and corresponded with his office. Yesterday was the first time I met him in person. He has an interesting proposition for you."

"And if you like the deal, Peter will take a one percent cut of the trade." Sign paused, looking at each of the men in turn. "Peter vouches for you, saying you have access to serious money."

"And what do you have to trade?" asked one of the FSB men.

"Technology that Russia doesn't have." Sign smiled. "Blueprints of Britain's latest prototype EMT weapons, Polaris submarine communications systems, and satellite interceptors."

"But they are just prototypes."

Sign shook his head. "Not anymore. The trials have been completed and approved by the British military and the COBRA committee."

The Russians glanced at each other. One of them asked, "How did you get these blueprints?"

Sign folded his hands. "I stole them via two generals on my payroll." He laughed. "I hope Peter didn't tell you I was a legitimate businessman."

"And your price for these blueprints?"

"That's for you to decide and for me to agree or disagree on." Sign took a sip of wine. "My business is a tricky one. Trust is non-existent. Proof of concept is the bane of my life."

"Meaning – how does a buyer know the technology works?"

"Yes." Sign's heartbeat had dropped by ten beats per minute. "So, here's the conundrum: how do I show you what I have; how do you decide if you like it; and how do I ensure that I'm not royally fucked over?"

The men looked at each other.

Sign waited.

The oldest FSB officer at the table said, "It is an impossible problem."

This was the moment Sign had been waiting for. The moment to lure in one of the FSB officers. He looked at Peter. "Who do you trust the most around this table?"

Peter glanced at each man. "I trust them all."

"I suspect that's not true but it doesn't matter. Regardless, pick one who can view the blueprints."

Peter said, "Boris. Simply because his forename is first in the alphabet of the men dining with us. But any of them would be up to the task."

"Boris it is." Sign stared at Boris. "You have a huge weight of responsibility."

Boris looked like a rabbit in headlights. "I'm not a scientist or engineer. How can I verify the blueprints?"

"You can't, but you know business. I will meet you in Vienna. Bring which ever experts you deem fit for the analysis of the prints."

Boris looked confused. "Vienna?"

"Neutral territory."

Boris shook his head. "My experts will memorise the blueprints and return with me to Russia. No money will be exchanged. Your theft will have been a waste of time."

Sign clapped his hands. "Bravo Mr. Boris." His demeanour turned serious as he analysed the men. "Just because Russian men play chess doesn't make you all chess masters." He tossed his napkin onto the table, his food uneaten. "Boris; expert analysts; Vienna; three days' time; a hotel of my choosing. You'll have one third of each blueprint. A supercomputer might be able to recall the data of each one-third. A genius or photographic mind or anyone on any form of spectrum will most certainly not be able to recall a trace of what I show you. You pay me ten million pounds for the traces. You take them home. You make a judgement call. Do you move your queen to take king? Or do you walk away? If the former, you get the rest of the blueprints for a serious price. If the latter, I have ten million quid for wasting my valuable time. What say you?"

The senior FSB officer in the room touched Boris' arm. "This could be a trap."

Sign snapped, "Gentlemen – if this was a trap, I wouldn't be in Moscow. On my own. I'm giving you the ability to neutralise what Britain, France, and America can throw at you." He stood and looked at Peter. "If I've wasted my time, do let me know. I have a private jet to catch."

Peter waved his hands up and down. "No need for any of us to get annoyed. I think Mr. Harcourt's strategy is sound for all sides."

Sign swivelled and said in a loud voice, "So, what's it to be?"

The door swung open with sufficient force to make it bang against the wall. Five policemen rushed into the room and grabbed Sign. Peter and the FSB men stood. The intelligence officers had grins on their faces. The senior officer said, "You talk of chess. Well, you've just been outplayed. We knew all along that you were an MI6 officer."

Sign looked at Peter. "Tut tut, Peter. Only you could have done this. And I thought we were friends."

To Peter's surprise, Sign laughed as he was led away.

For forty eight hours, he was interrogated by the FSB in its headquarters in Lubyanka Square, Moscow. He wasn't tortured – to have done so would have been a catastrophe for Russia, given Sign had diplomatic status and the FSB was fully aware that maltreatment would be dealt in kind by the Brits if they caught a Russian spy. But, for two days he was given no food or water, and in between harsh questioning he was made to stand while distorted noise was blasted from speakers. Sign was a thinker, not a man of action, yet he told them nothing.

On a road in Russia's north western border with Finland, Sign was guided to British authorities who were flanked by MI6 paramilitary operatives. It was dark; snow was falling. The senior FSB man who held Sign's arm was the man at the dinner who told Sign that he'd been outplayed. Ten yards from the British men, he released Sign's arm and said, "Never come back to Russia."

Sign turned to him. His exhausted face was highlighted by the headlights of the FSB and MI6 cars that were fifty yards apart from each other. Sign said, "You forgot the rule. Because you play chess doesn't make you a chess master. I've been running Peter for five years. I always suspected he was a double agent, though had no proof. So, for five years I've been feeding him crap. It was time for me to flush him out at our lovely dinner two days ago. You did the heavy lifting, for which I'm very grateful. Send my regards to Peter. He was my pawn. Don't be too hard on him. And don't be too hard on yourself that you've been sucker punched."

Sign smiled and walked to the British men.

CHAPTER 2

The morning after Sign was delivered over the Finnish border, Tom Knutsen and Helen Pope were in a stationary transit van in Unwin Street, Elephant & Castle, London. The two undercover Metropolitan Police officers shared the vehicle with hardened criminals who had concealed pistols. A shotgun was beside the driver. In front of them was another van, containing three more criminals. They were here to do a bank heist. Knutsen and Pope's role was to witness the crime. The gang lord who'd planned the heist wasn't present in the vehicles, instead monitoring the job from afar. The protocol was simple: he called them with the location of the robbery; they mobilised; the bank was assaulted. And he'd given them strict instructions that the assault was to take place with speed and absolute aggression. The guns were not here for show.

Knutsen and Pope had infiltrated the gang from different angles and timeframes.

With the permission of the Met, one year ago Knutsen had held up a post office in Canterbury. He was brandishing a disabled WW2 Luger pistol. He tried to fire a shot at the ceiling, knowing the gun wouldn't work, but hoping his theatrics would draw the attention of the Kent Police. He was arrested and incarcerated in Parkhurst Prison for nine months. The sentence was lenient because he'd not pointed his weapon at anyone, nor had he committed ABH or GBH on any of the customers in the post office. In fact, the witnesses declared in court that the medium-height, muscular, thirty seven year old seemed desperate and kind. He'd sat on the floor after his gun failed and told everyone around him that he was a good man from the wrong tracks. He gave no resistance when the police came. But his real ploy had worked. In prison he was in the A-list, because he was an armed robber. Serial killers are viewed as weirdos; paedophiles are killed if left alone with other inmates; teenage knife crime is viewed as kids brandishing weapons they don't know how to use; drug dealers are considered useful because they might get substances into the clink, but otherwise they're labelled parasites; and petty criminals are simply ignored. But major gun crime equals prestige. Quickly, Knutsen came to the attention of other armed robbers. His target was a criminal boss who was due for parole shortly. The Met and Knutsen knew the gang lord was pretending to be a reformed member of society. Once out, the gang lord would go back to his old ways. Knutsen had to stop that from happening. Knutsen assaulted guards and inmates in prison, but not to a pulp, even though he could have done so against the most hardened members of Parkhurst. Many times, he was put in solitary confinement. Eventually, he was summoned to the gang lord who gave him a simple command.

"You're a man who should be working for me."

When gang lord and Knutsen were out of prison, Knutsen had achieved his Met mission to infiltrate the gang. Now, he was about to commit a heinous crime, all in the name of queen and country.

Pope had different instructions, though no less arduous. Fifteen months ago she married Knutsen in a Brixton registry office. The plan was they'd divorce as soon as their undercover objective was complete. She visited Knutsen in prison, bringing contraband secreted in her private parts. Her visits were welcomed by many inmates, because Knutsen distributed the contraband to prisoners. Plus, Pope always dressed to kill during her visits. Other inmates in the visitors' reception gawped at her. She put a smile on their faces. Playing a bimbo was hard for her because in reality she was anything but. Prior to her undercover work, she'd had stints in the Met's firearms units, hostage negotiation, had been a detective in the serious crime unit, and had worked as a scuba diver, pulling bloated human carcases out of rivers and lakes.

When the gang lord had asked Knutsen to work with him, Knutsen replied, "Only if my wife is there with me on every job. She's a looker. She distracts people. Plus, she shoots guns better than any man I know. And there's one other thing. She works at a bank. You know the adage: if you want to rob somewhere, work there. Eventually you'll spot the cracks."

The gang lord replied, "Which bank?"

Now, Knutsen and Pope were brandishing pistols. Pope looked nothing like a bimbo. She was wearing jeans and a puffer jacket. Knutsen and Pope exchanged glances. They were married. And they now felt it was real. Knutsen nodded at her. She smiled.

The team leader got the call from the gang lord. The gang lord said, "Royal Bank of Scotland. 29 Old Brompton Road. But don't tell the others until you're there. Just get them to follow you. And make sure your route to the target is circuitous."

"Circuitous?"

"Don't go the most direct route."

"Why?"

"Just move."

The team leader looked over his shoulder. "We're on." Via his mobile, he relayed the instruction to the other van and drove out of Unwin Street, the other van on his tail.

Pope held her mobile phone out of view of the others and sent a text message to the Met's head of the Specialist Firearms Command. The message was *MOBILE TO TARGET.*

Clad in fire-resistant black overalls, Kevlar body armour, helmets, boots, communications sets, holstered pistols, and Heckler & Koch submachine guns strapped to their chests, eight members of the Met's elite SCO19 firearms unit waited fifty yards from the Royal Bank of Scotland branch. They were in a decrepit white van that had insignia on its exterior declaring the vehicle belonged to a plumbing firm. The bank knew they were there. Its staff had been replaced by plain clothed detectives who'd been given a twenty four hour crash course in how to run the branch until the heist took place. Only the branch manager remained on site, to ensure business was efficient and unsuspicious before the attempted robbery.

The Met paramilitary officers had rehearsed the drill twenty two times. The robbers arrive. SCO19 wait. The robbers enter, alongside Knutsen and Pope. The SWAT team still waits. Only when one of the robbers brandishes a gun and tells the fake bank staff to hand over cash or die will Pope run out of the building and wave her hands. That will be the trigger and the end of Pope and Knutsen's undercover assignment. SCO19 knew they could get to the building in six seconds flat. They'd deploy flashbangs. The criminals would be dead before their heads smacked the floor. Knutsen and Pope would walk away and vanish to their next job.

It took forty minutes for the vans to arrive in Old Brompton Street. The drivers remained in the vehicles. Alongside Knutsen and Pope, six armed criminals exited the vehicles, their guns hidden from pedestrians on the bustling street. The RBS branch was forty yards away. When the job was done, the vans would hurtle toward the front entrance and collect the robbers.

"This is the target," muttered the team leader.

Knutsen and Pope resisted every urge to panic. This wasn't the bank that Pope had allegedly worked in. That was two miles away. The gang leader who'd set up the heist probably didn't trust Pope and Knutsen, so had chosen a different target. They were fucked.

SCO19 waited. Knutsen and Pope would be in hoodies. No way of identifying them and the men around them. All SCO19 could rely on was Pope's signal to assault. The firearms officers were poised, breathing fast, their van filled with the musky scent of testosterone, their fingers on the triggers of their submachineguns.

Fifteen yards from the bank's entrance, Pope pulled out her mobile, desperate to inform SWAT of the change of plan. But the team leader spotted her action, slammed his hand on hers, and stamped on the phone after it hit the ground. He barked, "No calls now!"

Knutsen moved to her side and whispered, "Run. I'll go in with them."

Pope replied, "I'm going in."

"I thought you'd say that." They were by the front door of the bank as Knutsen pulled out his sidearm and pointed it at the criminals. "Police! Drop your weapons! You're under arrest!"

The team leader grabbed Pope, spun her around so that he and her were facing Knutsen, held a gun to her head, and shouted to his men, "Get out of here! I'll find my own way back."

His men sprinted to their vans. People in the street were screaming, some of them running, others ducking behind whatever cover they could find. Within seconds, the place had become chaos.

Knutsen was motionless as he kept his gun trained on the few inches that were visible of the team leader's head. "Attempted robbery is one thing. But if shots are fired, that puts you into a different league. Don't be stupid!"

The team leader laughed and walked back with Pope. "You set us up."

Knutsen was silent.

"That means you've got boys with big guns somewhere nearby. But I'm betting they're not near enough. The boss saw through you, I reckon."

No way could Knutsen take a shot at the criminal's head. The team leader's finger was on his pistol's trigger. A bullet entering his brain would most likely cause his finger to tighten and blow out Pope's brains. Knutsen lowered his gun and said, "Let her go and I'll let you go. I can't promise you that you, your men, and your boss will get away with this, but at least I can give you a breathing space."

"A breathing space. I like the sound of that." He shot Knutsen in the shoulder, causing the undercover cop to crash to the pavement and release his firearm.

Pope screamed and kicked her captor with her heels against his shins.

But the criminal held her firm. "Not my lucky day. Not your lucky day."

Police sirens were drawing close. And the van containing SCO19 was hurtling toward Old Brompton Road. They'd realised what was going on.

The robber said to Knutsen, "Time for me to go." He shot Pope in the head, killing her instantly. He spun around and ran.

Knutsen shouted, "No." He staggered to his feet and collected his sidearm. The criminal was twenty yards away, then thirty. Knutsen was right handed, but it was his right shoulder that had been hit and was now useless. He put his gun in his left hand and raised his arm. The action was excruciating. The criminal was now forty yards away, his head moving left and right as he was looking for side alleys to dash down and vanish. Knutsen wasn't going to let that happen. He took aim at the criminal's head, pulled the trigger, and hit him in the back. The team leader hit the ground and started crawling. Knutsen walked up to him, blood pouring down his chest, his breathing erratic. He pointed his gun at the robber's head and put two bullets in his skull.

He walked as quickly as he could back to Pope, knelt down, and cradled her head. It was a mess – nothing like the beautiful visage he'd admired since he'd worked with her. He doubted they'd have got divorced after this job. They were meant for each other, not just as cops, but also as civilians. He kissed her forehead, not caring that her blood was on his lips. He gently lowered her head and started sobbing.

CHAPTER 3

Two days' later, Ben Sign was in MI6 headquarters, Vauxhall Cross, London. He'd been summoned to one of the Babylonian-style building's conference rooms on the ground floor. The Chief of MI6, Head of Security, Head of the Russia department, and the service's senior legal counsel were facing him across an oak table. Sign felt like he was on trial by a kangaroo court.

All were silent throughout the meeting, save for the Head of Security; a man called Jeffery who alongside Sign was in the running to be the next chief of the service. Jeffery was a ruthless officer whose stint in operational security as a board director was merely a stepping stone up his career ladder.

Jeffery said, "At what stage did you suspect Peter was a double agent?"

Sign smiled. "From the outset."

"And yet you ran him against the Russians for five years."

"I ran him *at* the Russians. Your terminology needs to be more precise, Jeffery."

Jeffery flicked through a file on the table. "You had no proof he was a double, but you went on your gut instinct."

"Don't be crass. Gut instinct? Dear me. No – when I inherited him from my predecessor, I felt he was too good to be true. Plus, there was tangible evidence that the crap I fed him was being actioned on by the Russians. Everything I said to him was being passed by him to the FSB."

"And yet you failed to tell us about your suspicions."

Sign could see where this was headed. "It's always difficult to know who to trust at our level."

"Meaning?!"

"It's a statement, not an accusation." Sign smiled. "Sometimes senior MI6 officers use operational successes or failures to further their careers."

"You're suggesting I would have capitalised from the fact you were running a double agent?"

With sarcasm in his voice, Sign replied, "Heaven forbid, no. It had never occurred to me that you'd see this as an opportunity to better me in the application to be the next chief. You wouldn't stoop that low, Jeffery." Sign's tone hardened as he added, "I knew there was a mole in MI6. I thought it unlikely that the mole was cadre MI6. Most likely I thought it was Peter. But then again, it's always difficult to be certain. For all I knew, the mole could have been you, Jeffery."

The fury in Jeffery's face was obvious. "I have a distinguished..."

"Yes, we all have distinguished careers, blah blah. But some of us are not back-stabbing shits." Sign looked at the others, before returning his attention to Jeffery. "I'm not accusing you of anything untoward. But do I trust you? Not a fucking chance."

Jeffery composed himself. "Do you know what's happened to Peter?"

Sign shrugged. "I've been held in lockdown since I got to Finland. Most likely the FSB has promoted Peter and given him a medal."

Jeffery closed the file in front of him. "One day ago, a cardboard box was delivered to the British embassy in Moscow. Inside was Peter's head."

Sign digested the news, and showed no sign of emotion, even though he was shocked by the development. For all of Peter's treachery, Sign had liked him. "Peter's use to the FSB came to an end when he set up my Moscow meeting. But there was one more thing Peter could do – send a message to us that we must not spy on the motherland. Peter's head was that message."

Everyone before him nodded.

Jeffery smirked as he said, "Your actions got an agent killed."

It was time to take the gloves off. With an angry and strident tone, Sign said, "Jeffery – God knows how you've made it to the board of directors. You were never a good operator and your intellect is somewhat wanting. So too your compassion. Peter was deployed against us. I knew that and played along. No doubt, Peter hoped to receive Russian praise for what he'd done. He was many things, including being brave. Let's not be hypocritical. We deploy our agents against the Russians. And some of them are double agents. It's the endless game. I corrupted Russian Intelligence by using Peter. Read the Ukraine and Crimea files. What the Russians did there would have been one hundred times worse had I not planted the idea in Peter's head that NATO was about to strike." Sign stood and looked at the chief of MI6. "Your successor will be chosen by you and the Joint Intelligence Committee. I realize that this witch hunt today has smeared my name. Unfairly, I should add. But that matters not. May I suggest to you sir, that you choose your successor very carefully. Don't pick anyone in this room. And that includes me. Because as of now, you have my resignation."

"You executed a criminal!" The commissioner of the Met Police was sitting behind his desk. Standing to attention in front of him was Knutsen, wearing a police uniform that hadn't seen the light of day in years.

Knutsen said, "He killed my wife."

"Your fake wife."

"She was still my wife. Plus a fellow officer. What would you have done, Paddy?"

"You'll call me sir!"

"Okay Paddy sir."

"You're one of the best shots in the Met. You had a clean line of sight. Why didn't you shoot him before Pope died?"

Knutsen moved his legs apart.

"Remain at attention!"

"I can't. It's the shoulder. It hurts. Standing makes it worse for some reason. I'd like it on record whether you'd like me to stand to attention. I'm not saying it's torture by you or anything but I would like to hear your views on interrogations under duress... Paddy."

The commissioner sighed. "Sit. How is the wound?"

"They got the bullet out. Bit of reconstructive surgery and physio over the next few weeks. After that, I'll be punching above my weight."

"And how is your mental health?"

"Like most people, I get up in the morning and think, Not this shit again. What about you?"

The commissioner ignored the comment. "Why didn't you take the shot?"

Knutsen shrugged. "You give us elephant-stopper side arms. That's good if you're in an isolated field and chasing a guy with a bullet-proof vest. Bad if you're in Old Brompton Road with hundreds of people around you. If I took the shot, I'd have hit his head. He'd have involuntarily squeezed the trigger. Pope would have died. But it may not have ended there. The bullet could have exited his head, ricocheted off a wall or the street, and thumped into an innocent bystander. In fact, the power of these bullets is such that my shot could have gone through three or four bodies. Would you have liked that on your conscience?"

The Met chief hesitated. "No."

"I thought not. My wife's dead as a result of my calculated decision."

"Fake wife..." The commissioner held up his hand. "No need to correct me. I'm sorry."

Knutsen touched the arm of Britain's most senior cop. "Put me back in jail again if you want. I'll handle that. Put me in a noose if you want. I'll handle that, too." He bowed his head. "Helen Pope was more than a colleague. Least ways, I hoped it would pan out that way. I wanted to cook for her and take her to see me practise kendo."

The commissioner frowned. "That would have been an odd but endearing date."

"Yes, it would sir."

The chief drummed fingers on his desk and muttered, "What to do, what to do?" He looked at Knutsen. "CCTV has got you. Witnesses have got you. Point blank, you killed him."

Knutsen smiled, though his look was one of resignation. "In kendo, or at least the British version of it, we call it a death strike. When the opponent's on the ground, don't assume he won't get up. He will and he'll hit you with his bamboo stick bloody hard. Then you're down and he'll finish you off. I finished him off. I'll pay the consequences."

The commissioner walked to the office window and looked over the magnificent vista of London. With his back to Knutsen he said, "It is a shame. You were my finest undercover officer."

"People come and go."

"They do." The commissioner swivelled. "But I don't want your life defined by this event. You deserve far better." He patted Knutsen on the shoulder. "I'll sweep this under the carpet. In return, you'll need to leave. I can't avoid that. My sincere apologies. You will be a serious loss to my team."

Knutsen rose and nodded. He held out his hand. "Thank you Paddy."

Paddy shook his hand. "Thank *you* Tom. Don't let the bed bugs bite."

Knutsen smiled and walked out of the room. This was the end of his career as a police officer.

CHAPTER 4

Two weeks later, Sign entered a small house in Mayfair that had been converted into a place of business. It belonged to a former MI6 officer turned head hunter. Sign had an appointment with the recruiter. The receptionist asked Sign to take a seat, phoned her boss and told him that his guest had arrived. She instructed Sign to proceed to the lower floor for his appointment.

The head hunter was Robert Lask. When in MI6, he'd been an expert on China, and spoke fluent Cantonese and Mandarin. Prior to joining the service, he'd been an inspector in the Royal Hong Kong Police. He was a bit of a throwback to colonial days, plus had been a fairly average MI6 officer, but he was a decent bloke. Sign trusted him, though did think that Lask thought he was more important than he actually was. It was his job that had made him that way. Lask specialised in finding jobs for former MI6 officers and other members of the British special operations community. That included interviewing former chiefs of MI6. It gave him power and a sense of self-importance, wherein the reality was that Lask would never have made senior management.

Sign shook the fifty five year old's hand and took a seat on the solitary sofa within the ornate room. Lask remained behind his desk, looking like a judge at the bench.

"How can I help you?" asked Lask.

"I'm on the *rock and roll*."

Lask laughed. "Of course. What other reason would you have for being here?" He frowned. "But you were tipped for the top. What went wrong?"

"I saw the writing on the wall and jumped before I was pushed."

"But you were the smartest man in MI6. One of the smartest men in the country. You could have outgunned them."

"If I'd had the will." Sign smiled with resignation on his face. "I no longer wanted to belong to an organisation run by buffoons."

Lask rifled through papers. "I can get you a job in a jot. For someone of your standing, you'll be snapped up. Head of Security at Price Waterhouse Cooper, senior advisor to the Prime Minister, professor at Oxford – the list goes on and on. You do realise how important you are?"

Sign ran a finger and thumb alongside the cuff of his shirt. "I don't care about that. I want something smaller. Something that matters."

Lask was confused as he reached the end of the CVs in front of him. "I don't have anything that matches that brief."

"I thought not." Sign crossed his legs, clasped his hands, and stared at Lask. "I'm not here for a job. I'm setting up my own private consultancy. I need to employ someone to help me. Someone special. You can help find me that person."

"Consultancy of what?"

"Crime, espionage, mysteries. That's what I do."

"Yes, yes. That is you." Lask pulled out a box file. "And what are the credentials of the employee you seek?"

"Someone who has an edge. Aside from that, I won't know until I meet him."

Lask rifled through his papers. "I have an ex-SAS sergeant who spent twenty years in the Regiment. Tours in Iraq and Afghanistan."

"Happily married with kids?"

"Yes."

"Dishonourably discharged?"

"No."

"Then let's move on. Next."

Lask picked up a CV. "This guy might interest you. Former MI5 and…"

"Boring! Next."

Lask went through his pile of CVs. "I have MI6 officers."

"I don't want MI6. I want someone different from me."

Lask picked up the last CV. "What do you think about cops?"

"They're a different breed to us. But there are exceptions. What's interesting about this man or woman?"

"It's a man. He was undercover for years. He spent time in prison as part of one assignment. Was shot. He…"

Sign held up his hand. "Don't tell me anything else. I want to meet him. Arrange that meeting. If I hire him, you'll get your introductory fee."

The next day, Sign entered Simpson's In The Strand. It was lunchtime and the restaurant was bustling with businessmen, government mandarins, and generals. One of the oldest traditional restaurants in London, Simpson's was renowned for its carved meats, brought to the table on trolleys by expert waiters. Sign had been here many times, but not because of the fare. Like many others, he enjoyed dining in the establishment because it had wooden booths that allowed privacy. He sat in one of the booths. Tom Knutsen was sitting opposite him.

"Mr. Knutsen. You know who I am?"

Knutsen was wearing a blue suit he'd purchased from Marks & Spencer. He looked immaculate. Knutsen said, "Yes, I know who you are."

"What do you know about me?"

Knutsen replied, "Senior MI6, until recently. Lask said you were destined for the top. He said your career was remarkable. Then he shut his mouth and said the rest of your background was classified."

Sign nodded. "I haven't read your CV. Lask gave me the briefest of thumbnail sketches. Beyond that, there's a lifetime of experience that I refused to hear about."

"Why?"

"Because I wanted to get the measure of you in person." Sign gestured at a nearby waiter. "Would you like a cut of beef or turkey? They slice it with razor sharp knives."

"I'm not hungry."

Sign summoned the sommelier. "But you'll have a glass of Sancerre." When the wine waiter was gone, Sign asked, "How is your injury?"

"Fully recovered. I'm back on my dojo."

"Dojo. The *place of the way*." Sign drummed his fingers. "I wonder what Japanese martial art you study. Karate? Aikido? Judo? Wrestling?" He stared at Knutsen. "The problem with those disciplines is they're street-fighting arts. I don't think a man like you – undercover for most of his adult life – would wind down by doing something so eminently useful in his line of work. I think you'd want something more romantic, noble, disciplined. You'd want the counterbalance to the grimy life you've led. You study kenjutsu."

"We call it kendo. Yes. You're right."

"Bravo, Mr. Knutsen. You are therefore a noble warrior."

Knutsen laughed. "Does everyone in MI6 talk like this? You sound…"

"Old fashioned?"

"Something like that."

"I can sound like many things, depending on the circumstances. You of all people know we adapt."

"Chameleons."

"Yes."

They sat in silence for a moment.

Sign broke the silence. "You're educated."

"How do you know?"

"Your eyes and your self-confidence."

Knutsen nodded. "I gained a first at Exeter."

"So why join the police, unless you wished to be on track to being a chief constable?"

Knutsen didn't reply.

"I posit that you wanted to escape something and join a gang; the gang being the police. But when you joined, you realized something – you were always destined to be a loner. Uniforms and allegiance were not for you. Destiny and reality is a cruel fate. Unhappy childhood?"

Knutsen shrugged. "Unlike you, I wasn't born with a silver spoon in my mouth. My father died when I was young. My mother turned to drink and had barely a penny to her name."

Sign took a sip of his wine. "My father was a merchant navy sailor. He joined the navy age fourteen after being flip-flopped between different foster carers. He came from a very poor family. His mother died when he was seven. He never knew his father. As a child, my father suffered problems in his legs. Doctors put his legs in irons for a year. They were different days back then. He failed entry into the army, when conscription was still around. His feet were too flat. So, he travelled the world on a boat. My mother was brought up in London's east end. She had a big working class family. They're all dead now. They had very little money. But they were brilliant people and stuck together. My mother educated herself and became a scientist." Sign pushed his wine away. "I am not as I seem."

"You most certainly are not." Knutsen felt like he was in the presence of a huge force of kinetic energy. "Undercover work is shit."

"It is, and yet we chose that life."

"For a reason."

"Indeed." Sign wondered how far he should deploy his mental prowess. He liked Knutsen. But, he had to test his metal. "Did you want her to be your real wife?"

Knutsen bristled. "That's none of your damn business!"

"Correct response." Sign looked at the other diners. None of them had done what Knutsen and Sign had done. They were establishment, never having sacrificed their souls. Quietly, he said, "Dear fellow. You did the right thing. I did the right thing. The trouble is, the right thing eats us." He returned his gaze to Knutsen. "You are an expert shot, a warrior, a loner, a thinker."

Knutsen's chest puffed up with anger. "And I assume you have a healthy pension and a wife and kids to go home to somewhere near here."

"Actually, my wife was killed in Latin America. I have no children. I have very little money."

Knutsen's anger evaporated. "What is the job?"

"We become specialist detectives, operating in London."

"If you've got no money, how will you pay me?"

"By results." Sign leaned forward. "People want strange expertise that they don't like."

Knutsen smiled. "I'd never thought of it that way."

"Nor had I until now." Sign added, "It would be a fifty/fifty partnership. I'm too old for the dojo. You're not. But, as you know, on the dojo it's not about the fighting, it's about the analysis of the opponent. Together, we can do that analysis. But, if there's heavy lifting to be done, I'm not that man. You are."

"Where are your offices?"

Sign sighed. "I've looked around London. They're all too expensive. For now, we'd work from my home."

"Whereabouts in London?"

"West Square, Kennington. I recently bought the place off a superb former MI6 agent. He now lives in the States and is happily retired. Will Cochrane sold me his home for half its value."

"And this Cochrane character is no longer spec ops?"

Sign smiled. "He's done his time in the trenches. He's at peace." Sign tossed his napkin on the table. "We, however, are not at peace. Do you agree?"

"Yes." Knutsen was deep in thought. "Mr. Sign…"

"Ben."

"Ben – here's the thing. The Met commissioner got me off the hook for executing a piece of scum. But I had to resign, with no pension. I'm looking for a job with a salary. I'm broke. What you're offering sounds appealing, but it won't pay my next three months' rent."

"And yet, you could earn ten times that rent after just one assignment. I don't come cheap." Sign clasped his hands together. "I understand your predicament. Do you smoke?"

"No."

"Drink?"

"Yes."

"How much?"

"More than the British surgeon general recommends, but never to excess."

"Drinking is a man's prayer time. Doctors don't get that." Sign added, "I'd like to offer you the position of co-director of my business. You can stay at my place until the money starts rolling in. My bedrooms have en suite bathrooms. There is a sizeable lounge where we can conduct consultations with clients."

"Sir, I'm not…"

"Homosexual. Nor am I. This is business. You and I are out of work."

"Holmes and Watson?"

"Something like that, if you choose to draw parallels."

Knutsen asked, "Are you IT literate? Have you got a website? Twitter account? Facebook page? Advertising?"

Sign shook his head. "I have a black book. With your contacts in the Met, you'll add to that black book. Business will come to us. We don't need to prostitute ourselves by chasing petty divorce cases and the like."

"So, what would we be chasing?"

"Mysteries. But tell me something. Why should I go into business with you?"

Knutsen looked away. "You decide." He returned his attention to Sign. "Loyalty is key to everything, isn't it, Mr. Sign? If I join the business, I wouldn't do so half-hearted. As important, I don't have your abilities, but you don't have my abilities."

"True indeed." Sign held out his hand.

Knutsen shook his hand. "I can move in on Monday."

CHAPTER 5

The forty year old Englishman rang the bell of the Edwardian house in Godalming, Surrey. He'd watched the home for three hours and knew that the occupiers were at home. He was smartly dressed, an overcoat protecting his suit. His hair was cut to precision – shorter than a civilian haircut, longer than that of a military serviceman. This morning, he'd shaved with a cutthroat razor, after which he'd dabbed eau de toilette over his immaculate skin. Yesterday, he'd had a beard and his voice was that of a Belarusian artisan; the day before he was a Finnish drunk; today he was a gentleman. His true self.

A woman answered the door.

"Mrs. Archer. I'm sorry to turn up unannounced. I work with your husband. We have a crisis."

The wife looked uncertain. "My husband's at home. Who should I say is calling?"

"John Smith."

"Oh, it's like that, is it?"

"I'm afraid it is. My real name was buried a long time ago." He checked his watch. "I don't have much time."

She gestured him to enter the house while calling out, "Mark, we have a visitor."

Mark was a fifty one year old MI6 officer. He was reading a paper and was sitting next to a fire in a tastefully decorated living room.

Mark looked up as the man who called himself John Smith entered the room. "What do you want?"

Smith looked at Mrs. Archer. "I do apologise for asking this, but would you be offended if I asked you to give us some privacy?"

Mrs. Archer had been married to Mark for twenty three years. She'd accompanied him on four overseas MI6 postings. She knew what it was like to be married to a spy. She acquiesced and left the room.

The man sat opposite Mark and spoke to him for ten minutes.

Then he left.

Two days' later, the man who called himself by the fake name of John Smith waited in a hotel room in Mayfair's Duke's hotel. The senior MI6 officer wasn't wearing his suit jacket, but otherwise he was immaculately dressed. He was sitting in an armchair, two untouched glasses of beer were by his side. His fingers were interlaced while he was deep in thought.

Someone at the door knocked three times, paused for three seconds, then knocked again. It was the visitor Smith had been waiting for. He let the man in and locked the door.

The man was thirty six years old, wiry, of medium height, had shoulder-length black hair, and eyes that looked dead. He was wearing jeans, hiking boots, and a fleece.

Smith gestured to a spare chair and handed him one of the beers. "It's been two years. How have you been, Karl?"

Karl Hilt took a swig of his beer. "I've been doing private work since I left MI6. Pay's better."

Hilt had been a paramilitary officer in MI6, prior to which he was an SBS operative. He was an expert in surveillance, unarmed combat, weaponry, espionage tradecraft, and deniable assassinations. But what stood him out for Smith was he had no mercy. He was a highly trained psychopath who was kept on a leash only by virtue of the organisations he'd worked for. Now, he was off the leash. But Smith still needed him to have a master. For now.

"I want you to do a job for me. I'll pay you well. It will be UK-based."

Hilt nodded and said in his east London accent, "I'm between work at the moment. What do you have in mind?"

Smith didn't answer him directly. "Do you remember those guys you killed in Iraq?"

"Yeah. You were in a shit storm back then. They'd have cut your head off if I hadn't got into the house."

Smith nodded. "And you remember the last remaining member of that terror cell – the woman who came at you with an AK47?"

"I slit her throat."

"And you did so without blinking."

"She was a fanatical bitch. Wanted to put bullets in you and me."

"You could easily have disarmed her."

Hilt shrugged. "She could have been packing a secondary weapon, grenades, bomb vest, anything." Hilt smiled. "The point being – she deserved to die."

"Yes, she did."

"So, what's your point? Men, women, even kids who pick up RPGs and will one day soon be radicalised – I don't care who I've killed. Are you in or out of MI6?"

"Still in. But the money I'm going to pay you is mine and the job is private. Do you have a problem with that?"

"No."

"Good. There's a Metropolitan Police case that I have a particular interest in. I don't need to go in to details as to why the case peaks my interest. All that matters to me is that the case is open and is being investigated by a detective inspector called Katy Roberts." Smith handed Hilt a mobile phone. "That's deniable. It has one number stored in it. It's your link to my deniable phone. Keep tabs on Mrs. Roberts. Let me know of any developments."

"Where do I find her?"

"New Scotland Yard. I also have her home address." Smith handed Hilt a slip of paper. "For now, it's just surveillance and reporting back to me. But, if things develop in the wrong direction, I may ask you to up the ante."

Hilt smiled.

CHAPTER 6

Knutsen stood in Kennington's small West Square. The beautiful enclosure was surrounded by regal Edwardian terraced houses. Knutsen had a holdall slung over one shoulder. In his other hand, he held a small trolley case. Both bags contained all of his possessions. He pressed the intercom of the house containing Sign's apartment. The house had long ago been converted into four flats. Sign's dwelling was on the fourth floor.

The door buzzed and opened. Knutsen entered and walked up the stairs. He knocked on the door.

Sign answered and asked, "Did you bring your suit?"

Knutsen nodded.

"Good. We have a meeting this afternoon with New Scotland Yard." Sign showed Knutsen to his bedroom. "Unpack. I'm making a pot of tea. Let's convene in the lounge in fifteen minutes."

The bedroom was twice the size of the one Knutsen had been sleeping in within his former residence. A spiral staircase led to the attic that had been fully converted into a bathroom. He unpacked his clothes into a wardrobe and chest of drawers and examined the bathroom. It was state of the art – spot lamps in the ceiling, extractor fans in the shower cubicle and toilet area, and a heated towel rail. He exited his room, walked past the solitary toilet room that had come with the original layout of the property, and walked past Sign's bedroom. It too had a spiral staircase leading to a separate loft converted bathroom suite. Somebody had spent a lot of money converting this place. Sign was in the kitchen. By comparison to the other rooms in the property, it was tiny; no room even for a breakfast table. But it had an expensive gas oven and separate hob, a washing machine, dishwasher, Global knives on a wall-mounted magnetic strip, cupboards, and a wooden chopping board strewn with fresh vegetables sourced from Borough Market.

Sign handed him a cup of tea. "I guessed milk, no sugar."

"You guessed right." Knutsen followed him into the lounge. The place was twice the size of any lounge Knutsen had seen before. It was strewn with antiquities and other artefacts – a six seater oak dining table, a neo-classical era chaise longue, a sofa, gold-framed oil paintings on the walls, bookshelves crammed with out-of-print non-fiction historical and academic works, a wall-mounted Cossack sabre, Persian rugs, two nineteenth century brass miners' lamps within which were candles, a five foot high artificial Japanese tree with a string of blue lights around it, seventeen century Scottish dirks in a glass cabinet, a laptop on a green-leather covered nine drawer mahogany writing desk, lamps, seafaring charts, and so many other objects of interest it made the mind swirl.

On one of the shelves was a silk map that had been mounted between glass. It was the type worn under the garments of operatives working behind enemy lines. On its back were eight short paragraphs – in English, Dari, Pashwari, Tajikistan, Urdu, Uzbekistan, Turkmenistan, and Persian, together with the contact numbers of six UK diplomatic missions. The paragraphs asked for food and water, promised the reader that the bearer of the map wouldn't hurt him, and requested safe passage to British forces or its allies. On the front of the map was the title AFGHANISTAN & ENVIRONS, ESCAPE MAP.

Sign took the map out of Knutsen's hand and placed it back on the mantelshelf above the open fire. He said, "Different days for me back then."

The centre of the lounge was uncluttered. All it had was three armchairs facing each other, and tiny adjacent wooden coffee tables. Knutsen and Sign sat.

Knutsen looked around. The room seemed to him to either be an Aladdin's Cave or the result of an eccentric professor's penchants.

Sign followed his gaze. "I travelled the world. Many of these things are my purchases. But some were given to me. They remind me of good things." He took a sip of his tea. "This is our centre of operations."

"And we'll meet clients here?"

"I don't see why not."

Knutsen stared at Sign. "You could have been chief of MI6. Do you not worry that you could have done better than scratching a living with me?"

Sign replied, "No. I'd been thinking about resigning for some time. All my adult life I've worked alone or in small teams. As soon as I heard I was tipped to be the next chief of MI6, I feared that if I got the job I'd have to become a corporate beast – not just managing thousands of staff, but also liaising with all the other agencies, plus Whitehall and our overseas allies. I get easily bored with playing management and politics. Operating in the shadows suits me better."

That made sense to Knutsen. It was for similar reasons he'd gone undercover, rather than grabbing rank after rank until he headed up the Met or one of the county forces. "Tell me about the meeting with the Yard."

"I'll answer that indirectly and directly. Over the last few days, I've been making calls – to the chiefs of every police force in the UK, Interpol, the chiefs and directors of MI6, MI5, GCHQ, army, air force, and navy commanders, and twenty nine heads of foreign security and intelligence agencies. I've been setting out our stall; telling them that you and I are in business for any delicate work they need to outsource. Your former boss – the Met commissioner – has bitten. This afternoon he's sending a detective inspector to talk to us."

"What's the name of the inspector?"

"Katy Roberts. I don't know her. Do you?"

"No. But I do know *of* her. She's more than just a detective. She's Special Branch. And she's a rising star. What does she want?"

"I don't know." Sign checked his watch. "She'll be here in two hours. That gives us time for lunch. What say you to pan-fried guinea fowl, caramelised shallots, toasted carrots, green beans, and sautéed potatoes?"

"You've booked a table?"

"No, dear chap. I'm going to cook the dish myself."

Katy Roberts arrived on time after Sign and Knutsen had eaten and changed into their suits. Knutsen took her coat and asked her to take a seat in one of the armchairs. The men sat in the other chairs.

Knutsen asked, "How can we be of help, ma'am?"

"You don't need to call me ma'am. You're no longer a cop." Roberts had long hair that was dyed platinum. She wore no rings on her fingers, even though she'd been happily married for fifteen years. At first, Sign thought her elegant and beautiful demeanour was icy. He revised that assessment. No, she was an owl, he decided. She watches.

Sign said, "You know Mr. Knutsen is late of your service. I am Ben Sign."

"I know who you are." Roberts looked around the room, before looking at Sign. "You're a picky collector."

"*Picky*, yes."

"Why did you pick Tom Knutsen to work with you?"

"A raft of reasons, but in particular because he knows loss. I can't work with someone who doesn't understand emotional toil."

"Why?"

"Loss sharpens the senses and also allows us not to fear death."

Knutsen looked at Sign.

Roberts said, "An interesting perspective. And you think just because you were a high flying MI6 officer, you can help us out with difficult problems."

"I can but try."

Roberts huffed. "I didn't agree to this meeting. I told my boss it would be a waste of my time."

"I suppose, therefore, it could also be a waste of our time." His tone of voice was benign as he added, "I was recruited into MI6 because my DNA demands that I accurately read people. It's the key requirement of all MI6 officers. I've never arrested anyone, because I'm not law enforcement. But I have stopped covert nuclear programs, terrorist attacks, and wars. I wouldn't dare to presume I have your skills of detective work."

Knutsen suppressed a smile. He'd expected Sign to lambast Roberts, not flatter her. Then again, Sign was a gentleman when he needed to be.

Roberts said, "To my errand. We have the death of a senior MI6 officer. MI6 won't cooperate. It thinks it's simply a suicide. The victim has a wife. She has no idea why he'd have done something so devastating. We can't access MI6 or get in its head. You can."

"His name?" Sign was leaning forward.

"Mark Archer."

"Mark?" Sign was frowning. "He was ranked as an average officer, meaning he was exceptional by the standards of other special operations agencies. More importantly, he had a loving family and was a very stable man. Suicide makes no sense."

"That's what my boss thinks." Roberts tone softened. "He has a slush fund and is willing to pay you to do what he calls a *back channel investigation*. I thought he might be wasting his time. Maybe… I was wrong."

"It's a tremendous sign of intellect when one self-corrects." Sign was deep in thought. "Inspector Roberts – forget what your boss thinks. What do you think about Mark's death?"

Roberts had attended this meeting with a preconceived notion of what Sign would be like. She'd imagined he would be arrogant and condescending. But he was nothing like that. She knew he was treading softly with her. But that mattered not. What did were his impeccable manners and deference to her vocation. "The wife is hiding something. I've interviewed extensively. I applied every trick in the book. But I can't get through to her."

Knutsen asked, "What do we know about the wife?"

"Mrs. Archer has no criminal record. She has a daughter and son; both are at university. Due to her marriage to a spy, she's security cleared to the highest level. I saw no chinks in her armour." Roberts focused on Sign. "I'm told you can see things differently."

Sign waved his hand. "I'm an amateur, by your standards."

Roberts smiled. "Thank you for being so kind." Her tone hardened. "I'm out of my league. You, of all people, are not."

Sign stood and walked to the mantelpiece. "Your instincts may have been right. This could be a waste of time. Maybe it is suicide driven by any number of stresses – debt, marital problems, infidelity, the usual suspect list goes on. Or maybe he was murdered. If murder, then that is a police investigation. The only reason I should be involved is if the murder was carried out by a hostile foreign agency."

"It's not murder. He killed himself. Forensics is certain of that. So am I."

"How did he do it?"

"Fifty capsules of prescribed painkillers, washed down with a bottle of cheap vodka. He also slit his wrists in his bathtub for good measure."

"No bruising on the throat or blemishes on the inner mouth?"

"Meaning he was force fed the cocktail? No." Roberts elaborated. "The razor he used to slit his wrists was on the side of the bath. His, and only his, prints are on the razor. Mrs. Archer's prints and sole imprints are in the bathroom, as you would expect." She clasped her hands. "But even if a murderer was so ingenious to fake suicide without trace, he or she would not be able to eliminate their presence in the crime scene. Forensics is so good these days that a man in a disposable jump suit, face mask, and shoe covers would still leave traces of his presence. Mrs. Archer couldn't have killed him. She's not strong enough, plus there's zero evidence of forced death. It's suicide. But I don't know why. That's what I need you for."

Sign spun around. "Knutsen and I need to speak to Mrs. Archer. With your permission."

Roberts nodded. "You have my permission. The commissioner has authorised me to engage you both on thirty thousand pounds."

"Make it forty and you have a deal."

"Forty?"

"Try to find someone else who'll work for you and understands the secret world."

Roberts sighed. "My default position was forty. I can do that."

Sign strode up to her. "It's been a pleasure to make your acquaintance." He shook her hand. "We'll use our methods. But all formal communications will go through you. I don't want to liaise with anyone else in the police. Agreed?"

Roberts frowned. "Why?"

"Because I don't want to work with anyone I don't trust or respect. I can see into you. My evaluation is very favourable."

Hidden from view, Hilt watched Roberts leave West Square from the same position he'd seen her arrive. He called Smith. "During the last three days, she's either been at home or in the New Scotland Yard building. With two exceptions. I followed her to an address in Godalming three days ago."

"I know that address. What is the other exception?"

"She's just left a house in Kennington. She was in there for half an hour. The house is converted into four flats, but I know which flat she attended. Zoom camera. Saw which button she pressed to get into the communal entrance."

"Find out who lives there."

"Will do." Hilt ended the call and followed Roberts.

CHAPTER 7

Post dinner, Sign and Knutsen sat by the fire in the lounge. Sign said, "We are seeing Mrs. Archer tomorrow. When I called her she sounded understandably distraught. She can't believe her husband committed suicide, but she also knows that's what happened. She has two issues: one is grief; the other is bewilderment."

Knutsen asked, "You're certain it's suicide?"

"I'm inclined to believe the police know what they're doing, though I never discount anything until I'm on the ground. But if it is suicide, I can do something that the police can't. I can get into the minds of people, dead or alive."

Knutsen laughed. "Like a clairvoyant?"

"No. Like someone who knows the human condition, regardless of nationality, race, gender, age, religion, political beliefs, social status, or sexual persuasion." Sign look wistful as he added, "I like to think of the process as one of absorbing souls."

There was so much about Sign that Knutsen wanted to know. "Does it pain you to have that burden?"

"Absorbing souls?" Sign looked irritated. "It's like asking a shepherd if he's wracked with anguish because some of his sheep are mischievous or prone to stupidity."

"Fair point." Knutsen drank some coffee. "But you are a chameleon. I saw you change colours when Roberts was here."

Sign made a flourish with his hand. "Chameleon? Praying mantis. Whatever? You decide." Sign was distracted. "Thus far I have nine theories about Mark Archer's death. Eight are banal. One most certainly is not."

"You haven't even seen his dead body, or yet visited his wife."

"Body's don't talk and people lie. It is in the imagination that we begin to hypothesise." Sign added wood to the fire. "I need you to get a handgun. Something reliable. A Glock or similar. Can you do that?"

"Yes. Do you want me to get you one as well?"

"I don't carry guns unless absolutely necessary."

Knutsen frowned.

Sign elaborated. "We did things in the bandit zones of South Asia, Africa and Latin America that you wouldn't believe. I don't like those days. They stay with me. I held a gun when I was younger. Now I'm older. Let's leave it at that."

"But why do I need a gun?"

"In case my ninth theory is correct."

Knutsen said, "Okay." He paused for a moment before asking, "Are you religious?"

"No."

"Have strong political beliefs?"

"I've worked with too many politicians of different parties. They're all the same. All they want is power. No, I have no faith in one party versus another."

"Do you aspire to re-marry?" Knutsen expected a harsh retort.

But instead, Sign said, "Perhaps one day, but not for now. My wife's buried not far from here. I visit her grave when I can and talk to her. She's still my wife."

Knutsen wrapped his hands around his coffee mug. "There's a cold draft coming in to the room. We need to do something about that."

"I like the draft. I think of it as a messenger from the outside world, reminding me that all is not well." Sign smiled. "It comes from the extractor fans in the bathrooms. I suppose there might be one-way extractor fans on the market these days."

"I'll check it out." Knutsen checked his watch. "I've got to go out now."

"Excellent. It'll give me some peace from your questions. We're on parade tomorrow morning. Ten o'clock train from Waterloo to take us to Godalming. Then we'll see what we make of Mrs. Archer."

Forty five minutes later, Knutsen knocked on the door of a council flat in a high-rise tenement building in Brixton. A black woman, mid-forties, opened the door a fraction, but kept the security chain attached. When she saw it was Knutsen, she fully opened the door. Her eyes were bloodshot. She'd been crying.

Knutsen was worried. "Wendy. Is everything okay?"

Wendy couldn't stop the tears starting again. "He's not here."

"But the dojo starts at nine." Knutsen had driven here. Once a week, work permitting, he collected Wendy's son David and helped him with his martial arts training. It kept David off drugs and petty crime. "Where is he?"

"He'll... he'll be hanging out with those guys. You know the place. I thought he'd given up on all that. They're bad people, Mr. Knutsen. Tonight we had an argument. He laughed at me and told me he was going to see people who actually cared about him. He used bad language."

"Leave it with me."

Knutsen left and walked four hundred yards to a side alley off Brixton High Street. Wendy was right. Her eighteen year old son was there, hanging out with three men who were in their early twenties and had the physiques of basketball players. The older men were drug dealers. David was truly in the wrong company. Knutsen approached David and told him that he had to go or they'd lose their slot on the dojo. David feared Knutsen, though also highly respected him. But in front of the other men he tried to act defiant.

David said, "I'm not doing no training tonight. I'm working."

"With these idiots? And what are you actually *working* on? Construction? Taxi driving? Plumbing? Painting and decorating? Anything noble? Or are you just selling plastic wraps of hash, coke, and spice to kids? I don't call that work."

The tallest of the older men walked up to Knutsen and put his face millimetres from his face. "Back off, white boy."

David yelled, "Leeroy! No!"

Leeroy persisted. "You a cop?" His breath stank of fast food.

Knutsen held his ground. "I'm simply here to take David to his kendo class. He's improving. I don't want to see him fall behind."

Leeroy pushed him against a wall. "He ain't falling behind when he's with us, you cunt."

The two other older men pulled out knives. David looked terrified.

Knutsen said, "Calm down. I just want to help David. I'm not a cop.

"Yeah, all off-duty cops say that." Leeroy put his hand in his puffer jacket. "I got me a piece. Finger's on the trigger. If you fuck off, I don't put a hole in your gut."

Knutsen nodded, then head butted Leeroy, stamped on his chest and groin, advanced with lightning speed to the other men, dodged their knives, smacked one of them in the throat and jabbed the other with two fingers into his eyes. The men would live, though would need medical treatment. Knutsen said to David, "Let's go."

They walked out of the alley. Knutsen didn't care that the three men were writhing in agony on the ground.

Fifteen minutes later, they were in the Brixton martial arts gym. It entertained all sorts of fighting disciplines, including boxing, kung fu, and krav maga. But tonight was kendo night. Knutsen helped David get his armour on. He said, "Now we do a better class of fighting."

Knutsen geared up and stepped onto the dojo, facing David. Both were brandishing their bamboo swords. They bowed. Knutsen said, "Now, don't forget your feet and legs. The arms and sword are their slaves and are useless without them."

David lunged, trying to jab his sword at Knutsen's chest. Knutsen tapped David's sword to one side. Using both hands, David attempted to swipe his sword downwards. It was a move used by samurai to slice a man diagonally in half from shoulder to waist. It was also effectively used by Japanese soldiers against Americans in the Battle of Iwo Jima in WW2. Knutsen stepped sideways. David's attack didn't connect.

Knutsen discarded his sword and said, "First incapacitate, then execute. Show me where you want to strike."

David tried to slap Knutsen's abdomen. Knutsen stepped back, his hands behind his back. David dropped to a crouch and attempted to strike his ankles. Knutsen jumped, the sword cutting through air. David by now was angry and ill disciplined. He tried to hit Knutsen on the head. Knutsen dodged left, brought his arms in front of him, rushed forward, knocked David off his feet and punched his mask. "Now you've got a bloody nose and concussion. All I need to do is pick up my sword and cut you into pieces. Easy. Good job you're wearing protection."

David got to his feet. "Where did I go wrong, Mr Knutsen?"

"You had an argument with your mum and held on to the anger. Here we don't have anger. We have calm precision." Knutsen patted him on the shoulder. "You just had a bad night. I'll drive you home. But first there's something we need to do."

After leaving the gym, they stopped at a newsagent. "Why are we here?" asked David.

Knutsen walked David to a section containing cards. "Choose one. Inside you're going to tell your mum that you're sorry."

"Really, man?!"

"Do it."

David picked up a card. At the checkout, Knutsen gave him a pen and told him to write. After payment was made, they left.

Knutsen said, "One more stop."

Two shops next door was a florist. The shop was closed, but Knutsen knew the florist lived above the establishment. He pressed on the intercom. A woman answered. Knutsen said, "It's Tom Knutsen. I have a young lad with me. We need your help."

Inside the shop, the black woman kissed Knutsen on the cheek.

"How have you been doing, Maggie?"

The former meth addict smiled. "I breathe the free air. That's what you taught me to think."

"And it works." Knutsen pointed at David. "This gentleman went off piste tonight. He's now back on track and wants to make amends. Could you make us a bouquet of flowers? It's for his mother."

Maggie smiled. "My pleasure handsome. You want to stay here tonight?"

"Remember the rules. We always maintain parameters." Knutsen had killed Maggie's husband. He knew she was clean from drugs for two years. But like all addicts, her nervous system had been irrevocably changed by drugs. It meant she believed anything was possible, including sleeping with Knutsen. "Make the flowers pretty, Maggie. And find a good husband. Just avoid Internet dating."

Sixty minutes later they entered Wendy's house. Wendy was tearful as David handed her the card and flowers, hugged her, and told his mum that he was sorry.

Wendy made Knutsen a cup of tea, told David to go to his room, and sat with the former undercover cop in her tiny but pristine living room. "It's hard being a single parent."

"It is. Particularly when the child is a boy."

Wendy shook her head. "It makes no difference if it's a boy or girl. The challenges are just different, but equally hard. David needs a father. He's never had one. You're the nearest he's got."

The comment made Knutsen feel awkward. "I just want to help him out. In doing so, it helps me out. I have no children. You know that."

"What I know is that even when you can't move heaven and hell to train with him, you still lie to the probation service and tick the box that says he's been to the gym every week. You're a very good man."

"But David's not yet a man. He may look like one, but he's not."

"That's where you come in. You teach him." Wendy rubbed her eyes. "I couldn't bear it if he went back into prison."

Knudsen smiled. "I've eaten this evening, but I could do with a snack. Also, do you allow David to have a small, low alcohol drink?"

Wendy frowned. "Now and again."

Kendo is thirsty work. "How about I grab a couple of cans from the local off licence while you rustle up some crisps and salsa or whatever comes to hand. David and I will sit and have our beer and snacks. Alone, I'm afraid. It will be mans' talk."

"What will you talk about?"

"I will tell him about my father. He was conscripted into the army between '53 and '57. He served in Egypt and Libya. He wanted to know what makes the Japanese military thinking tick, particularly tactics and strategy in the medieval period. This brought him into contact with two experts in the arms and armour field. One was a curator of swords and spears at the V&A. The other was a representative of the Royal Armouries. My father's fascination about how swords and spears were employed in combat was underpinned by one thing: he wanted to understand discipline. He had a friend who he went to school with. The friend joined the merchant marine at the same time my father joined the army. Previously, they were inseparable. Both were highly intelligent. One stint of my father's tours was guarding the Suez Canal. My father spent hours there, hoping his friend would pass on a ship. His friend never did. But the possibility was there. They reunited after they were out of service. My father's friend had just got married. She'd died from malaria, age twenty two. My father taught his friend kendo. It saved his friend from depression or far worse." Knudsen smiled. "I want to tell David what I've just told you. And I think two thirsty men deserve a beer while I recount my history."

Wendy beamed, all traces of tears now absent from her glistening eyes. "You move your ass and get those beers, mister. And I'll do better than crisps and salsa. I do mean double fried chips and mayonnaise." She grabbed Knutsen's hand before he left. "Thank you for everything. And tonight will mean the world to my son."

CHAPTER 8

Accompanied by an icy wind, rain lashed the Surrey town of Godalming, as Sign and Knutsen walked from the train station to Mrs. Archer's house on Charterhouse Road. Both had umbrellas up and were wearing woollen coats over their suits. Due to the weather and the fact it was late morning, the pretty town was relatively quiet – London commuters had long since departed for work. Sign and Knutsen walked up the hill that took Charterhouse Road to the famous school bearing its name. The house was a detached four bedroom property, these days probably having a value of seven figures. There was no way that Mark Archer could have afforded that on his government salary.

Sign rang the doorbell. Mrs. Archer answered.

Sign said, "Mrs Archer – Ben Sign and Tom Knutsen. I believe you are expecting us."

She looked like she'd barely had any sleep during the night, though she was elegantly dressed, had applied makeup, and not one hair on her head was out of place. In a posh voice, she said, "Do you have any identification?"

Sign nodded and showed her his passport. "We're very happy to wait outside while you call Inspector Roberts to verify our credentials."

"That won't be necessary. Come in."

The men placed their umbrellas in a stand, hung their overcoats on a rack, and followed her into the lounge.

"Would you like tea?"

"That would be very gracious of you. Milk, no sugar." Sign sat on a sofa. Knutsen sat next to him, even though there were many chairs in the room.

When Mrs. Archer had left the room, Knutsen whispered, "Expensive gaff. Some of the furnishings and other stuff in here must have cost a fortune."

Sign placed a finger to his lips and shook his head.

Five minutes later, Mrs. Archer returned carrying a tray containing a teapot, cups and saucers, a small jug of milk, and a plate of biscuits. As she poured the tea, she said, "Inspector Roberts told me that you were advisers. She said you were to be trusted." She looked at Sign. "And she said you worked with my husband."

"I no longer work for The Office. And when I did, I knew of your husband, though our paths never crossed. We operated in different parts of the world."

After handing them their cups of tea, Mrs. Archer sat opposite them. She looked sorrowful as she said, "It's been an odd life. When Mark and I went on our first two overseas postings we made a mistake. In Kuala Lumper and Brasilia, like all newly-arrived diplomats, we were pounced on by the close knit expat community. They get so lonely and so bored. They want new friends. We thought it was great to meet new faces. The trouble is…"

"Postings last three years. Then people leave. We never see them again."

"Yes. You make a friend. But that friendship has a very short shelf life." Her hands were shaking as she sipped her tea. "So after that, on other postings, we kept our distance from expats and other diplomats. There was no point becoming their friends. For me, the only constant was Mark. He kept me sane."

Sign had a gentle smile on his face. "I'm so sorry for your loss. I'm also very sorry that we felt the need to meet you so soon after your husband's departure."

"Departure? Yes, he's gone. I'm not religious. I don't have a fantasy that I'll join him in heaven. What do you want?"

Sign gestured to Knutsen. "Tom is a former police officer. He's now my business partner."

"And what is your business?"

"To find the truth and then decide if the truth benefits good people."

"What an unusual remit." She raised a finger nail to her mouth, but quickly replaced her hand on her tea saucer.

Sign said, "Would you like me to fetch you a mug from your kitchen? You could pour your tea into the mug. Mugs are so much easier to hold when the nerves are playing havoc. And we don't mind. In our time, Knutsen and I have drunk out of tin cans, bowls, dirty glasses, you name it."

"I have standards." She placed her cup and saucer on a side table. She repeated, "What do you want? Be specific."

It was Knutsen who answered. "We want to know if your husband killed himself or was murdered. If he killed himself, we want to know why."

Mrs. Archer frowned. "But, I've already spoken to Inspector Roberts about this. I told her I'm confused. The police say there is no doubt that it was suicide." Her lip was trembling as she looked away. "But I can't understand why he did this." She looked at the men. "We have no debt. Our children are doing well at university. They have no problems – not that we're aware of. Mark has always been a loyal husband. He wasn't seeing another woman. I know that. Women can tell. He was extremely loyal to MI6. And he was happy. His last job was London-based. In headquarters. He knew it was probably the pinnacle of his seniority, that he wasn't going to go any further, but he didn't mind. He was content. No stress, he told me. Who cares about entering the vipers nest at the top of the tree, he recently joked. I was glad. We were too old to return to the overseas postings merry-go-round. At last, we could enjoy what we had. In England."

Sign asked, "Your children?"

"My son's at the University of East Anglia. My daughter's at Newcastle."

"Have they visited you since the tragic event?"

"Of course! They've returned to their studies, but they'll be back here once the body's released and I can have him buried."

"What are their thoughts about your husband's death?"

She slapped her thigh. "They're distraught! What do you expect?"

"As surprised as you?"

"Yes. They can't understand why this happened. The only reason they've returned to university is they have exams. Goodness knows how they're going to stay focused."

Knutsen leaned forward. "Doctors, and the police for that matter, don't fully understand mental health problems. But we do know that sometimes people are unhappy for no discernible reason. That's the hardest part – dealing with people who are clinically depressed. It's easier to deal with people who are down in the dumps because they're behind on their rent of are going through a rough patch in their marriage."

"*Down in the dumps*?" Mrs. Archer laughed as tears ran down her face. "I haven't heard that phrase for a long time." She withdrew a handkerchief, patted her face, and composed herself. "I must impress upon you both that my husband did not have clinical depression. Nor was he down in the dumps. He was the happiest I've ever seen him."

Sign said, "I need to ask you a hard question."

Mrs. Archer looked nervous, but nodded.

"Despite what the police think, is there any suspicion in your mind – even if just one percent – that your husband was murdered?"

She shook his head. "Forensics were here for hours. They said there was no doubt he killed himself. I found him." Tears were once again freefalling down her face.

"Take your time."

"I… I found him. In the bath. It's funny." Her voice was trembling. "He didn't normally drink to excess. The bath water was bright red with his blood. He'd slit his wrists. But all I could think about was that empty bottle of vodka by his side. I was cross that he'd drunk that much. Stupid me."

"You were in shock."

"Anyway. Why would anyone murder him?"

Sign wondered how far he should push her. "Your husband and I were MI6 officers. There are bad people out there who'd like to see us dead."

Mrs. Archer held her head in her hands. "You'll think bad of me, but I wish it was murder. It would be so much easier to rationalise. Suicide seems so…"

"Selfish?"

"Unexplained."

"And that's why we're here." Sign handed her a business card. "You can contact us anytime if something else occurs to you, no matter how trivial. There are three of us helping you – me, Knutsen, and Roberts. Don't trust MI6. Don't trust anyone in the police aside from Roberts."

"Why?"

"Because organisations don't like problems, particularly when they involve someone with your husband's security clearance and seniority. They find it an embarrassment. They fend off the media and the truth." Sign tapped Knutsen on the arm. It was the signal to leave. The men stood and walked to the hallway. Mrs. Archer followed them. After putting on their overcoats and retrieving their umbrellas, Sign said, "Mrs. Archer – once again, we are so sorry for your loss. I too lost my wife; Knutsen lost a woman who he hoped would give him happiness." He paused by the door. "Did anyone come to see your husband on the day before he died? Possibly a short time before he killed himself?"

She shook her head. "No one."

Sign and Knutsen left.

As they walked down the road, Sign said, "She's lying."

From the opposite side of the street in Weybridge, Karl Hilt watched Katy Roberts leave her house. He knew her husband was still at home. Probably he either worked from home or was unemployed. Hilt didn't care. He waited ten minutes. The street didn't have CCTV, but there was a chance that Roberts' house had security cameras. Given her occupation, there was a slim chance the cameras were hidden on the exterior and interior. Hilt wasn't going to take a risk. Face, ears, and eyes couldn't be exposed, due to modern recognition technology. He jogged across the road, donned a balaclava and sun glasses and ran to the rear garden. He'd brought equipment to force locks if necessary, but they were not required. The rear-facing kitchen door was unlocked. He entered.

The place was modest in size and indicative of a couple who had no children – no clutter, holiday postcards of trips to Thailand and other exotic climes were fixed to the fridge door by magnets, a Post-It note was stuck to the microwave saying *Don't forget – five minutes on full blast, then one minute rest*, and an empty pot of coffee was on the hob.

Hilt moved into the lounge. It contained one sofa, an armchair, a TV, and not much else. Katy Roberts' husband was on the sofa, watching a program about antiques. Hilt moved up behind him, placed his arm around the man's neck, and squeezed. He said nothing as Roberts' husband lost consciousness. For good measure, Hilt punched the man three times in the face.

He stood over him. The man's face was a mess. He was either passed out or dead.

Hilt moved on. He had to make the event look like a random burglary. In reality he was looking for anything that could be of interest to John Smith. He searched the lounge, found nothing of interest, and trashed the room. In the upstairs bedroom, Katy Roberts' wedding ring and other jewellery were in a box on a chest of drawers in the bedroom. Hilt took them all. He rifled through bedside cabinet drawers and found nothing. He opened all of the drawers in the chest and tossed underwear and other clothing onto the floor, to make it look like he was searching for hidden cash, spare car keys, or other valuable items. He ripped down wall framed photos of Katy and her husband, taken in various UK and overseas locations. He stamped on them, shattering glass and sending shards into the photos. He upended the mattress and used a hunting knife to slash it open. Duck feather spilled out. Reaching behind the heavy chest of drawers, he yanked it forward so that it crashed face down on the floor. The place was a mess.

The other two rooms on the level were a bathroom and an office. The bathroom was of no interest to Hilt. He entered the office. It contained a desk and laptop, table lamp, tray containing papers, and a small metal cabinet next to the desk. Hilt searched the tray. There was nothing of interest – just bills that needed to be paid and other household documentation. He threw the tray against the wall behind him, papers spewing out. Crouching down, he carefully examined each of the four drawers in the filing cabinet. There were a few sheets of paper listing birthdays and marriage anniversaries of relatives and friends of Katy and her husband, mortgage documentation, a will, a list of passwords for Tesco's online shopping, Amazon, LinkedIn, and Skype, a bundle of charger leads, and one business card.

The business card gave the names and address of Ben Sign and Tom Knutsen. The address corresponded to the one Hilt had seen Roberts attend to. He took a photo of the card, then tossed it onto the floor, alongside everything else from the drawers.

He walked back downstairs. Katy's husband was still sitting in the lounge, his eyes scrunched tight, his face covered in blood. He was moaning. Hilt ignored him and left.

Fifteen minutes later and three miles away from the house, Hilt called Smith. "She doesn't take her work home. With one exception. I found a business card."

"Ordinarily that's not unusual," said Smith. "But I'm listening because it's grabbed your interest."

Hilt explained.

Smith replied, "I don't know who Knutsen is. But I most certainly know who Ben Sign is. We may have a major problem. Meet me at four PM."

CHAPTER 9

In Epsom General Hospital, Katy Roberts sat by her husband's bed. He had bandages on his face and was conscious. Roberts had been told that her husband would need to stay in for at least two nights. The doctors weren't worried about the facial injuries; but they did want to monitor his breathing. The crush to his throat worried the medical staff, though they were confident he'd make a full recovery.

Roberts rubbed her husband's hand and said, "I need to step outside for a few minutes."

Her husband coughed and said, "Go home. No… no point you hanging around in this place. Plus, after what the burglar did to our house, the place needs tidying. You better put on your marigolds and get to work."

Roberts laughed. "Be Miss Dolly Domestic?"

"There's a first time for everything."

Roberts' voice trembled as she said, "He took my wedding ring."

"Don't worry about that, my love. It was just a cheap piece of shit I picked up in Dubai. They weren't real diamonds."

Roberts smiled. "You've always been a terrible liar. I know you spent a fortune on the ring. The diamonds were real. I had it analysed by a specialist for house insurance purposes."

Between more coughs, her husband said, "Good. Let's hope the insurance pays out. Then you can nip down to Hatton Garden and pick yourself up another ring."

This was the first time Roberts had seen her husband in a hospital bed. It broke her heart to see him so vulnerable. "Okay. I'll go home and sort the house. I can come back later tonight."

"No point. I'm so damned tired, for some reason. I'll probably be asleep."

She kissed him on the forehead and left the room.

In the corridor was one of her plain clothed detectives. She asked him, "Any updates?"

The detective nodded. "I've just got off the phone to Surrey Police. Because of who you are, forensics went through your place twice. They really pulled out the stops. Only your jewellery's missing. But the burglar made every effort to see if there was anything else of value in the house. We think he must have left on foot. Your laptop and TV weren't taken. No other electrical items he could have flogged. He only took what he could stuff in his pockets."

"He must have left some traces."

"Yes and no. We have size ten boot prints. Forensics is certain they're boots, due to the shape of the soles. But here's the thing – the burglar scraped the treads off, most likely with a knife. Also, most likely he wore plastic shoe covers. There are no finger or palm prints. He wore gloves."

"There should have been fibres from the gloves. And with modern forensics technology, prints can still be partially obtained – not just from the inside of gloves but also from everything they've touched."

The detective nodded. "We got traces of resin."

Roberts frowned. "He coated his hands in a resin compound, let them dry, then put gloves on?"

"Yes. I've never seen that done before. Forensics are both furious and fascinated as to how he came up with that idea."

"What else?"

"He wore a smooth jacket. No fibres were transferred when he grabbed your husband. He was immensely strong – the injuries speak for themselves. And he knew exactly what he was doing. He's been highly trained."

"Ex-military?"

"Could be. But military guys aren't trained to do this kind of stuff. Not that I know of."

"So, most likely a hardened criminal who's learned his trade on the street. A lot of effort just to steal my wedding ring. I wonder if he was hoping to find something more than that." Roberts sighed. "Okay, we're not going to catch this guy through forensics. My husband didn't see his face. The burglar didn't speak, so voice recognition is out. We just have to hope he burgles another place and makes a mistake."

"I'm sorry, Katy."

"So am I." Roberts left. Her priority was to clean her home and get her husband back when he was recovered. She called Sign and told him what had happened. "I'm probably going to be out of circulation for the next twenty four hours. Apparently the house is a mess. Plus, I need to be close to my husband."

Sign replied, "Of course. What's your address?"

Roberts supplied him with details.

"You're heading there now?"

"Yes."

"Do you have anything to eat this evening?"

"I… I doubt it. I don't feel hungry."

"Hang tight, inspector." Sign hung up and shouted to Knutsen. "Put on your scruffiest clothes. Make sure your car has a full tank. In one hour we're leaving. It's meals on wheels time." Sign entered the kitchen.

Two hours later, Sign and Knutsen were in Roberts' house. Knutsen was in jeans and a jumper. Sign was still in his suit.

Roberts was teary as she gestured toward the mess in the lounge. "Look what he's done to my home. I don't know where to begin."

Sign handed her a tray containing two casserole pots. "It's just basic fare that I knocked up in sixty minutes – beef casserole and wild rice. The casserole will need another hour in your oven. I do hope you're not vegetarian."

Roberts shook her head as she placed the dish in the oven. "This is more than I can eat."

"Good, because you've got two hungry labourers at your disposal who are going to need feeding. Mr. Knutsen – this is no longer a crime scene. Let's get it back in order." Sign slung his jacket over the sofa where Roberts' husband had been strangled. He rolled up his sleeves. "Let's look upstairs."

Roberts showed them the bedroom and the office.

Sign said to Roberts, "Could you make us a cup of tea?"

When Roberts was downstairs, Sign said to Knutsen, "You know London better than I do. And you know people. Call in some favours." He wrote on a slip of paper and handed the sheet to Knutsen. "This is what we need. And we need it in the next hour or two. Go."

When Knutsen was gone, Sign set to work. He cleaned up each room, with Roberts' assistance, and hauled the ripped mattress into the garden. He vacuum cleaned the house, head to toe, and used cleaning products to eradicate Roberts' husband's blood from the sofa. Bed sheets, underwear, and every other piece of linen were in the washing machine. Locks on the doors were checked and applied. Ground level garden lights were turned on. So too other exterior lights. But there was still more to be done that was beyond Sign's ability.

When Knutsen returned, he was carrying a bottle of wine and scented candles. Next to him were four men. Two of them were carrying an expensive double mattress. The other two had tool belts and other equipment.

Sign smiled at Knudsen. "Good man. I've taken it as far as I can. Over to you."

The men set to work. The mattress was placed on the bed. The old mattress was placed in their transit van. The tool-carrying artisans replaced picture frames, inserted new glass, and hung the pictures back up. Knutsen placed the bottle of white wine in the fridge, lit candles and shook hands with the four men. They left. Knutsen and Sign remained in the house with Roberts.

Roberts asked Knutsen, "How did you arrange this at such short notice? Who were those men?"

"Cutthroats and thieves." Knutsen laughed. "Something like that. I helped them get on the straight and narrow. They're good people."

"Who owed you a favour?"

"In different locations and time frames, individually they tried to kill me. Obviously it didn't work. They got a bit bruised. I forgave them and marched them off to the Job Centre. I suppose I should have arrested them. What would have been the point? Who else would have repaired your home so well at the drop of a hat?"

"No one else", said Sign. "You made them good men. A superb judgement call. Mrs. Roberts – would you object if I played mum and served up food and wine? Your home is once again beautiful and untarnished. While we eat and drink, I will regale you of an adventure I had in Paris that involved my discovery of a white severed arm clutching a black severed arm." He walked into the kitchen.

Roberts was emotional as she whispered to Knutsen. "Thank you both so much for doing this."

Knutsen smiled. "We had no other plans this evening."

"What did you make of Mrs. Archer?"

"Sign agrees with you that she's holding something back." He gave her details of the meeting.

"What's Sign going to do next?"

Knutsen shrugged. "No idea. But I know what I've got to do next." He checked his watch. "Later tonight I've got to meet a man about a gun."

At eleven PM, Knutsen was in a south London motorcycle shop that was in a converted railway bridge arch. Above the shop, day and night, long and short distance trains passed over the premises, producing noise and vibrations. The noise suited the proprietor. He didn't want complaints when tuning and revving his bikes. But there was another reason that the noise was his friend.

The proprietor – Jerry Logan - was a small, middle age man, bald, who had an aroma of metal and grease. Tonight he was wearing blue overalls that were splattered with oil. His face and calloused hands were dirty. He said, "I'd shake hands, but," he held up his palms, "I've been stripping down and reassembling an old Ducati. I'm hoping to sell it for a song. Haven't seen you in a while, Tom. How are things?"

Knutsen was cautious. Logan was a hardened criminal who'd done stints in prison. Three years ago, for reasons that weren't clear, he'd agreed to work with the police in an undercover sting. The targets were major drug dealers. He enabled Knutsen to meet the dealers. The sting went wrong. At the final meeting with them, Logan pulled out his mobile phone, pretended to read a text message, and shouted, "Shit! This guy's a cop. You're about to be busted!" The dealers fell for Logan's sleight of hand and ran, leaving a stash of drugs behind. Pointing a gun at Knutsen, Logan picked up drugs with a street value of half a million quid, and smiled. "They won't talk. You can't talk because you'll blow your cover. And I don't need to talk. See you sometime, pal." He later sold the drugs and bought the shop and some very rare bikes. His business had been booming ever since. But he wasn't completely legit these days. He still kept one foot in the criminal underworld by supplying discerning customers with weapons. Knutsen knew that.

"I'm out of the police. Doing a bit of private detective work."

Logan picked up a large wrench. "If you've got eyes on me, you're wasting your time." He lied, "I threw the drugs in the Thames. Can't have that crap on our fine streets, can we?"

"I'm not here about that. I need your help."

Logan used the wrench to tighten bolts on the Ducati. He placed the tool down and wiped his hands on a towel. "You want a gun?"

"Yes."

"Loud and proud? Or fuck-them-up small?"

The former meaning a shotgun, machine gun, or rifle. The latter meaning a handgun.

"A pistol, plus at least four spare magazines. Deniable, of course."

Logan said, "Step into my office." He led Knutsen to the back of the shop and into a small shooting range. At the end of the range was a target of a man. The only other items in the range were an eight foot metal cabinet and a desk. Both were flush against the right-hand-side wall. Logan opened the cabinet. There was an array of weapons inside. He withdrew four pistols and laid them on the desk. "Browning 9mm. Bit old school and kicks like a mule. But, one bullet makes a severe mess. A Makarov. Good for rapid firing, plus needs less maintenance compared to the Browning. The bullets sting like fuck, but a leg shot won't kill you unless you're lucky. A Sig Sauer P320-45. This will hit you like a rhino. And it's accurate. But it's loud. And" he prodded a finger on the last weapon, "a Sig Sauer P226. They come in a variety of calibres. This one's 9mm."

Knutsen looked at the weapons. "Where do you get these?"

Logan turned to him, his face filled with aggression. "It'll go bad for both of us if you're wearing a wire!"

Knutsen held up his hands. "Jerry – I'm here to make a purchase. I don't want anyone, least of all the police, to know I've been here."

"You'd better be telling me the fucking truth. What do you need the gun for?"

"At this stage, I don't know."

"Human target?"

"Come on, Jerry."

"Yeah, fair point. Urban or rural?"

"I genuinely don't know. Could be both."

Logan brushed his hand over the guns. "I get a lot of my weapons from soldiers who return from places like Afghanistan, Iraq, Africa, other places. Many of them are on their uppers. I give them a few hundred quid. It pays for their rent in a bedsit for a month or two. Or gives them a night out on the booze and coke. They're trophy weapons taken from their enemies, or they're nicked from their unit's armouries. But I also have other sources. The key thing is I don't buy or sell anything unless I think it's serviceable. I strip down every gun; sometimes I have to reconstruct them with new workings." He gestured toward his shop. "Just like my Ducati motorbike." He slammed his hand on the table. "Best you test all four and see what you think. Prices vary."

Knutsen picked up the Browning. "My father carried one of these." He got into a shooting stance and aimed the gun at the target.

"Wait!" Logan checked his watch. "Anytime now. Anytime now." A train passed overhead; the noise was easily sufficient to drown out gunshots. "You've got five seconds max. Go now!"

Knutsen fired three shots. My goodness, Logan was right. It kicked like a mule. But the target was shredded. "I'll take this."

"You sure? The others are more advanced."

"I know, but this one feels good in my hands."

"That's all that matters. Just remember, your Browning bullets will go through someone and won't stop until they've done with death."

"I'll need at least four spare magazines."

"I'll give you six for a total price of one thousand pounds."

Knutsen nodded. "Deal." He handed over cash and took the gun and magazines, which he secreted in his fleece jacket. He shook hands with Logan, not caring that engine oil made his hands mucky. "You inherited wealth from an obscure relative who lived in Latin America. It enabled you to finance this shop. That's the line. Get rid of the guns. You don't need them anymore. It's time to go legit." Knutsen walked out.

CHAPTER 10

It was eight AM. On the south bank of the Thames, Sign walked behind a man who was smartly dressed and holding a rolled-up umbrella. The man was approximately the same age as Sign. A few tourists were braving the cold air. Everyone else was office workers going to work. Still, the ordinarily bustling pathway was sparse of pedestrians.

Sign walked alongside the man he'd been following and matched his pace. "Thanks for agreeing to talk."

"I agreed to this meeting. But, we have less than a mile to cover whatever it is that's of interest to you. After that I walk into the temple. I understand that you no longer have a security pass to get in."

Colin Parker was referring to the MI6 headquarters in Vauxhall Cross. He worked there as head of counter-espionage. Despite being a senior posting, and a sexy-sounding title, it was a role that required him to sit in London and analyse files. Though Parker had entered the service out of Cambridge as a fast-stream spy, he knew that his current job was a career killer.

Sign knew that as well. "I wanted to talk to you about Mark Archer."

"His death?"

"What led up to his death."

Parker laughed as he carried on walking. "Who knows?"

"Why is the service being uncooperative with the police?"

"We haven't been uncooperative. On the contrary, we invited senior Met detectives to come into HQ to discuss Archer's death. They told us point blank that there was no doubt he committed suicide. What they wanted were two things: first to know if there were any skeletons in the closet; second, to know how to handle the media if it was leaked that Archer was MI6, rather than a diplomat."

"Were there any skeletons in the closet?"

Parker stopped walking. "Come on Ben. You of all people should know how this works. I'm only privy to matters that cross my desk – a Chinese spy tries to blackmail one of our officers, the Russians have set up an eavesdropping station in Pimlico, that kind of thing. What I'm *not* privy to is the machinations of our officers' private lives. You'd have to talk to security about that. And they won't talk to you or me. Their job is so dull that they've developed a them-and-us syndrome. Everyone in security realises they've been marginalised because of their mediocre performance as operators. You won't find a single friend there."

Sign had expected this response. "Were there any rumours about Archer, even if it's just unsubstantiated tittle-tattle?"

Parker continued walking. "If there were rumours, I wasn't privy to them. Service personnel don't gossip to me. They worry what I'd do with that information."

"Who were Archer's friends in The Office?"

"You know us lot, Ben. None of us like each other."

Sign saw the MI6 HQ ahead. "How well did you know Archer?"

"Not that well at all. Different departments; different postings."

"But your paths crossed?"

"Fleetingly."

"Have you been to his house?"

"No. Why would I?"

"Do you know his wife?"

Parker shook his head. "I heard she was a school teacher assistant before Archer swept her off her feet and made her feel like lady of the manor on overseas postings. You know how being a diplomat's spouse goes to some people's heads."

"She came from a humble background?"

Parker laughed. "Nothing wrong with that." He stood opposite the headquarters. "They were kindred spirits. Mark Archer had a brain and good education, though he too came from working class stock. Marrying a working class girl was his two fingers up to the establishment, is my guess." He frowned. "So you're now playing private detective?"

"I'm an advisor, currently to the Metropolitan Police."

"Needs must." Parker looked sympathetic as he said, "Personally, I thought you were the best candidate for chief."

"I thought I was the worst – people like us are bred and trained to run people and make them sacrifice their lives in hostile territories; we're not designed to manage an organisation."

Parker glanced at the temple. "It's turned into a feeding frenzy in there. Sharks turning on sharks. Your departure has created a void that can't be filled."

"That's no longer my problem, Colin."

"Soon, it won't be mine either. In six months, I'm out of here. My partner and I want to retire to our home in Normandy. I've had enough of this game."

Parker was about to leave, but Sign placed a hand on his arm. "Archer's home is way beyond his pay packet. I wondered if he or his wife had inherited the money to buy it. From what you've said about their backgrounds, that seems highly unlikely."

"We all accrue cash expenses on postings."

"A few thousand pounds here and there, yes. But Archer's house is worth at least one or two million."

Parker was motionless. "I did briefly meet his wife once. But not at their home. The Archers had laid on a barge trip down the Thames to celebrate their daughter's acceptance into university. Ten of us from the service were invited. God knows why. Probably just to make up numbers."

"A few people dropped out at the last minute?"

"There's no other explanation. The event was a bit tedious. Aside from Mark Archer, who I didn't really know, the only other people I knew at the event were my colleagues, and I barely knew them. But there was an odd thing."

Sign said nothing.

"It was the champagne. I know you don't have kids. I do. But if you did have kids and your daughter got into uni I'm guessing that, like me, you'd flatter her by laying on a few bottles of Prosecco and a two hundred pound plate of sarnies. Nothing less, nothing more. But here's the thing – Mark Archer had an on board personal chef who cooked lobster with caviar, truffles, and Wagyu beef that had been flown in from Japan. And there must have been a hundred bottles of Veuve Clicqout Brut flowing."

"Where did he get that money from?"

"My colleagues and I thought it must have been down to a soppy dad squirreling his cash away for his daughter's send off."

Sign shook his head. "It was a cry for help. You and others were invited to his daughter's celebration because you needed to be witnesses to his despair. But, you didn't pick up on that or help him."

"Help him?"

"Put him out of his misery." Sign spun around. Over the road was the motorcycle shop that Knutsen had visited last night. It amused him that Logan's gun range was so close to the epicentre of the world's most successful intelligence organisation. "Archer was on the take. The only explanation is that he was being paid good sums by a foreign intelligence organisation that wanted our secrets. He was a double agent. Towards the end, he wanted a way out. He wanted to be caught." Sign turned back to Parker. "This falls bang into the centre of your remit as head of counter-intelligence. Do some snooping for me, will you Colin?"

"So, that's why you approached me, of all people in the service." Parker banged his umbrella on the ground. "You suspected Archer was a double and you decided to use me to get to the truth."

Sign said, "The truth won't bring him back."

"So, what's the point?"

"The point is, there is the slightest possibility that a garbage man is at play."

"A garbage man? What does that mean?"

Sign handed him his business card. "Call me with any developments." He walked off.

CHAPTER 11

Sign stoked the fire in his lounge and poured Knutsen a glass of calvados. "Let me look at your gun."

Knutsen retrieved the weapon from his bedroom.

Sign held it in his hand. "A fine choice. One shot, anywhere in the body, causes massive trauma. It reloads quickly. It rarely malfunctions, providing it's kept clean. And it puts the jeepers into opponents." He laid the gun on a side table. "Drink up. We need to go for a walk. I need to do some late night shopping and could do with company."

They walked across Lambeth Bridge and into the heart of London. Sign explained that he needed to purchase some new brogues. Taking in Regent Street, Oxford Street, the City of London, and Saville Row, they stopped at thirteen shops. In each of them, Sign tried on shoes. It wasn't until they were in the last shop that Sign bought a pair of shoes. They returned on foot to West Square.

Inside, Knutsen rubbed his cold hands and asked, "What was that all about?"

"My previous pair of brogues was getting worn." Sign replenished their glasses. "Plus, I needed to think." He took a swig of the spirit. "We have a limpet."

"What?"

"You and I just walked an anti-surveillance route. The key is to draw any potential followers into a static environment. If they're following, they can't resist entering the static place – in our case shoe shops. Failure to do so could mean they'd lose us out a back door. Key to the technique is convincing the follower that we are oblivious to his presence and have a pattern of behaviour that makes sense. In our case, it was shoe shopping. And even though the route was convoluted, it didn't look suspicious because my pre-planned pattern was to seek out select shoe shops that sold particular brands of shoes. A double sighting of a man or woman is the tell-tale indicator that you're being followed. Tonight we had a limpet – someone who stuck to us. He was good. He changed his jacket three times, put on false glasses, removed false glasses, carried a cigarette, then a vaporiser, twice pretended to be on a mobile phone, different models of course, wore a woollen hat, didn't wear a hat, and never once engaged eye contact with me or you. But he was most certainly following us."

Knutsen was confused. "I've done anti-surveillance. Why didn't I spot him?"

"Because you weren't looking for him or expecting him." He picked up his landline and called Roberts to see if she was okay. She told him that her husband was on the mend and would probably be home later tonight. Sign relayed this update to Knutsen. "The limpet isn't police. I've got no evidence to support that assertion, but I can sniff a spook a mile off. He was western Caucasian, though not Mediterranean or Slavic in appearance, but that says nothing. People's appearances adapt over time. But my hunch is he's British."

"MI5?"

"They have to work in teams because they're so incompetent. And there was no team on our tail. No, this man was MI6."

"Freelance or cadre?"

"Impossible to tell at this stage."

Sign handed Knutsen his gun. "It may be nothing."

"Or something?"

"Yes. MI6 may simply be wishing to keep tabs on us."

"Or maybe Roberts' burglary wasn't random."

"The thought occurred to me." Sign was deep in thought. "Somebody has got wind that we're investigating Archer's death. The route to that is via Roberts' connection to us. Roberts left something compromising at her home, most likely my business card. It wasn't her fault. She didn't want anything that linked her to us being kept in Scotland Yard. I imagine the commissioner instructed her to that effect. The limpet is off the books. That means he's either a deniable agent or he's a retired paramilitary officer. If the former, MI6 has tasked him. If the latter, he's working for someone deeply embedded in MI6."

"Someone who wants to shut mouths?"

"Or someone who wants to open them for their last gasp before the hangman's noose."

"What do you mean?"

Sign didn't answer. "I think we should get a Christmas tree. It is the first of December, after all. Also, I've ordered peacock for the twenty fifth."

"Peacock for Christmas Day?"

"Yes, unless you have anywhere better to go. I wouldn't blame you. But if, like me, you're on your tod then we could have game, celery, plums, roast potatoes, a citrus-cherry sauce, a pud with brandy, and I'd go head to head with you on the Trivial Pursuit board game. I must warn you – I'm superb at geography and history, arts and literature, appalling at science and sport."

Knutsen laughed. "I haven't celebrated Christmas for a long time."

"Nor have I. Too busy being someone else overseas. I have fine vintners in Holborn and elsewhere who can recommend wines to match the peacock."

Knutsen sat and cupped his calvados. "I think we should invite the Roberts."

"Agreed. I'll play host and Santa."

Knutsen chuckled. "You're not like anyone I've ever met."

Sign gave a dismissive gesture with his hand. "One of the first components of being a successful MI6 officer is that we must keep the world off kilter. We must always wrong foot people, usually in a positive way. Secondly, we must believe in the impossible and achieve what others can't. Third, we mustn't give a damn about protocol or what others think." He smiled. "Life's more fun that way. The peacock's from Australia. Inspector Roberts' husband was nearly murdered. You were a highly successful undercover cop. I was tipped to be the next chief of MI6. And yet we are reduced to peacock, a trivial game, and some good plonk. Life doesn't get better than that."

"It doesn't." Knutsen stared at him. "You're lonely."

In a strident voice, Sign replied, "So are you. And the reason we're in this predicament is due to the nature of our jobs. They alienate us from normality. But we crave embracing human norms. Christmas is one of those norms." His voice quietened as he said, "We need to go old school tradecraft when it comes to protecting this flat. Carry your sidearm at all times when leaving the flat. I will rig the door to see if anyone has entered when it's empty. Also, I'll leave misinformation – a draft file containing papers that state that in our opinion there was nothing untoward about Mark Archer's death, another file containing details of a fake new case that we're working on – completely unconnected to MI6 or Archer, and I'll scatter other lies around this room."

"The limpet can't be working alone. He can't watch us 24/7."

"He can't. But my hunch is that he's the only person watching us."

"Why?"

"Because if there was a team on us, he wouldn't have needed to go to all that effort to change his appearance. A team would simply rotate its members, to avoid me getting a double sighting of one of them."

Knutsen weighed his pistol in one hand. "If I kill someone with this I could be sent down for life imprisonment."

"Let's hope it doesn't come down to that." He withdrew a sheet of paper from a stationary cupboard. "However, I have been busy." He handed Knutsen the sheet. "This is from the home secretary. You'll note it is countersigned by the prime minister and the commissioner of the Metropolitan Police. It gives you authority to carry a sidearm. You are able to use the gun only in accordance to the training you received as a cop. Specifically, that means you cannot use the gun unless you are facing someone who has a weapon and is threatening your life or someone else's life. The letter was produced in triplicate." He took the letter off Knutsen, placed it back in the cupboard, and produced one of the copies. "This one I laminated. Whenever you carry your gun, carry this as well. If you're stopped by police or security services who want to know why you're carrying a gun, show them the letter."

"How did you manage to pull this off?!"

Sign smiled. "I may be out of MI6, but I still carry some sway in the corridors of power. Let's leave it at that."

Knutsen folded the letter and placed it in a pocket. "The letter will give me some protection. But, real life situations involving guns can be unpredictable. If I shoot someone who I think is reaching for a gun, but it turns out he's reaching for a knife, I could still face a jury."

"Ah, but that's where I come in. I'm very good at making things seem different to how they are."

"Contaminate a crime scene? Plant evidence?"

Sign's face was mischievous as he said, "Hush now with such crude words. I would protect you from the law. That's all you need to know." He walked to a window and opened the curtain by an inch. "Is the limpet out there? Or has he gone to bed? It's too dark to know. So, there's nothing to be done right now. Tomorrow, I want you to find out when the Archers bought their house in Godalming. It needs a copper's methodology. I don't just want an online land search. I want to know who sold the house, how it was paid for, all details."

"And what will you do?"

"Tomorrow I have a matinee appointment at the Royal Festival Hall to watch the Philharmonic perform Sibelius' Lemminkäinen Suite."

Sarcastically, Knutsen said, "Nice to know you're busy."

"If I have time, I may also take in the Goya exhibition at the National Gallery."

"Jesus! Busy day for you, pal."

Sign smiled. "I'm also hoping to get an answer to something that's been nagging me."

Hilt called Smith at eleven thirty PM. "I'm clocking off. The house is in darkness. I'll be back on it tomorrow."

"Any unusual activity today?"

"No. They went shoe shopping. I followed them."

"Where did they go?"

Hilt gave Smith the details.

"Shit!"

"What's up boss?"

Smith said, "Sign always buys his shoes in one shop in Holborn. He sucked you in to an anti-surveillance route."

"It doesn't matter. He didn't clock me."

Smith exhaled deeply. "You're dealing with one of the finest minds. Not only that, it's a mind that's been superbly trained in our craft. He clocked you."

Hilt asked, "What do you want me to do?"

"Back off Sign and Knutsen. Watch Roberts and wait for my instructions."

CHAPTER 12

Sign was drinking a glass of sparkling water as he sat in the library of his club in St. James's. No one else was in the room. It was lunchtime and a weekend. The few club members who were in the building were dining. Sign tried to read a newspaper, but his eyes were not taking in words. Instead, his mind was racing.

Colin Parker walked into the room and sat in a leather armchair, opposite Sign. The MI6 head of counter-intelligence was wearing a sports jacket, shirt and trousers. The only reason he'd chosen the apparel was so he could conform to the club's dress code. Otherwise, today he'd have been in anything other than the formal attire he needed to wear during the working week. Quietly, he said, "This had better be worth my time. To be here, I had to lie to my wife and tell her that I'd like to take her clothes shopping. I've endured two hours of visiting shop after blasted shop. My frustration and boredom were real, but I made a show of ensuring she could see how agonising the jaunts were. She told me to leave her to browse while I get a drink. We were both relieved. So, I'm here and she's probably buying up half of Oxford Street."

"It's very good of you to come. I know weekends are your precious family time."

Parker checked his mobile phone. "I've got thirty minutes. Then I need to meet my partner in Selfridges."

Sign stood and walked to a trolley that contained tea, coffee, and snacks. He poured Parker a coffee and handed it to him. After sitting back down, Sign asked, "Were you followed here?"

"Impossible to know. It's heaving out there. Not ideal circumstances to run the drills."

"I'm sure. What have you found?"

"I've been through Archer's agent files. All of his reports were cross-checked by security and analysis. There's nothing untoward in any of them."

Sign was still. "You of all people know that files are stories concocted by case officers, to their pleasing. It's the beauty of our job. We go overseas alone, no one is watching over us, we meet our foreign agent, and we write up the contact in a way that makes us look glorious. We lie."

"You never lied, Ben. When things went wrong for you, you told the truth. And when things went unbelievably right for you, you heaped praise on your foreign agents, not you. It's one of the reasons we wanted you to head up the organisation. You were our best operator; but more important, your moral compass was exactly where it should be." Parker bowed his head. "Yes – the files only say what Archer wants us to hear. They're useless. He got intelligence out of his people, no doubt about that, but none of it was remarkable. Low-level shit about troop movements, political posturing, that kind of stuff."

"But there's one thing he couldn't lie about."

Parker frowned, wondering how Sign knew what he had to say. "Yes. Overseas postings. One can't lie about when and where one was deployed. His first posting was under second secretary diplomatic cover to Moscow. Three years later, he returned to London and was put on a year-long Russian language course. He'd told personnel department that he'd got a taste for Russia. Personnel loved that. It was at the time the USSR had imploded and Russia was seen as an unpredictable time bomb. Personnel needed people interested in what happens next with Russia. He was posted back to Moscow as first secretary."

"A prestigious job."

"Yes. Though, a weird thing happened after he'd completed that posting. Archer started messing up. We tried him in a variety of different London-based jobs. He was unremarkable in all of them. So, we thought a change of scenery was required. We gave him the opportunity to be head of station in Pretoria."

"Most people would have snapped up that promotion."

Parker shook his head. "He turned it down and asked to go back to Russia."

"As first secretary?"

"Yes. A sideways move."

Sign nodded. "He needed to be back in the motherland."

"It seems that way." Parker looked at Sign. "I know what you're thinking, but I have no proof that Archer was on the take from the Russians."

"Nor do I, but his suicide speaks volumes." Sign placed his fingertips together. "It's impossible to know for sure when the Russians got their hooks into him. My guess is they used Russian businessmen under the pay of the SVR to get Archer to take money. Probably they told him that he needed an alternate career if ever he decided to leave the diplomatic service. But the money would have been chicken feed. On the second tour, the Russians upped the ante. More money was paid to him. The money would have been for innocuous stuff – consultancy on Norway's position on the latest EU agricultural policy, that kind of thing. Then the businessmen really screwed him. They said they had a major client who wished to deal with him directly. If business came out of that contact, they'd get a ten percent introductory fee and would have no further dealings with Archer. The client wished to do business in the UK but had no idea how to navigate the minefield of our laws and regulations. The client, the businessmen said, was above board and wanted to invest billions in the more impoverished corners of Britain. This would be a huge feather in Archer's cap. But the client turned out to be the SVR. Russian Intelligence had him by the balls and paid him handsomely for the deal. He became their spy."

Parker rubbed his face. "You're speculating and imagining scenarios, but loosely this hangs together. The thing is, Archer was many things, but he wasn't stupid. Over years, he'd have known he was falling into that trap."

"He felt he needed the money." Sign received a call from Knutsen. He listened, thanked him, and hung up. To Parker, he asked, "What were the years of Archer's second posting to Moscow?"

"Two thousand and one to two thousand and four."

Sign ran his finger around the rim of his glass. "I have a bloodhound. He's very good. Today he's ascertained the exact details of the Archers' purchase of their home in Godalming. They bought it for two point four million pounds in two thousand and four."

Blood drained out of Parker's face.

"You should have spotted this, Colin. It's your job."

Parker's hands were sweaty as he said, "I can't spot everyone. We have thousands of staff. And half of them are scattered across the globe. Still," he looked wistful, "yes, it's my job. I should have spotted this."

Sign stood. "Not to worry, dear chap. Archer's dead and the overpriced house is just bricks and mortar that now need constant repairs by a widow who knew exactly what her husband was doing and indeed encouraged him to be a traitor, merely for financial gain." Sign paused. "Let's keep this between ourselves. Someone else in MI6 knew Archer was on the take. I wonder about that person."

"What do you mean?"

Sign said nothing, left the library, and exited the building via the basement kitchen back door.

Through binoculars, John Smith watched a man walk across heath on the Scottish island of Skye. Beyond him, mountains were being caressed by swirling mist. The air was thick with the scent of grass and other flora. The man was alone; the nearest habitation was five miles away. The man was carrying a shotgun and was oblivious to the fact that he was being observed. He was probably hunting woodcock or grouse. Smith didn't know or care. Smith was wearing a yellow waterproof jacket, with hood on. From one hundred yards away, he waved his hand and shouted at the man.

The man stopped, un-cocked his shotgun, opened the barrel, and cradled his weapon.

Smith ran to him, a smile on his face, rain cascading off his garments. "Sir, can you help me?"

The man was stock still as he eyed him with suspicion.

Smith got closer. "Car's broken down. Where can I get help?" Smith was thirty yards away.

The man gestured to an escarpment. "Get back on the road, walk six miles west, Eddy's got a garage, he'll help you."

Smith walked right up to the man and pulled down his hood.

The man looked shocked. "You! What are you doing here?"

Smith smiled. "Hello Arthur."

Arthur Lake slammed shut his shotgun barrel.

Smith said, "I need to talk to you."

"Can't it wait? I've got another week off before I'm back at The Office." Lake was head of an operational MI6 team in London. It was likely he'd soon be promoted to the organisation's board of directors. His previous overseas postings had been to Paris, Warsaw, Mexico City, and Washington. He was a rising star, considered by most intelligence officers to have an impeccable career.

Smith thought otherwise. "Is there anywhere dry we can go? I'd kill for a coffee."

They walked to the cottage Lake had rented for his hunting holiday. Inside the isolated one-bedroom stone house, Lake put his shotgun on the kitchen table and flicked on the kettle. Out of the slow cook segment of the Aga, the aroma of venison stew permeated the room. Peeled spuds were in a pan on the hob, waiting to be boiled this evening. Carrots and wild mushrooms were in a bowl adjacent to the oven. Lake hanged his sodden jacket on a coat rack that also contained anti-midge mesh smocks, camouflage jackets and trousers, and a six-foot walking stick with a ram's horn.

Smith sat at the kitchen table. "Is it your first time on Skye?"

Lake made no effort to hide the irritation in his voice. "I come here every year. It clears my head."

"How are the wife and kids?"

"What's this about?"

"I was passing by and fancied a chat."

"Bullshit." Lake handed him a mug and sat opposite Smith. The shotgun was between them. "Is there a crisis in HQ?"

Smith smiled. "I'm sorry to have intruded on your solitude. This won't take long." He wrapped his hands around the mug to take the chill out of his fingers. "There is an immediate crisis."

"What?"

"You."

Lake frowned. "You've come a long way if it's just to tell me that I'm no longer being considered for the appointment of director."

"Oh, it's nothing like that. As far as I know, you'll get the appointment next autumn."

"Has something happened to one of my team members, or one of their agents?"

"This is nothing to do with anyone under your control. It's to do with Washington."

Lake was about to drink his coffee. He lowered his mug. "Washington?"

"To be precise, your posting there in two thousand and nine."

"I don't understand."

"Actually, you partially don't". Smith drank his coffee. "You made a deal with the Americans. The CIA to be precise. They and you wanted to bring the so-called special relationship even closer. To do so, the Americans wanted you to plant rose-tinted intelligence into MI6 HQ. They wanted to be seen as a conjoined twin with MI6, thereby giving them complete access to our top agents."

"Now hold on a minute!"

Smith held up his hand. His voice was steady and calm as he added, "In itself, that's not a major sin. You were simply being asked by the Yanks to play spin doctor; be a de facto ambassador for them; promote the cause, and all that. It happens a lot. We've all been there – making judgements on our own when liaising with foreign intelligence organisations. Sometimes we overstep the line by the standards of the rule book, but the rule book is open to interpretation, isn't it?"

"You can drive a bus through the rule book."

"Precisely. So, no high treason there. Just a slap on the wrist. What did the CIA promise you in return?"

"It was just diplomacy."

"What did they promise you?" Smith repeated.

Lake sighed. "You know what it's like at this level. It's not just about support within MI6. As crucial is support from allies."

"If you want to get up the ladder. Yes." Smith ran a finger along the length of the shotgun barrel. "Excellent relations with the Americans, French, Germans, Canadians, Australians, and New Zealanders are crucial when one is being considered for a board level appointment. One person can't have all of that. So the board is put together like a jigsaw, each board member bringing an ally to the table. You'll bring the Americans."

Lake shouted, "And that's a damn good thing!"

"I didn't say it wasn't. But the process of getting there is pertinent."

"Meaning?"

Smith said, "When you were head of Washington Station, you cultivated the Americans, and they cultivated you. It was mutual. You knew what they wanted; they knew what you wanted. Your interests were selfish but they never compromised UK national interest. You trod a fine line, but the end game was sound. Relations with the Americans always ebb and flow. At the time you were in Washington, we were in an ebb. We need their intelligence as much as they need ours. You knew that. You tried to build bridges."

"How do you know all this?"

Smith didn't answer. "The CIA should be delighted when you're appointed to the board. So will MI6. You'll have brought a temperamental mistress back to bed so that you can make love to her."

Lake laughed. "That's one way to look at it."

"But, it's not the only way, because we have a problem."

Lake put his hands flat on the table. "I did nothing wrong. Yes, I bent a few rules. But the endgame was crucial. Still is."

"Ah, but you didn't factor in the possibility that you might be taken for an idiot."

"How dare you. Just because of who you are…"

"Yes, yes, And all that." Smith's tone was blasé. It steeled as he asked, "How are your wife and kids?"

"None of your damn business!"

"Toby and Ella are at the Cotswold School. It's one of the top ten schools in the country. You should be proud."

Lake didn't reply.

"And your loving wife is an entrepreneur, carving a cottage industry living from making bespoke perfumes. She'd be heartbroken if she knew you'd had an affair with a CIA officer called Frédérique Dubois."

"I didn't have an affair!"

"Yes you did!" Smith lowered his voice. "She was your CIA case officer."

"Liaison officer!"

"Call it what you will. You were told by the CIA only to speak to her. The duration of the affair was four days, within which you used her as much as she used you. Both of you understood the game. Frédérique Dubois is an interesting name."

Lake put his head in his hands. "She was from Michigan. Her family were Muskrat French."

Smith nodded. "Descendants of habitants, voyageurs and coureurs des bois in the Pays d'en Haut. It's a good cover for a French DGSE intelligence officer."

"What?!"

Smith swirled his coffee. "See, here's the thing. The woman you fucked moved on to pastures new. She turned up in England. She tried her tricks but we were wise to that and had her arrested. Right now she's in high security detention in Paddington Police Station. Soon, she'll be moved to one our UK black sites where we'll put the thumb screws on her. Frédérique is in fact Marceline Collobert. The French knew Frédérique was due to meet you. Probably they had that information via surveillance. They had Frédérique killed and dumped in a quarry. The Americans have only just discovered her body and put two and two together, with our help. Marceline was deployed against you, pretending to be Frédérique. You fell for it and thought you were talking to the Americans. Instead, you were informing the French about Britain's economic policies towards Europe, our military strategy against Syria, which UK politicians were in the ascendency, and ultimately whether we favoured France over America. Marceline has told us everything about you. She has more to say about the wider picture and we'll work that out of her. She was a Mata Hari, and you couldn't keep your dick in your pants."

Lake was incredulous. "I… I had no idea."

"You were trained to second guess! How could you have let this happen?"

Smith whispered, "If you try to defend your actions, your career will be ruined, you'll face imprisonment, your wife will divorce you, your children will be taken into protective custody, and they and your wife will suffer public humiliation from the press."

Lake started crying. "I had no idea. I had no fucking idea."

"I'm sure. But your actions have put Britain in a pickle with our European partners."

"Why are you here? Why not just send the cops and MI5 to arrest me?"

Smith touched his hand. "You have to think about your wife and children. They're all that matters now. A hearing and court trial – public or behind closed doors – will spew out everything you've done. You'll be a ruined man. I assure you that you'll have not one waking day left on this planet without feeling the weight of a cannon ball in your skull. You'll hate yourself. You'll miss seeing your kids grow up. You'll wonder how they are. They'll be confused at first, then they'll hate you. Your wife will ensure that. And she'll remarry. You will no longer be a father and husband. The world will think you're a traitor. France will think you're a fool. It fucked you. There's nothing Britain can do about that. We like France. You're a pawn. And a spent one at that. Marceline will die in prison. She never liked you, let alone loved you. She's gone." Smith stood. "There is only one way out. Nip this in the bud before the judiciary gets its hands on you. You have two hours to think it through before I call in the hounds."

Smith left and walked across the moor to his hire car. He needed to be back in London this evening.

Thirty minutes later, Lake placed the barrel of his shotgun into his mouth. His face was blotched, sweaty and covered in tears. His hands were trembling. He didn't want to do it, but Smith's words kept pounding his brain. Smith was right; there was no other way. He wanted to think something profound – anything about his kids, wife, job, youth. Anything. But all he felt was the pressure of massive depression. And it was unstoppable. His life was now useless and pointless. He couldn't bear the thought of his family being dragged through the muck because of him. But more important, he felt like scum. All the good times seemed like a distant memory – chatting up girls when at Trinity, a boozy and fun holiday in Ibiza when he was in his early twenties, being awarded a prize at school for his prowess in chemistry, catching crabs in rock pools with his dad, his mum making a Sunday roast every week because he loved the food and it tempered the feeling of angst about going to school the next morning, playing dragon hunt with his mates in the playground at nursery. None of it felt real now.

He sucked in deeply, the acrid taste of cordite hitting his nostrils.

He pulled the trigger and blew his brains out.

CHAPTER 13

Inspector Roberts pressed the door buzzer in West Square. It was five PM. Light was fading. Knutsen was at home. Sign wasn't. Knutsen ushered her in to the flat.

"When's Ben home?"

Knutsen looked at a seventeenth century German clock that had been given to Sign by one of his Iranian agents. Sign had arranged for the agent to escape Iran after his cover was blown. Sign had put him on a boat in Bandar Abbas and had helped the skipper – a Moroccan smuggler – sail the boat to Muscat. "He's due back anytime. I'll get the fire going. Blinking cold out there today."

Roberts sat in one of the armchairs and watched Knutsen assemble and ignite the fire. "How are you getting on with Sign?"

Knutsen laughed as he rubbed coal dust off his hands. "I've never met anyone like him before. He comes from a working class background but speaks like royalty. I've heard him on the phone to people. I'm no good at languages and accents, but I reckon he was speaking Chinese, Russian, Spanish, French, German, and in one instance English in a Geordie accent."

"He needs to be who he needs to be on any given occasion. But who is he really?"

Knutsen shook his head. "I reckon it will take me a lifetime to answer that question."

Sign walked into the room. "Mrs. Roberts. An unexpected but lovely surprise. Will you be staying for supper?" He put a bag on a table. "Sibelius' interpretation of Finnish life has invigorated me. This evening I stopped off at a trusted fishmonger and butcher and purchased some excellent herring and hare. One will be the starter; the other the main course."

The suggestion sounded intriguing. But Roberts needed to be home for dinner with her husband. She said, "Another time. I'm here for two reasons."

Sign slumped onto his chaise lounge. "One of those reasons will be to enquire about our research into Archer's death. The other will be to do with something bad, though the variables of what that might be are too vast to speculate on a specific."

"Archer."

"He was taking money from the Russians in exchange for supplying Western secrets. His wife supported this arrangement. Guilt overwhelmed him. He ended his life rather than furthering his duplicity. But..."

"But?"

"I suspect a trigger is at play, though have no evidence to support that theory."

"A trigger?"

Sign placed the tips of his fingers together. "When one is in an unhappy marriage, frequently one sticks one's head in the sand and hopes for the best. Things will muddle through - that kind of mentality. Then one day that person goes out for a drink with his or her pals. They have a gallon of booze and pluck up the courage to tell him or her to divorce the bitch or bastard. Usually, the unhappy person ignores the advice, though recognises its truth. It eats at the person. And sometimes the person wakes up and decides that he or she can't ignore the descent into Hell any longer. The person takes action. Foul words, violence, and divorce are common results."

"So, somebody triggered Archer's death?"

"Yes, but not a pal, or a bitch, or a bastard. This is somebody very clever. Somebody went up to the horse's nose and made it think differently."

"But as you say, you have no evidence of that."

"I do have my experience. When I asked Mrs. Archer if someone had visited her home prior to her husband's death, she lied and said no one had visited." Sign leaped off the chair. "I can smell a liar by looking at their face and listening to their voice." He chucked logs onto the fire. "What is the second reason you're here?"

"Do you know Arthur Lake? Our records show that he's a diplomat in the Foreign & Commonwealth Office."

"Why do you enquire about Lake?"

"He killed himself this morning. He was alone in a holiday cottage in Skye. His wife and children remained at home in London. My colleagues informed her of the death. She is devastated and can't give any reason why he would have taken his life."

"What else did she say?"

Roberts said, "She asked if he was killed. She said that her husband had been living a lie for decades. He wasn't a diplomat. He was MI6."

Sign nodded. "Lake was a high flyer in MI6. How did he kill himself?"

"Shotgun in the mouth."

"He was on a hunting holiday?"

"According to the owner of the holiday let, he went there every year to shoot game."

Knutsen asked, "Have forensics been to the scene?"

"Local police were reluctant to deploy forensics. But as soon as I heard Lake was MI6, I called in some favours. They flew over a couple of specialists and a detective from Inverness. The cottage has been thoroughly examined. So too, Lake's corpse and the gun. There's no doubt he killed himself."

Sign said, "Because…"

Knutsen finished what Sign was about to say. "Blood, brain matter, and bone fragments were on the ceiling, meaning the gun was pointing upwards. Cordite residue is in his mouth. The gun could have been forced into his mouth to make it look like a fake suicide, but that would mean he'd have had to have been restrained. Forensics would have looked for rope fibres, bruising from handcuffs, maybe even traces of some kind of head brace that would have locked him still when the gun was put in his mouth. They found nothing, correct?"

"Correct." Roberts looked at Sign. "Why would he take his life?"

"I don't know." Sign sat down and rubbed his eyes. "Our paths crossed a few times, but that's the extent of our contact." To himself, he said, "Come on Sign. Think. Think." He looked at Roberts. "I'm not aware of any chinks in his armour. He liked a beer at lunchtime, but only half a glass. He had an eye for the ladies, but only an eye as far as I'm aware. He was a devout Catholic and regularly attended church when he could. He had no enemies in The Office. He was the perfect example of someone who could make it to the top – a grey man who happened to be a superb operator. But, I'm missing something. Where is his body?"

"In a morgue in Inverness. It will be flown back to London once the inquest is closed in a day or so."

To Knutsen, Sign said, "That's too long. Check out the next available flight to Skye. You and I need to take a trip."

Knutsen used his mobile phone to check flights. "Eight AM tomorrow. Flight to Edinburgh, then we get a small propeller plane to Skye. We land at eleven thirty. I'll arrange for a hire car."

"Excellent. Make the bookings." Sign said to Roberts, "I'm certain that I won't find anything that contradicts your Scottish colleagues' findings. But I want to pursue my theory. This one's tougher. There's no lying wife in play."

"Your theory being the trigger for his suicide?"

"A man. A horse whisperer. Someone who talked to Archer and Lake and persuaded them to kill themselves."

Roberts replied, "It's just a theory. I'm not sure how long my boss will give you slack."

"Mrs. Roberts – in my career, not one senior MI6 officer has committed suicide. Yet, within less than a week, two have. It could be an anomaly. Or they could be connected. Ultimately, we could be dealing with murder."

Roberts was angry. "We know for a fact that Archer and Lake committed suicide!"

Sign's voice was quiet as he said, "Murder can take many guises. An MI6 officer can kill people with words. How is your husband?"

"Can we get back to business? He's fine. Thanks for asking."

"Good. Now, inspector, you are plummeting into a world that is hard to comprehend. But, with your permission, I'm giving you a portal into that landscape. We could be dealing with someone who is killing people by blackmailing them. And he's doing so with merely the power of suggestion."

"A serial killer?"

"Time will tell." Sign stared at nothing. "I wonder, I do wonder, if my theory is right. Is someone getting rid of people? If so, are they in his way? Or is he clearing up a mess? Maybe it's a combination of the two."

"Maybe there is no person. But if there is, maybe it's a woman."

Sign agreed. "I'm not discounting any possibility. If there is a person – a trigger, horse whisperer, garbage man; my labels but slap whatever label you like on the person – the person could be male or female, black, white, Asian, a UK national, or a foreign national. I'm using the gender 'he' as shorthand. But I have a feeling that he's a man and he's British."

"If he exists."

"Indeed." Sign walked to one of the windows and partially opened the curtain. He wondered if the limpet was out there. He closed the curtain. "We must brace ourselves for the possibility of more deaths of MI6 officers."

Roberts checked the time. "I need to head home."

Sign clapped his hands. "Do me a favour. Call your esteemed Scottish friends and ask them to check the UK flight rosters to any port in Scotland during the preceding twenty four hours leading up to Lake's death. Also, ferry tickets to Skye. I need names."

"You think the whisperer will be one of those names?"

Sign picked up Roberts' coat and handed it to her. "I'm most interested to know if he's not on any roster. That would make him invisible and highly trained."

The following morning Sign and Knutsen were in Skye. As Knutsen drove, snow was heavy. "Never been here before," he said, "and I'm not sure I want to be stranded."

Sign glanced at the SatNav. "Four miles to go. Can you keep the car on the road until we reach our destination?"

"I've done the advanced driving course."

"I've done a variation of that, refined to be offensive and defensive driving in hot and cold climes. Let me know if you want me to take over driving duties."

"No. You're okay."

Sign smiled. "It's a shame about the snow."

"What were you hoping to do? Trace footprints with a magnifying glass?"

"No. It just changes the image of the place. I wanted to see it how Lake saw it when he died."

"You want to get in his head?"

Sign didn't answer.

Fifteen minutes later, Knutsen drove the hire car off the road and down a track that led to the cottage where Lake had taken his life. A four wheel drive vehicle was parked outside the property. Knutsen stopped his vehicle next to the SUV. A Scottish man got out of the vehicle at the same time Knutsen and Sign disembarked.

The Scot said, "Mr. Knutsen?"

"That'll be me."

The middle aged man shook hands with Knutsen. "Spider McCloud. I'm the estate ghillie. My boss said you're with the police."

Knutsen nodded.

"Come in then, but don't take too long. Weather's closing in. You'll need to get a flight back before they close the airport." McCloud unlocked the front door and led them in.

Sign looked at the kitchen floor and ceiling. "He was sitting at the kitchen table when he pulled the trigger?"

McCloud answered, "Yes. I was the one who found him. We had new guests due to arrive and I needed to check everything was in order in the cottage. He was on his back on the floor, chair underneath him, shotgun still in his mouth. It was a right mess."

"Who owns the shotgun?"

"The estate. We're licensed firearms owners. And we're only allowed to lease shotguns to people who have licenses from the British authorities. Each year we thoroughly checked Mr. Lake's permit to see it was up to date and in order." McCloud sounded hostile as he added, "We're a professional bunch here, mister. It would cost us our livelihood if we bent rules."

"We don't doubt that." Knutsen looked at the large amount of bloodstains. "My goodness. It must have been a horrific sight for you to confront."

McCloud shrugged. "I shoot deer in season, string them up, gut them, and butcher them for sale in Skye. I've seen worse than a man's head blown off. Plus, I was in the Royal Scots Dragoon Guards in the first Gulf War. In '91 I was deployed in the 7th Armoured Brigade. I've witnessed what rockets and grenades can do to the insides of an armoured vehicle containing my pals. Still," McCloud hesitated, "that was a while back. Deer I can handle. They need to be culled to keep numbers to a manageable level. Otherwise, whole herds will die. But human bodies? I thought I'd left that life twenty five years ago."

"Sir, you are a brave man." Sign examined the floor. "You found him. What happened next?"

"I called 999. Two local police officers turned up. I know them well. They're nice lads, but too young to see stuff like this. Robbie threw up; Angus nearly fainted. But they manned-up. They put police tape around the house. Two hours later my boss called me and told me to stay here. Specialist police were coming from Inverness, he told me. When they arrived, they took my finger and boot prints. After that, they asked me to leave. Two hours later, they called me and said that the body had been removed and there were no suspicious circumstances surrounding Mr. Lake's death. I came back to the cottage and cleared up the mess as best I could. But," he pointed at the floor and ceiling, "I can't get rid of the stains. I've got professional cleaners and painters and decorators arriving this afternoon to deal with the rest. The next guests are arriving tomorrow. We can't cancel them. This time of year, the estate needs any cash it can get."

"Of course." Knutsen asked, "Were there any other boot or fingerprints that were unusual?"

McCloud laughed. "We don't take prints of our guests when they arrive. Anyway, you're the police. You should know what was and wasn't found."

Sign snapped, "We're specialist police. We've been asked to look at the suicide with fresh eyes. That requires us not to know details of what forensics found." He looked around the kitchen. "Aside from the mess that you discovered, was there anything that struck you as unusual in the room?"

McCloud rubbed his stubbly face. "Mr. Lake had venison stew on the go. And there were a brace of grouse and one woodcock hanging on the meat hook next to the Aga. They were fresh, caught that morning. I thought it was odd that a man who was going to kill himself would be preparing at least four days' worth of food. I took the birds and gave them to my wife. The stew I put in the bin."

Sign said, "In remote and interconnected parts of the world such as these, trusted men like you are paid to keep an eye on matters. On the day of Lake's death, did you see any vehicles go to the cottage?"

"I can't be in one place all the time. I have my rounds to do. Before coming to the cottage, I had to repair a fence, drive to Portree to get some food and cigarettes, and put turnips and other meal down for the deer. This time of year we don't kill deer; we feed them. They come down from the mountains because there's nothing to eat there in winter. I protect them now; I kill some of them in the warmer months. But they know me. I'm probably the only one around here who can feed them by hand. We're a family. No, I didn't see any visitors to the cottage. But I wasn't watching the cottage."

"Was Lake any different in demeanour compared to his last trips here?" Sign elaborated. "In other words, when you greeted him on arrival, did he seem different?"

"No. He always struck me as a private man who wanted a spot of solitude. He asked me about hunting and where were the best places to bag some game. If you ask me, he looked very happy to be here."

"Thank you very much, Mr. McCloud. You've been a great help."

McCloud checked his watch. "I need to check the upstairs boiler. It's been playing up lately. Is there anything else you need me for?"

"No. Carry on with your chores. We'll be here for five or ten minutes, then we'll take your sage advice and be on our way before the weather closes in." When McCloud was gone, Sign said to Knutsen, "Sit opposite me at the table."

Knutsen did so, wondering what this was about.

Sign grabbed a fire poker that was the length of his arm and placed it on the table. He sat. The poker was between them. "Imagine I'm Lake. Imagine you want me to kill myself. Imagine the poker is the shotgun. What would you say to me to ensure I put a gun in my mouth and blew my brains out?"

"I'd have to know your secrets; ones that you were deeply ashamed about. I'd confront you with those secrets to push you over the edge."

"That's half of the equation. When I was a youngster in MI6 I had a controller who was as wise as they come. And he'd been several times around the block in the Cold War. There was nothing he hadn't seen. He told me that if ever I fucked up and it came to the attention of a hostile foreign intelligence agency who tried to use my fuck up as blackmail against me, tell them 'publish and be damned'. It was sage advice. I'm bullet proof. Archer and Lake were not. But to know they were not requires an in depth understanding of their psyches. The whisperer knew exactly which buttons to press. He knew how to torture them."

"In plain speak, he knew them in person."

"Yes."

Knutsen inhaled deeply. "Ben – you could be so wrong about this. I know it's a massive coincidence that two MI6 officers killed themselves in the space of a week, but coincidences…"

"Are coincidences." Sign picked up the poker and put the tip into his mouth. "Boom." He put the poker back onto the table. "Archer ended his life in a haze of booze and drugs. It was still hard to do, but it's effective because not only does it shut down the body, it also makes the brain no longer care. But suicide by more immediate actions are incredibly exhausting. I've read about samurai who couldn't go through with committing harikari. They were dishonoured as a result, though cared for by the women folk in the tribe. The samurais would sleep for up to three days after sitting cross legged with a blade against their stomachs. It is that debilitating. Lake would have been in mental agony as he held the gun. And yet he still pulled the trigger. And we know that he hadn't planned to blow his head off. Food was prepared by him, he was out on a healthy walk and hunt in the morning, this cottage is his safe place once a year, and he has a loving wife and children."

"As far as we know."

Sign lowered his head. "I know his wife. She adores her husband."

"That could be the trigger."

"Adulation?" Sign replaced the poker next to the fire and gazed at the stunning mountain scenery outside. "The thought had occurred to me. There is nothing more beautiful than a person loving you unconditionally. It is rare, but in some cases it can breed a desire to stray from the path. It is possible that Lake had an affair."

"He felt claustrophobic?"

"No, he sought danger. It's an act of rebellion. He knew how good his wife is; therefore he wanted to taste a woman who was different."

"That sounds messed up."

"It is." Sign washed his hands in the sink. "I have an insider in MI6, but I doubt he'd find the glitch in Lake's history. So, infidelity is but one possibility. But actually the reason doesn't matter. What does is whether someone else knew exactly what would prompt him to put a gun to his head."

"What would you do if you were the whisperer?"

Sign smiled. "You don't want my mind in that space. Nobody does. It wouldn't be pleasant."

"Let me correct my question." Knutsen clasped his fingers on the table. "How would you kill me?"

"I'd tell you things."

"Such as?"

"Such as things I don't want to speak about." Sign's smile was the most glowing example of empathy. "Dear sir: you are the finest man. But to become that, we have to trip along the way."

"Such as executing a man because I fancied a bird who'd been clipped by that man."

"Clever use of language." Sign picked up the pot that had yesterday contained venison. "There are two breeds of man: those that solely care about themselves, and those who don't give a shit about themselves. You and I fall into the latter category. We look outwards, not inwards. We are the *publish and be damned* types. I couldn't kill you with words. Ditto, you couldn't kill me with blackmail. Basically, we don't care about any indiscretions. We just get on with the job in hand."

"And do you have any indiscretions?"

Sign waited five seconds before answering in a quiet voice. "Like you, I've killed people. I've screwed male and female brains. I've played chess on an international stage and at the highest stakes. And I've had to watch friends die. Friends from all over the world. All of that will stay with me for the rest of my life. But it can't be used against me. It is personal business. My business. If anyone tries to throw it against me I'll put a knife to their throat, and it won't be a bluff. Then I'd carry on with my life. My wife is always in my heart. I will never have another woman. She was the best. *Indiscretions* is the wrong word. *Bollocks to it all* is the right response if ever one doubts oneself. If Archer and Lake had fixed that phrase into their heads, they'd still be alive."

McCloud came downstairs rubbing his arms with a rag. "Boiler's sorted. Bloody thing hates the cold. I need to lock up, if you're finished here?"

"We're done." Sign winked at Knutsen. "We have to trade untamed beauty for a metropolitan bee hive. I know where I'd rather be. But work beckons. London it is."

CHAPTER 14

It was dark and rain was pounding the street in Weybridge. Hilt didn't care. He loved being wet. It was one of the many reasons that had got him through the hellish selection into the Special Boat Service and the resultant continuation training. In the course of his career in special forces and MI6, he'd spent nearly as much time in water as on dry land. And some of those waters had been icy oceans in January. He rang Smith. "Roberts is at home with her husband. There's no point me watching her tonight, unless you have specific instructions."

"No. Stay on her tomorrow. Any news on Sign?"

"He's got a guy called Tom Knutsen living with him. Knutsen's ex-Met police. But he's unusual – spent most of his career undercover. He resigned after executing a criminal."

"How do you know this?"

"Don't ask, don't tell. But I will say I have sources and techniques." Hilt walked away from the Roberts' property. "No doubt, Knutsen has gone into business with Sign. They're using their West Square flat as their base of operations."

"And Knutsen is down on his luck with cash, so Sign suggested he move in to the spare room. I'd have done the same, though God knows how Knutsen is putting up with Sign. Ben has so many brilliant facets, but he does tend to carve the world to his choosing." Smith was silent for a few seconds. "Knutsen was chosen by Sign to be his right-hand man. How old is he?"

"I'd estimate mid-thirties."

"Nearly fifteen years younger than Sign. Age is important. Sign wanted a younger business partner in case he needed to deploy him against men like you."

Hilt smiled. "I can deal with an undercover cop, with my right arm tied behind my back."

Smith's tone was icy as he said, "Ordinarily, yes. But consider this: Sign decides to set up business as a security consultant; Sign wants a shooter with a brain to help him run the business; he'd have tapped his contacts from his MI6 days to see who might qualify; he'd have been presented with candidates from MI6, MI5, SAS, and your old bunch. And yet he chose an undercover cop."

"He saw something different in Knutsen?"

"He saw something unconventional; someone who'd look at things differently compared to those who serve in spec ops, and someone…" Smith's mind tried to fill in the gaps. "Perhaps someone who'd lost someone."

"Like Sign and his wife?"

"Yes. Sign never makes mistakes when it comes to the people he works with. There's something unusual about Knutsen. Quite what it is, we don't know. But that doesn't matter. What does is he's proven he can be an executioner."

"Leave that to me. He won't know what hit him if he has a pop." Hilt got into his car. He was hoping to have a beer or two at home, watch *University Challenge* on BBCi catch up, before hitting the sack. Tomorrow he'd be up at six to watch Roberts. "Something else I've got to tell you. Roberts visited West Square yesterday evening. This morning, I watched Sign and Knutsen go to Heathrow airport."

"You were supposed to stay on Roberts!"

"Well, I decided to ignore you. I followed my gut. But what I didn't ignore from you is the certainty that I'd get sucked into an anti-surveillance choke hold if I got too close. So I used binos and a zoom lens camera. Sign and Knutsen got on a plane to Edinburgh."

Smith said nothing.

"Don't know why they went there."

"They went there to get an interconnecting flight to the Isle of Skye." Smith had anticipated this, but still the information was unsettling. In an authoritative voice, he said, "There is a tragedy in Skye that peaks Roberts' interest. She's continuing to liaise with Sign on matters that relate to matters that relate to me."

"Why don't you tell me what's going on?"

"That wasn't part of the deal." Smith added, "I want you to do something for me. It won't be pleasant. But it will be a puzzling message."

"What?"

Smith told him exactly what to do. Hilt had no problems with the instruction, even though he'd miss his favourite TV show.

Sign and Knutsen arrived back in West Square. Sign had barely spoken during the flights back to London. He was preoccupied and deep in thought.

Knutsen made a fire and asked, "What shall we have for dinner tonight?"

Sign was in his armchair. He looked up. "I'm sorry. I've been a tad distracted and hadn't thought about food. That's remiss of me. I'll put my coat on and nip out to the butcher and my vintner and pick us up two partridge and a bottle of Perdrix aux Choux."

Knutsen patted him on the shoulder. "It's time you let your brain rest. I'll order a Chinese takeaway."

Sign's voice was distant as he said, "Chinese food? Yes, I've had that many times – in Hong Kong, Beijing, Chengdu, and Xi'an, among many places in China. But I've not eaten it here."

"It will be different. You can thank the Americans for that. But at least it will allow you to rest."

Fifty minutes later, Knutsen handed Sign a plate containing Peking duck, pancakes, cucumber, and a soy sauce. Both men ate in silence in front of the fire, their plates on their laps.

When he'd finished eating, Sign said, "In 1995, I saw a Mongolian man attempt to ride his camel up a mountain in China. It was for a bet he'd made with four Chinese men. They thought he wouldn't make the summit. They were partially right. The camel dropped from exhaustion halfway up. The Mongolian man felt he had no choice other than to put his beloved beast out of its misery. He shot it dead, then carried on climbing. He reached the summit. We witnessed his achievement through telescopes. He descended and demanded payment for winning the bet. The Chinese men tried to argue with him, saying his camel failed him. But the Mongolian man stood his ground and said the bet was about him, not the camel. The Chinese men pulled out knives. I pulled a gun out and told them to pay up."

Knutsen laughed. "Is there *anything* in your life that is normal?"

"I suppose not." Sign chuckled, clapped his hands and said in a strong tone, "The Peking duck has reinvigorated me. There's a pub within walking distance that serves excellent real ales. What say you to a couple of jars and a game of darts?"

Hilt donned a black wig, glasses that had fake lenses, and a high vis jacket with the logo 'DHL'. He carried a small cardboard box within which were stones he'd picked up from a residential driveway. He walked down the street and rang the Roberts' doorbell. Given it was nine PM, cold, and dark, he expected Mr. Roberts to answer the door. Instead, it was Katy Roberts.

"Yes?" she said.

Hilt put on a Romanian accent. "I have a package for Elliot Roberts. It needs to be signed for."

Katy yawned. "Okay. I'll sign it." She held out her hand.

"No. It can only be Mr. Roberts. I'm under strict instructions and will get in trouble if he doesn't sign." He looked at the box. "It has a government stamp on here. Maybe passport? Bit too heavy for that, though. But it must be something important."

Katy was irritated. "My husband's in bed. He's not feeling well. Leave it at the local post office. He can collect the parcel tomorrow."

Hilt dropped his false accent. "Okay missy." He barged past her, withdrew a silenced pistol, and entered the house.

Katy screamed and tried to grab him. Hilt punched her with sufficient force to break her nose and slam her unconscious against the corridor wall. He walked upstairs. In the bedroom, he saw Elliot Roberts sitting upright in bed, a bedside light on. He was reading a book. Roberts' mouth opened wide as he saw Hilt standing in the entrance, pointing his gun at him.

Hilt said, "Night, night," and pulled the trigger twice. The bullets ended Elliot Roberts' life.

Hilt walked downstairs. He grabbed Katy Roberts' jaw and slapped her on the face. "Time to wake up." He had to repeat the action several times.

Five minutes later, she moaned, opened her eyes, looked horrified when she saw who was in front of her, and lashed out with her legs.

Hilt ignored the blows. "Nah, love. That's not going to do it."

Blood from her nose was drooling down her lower face. She spoke, despite the movement of her mouth causing agonising bolts of pain in her head. "What do you want? Money? Me?" She sucked in air and looked at Hilt with defiance in her expression. "You've been here before, haven't you? Bastard! Your DNA will be all over this house. We'll get you."

"We, Inspector Roberts? You haven't got any pals in your house tonight. And my DNA doesn't exist." Hilt's grip on Roberts' jaw tightened as he put his face close to her face. "Listen carefully, sweetheart. I've just made a delivery. It's upstairs. It might not be your kind of thing, but I don't care. I'm just the messenger. What I do care about is national security. You're interfering in that. Go back to PC Plod work. Zero contact with Sign and Knutsen. It's your choice, darling. But just remember – I can find you anywhere on this planet."

He slammed her head against the wall and left.

It was just after ten PM. The Metropolitan Police Commissioner was in the A&E reception of St. Thomas' Hospital. Britain's most senior police officer was unshaven and wearing jeans, boots, and a Christmas jumper depicting reindeer and snow. The jumper had been given to him by his children as part of their attempts to get him into the festive spirit. When he'd got the call about Katy Roberts, he hadn't thought to change. He just came straight over to the hospital. Given it was a Friday night, most of the people around him were injured drunks. The place stank of booze and disinfectant. Knutsen and Sign strode in and shook hands with the commissioner.

Knutsen asked, "How is she?"

"Mild concussion. Her nose needs realigning. But otherwise she'll live." The commissioner rubbed his eyes. "I've talked to her. She told me exactly what happened. When she came to, she found her husband. The doctors aren't worried about her physical health. But they are worried about depression… grief, call it what you want."

The men sat opposite him. Sign asked, "Was this a message?"

"Yes. To you. Back off or she dies."

Sign and Knutsen glanced at each other.

Sign asked, "What's your recommended course of action?"

The commissioner looked directly at Sign. "Last time I checked, Ben Sign is above the law. Rumour had it that I might be way down the ladder from you. That didn't happen. You resigned from your organisation."

"Rumour is a temperamental mistress." Sign showed the commissioner the palms of his hands. "Sir, I am now simply a humble civilian."

"Technically you are. But I know that you know people and stuff that's way beyond my pay grade." The commissioner sighed. "What happened to Katy?"

Sign pointed to Knutsen while keeping his eyes on the commissioner. "Who was Knutsen to you?"

The commissioner frowned. "A brilliant cop. Excelled in undercover work. The jobs he did would have broken most men. But he survived… until the end."

Sign nodded. "He was the man you sent in to do the laundry. We're dealing with a very similar man. He won't be law enforcement or a criminal. He will be paramilitary – probably ex-special forces, trained by men with my qualifications."

The commissioner glanced around, worried that the conversation might be overheard by the drunks in the room. "Formerly your lot?"

"Could be. But he could also be Mossad, Spetsnaz, SVR, FSB, DGSCE, BND et cetera. The list goes on."

"Katy said he spoke with a London accent."

Knutsen interjected. "I've heard Sign speak with a South African accent."

The commissioner stood. "Let's speak somewhere more privately." He gestured to the back of the waiting room. "I've got two of my best firearms officers in Katy's room. They'll kill anyone who shouldn't be in her room."

Outside the hospital, the commissioner stood in front of a placard saying 'Smoking Is Strictly Prohibited In The Hospital Grounds'. He lit a cigarette. Sign and Knutsen were with him. No one else was nearby. The commissioner said, "I authorized you to investigate the suicide of Archer. Roberts' husband was brutally assaulted and his home trashed. I authorised you to investigate Lake's suicide. Katy was assaulted, her husband is shot dead, and the killer tells her to mind her business because she's messing with national security." He looked at Sign. "What would you do if you were me?"

Sign answered, "If it is a matter of national security, you should go to the foreign secretary and ask him what's going on. If you get no joy from him, demand an audience with the prime minister. And if you get no joy from her, go to the attorney general. You of all people know that on UK soil we don't kill individuals unless there is an immediate threat to life. I don't think this is a UK organisation backing this."

"So, you think this is a foreign agency?"

"It could be. We kill people overseas. Foreign intelligence agencies kill people on our soil."

The commissioner inhaled deeply on his cigarette and blew out a stream of smoke. "If we've got a foreign individual or cell working our patch I need to involve MI5."

"I doubt that will be necessary."

The commissioner flicked his cigarette at the no smoking placard. "You MI6 people always hate MI5."

Sign shook his head. "We're just different breeds of animals."

"And MI6 always thinks it's superior."

"Just different." Sign touched the commissioner on the arm. "Sir: this must be stressful for you. When one of your own gets walloped, it's hard to see the wood for the trees. But I don't think we're looking at trees. I think we're searching for a solitary oak. That's the person who's doing this. But he has a helper. And the helper is the person who killed Katy's husband."

Knutsen said, "We call him the limpet. He's been following us. Sign spotted him."

The commissioner asked, "Is he watching us now?"

"Almost certainly." Sign looked away. Ambulances were parked nearby, others were delivering casualties to A&E. Aside from the glow from headlights and lamps, most of the surroundings were bathed in darkness. He asked the police chief, "Do you have any armed officers – plain-clothed or uniformed – around the exterior perimeter of the hospital?"

The commissioner replied, "No."

Sign looked at Knutsen. "Walk the perimeter. Kill anyone with a gun."

When Knutsen was gone, Sign said, "Knutsen will tackle the limpet. I will tackle the oak. In the interim, we have a problem."

The commissioner nodded. "Katy." He pulled out another cigarette. "You're thinking two things. First: will she be safe. Second: should I continue to deploy her as liaison with you."

"Correct." Sign sighed. "She won't want to go back to her home. Probably she'll sell the property. You'll be tempted to put her in a safe house, under armed guard. My suggestion to you is to ignore that gut instinct. Does she have relatives?"

"A sister in Northumbria. She's got a cottage in the middle of nowhere."

"Don't put her there. The limpet will find her."

"But the limpet didn't kill her." The commissioner couldn't fathom Sign's logic. "So long as she doesn't communicate with you and Knutsen, she's safe."

"No. She's a move on the chess board. It's too late for her now. She'll be made an example of, even if she never speaks to me or Knutsen again."

"I don't understand."

"Somebody persuaded Archer and Lake to kill themselves. I have a theory as to why, but I need more dead bodies before I can substantiate the theory."

"You want more dead bodies?!"

Sign nodded. "I'm dealing with a serial killer. The most superb one I've ever heard about. I can only beat him if he gives me a pattern. Even then, it's a major problem. How many serial killers are you aware of who've killed men with words?"

The commissioner lit his cigarette. "You're theory might be crazy."

"And yet Katy Archer's husband is dead." Sign pulled out a piece of paper and a pen. He wrote an address on the slip. "No safe houses; no relatives; absolutely nothing official or pertaining to family. The limpet will find them and kill her if I continue with my enquiries. But Katy Roberts is so deeply embedded in what's happening it's impossible to pull her out." He folded the note in half, obscuring the address he'd written on the paper. He waited, looking out into the blackness. The commissioner became impatient. Sign wasn't. He just stared.

Knutsen emerged out of the blackness. Sign walked up to him and asked, "What do you think?"

Knutsen replied, "If the limpet's here, we're dealing with a ghost."

"Then we're dealing with a ghost." Sign spun around and walked back to the police chief. He handed the note to him. "It's the flat below me. Students previously occupied the place. It's now empty. Knutsen and I will sort out the place. Katy will be safe there. Knutsen and I will ensure that."

"I'm going to take her off the Archer and Lake cases."

"Then you're signing her death sentence! And you'd be giving her no chance to obtain revenge against the two persons who killed her husband. What kind of life will it be for her to live in hiding with only SWAT operatives for company? She needs to be very close to Knutsen and I until we identify and destroy the two men who killed Archer, Lake, and Elliot Roberts. There is no alternative."

The commissioner said, "Maybe it's only one man. The limpet."

"You could be right. But I maintain my position that the limpet is hired help. No. We're dealing a far higher power. Almost certainly a senior, uber intelligent, highly trained spook. Knutsen and I call him 'the whisperer'. He's our serial killer."

"So, why's the whisperer doing this?"

"The million dollar question." Sign looked at Knutsen. "I presume Katy will be released from hospital tomorrow. I will make arrangements to secure the flat below ours. Call your pals to sort furnishings. They need to come over in two hours' maximum and set to work. A bed, chairs etcetera. It'll just be the basics. She'll make the flat look pretty in due course. Meanwhile Mr. Knutsen, do you know a trustworthy woman?"

Knutsen nodded.

"Good. Take her late night shopping."

Sign said to the police chief. "Whatever you do, don't take Katy off this case. I believe the whisperer has a kill list. This isn't over. Trust me."

The commissioner would have ridiculed Sign's comment under other circumstances. But Katy's plight was too serious to warrant macho jockeying. "The case remains yours, so long as you understand that you are part of the problem. The whisperer killed Katy's husband to warn you off. He fears you. No one else. That means he knows you."

Sign said, "Can I see Katy?"

The commissioner nodded. "In a couple of hours. She's in treatment right now." He checked his watch. "I need to head off. I'll tell the two SCO19 guys in her room not to kill you when you enter Katy's room."

Knutsen knocked on Wendy's door in the council tenement high rise in Brixton. When she opened the door, Knutsen said, "Hello Wendy. Sorry to turn up unannounced."

She smiled. "That's okay, Mr. Knutsen. Come in. I was just making a pot of tea. Take your shoes off though. I've just had a new carpet fitted."

Knutsen entered the tiny, immaculate apartment. Wendy's son David was sitting on the sofa, playing *Mortal Kombat* on his Xbox.

Wendy called out from the kitchen, "Milk, no sugar? Right?"

"That's right, Wendy." Knutsen sat next to David and watched the TV screen. He said to David, "Your opponent's got a massive uppercut. Go for his legs."

David smiled. "You telling me how to play this game, old man?"

Knutsen leaned forward. "That's it. Hit his shins now!"

David followed Knutsen's instruction. "Got him. KO, brother!" He paused the game.

Sign said, "I need to take your mother out for an hour or so after the cuppa. Are you going to be okay?"

"You mean, am I going to go out and hang round crack dealers?"

"Something like that."

"Nah. You beat them up big time. They think they're tough, until they meet real tough. I don't hang round those guys anymore. Dojo next Wednesday?"

"Bang on." Knutsen held out his fist. "Yes, yes, I know what you're about to say. White boys can't do this. But just man up and get over yourself."

David laughed and pressed his fist against Knutsen's fist. "You on a date with my mum? I'll kick your ass if you are."

Knutsen smiled. "No. Your mother and I are bonded by friendship revolving around our mutual concern about an errant boy."

"Errant? What does that mean?"

"Fuck up. And I'm referring to you."

"Yeah, I got that bit mister." David placed his controller down. "I wanted your advice. I'm thinking about applying for a job with the police. I've checked online and I've just about got the academic grades. But…"

"But you've got a petty crime record that disqualifies you from applying. It's just as well you know me." Knutsen pulled out his mobile phone and called the head of the Metropolitan Police Service. "Sir, I have a young man – age eighteen – who wishes to join your ranks. He's intelligent, physically very fit, now and again needs a clip round the ear, but is ready to be a man. The problem is, he's grown up around idiot boys. He'll be on your database for stuff he shouldn't have done. I know ordinarily that would mean he can't apply. But he's a great kid. And he knows the streets in south London like the back of his hand. And I reckon, if he's up for it, he could go into my former line of work."

Undercover assignments.

"Would you entertain his application? No other favours. He'll have to pass the physical and mental tests to get in to Henley. And if he doesn't pass those and the Henley training process, then that's as far as it goes. I just want to give the lad a break."

When the call ended, Knutsen said to David, "I'll help you with the application process. The god of police has just said that anything you've done in your past doesn't pertain to your future."

"Pertain?"

"Never mind. I'll also get you a dictionary." Knutsen smiled. "You've got a job interview coming up with one of the finest police forces in the world. You need to get a suit, shirt, tie, and black shoes. No gangster bling for you any more, Mr. Man."

David was overjoyed. He ran into the kitchen shouting, "Mum! Mum!"

Wendy was in tears as she walked into the lounge while holding a tray containing a pot of tea and cups. "I can't thank you enough."

Knutsen stood. In a formal voice he said to David, "Squeaky clean from now on in. You got it?"

David nodded, brimming with enthusiasm.

Knutsen held out his hand. "No fist pumps for you anymore, David. You've just graduated into manhood. That means we shake hands."

David shook hands, smiling as wide as a Cheshire cat.

"Get on your smart phone and research Wyatt Earp. He started out life like you, though in the States. His early life didn't go so well. The law wasn't his friend. But he became one of the best cops in America." Knutsen grinned. "The best cops are always the ones who know the wrong side of the law. Next Monday I'll buy you a suit. I'll be here nine AM sharp. Now, fuck off and download the Met application form."

David laughed. "I owe you one, man."

"You can call me sir. And I'll put you through hell to make sure you graduate top of your class at Henley Police Academy."

When David was in his bedroom, Wendy poured tea. Her hands were shaking. "You've no idea how much this means to me. Did you encourage David to apply to the police?"

"No. In fact, we never spoke about my job. Either it rubbed off, or he just wants to protect his mum."

"Whatever the reason, my goodness me, I couldn't have asked for better." Wendy asked, "Is that why you came over? David? Job applications?"

Knutsen sipped his tea. "Actually, I was as surprised as you at his decision. I need your help. And I'm out of my league on this one. There's a woman who's just suffered a bereavement – her husband. She'll want somewhere to stay but it must be her private space. I've got a flat sorted, but I've no idea what to put in it, aside from a bed and other furniture."

"She'll choose."

"I know, but this is an emergency. I need stuff – cosmetics, bathroom soaps, everything just to tie her over for the next few days."

"Where's the flat?"

Knutsen put down his tea and touched Wendy's hand. "I trust you so much that I can't tell you. It would endanger you and David. It's a police matter."

"She might be hunted?"

"Yes."

Wendy was deep in thought. "What colour is she?"

"White."

Wendy laughed. "Just because I don't have a cock between my legs doesn't mean I know what white girls like."

"Yeah, but you've still got a head start on me."

"When did her husband die?"

"Today. He was murdered."

"Fucking hell." Wendy patted her hand against her braided locks. "What hair colour is she?"

"Blond."

"Real colour or dyed?"

"No idea."

"Age?"

Knutsen shrugged. "Late thirties. Forties. Something like that."

"What scent does she wear?"

"Scent?!"

"Perfume."

"I don't know! I've only met her twice."

"So, you've not had sex with her?"

"No, Wendy!"

Wendy patted him on the hand. "Okay. I know exactly what we need to do. You're absolutely right. We need to create a private place for her. But it must also be a kind place. I'll get what you need to see her through the next forty eight hours. Most of it will be wrong, but that doesn't matter. No one complains that hair products are wrong when they go to their hotel room. There's a pharmacy down the road that's open tonight. We'll start there. What about her clothes?"

"I'm going to her house later. I'll collect them."

"Fold them carefully. It's awkward. You're going to have to get her knickers and bras. I suggest I come with you to her house after shopping and do that. You can tell her that a woman packed her undies. Would that be okay?"

Knutsen kissed Wendy on the cheek. "That would be more than okay. But I must warn you, there's blood in her bedroom."

Wendy shrugged. "Us women are used to far worse than that. Let's get this lady sorted."

Sign entered Katy's hospital room. The two firearms officers were clad in uniform and body armour and were holding Heckler & Koch submachine guns. Using his phone, one of them took a photo of Sign and sent it to the commissioner. Their boss replied and confirmed the man in the room was Sign.

"Could you wait outside the door?" Sign looked at Katy Roberts. "I'd like a moment alone with her."

The cops hesitated.

Sign said, "There's no window in the room. The door is the only way in and out. She's safe."

Reluctantly the officers complied.

Roberts was in a bed, sitting upright. Her nose was covered with a plaster cast. Her eyes were red and her hair dishevelled. She was staring at the wall and didn't seem aware that Sign was in the room.

Sign pulled up a chair, sat next to her, and held her hand. "Katy, it's Ben."

Slowly, Katy moved her head and looked at him. "Ben... Ben Sign."

"Yes, that's right." His tone was quiet and sympathetic. "I'm so very sorry to hear about your loss."

"Loss?" Roberts' voice was distant and weak. "I didn't lose my husband. I found him. In our bedroom"

"Yes you did."

"I… I need to make arrangements. Funeral."

"There's no rush for that." Sign chose his words carefully. "Your husband's in the care of police and specialists who are examining his…"

"Body."

"Yes. His body. Friends and family will help you with the funeral. And if you don't have many of those, Knutsen and I will help."

It was clear that Roberts was in deep shock. "I can't go back there. I can't. My home. How could I? It's not my home anymore. It's a murder scene. My husband… Elliot." She gripped his hand tight. "Is this what your world's like? Men coming into houses and talking about national security while murdering people?"

"Sometimes it can be. Katy, I need to ask you a question – aside from the Archer and Lake suicides, are you working on any other cases at the moment?"

Roberts shook her head. "The commissioner said I had to be ring fenced. Only work with you, he said."

"Have you done any other work recently that could be perceived to be an intrusion on national security?"

Roberts rubbed sweat off her brow. "No." She started weeping. "My husband was killed because of Lake, Archer, and my liaison with you. And I was… Jesus, I did unarmed combat training where I got a few bruises, but I've never been punched as hard as I was this evening. It was like a hammer hitting my face." She touched her nose.

"The doctors say your nose will be fine in a few hours. A day or two at worst. But it will hurt for a while."

"Hurt? I've got worse pain that will last far longer."

"I know." Sign recalled how he felt when his wife was murdered. It took him years before he stopped reaching out in his sleep, hoping to put his arm around her only to wake up in the middle of the night realising he was alone and she was gone. "I'm very sorry that I brought this on to you and your husband."

"You? You didn't do this. The person who killed my husband did this!"

Sign was motionless. "The police bereavement service will help you."

Roberts withdrew her hand from his. "Tea and sympathy brigade? They can't bring him back."

"No, they can't. I have two propositions that may help. I'm on very good terms with the landlord who owns the flats in West Square. The landlord has agreed to let you the flat immediately below mine. You're in danger. Knutsen and I will be on hand to negate that danger. You can have the flat for a few days or far longer if you choose. Right now, Knutsen is getting the place fitted out. And he's collecting your things from your house. A woman is helping him. Only she will handle your more delicate belongings, although Knutsen won't allow her to know where you're being re-housed. Would that be okay?"

Roberts nodded. "I need to clean up the blood and sell the house."

"We have people who can take that burden off your shoulders."

"Yes, yes. I'll move in to the flat." She was shaking. "What is the other proposition?"

"I wonder if you'd like to keep working with us to find the bastards who did this to Elliot?"

Roberts replied, "I'm in no fit state."

In numerous places around the globe, Sign had been in similar situations with his foreign agents. The agents were amateurs, recruited by him to spy on their countries. Sometimes their nerves would crack; other times they would be confronted by severe threats to their lives; and on a few occasions a colleague or family member of theirs had been murdered. One of the hardest parts of being an MI6 case officer was to persuade agents to carry on risking their lives. But judgement was needed. Sometimes the case officer needed to know when to back off and let the agent retire from the secret world. Sign wondered whether his judgement was accurate right now. Should he let Roberts retire? Or should he encourage her to get back to work?

He said, "You can't grieve until you know why this happened. On a battlefield, a soldier can't walk away, even though his mates have been destroyed. He has to continue fighting. Only later do the demons kick in. Before then, he has to kill what's in front of him."

Roberts looked into his eyes. "You send people to their deaths."

"Sometimes yes; sometimes no. Twenty four hours after my wife was murdered in South America, I had to go to Mumbai to meet a chemistry professor who was attempting to sell biological weapons to Yemen. I just wanted to sleep; let the world eat me up. The professor pulled a gun on me. I smiled. Part of me wanted him to pull the trigger. But then I thought about my wife and what she'd want. I knew she'd want me to stop my death and stop potentially thousands of deaths in Yemen. I put a knife in the professor's throat and held it there until he was dead. Blood was all over my arms. It was messy. I washed up and got on a plane to London. When I arrived, I was met by my MI6 boss at the airport. He told me to go to El Salvador and find my wife's killer. It took me three months. And along the way, I had to cut through a number of bandits. But when I found the identity and location of the killer, I spoke to him while holding a gun against his head. He was only twenty seven, but a ruthless gangster. He told me the reason he'd killed my wife was because she worked for an NGO that was funnelling food into his country but not to his criminal gang. I thought, my wife died for that? It felt such a waste. I shot him. I was a different man back then. When I returned to my London home, grief overwhelmed me and I collapsed. But I did at least have closure that the piece of scum who killed my wife was off the planet."

"Your accent has changed."

Sign smiled. "It bends with the wind."

"I didn't know you had a wife. I didn't know she was murdered."

"Why would you? For most of my adult life I've been kept secret. That might sound alluring. Quickly, it becomes otherwise. If you're secret, you don't exist. If you don't exist, you are not alive." Sign's accent returned to that of an aristocrat. "Grief is purgatory. And I died a long time ago. The question is, will you tread a similar path? Or will you give up on everything?"

"I... I..."

"Forget about the next few years. Time and grieving will deal with that. Focus on the next few months."

Roberts winced as she got out of bed. "I want to get out of here. I want to catch my husband's killer."

Sign looked at her while wondering if he'd just made a godawful mistake. "We'll get the doctors in here to make a final assessment. Once you're out of this silly smock and properly dressed, I'll drive you to your new home. It'll have to be a convoluted drive because I'm certain the killer is watching you, me, or Knutsen. But I'll get you there safe and sound. By the way, can you wash men's clothes?"

"What?!"

Sign winked at her. "I didn't say any of this came for free."

"You have to be kidding me!"

"I might be. That's for you to decide." Sign smiled. "I'll wait in the corridor with your burly bodyguards. Let me know when you're ready."

CHAPTER 15

John Smith met Karl Hilt in a grubby pub in north London. Most people would have wondered why someone of Smith's refinement would be in the establishment. But, Hilt understood – it was the last place anyone would expect to find Smith; therefore it made an excellent meeting location.

It was noon. The pub only contained four other customers and a bored-looking bartender. Smith was sitting by a corner table, half a glass of beer in front of him. Hilt sat opposite him and said, "She's out of the hospital. Eleven thirty last night."

"Armed police took her?"

"No. Sign."

Smith's expression was neutral as he said in his icy accent, "He has more skills than the police. He knew you'd be on her. I assume he put her in a car. Where did they arrive?"

"I lost them at Piccadilly Circus. I wouldn't have done if you'd given me a team. The place was heaving, but we could have still put a box around Sign."

Smith chuckled. "Piccadilly Circus? He's taking the mickey. It was theatrical and a finger up to you."

"Yeah, I know." Hilt added, "I went back to her house in Weybridge. She's not there."

"She won't be. I doubt she will ever go back there." Smith took a sip of his beer and winced. "The beer's flat, and this place smells like a fishmongers." He smiled. "But you and I have tasted and smelled worse."

"True. I once had to eat goats' balls in Afghanistan while pretending to be a U.S. Green Beret playing hearts and bleedin' minds with the locals." He leaned across the table. "Where's he taken her?"

Smith looked out of the adjacent window. "If he was dumb, he'd have taken her to a safe house somewhere in the country, or even overseas. But Sign is the opposite of dumb. He'd know you'd track her. And if I gave the command, you'd kill her. I know what Sign has done. He wants Roberts to continue to liaise with him on matters that are important to me."

"Murder? National security? What is this about?"

Smith returned his gaze to Hilt. "If you persist with those questions I *will* get you a team of men. And they'll put bullets in you."

"Alright, pal. I get your point." Hilt could easily kill Smith. But his employer's money was important to him. Plus, Smith's mind was beyond his reach. "Where is she and what's the next move?"

Smith smiled. "I will tell you what has happened since last night. Sign has decided that he only trusts Katy Roberts in the Metropolitan Police Service. He will have used his expertise in human character assessment to reach that judgement. Think of it this way – she's a pawn he's sent out on the chess board. She's too committed to the fight. He knows that. So, the best he can do is put knights around her. And the reason he's done that is not just because of chivalry. He needs her to flush you and me out. He's worked out that whether she's in the game or not, I can crush her. It would be a message to him. Where is she? Extremely close to Sign and this man Knutsen. What's the next move? Forget Roberts for now. She serves no purpose, unless things deteriorate. So, we have a change of plan. Put your energies into Sign and Knutsen. But take some time off first. I want Sign to get frustrated that nothing's happening for a period of time. In one month's time, I will do something that should peak Sign, Knutsen, and Roberts' interest. I will call you before that event and give you details of a specific location. That's when you're back on duty. Watch Sign and Knutsen. But keep your distance. If Roberts, Sign, and Knutsen do nothing it means Roberts is no longer the Met liaison to Sign; no one else in the Met has taken over her job; Sign and Knutsen are no longer advisors to the police. But, if they move after my next event, we have a problem."

"Shouldn't I just solve that problem?"

Smith smiled. "I know exactly what you're referring to. No. Taking Sign out of the equation would put me back to square one. I'd have to work out who has replaced him and is causing me problems. That person won't be as good as Sign, but he or she would be given infinitely more resources. I'd have a highly trained pack of dogs on my back."

Hilt had no idea what Smith was talking about.

Smith knew that. "I keep my own counsel. It's best you don't know what I know. That said, if I give the order, kill Sign, Knutsen, and Roberts."

Four hours later, Knutsen knocked on the door of the flat below Sign's flat. "Katy. It's Tom."

Roberts opened the door. Her face was ashen; eyes lids swollen; and her left arm was shaking.

Gently, Knutsen said, "Sign's cooking some weird Polish dish for dinner. We wondered if you'd like to join us?"

"What... what time?"

"About seven." Knutsen suspected that Roberts had no concept of time. "In three hours. That'll give you time for a nap, if you like; or a walk. When you're ready, just let yourself in."

"Shouldn't you be locking your door, in light of... of..."

"Circumstances? The two flats below you are empty. It's only you, me, and Sign in the block. This afternoon, I've got experts arriving to install higher security on the downstairs communal door. It'll be like Fort Knox. Once all the fittings are done I'll give you details – new security codes, keys, and anything else. We don't need to lock internal doors. But I wouldn't blame you if you bolted your door at night."

"I... I don't know if I'm up for company tonight."

Knutsen expected her to say that. "You need to eat. We don't need to talk. It's just a plate of food."

"I don't feel hungry."

"That'll be due to shock. But, you'll start getting dizzy if you don't get grub inside you. I tell you what – why don't I knock on your door at seven? You can let me know then whether you're up for a bite."

That evening, Sign served up plates of pierogi dumplings, bigos stew, and cabbage rolls. Roberts and Knutsen were sitting at his dining table. Roberts had made an effort with her hair and attire, her nose cast was off, but she still looked like someone had knocked her for six.

Her voice was barely audible as she said, "Thank you. The flat is nice. The food looks nice." She pushed a fork through the stew but didn't eat.

Knutsen looked at Sign and shook his head.

Sign said, "Mrs. Roberts - it would be vulgar for us to eat before you start eating."

She put her fork down and bowed her head. "Just eat."

"No. Tell me about Elliot."

Knutsen wanted to grab Sign and tell him to shut up.

She raised her head. "Elliot?"

"Your husband."

"Dead husband."

"He's still your husband and always will be. Tell me anything."

She was silent for a minute. "I met him at university. He… he wasn't much to look at really. But he was interesting. He used to do magic tricks in front of students in between lectures. Not for money. It was just fun for him. My girlfriends and I tried to work out how he did the tricks. We couldn't. He made me smile. We dated. Got married. No kids because there was a problem with one of us. He took me to Thailand, India in Spring to see the lakes fill up with rainfall in Rajasthan, so many other places. When he got home from work – he was a lawyer – he liked watching Eastenders. God knows why. He used to pat me on the bottom and tell me I was the greatest woman who'd ever existed. He lost his job but never got depressed about that. He had a smile. He only wanted sex when I wanted sex."

Knutsen blurted, "Ben you're intruding on her grief!"

Roberts shook her head. "No he's not. He's helping me. Elliot cuddled me." Tears streamed down her face as she said, "He took me to Mount Snowden once. By then we didn't have the money to fly off here there and everywhere. I didn't care. On the summit he picked me up and kissed me. I was on top of the world." She looked at Sign. "That was my husband." Her voice shook as she said, "Elliot was everything I needed. Now he's gone."

Sign clasped his hands, as if he was praying. "Have you thought about what kind of funeral you want?"

She shook her head. "It never... never occurred to me. Not at this age."

"Would you consider cremation?"

"We... we were never religious. Not that it matters, I guess. I don't know if religion dictates what kind of funeral you should have."

Sign said, "It doesn't matter what religion you do or don't follow. What does matter are memories. Perhaps you could scatter your husband's ashes on Mount Snowden."

"Yes. Yes, that would be perfect. Why did you cook Polish food tonight?"

"Because my wife was Polish. Today is the anniversary of her death." Sign smiled. "But her departure was years ago. I still love every second I spent with her. I too am not religious. It's odd though. I feel she's with me. I'm fascinated by my ignorance. I believe electricity is the key. It drives our bodies. I also hypothesise that it drives our souls, in life and death. If we can understand electricity, we can understand not only life and death, but also why we can feel people's presences when they're not around."

In a stern voice, Knutsen said, "Ben – back off from the intellectual and philosophical shit."

Sign didn't reply. He watched Roberts put a mouthful of food into her mouth.

She said, "Elliot is now a force of electricity. He's here. He transfers electricity to me. I transfer my electricity to him." She nodded. "He gives me his energy. Yes. Yes! He's with me."

"Always." Sign pushed Roberts' plate an inch closer to her. "If it doesn't pain you too much, perhaps you'd care to join Mr. Knutsen and me on a walk around the block after dinner. Christmas lights are in abundance, street lights are illuminated, cars will pass by with their headlights on. My wife is out there. So is your husband. And so is the woman Knutsen wanted to marry for real, outside of his former undercover work." He touched her hand. "Shall we join them and pay our respects?"

They ate in silence.

When Roberts finished her food, Sign asked her, "Why did you join the police?"

Roberts frowned. "I don't really know. It was a whim. I liked watching *Inspector Morse*, *Prime Suspect*, and other cerebral police TV dramas in the '90s. Maybe they rubbed off on me. I was intrigued by detective work."

"And you became the living embodiment of Morse and DCI Jane Tennison. A detective. But you went one step further – you joined Special Branch."

Roberts nodded. "The police's most secret unit. I was intrigued by the unit. They worked behind closed doors. Regular detectives and uniform weren't allowed in SB's offices. But, I never set out to be in SB."

"Perhaps you wanted to hide. More accurately, you wanted anonymity while performing a most noble task."

Knutsen muttered, "She just wanted a fucking job."

Sign ignored the comment. "Knutsen needed the same. He was never happier than when he was working alone; no other cop watching over him. His friends around him were armed robbers and killers. And the thrill of it was that one day he would betray them."

Knutsen looked at Sign. The former MI6 officer was right.

Sign continued. "I was the same. Though it is an organisation, the elegance of British Intelligence is that it gives vent for people like me. Spooks are a bunch of mavericks. Loners. Non-conformists. Rebels. People who spend years in the company of foreign spies who want to put bullets in the back of our skulls when our backs are turned. We'd rather all of that than spending one second in the company of our peers and bureaucracy. The three of us are different breeds of animal compared to normal people. Vive la difference." Sign's eyes widened. "And yet we wish to connect with normal folk. But how difficult is that? Angels or devils walking the Earth trying to make sense of the planet's populous. We try to make friends, but fail because we don't understand what friendship is. We marry. They leave us or die."

"Ben!" Knutsen wanted to guide Roberts out of the room and apologise for Sign's words.

Sign persisted. "But here's the thing: Knutsen successfully mentors a young man called David. The poor lad is from the wrong side of the tracks. Mr. Knutsen is in the process of solving that. You, Mrs. Roberts, take disabled children to a skating rink in Bedfordshire. You make them feel that anything is possible."

Quietly, she said, "I make them feel whole. How did you know that?"

Sign made a dismissive gesture with his hand. "What I know is irrelevant. What I don't know is most relevant."

"And what about you?" she asked.

Sign looked away. It sounded like he was talking to himself when he said, "Most foreign agents I've dealt with have been traitors to their country. Some of them have been double agents. It didn't matter to me. When I looked them in the eyes I saw mirrors to my soul. It sounds melodramatic, but it's the truth. They were like me. They were lost. I didn't care what head office said about the people I ran as a case officer. I knew the beating heart of my flock. HQ didn't. I bought a house for an impoverished Chinese man who earlier tried to garrotte me. He had a wife and four children. MI6 once wanted me to bludgeon a Venezuelan woman, shove her in the boot of a car, and get her to America. She was working for the Russians. British Intelligence and the CIA wanted to interrogate her. But, here's the thing – I liked her because she taught me how to climb the mountain of Pico Bolivar. And she fed me breads and meat at the summit. She knew that I knew she was a traitor to my cause. She had a fiancée and didn't want to die in an American or British black site. I told her she was free. And I also told her to take her beloved to Bolivia and start a family there. I lied to MI6 and said she'd never turned up to our last intended meeting." Sign looked at Roberts. "I could give you a hundred other examples. Nations rage against each other. But it needn't be that way with people. The trick is to know who can stop people slitting each other's throats. That's where we come in, even though it means we lose a little bit of ourselves with every kind deed."

"Because we lose a bit of what we want." Roberts nodded. "Connection with others." She breathed deeply. "You're putting my husband into that melting pot."

"Perhaps I am."

Tears ran down Roberts' face. "So, this is my destiny?"

"I'm afraid it is." Sign held her hand. "My destiny; Knutsen's destiny; your destiny. But, we hold on to hope and feel more than most. Elliot's death is the most agonising pain. Elliot's murder requires the most agonising vengeance. We can do the former; and only people like us can do the latter." Sign looked at Knutsen.

The former undercover cop nodded at him.

They took a walk around South London. Sign pointed at electric lights. Roberts smiled, cried, went stoic, smiled again, and cried again. When she was in bed in her West Square flat, Sign and Knutsen retired to their lounge. Knutsen lit a fire. Sign poured calvados.

Sign asked, "What do you think?"

Knutsen sat in his armchair. "You've made her think about grief differently by explaining to her that she must be cautious about grieving someone very unlike her."

"Yes."

"Not your finest hour."

"No. But necessary." Sign placed another log on the fire. "My finest hours are usually the worst. The moral compass spins in confusion."

"You did the right thing. And it was clever." Knutsen watched Sign and wondered how he'd managed to bear such tremendous ethical complexity throughout his adult life. There was no doubt Sign was an extremely good man who'd devoted his life to saving others. But, unlike soldiers who return from a battlefield, Sign's brain was constantly on the battlefield. He was permanently in war. "We need light relief while we drink. What's light relief for you? Chess?"

Sign sat opposite him, cradling his calvados. "No. Chess puts me back on duty."

"Cards?"

"My father taught me never to play cards. He said it led to drink and debauchery in ports. He was a very clever sailor."

Knutsen picked up a copy of the *Radio Times*. "There's a political debate on TV."

"Boring!"

"On one of the other channels there's a film about cowboys."

Sign narrowed his eyes. "Cowboys or homesteaders?"

"I never know the difference."

Sign smiled. "I do, but that's irrelevant. A cowboy movie it is. Did I tell you about the time I was in Oregon and…"

"Now that is fuckin' irrelevant. Just drink your drink and watch the damn movie."

Sign smiled. "Sage words. But before we switch the TV on, I need to tell you something. Tomorrow I want your help. But I won't blame you if you refuse."

"Refuse?"

Sign looked at the window. "We have to do something that may get both of us killed. What say you?"

Knutsen smiled.

CHAPTER 16

It was early morning as Sign drove his vehicle across Cambridgeshire and into Norfolk. He was alone in the car. The country road he was driving along was deserted. Rain was lashing his vehicle, though it was hard to predict if the inclement weather would persist – interspersed between the black clouds were patches of blue sky sending bolts of sunlight to the flat lands. High winds were moving the clouds at a rate of knots, changing where sunlight fell and darkness prevailed. The strength of the winds was sufficient to smack Sign's car a few inches sideways as he drove onwards. It wasn't a problem. Sign had driven through massive sandstorms in the Middle East, minus forty degrees frozen waste lands in Siberia, and on one occasion had managed to maintain grip of his vehicle after it had been rammed by a rhinoceros in Botswana. On all of those occasions he knew death was likely, but not from the elements or wild animals. There were worse things on his heels – men with guns.

Sign stopped his car and got out of the vehicle. Ignoring the weather, he stood on the empty road and opened an umbrella. He was wearing an immaculate suit. Fields were either side of him. There were no houses, no cars, no sign of life. He pulled out his mobile phone and held it to his ear. He didn't call anyone. No one called him. But he waited, tilting the umbrella slightly back so that his face and phone were visible.

From a distance of seven hundred yards, Hilt watched him through the scope on his high-powered sniper rifle. Hilt was prone, hidden in gorse on a slight rise that gave him perfect views of the road Sign was on. Hilt had followed him here from West Square. Hilt's crosshairs were on Sign's head. It would be so easy. Pull the trigger and put a savage hole in Sign's head. And if he missed, he'd shoot two of the tyres, move closer, and finish Sign off. If Hilt's boss gave the order, Sign was a dead man.

Hilt called Smith. "Sign's in Norfolk. His pal's not with him. I guess it's nothing work-related."

Smith was silent for three seconds. "The chief of my organisation has a country retreat in Norfolk. What is Sign wearing?"

"A suit."

"Stay on him!" Smith ended the call.

Hilt collapsed his customised rifle, placed it in a rucksack and turned, with the intention of sprinting to his car. As he did so, Knutsen punched him in the face. Hilt collapsed to the ground, rolled, and sprang to his feet. He dropped his rucksack and moved close to Knutsen, slamming a boot into Knutsen's ankle and slapping his palm into the ex-cop's face. Knutsen gasped for air as he hit soil and grass. Hilt wanted to thrust his hand against Knutsen's nose and force cartilage into his brain. But Knutsen grabbed his arm and forced him onto his back. Hilt lashed out with his free arm and legs. But, Knutsen held him in a vice-like grip.

"Who are you?!" asked Knutsen. "Who do you work for?"

Hilt used his knee to whack Knutsen in the balls, stood, and stamped on Knutsen's head. "You picked the wrong person, matey." He gripped Knutsen's hand and placed his arm in an excruciating lock.

Knutsen rolled so that his arm was travelling away from the lock, kicked Hilt in the chest, kicked him again in the eyes and throat, and dragged Hilt to the ground. He got an arm around Hilt's windpipe and muttered, "I can do this."

Hilt banged the back of his head against Knutsen's forehead, wrenched his arm free, stood and kicked Knutsen in the ribcage. Knutsen was momentarily giddy as he got to his feet. Hilt smiled and punched him in the stomach and mouth. Knutsen staggered. This is just the dojo, he told himself. Just the dojo. Stay up. Think it through. Find his weakness. Execute. He shook his head and wiped saliva from his mouth. Hilt rushed at him. Knutsen spun around, grabbed Hilt, and used the ex-special forces' momentum to pound him to the ground, a boot on the back of Hilt's neck. Hilt wasted no time, using his fist to repeatedly hit Knutsen on his shin. Knutsen recoiled, in agony.

Both men stood staring at each other, breathing fast, steam coming out of their mouths, sweat dripping down their furrows.

Hilt picked up his rucksack. "Another time, pal. Wrong day. Wrong place." He jogged off.

Knutsen was in a bad state as he limped down the escarpment to Sign's car. Blood was all over his face and arms. He'd been pounded in a way he'd never experienced before. He was gasping as he reached Sign. "The limpet... limpet."

Concern was all over Sign's face as he said, "Dear fellow. Let's get you in the dry." He guided Knutsen into the rear of the car and used bottled water to clean his wounds. "Anything broken?"

"No. No... I don't think so."

"What happened?"

Knutsen explained.

Sign felt immense guilt. "I didn't realise we were up against someone like this. Almost certainly, he's done the paramilitary course."

"Paramilitary?" Knutsen's entire body was in agony.

"MI6. It's our blunt instrument. Blunter than special forces. It's our last resort. Most people fail the course – even our SF." Sign paced outside the vehicle. "I shouldn't have put you up against the limpet."

Knutsen's eyes were screwed shut as he muttered, "You had to. My... my job was easy. You... you had to be the tethered goat. You could have been killed. He had a rifle."

"I suspected he was armed." Sign looked at the escarpment where Hilt had been hiding. When leaving West Square, Sign had told Knutsen to hide in the boot of his car. Sign knew that he was being followed out of London. On a bend in a road in Norfolk, he'd slammed the brakes on and told Knutsen to get out and run. The instructions were specific – Knutsen tries to grab the limpet and make him talk; Sign stands in the road, waiting for death.

Knutsen said, "I've never seen anyone do something as brave as what you did today."

Sign didn't care for the flattery. "We all fall down, one day." He smiled. "Are you up to another job?"

Knutsen rubbed his face. "Damn right."

"Good man." He pointed up the road. "We need to go thirteen miles that way. On the rear seat of the car is your suit, a shirt, tie, and your brogues. Get dressed, because the man we're meeting in thirty minutes won't take kindly to shabby attire."

"Dressed? Where?"

Sign chuckled. "It appears it's too harsh a climate at this time of the day for the Norfolk folk. No one's here. You might as well get on with it."

Ten minutes' later they drove away. Though he was now in formal attire and showed no external signs of the brutal assault he'd suffered, Knutsen was still wincing. Sign leaned across and opened the glove compartment opposite Knutsen. He withdrew a first aid kit and handed it to the ex-cop.

"There are painkillers in there. All you need to do is get through the next thirty or so minutes. After that, I'll drive you back to London. I have a friend who works as a doctor on Harley Street. He can prescribe you stronger pain killers if need be."

Knutsen put two paracetamol in his mouth and swallowed them down with a swig of water. "I'll be alright. I just don't like losing fights."

"You neither lost nor won. The same was true for the limpet." Sign turned into a narrower country lane, while glancing in his rear-view mirror. "Still, we'll have to be more careful next time. I don't like the fact that he has a rifle. And I don't like seeing a master of the dojo sitting in my car holding his seatbelt away from his chest because the strap is aggravating wounds." Sign stopped the car outside an iron double-gate. Beyond it was a gravel driveway that led to a small mansion. "We have arrived at the country retreat of the chief of MI6. He is expecting us. Still, the encounter will be tricky. I will do most of the talking. And I will do my best to counter any mind games he might throw at us. But if you see me faltering, play PC Plod and threaten him with a police investigation. On UK soil he is not above the law."

Two armed bodyguards opened the gates and waved them through. Sign stopped the car outside the front door. He and Knutsen exited the vehicle. The door opened. Two beagles ran out, tails wagging, and ran circles around the guests, sniffing their shoes.

In the doorway was the chief. "They're harmless. I need to walk them later, or they'll be the equivalent of children who've eaten too much sugar. Come in."

The chief guided them through the hallway containing shooting smocks, walking sticks, and a gun cabinet. They entered a large lounge. He told them to sit where they liked. The beagles followed them and rolled onto their backs in front of a log burner. A maid entered the room and asked them what they'd like to drink. Sign asked for tea; Knutsen wanted black coffee. Knutsen looked around the room. It was oak-panelled, crammed with books, paintings, and antiquities. But what grabbed his attention was a glass cabinet containing a samurai sword.

The chief was wearing tweeds, looking every inch a country gentleman. "You are interested in the sword, Mr. Knutsen. Its steel remains as sharp as it was in the Battle of Shiroyama in…"

"Eighteen seventy seven. May I hold the weapon?"

The chief delicately pulled out the sword and handed it to Knutsen. "The last man to have held this in anger is rumoured to have killed thirty six men in the battle. Treat this with respect."

Knutsen moved away from the chief and Sign. He gripped the sword's hilt with two hands and swashed the blade through air. "It's so delicate. I never knew." He handed the sword back to the chief, who replaced it in its cabinet.

The chief said, "All those years studying kendo and yet this is your first time holding a samurai sword."

Knutsen sat near Sign.

The chief sat opposite them. "What do you want?"

Sign replied, "Sir, we…"

"I am not your sir or your chief. You are no longer in MI6." He looked at Knutsen. "And you are no longer with the Metropolitan Police. You are civilians. Anxious ones, I will concede." He looked at Knutsen. "My name is Henry Gable. I am publicly avowed, so I'm the only person in MI6 who can be named. Given it's a weekend, on this occasion you can call me Henry. I answer to the foreign secretary and the prime minister. No one else. Even then, politicians come and go and most of them couldn't organise a piss up in a brewery. I control things. But not for much longer. We have people nipping at my heels, don't we Mr. Sign?"

"I'm not after your job. You know that."

"Yes, I do." Henry smiled at Knutsen. "And there is no route back for you into the police, young man."

"No." Knutsen felt uneasy.

Sign sensed his colleague's unease. "Mr. Knutsen is a highly decorated former undercover cop. He doesn't need to prove himself to anyone, including you and me."

Henry nodded. "Yes, but he did execute a criminal in cold blood." Slowly he turned his head towards Knutsen. "It takes a particular kind of man to do that."

Knutsen was about to reply, but Sign interjected. "Knutsen killed the man who killed the woman Knutsen was in love with. And the criminal was a piece of scum. Knutsen isn't by nature a killer. Let me ask you this, Henry: how many drone strikes have you ordered that sometimes missed their targets but not civilians; how many black ops assassinations have you signed off on; how many foreign agents have you sent to their deaths?"

Henry smiled. "I could ask the same of you."

"You could. So, let's cut the crap. The three of us know what it's like in the real world and what we have to do. We all have blood on our hands."

Henry was silent, though his gaze was penetrating.

Sign clasped his hands and lowered his voice. "I believe we have a situation that is beyond the purview of espionage."

"Elaborate!"

"Mark Archer killed himself because he was corrupt. Arthur Lake killed himself because he couldn't keep his dick in his pants. Detective Inspector Roberts' husband was murdered and Katy Roberts was told to back off consulting with us on the suicides due to *national security*. What can you tell us about that?"

Henry was unfazed. "I can tell you nothing, for two reasons. First, I have no insight on these matters. Second, even if I did it would be none of your business."

Knutsen said, "This is a murder enquiry."

"Conducted by one disgraced cop and one former MI6 officer who refused to toe the party line." Henry shook his head. "You have no authority over me."

"Not so!" Sign looked menacing as he added, "*You* have no authority over us. But we most certainly have authority over you."

Knutsen said, "Mr. Sign and I answer to the police and the judiciary. It wouldn't be difficult for me to arrange for you to be forced to testify in a closed court. Yeah, you'd pull in favours, speak to mates you went to uni with who now work as judges, blah blah. But here's the thing. I'd also pull in MI5 and Special Branch to a court room session. And they hate posh bastards like you who work for MI6. I'd set a ball rolling. They'd drag you through the dirt. I'm sure someone of your intellect would outsmart everyone in the court. But at what cost? You're due to retire shortly. Is this how you want to be remembered? Possibly covering up a murder in the UK?"

"Don't threaten me, Knutsen!"

"He's not threatening you." Sign drummed his fingers on a glass coffee table. "He's laying out the facts. I strongly urge you to cooperate with us. If you don't we will set wheels in motion."

Gable couldn't believe what he was hearing. "You come to my house and..."

"Yes, yes." Sign made no effort to hide his anger. "Elliot Roberts was unemployed. Previously he was a family lawyer. Nothing – *absolutely* nothing – he did in his life brought him anywhere near our world. He wasn't a national security threat. But he was a means to put the frighteners on his wife. And the only case she was working on was the suicides of two senior MI6 officers. So, in the presence of Mr. Knutsen, I'll ask you what you know about those suicides."

Gable looked confused. "Nothing. I was as shocked by their deaths as everyone else. If you have evidence that they took their lives due to past indiscretions, lay that evidence in front of me and the Joint Intelligence Committee. I can assure you that we'll go over the allegations with a fine tooth comb."

"What's the point? Archer and Lake are dead." Sign decided to soften his tone. "It is quite possible that you're not our enemy. On paper, why would you be? You're due to retire. The machinations of MI6 will soon no longer be your concern. But, there is a problem. What links Archer and Lake?"

Gable frowned. "Both senior MI6 men. But they had different career paths. I doubt they knew each other that well."

"Think, Henry! There must be something they have in common."

Gable shook his head. "If you were still in MI6 I could answer you. Given you're not, it's classified."

Knutsen pulled out his mobile phone and asked Sign, "Shall I call the commissioner? He can get a squad car here in minutes."

Gable waved his hand through the air. "That won't be necessary."

"It will be if I decide it is." Sign pointed at Gable. "Here's the thing, Henry. There's a possibility we're dealing with a serial killer. An unusual one at that. But to catch him I need to understand motive. Why did he or she want Archer and Lake dead? Why did he kill Roberts to try to stop the investigation? When we know the reason, we are closer to knowing the killer."

"Roberts' death may be completely unconnected!"

"Come on Henry. Our whole lives have been devoted to connecting the dots. Coincidences never factor."

Gable looked pensive. "Archer and Lake's deaths were by their own hand. How on Earth could they be murders?"

"Someone very skilled could have talked them in to taking their lives."

"It's possible." The chief frowned. "But if that's the case, who? Lake and Roberts never shared the same geographical targets. The Russians might have targeted Roberts to shut him up, but they'd have no bug bear with Lake."

"So, maybe we're dealing with someone closer to home." Sign leaned forward. "The motive might be personal, not professional."

"Your ideas are supposition."

"Yes, they are. But in the right hands, supposition is instinct that out-speeds deductive reasoning. A woman looks at a man and knows he's a wrong 'un. Only later may she be able to work out why she reached that conclusion. I'm thinking there's a wrong 'un out there. Why, who, and how, are eluding me, though I do have a thought. Who's on the shortlist to become the next chief of MI6?"

Gable looked mortified. "I can't give you that information!"

"You will give me that information. Or I hand you over to Mr. Knutsen. Trust me – he'll move faster than your bodyguards."

"You are both looking at a prison sentence!"

"That's alright. We'll share a cell with you. We can pass the time by playing board games and wondering how we all got locked up."

The chief smiled. "How is life out in the cold suiting you, Ben?"

"Just fine. Let me know how it goes for you after you retire in a few months' time. No more bodyguards; no chauffeur-driven limousines; no hotline to the prime minister; no invitations to banquets at the palace; no private jets to Washington DC; just you and your beagles. But the beagles are looking a bit old. They won't be around for much longer. I understand your daughters are married, with kids, and are living overseas. They won't see you that much. We all know your wife moved out a while ago. Rumour has it she's got a fella." Sign's tone of voice was cold as he added, "If I were you I wouldn't sit there all smug and gloating, asking me how it feels to be out of the fold. You'll know soon enough what it's like to have no power."

"Ah, Ben." Gable's eyes were twinkling. "You'd have made such an excellent chief. But you backed out of the game and decided to play private detective." He looked away, deep in thought. "I can tell you this for free. Alongside you, Archer and Lake were on the shortlist of candidates to be my successor. You know how it works – the candidates are chosen by me and the cross-party JIC. Each person is picked due to varying capabilities so that the final choice can reflect the current mood in Westminster and the mood of our closest allies. Archer was deemed unremarkable, but a safe pair of hands. That could have been useful. Lake was deemed a good operator, but perhaps too much of spy to be a manager. And you, Ben, were our best spy. But you did have a negative against your name. You were deemed by all to be cavalier. That negative could have worked exceptionally well in the current climate – keep our allies and detractors on their toes by having an unpredictable spy chief." Gable pointed at the samurai sword. "Knutsen will know that Shiroyama was the last battle of the samurai. They'd reached the end of the line. Technology was outstripping them. Guns and canons were the new way of things. I keep the sword to remind me of who I was and who I cannot be. It's soon going to be my end of the line. But you, Ben, were young enough and mentally adroit to adapt to the times. But you fucked it all up."

"I resigned." Sign pulled out a sheet of paper and a fountain pen. He placed both on the table in front of Gable. "Give me the shortlist names."

"I've already given you my response to that request."

"And I haven't accepted your response. How many are on the list?"

Gable shrugged. "I can tell you that. Seven in total. Thanks to you, Archer, and Lake, we're now down to four."

"Who's your favourite candidate?"

"Don't insult my intelligence, Sign!"

Sign stood, walked to the beagles and rubbed their bellies. "Okay, Henry. Let's do it this way. You call the foreign secretary or prime minister and get their permission to release the names to me. I call the home secretary and tell her that the chief of MI6 is obstructing a murder enquiry. She'd love that. You know how much she's hankering for a domestic scandal that will put her in the shining light as the woman holding the scales of justice."

Slowly and with a deep authoritative tone, Gable said, "Be *very* careful, Mr. Sign. I am adhering to security protocols. *You* have no proof that the suicides are linked, nor that Roberts' murder is linked to the suicides. You have everything to lose and nothing to gain by meddling in matters that don't concern you."

Sign faced him and smiled. "That's the beauty of my current position. I have nothing to lose and everything to gain. Make the call. The names may turn out to mean nothing. But I don't want it on your conscience if they turn out to be something."

"You are making a big mistake!"

The noise of Sign's voice made the beagles scarper as he said, "I am an official emissary of not only the Metropolitan Police but also our government. Make the call!"

Gable stood. "God help you, Sign." He walked to the adjacent conservatory and picked up the landline phone. He spoke for ninety three seconds, listened, and hung up. He returned to the lounge, sat, picked up the pen, hesitated, then wrote seven names on the sheet. "The prime minister has assured me that I will be immune from prosecution by revealing these names to you and Knutsen. Every phone call in and out of here is recorded by me. It's my insurance. If the PM denies the conversation I've just had with her, I'll publish and be damned."

Sign took the sheet. "Thank you, Henry."

Gable pointed at the sheet while looking at Knutsen. "I've just given you the names of our top seven spies. You and Sign have authority to read their names. But, if you want to share their names with anyone in the course of your investigation, you will need me, the foreign secretary, and the home secretary – all three of us, not just one – to vet that person and give you authority or otherwise. Am I clear?"

Knutsen nodded.

Sign folded the paper in half and placed it in the inner pocket of his jacket. "We fully understand."

"That includes the commissioner of the Metropolitan Police. He's security cleared, but not to the level of the UK intelligence agencies. You understand?"

"Yes."

Gable pulled Sign to one side and said in a quiet voice, "Ben – you could be making a huge mistake. Maybe your train of thought is skewed. This may all be nothing."

Sign nodded. "I'm aware of that. But since when did men like you and I believe in the impossible?"

That evening, Sign and Knutsen were back in West Square. Sign cooked guinea fowl encrusted with a marmalade glaze, butter mash potato, and vegetables drizzled with lemon juice. After dinner, Sign sat opposite Knutsen in the lounge. He stared at the sheet of paper.

"What does it tell you?" asked Knutsen.

Sign didn't answer his question. "When are you next on the dojo?"

Knutsen frowned. "Wednesday."

"Take Katy with you. Pair her up with David. They both have broken wings. Exercise and focus will help repair their ailments. Have you checked on Katy this evening?"

"Yes. She's ordered an Indian takeaway and is making funeral plans."

"Good. She's eating and is busy." Sign stared at the paper before placing it in front of Knutsen. "What do you see?"

The list read:

Ben Sign
Mark Archer
Arthur Lake
Edward Messenger
Nicholas Pendry
James Logan
Terry File

"I see a list of men."

Sign looked resigned. "One day we'll have a female chief." He took the sheet off Knutsen. "I see a kill list." He turned the sheet over and withdrew a pen. On the back he wrote:

MURDER VICTIMS
Mark Archer
Arthur Lake
Elliot Roberts
POTENTIAL MURDER VICTIMS
Ben Sign
Tom Knutsen
Katy Roberts
Henry Gable
Edward Messenger
Nicholas Pendry
James Logan
Terry File

Beneath that, he wrote:

Who is the limpet?

And:

Who is the whisperer?

He handed the sheet back to Knutsen. "Messenger, Pendry, Logan, and File. They may all be dead men walking. Or maybe one of them is the killer. The whisperer."

"Why?"

"Remember – he's cleaning out the garbage. I think he wants to be chief. He is eliminating the competition and ensuring that he does not inherit any bad apples. It is pure self-fulfilment. He wants the top job."

"Ben, this is a…"

"Stab in the dark? Yes, I know. But I was hired to investigate this case because I know the mind-set of a spy. This is what I'm doing. I'm ascertaining motive and methodology. But if I'm right, we have very dark waters to navigate. Right now, we have a number of low IQ sociopaths who are presidents around the world. That's one thing. But imagine if a supremely intelligent serial killer becomes head of MI6. He'd have at his disposal huge power and resources. I can imagine what he'd do with that power. He'd corrupt others and send our men and women to kill."

"Spies would become his army?"

"Yes. But it would be more complicated than that. He'd do what spies do best – he'd manipulate foreign powers; change landscapes; start wars; and he'd do it all purely for the thrill." Sign's voice quietened. "In my time, I've dealt with many, many, sociopaths and psychopaths. I've outwitted them all. But, a psychotic MI6 officer? That would be a whole new challenge for me."

"No one else is better suited to that task than you."

"If indeed it is a task. I could be so wrong." Sign frowned. "Do you think it would be a good idea to erect a cross on Mount Snowdon for Katy's husband? I have sway with the MP of that district. She'd give me permission for the construction."

"It would be inappropriate. Let Katy make her own plans."

"Yes, you're right." Sign touched the paper. "This is all I have to go on."

"But, your instinct tells you that all that's needed?"

"Yes."

Knutsen lifted the paper. "Tell me about the others."

"You could put a cigarette paper between their intellects. All of them are overachievers. Messenger is currently head of all European operations; Pendry is on the board of directors as head of communications; Logan runs Asia; File heads up the paramilitary wing."

"File runs people like the limpet?"

"Yes."

"Then, he could be our man."

"Maybe. The problem is, all operational MI6 officers use limpets from time to time."

"We could meet File and get his opinion."

Sign shook his head. "And tell him what? That a highly trained killer with an English accent has been following us and has killed a detective inspector's husband, allegedly for the sake of national interest. File would laugh us out of his home. He'd remind me that he has dozens of UK killers under his control; that he also has hundreds of foreign paramilitary assets overseas; that the killer may not be intelligence, but rather a regular criminal; and that this could be a foreign intelligence operative posing as a Brit. Plus he'd remind me that special forces types come and go. If the limpet is retired and reactivated, we can treble or quadruple the number of suspects. File would tell me I'm looking for a needle in a giant haystack. He'd be right."

"We should warn Messenger, Pendry, Logan, and File that their lives are in danger."

Sign looked weary as he rubbed his face. "Were it that easy." He sighed. "If we talk to all four of them, and one of them turns out to be the whisperer, we'd be signposting our knowledge of the kill list to the whisperer. No. We have to let things play out."

"Play out?"

"We need three of them to die; and one to stay alive. Whoever stays alive is the whisperer."

Knutsen was incredulous. "You want more murders to identify the killer?!"

"Logically, can you see an alternative?"

"Yes! Forget the investigation. Protect all four. Maybe some other evidence will come out in due course."

Sign looked wistful. "It won't. I believe we're dealing with a highly capable thinker and operator. The only way to flush him out is to leave him isolated. If he kills the others, he is the killer. If we warn him off he'll go to ground."

Knutsen desperately wanted to find a flaw in Sign's logic. He couldn't. "You might be sending your former colleagues to their deaths!"

"I know." Sign wrung his hands. "I hate this. But what else is there to do?"

Knutsen's mind raced. "Has it occurred to you that Gable might think you're the whisperer?"

"Yes. What do you think?"

Knutsen was silent for a moment. "I don't think you are. But it's hard to tell with you spooks. You're such thoroughbred liars."

Sign laughed. "Indeed we are. But I have no vested interest in the deaths of the men on the list, one of whom is sitting in this room. And both men sitting in this room are on the back of the paper as likely targets for assassination." He touched Knutsen's hand. "My agenda is to catch a killer, even if the killer is someone I know. It deeply saddens me that I have to await more killings. I am not the whisperer. Do you understand?"

Knutsen nodded. "I understand and trust you implicitly. So, what do we do now?"

"We wait."

CHAPTER 17

Four weeks later, Katy Roberts entered Sign's flat. She'd just returned from her husband's funeral and scattering of his ashes on the mountain. The funeral had been delayed because her husband's corpse was subject to a murder enquiry. She was wearing a light pink jumper and sky blue trousers.

Knutsen asked, "You didn't wear black at the funeral?"

"Should I have done?"

"No. You were celebrating Elliot's life, not his death. Your colours are perfect. Fancy a brew?"

Roberts nodded. "Where's Ben?"

"Tearing up half of London, I imagine." Knutsen grinned. "He's been going out of his mind with boredom during the last few weeks. The commissioner has threatened him that he might cancel the investigation and not renew his contract. Sign and I have been working on chicken feed – divorce cases, infidelities, financial fraud, basically anything to pay the bills. Sign is not in the best temper."

Roberts laughed. "I can imagine." A tear ran down her face, brought on by the fact this was the first time she'd laughed since Elliot's death. "Do you think I'll ever remarry?" She had no idea why she'd blurted out that question. Men, companionship, relationships of any kind were the last thing on her mind. Mind you, she cherished the contact she had with Knutsen and Sign. They helped her in the same way she'd help them if they'd gone through her ordeal.

Knutsen replied, "Don't ask me. I killed a man who killed the last woman I fancied. I'm not exactly a balanced example of wise relationship counselling." He smiled sympathetically. "Emotions run high at times like these. It's like hitting puberty again. The body and mind have no idea what the fuck's going on." He handed Roberts her cup of tea. "You're a good-looking woman, successful, and kind. Who knows what waits for you out there?" He felt he needed to change the subject. "Let's do some kendo practice with David this evening. I'll get Sign on the case for dinner after. The bloody guy needs a distraction."

"Yes to both ideas." She sat in Sign's armchair. "I'm selling my house. I'll find somewhere else soon, but if it's okay with you both I'd like to stay on in the flat while I'm in… transition."

"Of course it's okay. Look at it this way: when you're not around I'm cooped up with the fractious bastard. I welcome your company; so does Sign."

Roberts smiled. "You are the oddest couple. Chalk and cheese." She took a deep breath. "I'm going back to work. Do you think I'll be watched by the limpet?"

"Hard to say. If the whisperer's work is done, it may be that we're all out of danger."

"What does Sign think?"

Knutsen hesitated. "Katy, we're in possession of a list of names. Ben calls it a 'kill list'. He wonders if one of the names on the list is the whisperer. On the back of the list are the names of the people the whisperer has killed. Also, there is a list of the people he may kill. Me and Sign are on that list. So…"

"Am I." Roberts looked calm. "What is the kill list?"

"Seven names of predominantly current MI6 officers, one of whom was tipped to be the next chief. Two of them are the suicides, so they're out of the game. Sign is also on the list, because he was in the running before he resigned. So, he's also out of the game. That leaves four names – all men. One of the four could be a psychopath."

"That's if the whisperer even exists."

"Yes." Knutsen wondered if he should reveal more about what he knew. He made a decision. "Sign's idea going forward is… unusual. He wants to see if anyone else on the list is killed. That way he narrows down the list of suspects."

Roberts digested the information. "It makes sense, to a point. But surely there is a more humane route forward. If we can grab the limpet, we can get to his master."

"Make him talk?"

"Arrest him. Interview him. Throw the book at him. Offer him twenty years in prison with the chance of parole, if he cooperates, or life imprisonment with no chance of parole if he doesn't."

Knutsen admired the fact that Roberts would be willing to offer her husband's murderer a degree of clemency. Most people wouldn't have the balls to think that way. "It won't work. Sign thinks we're dealing with a highly trained black ops guy. The limpet will sit in your interview room, say nothing, and suck up a lifetime of jail. And when he's in jail, he'll be a massive problem. He'll end up running the place."

"So, you're suggesting we capture the limpet and torture him to get the name of the whisperer?"

"Yes."

Roberts nodded. "Just make sure I'm in the room when it happens. Come and visit me in prison if I get caught and you don't." She rubbed her eyes. "I'm going back to work because I want to keep the investigation into my husband's death open. If needs be, I'll put my bitch hat on. I'll tell the commissioner that if he doesn't renew your contract to continue the investigation then I'll cause him trouble. He'll capitulate." She looked Knutsen directly in the eye. "My husband's free. But so are the limpet and the whisperer. Where's the yin and yang in that?"

"We get the bastards."

"Yes. Only Sign can access the whisperer's mind. But we can get the limpet."

"Agreed."

Roberts looked around. "Where did he get all this stuff? All these antiques, paintings, books and other things?"

"He travelled the world. I think of him as a magpie – scavenging things in the same way he scavenged and collected souls." Knutsen laughed at the absurdity of his analogy.

Roberts didn't laugh. "You're right. Everything in this room is all he has. The souls never stuck by him. He's alone." She picked up a diary. On the inner cover were Sign's handwritten words 'My great, great grandfather's love letter to a woman he lost while he was at sea'. It wasn't per se a love letter, rather Sign's ancestor's diary while at sea on board a clipper navigating the waters around the Americas. But the diary was most certainly written for a woman. Roberts gently replaced the leather-bound journal back on the bookshelf. "Sign still seeks love."

Sign entered the flat while holding bags of groceries. "God damn, fucking shits out there have clogged up traffic. Just because there's a bit of rain it seemingly means they all have to jump in their cars and bring London streets to a damn standstill."

Knutsen winked at Roberts and whispered, "There is a reason why he has no woman in his life."

Sign placed his grocery bags on a table, and hugged Roberts. "Today was the day. My sincerest condolences." He stepped back. "Tonight I'm cooking Mexican food. Given it's a Wednesday, I'm guessing that you two are shortly off to bash each other over the heads with bamboo sticks. Does a late dinner at nine PM sharp suit?"

They nodded.

"Good, because I've got nothing else to worry about and do aside from solving why Mrs. Parson's husband was caught in flagrante with a gay Lithuanian man, why a rebel Tory MP adhered to the whip and voted against his fellow rebels, and whether an escaped London Zoo golden eagle, that's been terrorising small dogs in Hyde Park, legally constitutes a redefinition of assault versus natural predatory behaviour. I am bored."

Knutsen went up to him. "Katy's going back to work. She will ensure we're still on the whisperer case."

Sign looked at her. His demeanour and tone of voice changed - less strident; more thoughtful. "You wish to catch your husband's killer. You've enrolled Knutsen to help you snatch the limpet. Together, you'll aim to get the truth out of him. Who is the whisperer?"

. "Yes."

"We tried that already. Knutsen came out of the encounter battered and bruised. And for nearly a month I've seen no evidence that the limpet's been following us. We need another development. If that happens, we spring into action; he springs into action. At that point, you have my blessing to try to get him. But you'll have to be very careful. He'll try to kill you both. And he'll only talk if he's under extreme duress. Hurt him to the point he thinks he's going to die. Offer him medical assistance on the condition he tells you the name we need." He looked at Knutsen. "A leg shot might suffice. Be accurate. The limpet will know about battle injuries. He has to be convinced he'll bleed to death unless you apply tourniquets, give him morphine, extract the bullet, stitch him up, and place paddings on the wound. Search him thoroughly. He must have zero means to communicate with the whisperer. What you do with the limpet after that is of no concern to me."

Roberts asked, "And if we get the whisperer's name, what will you do?"

Sign slumped into a chair and placed the tips of his fingers together. "I'll put the whisperer out of his misery."

Hilt met John Smith in *Pizza Express* in Hertford. He ordered a mineral water but no food, sat opposite the senior spy and said, "I've been watching them."

"All three?"

"Yep."

"Good. You have a pattern of behaviour?"

"Tonight, two of them are going out. The other will stay in and cook. Least ways, that's how it's worked every Wednesday evening so far."

"Okay. Tomorrow morning I want you to do something very unpleasant. But it won't be unpleasant for you." Smith smiled, though his expression was cold. He handed Hilt a small rucksack. "In there are things you'll need. Did you get the rifle?"

"Yeah. Lee Enfield .303. Bit old school, but it will do the job."

"Old school is necessary. And you've put a message on the gun?"

Hilt smiled. "An engraved message on a brass plate on the rifle's butt."

"Good. Tomorrow, wear a face mask that covers your mouth and nose. I can't have one drop of your saliva or any other involuntary excretions on the weapon. Obviously wear gloves. And wear a coat that has a hood and won't release fibres – a rain mac or similar. Bottom line, there must be no DNA, fingerprints, or other suspicious traces on the rifle." He told Hilt exactly what he had to do in the morning.

CHAPTER 18

Snowflakes the size of saucers sank slowly downward as Hilt lay prone and trained his rifle on his targets. Two people were walking slowly along a street; houses and commercial buildings were either side of them. They were only fifty yards away. If they moved out of sight, Hilt would simply reposition and get them once again in his sight. Either way, they were dead if he wanted them to be. On top of the World War 2 rifle, Hilt had gaffer-taped a modern scope. He had no idea why Smith wanted him to do this job. He didn't care. This was target practice. Out of the rucksack Smith had given him, he withdrew a laptop and tiny camera. He attached the camera to his right eye and plugged a cable between it and a laptop. Into the laptop he wired a mobile phone that gave him Internet connection. The laptop was good to go; the camera was good to go. He Skyped Smith, looked at the targets through the camera and sniper scope, and asked, "Are you getting this?"

Smith replied, "Yes. Visual is good. Whatever happens, keep them in your sight." Smith walked along a street within a housing estate. It was early morning; people were leaving their houses to attend to their daily chores. He reached a detached house – modest in size and identical to all of the other houses surrounding the property. He was wearing a suit and overcoat, because he was due to be in work soon. He rang the doorbell and waited.

A man opened the door, chewing the last mouthful of a bacon sandwich that he'd prepared for breakfast. He looked shocked. "What are you doing here?"

"Hello Terry. We have an emergency."

"At the office?"

"Yes."

"You'd better come in." Like Smith, Terry File was smartly dressed, though he wasn't yet wearing his jacket. As they walked to the lounge, the head of MI6's paramilitary unit said, "I've got a meeting with the chief at ten o'clock. That means I have to catch the…"

"0817 from Hertford North to King's Cross."

File's eyes narrowed. "How did you know that?"

Smith shrugged as he waved a hand through the air. "You live in Hertford. It's the next available train into London. I need to be on that train because I too have meetings this morning in head office."

"What's this about?"

"It's about an assassination. Actually, potentially three assassinations. It falls right into your remit."

"You wish me to deploy some of my team to stop it happening?"

"It might be too late for that, but I do need your advice. I have data I need to show you. I'd value your opinion. I must warn you – it makes for uncomfortable viewing."

File sat in a chair. "In my time in this job, I've seen things you wouldn't believe – videos of beheadings, rape, genocide, and so much more. I doubt what you're going to show me will be more upsetting."

"This might be." From his briefcase, Sign took an IPad and its stand and placed both on a coffee table, facing File.

"Should I ring the chief and cancel our meeting?"

"That won't be necessary. This won't take long. You'll have enough time to get your train." Smith sat next to the coffee table. "The assassination attempts pertain to an MI6 officer and his affiliates. We need to move very fast on this."

File frowned. "Why didn't you just call me on the secure line, rather than come all the way up here? It would have been so much quicker."

"We have a breach of security. It's most relevant to the assassinations. Even secure communications might be compromised. This had to be dealt with face to face."

"Breach of security? What, exactly?"

"Someone is corrupting MI6. The Office doesn't yet know who. It may never know. But we do know lives are at stake." Smith held up his hand. "Don't worry. You're not a suspect. We know you're loyal to the cause. Plus, you're a devout Catholic. It would be inconceivable for you to betray your country and your ethics. The only thing that matters more to you than patriotism and your religion, is your family. You have a wife and a five year old boy, I believe."

File bristled. "I do. Why's that relevant?"

Smith turned on the Ipad and activated Skype. "There they are. Your wife; your son. How sweet – they're holding hands. As usual, your wife is walking your son to pre-school nursery. She'll drop him off, do some shopping, and return most likely around mid-morning."

File was incredulous. "What's going on?!"

"I told you – we're dealing with one or possibly three assassinations. The numbers will be down to you. What you're seeing is a video taken by my sniper. It's in live time. My sniper will kill your wife and child if needs be."

"You fucking…!"

Smith smiled. "You're a big man. You could probably overpower me and call the police. The problem you have is that my sniper is listening to our conversation. My orders to him are that if he has the slightest indication that I'm in danger, he must pull the trigger. First it will be your wife. The son will be utterly confused. Most likely he'll stay with his mother's body. But, if he runs, he'll make five yards or so before his head is blown off. And cops will be of no use to you. Their response time is three minutes at best. You of all people know that a bullet is considerably faster than that."

File looked at the screen and saw his wife and son walking down one of the streets they always took in the outskirts of Hertford, en route to school. "This could be a pre-recording from yesterday or any other school day."

"It could be but it's not. And you know that. Look at your wife's garments. Did she wear them yesterday, the day before, or anytime this week? And if she did, were they the same combination as she's wearing today."

File walked up to Smith and grabbed him by the chin. "Why are you doing this, you bastard?!"

Smith was unperturbed. "Because I want to remove you from the shortlist of candidates to be the next chief of MI6. Take your hand off me or they die."

File backed away, breathing rapidly. "You won't get away with this!"

"Well, we'll see. But your wife and son can certainly come away from this situation alive if you do the honourable thing."

"Honourable thing?"

Smith took a length of rope from his briefcase. He expertly tied a hangman's noose at one end, screwed a hook into the skirting board, attached the other end of the rope to the screw, and slung the rope over another screw-hook that he'd inserted into the wooden beam traversing the ceiling. He pulled up a dining chair directly under the noose. "You must choose - your life versus your wife and son's life."

File was shaking. "You... you can't."

Smith placed a finger on the screen. "My sniper has repositioned to get a clean line of sight of the final leg of your wife and son's journey. Ordinarily they'd reach school in about five minutes. That can still happen, but only if you comply. If you don't they'll be shot dead before they complete their journey. Get on the chair!"

File whipped out his mobile phone.

"By all means call your wife. She'll be dead before you utter a word to her."

Tears were running down File's sweaty face.

"Time is running out. What does your conscience tell you? How will you live with yourself if you let your family die to save your skin? In what direction is your moral compass pointing? What would God say about your decision?"

"You're... you're bluffing."

"I never bluff." Smith spoke to Hilt. "Shoot her in the ankle, then train your rifle on the boy's head."

File shouted, "No!" as he saw his wife collapse to the ground.

The boy was bent over her, clutching his mum.

Smith laughed. "She'll need reconstructive surgery. But she'll live. There might be some concerned civilians who come to her assistance. But," he looked at the screen, "That's not happening yet. Your wife's pulled out her phone. She'll be calling emergency services. After that she might call you. If so, I give you permission to speak to her providing you are on the chair with the noose around your neck. If you tell her to tell your son to run, he'll be killed first, your wife second."

File was gripping his head so hard that blood was oozing out of his skull. He screamed again. "You bastard. Bastard!" He stood on the chair. "May God have mercy on your soul, you piece of scum."

"The clock is ticking, Mr. File." Smith turned to the Ipad and said to Hilt, "Prepare to kill the child. We are moments away."

File's mobile rang. It was his wife. He answered the call. His voice was trembling as he said, "I love you, Debby. I love you and Thomas so very, very much. This is not what it seems."

Smith wagged a finger.

File ended the call and dropped the phone onto the floor.

Smith checked the phone to ensure the phone wasn't still transmitting. He replaced it back on the floor.

File stared at Smith. "You... you might kill them anyway."

"Tut, tut, Mr. File. I am not a monster. Once you're dead I have no interest in your wife and son. They'll be left alone."

"You are a monster!"

"Maybe. You have ten seconds to kick the chair away. If you don't, the fireworks begin in earnest."

File closed his eyes and started muttering a prayer.

"Your god isn't going to save your wife and child. Right now, I'm God. Move fast."

File was hyperventilating. He looked at the ceiling. "Forgive me, Lord." He kicked the chair away and dangled while choking and writhing. It took a minute before he went limp, dead.

Smith shut his IPad and called Smith on his mobile. "It's done. Get to the house asap. The woman and boy are of no use to us now. Leave them alone. Remember what we spoke about – sorting the house is vital. We'll only have a few minutes to get it done. I'll make a start now while you're heading here. Your gun is vital; so too eradicating all traces of our presence. Meanwhile, I'll plant the evidence." Smith smiled and set to work.

Roberts hammered Sign and Knutsen's door, her heart beating fast, face pasty and oily after a sleepless night. She was in her pyjamas and didn't give a hoot about her appearance. Sign and Knutsen were like brothers to her. They'd seen her in worse states.

Sign opened the door. He was unshaven and wearing a dressing gown. "Everything okay?"

Roberts was breathless as she said, "I've just had a call from the commissioner. There's been another suicide. In Hertford. Terry File. MI6 confirmed to the commissioner that he's one of yours."

Sign bellowed, "Action stations!" He grabbed Roberts arm. "Call for a Met car and driver. The car must not be unmarked. The driver must be expert. His number plate must be flagged as unstoppable by other squad cars. We'll need to break speed limits." He turned. "Mr. Knutsen – we have ten minutes to get shaved, showered, and dressed!"

Fifteen minutes later, Roberts, Knutsen and Sign were hurtling through London, heading north. The driver was a traffic cop. His vehicle's blue lights and sirens were on permanently.

Sign cupped a hand around Roberts' ear. "We can't speak openly here. The driver isn't security cleared. I'll tell you what you need to know when we're at our destination."

Normally the route at this time of morning would have taken at least seventy five minutes. But with the help of driving that entailed cars swerving left and right when they heard the vehicle's sirens, the cop driver utilising not only road but also pavements, and a driving speed that constantly produced an adrenalin rush for the car's passengers, they made it to Terry File's house in forty minutes flat.

All of them got out of the police car. The driver lit a cigarette and wandered over to the only other police officers who were leaning against their vehicle while drinking coffee. Next to their response car was a white van belonging to forensics. Alongside that was a black BMW. Colin Parker, the MI6 head of counter intelligence, was in the vehicle. He got out when he saw Sign.

Sign walked up to him while glancing at the house that was surrounded by blue and white tape with the words, POLICE LINE. DO NOT CROSS. "What happened, Colin?"

The senior MI6 officer replied, "File shot his wife while she was taking her kid to nursery. Then he hanged himself. Forensics is in there now. They've been here for an hour."

"The body?"

"Taken to Watford General Hospital. The media haven't been notified. But if some of them get wind of this I'll ruin their day."

Sign nodded. "What's your take?"

"Face value or instinct honed over decades? Face value is as follows: we found bank statements in a filing cabinet belonging to his wife. The wife had been running up credit card debts way beyond File's paygrade. They were financially crippled. She also had photos of her husband with another woman – nothing lewd; just street shots of them together in daylight. And her husband's prints and DNA are all over the Lee Enfield rifle he allegedly used to shoot his wife. He missed and hit her in the ankle. She's in the same hospital as her dead husband. She'll be alright."

"But what about your instinct?"

Parker rubbed his face. "Actually, *instinct* is the wrong word. *Intellect* and *covert experience* would be the right phrase." He nodded at the house. "Go in there and see what you think. Forensics will require you to wear head to toe white garments and gloves. See what you make of the suicide scene."

Sign asked, "Who do the police think you are?"

Quietly, Parker replied, "MI5. They know File was MI6, but I can't have them knowing that I'm also MI6. I suggest you adopt a similar cover story."

Sign agreed. MI5 was one step away from being a police agency. MI6 was nothing like that. It was a top secret spy agency and its members – past and present – had to remain in the shadows. Five minutes later, he, Knutsen and Roberts were in the house. Two forensics officers were also in there. They'd finished their job and were preparing to leave. On a dining room table were clear plastic bags containing the evidence they'd collected – the bank statements, rifle, rope that File had hanged himself with, File's mobile phone, his wallet, train tickets to London, shoes, and photos of him with the woman. Sign examined them all.

The forensics officers were removing their white overalls. Sign asked one of them, "What do you think?"

The female forensics officer shrugged. "Detectives will interview Mrs. File when she's out of surgery. Everything points to a domestic dispute. He may have been having an affair; Mrs. File found out; she got emotional and wanted revenge; she binged on her credit card, just to spite him; she confronted him and told him that she knew he was seeing a woman and that she's created one hell of a financial debt; he cracked and shot her with his rifle; then he killed himself." She frowned. "How would he be allowed to have a rifle?"

"He worked in MI6 special projects. The inscription to him on the gun suggests it was a gift – most likely from a foreign ally. Technically he shouldn't have kept the gun at his house. Sometimes guys like File break rules."

The forensics officer smiled. "These MI6 people make up the rules as they go along. Unlike you MI5 guys, they don't follow procedures and laws."

"Quite." Sign looked around. "Did anything strike you as odd in the house?"

"No."

"Fingerprints?"

"All normal. Fingerprints of the Files and their son – upstairs and downstairs. No other prints."

"And File's prints were on the gun?"

"Yes. Also his saliva was on the side of the weapon. He also had cordite on his forearms. It's not visible to the naked eye. But we have specialist equipment. Most shooters don't know they leave traces of their presence when they shoot guns."

"It was File's job to know such matters." Sign swung around and pointed. "The chair was here." To himself, he muttered, "Where, where?" He knew the answer and sat on a chair facing the place where File killed himself. He knew this was where the whisperer sat, because it was the exact spot Sign would have chosen under the same circumstances. He addressed the forensics officer. "You must have examined hundreds of domestic homes in your career. All of them contain tell-tale signs of the inhabitants. Also, they contain signs of visitors. Did the chair have File's prints on it?"

"Yes. Also Mrs. File's prints. It was a dining table chair, identical to the chair you're sitting on."

"So, it was well used." File drummed his fingers on the adjacent dining table. "Did you check for prints of any kind on the table and other chairs around me?"

The forensics officer checked her notes. "Yes. There were no prints whatsoever – not the Files' or anyone else. The table and chairs must have been cleaned recently, or not used for a long time."

"Yes, that makes sense." Sign stood. "Thank you, officer. As you say, this looks like a tragic falling out between husband and wife. There's no role for me and my colleagues in this matter." He left the house with his colleagues. To Knutsen, he said, "Wait here with Katy for a moment." He walked to Parker and said to him, "It was murder. Meet me at my flat at seven PM this evening."

Hilt watched Sign through high-powered binoculars. He cursed and called Smith. "The pain in the ass is on your back again. He's been to the house. Roberts and Knutsen are with him. They're all leaving now."

Smith replied, "Sign will know the scene was stage-managed. But he'll have no proof." He laughed. "That will considerably annoy him. He's digging a hole for himself. In the end, he'll be a laughing stock and his credibility will be shattered. Stay on him though. And watch out for Knutsen and Roberts. They'll try to grab you while you're watching Sign. They'll try to use you to get to me."

"Understood boss. If that happens, what are my protocols?"

"Kill them."

"No problem."

That evening in West Square, Sign paced back and forth in front of Roberts and Knutsen. He checked his watch. "We don't have long. In five minutes' time, the man you saw me speaking to outside File's house will arrive here. He won't be late or early. He's a very senior MI6 officer and is the only person at that grade that I trust. I won't introduce him to you as MI6. I'll leave it to him to decide how he couches his credentials. I'd be put in prison for blowing someone's cover without authority. But when he arrives, I am going to break other rules that are equally detrimental to my freedom. Win him over; charm him; show him you mean business." The downstairs communal intercom buzzed. Sign looked at Knutsen. "Do your usual security checks first. If all is good, let him in."

Two minutes' later, Colin Parker was in the room.

Sign gestured to the others. "This is detective inspector Katy Roberts of the Metropolitan Police Special Branch. You saw her this morning. She has been working with me for several weeks and is my sole link to the commissioner of her service. The gentleman sat next to her is Tom Knutsen. He has recently retired from the Metropolitan Police. When in service, he was a detective and an undercover operative. Their credentials are impeccable."

Parker nodded at them and slung his overcoat onto a chair. "You're all working on File's suicide?"

Sign pulled out a chair. "Take a seat dear chap. We're working on a pattern of behaviour. Archer, Lake, and now File. In a matter of weeks they took their lives."

Parker was impatient. "I know!" He sat.

"Would you like to tell Mrs. Roberts and Mr. Knutsen who you are?"

"I work in government service."

"They'll need specifics if they're to trust you."

Parker looked horrified. "Ben, what the..?"

Sign smiled. "They know I'm formerly MI6."

"Good for you. I didn't realise you were so loose lipped."

"Three deaths. But it's not just three deaths." He pointed at Roberts. "Katy's husband was murdered by a killer who I strongly suspect is working for the man who's orchestrating the suicides."

Parker looked at Roberts. "I'm sorry... I heard, but didn't know it was your husband."

"Why would you?" Roberts pointed at Sign. "Knutsen describes Sign as a magpie. He collects things. But only things of extreme value to him. He's collected Knutsen and me. Maybe he wants to collect you." She gestured to the antiquities, other artefacts, and books in the lounge. "As far as I can ascertain, there are four things that are vital to his life and work: trust, kindness, authenticity, and expertise. You won't find one item in this room that doesn't match all four criteria."

The accurate observation startled Sign. He decided to lighten the tone and opened a drawer in his wooden writing desk. "Thank you for being so flattering, Mrs. Roberts. But, I do have some things in here that don't quite match those criteria. An eighteenth century cutthroat razor used by a man who wanted to cut off my head," he rummaged through the contents of the drawer, "a leather sheaf containing a pin dipped in poison – I would have died in two seconds if the woman had succeeded in sticking it in me, a defused bomb inside one of my old mobile phones, a revolver that nearly blew my head off, and so many other things. He slammed the drawer shut. My Pandora's Box. But Mrs. Roberts is right – everything else, organic or inorganic, in my flat matches her criteria." He looked at Parker. "We're dealing with matters of national interest. That bothers me of course, though I'm no longer in that game. So, all a humble civilian like me can do is deal with the immediate problem. We're dealing with a serial killer. If we capture or kill him we…"

"Nip the bud before it grows into an oak." Parker looked at Knutsen and Roberts. He was silent. All were silent. Then he said, "I am head of counter intelligence at MI6. I am due to retire in six months' time. By declaring my status to you, the only things I have to lose are my pension and my dignity."

Knutsen replied, "We don't breathe a word to anyone outside of this room. That's how we're wired."

"It had better be." Parker addressed Sign. "You've spoken to the chief?"

"Yes."

"As cantankerous as ever?"

"Correct. But he did help." Sign pulled out an old school chalkboard that he'd rescued during a Pakistani bombardment of an empty Indian school. "I'm not supposed to do this." He winked at Knutsen. "But I'm going to." He started writing on the board, using chalk. "The outgoing chief gave me the list of candidates for the top job in MI6." He wrote the list. "One of them could be the whisperer."

Parker frowned. "The whisperer?"

"The person who whispers people to death." Sign drew two lines down the board, thereby dividing it into three columns. At the top of column one he wrote the title, *List of Candidates to be Chief of MI6*. He drew a line through Archer, Lake, and File. "That leaves me, Messenger, Pendry, and Logan on the list. I'm no longer in MI6, but could I be playing a canny game, hoping to get back into the organisation at the very top?"

Knutsen said, "No."

Roberts and Parker agreed.

Knutsen added, "You weren't anywhere near the death scenes when the suicides happened. I bear witness to that."

Sign put a line though his name. "So that leaves Messenger, Pendry, and Logan. All potential victims? Or, is one of them the killer? In the middle column he wrote the title, *Tangential Victims*. Beneath that he wrote the names Elliot Roberts and Debby File. "Any of us could join this middle list." On the right column he wrote the title, *The Murderers*. Beneath that he wrote the words 'whisperer' and 'limpet'. He looked at Parker. "The limpet, I am sure, is former paramilitary MI6."

"Shit!"

"Yes. But he's not the brains. He's an employee. An extremely ruthless one at that." Sign patted Roberts, Knutsen, and Parker on their shoulders. "Everything – absolutely *everything* – is kept within this room. Mr. Parker – would you care to help us with our investigation?"

Parker glanced at Knutsen and Roberts. "I have a day job."

"Which is vital to us. What does MI6 think about the suicides?"

"It thinks there's a conspiracy between Archer, Lake, and File. They got caught out by a foreign intelligence agency. They killed themselves rather than face the music."

"Idiots!" Sign started pacing again. "MI6 knows that's not the case. But it wants this to be swept under the carpet."

Parker bowed his head. "Ben – you know these are troubling times. We have an idiot savant U.S. president, problems in Germany, major problems with Russia, the possibility of nuclear war with North Korea, China breathing down our necks, Brexit, terrorism at the drop of a loony tunes hat, UK politics all over the show, and UK workers overseas looking at our shores as if they're stranded troops on the sands of Dunkirk. We need a new head of MI6. No one outside of the list is qualified for the role."

"MI6 could recruit someone outside of The Office; perhaps from the Diplomatic Service. It's happened before."

Parker shook his head. "Not in this climate. Right now we need an expert spy; a combatant. These are not times for diplomacy."

"And what about you, Colin? You could postpone your retirement. You are both senior and experienced. The only reason you're not on the list is because you're soon leaving the service."

Parker shook his head. "I've told you before – My partner and I have plans. We've bought a restaurant in France."

Sign stared at the board. "So, it's down to Pendry, Messenger, and Logan."

Parker said, "We could put protection around them."

"We could. But in doing so, we could be protecting the whisperer from himself. We'd never find out his identity." Sign walked up to Parker. "Are you prepared to help us?"

"Doing what?"

"Work from the inside. How do you get on with the head of security?"

Parker shrugged. "He's a bumptious plodder who has ideas above his station. But he does the job right. I can work with him."

"You'll need Gable's permission for this, but why don't you and the head of security interview and brief Messenger, Pendry, and Logan. Ostensibly it will be to flesh out their understanding of operational security and counter-intelligence. The meetings would be couched as part of the selection process for the next chief."

"The chief interviews are not scheduled until two months before Gable retires. You know how it works. There's a ring of steel put around the process to ascertain the next chief. Only a handful of people in MI6 are privy to that process. To interview candidates now would be premature and unprecedented."

"I know." Sign sat in his armchair. "But these interviews would be data sharing, not the real deal. Look at it this way: when an election is about to take place, MI6 always briefs potential foreign secretaries from all major parties, on the basis that elections can be unpredictable and whoever wins must hit the ground running. This could be a similar dynamic."

"It could." Parker was deep in thought. "I'll speak to the chief. I'm sure I can set this up. Presumably what you want me to do is get the measure of Messenger, Pendry, and Logan."

"Yes. See if one of them is a psychopath."

Parker laughed. "I'm good at my job, but a highly intelligent serial killer is hardly going to reveal himself to me."

"Ask them, 'What would you do?' questions. What would you do if you met an agent in Islamabad, and your agent was compromised? Would you save the agent or get out of there on the basis that you carry a treasure trove of secrets in your head? Work the angles; keep probing. Eventually the answers to your questions may paint a picture. We're looking for a narcissist; someone who only prioritises himself. The whisperer is ruthless and single minded. He doesn't care about others."

"Logan, Pendry, and Messenger are too bright to fall for that."

"Then set them up for a fall. Tell them these are troubling times. We need clear thinkers. People who are not afraid to make tough decisions. Lure the whisperer out with the backdrop of a world that's turned to madness. See if the whisperer bites and answers your questions truthfully."

Parker sighed. "I'll try. But let me put it this way: if I interviewed you under similar circumstances, you'd run circles around me, the head of security, the chief, the prime minister, in fact anyone in power."

"But, you're not interviewing me."

"Have you considered the possibility that the whisperer is as clever as you?"

"I've considered the possibility that his intellect outstrips mine." Sign said, "Give it a shot. Sometimes it's not about the answers, but rather the demeanour of the interviewees. Use your antennae. Who, sitting in front of you, could be a murderer?"

Parker stood and put on his coat. "I'd be going out on a massive limb for you all." He hesitated. "But I'll do it. Oh, and if I took your question literally, I can see two male murderers in this room." He left.

Sign said to Knutsen and Roberts, "Good. We have Parker on our task force. Now – I need to cook a stir fry. It's my own recipe, adapted from a recipe I received from a Chinese prostitute I rescued from a slave trade program. Mrs. Roberts – I suggest you stay for supper. There are no aromas of food coming from your kitchen and one can only eat takeaways now and again. Mr. Knutsen – shall we all eat our Chinese food while playing a board game? Trivial Pursuit?"

"No! You always win."

"Monopoly?"

"You cheat."

Sign considered the options. "Texas Hold'em poker. Five quid in loose change maximum per player. Winner takes all." Sign paused before entering the kitchen. His face and tone of voice were serious as he said, "Parker will not be able to achieve much beyond character assessments. Even that will be flawed because Logan, Messenger, and Pendry are chameleons. Parker's use to me is not to flush out the whisperer; rather, to tell him the net is closing around him. The whisperer will see through Parker and know he's working for me. We must pray nothing bad happens to Parker."

CHAPTER 19

Roberts entered the commissioner's office in New Scotland Yard. Wearing a smart black trouser suit with her ID badge pinned to her collar, and with her hair pinned up, she looked every inch the top detective the Met had to offer. Much to the consternation of the commissioner, she sat on the edge of his desk and addressed him. "Let's cut to the chase. I'm still grieving, but am rational. Knutsen's a power house. Sign's IQ is off the charts. And we have a fourth member of our team – an MI6 officer – who may be able to help. We also have a list of three people who may be potential victims or suspects. I can't tell you who's on that list – it's classified – but I can tell you we're making progress. Keep Sign and Knutsen on the payroll. If you don't, you may be compromising national security. I want your assurance that you'll keep us all on the case."

The commissioner partly wanted to bollock Roberts for being so impertinent. But secretly he loved the fact that she was back in the saddle. "I presume the three people on the list are MI6."

"Yes, but it's more complicated than that. There are other potential victims in play. Plus, we have a hitman in the mix – my husband's murderer."

The commissioner looked away. "I will renew Sign's contract from my slush fund. Stay on the case and stay focused. MI5 is breathing down my neck. They're gunning for an MI6 scandal."

"Just tell MI5 to fuck off. They're reasonably good at catching terrorists on UK soil. They're bugger all use for anything more cerebral." Roberts stood. "I want to interview Debby File."

"She's been interviewed already."

"But not by me. Where is she?"

The commissioner replied, "In the same hospital." He sighed. "You can see her. I'll notify the appropriate authorities." His eyes narrowed. "You have your war-paint on, and I'm thankful, but what's the devil in the detail?"

Roberts wondered if she should tell her boss the truth. She decided she should. "My husband put a flower in my hair on the summit of Mount Snowden and kissed me; I burned his body and tossed the remains onto the rocks. We bought a house that was to be ours forever; I've just sold it to an anonymous cash buyer. My stomach cramps at night. I smell him, even though it should be impossible to do so. So, the devil in the detail has a new face.- a murderer. I've put my affairs to bed. I need to catch the killer."

The commissioner stood, walked round his desk, and touched Roberts' elbow. Ordinarily it would have been an inappropriate action for such a senior officer to make. But, the commissioner was happily married and viewed Roberts as a daughter. "Time heals. Work helps."

"I hope so."

"Go interview Debby File and find out if something's amiss." The commissioner smiled sympathetically. "The anonymous cash buyer for your house was Ben Sign. He wanted the place off your hands as soon as possible. He paid more than the asking price. When the transaction's complete, he'll hopefully sell the place. He took a mortgage out against his pension."

Roberts was startled. "His pension? That could cripple him. I don't need his charity!"

"You don't. But you do need friends. Sign wasn't giving you charity; he was giving you closure, despite the cost to himself."

Hilt watched Roberts enter Watford General Hospital. The limpet was in a car, holding a zoom lens camera to his face. His handgun was tucked under his belt at the nape of his spine. He called Smith and told him what he was seeing.

Smith replied, "Let Roberts proceed. I've geared this to make it look like Debby File is integral to her husband's death. Lack of evidence to the contrary is all that matters to us. But stay on Roberts. I want to know where she goes next."

Roberts entered Debby File's hospital room. Aside, from File and Roberts, the room was empty. File was on a bed, her left leg elevated and held in place by straps. A plaster cast and bandages were on her ankle; a drip was by her arm, its liquid intravenously entering her forearm via tubes. Her auburn hair was matted, eyes bloodshot, face blotchy.

Roberts pulled up a chair and sat next to her. "I'm Detective Inspector Katy Roberts of the Metropolitan Police Service. I know you've been interviewed before, but I'm working a different angle. I'd like to talk to you."

"Detective Roberts – I have nothing to add to that which I've already said to your colleagues. I was shot in the ankle. My husband committed suicide. I never spent the things the bank said I spent on my credit card. If my husband had that rifle in our house, he must have kept it well hidden from me. My husband loved me and our son. He showed no signs of instability. He was a clever man. He'd have worked us out of debt. Why did he kill himself? It makes no sense."

Roberts pulled out copies of File's credit card statements. "These say you spent nearly twenty three thousand pounds in two days. None of the purchases were blocked by your bank, because the things you bought were typical of the kind of items you'd bought in the past – food at Tesco's, online shopping at Amazon, ditto M&S and Next, utility bills, and petrol. Plus, you paid a rather hefty bill for your car to be repaired at your local mechanics, on top of which you booked a holiday at your local travel agent for you and your family to spend four weeks in a series of luxury resorts in Asia. That holiday alone cost seven thousand pounds, factoring in business-class flights."

File shook her head. "I didn't buy any of those things. The last time I used my credit card was about three weeks ago. And that was to buy lunch at a pub. This must be a mistake."

"Your credit card statements are delivered to you once a month. It looks like you requested these copies in advance of your regular statements."

File looked confused. "I didn't request them. I'd never seen them before one of your colleagues showed them to me."

"And yet they were found in your filing cabinet. Could your husband have requested them?"

"No. We have separate bank accounts. He doesn't have authority to access mine."

"Are you sure your husband didn't see these statements?"

"No, I'm not sure! I don't hide things from my husband. My filing cabinet is unlocked. I didn't know the statements were in there! But he never snoops. Least ways, not at home." She started sobbing. "Anyway, why would he shoot me and hang himself over twenty three thousand pounds? It doesn't make sense."

"No, it doesn't. But it makes enough sense for a coroner's report to conclude that you and your husband were under marital stress. It will conclude that violence led to these outcomes." Roberts showed her the photo of Terry File and the woman. "Have you seen this before? It too was in your filing cabinet."

"No! No, no. no!"

"Do you know who she is?"

"I've never seen her before. My husband was faithful."

Roberts put the photo back in her pocket. "I believe you. The woman was one of his colleagues. They were working. I've no idea who took the photo."

File breathed deeply. "What's happening?"

"I'm trying to find out. Who's looking after your son?"

"My brother and his wife. They live nearby."

"Has your husband ever expressed suicidal thoughts before?"

"Never. He was happy."

Roberts nodded. "You are security cleared to know exactly the nature of his work?"

File replied, "He's been MI6 all of his adult life. His last job was head of the paramilitary unit. He didn't go out and do the 'guns and glory' stuff, as he used to call the work of his department. He merely managed his units from his office in HQ."

"Did he know how to use a gun?"

"Of course."

"How good?"

"If he wanted to kill me, he'd have done so." File winced as she adjusted position in her bed."

Roberts stood. "Nothing you've told me or my colleagues is admissible in a court of law. You're on morphine painkillers. Anything you say until you're off morphine cannot be deemed as evidence. But, for what it's worth, I believe you. Something's not right. There is a team working on your case. I'm part of that team. We have access to places that other police and investigators can't access." She paused before leaving. "I've recently gone through the loss of my husband. I suppose it varies per person, but if you're like me it starts bad, then becomes hell, but finally gets into the realm of being a new chapter in your life."

"Do you have children?"

Roberts shook her head.

"Imagine explaining to a child that their daddy isn't coming home. That new chapter you speak of may never come to me, let alone my son."

That evening, Parker was in Sign's lounge. Sign, Knutsen, and Roberts were also present. Sign had made mince pies and mulled wine. He handed out the food and drink to the team before taking his seat.

Parker said, "The head of security and I interviewed and briefed Messenger, Pendry, and Logan."

"All three of them together, or individually?" asked Knutsen.

"Individually. But we didn't have much time, given it was arranged at short notice. We had thirty minutes with each officer." Parker took a sip of his mulled wine. "Ooh, this is good. You've put something different in here."

"Ginger." Sign tapped his finger against Logan, Messenger, and Pendry's names on the chalkboard. "How did you couch the interviews?"

"As we agreed. I told them that the interviews were not part of the upcoming formal application process to become chief. I added that, if anything, today's meetings were designed to bolster their knowledge of security matters and thereby enhance their chances of success within the application process. I said matters were becoming urgent. All three of them were aware of the suicides of Archer, Lake, and File. We told them that MI6 is cooperating with the police but MI6 is also conducting its own investigation. I said that it was probable that the suicides were linked; that all three may have taken their lives because they were in some kind of conspiracy that compromised the integrity of MI6. Most likely they were blackmailed by a foreign intelligence agency. They cracked and took the easy way out."

"Good." Sign brushed chalk dust off his fingers. "Do you think they bought that falsehood?"

"Of course not. But not one of them indicated they knew I was lying."

"To be expected." Sign closed his eyes. "Logan, Pendry and File. Two of them may be potential victims. One of them may be the whisperer." He opened his eyes and stared at Parker. "Which one is the whisperer?"

Parker sighed. "I couldn't tell. Messenger has fourteen aliases. That means he's fourteen different people. Pendry has adopted the mantle of spin doctor. Anything that comes out of his mouth is utter shite. Logan is ruthless and arrogant. He prides himself on speaking five Asian languages with fluency. He keeps his cards close to his chest."

Sign repeated, "Which one of them is a killer?"

"Come on Ben! We're all in that ballgame! It's like gathering a bunch of lunatics and asking them 'Which one of you has been a naughty boy?'"

Sign ignored the astute comment. "Messenger is head of MI6's European Controllerate. Fourteen aliases is a heavy burden. At peak, I did sixteen. Managing that for years induces schizophrenia. Pendry is Head of Communications. That means he needs to speak to every component of UK government, together with the media and foreign governments. He's a political animal. Power has rubbed off on him. He knows how to manipulate the world. Logan is the dark horse. He thinks like an Asian. Family is essential; the lives of others are not. He'd happily cut out your eyes if it meant he could save his wife and kids." Sign wrote three words next to the suspects on the board. "Schizophrenic, megalomaniac, psychopath." He looked uneasy as he spoke quietly to the board. "Which one of you is the whisperer?"

CHAPTER 20

John Smith entered the chief's office in MI6 headquarters. The large room contained framed photos of every chief who'd served in the organisation since it was created in 1909. Typically, each chief served five years before being told to retire. The current chief was no exception. He had three months left in MI6 before he'd swap his cloak and dagger for something more benign. Smith was counting down the days for that to happen.

He sat opposite Henry Gable. "You wished to see me, sir. I have to say it's inconvenient. I'm running a misinformation exercise in parliament. MPs are nibbling at the false intelligence I've fed them. It should sway them on their vote on Syria."

Gable sighed. "Games, games. You were always very good at them. But yes – we need parliament to vote the right way." He ran a finger around his tea cup. "That's not why you're here. Archer's dead; Lake's dead; File's dead. That leaves you and two others in the running for my job."

"Who are the others?"

"You know full well who they are." Gable wondered how MI6 would fare if Smith was made chief. Still, Smith was exceptionally bright and ruthless. Maybe that's what the service needed right now. "I've been advised by an external agency not to protect you and the other two candidates. As contrarian as it sounds, the rationale behind that advice is that we must weed out the bad apples. Are you a bad apple?"

"Yes."

"Don't be flippant with me. Do you have any links to Archer, Lake, and File?"

"Of course. We've all gained seniority in MI6."

"And they're dead."

"And I'm not." Smith looked at the pictures of the chiefs. Soon, he'd be up there. "You'll be going out having hit the zenith of a remarkable stint of service. But you won't matter when you're gone. The service will put a picture of you on a wall. It's the equivalent of getting a gold pen at the end of a career where you've sacrificed everything and received little in return."

"So, why do you want the job?"

"I want to change things. Get rid of the pomp and bullshit in The Office."

"Do you now?" Gable chuckled. "You have ambitions above your station."

Smith shook his head. "You're in charge of a bunch of free thinkers who don't give a shit about what you say. Name me one other government organisation – Crown Service, military, Civil Service – that contains people like that."

Gable was silent.

"Free thinking is crucial. But I want us to adopt a U.S. model – more militaristic in chain of command; and I want UK special forces to report to the chief of MI6, not the director of UKSF. In fact I want the post of director scrapped."

Gable frowned. "You want control of the SAS, SBS, and SRR?"

"And MI5. It's about time those knuckle heads were merged with MI6. I'll sack most of them and get people with brains to replace them."

Gable said, "You'd be building a fiefdom."

"I'd be building a streamlined and efficient structure. Come on Henry. We both know this has been under consideration for a decade or so."

"And rejected. UKSF is very different from MI5, which in turn is very different from MI6."

Smith breathed in deeply. "MI6 sets the bar. It's gold standard. The others are not. With good selection and training, we can change that. I'll redefine the benchmark of excellence."

"Save your speech for the interview process." Gable sipped his tea while keeping his eyes fixed on Smith. "Why do you think Archer, Lake, and File killed themselves?"

Smith shrugged. "Logically, there's only one explanation – they did something wrong. A foreign intelligence agency knew that and decided to try to blackmail them. They'd have been wracked with guilt. They did the honourable thing and took their lives, rather than risk shame and prison. Which foreign agency did this is unknown. But, it will have been one of the usual suspects – Russia, China, maybe Iran. You know all this. My views are shared by you and other senior MI6 management."

Gable nodded. "Why this has happened is not the priority. What matters is that we get a new chief. Are you sure you don't have any skeletons in your closet?"

"I'm a career spy. If you raked over my past in the field, you'd discover actions of mine that might be morally ambiguous. That's true for all MI6 operatives. But, I've never passed secrets to foreign agencies without strict authority to do so from our service; I've never slept with a foreign spy; never taken cash; never misappropriated funds; never done anything that would compromise my application for your job. If I was approached by a hostile agency who thought it had dirt on me, I'd laugh and tell them to do their worst. They've got nothing on me. I'm armour plated. Clearly, Archer, Lake, and File were not."

"Yes." Gable addressed Smith by his real name and said, "As you've described, I think you would be a force for change if you were appointed. We shall see. You're up against two other highly qualified candidates. They're different from you, but they also have huge strengths. When you're interviewed for the job, I'll be there – alongside the prime minister, foreign secretary, members of the Joint Intelligence Committee, psychologists, police chiefs, and plus as you know we always throw in a wild card such as a senior former KGB defector. But know this: my voice will be heard. If I smell a rat, I'll exert my influence."

Smith smiled. "Of course, sir. You have nothing to worry about."

Two hours' later, Hilt sent Smith a text message with a photo.

This guy turned up at Sign's place last night. Knutsen met him at the door. Know who he is?"

The photo very clearly showed the man's face.

Colin Parker.

Smith texted back.

We have an insider helping Sign. Meet me in one hour at the safe house in Chelsea.

In West Square, Knutsen stood in front of the chalkboard. "You, me, and Roberts could individually follow Logan, Messenger, and Pendry."

Sign replied, "We'd be spotted by them."

"You wouldn't."

"Maybe; maybe not. Regardless, the risk of scaring them off is too great."

"What about their mobile phones? If we could get hold of them, I know a hacker in Peckham who could work wonders. I could insert tracking devices. Possibly even intercept devices to monitor their calls, texts, and emails."

Sign chuckled. "How very *Jason Bourne* of you. Alas, the real world of espionage doesn't work that way. When Pendry, Logan, and Messenger go to head office, they are required to hand over their mobile phones to security. The phones are examined with state of the art equipment designed by GCHQ. Any tracking or intercept devices will be discovered. We would have blown our game and made future steps considerably harder."

Knutsen paced. "There must be something we can do!"

Sign interlaced his fingers while deep in thought. "Let's presuppose that the whisperer is either Logan, Messenger, or Pendry. The end game is that one of them becomes chief. The whisperer has two chess moves that are difficult to defeat: first, he's killing the competition for the post; second, it's hard to resist the assumption that the shortlist is being murdered by a hostile foreign agency. But the third chess move plays to his strength but also his Achilles heel. Whichever man on the shortlist is left standing will know that he's the suspected whisperer. MI6 will wonder why he wasn't killed."

Knutsen disagreed. "MI6 is desperate for a new chief. Once that person takes office, he'll be protected day and night. The whisperer has done his work. He doesn't need to kill again."

"You think MI6 will turn a blind eye and move on?"

"Yes."

"I fear you may be right. However, there is something you're missing."

"What?"

Sign smiled. "You and I won't turn a blind eye."

At nine twelve PM, Smith and Hilt moved silently into the rear garden of a detached rural property in Oxfordshire. It was dark; they were wearing clear, thick, plastic black overalls. Underneath Smith's external garment, his suit, shirt and tie were visible. Beneath Hilt's overall, he was wearing a jumper and jeans. Both had shoes that were too big for their foot size, but had toilet paper stuffed inside them to compensate for the size-differential between foot and shoe. Over them were blue disposable covers of the type that doctors wear when performing surgery. They had Sellotape wrapped around their fingers, gloves on their hands, face masks covering their mouths and nose, and gaffer-tape wrapped around every thread of their hair.

A dog was barking nearby, but not at them. There were two other houses that were one hundred yards away. No other properties were within miles of the tiny hamlet. Bats were flying overhead, chasing midges in a star-encrusted sky. A fox screeched close to them, sounding like a woman or child screaming. It was probably just calling to its mate or cubs, or it was warning the barking dog to back off from its aggressive tone.

Hilt was the first to reach the rear kitchen door of the two bedroom property. Through the gap between the hallway and two doors, the lounge was partially visible. A middle age man was sitting on a sofa, watching a natural history program. There were no other signs of life. This was to be expected. Smith had told Hilt that the man lived alone and had a boyfriend who resided six miles away at the end of a country lane. Hilt tried the door. Locked. He used lock picks to open it. He entered, holding a silenced pistol. Smith was close behind him. Hilt wasted no time. He punched the man on the head, though not hard enough to render him unconscious, wrapped his arms around the man's arms, yanked him out of his seat, maintained his vice-like grip as they crashed against a wall and slumped to the floor, and wrapped his legs around the man's legs. The victim couldn't move an inch as Hilt held him in place.

"Hello, Colin," said Smith as he stood over the man.

Colin Parker looked shocked. Though most of Smith's features were covered, his eyes were exposed. There was no doubt it was Smith. "You!"

Smith sounded bored as he replied, "Yes, it's me."

"You're the whisperer!"

Smith laughed, though the sound was muted by his face mask. "The whisperer? Is that was Sign calls me?" He angled his head while thinking. "Actually, I like the name. It makes sense." He looked at Parker. "I've bought you a gift." From the small holdall he was carrying, he pulled out a one and a half litre magnum of Johnnie Black Label. "It's twelve years old. I believe it's your favourite tipple, though you're very cautious with booze – only a dram once or twice a week. You don't drink beer, wine, or any other alcoholic beverages. I always think that middle age is when men make steadfast decisions about what they like and dislike. It brings clarity to the mind, after years of putting up with shit we don't like. Regardless, your alcohol tolerance will be very low."

"What do you want?"

Hilt gripped harder. Parker gasped.

"What I want is for you to have a drink, in a slightly different way than normal. It's always good to try out new things, even at our age." He unscrewed the bottle's cap and crouched in front of Smith. Out of his bag he withdrew a plastic funnel that was attached to three foot length of rubber tubing. "You may be aware of this technique of supplying food and drink into someone. The Russians used it on prisoners in the Cold War. I must warn you, it will hurt."

Hilt adjusted position so that his hands were around Parker's head, while retaining the lock on his arms and legs.

"Open wide." Smith forced the tube into Parker's mouth.

Parker writhed, sweat pouring down his face, his eyes screwed tight.

But Smith's hand was steady. He pushed the heavy tube down Smith's gullet, and kept pressing until the tip of the tube was in his stomach. "There we go. That wasn't so bad."

Parker was in agony.

"So, here's the tricky bit. You're going to polish off this magnum in stages. What I need you to do is take a deep breath through your nose. Then I'm going to briefly block your nasal airway. Ready, steady, go."

Parker inhaled air.

Smith clamped his nose shut with forefinger and thumb and poured whisky into the funnel. He waited a few seconds before releasing his grip on Parker's nose. "Breathe now. We'll continue in a moment."

Smith repeated the process twelve times, before the magnum was empty bar a few drops. He pulled out the tube. "That should do the trick."

Parker was moaning but still conscious, though he was paralytic. Hilt released his grip on him and stood.

Smith said to Hilt, "Check his breathing." Smith put the tube back into his bag.

Hilt said, "Breathing's fine, for now. But he's blacked out."

"Good." Smith moved fast. He put Parker's finger prints all over the bottle and screw top, grabbed a tumbler from the kitchen and put Parker's finger tips around the exterior and his saliva on the rim, poured the tiny amount of whisky left into the glass, swilled it around, and placed the glass and empty bottle on a coffee table next to the sofa. He picked up Parker's mobile phone. "Key code protected. But here's the thing – Parker was never good with numbers. He's right handed." He grabbed Parker's right hand and placed his thumb against the unlock function. "There we go – thumbprint recognition. I'm in." He scrolled through the list of contacts. "Got you." He examined texts previously sent by Parker to his boyfriend. He wanted to see his style of language. He typed a text to Parker's boyfriend.

Feeling a bit down this evening. Got any whiskey? Am coming over. Don't say no. x

He sent the message. Within seconds the boyfriend was ringing. Smith ignored the call. "Car keys, car keys! Where would they be?" Smith found Parker's keys in a tray in the hallway. "Time for some heavy lifting." He placed the phone in Parker's pocket. "I'll bring his car to the rear of the house. Make sure you lock the kitchen door behind you." From the locked front door, Smith took out keys that were on the interior side of the door. He put them in Parker's other pocket. He smiled as he looked at Parker. "There we go – house all locked up, and you're about to make a journey to see your lover. Cops will take a dim view of that, given how much you've had to drink."

Smith left to get Parker's car.

Hilt hauled Parker onto his shoulder and walked out of the house. Previously, the former special forces operative had carried men twice Parker's weight over miles. This was child's play. Without dropping Parker, he stopped outside the kitchen door and used the lock picks to secure the entrance. He carried Parker to his car. The engine was running. Smith was standing by the car.

Smith said, "This is where I vanish. Over to you." He walked off into the darkness.

Hilt put Parker into the front passenger seat and placed a seat belt around his limp body. He got into the driver's seat and motored down the deserted country lane leading to Parker's boyfriend. It was dark, no street lamps. Hilt stopped the car two miles away from Parker's boyfriend's house.. He looked at Parker's comatose body. "Time for us to go loud, my friend." He put Parker in the driver's seat, no seat belt attached, sat in the front passenger seat, placed his foot on the accelerator, steered the vehicle until it got to sixty miles an hour, swung the steering wheel left, and leaped out of the car. Parker's vehicle smashed into a tree. Parker careered out of the car, via the windscreen, and smacked the ground. Hilt grimaced as he staggered to his feet. The landing on grass had cushioned his escape. But at that speed he still felt raw. Parker was motionless on the ground. The car was a wreck. Hilt ripped off a dangling piece of metal from the car and beat Parker around the head and body. Police forensics would never know what had really happened. The violence of Parker's ejection from his car would account for any bruises, broken bones, lacerations, and brain damage.

Hilt wiggled Parker's neck. It was broken. Parker's face was a bloody mess and swollen. One of his eyes was closed. The other was dangling by a thread and nestled on his face. His arms and legs were all at the wrong angles. Clothes were lacerated. Shards of glass were in his head and clothes. There was no breathing.

Parker was dead.

CHAPTER 21

The following morning, Sign was growing impatient as he kept glancing at his lounge wall clock. "Where is he? Parker was supposed to be here at eight o'clock." It was now eight forty five.

"Something must have come up," said Knutsen.

"Most likely. But he could have texted me."

Roberts asked, "Was it important for him to be at this meeting?"

"Yes!" Sign regretted snapping. "Sorry, Katy. I had an idea. Parker is integral to that idea. He could assemble a team of MI6 surveillance experts and get them to follow Messenger, Pendry, and Logan for a week."

"Would the chief allow that?"

"He wouldn't have to know. Parker could tell his team that it was simply a training exercise. All of the team members are cleared to know the identities of other MI6 officers, so technically Parker wouldn't be breaking rules. It's unlikely, though possible, that our three targets would spot the team. What's crucial is that the limpet *does* spot them. That way we take his eye off the ball. His focus will be on the MI6 team. Meanwhile we search for the limpet." He started pacing. "But I need Parker! No one else in MI6 would do this for me – they'd ask too many questions."

Roberts said, "Parker might say no. Technically he might not be breaking rules, but he's still deploying MI6 officers against high ranking officers. Parker's retiring soon. The last thing he needs is a disciplinary charge and a potential threat to his pension."

Sign waved his hand dismissively. "Parker will do it; and his pension is ring fenced, even if he steals the crown jewels." He checked his mobile. "Still nothing."

Knutsen said, "He must have needed to go to head office early."

"Yes." Sign rang Parker's mobile. It went straight to voicemail. He called the switchboard number of the Foreign & Commonwealth office. He asked for Parker. The call was transferred to Parker's office in MI6. His phone rang four times and went to voicemail. Sign hung up. "This is most unlike Parker. Things would be different if he was overseas – situations then are more fluid – but he runs a prestigious department in London. Every morning he gets the same train to London; every evening he returns home at the same time. It's his reward to himself after spending years in the field where there's no structure to daily life." Sign looked at Roberts. "Call the Met. Ask them to check their police national computer and incident logs to see if there's any reference to a Colin Parker of Oxfordshire." He gave her Parker's address. "I don't know his date of birth."

"I don't need it." Roberts was on the case. After she got off the call, she waited. "They're checking." Ten minutes later her phone rang. She expected it to be from the woman in Scotland Yard who was doing the checks. It wasn't.

A man asked, "Inspector Roberts?"

"Yes."

"I'm Superintendent Moore of Thames Valley Police." He was about to continue.

But Roberts interrupted. "I need to verify you are who you say you are. I'm calling your switchboard and will tell them to transfer me to you." She hung up, made the call, and listened as the call was transferred. "Superintendent – now we can talk freely. What do you have?"

Moore replied, "Colin Parker is flagged on our system as a senior government official whose wellbeing is vital. Last night he got drunk; *really* drunk. He drove a few miles and lost control of his car. He's dead."

Roberts looked at Sign.

Sign immediately knew something was wrong.

"Anything suspicious?" she asked.

"No. Traffic police and forensics have been all over the road traffic accident, plus detectives have examined his home. He got sozzled, got in a car, and drove. He wasn't wearing a seatbelt. Death was probably instantaneous. He was a mess when we found him."

"Where was he driving to?"

"We don't know. Toxicology reports show that he was at least twenty times over the limit. It's an open and shut case."

"Thank you, sir." Roberts ended the call and told Sign and Knutsen what she knew.

Sign was silent for a moment. He picked up his tea cup and smashed it against a wall. "Parker wasn't a heavy drinker!"

"Why was he driving at such a late hour?"

Sign rubbed his face, exasperated. "Because on one level it makes sense to MI6 and the police, if the latter were privy to what made him do something so stupid. Parker's been openly gay for years. He has a boyfriend in Oxfordshire. They've been steady for fifteen years and love each other faithfully, though now and again they throw their toys out of the pram and have a tiff. Passion is key. MI6 will think it was out of character for Parker to go on a binge and drive, but it will also conclude that passion corrupts every soul. However, what we're dealing with is murder."

Knutsen said, "You heard what Katy said. The police examined his house, car, and body. Nothing! This is not linked to our case."

"It has everything to do with our case. No doubt Parker was photographed by the limpet coming to our digs. The whisperer realised that Parker was my insider in MI6; my informant and pawn. This had to stop. Parker was force-fed booze. Either the limpet did it or the whisperer did it. My money is on the whisperer, while the limpet held Parker down. They'd have been wearing specialist clothing and other accoutrements to protect their presence in Parker's home. One or both of them would have driven him a few miles while Parker was passed out – I suspect the limpet drove and the whisperer wasn't present for the journey. Close to the death scene, the limpet put Parker in the driving seat while he was still blacked out. The limpet reached across from the passenger seat and drove at high speed. Parker wasn't wearing a seat belt. The limpet jumped. The car crashed. Parker flew through the windscreen." Sign shook his head. "If there were any indications of life, the limpet would have quashed them with a piece of metal from the car. Paint or splinters from that piece of metal would be attributed to the accident. There are no traffic cameras on the country lane he died on. No one would know the limpet was the driver. It's a perfect murder."

Knutsen walked up to Sign and placed a hand on his shoulder. "You've no evidence of this."

Sign shrugged off his hand. "Evidence?! I once caught a traitor because I'd noticed that he was wearing a green tie rather than his usual blue; I put a bullet in the head of a man who usually smoked Marlboro Lights but on the last day I met him was smoking the full strength brand – his cigarette contained a toxin aimed at me; I stripped a Russian woman and found an FSB wire, merely because she had an uncharacteristic twitch in her eye. She'd been forced to work for the FSB, under threat of death if she failed to comply. I got her out of Russia. She'd have been dead had I not noticed the tiniest minutiae. She's now happily married in France and is safe. I could go on and on with other anecdotes. Evidence is for cops. Don't put me in that category!"

Knutsen briefly glanced at Roberts. He said in a gentle voice, "Ben – Katy and I trust your instincts, we really do, and we'll back you up, but what you're suggesting sounds fanciful. I know he was your friend, but don't let that cloud your judgment."

"He wasn't a friend; he was a trusted associate. There is a difference. And I'm not being fanciful. This reeks of an assassination. I should know. I've conducted similar acts overseas." Sign walked to the window. Calmly, he said, "I thought I'd permanently given up violence. But it seems violence is coming for me. When bad men wish ill of you, you want it to happen when you're in your twenties or thirties, when you can still run half marathons and play rugger at the weekends. But at forty nine, those things become harder. My mind's agile and I can walk a fair lick, but I couldn't defend myself against the limpet."

"That's why I'm here."

"I know, dear chap." Sign smiled. "I'm sorry."

"For what?"

"Your first case in our business has thrown you straight in at the deep end. We're probably dealing with a serial killer who wants to be chief of MI6, together with a lethal assassin." Sign laughed. "You could have got a job with a local security firm."

"Where's the fun in that?" Knutsen saw the weight of the world on Sign's shoulders. "You once told me that anything is possible. At first, I thought you were spouting some mumbo jumbo positive thinking shit, like those alleged gurus do in California. Then I thought you were referring to negative stuff – how to kill someone; how to manipulate the Establishment; how to cover your tracks. Finally I realised your assertion was simply a statement of fact. Anything is possible. But, unless a person understands that, they won't even aspire to the near-impossible, let alone achieve it."

Sign nodded. "It is a mantra of sorts, but very few men and women have that gift. The problem is, you have men like me and the whisperer who strive to dally with the art of challenging the impossible. But that doesn't mean we're all good."

"You and the whisperer are very different. He's a psychopath; you're not."

"I'll let higher powers decide whether that assessment is accurate." Sign sat in his chair and interlocked his fingers. "Seven years ago I ordered a drone strike on fifty armed rebels. They probably had wives and kids. I've planted information on traitors, leading to their incarceration and probable execution; and I've shot people point blank. I may not like death, but it seems to stand by my side in life."

Knutsen repeated, "You're not a psychopath. You care. You're a good man."

Sign looked at Knutsen. "How's David and his mother?"

"The mother's clean. David has his first interview with the Metropolitan Police on Monday. I'm helping him."

"Will he get into the force?"

"We call it police service these days."

"Regardless of terminology..?"

Knutsen hesitated. "Hard to know. Standards required of new applicants have risen dramatically during the last few years."

"Bring them here before Monday. We'll do a mock interview."

"Them?"

"Yes. Mother and son." Sign seemed distracted. "I need to go to Oxfordshire. Not to the crime scene. That won't tell me anything that I haven't already deduced. But, I'd like to have a chin wag with Parker's boyfriend. You both need to come with me, though your role will be to see if you can spot the limpet. Bring a long range camera. See if you can get a shot of him. We'll leave West Square by the front door. Hopefully the limpet will follow us."

Two hours later, Sign rang the doorbell of a converted barn, eight miles south of Oxford. The property was in countryside. Flat heathland, fields, and a few trees were all that surrounded the house. A low mist hovered above the moorland, staying fixed in place because there was no wind. Frost covered the ground. There was no noise, aside from a couple of pheasants calling in the distance.

Sign waited. There was a possibility that Parker's boyfriend was out, though Sign had earlier called his employer – Oxford University – and had been told that today he was working from home. The boyfriend was a professor of English Language and Literature at Corpus Christi college. Today he had no lectures or seminars to conduct.

The professor answered the door. He was a lanky fifty seven year old, with a full head of medium length grey hair that looked messy, though had been fashioned that way to make him look contrarian. In all other respects he had the image of a country gentleman – tweed jacket, hunting shirt, corduroy trousers, and stout boots. He frowned as he looked at Sign, who was wearing a formal suit. "Do you work at the university? I vaguely recognise you."

"Not the university. We met once at a drinks function in the British Embassy in Jakarta."

The penny dropped. "You work with Colin. What do you want?"

"Can I come in?"

The professor looked annoyed. "I was just about to go on a walk. There's been a Richard's Pipit spotted near here. I was hoping to take my binoculars and see if I could spot him."

"Richard's Pipit – native to Asia, but sometimes strays west. That would be an extremely rare sighting."

The professor's face lit up. "Ah, you too study ornithology."

"Actually, no. But I do have a good memory. At some stage in my life I must have read about the bird."

The professor was enthused. "Come in, come in." He ushered Sign into his home.

Five hundred yards away, Knutsen and Roberts were in a car on the lane leading to the professor's house. Knutsen grabbed his camera and said to Roberts, "Time for me to leave. Lock the doors when I'm out. Keep the engine running. Any problems, get the hell out of here. Don't wait for me or Sign."

With sarcasm, Roberts replied, "How very chivalrous. Ladies first."

"Nah mate. I'm going to hide in the trees over there. You're exposed. As far as I'm concerned, that's good. If anyone's going to take a bullet in the back of the head today, it will be you. You're bait." He winked at her and left.

Sign sat in a leather armchair in a lounge that was crammed with books on shelves, academic papers in piles on the floor, art, and indoor plants. Logs were burning in the fireplace, a metal guard the only protection against a spark setting the barn and all its contents into ash. A lamp with a green shield was on a wooden writing desk. There was no computer on there; just more papers, pens, and other stationary. The only electronic item in the room was the professor's mobile phone, being charged.

The professor sat close to the fire. "You know my name?"

"Eduard Delacroix."

Delacroix nodded. "Because of my association with Colin, I've been assessed by your organisation for security clearance every five years. The last assessment was four months ago."

"It's not about that. Has anyone official phoned or visited you since last night?"

Delacroix looked shocked. "No! What's happened?"

Sign breathed in deeply. "Then, I have to be the bearer of very bad news. Last night Colin was in a car accident. He died."

"What?!" Delacroix stood and rubbed his face. "Dead? Dead?"

"He's dead. Is there anyone I can call on your behalf? Family, friends, colleagues?"

Delacroix was in utter shock. "How..? How did it happen?"

"He got blind drunk and drove over here from his home five miles away. It was a miracle he didn't crash his car within one mile of his house. He was coming to see you. His mobile phone was smashed in the impact, but the sim card was intact. Security services have analysed it. He texted you before he drove, saying he was coming over to see you."

"I know! I know!" Delacroix picked up his phone. "I got the message and tried calling him. Last night wasn't a good time for me. I had papers to mark."

"Colin's parents are deceased. He has no brothers or sisters. He has…"

"No next of kin! And I don't fucking exist. We weren't married. I'm just his gay lover." Delacroix punched a table.

Sign crossed his legs, his composure calm. "Legally, that's correct. You don't exist. But, I know the attorney general. I will impress upon him in the most forthright terms that all decisions about Colin's funeral and personal administration must be given to you. There will be no dispute on this matter. You were in a loving relationship for fifteen years. You know Colin better than anyone. It is your right to be sole guardian of his affairs."

Delacroix was breathing fast. "Tell me everything! Colin was an expert driver. You guys taught him all sorts of stuff. What happened?"

Sign told him what he knew.

Delacroix shook his head. "He wouldn't have got drunk. Not even in a fit of depression. I've seen him down – assets he'd lost in China; that kind of stuff. Whenever he was sad, he stayed sober. It was his way of coping."

"Sometimes people get drunk when they're elated."

"Not Colin. He was always in control." Delacroix ran fingers through his hair. "If anything, I was the emotional one. Colin was my rock."

"Has he ever come over to your place at short notice before?"

"Never! He was a creature of habit. Even though we only lived five miles apart, we had rules. He does his spy stuff in the week; I do my academic stuff; he drives up Friday night with a weekend bag; we go for a meal; Sunday evening he drives home." Delacroix had tears running down his face. "Did he..? Did he..?"

"He felt no pain. Death was instantaneous." Sign leaned forward. "My colleagues will ensure that a Thames Valley Police bereavement officer comes over to help you."

"Bereavement officer?! Will that person bring Colin back to life?!"

"No. You'll carry the burden of Colin's death for the rest of your life. Maybe one day you'll find love again, but I doubt it given your age and circumstances. You'll move into the top quartile of probable suicides. You won't notice anything around you. Your work will suffer. You might be sacked. You won't eat properly. Drugs or alcohol will temporarily numb the pain. Anything anyone says to you will be judged by you to be wrong. Your stomach will gnaw on itself. Ultimately, you will no longer be in charge of yourself. Hence the need for support."

"Fucking MI6 mind games!"

"My wife was murdered. Colin was murdered."

"What?!"

Sign remained calm, his tone measured and soft. "On the former point, my wife was raped and shot in Latin America. She was Polish. Rebels thought she was a Russian spy. They crucified her and put a bullet in her brain six hours later while she was still on the cross. It was a warning to others. They left her there. Vultures fed on her. I managed to get her bones and give them a burial. On the latter point, Colin's death isn't suspicious to the cops or MI6. He won't be afforded a full police investigation or post-mortem. And even if his body was sliced open, it would be near impossible to discern foul play. He was mashed up by the crash. However, I think a tube was pushed down his throat and into his stomach. He was force fed strong alcohol, probably his favourite whiskey. He never drove the car but it was made to look that way. He stood no chance."

Delacroix couldn't believe what he was hearing. "A tube down his throat will leave traces. Blood, maybe rubber, whatever."

"The potential traces will only be discerned by a top police forensics expert. Even then, there will be no evidence to prove murder. If I were the killer, I'd have made the tube out of the same material as the tyres on the car. The tyres were burnt out in the crash. A coroner would conclude that Colin inhaled their burning fumes in the last moments. Blood and rubber would be explained away."

"You're not a cop! How do you know these things?"

"It is precisely because I'm not a cop, and have conducted matters that would blow the minds of police officers, that I know these things." Sign's eyes didn't blink as he said in an authoritative tone, "You need a police bereavement officer here to help you get through your loss and to help you with all administrative matters. Do I have your permission to organise that visit?"

"Yes, yes." Delacroix's voice was distant. "Murder? Who would have done this?"

"There are a number of possibilities. The most likely possibility is one that I'm pursuing. I believe that Colin was the victim of a serial killer. A very unusual killer."

"Get the bastard!"

Sign nodded.

From his hidden position in the copse, Knutsen focused his camera on Delacroix's front door. His mobile phone had an ear piece and throat mic attached; the phone was dialled in to Roberts' phone. He said, "Sign's leaving. He'll be with you in a few minutes."

Roberts replied, "Okay."

Knutsen panned his camera to the right. He froze. "There's a man walking down the lane towards you. Opposite direction from Sign, but same distance."

Sign and the man were five hundred yards away from Roberts' car. Sign was walking from the north; the man was walking from the south.

"He's wearing jeans, boots and a jacket. Hood's up. I can't see his face."

Roberts sounded tense as she said, "Could just be a rambler. There's a country footpath off the lane, close to Delacroix's house. The man could be headed that way."

"Probably. But I don't like this. I'm moving position." Knutsen got to his feet and sprinted two hundred yards across heathland. He threw himself to the ground and trained his camera on the lane. Here he was more exposed. He muttered, "Come on you bastard – show your face."

Roberts said, "This doesn't feel like the limpet. He wouldn't do something like this."

"I know!" Knutsen was breathing fast. He swung his camera left. Sign was three hundred yards away from the car. Knutsen focused his camera back on the man approaching the car from the rear. "Get out of there, Katy! Pick Sign up. Don't worry about me. I'll make my own way back to London."

"No. I'm bait, remember. I'm staying put until you get that photo."

Knutsen cursed and moved to another location.

The man was a hundred yards from Roberts' car.

Knutsen made adjustments to the camera's lens. Given the angle he was now viewing the road, he was confident the man's hood would no longer expose his face.

The man was fifty yards from the car.

Roberts said, "I see him. He's in my rear view mirror. He's walking slowly. But his head's down. Can't see his face."

Nor could Knutsen.

The man was twenty yards from the car.

"Katy – get out of there. Now!" Knutsen dropped the camera, withdrew his pistol and ran across open ground towards the lane. He stopped in his tracks as the man turned to face him. They were one hundred yards apart. The man was wearing a ski mask. He put his hand inside his jacket, pulled it out – holding nothing – two of his fingers and his thumb positioned in a way to mimic a handgun. He was stock still as he turned towards the car and pretended to shoot Roberts. He turned toward Knutsen and repeated the action at him. If he'd had a real gun, both would have been dead. He turned and ran.

Knutsen pursued, firing warning shots in the air and shouting, "Police! Stop!"

Sign ran to Roberts when he heard the shots.

Knutsen raced past him while saying, "Limpet. Get Katy safe!" Knutsen continued his pursuit.

Roberts was in the driver's seat. Sign pushed her to one side, took control of the car, reversed it at full speed up the lane, performed a hand brake turn, drove for another hundred yards, then stopped, the engine still running. He'd performed the manoeuvre in five seconds. He waited, staring into the rear mirror.

Roberts said, "I can drive, you know?"

Sign ignored the comment. He muttered, "Come on Tom." In a louder voice he said to Roberts, "Call Delacroix." He gave her his mobile number. "Tell him who you are and that there is a threat. Tell him to lock every single entry point in the house and then stay away from windows. Tell him there's no threat to him per se, but we have a prowler in the vicinity."

When Roberts ended the call she said, "He's calling 999."

"It will be of no use."

Knutsen was breathing fast as he jumped over ditches and small bushes, his gun held at eye level, sweat pouring down his face despite the chilly air, muscles aching, and lungs feeling like they'd ingested battery acid. All of his senses were operating at optimum level. He swivelled left and right, searching for the limpet. He ran onward into an open field, rotated three hundred and sixty degrees, and stamped his foot on the ground.

The limpet had vanished.

Four hours later, Sign, Knutsen, and Roberts convened in the West Square lounge. They'd arrived ninety minutes earlier, had showered, changed, and made some calls. Sign lit a fire and poured three glasses of calvados, which he served with espresso black coffee and muffins. He sat in his armchair. Knutsen and Roberts took their drinks and sat near him by the fire. Sign was no longer in formal attire, though was smartly dressed in a shirt and trousers that had an immaculate crease down the centre. Knutsen and Roberts were in jeans and T-shirts. They didn't want to look like they were sitting in an officers' mess.

Sign sipped his calvados. "I've just spoken to Delacroix. Thames Valley Police are with him. He's in no danger."

"How do you know that?" asked Knutsen.

"Because he serves no purpose." Sign looked angry. "Katy's husband was killed in order to stop her snooping. It didn't work but it was a chess move. Delacroix isn't on the board. His death serves no purpose. The whisperer and the limpet will know that executing him won't stop us. No purpose," he repeated.

"What happened today?" asked Knutsen.

Sign placed his glass down. "It was a shot across the bow. It was another warning. The limpet deliberately showed himself on the lane. Normally, if he was going in for a kill, we wouldn't have seen him. Instead, he sauntered up the route, not a care in the world, and pretended to put bullets in your brains." Sign lowered his head. "If he'd pulled out his gun, you'd be dead."

Roberts said, "Why did you push me out of the driver's seat. I could have got us out of there!"

Sign lifted his head. His voice was loud and aggressive when he said, "Because I've done escape and evasion in Tehran, Moscow, Beijing, Kabul, Nairobi, New York, Melbourne, and a hundred other places! You haven't! I was saving your life! If you want to get all girl-power on me, go ahead, but try a few years at the real sharp end before you earn my respect."

"Ben?" Knutsen was worried about the outburst.

Sign maintained his aggressive tone. "Let me make this simple for you both. We're dealing with two people who want us out the way. I don't care if you like me or hate me. I don't care if you think I should drive or you should drive. I don't care who carries a gun and who doesn't. But let me tell you this: I damn well care if one of you gets hurt." He stood and chucked a log onto the fire. "We're dealing with highly trained psychopaths. It would be remiss of me to allow your egos to get in the way of your lives." He watched the wood burn. In a quieter voice he said, "Mrs. Roberts – you have skills and contacts that I do not have. Plus, you have a police badge. It opens doors. You are crucial to this investigation."

"Don't patronise me!"

"I'm not." Sign smiled. "I'm putting you in your place."

The comment was met with stunned silence by Roberts and Knutsen. Then both couldn't help laughing. It was as if a pin had burst a balloon.

Sign didn't laugh. "Parker's death has set us back. Henry Gable won't further help me – I can assure you of that. Ergo, I might be of use to you because I think like an MI6 officer; but I no longer have access to MI6." He stared at Roberts. "You see? I have limitations." He asked the Special Branch inspector, "What am I missing in this case? Don't mimic my style of thinking. Instead, think like a police detective who's investigating a series of murders."

Roberts considered the question. "In murder cases, detectives want to ascertain motive. It brings us closer to narrowing down a list of suspects. But, in this case it's weird. You've ascertained that the suspects are Messenger, Pendry, and Logan. One of them might be the whisperer. The other two could be dead men walking. The suspects might be the murderer's kill list. I've never worked a case like that. I don't know any detective who has."

"What do we do next? Parker's of no use to us, God rest his soul."

"You could separately meet Messenger, Pendry, and Logan. It would be easy for you to get their DNA. Just a handshake would suffice. If there are any more murders, we could see if DNA links the crime to the murderer."

Sign shook his head. "There's been no DNA at any of the previous crime scenes. The whisperer and the limpet have been meticulous about that."

Roberts' voice trembled with emotion as she said, "Interview them anyway! Use your brilliance to ascertain who's the killer."

"That won't work. Remember – we're dealing with a schizophrenic, a megalomaniac, and a psychopath – respectively, Messenger, Pendry, and Logan. They will all appear to me to be the killer. Alas, I won't be able to discern one brute from the others."

"Then we maintain our focus on the limpet. We grab him and make him talk."

"Therein is the problem." Sign prodded a finger on a coffee table. "If I was faced with a similar problem in Ankara or Casablanca, I could torture the limpet to within an inch of his life. I'd get the whisperer's identity. Then, I'd kill the limpet. But both of you are schooled in the art of following United Kingdom rules. You're police officers. You don't have what it takes to be unconventional."

Knutsen wasn't having any of this. "I'm *ex*-police. And Katy is Special Branch. We don't follow rules."

Sign smiled. "I hoped you'd say that." He stood and stoked the fire. "But, I must warn you that it's an unpleasant business seeing a man gasp for air as water is poured down his throat, or screaming for his mother as his fingers are cut off and seared with a car cigarette lighter. It's not like the movies. Most tough guys are not defiant at that moment. They just want the pain to stop." He turned to his colleagues. "The limpet, however, will be defiant until the very end. It will be a matter of pride, as well as training. We would have to do things to him that would make a billy goat puke. My question to you is whether you could endure that experience."

Knutsen and Roberts glanced at each other.

"Also, it would be highly illegal." Sign re-took his seat. "Don't worry. I need to explain something that will resonate with your exemplary service to our country. The torture methods I've described are not for us. Not for me anymore, at least. I've had the opportunity to conduct extreme surgery on people in order to extract secrets from them. In all cases, there was a ticking time bomb to be discovered, so to speak. But in recent years I chose not to take that route."

"You chose the high ground."

"I chose the moral compass. If a state or its associates torture someone, we define our country by that action. We must do unto others what we wish to be done to ourselves. In the case of Great Britain, we must be gentle men and women, and humanely kill people who aim to hurt us."

Knutsen said, "Other cultures and states would disagree with you – Native American Indians, Russians, Germans, Japanese, Chinese, parts of Africa, et cetera."

Sign nodded. "Correct. But, for the most part, that was in the past, though I concede that those countries and territories' DNA permeates through to the current generations of your examples. But savagery, driven by survival or unnecessary aggression is not us. Agreed?"

"Yes."

"Of course."

Sign's brain was thinking on multiple levels. "We must find the limpet's most sensitive nerve ending and press it hard. The limpet is being paid by the whisperer. We could pay him more and try to get him to turn on his master. It won't work. The limpet's reputation would be in tatters. He'd never get another job. Speak or be damned in prison for thirty years or more, is another option. That won't work either. The limpet would keep his mouth shut and escape or become a hero inside the penitentiary's walls. But, there is one thing we could take away from him – his pride. He won't like that one bit, particularly if he's facing life in prison."

Roberts was following his logic. "If he goes to prison a hero, he breezes through jail time. If he goes in a loser, welcome to hell."

"Correct. I have an idea, but it's a useless idea unless I have the limpet's name." Sign rubbed his face. "This would all be so much easier if I was wrong about the whisperer. All I'd have to do is get the three MI6 officers twenty-four-seven armed protection."

Knutsen said, "That still might be an option. We'd be protecting a shortlist of candidates for chief. If the whisperer is one of them, there's no guarantee he'd be selected for the post."

"Are you willing to take one-in-three odds?" Sign stared at the names on the board. "Let's say Logan is the whisperer and he isn't appointed chief. Messenger gets the job. What would Logan do? He'd use the limpet to circumvent or neutralise Messenger's bodyguards and he'd kill him. MI6 would be forced to then replace Messenger with either Pendry or Logan. Logan would kill Pendry. He'd then fake an attack on his life to make it seem that the whisperer is an external force. He'd play the victim. Logan would be heralded a hero by his peers for surviving an assault from a hostile foreign agency. No – none of this will end until the whisperer gets what he wants."

"Power over MI6."

"I would think more than that. Power over the whole UK special operations community." Sign said with authority, "I've thought through multiple options – bugging the shortlist's homes; examining their mobiles; the three of us following them; grabbing one of them and making him contact the others with false information; producing to them a fake doctor's analysis of Henry Gable's health, showing he has stage four cancer and will be leaving his post in a matter of days, thereby accelerating matters and perhaps getting the whisperer to make a wrong move; and many other chess moves. Mrs. Roberts – pretend you didn't hear what I'm about to say next. I've even thought about killing Messenger, Pendry, and Logan. Two innocents die. One killer dies. But, I can't bring myself to do the latter option. And the other options won't work. Pendry, Logan, and Messenger are too clever and attuned to the nuances of tradecraft. They won't make mistakes. They'll see through any bluffs and intrusions on their privacy."

Knutsen said, "I've had to sacrifice people for the sake of the bigger picture."

"So have I," said Roberts. "Maybe killing the shortlist is our only option."

Sign sipped some more of his calvados. "Remember – we are defined by our actions." He looked at Roberts. "If we kill the shortlist, we will never find out the limpet's identity; the man who killed your husband."

Roberts bowed her head.

Sign smiled sympathetically. "Katy, we must find the limpet. I must give you peace."

She raised her head. "I… I just want to know what's going on. And when I know what's going on, I'll pull out my police ID and throw the law at the people responsible for Elliot's death."

Sign clapped his hands. "That's my girl."

"Woman."

"Detective." Sign was being mischievous, but for the right reasons. He wanted fight back in Roberts. "I guarantee you – you'll be the one to arrest the limpet." His voice trailed as he said, "But we must get a photo of the limpet's face."

Roberts said, "Knutsen and I have both seen the limpet's face. We could try a sketch artist."

Sign was dismissive. "You only saw the limpet briefly and under duress. Sketch artists are notoriously inaccurate because the victims describing the perpetrator are inaccurate. Compound that with the fact that we're dealing with a special operative who won't be on the police radar. He's not a common criminal. But, that doesn't matter. If I get his face, I get his name." Sign's voice rose as he said, "Tomorrow I'm going to meet Messenger, Pendry and Logan. At least I hope I will. I will call them this evening and tell them it's an emergency. Mrs. Roberts – the meeting location has good cameras." He gave her details. "But tonight I want you to check they are all operable, and recording devices are intact." His voice turned grave as he said, "The MI6 officers are of no use to me tomorrow. All that matters is that we spot the limpet. But that is very high-stakes territory. One or all of us could die."

Hilt finished his shift watching West Square. He drove in early evening London traffic. It was dark, though the city was bathed in the glow of artificial light from car headlights, street lamps, shops, homes, and office buildings. He felt tired, having been surviving on four hours sleep per night during the last few days. He ignored the sensation. In his view, a full night's sleep was overrated. Many times, in MI6 and the SBS, he'd spent months on deployment, operating with far less sleep than he was getting now.

He parked his car and entered the one-bedroom flat he'd been renting in south London since he'd been commissioned by Smith. His real home was eighty three miles north of here. He locked the door and placed two wedges under its base. After withdrawing his handgun and placing it on a table, he had a shower, put on a clean T-shirt and boxer shorts, shoved his worn clothes in the washing machine, and grabbed a beer from the fridge. He slowly supped his drink as he checked the workings of his pistol and sniper rifle. Adjacent to them were three mobiles phones, all being charged via a socket with an adaptor. One of the phones was his hotline to Smith. He finished his beer and rang the MI6 officer. "Nothing's happened since they visited Delacroix. They tried to get a photo of me. I made sure that didn't work. They're back in West Square and it doesn't look like they're going anywhere. I've called it a day."

"They've got nowhere to go to tonight. Nowhere that bothers me, at least. Tomorrow is a different matter. Sign has just called me. He wants to meet me and two of my colleagues at ten AM tomorrow. If I go, there is a possibility I will be arrested or killed."

"Then don't go."

"Were it so simple. Sign has constructed a double-spring trap. I'm damned if I go one way and damned if I take the other route."

Hilt frowned. "I don't understand."

"Sign is trying to identify me. There are only three possibilities, and I'm one of them. He's summoned his list of suspects to tomorrow's meeting. I've made you aware of the consequences. If I don't go and the other two attend his meeting, I have a red flag draped over me. So, I will go. Take precautions. Don't go in unless you see Knutsen or Roberts enter the building. But don't take a gun or knife. There is a security scanner at the entrance. Rely on your training and ingenuity. If Roberts or Knutsen approach the meeting, this is what I want you to do." He explained what he had in mind. "Protection and extraction are key." He ended the call.

Hilt lay on the single bed. No duvet was required – he liked feeling cold when sleeping. He closed his eyes and did what he always did when trying to get to sleep – imagining people he wanted to kill. It was his version of counting sheep jumping over a fence. Most people who'd crossed his path had ended up dead; but, there were some who'd escaped his wrath. He knew who they were. As he was blissfully drifting off to sleep, he imagined shooting a Taliban leader who'd executed one of his colleagues, a Russian mafia gang lord who'd set twenty of his armed henchmen on Hilt in Murmansk, a barmaid in Berlin who'd slept with him and tried to stab him, a highly dangerous American computer hacker who'd escaped death by creating a confusing maze of false identities and addresses, a few pricks in MI6 who thought he was too unhinged to maintain his security clearance, and many others. Ultimately, he was at peace as he imagined killing Sign. He had no personal grudge against the man. Their paths hadn't crossed in MI6. But, he knew Sign was coming to kill him.

Right now, that made Sign Enemy Number One.

CHAPTER 22

At seven AM, Sign, Knutsen, and Roberts were in Sign's apartment. As instructed, Knutsen and Roberts were wearing robust clothing that would enable them to move fast. Sign was wearing a suit. He'd prepared coffee and croissants for breakfast. It was nearly daylight, though the sky was moody and rain was lashing windows. Roberts couldn't help yawning. Knutsen was bleary-eyed and unshaven.

Sign said to them, "Grief and anxiety are bad bedfellows. But we must be alert now. Strong coffee will help. You can sleep later."

"If we're alive." Knutsen rubbed his stubble and looked out of the windows. "It's a piss poor day to die."

Sign was full of energy, despite having had no sleep. And he'd taken care over his morning ablutions. "It's my job to ensure that I might die today and you won't." He handed Roberts a sealed envelope. "In the event of my death, open that. It contains specific instructions, the contact details of a man, a letter of introduction, and my signature. Don't take the envelope with you today. If the limpet grabs you he will strip search you. Hide the envelope somewhere outside of West Square. Don't tell me the location." He turned his attention on Knutsen. "Sir – today is about a sleight of hand. I want the people meeting me to see one thing, wherein what's actually happening is a wholly different matter. Katy's job is to act like an arresting officer. Your job is to focus on the limpet. No guns can be taken into the building. But you're a dab hand at unarmed combat. If you have to tackle the limpet, hurt him but don't kill him. Dead people can't give us answers. And most important – let him escape."

Roberts asked, "Shouldn't we swamp the building with plain clothes Met officers?"

Sign shook his head. "The whisperer will spot them in a jot; so too the limpet and the other two MI6 officers. Logan, Pendry, and Messenger will tell me they had to abort the meeting due to the hostile nature of the meeting location. And they will be right to say that. The whole exercise will have been a waste of time." He looked at Roberts. "But, I do want them to see you. And I want the whisperer to feel smug because you're all that I've got."

Hilt sat in front of a mirror in his flat. He applied makeup to his face, making his complexion look paler than normal, and a fake moustache and grey wig. He dressed in cheap clothes that looked like they were bought in the 1970s and sprinkled sugar on his jacket's lapels to make it look like he suffered dandruff. He took a swig of Special Brew lager, gargled and spat the mouth-full out, ensuring that some of the spit dropped onto his clothes. He picked up a wooden walking stick and left the flat, limping as he proceeded to central London.

At 0955hrs, Pendry walked through the huge pillars that fronted the entrance to the British Museum in Covent Garden. Hilt watched him. From a different location, so did Roberts. Knutsen was nowhere to be seen. At 0956hrs hours, Messenger arrived at the location and entered London's largest museum. Hilt remained static; so too Roberts. Logan was the last to arrive. Once he was in, Roberts ran to the entrance. Hilt hobbled there, pretending he was disabled.

Hilt approached the ticket counter and purchased an entrance ticket to the establishment. He handed the ticket to an official who was standing next to the museum's metal detector.

The official asked him, "Is there any metal in your walking stick?"

Hilt shook his head. "Just wood and rubber. I can't manage without it."

The official could smell the alcohol on Hilt. "We have disabled ramps and wheelchairs if that would help?"

"Nah thanks. Fell over outside the boozer last week. It's just temporary. The stick will be fine." He emptied his pockets of all metal items, winced as he took off his belt and watch, and placed all items into a tray. He hobbled through the X-ray machine, collected his belongings, and continued onwards. He knew Sign was already in here.

He spotted Roberts, but couldn't see Knutsen. Most likely Knutsen had entered the museum earlier. That didn't matter. Only Roberts could throw the law at Hilt's paymaster. He followed her. She was walking at a leisurely pace, pretending to read a museum brochure. The building was at half capacity, but that still meant there were hundreds of tourists in the venue. Hilt moved closer to Roberts, fearful he'd lose sight of her. He passed displays of Greek artefacts, Buddhist art, French ceramics, and Roman sculptures. Roberts entered the huge reading room in the centre of the museum. Hilt followed.

In the north end of the circular reading room, Sign stood in front of Messenger, Pendry, and Logan. All of the men were in suits. Sign's guests looked pissed off.

"What's so urgent that we had to be summoned here?" asked Messenger.

"And who are you to summon us?" asked Logan. "You're no longer one of us."

Pendry was silent, though looked hostile.

Sign looked around before he returned his gaze to the men. "It is possible you're being targeted for assassination."

All three laughed.

Pendry said, "We take precautions."

"Of course." Sign scrutinized each man.

Messenger, the schizophrenic. A medium-height man who today was playacting the façade of being a well-groomed gentleman, but tomorrow could transform himself into a Russian bar brawler, if the need arose.

Pendry the megalomaniac. A tall spin doctor who schmoozed which ever government was in power, and all because he wanted to run the country via the power of suggestion.

Logan the psychopath. A short man whose muscularity was that of an Olympian weight lifter and whose spine was reinforced by steel after an accident in a rugby match. He'd had problems getting through the museum's metal detector, just as he always had problems at airports. Logan didn't care. He always got to where he needed to be and he always got what he wanted.

Sign said, "I am authorised by the commissioner of the Metropolitan Police to investigate the deaths of Mark Archer, Arthur Lake, Terry File, and Colin Parker. There is a fifth death of a man who has no connection to our service. It is most likely related to the other deaths."

"*Our* service?" Messenger chuckled. "You are a private detective. You're no longer one of us."

Sign was unperturbed. "Be that as it may, I retain authority." He lowered his voice. "I am not here to antagonise you. I'm here to say that there's a killer on the loose. Most likely it's a foreign operative. He or she is killing the shortlist to be chief; also, anyone who gets in the way of the objective. I asked you here because I felt duty bound to warn you that your lives are in danger."

In a sarcastic tone, Logan said, "How very *noble* of you. Are you close to identifying the identity of the assassin?"

"No. And that's why I'm here."

Messenger's eyes narrowed. "You're not here for that. Something else is going on."

"Yes. I'm getting a whiff of bullshit." Pendry crossed his legs, clasped his hands, and said calmly, "Mr. Sign is attempting to play games with us."

"Poor Mr. Sign," Logan said in fluent Chinese. "The only reason I'm here today is because Pendry and Messenger called me to say you'd summoned them as well. We're busy people. We do the games, not you."

In impeccable Mandarin, Sign replied, "You decide if your death is a game." He switched to English, his voice cold and clipped. "There is the possibility that one of you is the killer and there is no hostile foreign agent in play. Somebody in front of me wants to kill off the competition for the post of chief."

Logan slapped his hands. "Bravo, Mr. Sign. I hope the commissioner is paying you handsomely for that absurd analysis."

Messenger looked less cavalier as he glanced at his colleagues. He returned his gaze to Sign. "It's preposterous, but feasible."

"It is." Sign saw Roberts approaching the group. He frowned, knowing the expression would be noticed by his guests. Roberts walked right up to him. "Katy – what are you doing here?"

Roberts showed him her police ID. "I'm here on official police business. The commissioner sent me."

Sign said to Messenger, Pendry, and Logan, "Gentlemen – leave now. I don't know what's going on."

"Stay where you are!" barked Roberts.

Hilt wasted no time. He dropped his cane, ran, knocked over Roberts, and grabbed Pendry. "Time to get out of here," he muttered to the MI6 officer. With his vice-like grip, he frogmarched Pendry away from the others.

Like Hilt, Knutsen was wearing a disguise. He'd been in the reading room for ninety minutes, waiting for the limpet to show up. He dashed toward the limpet and Pendry, ripped off Hilt's wig and fake moustache, and yanked his head back.

Hilt released Pendry and punched Knutsen in the face. Tourists were screaming. The room was turning into chaos as people ran like headless chickens. Knutsen struck Hilt in the chest and shin. Hilt staggered, regained his footing, and flicked his heel behind Knutsen's ankle while at the same time slamming his palm into Knutsen's jaw. Knutsen flipped onto his back. He gasped for air, rolled as Hilt attempted to smash his foot into his skull, and got back to his feet. Hilt and Knutsen stood before each other breathing fast.

Sign called out, "Knutsen – forget him! Protect Pendry!"

Knutsen grabbed Pendry and backed away from Hilt, toward Sign, Roberts, Logan, and Messenger. Roberts had withdrawn an extendable nightstick. She stared at Hilt, silently daring him to come close.

Hilt turned and ran, easily knocking unconscious two museum security men who'd entered the room. He kept running until he was out of the museum. Then he vanished.

Sign acted furious with Roberts. "What just happened?"

"I'm here to question Pendry, Messenger, and Logan."

"Are you now?!" Sign strode right up to her. "To do that, you'd need to have written authority from the foreign secretary or the prime minister. Let me see your paperwork."

Roberts hesitated.

"You don't have such paperwork, do you?"

Pendry brushed his hands over his jacket, but looked calm. He said to Messenger and Logan, "We leave separately, but we most certainly leave now." To Roberts he said, "Detective – your actions will cost you your career, if I have anything to do with it. Look on the bright side. You can sit at home and cry into your vino as you recall the death of your husband. Goodbye."

Pendry left first.

Then Logan.

Messenger was about to leave. He walked up to Sign and whispered, "If you're right and the killer's one of us, I don't think you'll have any chance of identifying that person. But, if I can help, call me." He left.

When Messenger was out of the room, Sign said to Roberts, "Set to work. When you're done, meet us in West Square."

Roberts walked away.

Sign approached Knutsen. "Are you okay, dear fellow?"

Knutsen rubbed his jaw while feeling pain all over his body. He stamped his foot on the floor. "The dojo has a bit of spring in it. And when I'm there I'm covered in armour. Not the same here. But I'll live." He winced as he placed his hand on his back. "I hope there's enough hot water in the flat's tank. I'll be using all of it because I need a very long bath."

Hilt was ten miles away from the museum when he called Smith from a payphone. "They've got my face!"

"I know. You have only two uses to me now: I want you to vanish and keep your mouth shut. I presume you no longer have any alias passports?"

"No. All confiscated when I left The Office."

"Okay. Lay low."

"I can deal with them if they come for me, though Knutsen's a handful. And Roberts might bring in SWAT, in which case I'm screwed."

"Roberts and Knutsen are not your problem. It's Sign who you should be worried about. He'll find your weakness and make you talk."

Hilt shook his head. "I've been through worse before and kept my mouth shut. Plus, I'll take them down before it gets to that."

"Make sure that happens. Just don't let Sign get close to you. I'll give you an extra payment when this is done. For now, don't speak to me until I call you." Smith ended the call. He cursed and called his deputy in MI6. "I won't be in today. Something's come up. Make sure you nail that problem in Cambodia." He took the tube and a taxi to his house in Richmond. His wife was at home and was surprised to see him. He muttered to her that there was a crisis at work and all essential staff had been told to vacate HQ for a few hours. He went into his living room. It contained framed maps of parts of the world, photos of him shaking the hands of three world leaders, decanters of fine brandy and single malt whiskey, and furniture that had been procured from an antiques dealer in Berlin. He sat on a sofa and clasped his hands, deep in thought. Hilt had done the right thing in the museum. But, in doing so it had compromised him. There were two others on the list who needed to be killed. Smith smiled and breathed in deeply. He had no need to worry. He'd outplayed Sign.

Sign tossed logs onto his living room fire and looked sympathetically at Knutsen and Roberts. "You did well today."

Knutsen looked exhausted. "What will you do now?"

Sign looked at the photos Roberts had obtained from the museum's cameras. The limpet's face was visible from several angles. "Inspector Roberts has run these photos through UK national police databases. It's taken her six hours to be ninety percent sure that the limpet has no criminal record and isn't on a list of criminal suspects with no formal police record. That comes as no surprise." He stared at the limpets face before sliding the photos into a beige A4 envelope. "The police can be of no use to us on this. But I have an idea. I need to meet someone who might know who this man is. But that can't be done until tomorrow morning."

"Why the delay?" asked Roberts.

"Because the man I need to meet is currently travelling back from India and he doesn't touch down in Heathrow until seven AM." Sign's demeanour changed. He smiled, clapped his hands and said, "Our local pub is trialling a new ale. Why don't we brave the weather and see what we think of the beer?"

At seven AM the following morning, Sign waited in the Arrivals section of one of Heathrow's terminals. Despite the hour, the airport was bustling. Around him were chauffeurs holding placards with names written on them. Announcements about flights were regularly made over speakers. People were staring at monitors. Others were waiting alongside Sign and the chauffeurs at the metal fence, scrutinising each face that was emerging from the British Airways flight from Mumbai. None of them looked happy. They were saving their smiles for when they spotted the person they were here to meet.

Sign saw the individual he was waiting for. He was a tall, middle-aged man, immaculately dressed in a suit, and was clean shaven. He must have shaved on the flight just before the plane entered UK airspace. He was pulling a trolley bag and seemingly had no escorts. Sign looked at other passengers. Yes – one younger men and one woman worked for him but they were keeping their distance and were wearing less formal attire. The woman was carrying a diplomatic bag. Almost certainly, guns were in there.

As the middle-aged man exited the barrier and traversed the concourse, Sign casually walked behind him, then alongside him. "Hello Freddy. There's nothing to worry about. I just want to talk."

Freddy Vine glanced over his shoulder, gave the slightest shake of his head at his colleagues, and looked at Sign. "I heard you were out of the community. What do you want with me?"

"I need your help. This will only be a quick conversation."

General Vine was the Director of United Kingdom Special Forces. He said, "In two hours' time I have to brief the prime minister. *Quick* is good. We can talk in my car."

Ten minutes later they were in the rear seats of a black BMW, stationary in one of the airport's log-stay carparks. The special forces woman and man were in the front of the car. Sign handed Vine the envelope containing pictures of the limpet. "This person has access to a target of significant interest to me. I believe the man in the photos is a British former special forces soldier. It's possible he was latterly MI6 or MI5 paramilitary. I don't know him. But I want his name."

Vine looked at the photos. "Are you acting freelance now, or do you have official authority?"

"I have the authority of the prime minister, the foreign secretary, and the commissioner of the Metropolitan Police."

Vine's expression was neutral. "I'm responsible for the SAS, SBS, SRR, 18 Signals Regiment, Special Forces Support Group, and the Joint Special Forces Aviation Wing. Combine them and you have thousands of men and women. Multiply that with former operatives of this man's apparent age," he tossed a photo onto his lap, "and you have ten times that number. Plus, I have no access to MI6 and its paramilitary work. This man could be a ghost."

Sign placed a hand on the general's arm, not caring that the act made Vine bristle. "A photo gives me a name. You'll have records. I'm not getting any help from MI6."

"The prime minister could order that assistance!"

Sign removed his hand. "She could. But in doing so she wouldn't know who was paying the man in the photos. He'd go to ground. National security is at stake. It is possible that the next head of MI6 is a serial killer who's contracted the man in the photo."

"Where did you get these photos and when?"

Sign told him what had happened at the British Museum.

"I don't know who he is, but then again I've only been in this job for two years." Vine leafed through all of the photos. "Caucasian; adept at disguise; presumably adept at surveillance; and unarmed combat given he managed to get away – he could be one of ours. But he could equally be American, French, German, or Russian."

"I know." Sign wondered if Vine was going to cooperate. "But, I think he's British."

"Why?"

"A hunch."

Vine laughed. "A hunch?" He placed the photos into the envelope and sighed. "I'll do what I can to help identify him, *if* he is or was one of my boys. But I can't tell you how long that will take. It could be a matter of hours; or it could be days if we need to talk to former operatives to see if one of them knows who the man is. And if one former operative does recognise him, there's every chance he won't tell me his name and may call the man to warn him off."

"I concede it's a risk. If I were you I'd pre-empt any conversation with a statement."

"A statement?"

"Tell your former colleagues that the man in the photo has betrayed the special forces community." Sign opened the door. "I'm not exaggerating, Vine. Do what I tell you to do. This *is* a matter of national security. If you don't cooperate, I'll ensure you're out of a job by tomorrow." Sign exited the car.

Mid-morning, Sign was back in West Square. He told Knutsen and Roberts about his encounter with Vine. "The general will do what he can. He has no alternative. But we must now wait."

"Wait?!." Knutsen paced the room. "The limpet is probably now long gone. And the whisperer will be laughing at us.!"

In a calm tone, Sign responded, "You are right, dear fellow on both counts. But we have something on our side that the whisperer doesn't – time. The clock is ticking before the appointment of the next Chief of MI6 is announced. The whisperer must attempt to kill the last two on the three-person shortlist. But we have muddied the waters. He's going to find murder a far harder task now that I've confronted them."

Roberts said, "The whisperer must be Pendry. He was the one who was grabbed by the limpet."

"Most likely." Sign didn't say what he was thinking. The intercom buzzed. Sign smiled and said to Knutsen, "That will be your young lad David. Show him in. And show no mercy."

When David was in the room, Sign slid a desk into the rear of the lounge, placed three chairs behind it, and put a chair in the centre of the room, facing the desk.

Sign looked at the nineteen year old black man. "Sit."

David sat in the solitary chair. He was wearing a suit that Knutsen had bought him. Sign, Roberts, and Knutsen sat behind the desk.

Knutsen said, "You have your first interview with the Metropolitan Police in two days' time. You have to pass that interview if your application to become a police officer is to progress. We're here to help you prepare for the interview. For the next hour, I am not Tom Knutsen. I am not your friend or mentor. Understood?"

David nodded.

"Yes or no?!"

"Yes." David was perspiring.

Roberts asked, "Why do you want to become a police officer."

David's voice was trembling as he answered, "I want to help my friends. Well, at least I thought they were my friends. I want to set them an example. Get them off drugs and crime."

"Wrong answer!" Knutsen slapped the table. "As a police officer you'll be helping a whole community, the vast majority of who you won't know."

"I... I hadn't thought of it that way."

"Think of it that way." Knutsen nodded at Roberts.

She said, "A police officer enters homes she or he has never entered before. They meet people they don't know. Some of them are liars. Some of them are criminals. Some will want to put a knife in your gut. But some of them will be good people. How are you going to spot the differences?"

David replied, "I... I know my neighbourhood. I know which bros are on the take, their mums and dads, their friends, and I know the streets."

Roberts shook her head. "If you join the Metropolitan Police you may be stationed in a part of London you don't know. You'll have to start from scratch. You'll need to use your brain, knowledge of the law, and your ability to read people."

David was lost for words.

Sign interjected. "Don't be nervous, David."

David frowned. "You a cop as well, mister?"

Sign gave him a half truth. "I work for the Metropolitan Police commissioner. No one else." He placed his hands on the desk. "Nerves are good. It means you respect this forum and it means you're not cocky and arrogant. But you need to get a grip of your nerves. We can't have nervous cops on our streets, can we?"

"No... no sir."

Sign stared at him. "Remember Mr. Knutsen's kendo training. Breathe properly. Always remain in control. Stay poised. Do not let your mind tell you that you've lost before you even raise your sword against your opponent. Believe in the truth. And if it helps, imagine the three of us are naked and sat on the loo."

Roberts suppressed an urge to giggle.

Sign continued. "Be calm. Don't go to the other extreme. Many cops are confident bullies. Don't be like them. Take the professional route. Be the man on the dojo." He glanced at Knutsen.

Knutsen nodded. "He's giving you good advice."

David hesitated. "The truth? The truth is I don't want to be a bully. I don't want to hide behind a uniform and rough people up. I want people like my Mum to make better decisions when they were younger."

Sign glanced at Knutsen and Roberts. "That is a good answer." He returned his attention to David. "You're no longer perspiring. Your voice now sounds confident. Your eye contact is good. My job is done. My colleagues will continue the interview. I will take my leave."

Knutsen and Roberts spent fifty minutes barraging David with questions. They also gave him hypothetical scenarios and asked him what he would do in such events. A mugger is stabbed with his own knife by the victim – do you first attend to the mugger or the traumatised victim? You witness a police officer, who once saved your life, steal cash from a drugs bust – do you report him to your superiors? An armed robber takes a hostage in an off-licence and you are first on the scene – do you request that you're taken hostage in exchange for the victim being released? A terrorist is about to blow himself up in a crowded location – do you kill him? The list of questions and scenarios were relentless. David didn't get all of the answers right. It would have been impossible for him to have done so without extensive police training and experience. And as every police veteran will agree, there are always situations that no police officer is prepared for. But that wasn't the purpose of the interview. What Knutsen and Roberts were looking for in David were thoughtfulness and swift decisiveness.

At the end of the interview Knutsen smiled. "David – you'll do an excellent job in your real interview. When you get home, hang your suit up and make sure it's free of fluff, wash and iron your shirt, polish your shoes, get rid of that goatee beard thing you've got going on, and – most importantly – be proud of who you are."

After David was gone, Sign re-entered the room and addressed Knutsen and Roberts. "General Vine has just called me. I know the limpet's name. He is Karl Hilt. He's a former Royal Marines commando and subsequently a Special Boat Service operative, before joining my lot and becoming a covert paramilitary operative. He left MI6 two years' ago. Now he works freelance."

Roberts asked, "What do you know about his character?"

Sign sat in his armchair. "Vine said he was an extremely effective operator in special forces. But, he's a psychopath; or a sociopath; or whatever label we can slap on him. That trait served him very well in behind-the-lines work, including with MI6. Regardless, Vine has told me to be very careful with him."

Knutsen asked, "What do we do next?"

"We hunt him down and make him talk."

CHAPTER 23

Four days' later Hilt checked into a hotel in Norwich. He felt grubby and exhausted. He'd walked and jogged one hundred and twenty miles from London to Norfolk and his only rest had been a few hours' kip in some ditches. He knew he couldn't go anywhere near his home, so he'd chosen Norfolk because there was a Cromer-based trawler captain he knew who might take him to Scandinavia. But the captain wasn't due back from his North Sea fishing trip until tomorrow and Hilt was on his knees. He needed a proper bed, But, in taking a room in the hotel, he knew that he was probably signing his own death sentence. In the bedroom, he showered and shaved, then sat in a chair, his gun on his lap. He stared at the door, desperately trying not to sleep. But fatigue started to overcome him. His head started nodding; eyes shutting and opening; nose sporadically snorting; and his mind was telling him to rest because he was too old for this lark. His gun fell off his lap as he slouched, deep in sleep.

Roberts ran up the stairs of West Square and hammered on Sign's door. Knutsen answered. Breathless, Roberts exclaimed, "We've got him! Hilt. He's checked in to a hotel in Norwich. He used his own ID. Must mean he doesn't have other ID. Hotel cameras picked up his face. There's no doubt it's him."

Knutsen ushered her in and called out to Sign.

Sign entered the living room. He was in a bathrobe. Roberts repeated what she'd told Knutsen. Sign said, "Norfolk will be the first stage of Hilt's escape route."

Knutsen frowned. "Escape?"

"Yes. Hilt's now of no use to the whisperer. He's been told to get out while he can. I imagine he didn't use any form of transport to get to Norfolk. He's tired and he's waiting for an asset to get him to," he looked at a framed map of the world, "somewhere. My guess is that his destination isn't the Netherlands or Germany – the crossings are too heavily policed. And if he wanted to take conventional ferries into Europe he'd have gravitated to Lowestoft. No. He's going to Denmark, Norway, or Sweden. And he's going there via unconventional transport. After that, who knows?"

Roberts was confused. "He'll have known that checking into a hotel might have blown his location. Why not check into a B&B where there are no cameras. It would have been far harder for us to trace him there."

Sign agreed. "He doesn't like you, me, and Knutsen. He's baiting us. He wants us to enter his room. Then he kills us and leaves."

Roberts pulled out her phone. "I'm calling SCO19. They'll arrest or kill him."

Sign shook his head. "It would take weeks for SWAT to rehearse how to take down a paramilitary spy. They're not trained for this."

"Then who is?"

"MI6. But they're not at my disposal." Sign rubbed his face. "Special forces could be an option, but there is a significant risk that they won't want to kill one of their own."

Knutsen asked, "What about foreign allies? Could they help? They'll be impartial."

Sign smiled. "It's a good thought but flawed. A foreign paramilitary unit would have to know what's at stake in order for them to risk a severe diplomatic row if they hit a UK national on UK soil. To get a foreign ally's help, we'd have to tell them that the next Chief of MI6 is a murderer. That information would escalate beyond our control. We're looking for the whisperer. We are most certainly not looking to lose the allegiance of a partner country." Sign pointed at Roberts. "We take Hilt down ourselves. I've no time to tell you how. I'll be there. I'll do the thinking. Give me five minutes to get dressed. Then we get in the car to Norfolk. Bring guns. Also handcuffs or rope."

When he was out of the room, Roberts muttered, "Arrogant prick!"

Knutsen was shocked. "Sign? He gave you a place to stay after your husband was murdered. He helped you get back on your feet. He helped give me purpose. He helped David. For very little money, he's helping UK national security. He's not arrogant. He was the brightest star in MI6. He's gone into problem-solving mode. Don't mistake that for arrogance. He just thinks better than us. You want to slap a label on him then I'll give you one – he's lonely. No man is an island and all that. He's been adrift since his wife was murdered. And I'll tell you this – he'll take a bullet for us without blinking. He wants to be with her again." Knutsen stood. "Don't ever speak about my friend like that again!"

Roberts paled. "I… I hadn't thought about it that way."

"Then, don't think!" Knutsen knelt before her. "You've been through so much. Goodness knows how you've coped. Always remember who your friends are. Sign is the best of them." Knutsen smiled. "He can, however, be a pain in the ass."

As he stood, Roberts laughed and said, "He most certainly can. But you're right. He's done more for me than anyone else."

"Including your husband?" Knutsen looked aghast. "Sorry, that came out wrong. It was a dumb thing to ask."

Roberts looked at the floor. Quietly she said, "It's okay. Elliot and I worked. Good marriage. Barely a bad word between us. He remembered anniversaries and birthdays. He was charming with my family and friends. He never did anything bad to me. He was a very proper man. But..." her lips trembled, "but..."

"There sometimes is a *but*."

She raised her head. "It's hard for women. Sometimes, when the best thing is looking you in the face, you want something else."

"You cheated on him?"

"No. Nothing like that. I thought of him like a superb brother. Not a lover. Does that make sense?"

"Yes." Knutsen stripped his pistol, cleaned the working parts, and reassembled the gun. "We all have to forget the past. The next few hours will define our future. We have to put our faith in Sign. SCO19 might have been the best solution. Then again, I'm not a spy. I don't think like Sign. Nor do I have his training."

"You over estimate him."

"Maybe."

Sign entered the room. He was wearing corduroy trousers, hiking boots, and a green fleece jacket.

Hunting, shooting, and fishing in Norfolk was what immediately came into Knutsen's mind when he saw Sign's garb. "Do you have any clothes that are twenty first century?"

Sign laughed. "Would they keep me warmer than those manufactured in the last century?" He poured himself a coffee. "Clothing manufacture is about fashion, not necessity. Still, people who need warmth within rugged environments are sucked in by alleged advances in clothing technology. It's a racket. Did you know in 1924 the British mountaineer George Herbert Leigh Mallory is probably the first man to scale Everest? He did so in clothing that by today's standards would be deemed nonsensical. It wasn't. I'm certain he reached the peak."

Knutsen was having none of this. "We don't know if he reached the peak. In any case, he died on the way down. His body was only discovered in 1999. I don't think his clothes were good enough."

Sign sat. "Or he was simply exhausted and suffering from altitude sickness." He smiled. "I've traversed Siberia during winter in little more than a shirt and trousers. I concede, I've never suffered altitude sickness. I did, however, have a pack of dogs on my heels. Men do what they have to do under the circumstances." His expression steeled. "I know what I'm doing. Clothes don't stop a bullet. If either of you think you know better, try swimming two miles in December from St. Petersburg to a British submarine."

Knutsen and Roberts were silent.

Sign said, "Now! Get dressed. Think like Mallory. We can ascend in whatever attire. But we may not make it back to base camp. We depart in five minutes."

John Smith watched Logan's home. He knew Logan was in there. It was Saturday. Logan had a rare day off. Given he had a six month old baby, that meant his wife would do anything to have a few hours respite from childcare. She'd be out of the house as soon as possible. Smith waited for ninety minutes. Logan's wife exited, holding a supermarket 'bag for life' and an umbrella. She looked tired but happy. Even an hour or two of buying baby food and other essentials would give her the head space she needed. Probably, when she returned home she'd feed her family, put her son to bed, and then collapse on the sofa. Smith waited until she was out of sight and then entered the house. He could hear Logan in the kitchen, washing dishes. He moved silently into the adjacent lounge. Logan had his back to him. His son was in a playpen, lying on his back while fiddling with toys that were too big to choke on. Smith stood by the playpen, staring at the child. He had no affinity to children. As far as he was concerned, they were not only a waste of time, they also produced emotions in their parents that ultimately messed with their minds and supplied them with an early grave. He knew that because his parents had worked themselves to the bone to support him. Like all children, he'd been selfish as a child. His highly educated and intelligent parents got through parenthood like any other mum and dad – they blagged it, taking each day as it came. Lack of sleep was a killer in the early days; so too lack of cash. In an attempt to keep things afloat, his dad had dragged his tiny family to tax havens around the world, every time telling his wife that his new job would make them millions. It never worked that way. His dad ended up bankrupt. His wife divorced him. Dad died of a broken heart. Mum killed herself. And before then, Smith had been schooled in Dubai, Isle of Man, Bermuda, and Vanuatu. Friends came and went. Childhood was a waste of time. Still, MI6 liked the fact that he'd had an unconventional upbringing. The organisation thought it made him well equipped for the work of a spy who had no connection to the normal world.

Smith pulled out a pistol and held it against the baby's head. "Mr. Logan! I urge you to desist from you chores."

Logan ran in to the room.

Smith smiled. "Hello Logan. The gun is loaded. If you don't do what I say, I will kill your son."

Logan's face flushed red. "Sign was right! There was always a killer!"

"We do what we have to in life." He placed the muzzle of the gun in the baby's mouth. It thought it was a toy. The boy gurgled. With his left hand, Smith withdrew a piece of paper and a pen and placed both on an adjacent table. "Sit down and write what I dictate. I'll stay here until you're done. Your baby's head will be mash if you make one error."

At midday, Sign, Knutsen, and Roberts stood outside the Holiday Inn in Norwich.

Roberts said to Sign, "The hotel concierge says Hilt's in his room. He has a 'Do Not Disturb' leaflet on his door. I've given the concierge your name and instructed him that you have police authority to approach the room. Are you sure this is a good idea?"

Sign shrugged. "Time will tell. But I don't think going in guns blazing will help. If anything, it will antagonise him and force him to keep his mouth shut. He'll stay silent out of principal. A more subtle tactic is needed. I want you both to stay outside in case he bolts."

Knutsen shook his head. "That will be a lottery. There are too many entrances and exits to cover."

"Try your best." Sign walked in to the hotel.

Knutsen muttered, "He's making a huge mistake doing this alone. He's unarmed. We can't back him up. All he's got is…"

"His brain." Roberts stared at the hotel. "This is what he does – going in to situations without a safety net. It's ingrained in him." She turned to Knutsen. "I'll take the north side of the hotel. You stay here. When he gives the signal, we move like fury."

Sign took a lift to the third floor and walked down the corridor. He knocked on a room door. "Karl Hilt, this is Ben Sign. You know who I am. I am alone and unarmed. But, I do have police officers surrounding the hotel. I'd like to talk."

There was silence for two minutes.

Sign spoke in a louder voice. "I know you're in there. And I know you're desperate. I have something that will help you."

The door opened a few inches. Hilt was there, his gun pointing at Sign. Hilt said, "If you've got others with you, you'll go down first."

"I agree to those terms."

"And it will be a head shot, in case you're wearing a bullet proof vest."

Sign patted his chest. "No vest. No wire. No recording device whatsoever. No pistol. No explosives. No tricks. But, I do have a piece of paper I'd like to show you." He pulled out a letter. "May I come in?"

Hilt fully opened the door, grabbed Sign by the back of his neck, flung him onto the bed, and stood with his gun in two hands. It was pointing at one of Sign's eyes.

Sign sat up. "There's no need for violence. I wouldn't be able to compete with you." He gestured to a chair. "May I sit there? I'd like you to sit opposite me. By all means keep your gun trained on me if you think it's necessary. I suspect you already know I can't hurt you. But I'll leave it to your intellect to decide whether I'm a problem or a solution."

Hilt hesitated, then nodded. "Get in the chair." He pulled up another chair and faced Sign. His gun was still in his hand but not pointing at Sign. "Why and how would you help me?"

Sign was calm. "You're in a bit of a pickle. No doubt you're here because you have an exfiltration route planned across the North Sea. If you haven't, that's bad luck because you've got nowhere to go in the UK. You've been hung out to dry by your paymaster. For people like us there's nothing worse than when you've been stabbed in the back by one of your own."

Hilt chuckled. "It comes with the territory."

"Yes. And I know you don't care about that. It's what you're trained for. Probably, abandonment is in your DNA. After all, your parents gave you up for adoption when you were four. But, you didn't get adopted. Instead it was foster care nearly every year until you were eighteen and enlisted in the marines. The commandos were the family you always wanted. The problem was that you could never really fit in with all the camaraderie and discipline. It was too late for you because you were a loner and had no trust. Nevertheless, you were top of your marine class and served with distinction. But, you wanted something different. Special forces appealed to you because you thought it might be a job where you could work alone. You made it through the excruciating selection process and were set to task for many years. Alas, you didn't find solace in the Special Boat Service. There was still a chain of command. And you had to work with colleagues. Family, you concluded, was not for you. And that's why we picked you up. MI6 gave you precisely what you always knew – you had no family, nor any substitute families. You could now work alone."

Hilt was silent, though anger was evident in his face.

Sign crossed his legs. "It's not your fault that you are a sociopath. When a child gets no love – from parents, foster parents, teachers, social workers, aunts or uncles, siblings, anyone – as a result, they don't trust love."

"Thanks for the therapy session, *Dr.* Sign." Hilt waved his gun. "But, I'm a grown up. And I'm the one who can end your life."

"Yes, of course you can, dear fellow. This is the problem," He handed the letter to Hilt.

It took thirty seconds for Hilt to read the two page document. It was written by General Vine, was classed top secret, and had the word *Draft* printed at the top. Within the letter it said that Hilt suffered mental illness, was a coward in action, had allegedly slept with a fourteen year old girl, and was dishonourably discharged from the military.

Hilt tossed the letter aside. "These are all fucking lies!"

Sign smiled. "Of course they are. But who did you think you were dealing with?"

"Vine didn't come up with this! You did this!"

Sign said, "You're going to prison for the murder of Elliot Roberts. I would imagine the sentence will be approximately twenty five to thirty years. Here's the thing – prison officers and inmates respect courage. You'll get extra rations; you'll be treated well; you'll be able to run a fiefdom. But, if I put a copy of that letter into the system you'll be a nonce. Your life will be hell. So, I'm sat here wondering what to do. Letter or no letter? No letter means you'll probably be out on good behaviour in fifteen years. In court a brilliant defence lawyer will cite your appalling childhood, the traumas you've suffered in combat, and the fact you were paid to kill Elliot by a man who is infinitely worse than you. Alas, the letter will not go well for you."

Hilt stated, "If I do anything to you, a copy of this letter will go straight to the courts and prison."

"Yes." Sign looked out of the window. "You could shoot your way out of this situation. You'll die. The papers will say the police killed a paedophile. But if by some miracle you make it to a boat that can take you across the North Sea, know this – there is a British frigate sitting there, waiting to check every boat that heads out of East Anglia. And on the frigate are thirty marines. They won't like you at all."

Hilt frowned. "You're bluffing!"

Sign pulled out his mobile number and extended it to Hilt. "Vine's number is in my contact list. Call him. Ask him security passwords to verify he is who he says he is. Also in my contacts list are the Minister of Defence, the Foreign Secretary, the Head of MI6, the Metropolitan Police Commissioner, and the Prime Minister. Ask them if I'm bluffing."

Hilt didn't take the phone.

Sign leaned forward. "There will be no letter if I get a name. I want to know who in MI6 killed the competition."

Smith watched Logan write his signature at the bottom of the sheet of paper. Smith withdrew his gun from the baby's mouth and looked at the sheet. It read as follows:

To whom it may concern

My name is James Logan. I am a senior official in British Intelligence. It was probable I would be the next chief of the Secret Intelligence Service. But, to attain that post, I knew I was up against strong competition, as well as external forces. The other men on the shortlist for chief are Mark Archer, Arthur Lake, Edward Messenger, Nicholas Pendry, and Terry File. All but Messenger and Pendry were killed by my hand. I would have killed Messenger and Pendry but my identity has been discovered by former MI6 officer Ben Sign. My tactic has failed. I also confess to instructing a subordinate to kill Elliot Roberts, the husband of a Special Branch Detective who has been helping Sign, and murder Colin Parker, a high ranking counter-intelligence officer. I'm writing this letter under duress. Ben Sign is pointing a gun at my child. He is forcing this confession out of me.

Nevertheless, I will accept whatever punishment is owed to me.

James Logan

Smith grinned as he placed the muzzle of his handgun back against the baby's head. "Him? Or you?"

"You bastard!" Logan was sweating.

"Live with what you might see for the rest of your life, or end the pain. You choose!"

Logan shook his head. "How could you do this?"

Smith cocked the gun. "Bye bye baby."

"No! No!"

Smith walked to Logan and shoved the gun in his mouth. "That was the right decision." He pulled the trigger. Logan was instantly dead.

Sign called Roberts. "Bring one of your colleagues. He's ready to come in. He won't hurt you. I have the name."

Knutsen and Roberts were in the room within eighty seconds. Both trained their guns on Hilt.

Roberts' stomach knotted as she looked at the man who'd killed her husband. "Why did you let us find you?!"

Hilt smiled. "I didn't want to run anymore."

"Liar!" Roberts stepped forward,

Hilt tossed his gun onto the bed. "I'm sorry about the loss of your husband. Life ain't fair, is it? If it's any consolation, pretty much everyone I know is dead. All I have left is a job. The jobs usually include bullets or knives. That's my path. Shit happens." He looked Roberts directly in the eye. "I came here because I want to reach the end of that path. I was going to get on a fishing boat tomorrow. But, then what? More of the same old crap. Reinventing myself. No ID I can use. One day being caught out and smashed up in a prison cell in Moscow or Beijing. I could have done that ten years ago. Now, I'm not so sure. See, the thing is I've got a bit of a medical situation. Only found out three months ago." He looked away, his smile no longer on his face. "If you're a betting person, don't put a wager on me making it past the next few weeks. Lung cancer's a fucker. I've never smoked. Probably it's all that nuclear, biological, and chemical training they put SF through. Respirators aren't faultless. Guess I got some filth in my airways." He stood and then laid on his front with his hands behind his back. "It's muscle memory. Leg it to an escape and evasion route. Get to Scandinavia. Go on foot and other means across Europe. End up in Thailand or similar. Then you realise you're not that person anymore." He looked over his shoulder. "Get it done!"

Roberts put her foot on his back and attached handcuffs. "You're under arrest for the murder of my husband." She looked at Sign. "How did you know?!"

Sign clasped his hands. "I didn't know about his cancer. But I deduced he'd come here because it was his last stand and a cry for help. It's like an old wolf who wanders from the pack because it knows something is wrong with its health. It chooses a place to die." Sign stood and walked out of the room while saying, "Do your police thing and get Hilt to a secure facility. He won't try to escape."

Ten minutes later, police were on the scene. They escorted Hilt to Norwich police station where he was placed in a cell. The custody sergeant refused the Metropolitan Police's request to transfer him to a London police station, on the grounds that Hilt might do severe damage to the officers transporting him. The Metropolitan commissioner tried to object, but the sergeant told him that custody sergeants can only be overruled by the home secretary. Hilt was to be kept in Norfolk, awaiting trial. A doctor and nurses visited him in his cell and did tests on him. They concluded he'd be dead before a court verdict was issued.

When Sign, Knutsen, and Roberts were back in London, Roberts received a phone call. After she ended the call, she said to Sign, "James Logan has written a letter stating he did the murders. Then he killed himself. His wife found the body. Logan wasn't the name Hilt gave you. The limpet lied."

Sign looked distracted as he strolled alongside his colleagues into West Square. "He didn't lie. The whisperer cast him aside, like a rabid dog. He wouldn't protect him now." He stopped and turned to Roberts. "By all means slap me if you wish, but I do feel sorry for Hilt – his upbringing and adult life have been hell. It would have been good if we could have turned back the clock and given him a proper family."

Roberts stared at him. First, she looked angry. Then sad. "Yes. I know all about living with grief. It corrupts the soul."

Knutsen said, "We all know how that feels." He placed his hand on Sign's arm. "What next?"

Sign stood outside the entrance to the apartment block. "Logan isn't the whisperer. Nor did he commit suicide. He was executed in the same room as his baby. What I would have done if I were the whisperer is tape bin bags to my arms so that I could dispose of cordite residue on my forearms, wear gloves, plastic shoe covers, hold a gun to the baby's head, and force a false confession out of Logan. When he'd finished the note, I'd have placed the gun in his mouth. Logan would have put his hands around the weapon, out of fear. I'd have pulled the trigger, knowing that Logan's prints were now on the gun and that cordite would be on his arms. Police forensics would see the case as cut and dry. And there'd be no trace of an external party in the room."

Roberts asked, "How do you know this stuff?"

"Life and death." Sign looked at Knutsen. "I need you and your skills today. You and I aren't going in to the apartment. However, Mrs. Roberts is going into her flat."

Roberts looked furious. "Don't leave me out of this!"

Sign leaned toward her and whispered into her ear. "I cannot compromise you or your profession. Knutsen and I are unconventional. But you have a career and life to protect. You can argue with me as much as you like, dear lady. But, on this matter I must hold fast." He patted Knutsen's arm. "Let's finish this awful affair."

Sign and Knutsen spun on their heels and walked away.

They traversed London via tubes and a taxi. On arrival, the residential house before them was where the whisperer lived. It was seven PM and getting dark. The house had internal lights on. The whisperer and his wife were easily visible in their dining room.

As they stood on the street, Knutsen asked, "What are we going to do about his wife?"

"We need her as a witness. There are two scenarios: she's either complicit in what the whisperer has done; or she's not complicit, in which case we need her to hear what's happened. Either way, she won't want prison. Regardless, here." He handed Knutsen a recording device the size of a cigarette lighter. "This is state of the art MI6. Turn this on as soon as we enter."

Knutsen laughed. "You spooks are so out of touch with technology. We could have just used a mobile phone to record everything that's said. It can be saved to Cloud forever."

Sign looked puzzled. "I've no idea what that means." His expression steeled. "Onwards."

Sign rang the front door bell.

The whisperer's wife opened the door.

Sign said, "We're colleagues of your husband. There is urgent business to attend to. May we come in? We're sorry if we are intruding on your dinner."

She answered, "The dinner is in the oven. Casserole. It won't be ready for a couple of hours." She called out to her husband. "Two men are here. They say they know you. I'm not letting them in unless you say it's okay."

The whisperer appeared in the hallway and asked, "What do you want, Ben Sign?"

"I need to talk to you about Logan. He's killed himself and confessed his direct involvement in criminal matters that affect national security. My investigation is now closed. But, I need you to hear from me what has happened."

The whisperer nodded. "Come in. And congratulations on a job well done."

Sign and Knutsen entered the house.

CHAPTER 24

The whisperer gestured Sign and Knutsen to the dining room table. The whisperer sat opposite them. He was wearing the suit he'd worn to work. He asked, "Would you like my wife to leave the room?"

She was leaning against the wall, watching the three men.

Sign faked a gentlemanly smile. "That won't be necessary. She's security cleared to know all about your work."

"She is. So let's get on with it. I need to shower and change into more comfortable attire before dinner."

Sign nodded. "I quite understand, dear chap. And once again, sorry for the intrusion. We're here because we want to protect you. When MI6 learns tomorrow of Logan's betrayal, it will be in a mess. Henry Gable won't be able to control that mess. He's not up to the task. The Metropolitan Police has no jurisdiction over the intelligence agencies. It can't step in to keep a steady ship. MI5 are a bunch of quasi-cops. They don't understand espionage. The announcement about Logan will have to be made to all MI6 staff. But the announcement will rock the morale of the service."

"Cambridge Five springs to mind." The whisperer's tone was calm and precise.

"Exactly. It took decades for us to get over that sucker-punch. During the Cold War, we couldn't afford that catastrophe. Now, the world's a more dangerous place."

The whisperer sighed and drummed his fingers on the table. "Spare me a lecture on the obvious."

"We need leadership. You can give that. So can the only other candidate left alive for the post of chief. One of you has to step up to the plate."

The whisperer was more benign as he answered, "I'm ready for the challenge."

"I feared you would be."

Knutsen's handgun was hidden from view under the table and pointing at the whisperer's stomach. Everything being said was being recorded by the electronic device in his jacket.

In a louder voice, Sign said, "Logan didn't kill Mark Archer, Colin Parker, Arthur Lake, and Terry File. Karl Hilt killed Elliot Roberts. Hilt is now in custody. He has a fatal illness and has nothing to lose. You employed him. *You* are the serial killer. You are what I call the whisperer. You are Edward Messenger."

Messenger laughed. "This is the stuff of fantasy!"

"No, it's not. Hilt has confessed."

Messenger shook his head. "This man Hilt has been briefed by Logan to give you my name. Probably Logan knew Hilt had cancer. It was Logan's parting shot."

Sign glanced at Messenger's wife. "Mrs. Logan. You're a nurse. Can you tell me how many fatal illnesses there are?"

She went pale. "Tens, hundreds, thousands. It depends on the quality of the treatment, how far advanced the disease is, the age of the patient, their immune system, and other factors."

Sign's expression was cold as he returned his attention to Messenger. "Thousands of possibilities. I didn't tell you Hilt had cancer. But he does."

Messenger breathed in deeply. "An educated guess. My wife and I have an agreement not to talk about her day job. My parents are dead. It's stressful to know what my wife goes through every day."

"Rubbish!" Sign slapped his hand on the table. "You've seen more death than she has. And you've dealt it out throughout your career. You understand death as well as me. You're not squeamish. But, you are stupid. There's no possibility of you knowing Hilt had cancer unless you knew Hilt and you knew his condition. Hilt will testify against you to get a lesser sentence. A resourceful man like him would never have trusted a Machiavellian man like you I guarantee you he'll have concrete evidence of your contract together and he'll have kept the evidence hidden from you. Who knows? Photos; recordings; bank transfers; phone calls; evidence in a closed court of where your paths crossed in MI6. You put him out to an unsavoury pasture. Now, he's doing the same to you. He'll crucify you in court."

Knutsen said, "I'm a former police officer. But, I still work for the police. What you say next will be used in court."

Messenger was silent but let out a groan after his wife walked up to him and slapped his face.

"How could you?!" She said to him. "How could you?!"

Slowly, Messenger raised his head and rubbed his face. He looked at his wife, then Sign and Knutsen. He bowed his head and said in a quiet voice, "Pendry is going to die."

Sign frowned. "You're going to jail. You won't be able to touch him."

Messenger rubbed his eyes and smiled. "I'm not, as you describe, stupid. I'm smarter than you. It's all about chess. The others had to be dealt with expediently. But after I got Logan to confess, I had to deal with Pendry differently. I saw him for a cup of tea yesterday in the MI6 canteen. When he wasn't looking, I placed a liquid nerve agent in his tea. The agent was designed at Porton Down. It's ingenious. Under our instructions four years' ago, the boffins constructed a deadly liquid that assaults the body. But it was crucial the effects weren't immediate. It means you can have a Russian, or whoever, visiting the UK, be infected with the nerve agent, fly back to Russia and not start getting ill for a few weeks. As a result, no one can categorically trace the poisoning to the UK, even if there are suspicions from other states. Ergo: bad guy dies; no diplomatic fallout." Messenger retained his smile. "Pendry is a dead man walking. He'll feel fine now. But soon he'll start frothing at the mouth. Not even Porton Down can reverse the effects. Our most lethal scientific research and development facility has created a poison that they cannot counteract. There's an irony there."

Sign was motionless. "Pendry will die, but you will not be made chief. You'll go to jail for multiple life sentences."

Messenger looked resigned to his fate. "I'd have made an excellent chief. The others on the shortlist weren't a patch on me." His expression turned menacing as he looked at Sign. "You too would have made a superb chief. But, you took yourself out of the equation. So, it was down to me to step up to the plate. And sometimes in life we have to do rough things to allow the little people to sleep peacefully in their beds."

"Serial killing to obtain power is *not* part of the job description of an MI6 officer." Sign looked at Messenger's wife. "Did you know anything about what your husband has done? Or, did you have any suspicions?"

She was tearful as she replied, "No. No… I never knew what he did at work. This is awful. Edward – how could you have done this? We were happy. We didn't need you to get a pay rise. I didn't need you to be chief."

Messenger looked at her. "You weren't enough for me. I needed a mistress. The position of chief was my mistress." He smiled and returned his attention to Sign. "I won't spend the rest of my life in prison. So, how do we resolve this situation?"

Knutsen gripped his handgun.

Messenger was calm as he said to Knutsen, "You're pointing a handgun at me, under the table. Did you expect me not to anticipate that? And did you expect me not to be doing the same to you? I believe they call it a Mexican standoff."

Sign snapped, "If you kill anyone in this room, it will go bad for you."

Messenger pulled his hand out from under the table. He placed his pistol on the table. "For the sake of the recording device that no doubt one of you has on his person, I employed Karl Hilt to watch you and kill Katy Roberts' husband and Colin Parker. I forced Mark Archer, Arthur Lake, and Terry File to commit suicide. I shot James Logan after forcing him to write a false confession. I made that murder look like suicide. And I poisoned Nicholas Pendry. I did all of this because I wanted to be the only remaining candidate for the top job in British intelligence." He picked up the gun.

Knutsen shouted, "No!"

Messenger blew his own brains out.

Three hours later, Knutsen and Sign were back in West Square. In the lounge, Knutsen lit a fire. "I'll get Katy," he said.

When she entered the bachelor pad, Roberts was fully clothed. "What happened?"

Knutsen explained everything.

She looked at Sign. "Will you take over as chief of MI6, even if briefly?"

Sign was in his armchair. "No. I like this job. I like working with you both."

Roberts touched his hand. "I'm moving to New Zealand. It will be a new life. You and Tom will be on your own." A tear fell down her cheek.

Sign gripped her hand. "Damn right you should go to New Zealand." He smiled. "Don't look back."

"Never."

Sign rose and kissed her on the cheek. "Knutsen and I will be alright. You'll be alright." He walked to the window and stared through it. "It's what's out there that worries me." He turned rapidly. "Mr. Knutsen, if you please! Three glasses of calvados immediately. Tonight we celebrate. Tomorrow may bring ills. I've received a letter. Knutsen – you and I have a new case."

THE END

THE FIFTH MAN

A *Ben Sign* Espionage Story

By

Matthew Dunn

FORMER *MI6 SPY* AND *BEST-SELLING* AUTHOR

CHAPTER 1

The Argentinian spy boat was anchored one mile off the Falklands Islands capital, Stanley. The vessel was thirty three yards long, resembled a fishing trawler, and had a crew of three men and one woman. It had been scouring the western and eastern isles of the Falklands for two months. Soon, it was due to return to the Argentinian port of Rio Grande, where the boat would be refuelled, fresh provisions would be taken on board, and the crew would rest for a few days. The boat had long-range telescopes, communications equipment, and thermal imagery. Its movements around the islands were random. Sometimes it would anchor, other times it would circumnavigate the islands, and sometimes it would only travel a few hundred yards before coming to an unanchored stop. Its purpose was twofold: first, to monitor British military movement on the islands; second, to annoy the islanders. Argentina wanted the Falklands back. It needed to show the islanders and UK military bases that it was watching them. But the boat posed no threat. The British military were aware of its presence; so too the islanders. They thought the boat was a joke. The UK navy couldn't be bothered to send a frigate from Portsmouth all the way towards the Antarctic to clear out the spy ship. What could the boat learn, reasoned the British commanders on the islands? That the Falklands only has a population of just over three thousand? That it rears sheep and exports fish? That a land invasion by Argentina would be met by fierce resistance? But the boat remained on duty, taunting the inhabitants of the islands. It was an Argentinian folly. However, the crew were not without teeth. They had guns. And they were firearms trained to the highest standard.

Tonight, the boat rolled in choppy seas. Two of its crew felt nauseas and were trying to stop themselves from vomiting. Only the captain of the vessel was a qualified sailor; the others were technicians. But, all of them had been taught how to master the boat should there be an emergency. They'd been told to watch the islands, but hadn't been given clear instructions as to what purpose their duty served. To them, the job seemed pointless. They were antagonists, they'd concluded – sent by their government to stir up shit and provoke the islanders and the UK military. Still, they had to do the job, no matter what the job. And they'd been told to kill anyone who tried to get close to their vessel.

It was getting dark and snow was falling. The skipper flicked on interior and exterior lights. He didn't care that it would make the vessel visible to others. He did care that if they remained invisible they might be accidentally struck by another ship. He walked on deck, pulled on a hemp seaman's jumper, rubbed ice off his beard, and lit a pipe as he gazed at the shores of the islands. Stanley was a mile away, its lights easily visible, the only sound to be heard was the slap of waves against the vessel and the boat's frame creaking with each movement. It was seven PM. Soon the crew would take it in turn to take over the night vigil for two hours per person while the others slept. It was a slog, no matter who went on shift first. They always woke up exhausted in the morning. It wasn't just the shift rotations and sea sickness that caused them shallow sleep; they never truly rested because there was always the threat that a British fighter plane would blow them to smithereens.

Still, tonight seemed like every other night. Boring. Lonely. Pointless.

The only silver lining was that tomorrow they'd be sailing back to Rio Grande – earlier than planned because the boat needed some urgent maintenance. The captain couldn't wait to turn on the engines and get home. He'd see his wife and kids for a few days, then motor back to the islands. His family thought he was a hero for doing a top secret job. He thought he was a fraud = a covert operative with no real mission.

He wished something would happen before he left – a British navy attempt to board his vessel; an aerial bombardment; commandos clambering up the sides of the boat; a diplomatic incident that would put his job front and centre of the world's press. Anything to relieve the tedium.

In one hand he held a telescope to his eye. In the other hand he gripped a semiautomatic pistol. It had never been fired in anger. He'd relinquish a month's salary to engage the enemy. The Brits had killed his father in the war. Payback was why he was here. But, so far it seemed he was on a fool's folly. Still, he kept grip of his pistol, willing soldiers, sailors, or islanders to attempt to take him and his crew on.

The pub in Stanley was modest in size and a popular venue for local islanders. It was off-limits to British military personnel who were garrisoned on the Islands' various bases, for no other reason than the military wanted to respect the islanders' privacy and community. "This is their homeland, not ours", the highest ranking officer told new military arrivals. "We are here to protect them. But we are not here to turn their town into a place for drunken squaddies to let off steam." Still, the islanders would have welcomed army, navy, or air force personnel into the boozer. Their attitude was *Britain first; Argentina last.*

The pub had Union Jacks hanging from the ceiling, a tiny bar with six barstools, pictures of the Royal Marines and Parachute Regiment marching across the islands during the war, three corner tables, a wooden floor, a *No Smoking* sign that was ignored by all, an old terrier dog that had lost one of its rear legs after stepping onto a mine that had sunk in a minefield and had shifted sideways with the earth – as the soil does in The Falklands – outside of the minefield, a painting of Margaret Thatcher, another of the current Governor of the archipelago, and an overhead fan that was only turned on in the summer or when the room was too clogged with tobacco smoke.

Sally was working the barmaid shift tonight. She'd lived on The Falklands all her life and had never visited anywhere else. But she wasn't naïve. The Internet kept her abreast of the outside world and she had virtual friends on Facebook who lived all over the world. She was twenty seven, pretty, and took shit from no one. Her father owned the pub. Normally he'd be here cleaning the place or checking the week's takings. But tonight he was out helping a mate to get one of his sheep to give birth, even though the unborn lamb was in the breach position.

Sally cleaned glasses while standing behind the bar. Four male islanders were on the other side of the bar, sitting on barstools.

Eddie Wilson. Thirty three years old. Fisherman. Not married and always hitting on Sally, though she was having none of it. Smoker, but not in the day. Facial skin as tough as leather. Hands that were calloused and as strong as a vice. Black hair that tonight was mostly hidden by a woollen hat. A permanent smell of salt and fish on him, no matter how many times he bathed. And a scar on his jaw from when his boat rolled in a swell, he lost his footing, and he accidentally tore a chunk out of his face with the fish hook he was holding. Wilson had splashed sea water on his face, showed no sign of pain, and carried on helping his fellow fisherman to haul the net containing their latest catch.

Rob Taylor. Twenty nine years old. Farmer on his dad's place ten miles west of Stanley. Due to get married to a local girl next summer. Big guy. Fearless and fit because he had to work fourteen hour days in any weather condition. Quiet. Nothing but kind to his childhood sweet heart. But if men got on the wrong side of him when he was drunk, he'd punch them across the room. Nobody in their right mind crossed Taylor. The story goes that a couple of years back one of his dad's sheep got lost. Taylor found the beast at night, bleating on an escarpment, totally exhausted and scared. Taylor lifted the sheep onto his chest and carried him for miles across treacherous terrain. It was a Herculean effort. Back at the farmstead, the sheep was revived, Taylor jumped into his pickup, drove to Sally's bar and challenged anyone in the tavern to an arm wrestle. No one – not even Wilson – took up the offer. Taylor had that look in his eyes. People let him be when he got like that.

Billy Green. Former Royal Engineer army commando corporal who was stationed here in 2009. Thirty four years old. Stayed on the islands after his tour ended because he'd got a local girl pregnant. Tough guy. Not big, but his body had the sinewy strength of high tensile wire. Devoted father, though he'd never married the girl he'd slept with. Blonde hair. Two missing teeth after he'd been in an altercation with five US Marines in a pub in Newquay – the marines had significantly worse injuries. Fearsome temper. A deckhand on Wilson's boat. An enthusiast of epic cross country runs, when he wasn't hungover. And rumour had it that he'd shot several Iraqis in cold blood when on tour in the second Gulf War.

Mike Jackson. Thirty one years old. Divorced. Short and prone to fat, but with the lung capacity of a race horse. Part-time lighthouse keeper at Cape Pembroke, east of Stanley, part-time fireman, part-time coastal repair volunteer and lifeguard. Wicked sense of humour. Bald as a coot. Never touches strong liquor but can out drink any man on the Falklands when it comes to beer. Church goer. Mouth like a sewer. Always taking the piss out of others, none of whom touch him because he rescued two girls when their dingy capsized a year back, single handedly put out a peat fire that threatened to scorch a mile of the islands, and stopped Wilson's ship from sailing perilously close to jagged rocks when its navigation system failed in a storm. But there was a side to him. He'd nearly strangled to death an off-duty local cop who'd cheated him in a game of poker. The cop didn't press charges and transferred to another station.

Now, Wilson, Taylor, Green, and Jackson were supping beers. They'd downed tools for the evening. This was their time. They were extremely close friends; the only friends they knew. Often they wouldn't engage eye contact with each other; rather they'd stare ahead at Sally and just order more drinks while they muttered brief sentences to each other. This was man-time after a hard day's work. It wasn't social. It was solace.

Sally poured them four more pints. "You all look like you've got stuff on your minds."

Wilson replied, "We're fucking knackered, gorgeous. What do you expect? You got any sarnies?"

Sally shrugged. "Nothing special – ham and pickle; cheese and onion; corned beef; tuna mayo."

"We'll have all of them." Wilson swivelled in his chair and eyed the two men sitting at the table behind them. "You alright, Carl, Nick? Got that fence fixed yet?"

The men nodded while drinking their beers. Nick replied, "Yeah, thanks for the wood. You going out tonight? Weather's turning. Bit choppy they say. And a blizzard's coming in."

"Tell me about it." Wilson swivelled back to the bar. "I reckon that Argie spy boat's having a hard time of it, if it's moored up somewhere."

Jackson had just come off his lighthouse shift. "Tonight the fucker's anchored a mile off here." He laughed. "The crew will be spewing their guts up."

"I hope they choke on their vomit." Taylor downed his pint in one go and shoved his empty glass towards Sally. "It's about time something should be done about those cunts."

Sally wasn't perturbed by the language. She was as tough as any man and could swear like a trooper. Plus, the four men in front of her were loyal customers. Even when they got blind drunk, the only time she told them to leave was when it was closing time. Bad blood on islands with as small a population as the Falklands were not only bad for business; it was bad for survival. Islanders relied on each other to help out on small matters and major catastrophes. While they could be obnoxious, Wilson, Taylor, Green, and Jackson and others like them would jump into their cars in a second and come to Sally's aid if needs be. And she'd do the same for them.

She slid four pints across the bar. "The Argie boat isn't doing us any harm. It's just watching."

"Watching us," muttered Green. "How would you like it if a stranger watched you while you were having a shower?"

Sally grinned. "I don't think it's quite like that."

"Yes it is. They're always *fucking* watching. Knowing our private business. Bunch of fucking parasites."

They drank their beers in silence for a few minutes.

Taylor spoke next. "I'd like to bash their heads in, point their boat at Argentina, set the throttle, get off the boat, and wave them goodbye."

Wilson chuckled. "If you bashed their heads in they'd be dead."

"Fucking right."

Sally could tell the men's mood was changing. "Give me a few minutes. I'll get the sarnies." She returned with a large baking tray within which was a selection of the food.

The men responded with genuine warmth, all saying nearly the same thing.

"Nice one, gorgeous."

"Nice one, Sal."

"Nice one."

"Yeah, nice one, love."

They woofed down the food, burped, and thrust their empty glasses across the bar. Sally set to work and poured four more drinks.

Wilson said, "I reckon tonight we should do something about those bastards." His tone of voice and expression were cold.

Taylor. "Ram the fucker."

Green. "Put a hole in it."

Jackson. "Sink it or put the shits into it enough so that it buggers off and never comes back."

Behind them, Carl and Nick could hear their conversation. Carl said, "It's just beer talk, lads. The army has got the boat covered."

Green slammed his glass on the bar. "The army?! I was in the army. What use is the army against a boat that's in water that will kill you in seconds if you swim in it? More to the point – where's the fucking navy? Haven't seen those guys around here for a long time. Nah. To get something done it has to be done by local boys."

Nick called out, "So what's the plan?"

Wilson looked at his three friends who nodded. "Tonight we're going to have as many ales as we can before closing time. Then we're going to sail out and get rid of the fucker once and for all."

Sally placed a hand on his hand. "Get as drunk as you like in my pub. But out there it's dangerous and you're not thinking straight." She winked at him, hoping it looked flirtatious. In truth she was trying to calm him down. "The girls in Stanley would hate it if they lost a good man."

Her tactic worked for a while. The men changed subject and talked about anything that came into their brains. Football. Women. Fishing. Farming. Gossip about neighbours ten, twenty, or a hundred miles away. Vehicle repairs. Property repairs. Shipments of provisions to the islands. Funny stories from their youth. And their concern about some of the elderly on the islands and what the four of them should do to help them via odd-jobs and food runs.

They were good men. Tough and coarse, for sure. They had to be. Their livelihoods and existence were merciless. And right now they were really drunk. But say a bad word about these four men to any islander and they'd pin you up against a wall and threaten to kill you. And they'd mean it. Wilson, Taylor, Green, and Jackson respected everyone on The Falklands. In turn, they got respect back. Loyalty holds the islands together. The four men had loyalty imprinted in their DNA.

Closing time. Four very inebriated men.

As they stood to leave, Carl called out in a sarcastic tone, "I hope you're not going to drive."

Wilson replied, "Of course we are. We're too pissed to walk."

Standing alongside his battered Land Rover, Green said to his friends, "I'll meet you on the trawler. First I've got to make a drive."

His friends frowned. "A drive?" said Taylor.

Green nodded as he looked toward the port. "I'm not going out there unless we have protection. I know a man who's got guns. He owes me a favour. I'll be back with the guns in a jiffy. Or it might take an hour or two. I suggest you get your heads down on the boat while I'm gone. When I'm back, we sail and sock it to the Argies."

Three hours' later, Green was on board the trawler. He'd brought with him five British Browning handguns and two SLR assault rifles, all found on the battlefields in '82. Wilson started the boat's engines and drove faster than he normally would out of Stanley. He didn't care that he was breaking speed rules. The harbour master would be in deep sleep at home by now; and the lighthouse was un maned and automated at night. Stanley had shut up shop for the night. Only the men on the boat were awake.

Wilson called out to Green. "Crack open the emergency rations. We need something for the journey."

Green opened a box and withdrew cans of strong lager, which he distributed to each man. They swigged from the cans, some of the drink splashing down their chests every time the boat struck head-on a wave. The weather was becoming treacherous – snow and wind – but Wilson kept a firm grip on the wheel with one hand while drinking from the other. Visibility was non-existent and the rapid descent of snowflakes played havoc on his drunken eyes. But he knew these waters so well that for the most part he could drive his vessel blindfolded. In any case this journey was easy. Normally he'd drive his vessel fifteen or twenty miles out to find fishing grounds of cod and other species. This was only one mile out and one mile back in.

Green stood alongside the skipper, raised his can, and shouted, "Lads, we're off to war!"

They all laughed.

The Argentinian on duty on the spy ship saw the lights of the trawler draw closer. It wasn't unusual, he reasoned, for a fishing boat to be out at night – often that was the best time to make the best catches – but something wasn't right. The spy ship was lit-up like a Christmas tree. Even in these conditions the trawler would be able to see the Argentinian vessel. And the trawler was travelling at speed, heading directly toward the spy ship. The watchman estimated it was five hundred yards away. But, it was difficult to tell. The snow blizzard was playing havoc with his eyes and despite the months he'd been working this detail at sea, he still couldn't master judging distances at sea and in a part of the world where clear air made something look to be a mile away when in fact it was ten miles away. He waited. The vessel was drawing closer, its bow rising and falling, spray spurting from the vessel's sides.

In Spanish he muttered, "Shit", ran into the boat, went to the captain's cot, and woke the man. "Boat approaching fast. Looks civilian, but I can't be sure. Small. Travelling at speed, straight at us!"

The captain rubbed his face, got on his feet, and shouted, "Everyone up! Ten seconds! Weapons at the ready!" He pulled on his cold weather gear. The others who'd been sleeping did the same. They grabbed their handguns and assembled on deck. The captain looked through a telescope. In a loud voice, he said, "Trawler. Three fifty yards. It can see us. We can see them. Prepare to pull up anchor on my command. Weapons by your sides at all times. This could be a raiding party, disguised as fishermen. If they get too close, you know the drill – shoot to kill and flee."

Wilson gunned the vessel to its maximum speed, aiming it at the spy ship's starboard side. He knew his boat's bow was sturdy enough to withstand the impact. He also knew the spy ship was weak on its flanks. He was twenty yards away. His friends were on deck with their weapons.

Shots rang out and all went to Hell.

CHAPTER 2

Two men resided in the fourth floor apartment of a converted Edwardian terraced house in West Square, Southwark, London. The three other apartments in the building occasionally contained students and London workers. But for now they were empty.

The top floor flat contained two bedrooms, a tiny kitchenette, bathroom, and a large lounge that was brimming with antiquities sourced from Burma, Mongolia, France, Patagonia, and Japan. Three armchairs were in the centre of the room – two facing each other next to a fireplace; the third on the other side of the room. On the walls were paintings, framed military maps of various parts of the world, bookshelves containing academic journals, leather-bound out-of-print works of fiction, poetry, non-fiction, and a diary written by a British naval officer during his voyage to America in 1812. Persian rugs were on the floor. The curtains adjacent to the double window were heavy and crimson. The mantelpiece above the fireplace had candles, oil lamps, a revolver that had belonged to a Boer soldier, and an Arabian dagger that had its tip embedded in the mantelpiece's wood and was vertical.

Today, the fire wasn't lit. It was summer in the UK. Tourist season in London. But the property was sufficiently set back from the hustle and bustle of the south bank and all its trappings. Very little could be heard aside from the muffled sound of traffic. It was an oasis of sorts. A place where the occupants could collect their thoughts. It was also their command centre for private detective work that ranged from mundane and routine to matters of national and international security.

Ben Sign was cooking lunch in the kitchen. Partridge, rosemary potatoes, steamed vegetables, and a lemon and orange sauce were on the menu. Sign was forty nine years old, a former MI6 officer who was tipped to be the next Chief of British Intelligence but resigned because he didn't like bureaucracy and following rules, had joined the service after graduating from Oxford University with a double first, had seen plenty of action, but now preferred to use his mental prowess to solve problems. Tall, a widower, no children, kind but - when needed – had the ability to deploy a razor-sharp ruthlessness, Sign was regarded as the finest spy Britain had to offer. He'd thrown it all away and had set up the private detective consulting business. In doing so, he had the support of the prime minister, foreign secretary, home secretary, and commissioner of the Metropolitan Police. It was lovely to have such senior endorsements. But for the most part it didn't help him pay the bills. He wasn't wealthy and right now he and his partner were working for a client who thought her husband was cheating on her. A tedious case, but it would ensure that the next three months' rent was taken care of.

His business partner and co-lodger was Tom Knutsen, a former Met undercover cop who'd joined the police after graduating with a first from Exeter University. Knutsen's belief that the police would be a place where he could quash his tendency to be a loner proved to be a false hope. He'd quickly realised that mass camaraderie and a uniform weren't for him. His superiors also realised that. He was given specialist training and told to infiltrate major criminal gangs in London and elsewhere. Like Sign, it suited him to work in places where he could be killed if his real identity was established. The thirty five year old was resigned to being alone in the world, with one exception – he was increasingly coming to the conclusion that Sign was the only man he could relate to. Sign was older than him, spoke like an aristocrat even though he was born into poverty, was a man of contradictions, had immensely powerful associates and yet was just as happy conversing with the average man on the street, and treated Knutsen with the utmost respect. Sign could also be a belligerent so-and-so whose vast intellect and cut-to-the-chase attitude sometimes hardened his soft interior. That didn't matter. In a deeper way, Knutsen was like Sign and vice versa. They were becoming friends.

Knutsen was in the lounge, sitting in his armchair, listening to Sign cursing in the kitchen about rubbish cases, idiots negotiating Brexit, the dire state of American politics, the incompetent police detective who'd arrested the wrong man for the murder of a boy in Islington, how long it would take the police to identify and capture the real murderer – who Sign had identified by spending two seconds looking at a newspaper archive, and why the world was run by idiots.

Knutsen called out, "You're having one of your moods."

"I'm bored!" Sign served up the food and brought it in on trays. They ate on their laps in their armchairs. "It's been months since we've had a decent case."

Knutsen shovelled the food into his mouth. The meal was delicious. "Since we set up shop six months' ago, we've only had one decent case."

"True."

Their first proper case – to catch a serial killer forcing senior MI6 officers to commit suicide, purely by the power of suggestion.

Sign looked irritated. "Perhaps I should call my *friends* in government and ask them if there's anything they'd like us to do."

"They'd have called you. They have no use for us at the moment."

"Damn fools!"

Knutsen smiled. He liked it when Sign was riled. "Maybe they've got someone better than us to advise and consult on near-intractable problems."

"Nonsense! I know their advisors. All of them have an agenda to either go into politics or earn a lot of money. Or both. They have the wit to feather their own nests but they don't have the intellect to problem solve for a few bob."

"A few bob?"

"You know what I mean."

They finished their lunch in silence. Knutsen washed up. It was their rule. Whoever cooks, the other washes up.

Back in his seat, facing Sign, Knutsen said, "I've often wondered why you chose me to be your business partner. I don't care one way or the other what your answer is. But I must admit it has intrigued me."

Sign waved his hand dismissively. "MI6 officers hate each other. It has to be that way. We are not selected to hunt in packs. MI5 officers are wannabe spies, wherein in fact they are glorified cops. And mainstream police can't think outside of the rule book."

"I was a cop."

"Technically, yes. In reality you were a lost soul who killed the man who killed the woman you were going to propose to."

Knutsen looked away and quietly said, "Yes".

Sign leaned forward and placed his hand on Knutsen's forearm. "Dear chap, I hired you because you were a solitary hunter who'd lost his way in the wilderness. That was far more interesting to me than hiring tired ex-cops, unimaginative special forces types, or Machiavellian former spooks with egos the size of planets."

Knutsen angled his head. "A pity case?"

"Necessity. I needed the right man for the job." Sign's expression steeled. "It's what spies like me do – find the correct person for the task in hand."

Knutsen nodded slowly. "I just wish we could flex our attributes on something other than divorce cases, financial fraud, and petty street gang crime."

The communal entrance downstairs intercom buzzed.

Knutsen frowned. "Are we expecting a client?"

"Not to my knowledge."

"Amazon deliveries?"

"You know I hate the Internet." Sign stood and pressed the button that opened the communal entrance.

Thirty seconds later there was a knock on the door. Sign opened the entrance. A man was standing in the hallway – late forties, cropped but stylish silver hair, medium height, slight build, tailored charcoal grey suit, highly polished black Church's shoes, and a silk tie that was bound in a schoolboy knot over an expensive shirt with cutaway collars. Sign immediately suspected he was a military officer. The man was holding a leather briefcase.

The man said in a posh but clipped accent, "Sir, I'm here to speak to Mr. Ben Sign. I apologise for turning up unannounced."

"I am Mr. Sign. How did you know I was going to be here?"

The man gestured toward the communal front entrance. "I have men. They told me that you and your colleague Tom Knutsen were at home because…"

"They've been watching my home. Sir – you have my name. If you wish to talk to me in the comfort of my home, I will need your name and position."

The man hesitated. "Colonel Richards. I am commander of all military bases on the Falklands Islands."

Sign gestured for Richards to come in. He patted the armchair used by all clients who visited the flat. Sign pointed at Knutsen. "This is Tom Knutsen, my business partner. You may speak freely in front of him."

"I would rather speak to you alone." Richards sat in the chair and crossed his legs.

"Both of us or none of us!"

The colonel bristled. Clearly he wasn't used to being spoken to that way. He held Sign's gaze. "As you wish."

Sign sat in his armchair and interlocked his fingers in front of his chest. "Are you army or Royal Marines?"

"Royal Marines. Plus I did three years in the SBS before returning to regimental duties and gaining promotion. I struggle to understand why what unit I hark from matters to you."

"I wish to have the measure of you before we proceed. What do you plan to do when you retire from the marines?"

"Sir, could we get to business?!"

"What do intend to do when you retire?" Sign repeated.

"I… I have been offered a senior position in BP. Also I'll be sitting on the board of directors for a golf club, a charity, a London museum, and a national haulage company."

"All positions requiring energy and youth. You're retiring imminently. Correct?"

"In two months' time. The Falklands is my last posting. My successor is an air commodore in the RAF."

Sign closed his eyes. "So what brings you to England at a time that presumably is very busy, given you're preparing to hand over the baton of command?"

"I came to London to see you. But what drove me here rests in the Falklands." Richards opened his brief case and withdrew a brown file. "I want you to have this, but first let me give you some context to its contents."

Sign opened his eyes and held up his hand. "If you have a case for us, remember it is our prerogative to decide whether we take it on."

"Oh, I think you'll take this on. It's gold dust. And it could lead to war. In fact we want it to lead to war." He eyed Knutsen and Sign. "Gentlemen – I'm not here to waste your time or my time. You've been recommended to me by the chief of defence staff."

Sign chuckled. "How is the general? Last time I saw him I had to instruct him to stop flirting with Russian agent provocateurs, or I'd ensure he lost his job."

Richards looked unsettled. "I... I...Well, he speaks very highly of you. Maybe he owes you a debt of gratitude."

"He owes me more than that. Now, you came here to see me, but the matter pertains to the Falklands and war. Proceed."

The colonel waved the brown file. "It is winter in the Falklands."

"Yes, Yes! Get on with it."

The colonel composed himself. "For two months there's been an Argentinian spy ship circling the islands. Its intentions seem to be pure observation, though goodness knows what they hoped to spot."

"It's provocation. They knew you knew who they were. They were hoping to kick the hornets' nest."

"That was our conclusion, Mr. Sign. And the islanders knew about the boat. For the most part they ignored it. The vessel kept its distance, didn't interfere with local fishing boats, and was viewed by British military and islanders as a useless piece of junk. But, three nights ago something changed."

Sign looked at Richards.

The colonel continued. "Four local lads – two fishermen, a farmer, and a lighthouse keeper – got drunk in a bar in Stanley. In front of witnesses, they bragged they were going to sail out and confront the spy ship. We know that's what they did because we've been monitoring the spy ship with an RAF drone, ever since it arrived. Via drone feed, we saw the locals' boat get close to the spy ship. But then we lost visual of both boats because a hellish blizzard kicked in. When the blizzard abated, we saw that the spy ship was gone and the locals' trawler was drifting close to where we'd last seen it. We sent one of our crafts out to check the local boat. No one was on the vessel. It was Mary Celeste. Of course, my men did a search in the waters around the trawler, but they found nothing. We towed the boat back into Stanley. Military and local police examined the vessel. There was fish blood on the vessel but it was impossible to ascertain if there was human blood."

Knutsen asked, "Evidence of gun fire?"

"Yes. The boat had bullet holes in its cabin. Aside from that the vessel looked like any other sea trawling boat, with the exception that there were guns on board. We think the guns had been fired on that night. They were scattered on the deck." Richards inhaled deeply. "We assumed at the time that the Argentinians had engaged the drunken idiots, killed them, and taken their bodies back to Rio Grande."

Sign said, "And they boarded the boat and intermingled any human blood traces with fish blood."

"Yes. Or they scrubbed the boat clean of the lads' blood."

Sign clasped his fingers together again. "But, it doesn't end there."

The colonel nodded. "The Argentinian ship is gone. It has not returned. But two nights ago four things did return, washed up on Stanley's shore – the bodies of the four locals. All of them had shots to the head and chest. We had to do an emergency post mortem. There is no doubt they were killed by bullets. And we are one hundred percent sure that the bullets were manufactured by Argentinian munitions companies. They were shot by the crew of the spy ship and their bodies were dumped in the sea. The tide brought them in."

Sign said, "The Argentinian military slaughter four civilians. It's an act of war between Britain and Argentina, but only if you have more proof of what happened other than bullets. Tis a shame your drone lost visual. You should have had men watching the spy ship, not artificial intelligence."

The colonel agreed but didn't say so. It was his decision to deploy the drone. "I want you to investigate the murders."

Sign looked at Knutsen, then Richards. "Why? You have the military police and local police at your disposal. Also, you could probably get detectives from Scotland Yard, or operatives from MI5 and MI6 to fly down. You have expert resources at your disposal."

The colonel shook his head. "The police will look at this as a murder investigation. It is not. It's far greater than that. Potentially this is war. The police can't be involved."

Knutsen asked, "And MI6 and MI5? The police might not have a grip on national security but the intelligence agencies do."

The colonel sighed. "There is a complication, and it's a delicate one. Is this a murder investigation, conducted by the police? Or is this a potential act of war, investigated by MI6? At the moment I don't know. What I do know is two things: first, I need someone to investigate this very discretely; second, I want proof that the Argentinians slaughtered the islanders. That's where you come in."

Sign said, "That makes no sense. We can't investigate a case of murderers who've fled back to their home country, and four dead bodies whose cause of death has already been accurately ascertained."

"That's not why I'm here." The colonel spoke calmly as he said, "Before the drone lost visual we had thermal imagery of the islanders' boat. There was no doubt – no doubt whatsoever – that there were five men on the trawler. Only four are accounted for."

Knutsen frowned. "Who is the fifth man?"

"We don't know. No one knows."

"How did the fifth man escape?"

"He used the emergency raft to get back to shore. We found it two miles away from where his friends were washed up. Gentlemen: I need to identify the fifth man. He wasn't in the pub that night. His evidence will enable us to go to war with Argentina. He will still be on the islands, somewhere. My men and the police can't try to find him. This is too delicate a matter. No doubt the fifth man is petrified. His testimony will mobilise an armada of British ships, an army, and a strike force of fighter planes. Find him and we have legitimacy to knock the Argentinians for six. What say you?"

Sign was quiet for a moment. "We'll take the case. All expenses paid for. We'll take one of your planes from Brize Norton to the Falklands. We'll be in civilian attire but I know how it works on that military route. For the sake of anyone asking, I will hold the rank of general; due to his age Mr. Knutsen will hold the rank of colonel. We are special investigators and are not to be obstructed by anyone in the British military. Understood?"

"Yes."

Sign checked his watch. "Time is against us today. But we can be on the first available flight tomorrow. You will pay us one hundred thousand pounds for this case."

"What?!"

"Half in advance; half upon completion of the job. And you will pay all expenses." Sign stood and held out his hand. "We have a deal, do we not?"

"One hundred thousand?!"

"We have a deal sir!"

The colonel slowly stood, looked confused, then nodded and said in a quiet voice, "Yes, we have a deal." He shook hands with Sign. "I will text you details of the flight times." He nodded at Knutsen. "Good day to you Mr. Knutsen." He nodded at Sign. "And good day to you sir." He walked out of the flat.

Sign opened the file. There was very little inside – birth certificates of Wilson, Taylor, Green, and Jackson; their addresses and employment history; a photo of Wilson's trawler; an aerial photo of the spy ship; the post mortem report on the deceased; a thermal image of five men on Wilson's boat before the blizzard hit the vessel and its surroundings; statements from Sally and the two other people in the pub on the night the four men got drunk and sailed their ship, and a photo of the four dead men on the beach. Sign handed the file to Knutsen. "Take a look and tell me what you think."

After Knutsen had carefully looked at the contents, he asked, "Do we trust Colonel Richards?"

"Of course not. We don't know him. But, I believe he's told us the truth. And he knows that if he tries to spin us a lie, then I will make his pension vanish. He's playing a straight bat."

Knutsen leaned forward and stared at the file. "All this tells us is what we already know. If the spy ship comes back, we could get the SBS to board the boat – Richards will have sway with his former unit – and arrest the Argentinians. We could interview the prisoners and get them to confess to what they did."

"The spy ship won't come back to the Falklands."

Knutsen's mind was racing. "Could you and I go to Rio Grande and try to find the spy ship? It's possible its crew are still near to the boat."

Sign shook his head. "A daring thought, but alas it wouldn't work. Upon their return to Rio Grande, the crew would have been debriefed about the incident. The Argentine intelligence services would have immediately recognised the severity of the situation. They'd have dispersed the spy ship crew and ensured they were as far away from Rio Grande as possible. The boat will have been destroyed."

Knutsen drummed his fingers on the arm rest. "So, all we have to go on is the fifth man. With a population of over three thousand in the islands, that's going to be needle in a haystack territory."

Sign stood. "We must endeavour to find the needle. Mr. Knutsen, tonight I will be viewing Mozart's Don Giovanni at the Royal Opera House. Would you care to join me? It's a black tie event."

"I don't have a tuxedo or whatever it's called by you posh types. Anyway, I've got a date with two cans of beer and the final episode of Masterchef." He grinned. "I'm trying to pick up some tips so that I can cook better stuff than the shit you serve up."

Sign smiled. "A laudable venture." His expression changed. "This afternoon, pack your bags. You'll need cold weather hiking gear and a suit."

"A suit?"

"Don't forget, we are high ranking military officers. We will travel in suits and when we arrive on the islands it will be military protocol for us to be invited for cocktails in the officers' mess in one of their establishments. For obvious reasons you can't travel with your handgun, but I will procure you a pistol when we arrive on the islands."

"Why would I need a handgun? We're not at risk. All we're trying to do is identify the fifth man."

Sign placed his hand on Knutsen's shoulder. "Were it that simple. There is a gun fight between two boats. The islanders lost because they were facing professionals who knew how to kill and vanish. But in that melee, the Argentinians must have realised that there was one islander they hadn't killed. That person escaped, most likely during combat. The spy ship had no chance of pursuing the fifth man while rounds were crossing decks. Probably the fifth man used the trawler as a shield while he rowed to shore as the battle raged. Here's the problem: the spy ship will have been decommissioned, its crew will have been laid out to pasture, but there is still a loose end."

"The fifth man. If he speaks, there's war."

"Exactly. Argentina will send new spies to the Falklands – paramilitary or special forces types. Probably no more than four of them. A greater number would arouse suspicion. And this time they will be on terra firma. They will have one purpose: kill the fifth man. We need to find him before they do. And that, Mr. Knutsen, is why you'll need a gun."

CHAPTER 3.

Four AM.

Sign and Knutsen were in their flat's hallway, their luggage at their feet. Knutsen looked bleary eyed, but alert. Sign looked like he'd had the best sleep in a long time. They were about to embark on a case. This was what Sign lived for.

"Have you ordered a cab?" asked Knutsen.

"We have a limousine. Military. It will take us to Brize Norton."

Two hours later they were in the West Oxfordshire RAF air base, exiting the limousine. They showed their passports to the security gate and walked to the main terminal. Inside were numerous military personnel. Those travelling were in civilian attire – that was the security protocol. Those not travelling were in RAF uniform. Sign had been told by Colonel Richards that an RAF corporal would meet them in the departures section of airport. The place was bustling. Knutsen wondered how the corporal was going to identify them amid the throng of people. Sign was unperturbed. He knew that Richards would have a photo of him that had either been given to the colonel by Sign's senior government allies, or had been covertly taken by the colonel's men outside Sign's home. The photo would now be in the possession of the corporal.

A wiry, thirty-something man in uniform came up to them, big grin on his face, and one hand holding a cluster of small documents. He saluted Sign and Knutsen. "General, colonel: Corporal Bainbridge. I have your tickets. Can I take your bags for you?"

"We'll carry our own bags," replied Knutsen.

Bainbridge led them to the check-in counter. He said to the woman behind the counter, "Two VIPs travelling today, Helen." He handed her their tickets. Knutsen and Sign gave her their passports.

She asked them, "Have you travelled this route before?"

Knutsen replied, "No."

Sign answered, "Yes."

She looked at Knutsen. "You'll fly to Ascension Island. There's a swimming pool there and a restaurant. Not much else aside from military and GCHQ instillations. It'll be very hot, so I hope you've packed your swimwear. You'll be there for about three hours. Then you'll head south to the islands." She smiled. "Different ballgame there at the moment, sir. Its winter and it's been chucking it down with snow. Don't be surprised if your flight is delayed."

Thirty minutes later, Sign and Knutsen boarded the flight. It was a civilian aircraft and was crammed with passengers – some of whom were soldiers and sailors returning to base after holiday leave, others were new entrants to the islands' military facilities. The plane had no first, business, or economy class. Instead, it was like a bus. Sign and Knutsen were however positioned at the front of the plane, both seats either side of them were empty.

Eight hours and thirteen minutes later they touched down in Ascension Island. It had been the staging post for troops and convoys on route to combat the Argentinian invasion of the Falklands. Ever since, it retained a military presence and was a place for planes to refuel. Knutsen put on sunglasses as he and Sign walked off the plan and across tarmac.

Knutsen said, "This is not what I expected. The island looks like a shit hole."

Sign replied, "The island's volcanic. There's not much more here than unforgiving shale and the sound of planes coming and going. Still, make the most of the sunshine."

They dined in a military cafeteria. The food was basic and designed to inject as many carbohydrates into hungry young men and women. Knutsen expected Sign's refined tastes to be repulsed by the fare. But instead Sign polished all the food off and rubbed his belly. "A man must eat whatever is offered to him when travelling," said Sign, reading Knutsen's thoughts. "I've eaten considerably worse in impoverished places where kind souls wanted to feed me their last morsel, rather than take the food for themselves. One must always be courteous."

Close to the cafeteria was a small swimming pool. It was within eye shot of Knutsen's table. He could see six Royal Marine commando trainee officers doing laps, jumping out of the pool, doing press ups and star jumps, jumping back into the pool, and repeating the process.

Sign followed his gaze. "Youngsters on a jolly. It will be bought and paid for by the marines. They'll be following the epic seventy five mile route across the islands that 45 Commando took in horrendous weather and with one hundred and twenty pounds on their back in order to engage the enemy." Sign smiled. "It will be deemed by their officers to be a character building exercise for these young men. The reality is they will be tested and at least one of them will twist his ankle on baby heads."

"Baby heads?"

"Much of the Falklands is covered by inflammable heathland. Some of it clusters into vast fields of uneven balls the size of heads. The only way around these stretches is to climb mountains. These lads will take the straightest route. They will suffer torn tendons or broken bones or both. The others will have to decide whether to casualty evacuate the injured party or press on. They will press on. Look at them – no more than twenty years old. Machismo will take a hold of their decision-making. It won't cross their minds that an injured party may not be able to return to training when back in England."

Knutsen looked at the young men. "How do you deduce all this?"

"Imagination and logic." Sign dabbed his napkin against his mouth. "Let's leave the boys to their pool exercise. I fear, no swim shorts and a dip for you, Mr. Knutsen."

"I wasn't going to take a dip, anyway." Knutsen frowned. "Why hasn't the fifth man come forward as a witness?"

"You tell me."

"He's scared. He may have concluded that the Argentinians may come for him. He may fear local police action against him for the reckless events of that night. Maybe he's in shock. Possibly he's protecting the families of the dead men, not wishing to bring dishonour on their names. I don't know. But I do know he's petrified and won't be easy to find."

Sign nodded. "We won't be welcomed by the islanders. "For them, this is not only a tragedy, it is also an embarrassment. Four of their own got slaughter by Argentinians. We must tread carefully. They will be feeling raw and angry."

Knutsen agreed. "Providing they know what happened and that the men are dead."

"They know. It's a close knit community. Richards wouldn't have been able to withhold this information from them." Sign stared at the volcano. Quietly he said, "Richards wants this situation to erupt, but on his terms. He doesn't want the islanders to take the law into their own hands. I very much doubt the islanders know about the fifth man. Finding him gives Richards control of the situation and organise a strike force against mainland Argentina. But if the islanders speak to the fifth man, Richards loses control. The locals will be baying for blood."

"They'll already be baying for blood if what you say is true. The Argentinian occupants of the spy ship killed four of their own. That in itself is enough to get them hot under the collar."

Sign shook his head. "The islanders know that Wilson, Taylor, Green, and Jackson were drunk that night. They also know that the men deliberately sailed out to provoke the spy ship. The islanders will have some sympathy with the men's actions, but they will also think they were stupid. But the fifth man can put a new slant on events – he can tell the islanders that they were executed in cold blood."

"And that paints a whole different picture."

"Yes. Richards wants to keep a grip on that information. If he can't he loses control of the situation and the Falklands." Sign checked his watch. "We depart in ninety minutes. While we're here I'd like to take a walk and examine Ascension Islands flora. I will meet you at the hanger for boarding."

Two hours after landing in the Falklands, Sign and Knutsen entered the officers' mess in RAF Mount Pleasant. They were here by invitation of Colonel Richards. As they walked toward the bar, Sign muttered to Knutsen, "Keep your cover vague. If someone asks, and they will do, say we're in a *specialist unit*. You were commissioned into the Parachute Regiment after graduating from Exeter University. There are no paratroopers based on the islands at present, so it's unlikely anyone here will know someone in your alleged old unit. But if by bad luck they do, say that you were pulled out of the paras after training and had to undergo selection for *special duties*. That should shut them up. I will adopt a similar cover story, though I can reel off a list of genuine contacts in the military. Attack is the best form of defence and all that. If they start asking too many questions, turn the tables and start asking them questions."

Knutsen replied in an irritated tone, "I was an undercover cop, you know. I spent years gaining the trust of criminal gangs and other shit. I do know how to bluff and lie."

Sign chuckled. "I'm sure you do."

They entered the bar. There were four RAF officers, three infantry officers, Richards, twenty five year old daughter, and a barmaid. Richards whispered in the ear of the barmaid.

In a commanding voice, the barmaid said, "Lady and gentlemen, please welcome General Sign and Colonel Knutsen."

A waiter appeared, holding a tray of cocktails. Knutsen and Sign took their drinks and introduced themselves to the officers. Like Sign and Knutsen, the officers were dressed in immaculate suits. Richards' daughter was wearing smart but unfashionable trousers and a blouse. Knutsen correctly assumed she was used to military life and all the rituals it brought, and that she'd change into something more flattering when she returned to her quarters. She was eying Knutsen, with a slight smile on her face. Knutsen knew the look. He felt uncomfortable. The last thing he needed was a twenty five year old getting the hots for him. Knutsen and Sign made a beeline for the colonel.

Quietly, and out of earshot of the others, Sign said, "Thank you for getting us down here and for the invitation. Tomorrow, Mr. Knutsen and I will set to work."

The colonel was on his third cocktail. His face was slightly flushed. "You were lucky. The snow storm has now kicked in with a vengeance. Flights have been cancelled. You won't get out of here for at least a week. How are your quarters?"

Their quarters being in the officers' section of Mount Pleasant.

"Perfectly serviceable, but not sustainable." Sign looked around the room, taking in everything he saw – framed photos of the queen, of previous military commanders of the Falklands, vistas of the islands, its mountains, and the men and woman in the room. Within ten seconds he'd correctly assessed every person's strength and weakness. He looked back at Richards. "Mr. Knutsen and I desire a cottage to rent, away from the military base. Can you arrange that?"

The colonel frowned. "You have everything you need here – a gym, restaurant, bar, shops, many other facilities. I would think…"

"I would think that I know my own mind." Sign gestured toward the others in the room. "Your facilities are for those men, not men like us. Mr. Knutsen and I must work under the radar. A cottage will be all we need, thank you. Two bedrooms; a log burner or open fireplace; a serviceable kitchen; and mobile phone reception. We will also need a four-wheel drive vehicle that is man-enough to drive over snow."

"I…"

"And we will need all of that by tomorrow."

The colonel nodded. "Yes of course. That can be arranged."

"Arranged by you. I want to keep knowledge of our presence on the islands to a minimum. And tomorrow morning, after we've checked out of your salubrious establishment, we will need to be taken by you and you alone to the beach where the dead men were washed ashore. Are we clear on all matters?"

The colonel had given up all hope of flexing his rank. Sign was too powerful and way above Richards' pay grade. "Yes. Ten AM sharp. I'll knock on your doors and escort you to our vehicle."

"Excellent." Sign turned to Knutsen. "Time for us to mingle. Be careful with the colonel's daughter. She's intrigued by you."

That night, Knutsen struggled to sleep. He got out of bed, put on his outdoor hiking gear, and walked through the military facility. Even though it was two AM, there were soldiers, sailors, and other staff milling about. They ignored him because they were used to strangers coming and going in the base. Plus, even if they suspected he was a high ranking officer, they didn't have to bother with salutes or standing to attention or calling him sir, given he wasn't in uniform and had no tabs on his civilian attire to declare his rank. Knutsen was glad he was left alone. He wanted to clear his head after the exhausting flight and from the two cocktails he'd had in the officers' mess. He walked outside, near to the runway. The strip was empty; snow underfoot was at least ten inches deep. That would change – snow was pouring out of the sky, only visible in the beams from lights on the airstrip and exterior walls. It was bitterly cold; so cold that Knutsen felt that every time he breathed his lungs were being filled with ice cubes. He'd travelled overseas before, though not as much as he'd liked – a trip to India with some pals when he was at university, family holidays to France with his poor parents when he was a kid and before they died, and Metropolitan Police assignments to track British criminals in Spain and other parts of Europe. The trouble was, in his adult life he'd been too busy getting under the skin of the darkest parts of London to find time to go on holiday. Plus, who would he go on holiday with? Six months ago, the woman he loved was killed in the line of duty. They'd never dated. He'd never told her he loved her, though she probably suspected she had his heart. It was too early to think about finding a nice woman who'd be thrilled at the prospect of sharing a hotel room with Knutsen in Switzerland, ride a gondolier with him in Venice, eat crab and shrimp in street markets in Hong Kong, or swim with turtles in the Maldives before returning to their beach hut and making love. Maybe that day would come; maybe not. Right now, Knutsen was at a time in his life where he needed to be distracted by work. He also needed male friendship. By pure chance, Sign had come along. He'd offered him a job and lodgings in West Square. Sign was in almost every respect different to Knutsen. At least it seemed that way on paper. Sign spoke like a man in command of everything around him; Knutsen was quiet. Sign liked classical concerts; Knutsen liked Nirvana and other grunge music. Sign socialised with prime ministers and kings; Sign taught kendo to a kid from the wrong side of the tracks in Brixton. Despite his petty crime record, that young man was now a cop in the Met, thanks to Knutsen. Sign wore suits purchased on Saville Row; Knutsen had one suit from M&S. But as he'd got to know Sign, Knutsen had begun to realise that they had far more in common than he'd thought. They'd both repeatedly risked their lives in undercover operations. They were both reluctant loners who, until recently, had failed to realise the pleasure of companionship, until it finally hit them in the face – both men were surprised at how the recent lodging arrangement in West square had lifted their spirits. They were quick thinkers. Knutsen didn't profess to have Sign's intellect, but you don't get a first class degree from Exeter through want of IQ. Sign was courteous; so was Knutsen. They could talk for hours, or they could sit in their armchairs in silence. Knutsen had often tried to pigeonhole Sign's character. It was an impossible task. Sign was a chameleon and unpredictable when working. But in West Square, Sign was himself. He cooked, he stoked the fire in winter, he wore jeans and a T-shirt, he laughed, he regaled Knutsen with his exploits in MI6 – never from an egotistical perspective, always humbling his magnificent successes. And Knutsen would eat Sign's sumptuous food and tell him about the London Sign didn't know. They were fascinated by each other – not in an emotional way; both men were straight; but in an intellectual way backed up by their life experiences. Key to Knutsen and Sign was that West Square was their safe place. If there was one label that Knutsen could slap on Sign it was that the former MI6 officer was like an older brother – one who'd been separated from birth from him, educated differently, taught how to be posh, and had risen through the ranks of government while Knutsen was playacting a gangster in Tower Hamlets and elsewhere. There was no doubt that Sign's persona was that of an aristocratic commander from the nineteenth century, and yet he was full of contradictions. It always made Knutsen laugh when Sign would rifle through the Radio Times after dinner and say, "EastEnders is on in ten minutes. We mustn't be late. I want to find out whether that woman really is cheating on her husband".

Knutsen trudged through the snow and looked around. He'd never been anywhere like this. The remoteness of the islands and proximity to the South Pole made him feel exhilarated. He stopped walking and closed his eyes. There were some sounds from the military base, but aside from that all was silent. And this was Stanley – the capital of the islands, with a population of approximately two thousand, on an archipelago that's total population was three thousand. Sign had told him that beyond Stanley it was commonplace for islanders to live ten or so miles apart from each other. There the silence would be deafening.

Knutsen opened his eyes. Despite the severity of the cold, the air smelled fresh and pure. Tomorrow he'd see the islands in daylight. But for now the former policeman in him tried to get the feel of the place. Was this a zone where a crime would not go unpunished, because everyone knew each other's business? Or was this a territory where one could easily murder someone, bury the body, and nobody else would be any the wiser? Knutsen wanted to know the answer. He turned and walked back to the barracks. He didn't know if he'd be able to sleep. But he did know that he'd get hypothermia if he stayed out here too long.

CHAPTER 4

The following morning, Sign and Knutsen were sitting in a jeep that was heading west from Stanley. Richards was in the driving seat. No one else was with them. As they drove through Stanley they passed a small supermarket, post office, iron mongers, petrol station, vehicle repair shop, and two pubs.

Richards pointed at one of the pubs and shouted above the din of the vehicle's racket and external weather. "That's where the men drank before they got slaughtered." He carried on driving along the coastal route out of Stanley.

Richards was in uniform. Sign and Knutsen were in hardy outdoors gear and hiking boots. Snow and wind were striking the vehicle. The temperature was minus ten. The vehicle was shaking and skidding so badly that Sign and Knutsen had to grip their seatbelts to stop their bodies slamming against the doors.

Richards stopped the vehicle. "We're on foot now. Two hundred yards to the beach. Watch your footing."

He got out of the vehicle. Sign and Knutsen followed him. The beach was partially clear of snow, due to the sea washing over the rock and sand. But snow and hail was still pouring down, hitting the men's faces with the ferocity of a swarm of locusts. They
trudged across the beach until Richards stopped and pointed.

"This is where they were washed up. It wasn't unusual they were so tightly grouped. The tides here can be precise. They were caught in a rip tide and funnelled onto the beach."

Sign asked, "Was there any possibility they were placed here?"

Richards shook his head. "The post-mortem proved they'd been in the water for many hours. They were bloated; their lungs were full of liquid; their gunshot wounds were quarterized by the cold; they had blows to the body that had come after death – most likely due to hitting rocks on the seabed as they were washed ashore; and most of their limbs were broken from the mile-long journey to the beach. We consulted with our naval friends. They confirmed that on that night a man dumped next to the spy ship would have been brought in to this place. It's all to do with currents and weather and other stuff I don't understand. There is no doubt they were dropped in the sea and ended up here."

Knutsen knelt down and touched the sand. "There is proof positive they died from gunshot wounds?"

"Yes."

Sign looked out to sea. "And no sight of the spy ship since?"

Richards followed his gaze. "None whatsoever. We've tripled our efforts to monitor the archipelago's coastline. Plus, we're getting help from the GCHQ post in Ascension. It would be wonderful if the boat came back. The SBS have got ten men doing a three month training exercise in Antarctica. They could be with us very quickly and board the ship. I've put them on alert. But I don't think the boat's coming back."

"I know the spy ship's not coming back." Sign crouched and placed his hand on the beach. "Who found the bodies?"

"Two local teenagers. They called the police. The police called me."

"Why?" asked Knutsen.

It was Sign who answered. "Because word had got out that the men were going to do something silly to the spy ship. The police realized they were out of their depth, that this was probably a military and political matter." He looked up, uncaring that his face was being smothered by snow.

Knutsen stared at him, wondering what was going through the man's mind. Sign was immobile, seemingly oblivious to those around him and the adverse weather conditions.

He lowered his head and looked at Richards. "We need to see the bodies."

Richards frowned. "What purpose would that serve? Neither of you are medically trained, and you have excellent post-mortem reports to draw upon."

"The bodies! Where are they?"

The colonel rubbed snow off his face. "King Edward VII Memorial Hospital, in Stanley. It was where the post-mortems were conducted. Their families want the bodies released in the next day or two. Wilson and Green are to be buried at sea. Their families and friends think that's fitting given they spent most of their working days at sea." Richards smiled. "Let's hope they're not washed ashore again. Taylor and Jackson are to be buried in the cemetery."

"Then we have not a moment to lose." Sign walked toward the jeep.

As they drove to Stanley, Richards said, ""I've secured you a two bedroom cottage. It's twelve miles south west of Stanley, near Bluff Cove. It has Wi-Fi, a log burner, you might have occasional problems with mobile reception though there is a landline, and overall it's a perfectly serviceable property. I picked it because it not only has road access to Stanley, but also the other parts of the islands."

"Where the fifth man may be hiding," said Knutsen.

"Precisely." The colonel drove into Stanley. "You'll have a four wheel drive at your disposal. As you requested, it has no military markings. Petrol is available at the RAF base or at the garage in Stanley – nowhere else, though people help each other out on the islands so if you get stuck a farmer will always donate some fuel. Trouble is, you might be twenty miles away from the nearest farmer if you're driving west. Keep on top of your fuel. And today one of you needs to go the grocery store in Stanley and pick up enough provisions for a week. Don't assume shops are open in Stanley every day. In conditions like this, they close if they can't get their deliveries. Always remember that you have Mount Pleasant as a bolt hole, if things go wrong." The colonel stopped his vehicle outside the hospital. "I don't know if either of you are familiar with this type of climate. It can kill you quicker than a man can make a decision." He looked at the men and smiled. "It's not all bad. Bluff Cove is spectacular. It's where the penguins congregate."

They exited the vehicle and walked in to the hospital.

Ten minutes' later they were in a sterile room containing slabs and freezers with bodies inside.

Richards introduced Sign and Knutsen to the only other person in the room – a female. "This is Dr. Carter. She trained and worked in London, and subsequently worked in Mumbai, Washington DC, and Melbourne. But she's an islander and the temptation to return to her roots was ultimately too great."

"My mother had stage four cancer. I wanted to be with her before the end." Carter had an icy demeanour and tone of voice. On the slabs were four bodies, covered with sheets. She pulled off each sheet. Wilson, Taylor, Green, and Jackson were there. "They were fit men. No signs of any pre-existing underlying illnesses. Toxicology reports show they were ten times over the limit, but the reports won't be wholly accurate because they'd been dead for at least twenty four hours before I set to work on them."

Sign and Knutsen stood next to Wilson's body.

Sign asked, "Can you be certain they died from gunshot wounds? Is it possible they drowned and were then shot?"

The doctor answered, "An interesting question."

Richards interjected. "Why would the Argentinians shoot them if they were already dead?"

"To provoke us." Sign leaned forward to get a closer view of Wilson's wounds.

The doctor said, "There is no doubt they were killed by bullets. I extracted the bullets and gave them to Colonel Richards. I believe they are now with ballistics experts in England. I can give you chapter and verse on how I know they died from bullets, and that any subsequent non-bullet wounds or water in the lungs came after death. But it's all in the post-mortem reports." She looked at Richards. "If you need a second opinion, you'll need to fly someone in asap."

It was Sign who answered. "That won't be necessary." He examined the other bodies before returning to Wilson. "He was the skipper of his boat. He was at the helm. He took a bullet to his arm and another to his chest. He turned to flee. That's when he was shot in the back of the head."

Carter was impressed. "You've seen gunshot wounds before."

Sign ignored the compliment. "Taylor, Green, and Jackson were killed while facing their assailants. They were brave men."

"Or drunken fools." Colonel Richards frowned. "I still don't understand why the bodies were thrown into the sea. The captain of the spy ship would have known that the tides were such that night that the dead men would be washed ashore."

"Once again – provocation." Sign stood upright. "He or she wanted the bodies to be found by you. The captain was smart. He realised the enormity of the event but he also realised the opportunity the situation presented to Argentina. This was a shot across the bow, but it wasn't an act of war unless there was proof. He may or may not have been aware of the drone surveillance, but being an expert in long range spying I suspect he knew that the blizzard was shielding coverage of the incident. So, it was a win-win outcome for the spy boat. Provoke the islanders and Britain, vanish, and the task of the spy craft is complete. And I'd hazard a guess that the crew of the spy boat couldn't wait to get back to Argentina, having completed their thus far mundane task with a bang. Argentinian intelligence services would have embraced them. The killings weren't scripted by the intelligence services there. But in that brief explosive encounter, the spy ship had achieved considerably more than months of the ship slogging around the islands." Sign went to Richards and whispered out of the doctor's earshot. "The fifth man is the fly in the ointment. The Argentinians thought they'd got away with the perfect set of murders. But they only saw the fifth man when it was too late. The fifth man was on a dingy, heading for shore. He was too far away. The skipper of the spy ship couldn't risk pursuit, so close to Stanley. This is the loose end the Argentinians will wish to burn."

The colonel nodded. "And they know that there are two possibilities. First, the fifth man came forward to local authorities, told us that he and his pals tried to commit murder, and supplied us with the evidence we need to go to war. Or, second, that he was petrified he'd be thrown in jail so went to ground. They'll suspect he's laying low. They think he's not come forward."

"I agree. But they won't risk the possibility that he may have a change of heart. And they'll know you will have brought in specialists to hunt him down."

"Which is why you didn't want to stay in Mount Pleasant?"

Sign nodded. "Knutsen and I have to be off the radar." Sign spun around and said in a loud voice, "Doctor – thank you so much for allowing us to intrude on your excellent medical facility. I can see that no stone has been unturned in the examination of these unfortunate souls. I believe that funeral logistics are being attended to. We will bother you no more and will allow you to complete your case. Good day to you madam."

Sign strode out of the room.

CHAPTER 5

Knutsen turned off the jeep's engine and looked at Sign. "Are we sure about this? It's in the middle of fucking nowhere!"

"Language, young man. It will suit our purpose." Sign got out of the vehicle and approached the door to the cottage that Richards had secured them. It was an isolated property, a crumbling disused stone sheep pen was twenty yards from the house, all around it was rolling heathland, the sea was thirty yards away, below an escarpment, and there was not another dwelling in sight. There was no evidence of animal life. The snow had forced all fauna into their nests or burrows.

Knutsen joined Sign at the front door.

"It's locked," said Sign.

"I know. Richards said there's a key in the combination lock next to the door. Shit, shit, shit! He gave me the combination but I can't remember it. All I remember is it's four digits."

"Call him."

Knutsen tried. No reception. "Now what do we do?"

Sign stood in front of the lock. "We improvise and use our imagination. Ninety eighty two – the year of the war." He tapped the numbers in to the keyboard. "No. Sixteen ninety – the year that English captain John Strong is officially recorded as discovering the islands. No. Eighteen thirty three – the year Britain reasserted its rule over the islands after French, Spanish, and Argentine settlements on the islands. No." Sign was getting frustrated. "Two thousand and thirteen – the year the islanders held a referendum on sovereignty and overwhelmingly voted to remain British." The number didn't work. "Damn it!"

Knutsen tried not to laugh as he took Sign's place in front of the keypad. "Let's see if this works." He typed in zero zero zero zero. The safe unlocked. Knutsen giggled. "I can't believe I forgot that code."

"Forgot indeed. Very funny, Mr. Knutsen!"

They entered the cottage. Its thick stone walls protected them from much of the sound of wind and precipitation outside, but it also insulated the cold. Sign prepared the wood burner while Knutsen opened curtains and followed the absent owner's written instructions to turn on the water supply and electricity. Knutsen checked the telephone landline – it was working. But, Richards was right – there was no mobile reception here. Once the fire was lit and the cottage's essential services were up and running, Knutsen and Sign examined the property.

Sign said, "Kitchen – electric hob, not ideal. I prefer gas. Knives are cheap junk and blunt. But there is a steel. I will sharpen them. Pots and pans are as bad as can be; none of them non-stick. But there is a slow cooker. I can improvise with that. Plates – fine. Cups – fine. Glasses – fine. Drawers - stocked with utensils and towels. Okay, I can work with this. Let's go upstairs."

The two bedrooms were intersected with a bathroom that contained a toilet, sink, and bath. No shower.

Knutsen said, "I haven't had a bath since I was ten years old. I'm a shower kind of guy."

"We must improvise. When you go to the store, buy the usual bathroom necessities but add on bath foam, or whatever it's called. Are you squared away on the boiler?"

"The boiler?"

"This is not West Square. To get hot water we need to plan at least twelve hours in advance."

"I'll look in to it."

Sign smiled. "I'll take this bedroom."

"It's the smaller of the two. Are you sure?"

"It has a view of the cove. I'm hoping to see the penguins congregate. Did you know, they get cold, just like us?"

Knutsen sighed. "No I didn't. I'm off to the grocery store in Stanley. Back in an hour or two. Don't do anything stupid while I'm gone."

"Such as?"

"Such as visiting your cold friends in Bluff Cove."

"Ha!" Sign slapped his thigh. "When you're in the store see if they sell seal blubber. It's just occurred to me that it might make a more nutritious and tasty substitute for sunflower oil when cooking."

Knutsen gave him a withering look. "Given what I know about this place so far, don't be surprised if we're having beans on toast tonight."

Ninety minutes' later Knutsen returned. He brought in four boxes of groceries.

"Did you source some blubber?" asked Sign.

"Fuck off." Knutsen placed the boxes in the kitchen. "The shop was surprisingly stocked with a variety of stuff. Alongside veg, herbs and spices, bread, tinned stuff, wine, beer, and toiletries, we've got steaks, chicken, cod, lamb, a joint of beef, mince beef, zebra trout, and brown trout." He started unpacking the boxes. "They didn't have your favourite drop of calvados. So, I bought a bottle of brandy instead. Hopefully your gastronomic skills and palate will be able to make something of it all."

"Splendid, dear chap." Sign placed a hard plastic case on the kitchen table, next to the boxes. "While you were gone, Colonel Richards popped over. He gave me this. He opened the box. Inside was a Glock 37 handgun, cleaning kit, and four spare magazines. Sign expertly stripped it down, reassembled it, checked its workings and handed it to Knutsen. "It's a .45 calibre weapon. You'd be able to kill an elephant with this thing. The magazine holds ten rounds. The gun has been cared for – there's not a speck of dust in its mechanics."

Knutsen weighed the gun in his hand. The last time he'd held a gun this powerful was when he was on an undercover assignment to take down a gang lord. His police partner – the woman he was secretly in love with – was his fellow undercover colleague. They'd married prior to the assignment, purely as a façade to give credence to their fake backstory. But Knutsen was convinced they'd never get divorced after the job. Alas, she was killed when they took down the gang leader. Knutsen had used a gun as powerful as the one he was now holding to blow her killer's head to smithereens.

Sign knew all of this and could tell what Knutsen was thinking. "Sometimes we need a sledgehammer to crack a nut. But on this occasion it is possible we may have formidable opposition. We need to find and protect the fifth man. One shot from your gun, *anywhere* in the body, will immobilise the enemy."

Knutsen ensured the safety gadget was engaged and placed the gun between his belt and the nape of his back. "What about you? Did Richards give you an identical model?"

Sign waved his hand dismissively. "You know I no longer use weapons of any sort. The days of violence are behind me."

"So I'm the dumb grunt shooter, and you're the thinker?"

"Incorrect. You are also the thinker. But you carry the gun because your youth means you are better equipped to deal with trauma. One day the trauma will catch up on you, but not yet. When it does, you will be where I am and will never want to pull a trigger again." Sign riffled through the food. In a strident and jovial voice he said, "You've shopped like a queen." He winked at Knutsen. "Lunch will be baguettes with melted cheese and salad. Dinner will be zebra trout with Parma ham, chives, sautéed potatoes, broccoli, carrots, and a drizzle of white wine jus. It's a shame you couldn't source seal blubber. It would have given a lovely shine to the jus. Regardless, while I'm cooking you can do some target practice outside. Just don't shoot any sheep."

Colonel Richards called the British chief of defence staff on a secure military phone. "Sign and Knutsen have arrived. They've demanded that they stay in a cottage, not Mount Pleasant. I've given them a vehicle and a weapon. Sign won't take orders from me."

"That's because when he was office he was infinitely superior to you. Plus, he doesn't take orders from anyone. Will Sign and Knutsen do the job?"

"I'm sure of that. They've distanced themselves from military command and I understand why. They want to work this in their own way. The remit is clear: find the fifth man and make him talk. They can't fly out of here for at least a week. The weather has grounded our planes. They're going nowhere."

"Good." The chief asked, "Everything is in lockdown?"

"Yes. Local police have washed their hands of the case. The hospital obviously knows about the gunfight but don't know details, and I've told the doctor who did the post-mortem that she'd spend a lifetime in prison if she breathed a word about the dead men, given the military now has jurisdiction."

"What about the dead men's families?"

""I've told them that the men drowned on a routine fishing trip."

"They will be suspicious, given the men bragged that they were going to confront the spy ship."

Richards shook his head. "I gave them photos, showing that the spy ship was nowhere near the men's trawler when they died. Obviously, the photos were doctored and taken days before the incident. But I did give them copies of the real toxicology reports. They know the men were blind drunk, the weather was awful, they fell overboard. The families are angry with the men's stupidity. There's no suspicion."

"And within the military?"

Richards replied, "Only a handful of people know about the incident. I've briefed them and laid down the law about national security, blah blah blah. Most important, I've told them about the sensitivity of the situation and that this may lead to war. Sir – are you making preparations?"

"Yes. To kick Argentina in the balls I will be using navy frigates and destroyers, 42 and 45 commando Royal Marines, 2 Para, navy and RAF helos and fighter planes, and I will position a Trident submarine off Argentine's coast. The end game will not be to take Argentina. We don't want their country. But it will be a massive *fuck off and leave us alone.* Nobody messes with Britain and its piss poor protectorates."

Richards smiled. "The number of civilian casualties will be immense."

"Are you worried about that?"

"No."

"Nor am I. The Argentines should have voted in a better government. So, let Sign and Knutsen do their thing and once that's completed we do our thing. Agreed?"

"One hundred percent."

"Alright colonel. Do your job. Make preparations for my task force to use your islands as a launch pad, keep an eye on Sign and Knutsen, and get me the fifth man. His evidence means I can strike Argentina and ensure they don't touch the Falklands." The chief hung up.

It was evening. Knutsen walked toward the cottage, his gun in his hand. It had been dark for two hours, but that had suited Knutsen because he'd wanted to do his target practice with the only light coming from the multitude of stars that resembled large jewels in the crystal clear sky. Since mid-afternoon, snow had stopped. But it had started again with a vengeance. He entered the cottage, stamped his boots on the internal doorway mat, placed his sodden fleece by the log burner, and rubbed snow off his face and hair. The gorgeous smell of Sign's cooking was permeating the lounge. Knutsen went into the kitchen. "It's getting shit out there again."

Sign was dashing between pots, stirring some, dipping his fingers in another and tasting its sauce, and checking the oven containing the zebra trout stuffed with lemons and encased in clay he'd sourced near the beach. "Food will be ready in ten minutes. That should give you enough time to clean your gun."

Knutsen returned to the lounge, stripped down his weapon, cleaned and oiled it, and reassembled the pistol.

Sign emerged from the kitchen holding two plates of food which he placed on the small table. From his pocket he withdrew knives and forks which he positioned next to the plates. He dashed back into the kitchen and returned with a bottle of white wine and two glasses. "Let's eat and be merry."

After the meal, Sign washed up and prepared two fresh coffees and two glasses of brandy. The men sat by the log burner.

Sign said, "Tomorrow we set to work. This will be delicate. We must enquire about matters that we don't want the islanders to know about, and yet to get to the truth we must speak to the islanders. It is an amusing yet complex spin on investigative procedures."

"Richards has covered up the killings?"

"No. He's blurred lines. It would be impossible in a place with such a small population to hide the deaths of four of its brethren. Richards has given the islanders part truths and part lies. I advised him to do so."

"What's the point? It's not like the islanders are going to raise a militia and invade Argentina."

Sign smiled. "The point is we don't want the islanders growing antagonistic towards the British military. If they knew that four of them had been slaughtered by Argentinians, they'd be baying for blood. A British military delay in action against Argentina would be deemed bad form by the islanders."

"Bad form?"

"You have to remember that we're in a delicate ecosystem. The islanders want the military to protect them. But they also have lives to lead. Every year, the military causes problems to their livelihood – accidental fires that scorch acres of rich farmland, landmines killing sheep, drunken liaisons between squaddies and young lasses, the list goes on and on. In equal measure, the islanders respect and reluctantly tolerate the British military presence. They'd rather the RAF, army, and navy weren't here; and they'd rather they were here. It's a delicate balance."

Knutsen sipped his coffee. "That's a bit of a mind flip."

"It's complicated. Unlike in our colonial days – when, like it or not, we always knew there was the inevitability of self-determination by our conquered countries' indigenous populations – here we are protecting British people who live on the other side of the world. It's hard for them; it's hard for us. We must muddle through. And in our case we must tread very carefully."

"Is Richards treading carefully?"

Sign placed his hands around his brandy, to warm the glass before imbibing. "He's an action man who's past his prime. He still clamours for blood and glory, though he won't be leading the charge. But he can instigate carnage. In his mind it will be his last volley. He wants war – every military person does. This will be his swan song. He *is* treading carefully by engaging us to get the evidence he needs. Thus, he is manipulating us for his own ends."

"You don't strike me as someone who can be manipulated."

Sign took a swig of his brandy. "I am several steps ahead of Richards. I'm several chess moves ahead of the Argentinians and the British chief of defence. No one manipulates me."

"Steps ahead? What do you mean? We haven't even started the investigation."

Sign looked at the fire. His voice was distant as he said, "Some people see what they want to see. That's when they're vulnerable. It's the time when a clever predator strikes them down." He looked at Knutsen and smiled. "Dear chap, we have a busy day tomorrow. Let's lighten the tone tonight. May I suggest we take a stroll to the cove? I wish to show you something."

Adorned with their hardy hiking gear, they strode to the cliff edge. Snow was falling rapidly but the flakes were small. Visibility was still good due to the stars and a moon that was three quarters visible, The air was thick with the smell of grass, heather, and the salty smell of the sea that was washing the beach.

Sign pointed at the beach. "Do you see them?"

Knutsen looked at the beach. There were hundreds of penguins there, not moving, just standing immobile, shoulders hunched, looking miserable.

"It's like Dunkirk is it not?"

Knutsen hadn't thought of it that way. "They want to leave but they don't know how to leave."

"Just like us, the military, and the islanders."

"And yet they embrace this climate because it produces fish they can feed upon. They are hardy folk." Sign put his hand on Knutsen's shoulder. "They hunt where the food chain exists. Clever. We must be equally clever. Come – let's retire to our quarters."

CHAPTER 6

Nine AM. Eight miles outside of Buenos Aires.

Major Alejandro Casero was in a safe house owned by his employer the Federal Intelligence Agency, Argentina's primary spy and security organisation. For the past two years he'd been running a top secret fifteen-person strong black operations unit called Special Projects. The unit was responsible for surveillance in hostile locations, infiltration of large criminal gangs, destruction of material assets purchased with dirty money, and the executions of key wanted individuals. The executions were always made to look like revenge attacks by rival criminal or spy organisations. Special Projects worked off the grid. They were not answerable to the FIA. Even Argentina's judiciary was not aware of its existence. In fact, Casero had a very simple chain of command – he reported to Argentina's president; no one else.

Casero was thirty seven years old. Before joining FIA he was a special forces officer. In large part, he'd been responsible for handpicking the current members of Special Projects. He'd drawn people from the ranks of FIA, military intelligence, special forces, and specialist police units. The people he'd selected not only needed to have outstanding skills; they also needed to be grey men and women who could blend in anywhere. The frontline Special Projects field operatives were experts in unarmed military combat, small arms, explosives, covert infiltration, exfiltration, communications, deep cover, sniper skills, and every other attribute required for an elite assassination unit. They also needed to look and sound the part. Special Projects were masters at disguise. They could pass as a drug gang member from Colombia and could just as easily convince someone they were French, German, or British white collar businessmen. All of them were highly educated. Fluent English, no accent, was a prerequisite for entry into the unit. Within the team, other fluent languages spoken were Portuguese, and most other European languages. They could also vary their accents to mirror regional variants in tone. All of them had mastery of the Falklands Islands accent, which sounded a close match to that of New Zealand.

Selection into Special Projects was merciless, regardless of the gender or age of the applicants. Candidates were put through a month of hell – forty mile mountain walks carrying sixty pounds of weight on their backs, two mile swims in clothing, minimal sleep, escape and evasion exercises with dogs and armed men on their heels, twelve hour interrogations, and daily ten mile runs in sodden clothes and boots. After that, continuation training and selection kicked in. They had to prove that they could acquire all the skills needed to be a Special Projects member. Three months later, the tiny number of successful applicants were allowed into the unit. There wasn't a graduation ceremony or any form of celebration. Casero would simply look at them while sitting behind his desk and say, "You're not in any recognisable unit now. Ditch lovers, husbands, wives, anything that ties you to your old life. But don't think you've got a new family. Special Projects needs brilliant loners, not team players seeking camaraderie."

Now, Casero entered the dining room of the safe house. Three members of Special Projects were in there – Javier Rojo, Maria Fontonia, and Zaia Sosa. They were sitting at the table. Underneath their civilian clothes, they had handguns strapped to their waists and back-up pistols attached to their ankles. Casero hadn't chosen them to be here because they were better than their peers in the unit – all members of Special Projects were exemplary. Rather, he'd picked them for the assignment because they looked Anglo-Saxon.

Rojo was a thirty six year old male. He'd spent five years in the French Foreign Legion's elite parachute regiment before returning to Argentina and joining special forces. He was medium height, had the strength of an ox, shoulder length blonde hair that he tied into a ponytail, a goatee, blue eyes that were penetrating and sexy, and a permanent slight smile that either suggested he knew something others didn't or he had a mischievous inner joke about the world. He was the first person Casero had recruited into the unit. Since then, Rojo had worked cases in Argentina, Chile, Paraguay, Bolivia, Venezuela, Mexico, and the United States. Though he wasn't university educated, he had a razor sharp brain, hidden behind his façade that some interpreted that to be of a cage fighter, others a slacker surfer dude or a guy that had just got out of a long stint in prison.

Fontonia was a thirty three year old female. After graduating with politics and economics at Harvard University, she'd joined the police. She could have made a career of it, rising to the top. Instead, she'd volunteered for the serious crime unit. It was a job that required her to wear Kevlar vests and carry a gun, while she and her assistants stormed houses, ranches, and any other place that held criminal targets. She'd lost count of the number of people she'd cuffed or shot. Despite her magnificent track record of takedowns, at heart she was a superb investigator. None of her arrests and killings would have happened had she not devoted weeks or months identifying the men she wanted to arrest or kill. But, she'd grown bored of the police. That's when Casero had identified her as a potential candidate for Special Projects. When he first interviewed her to see if she was suitable for selection, he was struck by her presence – she wasn't particularly beautiful, but nor was she plain. Brunette, average height, average build. Perfect for blending in. But when she talked everything changed. She spoke with a tone that was mesmerising. Casero knew that he was in the presence of someone special. And that's what he searched for in all of his candidates: something special.

Sosa was a thirty six year old woman. Tall, facially looked a bit like the actress Jodie Foster, and liked to wear dowdy clothes just to stop men gawping at her. She'd obtained the highest grade in her year when studying at Argentina's top university - Universidad de Buenos Aires – and had been snapped up by the Federal Intelligence Agency when she applied to be a field operative. After training and mentoring, she'd run some of the FIA's most sensitive cases, taking her all over South America, North America, and Europe. Things changed for her when a low level FIA analyst had booked her on a series of flights that ultimately took her to Tokyo. She was carrying twenty thousand dollars in cash to meet one of her agents in Japan and pay him the money. Unfortunately, the route she'd taken had been identified by Japanese security services as that typically taken by white collar drug dealers. She was arrested, put in prison, and severely interrogated for three days. Her profile didn't help her case – she was travelling under business cover. The twenty thousand dollars in her handbag also didn't help. But, she stuck to her story and was released. When she got back to the FIA headquarters in Buenos Aires, she pinned the analyst up against a wall by his throat and said to him, "You idiot. You're paid to know about drug routes. You nearly got me killed." She was sacked for the assault. That's when Casero stepped in. He met her at her apartment and said, "I have a job for you, if you can prove yourself to me. But, I don't believe you've ever killed anyone. Do you have a problem learning how to kill?" She'd pulled out a gun and placed it against Casero's head. Casero could have easily stopped her from doing so, but he didn't. He was testing her. She'd said, "When you have nothing, pulling a trigger is the least of your problems." Casero told her to report to him the next morning. She'd passed selection and subsequently executed fourteen men and women on behalf of Special Projects.

Now, Major Casero stood in front of Rojo, Fontonia, and Sosa. They watched him, silent. He said, "A new job. I'll be with you in the field. So, we're a four person deployment. We work alone and with different angles. But we must stay in contact with each other. We need to find someone and neutralise that person." He tossed brown files at the operatives. "Rojo: you're a shipping insurance guy, seeking evidence on a series of drownings. You want to pay the insurance money. You are a good guy. Fontonia: you are an investigative journalist. You are looking for evidence to support a rumour that Argentina is making provocative military gestures against Great Britain. You are tough but fair. Sosa: you are in the early stages of pregnancy from a one night stand with a man who died at sea. You want to track his friends and family. You are emotional and scared."

The unit didn't flinch.

Sosa asked, "And you?"

"I am a British intelligence officer, sent from London without the knowledge of the UK military bases in the target location."

"Meaning The Falklands," said Rojo.

"Correct. I will be investigating a situation that will enable the British government to go to war against Argentina. It will be a discrete role. The islanders will help me."

Fontonia said, "You're playing with fire."

"*We're* playing with fire. It is ever thus in the unit." Casero sat at the table and prodded one finger on each file. "Choose your passports with care. You can't be British because I've already taken that nationality. But you can be Australian, New Zealanders, or white Africans. You must not be Americans or Canadians. And the three of you must be different nationalities. There must be no crossover. We work different angles."

"What's happened," asked Rojo.

"We had a vessel monitoring the Falklands. A stupid idea, as far as I'm concerned. A few nights ago, the vessel contacted HQ and said they were under heavy fire from a local fishing boat. Our boat tried to return to Rio Grande but it sunk on route due to damage to its hull. We have recovered the boat and its dead crew. It is clear that our spy ship killed the four men who attacked them, then dumped their bodies in the sea. We know this because of the penultimate transmission we received from our sailors." Casero withdrew a slip of paper and read its contents out loud. "Four hostiles in the sea. Shot dead. We're returning to homeland now. Heavily damaged. British military weapons found on the vessel. Gunshot wounds to our crew. Stand by. Message ends." Casero put the slip of paper back in his pocket.

Sosa asked, "What do you want us to do? Take on the British army out of retaliation?!"

"No." Casero looked serious. "Our spy ship reacted valiantly to the attack. Some people in our nation think it's a victory. I disagree. It's not yet an act of war but it might be due to one other factor."

"Meaning," asked Fontonia.

Casero replied, "It's public information that four Islanders died in a drowning incident that night. It's a cover up. I know for certain that the British don't want the islanders riled by the knowledge that the men were shot by Argentinians. I also know that the British are searching for reasons to justify an assault against us. The dead men's details are in your files. They are Eddie Wilson, Rob Taylor, Billy Green, and Mike Jackson. Only Green wasn't a native islander, though he assimilated into the community. I want you to memorise everything in the files, then burn the papers."

Rojo flicked through his file. "We have no mission. Three Argentinian men and one Argentinian woman die at sea, close to our coastline, due to gunshot wounds, a deficient boat, drowning, or a combination of all of those factors. Four islanders are killed by our guys one mile out from the Falklands. Our people were simply defending themselves."

Casero shook his head. "We were in British waters. The islanders were drunk. We were professionals. We didn't defend ourselves; we expertly murdered them before limping towards home."

Fontonia said, "There's something you haven't told us."

Casero eyed them all. They were such bright people. So ruthless. And even though he only thought of his unit's members as loners, he still felt a duty of care over them. They were his family. He'd assembled them. He'd stripped everything they held dear away from them. He'd recreated them. "I'm coming on this mission with you because it is of vital importance. Yes, there is something I haven't told you. It's not in your files. On the night the islander's trawler attacked our ship, it is clear that four islanders were killed by our people. But before it sunk, our vessel sent its last transmission. It said, *"There was a fifth man on the islanders' boat. He escaped back to the islands on an emergency raft. We couldn't pursue. He is a witness to what happened.* The message ended there. We estimate our boat got flooded and sank minutes after. The signals man must have been terrified. We don't know the identity of the fifth man. He is the key witness. His testimony will bring war. We must do everything we can to stop that from happening."

Sosa nodded. "We find the fifth man and shut his mouth by putting two nine millimetre bullets in the back of his skull."

CHAPTER 7

Ben Sign cooked bacon, scrambled eggs, beans and toast. Knutsen was outside, doing an early morning run. When Knutsen entered the cottage he was breathless. It was impossible to tell whether his saturated T-shirt was soaked with sweat or snow or both.

"Smells good," said Knutsen. "I need a quick shower."

Ten minutes later they ate in the lounge, both men wearing their hardy outdoor gear. Sign had also prepared a pot of tea. He said, "This is rustic fare but it was all I could muster. Plus, we are in a rustic place so needs must. How far did you run?"

"Six miles, along the coastline."

"In future conserve your energy and be conscious that a twisted ankle will not serve us well. Plus, remember that people may come to kill us. I need you alive and upright."

Knutsen laughed. "This coming from the man who once trekked eighty miles across a desert to rescue a Syrian child while being pursued by rebels."

"It was eighty three miles and I was younger then." The forty nine year old shoved bacon into his mouth. "I've done worse journeys. On all occasions, I was lucky. Minimise risk, Mr. Knutsen. We may have plenty of opportunity to expand our lungs and hearts while on active duty. Pointless jogging in the snow is not advisable."

Knutsen ignored the comment. "Active duty today?"

"We must talk to Sally. She runs a pub in Stanley. She is young, quite pretty, and loyal to other islanders. She won't fall for your charms."

"The thought hadn't occurred to me." Knutsen frowned. "How are you feeling, being here?"

Sign stared at him. "Because my wife was Argentinian? And because she was killed in El Salvador?" He looked out of the window. In a distant voice, he said, "I think about her every day. I can smell her hair on the sea breeze. I feel her homeland. I imagine her growing up there – childhood escapades, family barbeques, college, early romances, and friendships. Then there is the reality of what I experienced. I met her in Buenos Aires when I was in MI6 and she was an NGO worker. My goodness me, she was a stunner. Extremely bright. Full of laughter. I'd never met anyone like her. We got engaged. I met her family. The women were lovely. My fiancée's brothers said they'd slit my throat if I did anything wrong to their sister. They were happy days. We married. She was murdered in Central America. And that is that. I'm still and always will be mourning. But, to answer your question, she is not truly here. She is buried near West Square." He looked at Knutsen and said in a firm voice, "It does not sadden me to be in a location close to my wife's birthplace. You and I know that the demons of loss always remain. The tactic is to keep the demons in a locked cage." His expression and tone of voice changed. "Now, sir – we must change the conversation."

Knutsen didn't speak for a minute. Instead he thought about Sign. He'd never met anyone like him. And having worked with him for six months he still couldn't pinpoint his character. Sign was brilliant, charming, temperamental, unconventional, powerful, lonely, and loyal to the bone to those who invested their trust in him. Right now, the only person Sign trusted was Knutsen. Still, every day Knutsen was learning more things about Sign that put off-kilter his previous preconceptions of the man.

"You'd have made a superb chief of MI6," said Knutsen.

"Different topic!"

"You should get married again."

"That would mean you'd have to move out of West Square and live with your criminal pals in some god-awful part of London."

"You could give up detective work and do consultancy to the prime minister. I hear there's good money in that."

"No fun. Plus, where would you rather be with me? The corridors of Westminster or hunting down a lead near the Antarctic?"

Knutsen smiled. "You really know your own mind."

"No I don't. Slice my brain open when I'm dead and somehow tell me what you see." Sign polished off the rest of his breakfast. "We should head down to Stanley. The pub opens early to serve breakfast diners. Sally will be on shift."

Forty five minutes later they were in the pub. The tiny pub was empty. Only Sally was there, washing glasses and attending to other duties behind the bar. Sign and Knutsen approached the bar.

Sign said, "Pretty lady – we wish to speak to an employee of this establishment. Her name is Sally. I presume you are Sally."

Sally eyed them with suspicion. "Who are you?"

"My name is Ben Sign. This is Mr. Tom Knutsen. We are from London. And we are at your service. We are private investigators and we wish to further establish the circumstances surrounding how Eddie Wilson, Rob Taylor, Billy Green, and Mike Jackson drowned. I'm led to believe they were drinking in your fine establishment on the night they died."

Her suspicion didn't ebb. "Who's employed you to investigate their deaths?"

A clever question, thought Sign. "We represent a British law firm. For now, our client wishes to remain anonymous. That will change when they release their report. Essentially our client is looking for evidence that the fishing rights of Falkland Islanders are being violated by Latin American countries. Moreover, our client wishes to prove that offshore drilling rights for oil or gas must remain in the hands of islanders. In the case of Wilson and his friends, our client wishes to establish whether their deaths were as a result of trying to gain justifiable dominance over fishing grounds that were being illegally used by non-Falklands vessels. Perhaps that's how the accident happened. If so, we can use their deaths to build a case that bolsters and enforces the protection of your waters. Probably, that will ensure that a Royal Navy frigate is permanently stationed here."

Sally placed down the glass she was cleaning. "How do you get paid? How does the law firm get paid?"

"We are on a retainer with the law firm. Our client gets paid upon results by the British government. If the Falklands loses a penny because of Argentina, the British will take action. We represent you."

Sally's expression softened. "Do you have a badge or something? Anything that proves who you say you are?"

Sign shook his head. "We're private investigators, not the New York Police Department. You must make a decision. Do you trust our credentials? Or do you think I'm spinning you a lie?"

Sally poured three cups of coffee and nodded at one of the two tables in the pub. "Sit there." She brought the coffee and placed it in front of the men. "Breakfast service has been shit this morning because of the weather. Deliveries haven't come through; people are staying at home; and I'm the only sucker who's come out in the snow to serve no one breakfast. You're my first customers. Your coffee's black because there was no milk run this morning. Drink it or leave it. I don't care."

"Marvellous." Sign cupped his hands around his mug. "Coffee should always be black, softened with a little cold water to prevent burning. The taste is infinitely superior to coffee polluted with cows' milk." He sipped his coffee, showing no indication that its scorching heat was burning his lips and that the liquid tasted foul. "Would you be so kind as to tell us what happened that night?"

Sally told them what she knew.

Knutsen asked, "How drunk were they?"

Sally shrugged. "I've worked this place for six years. You pick up on things. I've seen people get drunk on just two pints if they're in a bad mood. I've seen people neck a bottle of whiskey and walk out without any symptoms, because they're in a good mood. But on that night," she hesitated. "On that night, Wilson and his mates were in an awful mood but just kept drinking. It was man stuff. Adrenalin I guess. They wanted a fight. They were drinking to give them courage and anger. You know how it is when men drink like that. Their sentences get shorter. They become more certain. Then they take action."

Knutsen nodded. "What did they take action against?"

Sally wafted her hand in the air. "A load of silliness. We've had an Argie ship watching us for a few months. It never bothered us. We thought it was a joke. But male pride's a funny old thing, isn't it. Wilson, Taylor, Green, and Jackson got it in to their dumb heads to sail out and do something about the Argie boat. God knows what they were going to do. I bet even they didn't know what to do. Four pissed blokes, a boat with an engine, end of."

Sign looked away, faking agitation. "But, they fell off their boat and drowned. That's a serious matter."

"Who's to say they weren't pushed off?"

Sign looked at Sally. It was imperative that she didn't know the truth – that they were shot by the Argentinians. "We take violation of sovereign waters very seriously. The Argentinian vessel you referenced may have caused your friends to change course and inadvertently get caught up in a rip tide. Who's to blame? The Argentine vessel? Four drunk islanders? My client will err towards the former option. Wilson was an expert skipper. Yes, he was inebriated and the climate that night was atrocious, but five percent of his faculties would have been compos mentis."

"He'd have known what he was doing, a bit anyway," Knutsen said in plainer language.

Sign asked, "Who else was in the bar that night?"

Sally grew suspicious again. "Why do you want to know?"

"I'm merely trying to paint a picture of the scene in here before the men went to their boat."

She looked away, conflicted. After a twenty seconds she said, "Carl and Nick. They're sheep farmers. Carl works his farm six miles from here; Nick's place is eight miles away."

Sign nodded. "I presume they know Wilson, Green, Taylor, and Jackson?"

"Of course. Everyone around here knows each other."

"Were they friends?"

"They weren't enemies. Now and again they helped each other out with work. But I wouldn't say they were friends. Just acquaintances, I guess."

Sign paused. He was about to nudge his questions to a new level. "Is it possible that Nick or Carl joined Wilson and his friends on the boat that night?"

The question confused Sally. "Everyone on that boat died. And Nick and Carl are still very much alive." She laughed. "Carl's seventy years old and suffers from arthritis. He wouldn't have been able to walk onto the boat, let alone stand on the damn thing. Nick's younger but gets seasick just by looking at water. Neither of them would go anywhere near a boat. Plus, they stayed here 'til closing time. I saw them drive off towards home. Speak to them if you like. I'll give you their addresses. But, they'll tell you exactly what I've said." Her expression turned serious. "You promise me you're asking these questions for the benefit of our islands?"

Sign replied with the truth. "I can assure you I am." He was about to ask another question.

But Knutsen interjected. "Did they ever come in here with a fifth friend?"

Sally frowned, deep in thought. "No. I don't remember that ever happening. It was either the four of them, or two or three of them. They seemed to have got their tracks aligned, as us publicans like to say. Just the four of them. They didn't need another drinking partner. I can tell when men have long ago decided who they want to drink with. They stick with it. No deviations. No new friends. On a Sunday here we do a roast. Alongside the trimmings, we serve roast chicken, beef, gammon, and turkey. Wilson always has beef; Taylor, chicken; Green turkey; Jackson gammon. They've been doing that every week for years. It says something about their characters. They know what they like and dislike. And when they find something they like it becomes etched in their brains. Foods, friendships, routines, clothes they wear, you name it. They knew their own minds."

"They were loyal to their tastes," said Sign.

"Yes." Sally had a tear running down her face. "They were such loyal customers. More than that, they were good men. Helped me out. Helped others out. No fighting. They swore like troopers, but never at anyone. Now and again they got drunk and drove home way over the limit, but they'd drive carefully, sleep it off and be up and at 'em for work at four AM. They were hard men but you'd want them by your side if shit hit the fan." She wiped away her tear. "Excuse my language. I'm just saying they are missed."

Sign withdrew a pristine white handkerchief and handed it to her. "My dear – Mr. Knutsen and I have been around death all of our lives. It never gets easier to deal with the consequences of loss. If anything it gets harder."

She took his handkerchief, dabbed her face, and handed it back to him, her mascara smudged below her eyes. "You knew I'd cry. Your handkerchief was washed and ironed this morning."

"Nonsense. I carry a handkerchief at all times. I'm prone to hay fever. I sneeze when the pollen count is off the scale."

"In winter? In the Falklands?" Sally laughed, though was still emotional.

"Alright. Maybe I carry the handkerchief because Mr. Knutsen is accident prone. He's always falling over and grazing his knees. I have to dab the blood off him."

The comment cheered Sally up. "Your friend doesn't look accident prone." She breathed deeply.

Sign leaned forward and said in a sympathetic tone, "My dear – is there anyone you know who might have accompanied the men on that fatal night? A fifth man. We believe he might have survived. We'd dearly like to speak to him. He's not in trouble. On the contrary, his evidence might prove invaluable to further our case."

Sally took a swig of her coffee. "I just don't know. Wilson and Green divided their days at sea and in my bar. Wilson had the hots for me. Maybe that's why he kept coming here. Green isn't an islander but you wouldn't be able to tell that. He's got a kid on the island though he never saw her. Taylor worked the land and had the stamina of a huskie. Ditto lighthouse keeper and part-time fireman Jackson. Like I said, they were hard men. They slotted together because they saw themselves in each other. Least ways, that's my take. I can't imagine they had room in their minds for a fifth member of their gang. They were too close knit."

Sign asked, "What about suppliers? Someone who gave Wilson and Green their fishing nets; a man who supplied meal for Taylor's sheep; anyone who sorted the electrics in Jackson's lighthouse; or variants therein; anything that springs to mind?"

"Someone who was useful to the men," said Knutsen.

Sally upended a beer map and withdrew a pen from behind her ear. "Good luck. In the Falklands, everyone not only knows everyone, we also make sure we're all taken care of. But, I don't know who Wilson and his friends used to support their businesses. It might be someone near here on the east island. But it could also be someone on the west island. If so, be careful visiting that place. It's mostly uninhabited. You might die if you go there – no petrol, no food, no water, just penguins." She wrote on the white underside of the beer mat. "This is Carl and Nick's addresses. You can say that I sent you. They won't mind if you do that. They *will* mind if you turn up saying you're busybodies from London." She handed the mat to Sign. "Be careful. We love and trust the British. We also hate them nearly as much as we hate Argentina." She stared at Sign with piercing eyes. "Does that make sense?"

"It does indeed." Sign stood and extended his hand. "We are here to help."

Sally shook his hand and glanced at the bar. "Breakfast was a waste of time. I'm on a split shift. My dad's doing the midday roster. I'm back on this evening. When I'm between shifts, I'll have a spliff and a couple of hours sleep."

"A spliff?"

Knutsen explained. "A cannabis cigarette."

Sally looked tired. "Don't judge me for that."

Sign was utterly sincere when he said, "I never judge hard working honest souls. Mr. Knutsen! We must leave this young lady to her duties. Thankyou Sally. Let's hope the weather abates and allows you more custom later today."

She shook her head. "Don't hold your breath. This weather's not going anywhere soon." She smiled. "Take my advice – you can tell Carl and Nick that I gave you their addresses but don't say you're PIs from London. They'll clam up. Just so we reading from the same page, come up with another story."

Sign replied, "We're scientists, based in South Georgia. We've been tasked to investigate the deaths and whether they're related to aggressive intrusion of fishing rights and whether such intrusions are causing Falkland Island sailors to take unnecessary risks with their boats."

"Why didn't you spin me that lie?"

"Because we trust you and want you to know the truth. I judge you to be the eyes and ears of Stanley. Probably you don't have your finger on the pulse on matters further west on the islands. That doesn't matter. But if anything else does occur to you please let us know." He handed her a slip of paper. "We can be contacted via RAF Mount Pleasant. The number on the paper is not widely known."

Outside the pub and while standing next to their jeep, Knutsen said to Sign, "I don't think she was lying or holding back."

"I agree. But, we bounced her today and she was fatigued and emotional. Sometimes, what's important is not just what we remember, but what we forget."

"True. And she's a dope smoker – she'll forget quite a few things."

"Give her time. The important thing is that if anything does occur to her about a fifth man, I know she'll call us."

Knutsen wasn't convinced. "She might get wasted off shift and forget things in her private life. But in the pub she'll be on point. She has to be. She knows everything that goes on in the bar. She hasn't forgotten anything about Wilson and his mates."

"I fear you may be right, sir. And that takes us back to the starting line. We must visit Carl and Nick."

Knutsen drove six miles west out of Stanley. Though the four wheel drive was designed for treacherous conditions, Knutsen still had to drive slowly and with skill to avoid careering off the road. The windscreen wipers were on full and the pathetic heater was on maximum. Steam was coming out of the men's mouths. The land around them was becoming increasingly rugged, visible only between small breaks in the snowfall.

Sign had a military map on his lap. For the most part, GPS was useless in a Falklands winter. "Turn right here. Follow the track. Carl's place is four hundred and fifty yards at the end."

At the end of the track was a house and barn. Knutsen stopped the jeep outside the house and said, "I hope he's not miles away, tending to his sheep on the mountains."

"I doubt that's the case. I would imagine his sheep are in the barn. Even sheep feel a chill."

They approached the house. Sign knocked on the door.

A woman opened the door. "Yes?"

Sign gave her a variation of the line he'd given Sally and concluded, "We want to help the islands and Mr. Wilson, Taylor, Green, and Jackson." He also embellished and elaborated, "Our client's based in London but we're from South Georgia."

The island nine hundred and sixty miles east of the Falklands.

She looked dubious. "No one lives there. No one *can* live there."

"We do. We're from the British Antarctic Survey's base on Bird Island. We're scientists. Our client reached out to us because we have mutual interests and because we were closer to the source of the problem – namely the deaths of four Falkland islanders. Is your husband at home?"

"He's on site. You'll find him there." She nodded at the barn and withdrew into the house, closing the door behind her.

Sign and Knutsen entered the barn. As Sign had predicted, the place was full of sheep, eating grass, some of them baaing and bleating, all of them contained in pens. There were seventy of them, with blue dye markings on them identifying they belonged to Carl's farm. Sign and Knutsen walked down the central aisle, pens either side of them. Alongside the cacophony of noise, the stench of cooped up wildlife was palpable. There was no sight of Carl.

Sign spun around three sixty degrees. "There will be a private place here. One that Carl doesn't want these sheep to know about."

Knutsen jogged back down the aisle, looked up, saw nothing of interest, turned around, and pointed at the other end of the aisle. "Outside. I'm guessing an annex."

"Yes."

Both men exited the barn. Knutsen was right. There was a small outhouse, attached to the barn. They entered. An elderly man was inside, his back against them. A tethered lamb was in front of him. The man held a pneumatic pistol against the lambs head and pulled the trigger. A six inch metal spike exited the pistol and penetrated the lamb's brain, before retracting into the gun. The lamb's death was instant. The man used ropes attached to the ceiling and a motorised winch to raise the lamb. It was now dangling mid-height in the room.

"Carl?"

The man turned. "Who's asking?"

Sign gave him the same story he'd given Carl's wife. "We can wait for you in our car if now's an inconvenient time?"

Carl shrugged. "You can talk here, so long as you're not squeamish." He picked up a razor sharp knife, slit open the lamb's belly, placed his hand inside the creature, and yanked out its innards, all of which went into a bucket. He lifted the bucket and put it to one side. "Nothing goes to waste. I'll mince the guts and organs up. It'll feed my dogs for a few days. You want to know about Wilson and his friends? There's nothing I can tell you that Sally hasn't already told you. Damn fools were drunk that night and got in their boat. I heard they fell overboard, a mile out at sea. Must have been a swell or something." He started using the knife to remove the lamb's coat, slicing portions underneath the wool, ripping parts, then repeating the process. He winced and held his wrist. "Bloody arthritis. There were times when I could do this job in minutes. Now it takes me an hour."

Knutsen said, "Let me do it for you. I'm handy with a knife."

Carl shrugged. "Can't say I couldn't do with the help." He handed Knutsen the knife. "But it won't be just a case of skinning the lamb. You'll have to butcher it as well. Follow my exact instructions. Don't mess it up. The meat will be exported for a pretty price but I only get paid it the joints are perfect." He sat on a stool and used a cloth to wipe blood off his hands.

Forty five minutes later the job was done. The joints of lamb were laid out on a large wooden chopping board.

"Not bad for a beginner," said Carl. "These will sell. Here," he tossed Knutsen a leg, "put that in a roasting pan. It's for your troubles."

"Thank you, sir," replied Knutsen.

"Call me Carl." The elderly farmer rubbed his ankles. "My son's taking over the farm. He's in Scotland at the moment, finishing off his PhD. But next week he'll be done and will be returning home with his wife and kids. Mable and I have enough rooms. He's a good lad. He knows about farming. His PhD was in ethical farming, or something like that. I don't care. What I do care about is that he's got the muscle I once had." He stood and placed each cut of meat on trays, which he wrapped in cling film and labelled. "Four men died in an accident. The Argie boat that's been spying on us might have made them change course and make a mistake. But, I don't know. I know nothing about the sea. As far as I'm aware, the Argies have buggered off. They might have been nowhere near the boat that night."

Sign said, "We're trying to solve the deaths. Is it possible that Wilson and his friends had a fifth man with them that night?"

Carl looked nonplussed. "It's possible I suppose. But, I don't know who."

"Maybe a man who had access to guns. There were weapons on board Wilson's boat."

Carl looked stern as he said, "Help me bring the trays of meat into the house. I'll show you something."

After the meat was placed into the kitchen chest freezer, Carl guided them to his home's shed. "You talk of guns. We all have guns. Look at this." He opened a steel cabinet. Inside were three shotguns and a bolt action hunting rifle. "The shotguns are for bird game, when in season. The rifle's only used in bad situations – a lamb's got stuck up a mountain, I can't get to him, he can't get down, he's injured and in agony, that kind of thing. The kindest thing is to end his misery." He shut the cabinet. "Everyone around here has guns, for the same reason."

Sign asked, "Do you have weapons from the Falklands War? Trophies?"

Carl shook his head and genuinely looked upset by the question. "After the war we worked with the army to clear as much shit from the islands as we could. It was only the landmines that proved a bugger. None of the islanders were trophy hunters. We wanted our islands clean again. Why do you ask?"

"Because Wilson, Taylor, Green, and Jackson sailed out to confront the Argentinian spy ship, armed with five British Browning handguns and two SLR assault rifles. The weapons were almost certainly picked off the battlefields during or after the war. We are not talking about two shotguns and a hunting rifle. We're talking about military-grade devices that are designed to kill humans."

Carl looked puzzled. "I don't know anyone who'd store stuff like that. We're honest folk. We look after our animals. We feed them; shelter them at this time of year. We cull them when it's time. We shoot geese or whatever when it's that time of year to put something on the table for Christmas. But we *don't* keep military weapons. Least ways, not to my knowledge."

"Someone did. And I think that person is now very scared. He supplied his weapons to Wilson and his friends. He went out on the boat. They had an accident. Wilson, Taylor, Green, and Jackson drowned. The fifth man panicked and rowed ashore. He's in hiding because he supplied the guns and is worried he might get in trouble. The truth is, he's not in trouble. He's a witness. If there was a swell, as you suggest, or a large wave, or similar, and Wilson had to bank his vessel hard left or right to avoid the Argentinian ship, we need to know. Our client is a law firm. They'd say it was manslaughter by an illegal invasion of sovereign waters. But we need evidence. The fifth man can give us that." Sign stared at Carl.

Carl sighed. "I'd like to help. I really would. Did Sally give you Nick's address?"

Sign nodded.

"He's a lot younger than me. He's more likely to know the type of man that would store military weapons."

Five minutes later Knutsen and Sign were in their vehicle, driving west. Knutsen asked, "Do you think Carl's right – we're looking for a younger man? It would make sense. Older men wouldn't hoard military weapons unless…"

"He'd served in the war and wanted mementos. We must ask Richards to check his records to see if any veterans settled here after '82."

Knutsen thought it through. "The average age of British soldiers who fought in the war back then must have been at least twenty five. The government didn't want to send rookies to recapture the islands. That would make most of them in their mid-sixties now."

"Let's keep options open. The fifth man could be a trophy hunter. He could be a veteran. He could be the son of a veteran. He could be an islander or a foreigner. One thing's for sure – we're no nearer to identifying him. But I wonder…" Sign's voice trailed.

"What?"

"It's just an idea. I wonder about his profile. It is possible he's a loner. That would mean he doesn't live in Stanley. And that means our search is considerably narrowed down."

"A loner?"

Sign said, "Show me your weapon."

Knutsen placed his pistol in Sign's hand.

Sign checked its workings. "You cleaned and oiled it last night. You care about this weapon, but not because you love it; rather, because you don't want it to fail you. It is a tool that must be effective in extreme circumstances." He handed the gun back to Knutsen. "The weapons found on Wilson's boat were, according to Colonel Richards, in immaculate condition. Their owner made sure of that. But, why were the guns so cared for if he was just a trophy hunter? No. He wanted military grade weapons to be in their prime in case he needed to use them. I doubt he's a Falklands War veteran; or the son of one. I think he's an islander. And I think he has few friends and is a survivalist."

Knutsen stopped the jeep, tucked his handgun into his belt, and looked at Sign. "You're making huge assumptions."

Sign chuckled. "No. I'm tickling the possibilities of the truth. The fifth man was not like Wilson, Taylor, Green, and Jackson. He wasn't the kind of man to prop up a bar every night with his pals, while bantering about this woman and that and who he wanted to fight. He's thoughtful. He's a loner. Most likely he's perpetually paranoid. That would explain why he ran from the crime scene and has gone to ground. He's the type of man who thinks everyone is out to get him. But, he will have a connection to Wilson and the others."

"Maybe they had something on him." Knutsen started driving. "It's possible they blackmailed him to give them his guns and join them on the ship."

"No. That doesn't wash. Remember – loner, survivalist, paranoid, immaculate military weapons. He gave them his guns and went with them that night because he wanted to take the fight to the enemy. Alas, the poor fellow was not up to the task when hellfire unleashed. But his heart was in the right place. You must remember that the islanders live in constant fear that their land will be invaded and rebranded Islas Malvinas. Sometimes the islanders get to breaking point. The fifth man could never be blackmailed by Wilson or anyone else. Figuratively, he had his back to the wall with a gun in his hand. I think Wilson or one of the others went to him that night and explained the situation. The fifth man finally saw a means to hit back at his paranoia about Argentina. He supplied his troops with good war guns and he went to battle. It was a battle too far. Fight or flight. The fifth man chose flight." Sign smiled. "But, I concede that everything I've just said may be utter balderdash."

"It makes perfect sense. The fifth man was scared. And when it came to it he was a coward. Men like that treasure guns. He's a good guy who just wants to be left alone."

"Correct. Give me five minutes with him and I'd talk to him about a different way of life. It would work. He'd finally be happy." Sign looked at his map. "Seven hundred yards, take a left, slight incline."

They stopped outside a house that looked similar to Carl's place; ditto there was a nearby barn and a garage. Knutsen knocked on the door. No answer. They tried the barn and the garage. Both were locked. Knutsen tried the house again, but still there was no answer.

Sign withdrew a pair of binoculars from his jacket and scoured the hills around the farmstead. "There. On the escarpment. I'd say about five hundred yards away. It will be Nick. It looks like he's making repairs to some kind of shed on the hill. It must be where he stores food for his cattle. We'll meet him there. Watch your footing."

"Baby heads," stated Knutsen.

"Yes. Baby heads. Also bogs and the possibility of unexploded landmines."

They trudged uphill. Snowfall remained heavy and due to the amount of snow on the ground it was impossible to see any dangers under foot. Twice Knutsen lost his footing and Sign had to grab his jacket to prevent him going face down onto the grounds. They were breathing heavily as they neared the shed.

The man looked at them, looked right, and ran, shouting, "You fucking bastard!"

Knutsen whipped out his gun.

Sign placed his hand over the muzzle. "Calm, my friend. All is not what it seems. Look what he's running to."

Nick stopped and picked up a sheep. He walked back to the shed and put it inside. Sign and Knutsen approached him. Sign asked, "Nick?"

Nick was leaning against the shed, exhausted. "Yeah. That's what my friends call me. Who are you?"

Sign delivered their cover story, the reason they were visiting the islands and added, "We've spoken to Sally and Carl this morning. They both advised us to speak to you."

Nick was still sucking in air. He slapped the shed. "I got all of my sheep into the barn, except this fucker. Couldn't find her. Bastard. But she ain't going anywhere now until the snow melts." He stood upright, his breathing now normal. "I'm not having this conversation out here. We'll freeze our tits off. I'll be making a brew in the house. Join me if you want. Don't if you don't want."

Sign and Knutsen turned with the intention of walking back to the house.

But Nick said, "Not on foot. Too dodgy. You can hitch a ride with me. They followed him to the other side of the shed. Parked there was a large quad bike with a plinth on the back. He pointed at the plinth. "Sit there. I'll just be a minute." He entered the shed and re-emerged carrying the sheep. "You're going to have to earn your brew by helping me get this fucker down to the barn." He placed the sheep on Sign and Knutsen's lap. "Grip her hard, stroke her face, and don't take any shit from her. She's strong and can be a right cunt." He carefully drove them into the valley, placed the sheep into the barn containing the rest of his flock, and drove them to his house. When they were all inside, Nick put on the kettle and removed his oilskin jacket. "Sit in the lounge." He made a fire, returned to the kitchen, then brought out three mugs of tea on a tray containing a jug of milk and a bowl of sugar cubes. "The milk's goat's milk. Blokes like you will either like it or hate it."

"I'll take my tea black," said Knutsen.

"Goat's milk! Wonderful!" said Sign as he added a dash to his tea. Sign was partially lactose intolerant. Goat's milk was the last thing on earth he'd want to consume.

Nick sat down and gulped his tea. "So, your scientists playing cops, right?"

Knutsen laughed. "We're not playing cops. The police and coastal services know how Wilson, Taylor, Green, and Jackson died. They drowned. It was an accident. But, we're experts in all matters maritime. In particular, we specialise in the Antarctic and its surrounding waters. Our client – the law firm my colleague mentioned – engaged us because it wants to draw upon our expertise to see if there was anything that helped facilitate the accident – an unusual rip tide, a freak wave, a swell, other potential factors."

"Or whether it was just four pissed blokes who shouldn't have been out at that time of night in that weather." Nick drained the rest of his tea and held his hands near the fire. "They were on a mission to get really drunk that night. I'd lay money that they took beer with them on the boat, maybe spirits too. I don't know much about our coastline but I do know it can get shitty at this time of year. If those idiots were out on deck, swigging their beers, all it would have taken is for a wave to tip them over the side of Wilson's tin-pot piece of junk. And then they'd have stood no chance. A mile out, I've heard. An Olympic swimmer wouldn't have been able to make it to shore. He'd have died from the cold. Wilson and his drunken pals, probably dressed in cold weather gear, wouldn't have got more than a few yards. And they would be hypothermic. No chance they'd have been able to get back on the boat. I've seen Wilson's trawler. There's no ladders or ropes on the hull. If the boat tips you into the water, you're fucked."

Sign said, "Your hypothesis sounds completely laudable. We wonder, however, whether there were extraneous factors that may have prompted the accident. *Human* factors that caused Wilson to go against his instincts and change course, thereby putting the boat at risk of the sea and the weather."

Nick smiled. "You mean like another boat blocking its way or driving right at it?" Nick looked serious. "We've had an Argie boat patrolling our waters these last few months. It's gone now. Last time it was spotted was on the night of the drownings. Maybe it was involved, maybe its disappearance was a coincidence, or maybe it wasn't involved but witnessed the drownings and its crew freaked out and left. Who knows?"

Sign asked, "Did you know the deceased well?"

Nick shrugged and said nonchalantly, "I saw them a lot in the pub, but never drank with them. Rob Taylor helped me a few times with repairs on my farm. But he wasn't a mate. I paid him for his work. Mike Jackson helped put out a fire on my land after four dumb-witted squaddies stopped on a march and lit a calor gas to make a brew. They set the heath on fire. But Jackson was just doing his job as a fireman. Aside from that, I had little dealings with them. Jackson was a part-time fireman. His main job was operating the lighthouse. Wilson and Green were fisherman. Lighthouses and fishing are of no interest to me apart from what catches are brought in. On a Friday I like to buy a nice piece of cod from the store in Stanley. We were blokes who drank in the same boozer. Nothing more to it than that."

"Carl said the same. And yet you are friends with Carl and drink with him." Sign leaned forward. "I wonder what differentiates Carl from Wilson and his friends."

Nick looked nonplussed as he said, "Carl's my dad. My brother's going to help run his farm. The old man's getting a bit creaky."

"Of course he's your father. I knew that the moment I saw you. It's very kind of you to share a pint or two with your dad after a hard day's work. He will be most appreciative. But, mapping the family connections of the Falklands is not why we're here. We have a lead. There was a fifth man on board Wilson's vessel that night. He escaped. We'd dearly like to talk to the chap. He's a witness."

Nick frowned. "A fifth man? Are you sure?"

"The British military are cooperating with our investigation. They had thermal imagery of Wilson's vessel before the snow blizzard cut out all visuals of the boat."

"Maybe the man also drowned."

"It's possible, although Wilson's vessel's escape dingy was found two miles on shore from Stanley. And it was dragged over the beach and hidden in bracken. It would have been impossible for the sea, regardless of conditions, to have positioned the dingy in such a way. Do you have any idea who the fifth man may be?"

"Was it you?" asked Knutsen.

Sign immediately said, "Forgive my friend's direct approach. We are merely here to ask for any insight you may have."

Nick looked angry, but Sign's interjection softened his demeanour. "I don't do sea. I fucking hate the stuff. You can put me on a plane or a tractor or a bus, but never put me on a boat. You'd see the contents of my guts if you did." He stared at the fire. "A fifth man? That would be unusual. Eddie, Rob, Billy, and Mike kept themselves to themselves. They were close knit. Didn't need anyone else."

"What about a man who could supply guns – *military* guns. You know they went out that night to confront the Argentinian vessel. They got help from the fifth man. I think he gave them weapons that he'd stored since the war."

Nick looked genuinely confused. "Military guns? I mean, it's possible, but everyone I know has no need for that stuff. Most of us in the sticks have a shotgun or two. But that's about it. We're farmers. I was too young at the time to remember this but my dad told me that it took an age to get rid of all the shit that was left here after the war. What I do remember is that years later we were still finding shit – landmines, machine gun belts of bullets, grenades, guns, ration packs, army ruck sacks, artillery shells, you name it. The army helped us whenever we found something. It wanted the islands as clean as we did. They were worried about accidents to their men, islanders, and to our cattle. Do you reckon it might be a serving squaddie who went with them on the boat? Maybe he gave them the guns?"

"No. The handguns on board Wilson's vessel were Browning 9mm. They are still used in the British army but are being phased out. And I know for certain that there are no Brownings in the military base on the islands. The assault rifle on the boat was an SLR. That gun has long ago been decommissioned. It is highly improbable that a serving soldier would have access to these weapons. The person we're looking for is an islander." Sign looked around. "Do you live here alone?"

"Yes. I had a girlfriend who moved in for a month. But she was from Stanley. She told me she felt too isolated out here. She moved out last year. So, it's just me and my bloody sheep."

Knutsen laughed.

Sign said, "It's possible we're looking for someone who lives on his own in a place like this; maybe further west; possibly even on the west island. If anything occurs to you, would you be so kind as to give us a call?" He handed Nick a slip of paper containing the Mount Pleasant phone number. "We're not here to cause any problems. On the contrary and as we told your father, we're here to help."

Nick took the paper and placed it in a pocket. "Nothing springs to mind. But I can put the word out."

"I'd be eternally grateful if you didn't. The fifth man is obviously scared. We need him to feel safe. Word might get to him. Then, he might run."

Nick nodded. "If he gives you evidence that the Argie boat was somehow involved that night, what will you do with the evidence?"

"It will be escalated up the food chain – the commander of the military base, the governor of the islands, the British chief of defence staff, foreign secretary, and ultimately the British prime minister. They will decide what to do. Rest assured, if an Argentinian vessel was in any way involved in the death of four British citizens – whether by accident or by a provocative manoeuvre –action will be taken."

Nick stood. "I've got to feed my sheep. You might be on a wild goose chase. I still think this might be four pissed blokes falling off the side of their boat after a wave hit them, or something."

Sign replied, "You may be right, sir. Or you may be wrong. Please do call us if you think of anything that could bring this case to a close."

Outside, Sign and Knutsen watched Nick go into the barn.

Knutsen was frustrated as he said, "We're getting nowhere!"

"Keep calm, dear chap. Turn your thinking on its head. Every time we come up against a roadblock, it enables us to further narrow our search."

Knutsen replied with sarcasm. "How very *glass half full* of you." He got into the jeep. When Sign was sitting in the passenger seat, Knutsen said, "Look. Maybe Nick's right; that this is a wild goose chase. It's possible that Green supplied the guns. He's an ex-soldier. He could have had access to military weapons."

"No. He was a Royal Engineer commando, stationed here between 2009 and 2011. For the same reasons I articulated to Nick, Green was too young to have access to Falklands War British guns."

"Maybe he found them on one of his patrols. Kept them as souvenirs."

"Highly improbable. And you're forgetting about the fifth man. He was there on that night for a reason."

"Maybe there is no fifth man!" Knutsen started the engine.

Sign placed his hand on Knutsen's forearm. "Hold your nerve and hang tight onto your faculties. There is no doubt there was a fifth man – the drone footage Richards showed us; the dingy on the beach; guns on board Wilson's vessel that honest fishermen, farmers, and lighthouse keepers would have no means to ordinarily access. We are painting a picture of the fifth man. And like the slow darkroom exposure of a photograph, we are gradually getting a clearer image of our petrified witness."

Knutsen gunned the engine and drove. "Where to?"

"It's getting late. It's not recommended to be out on the roads after dark. Let's head back to the Bluff Cove cottage."

An hour later they arrived at the cottage. Knutsen stoked the log burner and bathed and changed clothes. Sign made a casserole, put it in the oven, parboiled some potatoes and beans, and set the potatoes aside for roasting thirty minutes prior to eating, and the beans aside for a three minute flash in a pan with a little water and butter when needed. When Knutsen was out of the bathroom, Sign too washed himself and changed out of his sodden clothes. Both men loaded their snow-caked garments into the washing machine. Later, the clothes would dry on a rack in front of the log burner.

After eating and cleaning dishes, Sign and Knutsen sat in armchairs in front of the fire. Both had a brandy. Lamps were on, but no overhead lights because they were too fierce. Sign and Knutsen liked the ambience of subtle lighting. The cottage was warm, despite high winds and snow battering the exterior of the property. It was now dark. If either man had stepped outside, they wouldn't be able to see anything but black. The glorious stars frequently visible in the southern hemisphere were shielded tonight by the snow clouds.

Sign opened the log burner and placed a piece of wood inside. He looked at Knutsen. "Sir, you got a little riled today."

"Riled?"

"Well, you nearly shot a man who was trying to rescue a sheep. And later you thought our investigation might be a waste of time. It doesn't take a rocket scientist to spot your current state of mind."

Knutsen bowed his head. "This island stuff is not something I'm used to. And the bloody snow – I used to love the stuff. But here it's ridiculous. No matter what we wear it's fucking freezing. And the people here all claim they know each other, but when push comes to shove it seems they don't. I'm a fish out of water."

"Mr. Knutsen. You were once the most highly decorated undercover police officer in the Metropolitan Police. You infiltrated highly volatile places that others couldn't."

"That was London and parts of Europe. Not places like this."

Sign had to gee Knutsen up. "You've been cold before, yes?"

"Many times – on London streets playacting a homeless man, chasing a criminal in a sewer in winter, doing all night surveillance on roof tops, so many other experiences."

"And you've dealt with the complexities of the human condition – whether criminal or otherwise. I'd hazard a guess that when you infiltrated the gangs in London, sometimes people were not as they seemed. You'd meet diabolical men. But you were also confronted with compassion and uncertainty. Some of the gang men were good. You didn't want to arrest them or shoot them."

"Yes."

Sign leaned forward and tapped his glass against Knutsen's glass. "Mr. Knutsen, men like you and I are not fish out of water. Instead, we're fish who deliberately swim in the wrong waters. Imagine the Falklands as Great Britain in winter. It has an epicentre – in this case Stanley – and it has countryside on its borders – in this case the hills and mountains of the east and west islands. The people here don't know us and are suspicious. You experienced suspicion when infiltrating the criminal underworld in London. We are unravelling a complicated knot. It takes patience. And you've had an exemplary career requiring patience. I heard from your previous commissioner that you had to bide your time for fourteen undercover months to simply get the mobile phone number of a major criminal." Sign sipped his brandy while keeping his eyes on Knutsen. "Never underestimate yourself again. You know this kind of territory. You know this type of people. Remember who you are. And remember what you've achieved in dreadful environments."

Knutsen looked up and smiled. "I guess it's because I can't get it out of my head that the Falklands are the other side of the world."

"Then, do a mind trick on yourself. Imagine they're the Scottish Highlands. Stanley is Inverness. Everything west is mountainous bandit country."

Knutsen laughed. "Yeah. When you put it that way it works." He sipped his drink. "I'm not like you. I worked a patch. I didn't travel the world undercover."

"Stick with me and you may well do. You are eminently well equipped to do so." Sign had achieved what he needed. "Now, Mr. Knutsen, tomorrow we must visit the homes of Wilson, Taylor, Green, and Jackson. At some point we will also need to speak to their families. But tonight we are housebound. I note there's a stack of DVDs next to the television. I wonder if we might watch The Imitation Game. It is historically flawed but nevertheless is a fine drama with near-perfect characterisation."

Knutsen looked at the stack. "I'd prefer Goodfellas."

"Heaven forbid. What about When Harry Met Sally?"

"Are you serious?"

"Of course not. I have my eye on The English Patient."

"Nah. Too maudlin." Knutsen now felt fully relaxed. "I tell you what, why don't we just sit here and swap war stories."

Sign smiled. "That would take us one or two steps back in the past. I believe a man should always step forward. The solution to this evening's entertainment, on such a dreadfully inclement night, is I believe to play a board game. There is a tiny selection on the mantelpiece. Would you prefer Monopoly, Scrabble, or Trivial Pursuit?"

"You'll beat me in Trivial Pursuit and Scrabble. And I know you – you'll cheat in Monopoly." Knutsen drained the rest of his drink. "Monopoly it is. But no way am I letting your conniving ass be banker."

CHAPTER 8

Major Casero arrived in Mount Pleasant via a direct flight from Santiago, Chile. If any official at the airport asked him why a 'British' man had flown to the islands from South America, he'd say he'd been on British government business in Panama. Then he'd keep his mouth shut. But, he wasn't challenged at the airport. Rojo was already on the islands, having taken the earlier flight from Santiago. Fontonia and Sosa were due to arrive in an hour, having flown up to Heathrow, and taken a coach and taxi to Brize Norton, before boarding a flight back down south. It would have been an exhausting journey, but the women were used to such hardships.

As Casero exited the airport he checked his watch. He had time to book in to the Southernwind hotel in Stanley, shower, and get changed. He picked up his hire car and drove into the tiny capital. Rojo was staying in a bed and breakfast, one mile outside of Stanley. Fontonia and Sosa would be staying in cottages. It would have been easy for the team to covertly infiltrate the islands via boats or scuba gear, once they'd been offloaded by a fake fishing vessel or a military submarine. But they needed to look the part, if ever challenged on the islands by police or the army. Possession of air tickets was vital. So too possession of fake passports that matched the Anglo-Saxon names on the air tickets. Thankfully, Casero, Rojo, Fontonia, and Sosa could bluff the rest in their sleep.

Casero was a British government official who was on top secret business.

Rojo was a white South African insurance official.

Fontonia was a Kiwi investigative journalist.

Sosa was a pregnant Australian who divided her time between Melbourne and the South Pole. She was to pose as an engineer who'd visited the Falklands and had a fling with one of the drowned men.

All of them were allegedly here to work out what happened on that tragic night.

In truth, their agenda was the same – find the fifth man and kill him.

After Casero had checked into his hotel and washed and changed, he lay on his bed and slept for two hours. The rendezvous was not until 1000hrs. He had time to re-charge his batteries. At 0900hrs, he exited the hotel and drove northwest. The ground was still thick with snow, but thankfully the air was clear. He spotted three vehicles adjacent to the bleak coast, stopped by them, and got out. The occupants of the other vehicles also got out – Rojo, Fontonia, Sosa.

Casero walked up to them. In perfect English, he asked, "Any problems?"

They shook their heads.

"The cache?"

Sosa replied, also with pitch-perfect English. "We've dug it up, got what we needed, and re-sealed the cache."

The cache was one of many planted by Argentina in the remote parts of the Falklands. All of them contained items of use to special operatives. The one Sosa dug up was no different. She placed her small rucksack on the bonnet of her car and withdrew items. "Four cell phones and chargers."

"Use the word 'mobile'" snapped Casero. "We are not Americans."

Sosa was unperturbed. "Four Sig Sauer handguns with extra magazines. Maps. Ten thousand British pounds each. Thermal binoculars. Bullet proof vests. And these," she picked up one of four identical items, each the size of a packet of cigarettes. "Cameras. They have a far greater range than mobile phone cameras, and images can be uploaded onto our phones and shared." She leaned against her car. "The vests are merely damage limitation. If you get shot in the upper body with anything as powerful as these," she lifted one of the handguns, "you'll most likely end up with a cracked sternum or broken ribs. The vests are too thin to fully protect us from military or police weapons. But, they give us a chance to escape or take down the enemy."

Casero asked, "Have the phones been programmed?"

Sosa nodded. "There are five contacts in each phone. Four of them are identified by letters. Casero is 'A'. Rojo is 'B'. Fontonia is 'C'. I'm 'D'." She'd put different coloured stickers on each phone in order to remember which phone belonged to whom. She handed the phones out. "The fifth contact is our way to get out of here. It's listed as 'Travel Agent'."

The team collected every other item.

Casero was pleased. Everything was on track. "Work the angles. And remember – other people might be looking for the fifth man. If you establish who those people are, identify them, take photos of them, share the images with the rest of us, follow them, and neutralise them once they've led us to the target. Hopefully it won't come to that. Let's hope we can find the fifth man before anyone else does."

Fontonia said, "Maybe the fifth man has given himself up and is under heavy protection in Mount Pleasant or has been taken off the islands by the Brits to another secure location."

Casero checked the workings of his handgun. "I very much doubt that. At best what happened when our ship was attacked would prompt a major diplomatic incident between Britain and Argentina. At worst we'd now be at war. The fact that nothing's happened means the fifth man's gone to ground." He placed his pistol in a pocket. "We find the fifth man. We kill him and anyone around him. Whoever makes the kills summons the rest of the team. We dispose of bodies. We exit via the trawler, codename 'Travel Agent'."

The trawler was an Argentine boat that belonged to FIA. It was anchored thirty miles off the islands. It would come to shore once the assassination was done. Casero, Rojo, Fontonia, and Sosa would swim a few hundred yards to the boat and get on board. The swim would be agony, but they could do it. Then, they'd go back to Argentina.

Casero looked at his team. "Let's hope the next time we see each other is when we're mopping up and getting out of here." He stowed his equipment in his car and drove back to Stanley.

Over the next four hours, Sign and Knutsen searched the homes of Taylor, Green, and Jackson. There was no need to force entry into the properties – Colonel Richards had given them keys. They found nothing of interest.

The last property to investigate belonged to Wilson. His home was a small house near the Stanley quay. They entered. It was clear there was no woman's touch in the place. The tiny kitchen's sink was crammed with dirty dishes. On the adjacent surface were empty foil ready-meal containers and pint glasses. Half-drunk bottles of cider and ale were on the floor. There was one upstairs bedroom. The bed's duvet was twisted and looked like it hadn't been washed in an age. The room smelled of fish and musk. The bathroom toilet was dirty. The sink contained whiskers from Wilson's shaving. By the taps were one toothbrush and toothpaste, a razor, and shaving foam; nothing else. The adjacent shower only contained one bottle of shower gel. The downstairs lounge had a sofa, a TV positioned on top of a chest of drawers, lobster pots hanging from meat hooks attached to the wall, rolled up maps of the Falklands' coastline, an overflowing ashtray, a rack that had dank-smelling cloths on them, and a mantelpiece that had a framed photo of four men huddled together, arms on shoulders, smiling, on board Wilson's boat.

Sign picked up the photo. "Wilson, Taylor, Green, and Jackson." He turned the picture around. There was a label on the back. Handwritten on the label was 'Feb 2017. Beers and fishing day'." Sign opened the frame and withdrew the photo. There was no inscription of any kind on the front or back.

Knutsen was rummaging through the chest of drawers. "Bills. More bills! Phone charger leads. A bottle of aerosol deodorant. Passport in Wilson's name. Bank statements. Loose coins. Cream for cracked heels. First aid kit. Packet of condoms – unopened. Tea towels. Nothing else."

Sign said, "Take the bills and the bank statements." He looked at the photo. "I wonder who took this shot." He carefully rolled the photo up and placed it in his fleece pocket. Leaning against the wall in the corner of the room was a shotgun. Sign examined the weapon. "This hasn't been fired for a long time." He put the shotgun back against the wall. "There's nothing more we can do here."

Knutsen placed Wilson's paperwork in his backpack. "If only we had the murdered men's mobile phones. We'd be able to find the fifth man in seconds."

Sign shared his frustration. "Navy divers searched the seabed underneath Wilson's boat. It was a futile task. Tides and currents could have taken the mobile phones anywhere, *if* they were thrown overboard after Wilson and his men were killed. There are two other possibilities: the Argentinians took the phones back to their country; or the fifth man took them because he didn't want the police to know he'd been roped into the mad escapade that night."

"The police analyse the phones. They identify the man who supplied the men with military weapons."

"Yes, but would he have had time to get their phones, with the spy boat so close? His priority was to escape." Sign moved to the centre of the room, staring at nothing while deep in thought. "It remains a hypothesis. And by definition, a hypothesis is an idea that can only be proved or disproved by evidence. We need more than evidence. We need fact. My hypothesis is that the fifth man is a loner and a survivalist. He is an islander; not an ex-military foreigner. He is fit. I posit that he may be in his thirties or forties, no younger, though folk around here are hardy so it could be he's in his fifties or sixties. I will tag another label to my imaginary profile of our quarry: he knows seamanship. Getting an emergency craft off deck and into the sea while under gunfire, boarding the vessel, and rowing it to shore, is no mean feat."

"So, he's a fisherman." Knutsen wanted to leave the house. There was no heating on. It was at least minus ten degrees.

"*Maybe* he's a fisherman. Certainly he knows the sea." He nodded his head, his voice quieter as he said, "What bothers me are the missing phones. If the Argentinians have them why haven't they done something about the fifth man?"

"Killed him. In which case the police would be aware that there's been another murder of an islander."

"Precisely. It would have been impossible for the spy ship not to have spotted the fifth man on Wilson's vessel. And it would have been impossible for the spy ship crew not to have seen him escape. But they had work to do. They had to cleanse Wilson's boat, dump the bodies into the sea, and get back to Argentina. They couldn't risk chasing the fifth man to shore." Sign frowned. "Why isn't the fifth man dead? It's because he hasn't been identified. If the Argentinians knew who he was he'd be shot by them in a nanosecond, so to speak. They absolutely *must* cover their tracks about what they did that night. The consequences for them if they didn't would be awful. The mobile phones may have been tossed overboard by the Argentinians, or they may - by some miracle - have been grabbed by the fifth man while bullets were raining down on him. Most likely they were taken by the Argentinians." Sign looked at Knutsen. "Maybe the evidence never made it to Argentina. Maybe the boat was damaged in the gun fight. The spy ship sunk somewhere between the Falklands and Buenos Aires. Argentina doesn't have the phones. The fifth man doesn't have the phones. They are forever lost." He looked grave as he said, "But Argentina will want the fifth man as much as we want him."

"Maybe they don't know about the fifth man."

Sign shook his head. "With the technology on their boat, the Argentinian spies wouldn't have missed a thing. They'd have seen the fifth man rowing to shore." He ran fingers through his hair. "This is so terribly annoying and dangerous."

Knutsen was puzzled. "Dangerous."

Sign snapped, "Idiot Richards and his idiot boss, the chief of defence staff, are gunning for a fight with Argentina. In turn, Argentina will pull out the stops to prevent that from happening. We and the fifth man are in the middle."

Knutsen walked to the front door. "There's an Argentinian special forces assassination squad here now, isn't there?"

Sign walked past him and out of the house. "Yes there is."

That evening Sign prepared a beef bourgeon and placed it in the oven, while Knutsen analysed Wilson's bank statements and bills. Sign walked out of the cottage and looked at Bluff Cove. He knew the penguins would be there, huddled together. He imagined they be feeling miserable as they tried to sleep. But he couldn't see them or anything else beyond the cottage. It was dark and the moon and stars were hidden by cloud cover; and there was no artificial light for miles around his temporary accommodation. Snow was falling fast, but Sign didn't notice the weather. All he could think of was that somewhere out there was the fifth man. He imagined the man was lonely and frightened. The fifth man couldn't trust anyone, least of all the police and the British military. Sign was convinced he'd not only supplied guns to Wilson and his friends, he'd also engaged the Argentinians. Post combat trauma was likely. Sign knew all about that.

He shivered in the cold, bleak weather. But he stayed for a few more minutes, collecting his thoughts. He wondered if what he and Knutsen were doing had moral purpose. There was a case to be made to let the fifth man stay off the radar in order to avoid a British assault on Argentina. Sign didn't want war. He'd seen too much death in his career to revel at the prospect of witnessing more death, thanks to his actions. But, if his hunch was correct that there was an Argentinian death squad on the islands the fifth man was a dead man walking unless he and Knutsen could get to him first. Sign was adept at looking at the big picture, protecting the national interest of Great Britain. But, so often in the front line field of special operations in came down to protecting those around you – your foreign agents, colleagues, civilians who'd helped you. Sign didn't know the fifth man, but he did feel a connection to his plight. On that basis, Sign and Knutsen's job in hand had integrity and honour. What Sign didn't yet know is what he'd do when he found the fifth man. Hand him over to Richards? Or debrief the man and tell him how he could go into permanent hiding? The latter option would involve him having to lie to Richards and his boss. Still, Sign had never been averse to lying to people in power.

He re-entered the cottage. The smell of the casserole pervaded the lounge and kitchen. Knutsen was sitting in front of the log burner, clutching Wilson's papers.

Sign sat opposite him. "What do you make of the documents?"

Knutsen sighed. "For the most part there's nothing that leaps out from the invoices and bank statements. It's all standard stuff – debit card transactions for the grocery store in Stanley, purchase of petrol, vehicle repairs, rent and utilities, bank transfers to suppliers – all of them fishing related, cash withdrawals, itemised sales of fish, tax returns, purchase of clothes, and on and on. In other words, regular stuff that a single guy would do with his cash and fishing income."

"The cash withdrawals – what was the pattern of behaviour in terms of typical amounts withdrawn?"

Knutsen smiled. "Twenty pounds here, thirty pounds there. But you've spotted the one thing that has perplexed me. On the day before his death he withdrew five hundred pounds. At six PM on the evening of his death he withdrew a further five hundred pounds. I'm guessing five hundred pounds per day is his maximum withdrawal limit permitted by his bank."

"Yes. But, he needed a thousand pounds in cash and he needed it urgently. The money won't have been for a knees-up in Sally's bar on the night of his murder. The amount is too exact and way beyond what four men could spend in one night in a modest coastal pub."

"Maybe he had medical bills to pay."

"With cash? No."

"Purchase of illegal narcotics? Sally said she smoked cannabis between shifts. Maybe there's an underground cottage industry on the islands. Or Wilson and his mates were smuggling in drugs and needed to pay their suppliers."

Sign waved a hand dismissively. "One thousand pounds wouldn't cover the costs of a covert return trip in Wilson's boat to South America to buy drugs. And with a population of approximately three thousand, the islands simply don't have enough people who ingest narcotics to demand such a trade. If, on the other hand, a small number of islanders are growing cannabis locally, one thousand pounds strikes me as a significant amount of money to buy – as, I believe, you cops and criminals call it – weed. Am I correct?"

Knutsen shrugged. "It's possible to spend that amount of money for personal use. Cannabis takes a while to grow and harvest. When it's cropped, it can take months for the next batch to be ready. Maybe Wilson was bulk buying to see him through the winter and spring."

"From what we know about Wilson, he doesn't strike me as a druggy. Drink was his tipple of choice. And he had no traces of narcotics in his system when the post-mortem was conducted. And his lifestyle – hardworking, hard drinking, up at four AM to strike the fishing grounds. No. His profile doesn't match that of a drug user."

Knutsen laughed. "You don't know much about drug users."

"Maybe not. But, there is one thing notable about the transactions. They were urgent."

"Five hundred pounds one day. Five hundred pounds the next."

"And both within a forty eight hour period that culminated in his death. The coincidence is too great. This is not about drugs. But I do suspect it is to do with something else illegal."

Knutsen put the papers to one side.

Sign was deep in thought. "We have no facts. All we can rely on is our imagination. Let's suppose that Wilson got it in to his head that he wanted to confront the spy ship. To do that he needed guns. There was a man on the islands who could supply the guns. But he wasn't Wilson's friend. He was the fifth man. And the fifth man wasn't going to part with his guns and assist him unless there was a business transaction to be had. The man demanded one thousand pounds, payable on the night he delivered the guns and joined Wilson, Taylor, Green, and Jackson on the trawler."

"It holds together, but it is only a hunch."

"I prefer the word *theory*." Sign stared at the fire. In a quiet voice he said, "My experience in life has not been a cold-hard-facts-police-procedural approach towards the problems I confronted. The issues I faced overseas were far more nuanced. And, I worked alone in hostile territories. I had no team of analysts and cops to support my work. I had to make my own judgements. Very often that meant that I had to deal with the realms of the possible. And the starting point for that approach rested in my head." He looked at Knutsen. "My instincts are telling me that the one thousand pounds was a cash-for-guns transaction."

"If that's true, why did the fifth man join them on the boat that night? Why didn't he just give Wilson the guns and tell him to return them when the job was done? Or, maybe the guns were sold to Wilson and didn't need to be returned. Either way, I don't understand why he risked his neck that night by joining a bunch of drunken blokes who were not his mates."

"When we find the fifth man, we will pose that question to him. For now, there are many possibilities. What would you say is the strongest reason for him being there during the battle?"

"It could be he didn't trust Wilson. Maybe he was only going to be paid after the job. So, he tagged along to keep an eye on his guns and Wilson. But, I think the strongest possibility rests on a more simple and immediate imperative – the fifth man wanted a fight with the Argentinian spy boat."

"Bravo, Mr. Knutsen. Simplicity is usually the route to the truth. Almost certainly you are right. Testosterone-fuelled aggression came in to play, requiring the fifth man to join the combatants. His anger against Argentina would have been simmering within the fifth man for years but not bubbling over. Until now. The spy boat was a tipping point."

"He lost the plot."

"Yes." Sign stood when the oven alarm pinged, telling him their dinner was ready. He seemed distracted when he said, "However…"

"What?"

"Oh, it's probably nothing."

"There's something you're not telling me," said Knutsen in a firm voice.

"I have a theory I've been carrying in my head ever since we first met Colonel Richards in London. It may amount to nothing or something." Sign held up his hand before Knutsen could ask more questions. He smiled. "We must eat, dear chap. There is nothing more that can be achieved this evening."

"What are our tasks tomorrow?"

Sign folded his arms. "This is indeed a difficult case. Sally, Carl, and Nick have not proven instructive. Nor should they be. They were simply witnesses to Wilson and his friends' behaviour in the bar. But, it is nevertheless regrettable that they have no inkling as to who may have joined the men on that fateful night"

"Could we ask the police to tell the islanders that any person involved in the escapade will not be prosecuted? Maybe the fifth man would then come forward."

"Were it so simple. Richards wouldn't allow that to happen. He wants secrecy. In conjunction with the Ministry of Defence in London he's preparing not only for the protection of the islands but also to use the archipelagos to be used as a launch pad for hostilities."

"How do you know this?"

"Logic and my analysis of Richards. But, Richards is also hampered by his impotency in this situation. He can't go public on anything. We're here because he can't use the police and military investigators. If he does, the cat will be out of the bag. As it is, Sally thinks you and I are merely meddling private investigators from England; Carl and Nick think we're scientists from South Georgia; and Richards has agreed to our cover as high-ranking army officers visiting the islands for an unspecified task." Sign kept talking as he went into the adjacent kitchen and served up dinner. To accompany the beef bourgeon he'd prepared double-fried chips, diced cabbage mixed with crispy lardons and chillies, and slithers of boiled carrots. "Tomorrow we must meet Richards." He returned with two plates of the food and cutlery. "As usual, we eat on our laps, in front of the fire."

Knutsen asked, "Why Richards?"

"Oh, just to see if there's something he's not telling me."

Knutsen ate a mouthful of the casserole. As usual Sign's food was delicious. Knutsen wondered how Sign conjured up such world class cuisine, even in locations where local produce was basic and limited. "You must have some other ideas as to what we can do. Use that brilliant brain of yours." The latter comment was said with sarcasm.

Sign breathed in deeply. "It is for you to decide whether I'm brilliant or stupid. But I can tell you categorically that I'm not a magician. I can't conjure something substantial out of something insubstantial. I'm running out of options to source the fifth man."

Knutsen replied, "If this was a police operation, faced with the same problems in a murder investigation, we'd do door-to-door. Maybe that's what we should do – simply knock on every door on the islands until we get answers."

Sign ate his food. "It would be relatively easier in the western areas of the islands, where the population is spread out. Not so easy in Stanley. The population of the Falklands is just over three thousand, on top of which are military personnel. But, restricting our search to islanders would mean we'd have to ascertain how many houses we'd have to knock on and how many interviews we'd have to conduct. Let's make an assumption that the average household on the islands contains three people. It won't be accurate because some houses will contain four or more people and others will only contain one. But the mean of those variables gives us approximately a headcount of three per property. So, we'd have one thousand houses to visit, spread across the islands, in the bleakest winter the Falklands has known for years. We could possibly do a maximum of ten households per day in Stanley. With its population of two thousand plus, divided by three, further divided by ten, it would take us sixty six days to cover Stanley. Then there's the remaining one thousand people spread across the islands. We'd be lucky to interview more than two or three in a day." He was silent while finishing his food, before placing his empty dinner plate to one side. "Door-to-door would take us a minimum of three months. More likely six."

Knutsen placed his empty plate on top of Sign's plate. "It's still worth a thought." He smiled. "After all, we're not going anywhere for now. All planes out of here are grounded. We're trapped."

"We don't have the luxury of time."

Knutsen placed another log in the fire. "Maybe the fifth man has left the islands on a plane."

Sign shook his head. "Since the night of the murders there have only been four flights that have landed on the islands. Two were from Brize Norton. You, me, and Richards were on one of them. There have also been two flights from Santiago. The planes have left but were not allowed to carry passengers due to the severity of the weather. Since those flights, all incoming and outgoing flights have been cancelled until the weather clears. There is the option that the fifth man is a sailor and took his boat to Argentina, but…"

"He'd be sailing to the last place on Earth he'd want to be."

"Yes. The fifth man is on the islands. Now, no one can come in; no one can get out. We are on Alcatraz until flights are resumed."

Knutsen rubbed his face. "We should check the flight manifests of the incoming planes from Santiago and Brize Norton. If, as you suspect, there's a four person assassination unit looking for the fifth man, they'd have been on one of those flights."

"I will be requesting that data from Richards tomorrow." Sign stared at the burning logs. "We have different agendas but I sympathise with the Argentinians. They are in the same mire as us. How do they find the fifth man?"

"They'll know Wilson, Taylor, Green, and Jackson's names. The drunken idiots would have been carrying their ID on them. When the Argentinians boarded Wilson's boat, they'll have searched them before chucking the bodies overboard. No wallets or any other forms of ID were found on their bodies. That means the assassination unit has the same starting point as we have – the identity of the dead men. Nothing more, nothing less."

"Correct. So what do they do?" Sign bowed his head and was silent for a minute. "The Argentinian unit will be on the islands under alias. The operatives will have been chosen for their looks and their command of language. They'll be posing as British, South Africans, New Zealanders, or Australians. Maybe the unit will take one nationality apiece."

"Why not United States nationality?"

"They'd stand out too much if the posed as north Americans. There are no legitimate US citizens working on the islands. Nor does the States have a reason to deploy workers here. The Falklands is a thoroughly British protectorate with solely British interests in trade and security."

Knutsen said, "Put bluntly, the States and its businesses can't be bothered with the islands."

"You could put it that way. I'd put it in more polite terms. The United States simply cannot see any business opportunities here. It knows that Britain would squeeze them out. Thus, an American on the archipelago would stand out like a sore thumb. However, there is a track record of South Africans, Kiwis, and Australians working here in a variety of temporary roles – engineers, traders, lawyers, insurance experts, vets, geologists, builders, et cetera." Sign listed his head. "When I see the flight manifests, I'm eighty percent certain I'll be able to identify the assassination squad. The question is: what do we do with that information?"

"If we have their fake names, we could take them to the governor of the Falklands and advise him to expel them."

Sign shook his head. "On what basis? That they may or may not be assassins? If they were legitimate Australians or whatever, we could risk opening up a can of worms. We need to keep this investigation discrete. That's why Richards brought us in. The governor knows about the murders. I very much doubt he knows about the fifth man. He will most certainly not have deduced there is a strong probability that Argentina has sent covert operatives onto his islands. Even Richards won't have thought that far ahead."

"Will the Argentinian unit be operating together?"

"No. Not until the last minute. For now they'll be in investigation mode. That means they'll be in a divide-and-conquer drill – each of them pursuing their own leads, minimal contact with each other unless something urgent arises, lodging at separate properties. Their drill will change when they identify the fifth man. That's when they'll come together in order to eliminate him and escape the islands."

Knutsen drummed his fingers. In a forthright voice he said, "If we come onto their radar, they'll come for us; probably torture us to find out what we know."

"If they attempt that, you kill them." Sign's eyes were twinkling as he smiled and added, "I gave you a gun for a reason. And remember – outside of Stanley, everything is bandit country. Bad things can happen west of the capital and not be discovered for weeks, months, or ever. If they come for us, gun them down. You and I will deal with the bodies."

"Richards has authorised this?"

"Not in so many words. He gave me the gun you're carrying in order for us to protect ourselves. But, the word *protect* is open to interpretation. That said, I'd prefer an outcome wherein anything extreme we do does not come to the attention of the authorities – Richards included."

Knutsen laughed. "This will be a first – me taking on a highly trained hit squad."

"You are up to the task." Sign placed his hand on Knutsen's shoulder. "You will not be alone. I will be there to help." He stood and said in a serious tone of voice, "Mr. Knutsen, we are swimming in murky and dangerous waters. Instead of swimming for shore, we must venture further away from safety."

"Only you could come up such a melodramatic statement." Knutsen's expression became serious. "That said, I get the point." He looked out of the window. There was nothing but black out there. To himself, quietly he said, "I didn't expect to die in a place like this."

CHAPTER 9

The following morning Casero woke up in his hotel, showered, shaved with a triple blade razor, and dressed into a two hundred pound white shirt, one thousand two hundred pound Saville Row charcoal suit, immaculate leather black shoes, and a silk tie befitting of British government mandarins and generals. Before arriving in the Falklands, he'd ensured his hair was clipped in the style of English army officers – not long, but not too short; rather that of a man who was posing as a gentleman in important service. He applied dabs of Harvey Nichols aftershave to his throat, placed his fake passport into his pocket, grabbed his wallet and car keys, donned an expensive heavy woollen overcoat, and stood in front of a full-length mirror. He smiled. He looked every inch the persona he wished to convey.

He left the hotel and drove across Stanley. The house he was seeking was almost the last property on the outskirts of the capital; overlooking the sea, modest in size, a small garden in front. He stopped his hire car outside the home's fence, got out, and rang the front door bell.

A woman in her sixties opened the door. "Yes?"

Casero spoke with impeccable English, with an accent that suggested he'd been schooled in Eton or Harrow before receiving further education in Oxford or Cambridge. "Mrs. Wilson. My name is Peter Sillitoe. I am a representative of Her Majesty's government. I have flown to the islands from London with the express intention of speaking to you about your son's tragic death. May I come in?"

The woman looked confused. "What's there to talk about? My son drowned with his friends." Her bottom lip trembled. "I had to identify his body. The police interviewed me. Then the army. I had to bury him. What more can I do?"

"My sincerest condolences, Mrs. Wilson. This won't take long, I can assure you. I'm not here to cause you further anguish. Nor do I wish to besmirch your good son's name. I represent a government department that wishes to ascertain whether your son's accident was in any way prompted by the presence of a nearby Argentinian ship. Do you know what I'm referring to?"

Wilson's mother nodded. "We all know about that boat. It's gone now. Hasn't been seen since Eddie died." She looked back down her hallway, seeming uncertain. "Alright. Come in." She led Casero into her lounge. "Would you like tea?"

"That's very kind but I had a cuppa just before coming here." He sat on one of the chairs.

She looked suspicious as she sat near him. "Which British government department do you work for?"

Casero looked away. "It's delicate." He reengaged eye contact with her. "Let's just say I deal with problems that are of interest to our prime minister."

"You're a spook then?"

He smiled. "Were it so easy to be candid." His expression turned serious. "I don't represent the military bases here. Nor do I represent the governor of the islands. In fact, they don't know I'm here. I am an emissary and guardian of London's gates. If you talk to me you are talking to power."

"How can you prove you are who you say you are?"

Casero waved a hand dismissively. "I can't. There are numbers you could call in London. They're freely available on the Internet. Alas, it is government policy not to respond to any enquiries pertaining to members of staff. You must trust me, or not. All I can say is that I'm here to help."

Mrs. Wilson picked up a framed photo from the adjacent coffee table. She stared at the picture. "My boys." She wiped a tear away. "My son. Bob Taylor. Billy Green. Mike Jackson. They were so close in life. Together in death." She placed the photo back on the table. "They were good lads. They didn't deserve this."

Casero looked at the picture, memorising their faces. "What did the police tell you about the incident?"

"You should have all the facts!"

"I do but sometimes facts overwhelm nuances. I'd dearly like to know your take on matters." He placed his fingertips together and was silent as he waited for her response.

She breathed deeply. "I don't know anything more than you know. That bloody Argie spy ship has been nipping at the islands' ankles for a couple of months. It annoyed everyone here, though didn't cause us any harm. But it was like, you know, an insult to us. Eddie in particular hated it being in his fishing waters. I could see he was getting more and more angry with it being here."

"How often did you see Eddie?"

"At least once a week. My husband passed away two years ago. Eddie came here to check on me and do work around the house if needed."

"So, you were gifted with a good barometer for his temperature?"

"What?"

"You could tell his mood."

"Yes, yes." She wrung her hands. "But, he was a quiet lad and didn't give much away in words. I could tell, though, from his eyes and the odd comment he made. He wasn't happy with the Argie ship. He blamed the British military for doing nothing about it. After his death, the police and military didn't tell me anything about why he was out on his boat that night. He fishes when he has to but for the most part he had a routine – night fishing, day fishing, twelve hours rest in between. One day off a week if he can get it. And he was getting drunk in Sally's pub in Stanley on the night of his death. As you know, Rob, Billy, and Mike were with him. Eddie never drinks before sailing. It makes no sense for him to have suddenly decided to do a night fish. Anyway, Rob and Mike aren't fisherman. I can't see why they'd have been on the boat with him, hauling in nets."

"And that is why I've been sent to see you. The police and military are in no doubt that this was a tragic accident. I agree with their conclusion. I'm sure it would give you greater peace if there was a better reason for your son's death than simply a drunken slip into the water. Did the coroner tell you about weather conditions that night?"

She nodded. "She told me that the navy said the weather was atrocious that night; that there were swells and fast tides. They should never have gone out that night."

Casero chose his next words carefully. "Do you think the Argentinian ship was in any way responsible for the accident? Maybe it crossed your son's path and caused him to make an emergency manoeuvre. Or something similar."

Floods of tears were coursing down Mrs. Wilson's face. "I don't think so. Eddie knew these waters. My guess is he and his friends went out there on some drunken rampage, got close to the spy ship, went on deck with beers, and started hurling insults at the Argies. They got hit by a wave or whatever. That's when they went overboard."

"I regret to say that we agree with your analysis. As you say, The Argentinian boat has gone. We know that." Casero chose his next words carefully. "It is a shame that there were no witnesses to the incident. The Argentinians on their ship may have seen what happened but they are of no use to us. We've made a formal request to the Argentinian government for assistance. Predictably they denied having a spy boat in the islands' waters. I wonder though." Casero faked a look that suggested a thought had just occurred to him. "Would it be possible someone else was on Eddie's boat when the tragedy occurred? Maybe that person also drowned but his body was washed out to sea. Or maybe he survived but is either too embarrassed or traumatised to come forward to local authorities."

Mrs. Wilson looked perplexed. "Another man? None of you lot have asked me that question before. I don't think so. Can't see how that could happen. Eddie had three friends. That's all he needed."

"Did he ever mention anyone else to you – an islander whom he had dealings with?"

She looked exasperated. "Everyone here has dealings with other islanders. We're a small community. We rely on each other."

"In particular, I wonder if there was anyone that Eddie knew who would be keen to join his crew in order to taunt the Argentinian boat. It would probably be a male; someone who hated the spy ship; maybe a drinker, maybe not."

"You're talking about every man on these islands. But, no. Eddie never mentioned to me anyone who might be the type to join him, Rob, Billy, and Mike. Why do you think there might have been someone else on the boat?"

Casero shrugged. "I don't. It's just wishful thinking on my part. I have to pursue every line of enquiry. I fear that when the weather abates I must fly back to London and advise my masters that there is nothing to report." He stood. "Once again, I'm so sorry for your loss. And I'm sorry to have intruded on your grief. Thank you for your time Mrs. Wilson."

When he was in his car, Casero called Fontonia. "I have a lead - Sally who runs a pub in Stanley. The men were heavily drinking in the bar on the night of the incident. See if she knows anything about a fifth man."

Sign was wearing a suit as he attended the headquarters of RAF Mount Pleasant. After getting through security checks, he was ushered to a room where he sat and waited.

A young RAF woman opened the adjacent door and said to Sign, "The colonel will see you now." She left the door open and exited the room.

Sign entered Colonel Richards' office. It was large and contained an oak desk at the far end of the room, behind it were windows overlooking the runway, chairs facing the desk, and wall-mounted pictures of previous military commanders of the base.

Richards was sitting at his desk, rifling through paperwork. "Mr. Sign. What do you have for me?"

Sign sat on one of the seats. "I'm not here to report progress. Instead, I'm information gathering. I'd like the flight manifests of every plane that landed here after the death of Wilson and his friends."

Richards frowned. "What use would they be to you? You should be concerned about who's left the islands after the incident, not who's come in."

Sign lied. "I'm wondering if someone came in to help the fifth man. Maybe a relative or friend. No one has been able to leave the islands since the gun battle. Thus, if a relative or friend of our mysterious witness came here, then that person is still here. He or she won't be able to leave until the RAF permits flights to recommence normal duties. I'm particularly interested in passengers who may have a connection to the islands. That means most likely the person was on one of the two Brize Norton flights that left England after Wilson, Taylor, Green, and Jackson were murdered. But – belt and braces – I'd also like to check the manifests of the two Santiago flights that arrived before lockdown was imposed."

Richards was unconcerned with the request. "As you wish. I can't see the point, but I suppose you have to check all angles." He made an internal phone call. "Flight manifests for the four planes that arrived before we suspended passenger flights." He hung up and looked at Sign. "Have you made *any* progress?"

Sign smiled. "None whatsoever. Knutsen and I have interviewed some locals but so far we've not ascertained any new data."

"I paid you to get quick results!"

Sign held the Royal Marines commander's gaze. "*You* didn't pay me. The Ministry of Defence paid me. The MOD reports to the minister of defence who in turn reports to the prime minister. Shall I call the PM and tell her that we have a problem? She'll do what I tell her to do. She'll ignore you and the chief of defence staff. You'd be on the next flight out of here, enjoying early retirement and beekeeping in Surrey, or such place."

Richards' face reddened. "You have no right to talk to me like…"

"Yes I do, Richards." Sign maintained his calm persona and tone of voice. "Know your place. You brought me in to solve this riddle. But, I am not your employee. Until this case is closed you are *my* employee." Sign crossed his legs and clasped his hands. "If I find the fifth man what are your plans?"

"That's classified!"

"Not from me. You've already told me that you're planning war. Your islands would be the launch pad for a strike on Argentina. It would be a nice feather in your cap before you retire. The chief of defence will no doubt promote you to brigadier before you leave government service. That will be a nice hike in your pension. You have a vested interest in the death of Argentinians."

Richards sighed. "If you get a testimony from the fifth man, one that clearly identifies the Argentinian ship as the perpetrators of murder, we will punish Argentina. There will be air strikes on their military bases, naval bombardments of ships and docks, and air strikes on communications systems. Then, we will back off because the point will have been made. It will be a sledgehammer to crack a nut. The end game is, for once and for all, to get Argentina to forget the phrase *Islas Malvinas*. We maintain our security and strike capability in this part of the southern hemisphere. The Argentinians fuck off for good."

"It is ever thus that countries like Britain want to carve up the world according to their perceived needs." Sign was nonchalant as he said, "You pretend that you want to protect a few sheep and their owners, wherein the truth is you want a military platform. To you the Falklands is in essence a massive, static, aircraft carrier."

"And I have no problems with that. It's my job."

"Indeed it is." Sign decided to change tack. "My job is different. Knutsen and I will continue our investigation until we solve this problem. The task in hand is difficult. We just need to find an access agent."

"Meaning?"

"Someone who knows who the fifth man might be. That person can then facilitate a meeting with the fifth man. Depending on circumstances, that introduction will either be done with or without the access agent's knowledge that Knutsen and I will be there to pounce on our target."

Richards sighed. "I can't be bothered to ask you what that spy stuff means. But I can be bothered to tell you that we need fast results. What are your next steps?"

"Knutsen and I will continue interviewing locals. But in tandem the flight manifests may speed up matters. I presume there is still no sight of the spy ship, or any other Argentinian presence in our waters?"

"Correct."

"So, the islands are safe."

"For now."

Sign nodded. "Good. Are you still deploying army routine foot patrols on the islands?"

"Of course. A bit of snow doesn't stop our security protocols."

"Cancel all patrols. Restrict your men and women to your bases. And tell the police not to do routine patrols; rather to only respond to emergency situations."

"What?! That would be absurd! It would serve no purpose."

Sign said, "It would produce an aura of calm. The fifth man will continue to lay low if he thinks he's being watched by authorities. I want him to think that the weather has gotten the better of your men and that they are putting their feet up in their barracks. Ditto the police. I want them to be brewing tea and coffee in their station and playing cards to kill time."

"I have no jurisdiction over the police! The governor of the Falklands is the only person who could issue such an order to his law enforcement officers"

"Technically you have no jurisdiction over the governor. In practice you do. Tell him to stand his officers down from all but the most critical incidents. Lie to him. Say to him that there is a team of investigators on the islands searching for a wanted man who's fled from England to the islands. Tell him that a lack of police presence will allow us to do our job. Do not name me or Knutsen. Conclude that this is only a temporary situation until the man is captured."

Richards was incredulous. "You're telling me – the military commander of the Falklands – and the governor – the highest ranking politician on the islands – to not do our jobs over the coming few days or weeks?!"

"Yes." Sign elaborated. "The weather is atrocious. It would not seem odd if locals saw the suspension of routine military and police patrols. But, the locals are hardy folk. They'd think you're weak and would laugh at your inability to continue normal business while they carry on with work regardless of conditions. If my assessment is correct that the fifth man is a local, he too will think it's a joke that an eight man unit of British soldiers thought it was too treacherous to venture out of Stanley, that your helicopters won't take off, that police are worried about getting their cars stuck in snow drifts. The fifth man needs to make a living, doing whatever it is he does. Zero sight of military personnel and cops with the power to arrest will induce complacency in him. In other words, he will come out of hiding."

Richards couldn't believe he was hearing this. "I could be court martialled for issuing such an order and for lying to the governor."

"I will make a call to the powers that be to ensure you are not chastised. On the contrary, I will say that you came up with this ingenious plan whilst cognisant that there is currently no threat to the Falklands. In Whitehall, you will be lauded as brave and smart. It will be another feather in your cap."

Richards looked confused. "I... Of course I have authority to do this. But, to all intents and purposes you're making the islands a lawless territory."

"Only for a brief period. Once we get the fifth man, we bring him in, normal duties resume, and you can have your war. And if you want your war, you have no alternatives. The fifth man is key. Without him you have nothing other than speculation. No fifth man, no war." Sign was silent as he stared at Richards.

Richards bowed his head for twenty seconds. He looked up and said in a quiet voice, "You really are a piece of work. I'll do it. Just make sure you make that call to Whitehall. The flight manifests are with my secretary in the adjacent room. Unless there's any further business to discuss, I bid you good day!"

Mrs. Wilson was outside her house, using a shovel to shift snow from her driveway. The task was backbreaking, compounded by the arthritis in her wrists and fingers. She was making little progress. But the job had to be done. She had a two wheel drive vehicle in her garage that, with the flick of a dashboard switch, could be transformed into four wheel drive. Alas, the switch no longer worked. Snow was a major problem. The roads in Stanley were regularly cleared. But that was of no use to her unless she could get her vehicle out of the driveway. She winced as she persisted with the task. She knew it was fruitless. There was at least a ton of snow to clear and more of it was pouring from the sky. If only Eddie was here. He'd have gotten the job done in a jiffy.

Knutsen stopped his vehicle on the road by her house. He got out and approached the woman who was oblivious to his presence. "Mrs. Wilson?"

She stood up and turned toward him, wincing as she rubbed her back. "Yes. Who are you and what do you want? I'm busy."

"I can see that. My name is Tom Knutsen. I'm a scientist, working with the British Antarctic Survey in South Georgia. I specialise in the southern hemisphere oceans."

"What's that got to do with me?"

"I've been sent here to see why your son and his three friends fell off their boat on the night they died. If it was a human error, then the matter is out of my field of expertise. If, however, it was down to a natural phenomenon such as a swell or a tidal wave, then I'd be interested to ascertain why we were unable to predict such changes in sea behaviour."

Mrs. Wilson was angry. "Do you think I have a clue what the sea was doing when my Eddie died?! Fishing's been in my family for generations. But I've never been on a boat. I've got other things to worry about. You're speaking to the wrong person."

"I do apologise. I wonder if you have a theory about Eddie's death."

She walked up to him. "My husband – Eddie's dad – is dead. The sea got him. He died in bed in this house; but he might as well have been swallowed up by the waters out there. A lifetime of working the nets will do that to a body. He died a smashed up man. Eddie knew what he was getting into when he took over the business. He knew the risks. Fancy scientists like you don't know what a hard day's work is. The sea's a cruel mistress, my grandfather used to say. He was right about that." She continued shovelling snow, her teeth gritted as she struggled with pain.

Knutsen placed a hand on the shovel. "Let me help you. In return, I could do with a cup of tea."

She was hesitant. Then she handed Knutsen the shovel and entered her house.

It took Knutsen thirty minutes to clear the driveway.

Mrs. Wilson came out with a mug of tea. "Thank you." She handed the mug to Knutsen and sighed as she looked upwards. "Another night of this snow means that what you've done will have been pointless."

Knutsen drank the hot brew while breathing fast. "You could grit and salt your driveway. Or you could park your car on the road."

Mrs. Wilson stood next to him and looked at the nearby road. "Grit and salt don't do anything when the weather's this bad. Only snowploughs can keep the roads clear. Yes. I'll park my car on the road. I wish my husband and Eddie were here."

Knutsen looked at her.

She didn't look at him. Instead, she looked at the sea. "Why are so many people interested in my son's death?"

"I didn't know they were."

"Police; army; this government bloke this morning; you. My son drowned because…"

"The sea is a cruel mistress." Knutsen slammed the shovel into the bank of snow adjacent to the driveway. "Out of interest, who was the government man who came to visit you this morning? I thought I was the only one investigating the sea conditions on the night of your son's accident."

Mrs. Wilson shivered. "He wasn't a scientist; I can tell you that. I don't quite know what he wanted. London government type. He was more interested in the Argie spy ship. I reckon he was a British spook."

Knutsen faked a relaxed demeanour. "Oh, that makes sense. I know London was worried that the Argentinian ship might have sailed in front of your son's trawler on the night of the accident. I don't think that's what happened. But before I leave the islands I need to file my report to the British Antarctic Survey. If British Intelligence is investigating the Argentinian ship, a copy of my report will need to be submitted to them. He was probably using a fake name but did the man who visited you this morning give you any form of identification? I may know him."

She frowned. "Why would he give me a fake name?"

"Standard practise. Don't worry. It just means he wants to be anonymous. And he's obviously trying to do the right thing by you."

This line seemed to placate Mrs. Wilson. "He told me his name is Peter Sillitoe."

"That name doesn't ring a bell. Then again, lots of people come and go through the islands. That said, I'm staying in the officer's quarters in RAF Mount Pleasant. Maybe he's staying there as well. What does he look like?"

She shrugged. "Mid to late thirties, I'd say. About your height. Well dressed. Well spoken. Brown hair cut like, you know, army officers have it cut – not like squaddies. Clean shaven."

Knutsen smiled. "That sounds like most people in the officers' quarters. Did he give you his mobile number?"

"No."

"That's a shame. If he comes back could you ask him for his number? I'd like to swap notes with him on this case."

Mrs. Wilson nodded.

Knutsen gave her a slip of paper containing his mobile number. "If anything occurs to you please don't hesitate to call me." He walked down the driveway. "And don't forget to put your car on the road."

As he was driving back to his cottage, he called Sign. "Are you still with Richards?"

"No."

Knutsen told him who he'd just visited. "Does the name Peter Sillitoe mean anything to you? He's allegedly British Intelligence. I presume MI6. He visited Wilson's mother this morning."

"No, but if he were MI6 he'd be using an alias."

"Did you get the flight manifests?"

"Yes, but if you're expecting me to find the name Sillitoe in there you'll be mistaken. He'll have travelled in here under one alias and he'll be operating on the ground with another alias. Meet me at the cottage. We've work to do."

An hour later Knutsen arrived at the Bluff Cove cottage. Light was fading. The temperature was minus fifteen degrees Celsius. As he entered the warm interior of the house, Knutsen could smell the rich aroma of food. The log burner was lit. Sign was sitting next to the fire, wearing his suit trousers and shirt, no tie. He was analysing the flight manifests.

"What's on the menu tonight?" asked Knutsen.

Sign didn't look up. "Chicken pan-fried in butter, with herbs, salt and pepper, and a sprinkle of paprika. I've made a red wine sauce, with sweated onions and seasoning, that's been simmering and reducing for the last hour. Thirty minutes prior to plating up, I'll also be cooking spicy sautéed potatoes and vegetables."

Knutsen sat opposite him. "Is there anything interesting in the flight manifests?"

Sign nodded. "In the two Brize Norton flights to the islands, the majority of passengers were military personnel. I've spent the afternoon on the phone to Richards' secretary. She's confirmed their identities. Over and above that, fifteen passengers are islanders. All of them booked their return flights to England months in advance. They're of no use to me. That leaves five passengers who made bookings at short notice – you, me, and Richards, on the first flight, and two women on the second flight."

"The women?"

"A New Zealander called Helen Lock. When she arrived at Mount Pleasant she told immigration that she was a freelance journalist. The other woman is an Australian engineer called Michelle Chandler. She works in Melbourne and the South Pole. Apparently she's here to look up old friends."

"Did they sit together on the flight?"

"No." Sign glanced at the second of the two folders. "The Santiago flights are also illuminating. Once again, many of the passengers are British military personnel, returning to the islands after rest and recuperation. But on the first flight there were eighteen civilians. Twelve of them are islanders; flight bookings were made well in advance of the murders. Of the remaining six, two of them were Chilean holiday makers in their seventies; here to take photos of the star constellations."

"They picked the wrong time of year for that."

"They picked the right time of year to see the most beautiful images of stars. No one predicted the weather would be this bad. Nevertheless we can discount them, due to their age."

"And the remaining four?"

"A Chilean clothes manufacturer who's been trading with the islands for over a decade; a Peruvian timber merchant who's here to sign off on a bill of sale – he has one arm after a logging accident in 2005; a French author who is here to conduct a series of interviews with the governor in order to produce a biography of the man – the interviews were set up eight months ago. None of these people are of interest to me. But, the fourth person is of interest. His passport says he's South African. He's never been to the islands before. He told immigration that he was an insurance expert specialising in shipping. He's here to investigate an insurance claim. His name is Max Bosch. He stands out."

"The other Santiago flight?"

"A similar ratio of profiles. There's only one person of interest. A British diplomat. Name: Henry Parker. I've never heard of him, but that means nothing. If he's Foreign & Commonwealth Office, or another department, there are tens of thousands of people I've never met or heard of. Diplomats are so spread out across the world that for the most part their paths never cross. If, however, he's MI6 and using diplomatic cover, his name will be false. I'd have no way of confirming he's British Intelligence unless I saw his face. He gave immigration no justification for why he was here."

"That must be Sillitoe."

Sign placed the manifests down and sighed. "Sillitoe; Parker – what difference does it matter what he calls himself? Tomorrow he'll use a different name. And that is the issue. If, as I suspect, Lock, Chandler, Bosch, and Parker/Sillitoe are the four person Argentinian assassination unit, while they're on the islands they'll be using whatever names suit them, depending on who they're talking to. It is unlikely that we'll get to them through their names. Their tradecraft will be too good. I expected as much. But my work today has not been a waste of time. On the contrary, it has been instructive. I wanted to see if four people came in to the archipelagos at short notice, bearing passports of nationalities that wouldn't stand out in the islands. Two men and two women did precisely that. Of course, I can't be certain that they are an Argentinian team. But, if I was deploying four killers into the Falklands, I'd make sure my operatives had similar covers. And I'd have to cross my fingers and wish for luck, because the only thing going against the team is they had to deploy at short notice."

"If there is a team on the ground, maybe they came in by other means – boats, submarines, small planes, that kind of thing."

"They wouldn't risk that. If they got stopped and questioned by military or police patrols, they'd want to prove they entered the islands by legitimate means. If they couldn't prove how they got here, this whole situation would be blown wide open. Argentina and Britain don't want what happened on the night of the murders to be made public. One or more Argentinian spies caught on the islands would be information that would eventually get out and would spread like wildfire – not just here, but across the world." Sign smiled. "It is, however, unfortunate they couldn't predict that I'd be here."

"What do you mean?"

"Today I told Richards to cancel all routine army and law enforcement patrols across the islands. To all intents and purposes, you and I are currently the only law in the Falklands. If the Argentine squad had predicted that, they wouldn't have had to enter the islands via planes and fake passports."

Knutsen frowned. "Why did you do that?"

"To make the fifth man feel safe. The last thing he needs is to get twitchy every time a patrol passes near his property. He's been in hiding. I want that to stop."

"But, you could be putting a death sentence on him! If we don't get to him first, the Argentinians will kill him!"

"If we do nothing, the assassination unit will inevitably get to him. We have to take a risk." Sign stood. "I shall get changed into my scruffs before dinner." He paused at the base of the stairs, turned around, and looked at Knutsen. "If only this investigation could have been handed over to the local police. They'd have canvassed the entire islands, appealing for witnesses who could help them with their murder enquiries. Specifically, the police would spread the word that they suspect there was a fifth man with the group and that he should not fear coming forward and telling them what he knows. Alas, matters are significantly more complicated. The islanders knew about the Argentinian spy ship. Some of them knew that Wilson and his friends went out that night to confront the boat. So far the islanders have bought the line that the men drowned due to a drunken accident. To tell them the truth would cause widespread outrage on the islands. But in doing so it would push the fifth man further underground. He's scared for his own skin. So, this is not a police matter; it is an issue of national security. Thus, you and I must be unconventional. And that means we have to play with fire. I have no choice other than to fuel the fire with risk."

At ten thirty that evening, Fontonia entered the pub in Stanley where Sally worked. She was wearing waterproof trousers over her jeans, hiking boots, ski gloves, a woollen hat, and a jacket of the type used by Arctic and Antarctic explorers. There were seven customers in the tiny establishment. Two of them were sitting at a table, playing cards; another three were playing darts; the remaining two were standing by a window, chatting and quaffing their ales. No one was sitting in one of the four barstools that Wilson, Taylor, Green, and Jackson always used when drinking here. Music was playing in the background, but it was quiet. The whole ambience in the room was subdued.

Fontonia sat on a barstool, removed her gloves, and addressed the young woman working behind the bar. "Can I have a double whiskey. Nothing expensive. I just need something to warm me up."

Sally smiled and poured Fontonia her drink.

After paying, Fontonia sipped the spirit and faked a shiver. "God, that's better. I'm not used to this climate."

Sally asked, "Have you arrived in the Falklands recently?"

Fontonia smiled. "You can tell from my accent that I'm not from the islands? Well, you're right. Yeah, I got here a few days ago for a job interview at the military base." She swigged her drink. "Logistics manager. They want someone who can help run the base. I doubt I'll get the job. The guy who interviewed me seemed like a right knob."

Sally laughed. "Where are you from?"

Fontonia drained her drink. "Grew up in Tasmania. But I moved around a lot with work – England, the States, Germany, Hong Kong. Recently I've been living and working in Bermuda. Met a guy there. He moved in with me. A month ago I found out he'd been cheating on me. I kicked him out and applied for the job down here." She slid her glass towards Sally. "I need a change of scenery. But, if this is what your winters are like, I'm not sure I chose wisely."

Sally empathised. Her last boyfriend had cheated on her. "Do you want another drink?"

"One more. After that, I have to hit the road and the sack. I've got a second interview tomorrow morning with knob-face." She downed her drink, stood, and shook hands with Sally. "Thanks for the drinks. My name's Debbie. Wish me luck for tomorrow."

"Good luck and it was nice to meet you. My name's Sally."

Fontonia left the pub and entered her nearby car. She watched the pub. Over the course of the next thirty minutes, the customers she'd seen in there left the establishment in dribs and drabs and drove away from the building. At eleven thirty, Sally exited the bar, locked up, and drove south through the small capital.

Fontonia followed her, while keeping her distance. It wasn't a difficult job. Snow was still falling, but it was lighter compared to earlier in the day; thus visibility wasn't too bad, despite it being night. There were no other drivers on the coastal road. All Fontonia needed to do was follow Sally's vehicle's taillights.

Sally stopped her vehicle outside her house. The property was a small wooden building with a slate roof. It was facing the sea. There was another vehicle parked outside. Who did the second vehicle belong to? Fontonia thought fast. Husband? Unlikely because of Sally's age and due to the fact she wasn't wearing rings when she'd seen her in the bar. Then again, she could have removed her engagement and wedding rings in order not to get them scratched and dirty when working. Boyfriend? A possibility, though islanders don't like gossip. Two unmarried people cohabiting together could be deemed inappropriate by Falklanders. There was a possibility she was wrong. She didn't discount the option. A strong, youthful boyfriend could pose a problem. The third option was that Sally was cohabiting with a family relative. This seemed a more likely scenario. Unless Sally had inherited money from deceased parents, she wouldn't be able to afford to run the pub. Somebody else was the owner of the pub. Most likely it was her mother or father. It was impossible to guess which gender lived in Sally's house. But, Fontonia was sure about one thing – only one other person lived in the house. It was too small to contain three people. She decided that the most probable scenario was that one of Sally's parents had died and that the other was the owner of the pub. She or he was in the house. That was for sure. Lights were on inside the property before Sally got home. It wouldn't have been due to Sally taking security precautions before her evening shift. Burglary didn't exist on the islands.

Sally entered her home.

Fontonia waited a few minutes.

She got out of her vehicle, approached the front door and turned the handle. It was locked. She looked left and right. Some of the houses on the street had internal lights on. She wasn't worried about CCTV – it didn't exist on the islands, outside of RAF Mount Pleasant. Nor was she overly worried about prying neighbours. It was too dark for her to be visible. Nevertheless, she decided to minimise risk and not force entry into the front of the house. She walked to the back of the property. The windows were double glazed. They could be smashed with repeated swings of a sledgehammer. But Fontonia wanted her entry into the house to be a surprise. She tried the rear door. It too was locked. But this time she wasn't worried about being randomly spotted by a neighbour. The back yard was in complete darkness. She withdrew from her pocket a leather pouch, unfolded the pouch, and ran her fingers over the small tools that were aligned inside the bag. She didn't need light. She'd memorised the exact location of every item in the container. Fontonia was adept at picking locks. It was a difficult task for two reasons: First, one had to identify what kind of lock was in situ; second, one had to crack the damn thing. Sometimes the process required using three or four tiny instruments to gently nudge the different internal lock's levers out of place; other times it a more brutish approach of using a specialist drill to bore out the lock and render it useless; on occasions one had to use a different kind of drill to dig a hole around the lock and then remove it; and worse-case scenario one had to use a lever to force the door until the lock broke free from the door frame. On this occasion, Fontonia was fortunate. The lock was a simple design and was easily picked. And it was done silently. That was good. She entered the house.

She could hear music in the lounge. Sally was in there, smoking a cigarette while watching a YouTube video of a rock band. She was on the sofa and had her back to Fontonia. The Argentinian assassin ignored her and walked up the stairs.

There was a bathroom and two bedrooms upstairs. The bathroom was in darkness; so too one of the bedrooms. But the other bedroom had a dim glow of light emitting into the hallway from the room. She could hear keyboard tapping. She got prone and crawled to the edge of the door. Very slowly, she peered around the doorframe. A man was in the room. He was hunched over a laptop that was on a bedside table. He wasn't facing the door. Even if he was it would have been unlikely he'd have seen her. The hallway was dark; and people don't tend to look at the first six inches of the base of an entrance. Making no sound, she stood and moved fast.

She ran into the room, grabbed the man's jaw and head, and twisted his head until his neck snapped. Almost certainly he was dead. But to be sure of death, She grabbed a pillow from the adjacent bed and held it firm over his mouth for three minutes. She tossed the pillow back onto the bed.

The man was in his late fifties or early sixties. Most likely he was Sally's father, Fontonia decided.

She walked downstairs. Loud music was still playing from the TV. Despite the noise, she moved carefully as she approached the sofa where Sally was sitting. Fontonia's breathing was calm. Her pulse rate was a mere sixty beats per minute. It had to be that way. Heightened emotion or fear were enemies of the job in hand. This was purely business, she always told herself. Emotion only came into play when she was back in Buenos Aires and dating a guy or watching a sad movie.

She grabbed Sally by the chin, hauled her backwards over the sofa, slammed her to the floor, stamped on her face and chest, and punched two fingers into her eyes. Sally was screaming and immobile. Fontonia put one of her ski gloves into Sally's mouth. Now all that could be heard were muted gasps of desperation and pain. In any case, the neighbours wouldn't have heard the brief screams. The music was too loud.

Fontonia grabbed a wooden chair, lifted Sally on to it, and expertly tied her hands and legs to the piece of furniture. She removed the glove and said, "I don't like screaming. Nor should you."

Sally was in shock. Her body felt like it had been hit by a bus. Her vision was blurry, eyes throbbing. She blinked rapidly while breathing fast. Every breath was excruciating. Her face was as bloody and swollen as a boxer's face after doing twelve rounds with a superior fighter. Her head was pounding and her mind was confused.

Fontonia turned down the music and sat on the rim of the sofa, facing Sally. "Remember me?"

Sally blinked faster. Her vision was blurred. "I… I remember your voice. Woman from the bar."

"Woman from the bar." Fontonia laughed. Her voice was cold when she said, "Not everything is what it seems."

"Please! Please! Why?"

"I'm just here to chat. You have something I want – information."

"Don't hurt me again. I've done nothing wrong!" Sally's vision was returning to normal, though her eyes were still in awful pain. "Who are you? What do you want from me?" She twisted her head and looked at the base of the stairs. "Dad! Dad! Help!"

Fontonia smiled. "Your father is unconscious. I did that to him. And I'll do the same to you unless you cooperate with me."

"You hurt my Dad?" Sally whimpered. "No, no, no, no!"

Fontonia picked up Sally's half smoked cigarette and took a drag on the tobacco. "So, this is how it works. I ask you a question. You answer."

Sally was still sobbing, even though her tears stung like Hell as they coursed down her bruised face and intermingled with blood. "Let me go. I don't know anything about anything."

Fontonia stubbed the cigarette out. "A few days ago four men died while sailing a trawler. They were washed up on a beach near Stanley. You know those men."

"Debbie… Debbie, I…"

Fontonia snapped, "My real name's not Debbie. Come on Sally! Work out a lie when one slams you in the face! Stay focused! If you do, I'll leave you alone. You knew the men, yes?"

Sally's head slumped.

"Head up! Look at me!"

Sally lifted her head. In doing so, pain shot down her spine. "I knew the men. They used to drink in my pub." She was shaking with uncontrollable emotion.

Fontonia lit a fresh cigarette from Sally's packet and placed the cigarette in her mouth. "A couple of puffs might calm your nerves."

Sally inhaled smoke, coughed, and spat the cigarette onto the carpet.

Fontonia used the soul of her boot to extinguish the cigarette. "We must be careful. We don't want there to be an accident."

Sally was moaning. "Who are you?" she repeated.

Fontonia's tone of voice remained calm and icy as she replied, "Who I am is of no relevance to you. And who you are is of no relevance to me. All that matters is what you know about the four dead men."

Sally shook her head while continuing to shake. "What's there to say? Eddie Wilson was a fisherman. Billy Green also worked on Wilson's boat. Rob Taylor was a farmer. Mike Jackson divided his time between being a lighthouse keeper and a fireman." Defiance entered her demeanour. "Are you telling me the truth about my Dad? If you are I'll make sure you rot in hell. The police and the military here know me and my Dad well. You'll never get off this island. They'll put you in prison for life. Or they'll shoot you on sight."

"Let them try. Maybe I didn't hurt your father. Maybe I just tied him up and gagged him. Either way, one thing's for sure – he can't help you now. Tell me more about the men."

Sally breathed deeply. Though she was still in shock, she tried to summon strength in order to get out of this situation. Anything she said about Wilson and his friends couldn't hurt them. They were dead. Compliance with the woman in front of her was her only option. Survival was all that mattered now. "They used to come to my pub. They used to sit at the bar. They didn't talk much. They'd usually stay until closing time. Then they'd go home."

"Who else drank with them?"

"No one."

Fontonia slapped her hard on the face. "Who else?!"

Sally was wincing as she repeated, "No one. There'd be others in the pub, but the men would never mix with them. Wilson, Taylor, Green, and Jackson only ever drank together."

"Before they died, they were in your pub. What did they say?"

Sally stared at her.

"What did they say?!"

Sally wished she could rub her eyes. "There's been an Argentinian ship watching the islands for a couple of months. We all knew about it. Wilson and his mates got drunk that night. They said they were going to drive Wilson's boat out to the ship and once and for all get rid of it. I told them not to do something so stupid. They left. That's the last time I saw them. And that's all I know!"

Fontonia withdrew a hunting knife and tossed its hilt back and forth between her hands. "On the night they died, there was a fifth man on the boat. Who is he?"

Sally stared at the razor sharp blade, her eyes wide with fear. "I don't know!"

"Yes you do," said Fontonia in a slow and deliberate voice.

"I'm telling you the truth! You're not the first person to ask me this."

Fontonia held the knife in one hand. "Who else has approached you on this matter?"

Sally kept her eyes on the knife. "Two detectives from London. At least, that's who they told me they were. Do they work for you?"

"Give me their names and I'll let you know."

"Ben Sign and Tom Knutsen. They said they were staying at Mount Pleasant."

"Ah yes. They're colleagues, though are working through this matter from different angles. I hope you cooperated with them."

"I told them what I told you; that I know nothing about a fifth man! Who do you all work for? Military? Intelligence? Police?"

"Something like that." Fontonia said, "Tell me about someone Wilson or his friends might know who has access to guns."

"What?"

"It's relevant to our investigation."

Fresh tears were streaming down Sally's face. "Lots of people on the islands have guns. Hunting rifles. Shotguns. That kind of thing. They have to register them with the police. It's all tightly controlled."

Fontonia smiled. "Shotguns and small calibre hunting rifles would be no match for a ship. I'm wondering if there's a man on the islands who has access to military-grade weapons. You may know that person."

Sally's head slumped again. "Don't know. I don't know."

"Yes, you do. You just need something to jolt your memory." Fontonia walked up to Sally and placed the tip of the knife against her stomach. "If I put this knife into your gut – and, trust me, I'm very willing to do so – I will ensure that I miss your vital organs. I will have done you a kindness. It would be possible that you could survive the wound. But, there would be a downside. The knife will have penetrated your stomach lining. You'd have massive internal bleeding. And if the knife was pulled out without an expert medical team present, you'd bleed out within twenty minutes. Or die from shock. RAF Mount Pleasant has a superb unit of combat paramedics with access to helicopters. They're on permanent standby. If I called the base, the unit would be here in minutes. They'd treat you here and evacuate you to the base. They have surgeons on the military compound. They'd treat you as if you were an injured war combatant. You wouldn't get better medical care anywhere else in the world. I'd make that call, providing you cooperate with me." Fontonia angled her head. "Do you want me to put the knife in you and take your chances? You decide. Who on the island has access to military grade weapons?"

Sally was petrified.

Fontonia stared at her.

Sally sucked in air. "Terry…"

"Yes?"

"Terry Maloney."

"Where does he live and why does he have the weapons?"

Sally gritted her teeth and closed her eyes. "He's got a farm and shooting range in Goose Green west of here, halfway across the east island." She tried to move her hands but they were bound too tight. "He's an islander but is contracted to the army. He lets them use his range for target practice."

"That's good Sally." Fontonia crouched in front of her. "Do you think Maloney might have been the fifth man on the boat?"

"I… I don't know."

"Have you met him?"

Sally shook her head. "My Dad told me about him. My Dad and some other men once went up to the range to deliver sandbags and help make repairs to the shooting range. It was a cash in hand job. That's the only contact my Dad had with Maloney. Seems like he keeps himself to himself. He's never been in our pub."

Fontonia sliced the knife through three inches of Sally's jumper, ensuring that she avoided Sally's skin.

Sally rocked back.

Fontonia grabbed the chair to avoid Sally crashing onto her back. She sat back down on the edge of the sofa. I think you're telling me the truth." She faked a look of sympathy. And she lied. "Your father will be okay. You must understand that people like me are investigating a matter that affects Western security. I'm not from Tasmania. I work for the Australian government. And in turn we're cooperating with other nations. Sign works for the Brits. His angle is obviously to protect the islands. Knutsen works for the Norwegian government. His angle is to ensure Argentina doesn't inadvertently discover that Norway has a top secret listening post in the Antarctic. And my employers' interest is to ensure that Australian mining rights in the Falklands' waters are not jeopardised by covert or overt military action. To get to the truth of what happened that night, all of us need to take desperate measures." She sighed. "If you want peace and stability on the islands, it's best that you don't breathe a word of our conversation this evening. Tell your father the same. If you say anything, it would go bad for everyone you know who lives here."

"Why are you telling me all this?!"

"Because I want you to know that a few aches and pains in your body have not been for nothing. On the contrary, you've done a service to the Falklands. I'm going to cut you free and leave. You'll never see me again." Fontonia moved behind her.

Relief overwhelmed Sally.

Fontonia withdrew a standard-sized hammer from the inside of her jacket and repeatedly smashed it against Sally's forehead and the crown of her skull. She did the same against her stomach, the base of her spine, the parts of her abdomen where her kidneys and liver were located, and against her chest. It was impossible to tell whether Sally died from shock, a heart attack, brain damage, or organ failure.

But, she was most certainly dead.

And there was not a drop of blood on the chair or floor. The only blood present was soaked into Sally's clothes. She secreted the hammer in her jacket and searched the lounge, hallway, and kitchen. She found what she was looking for: the keys to the old Land Rover that Sally drove. Her father's vehicle was too modern and therefore of no use. She went upstairs and lifted the dead man onto her shoulder. It would have been easier to have dragged him downstairs, but that would have meant that a strip of the fibres in the room and stairs carpet would possibly be facing the same direction. A clever forensics analyst would be able to tell that a heavy object had been dragged in one direction. So, she carried him downstairs and gently laid him next to Sally. She went outside, entered the Land Rover, and reversed it up the driveway adjacent to the house. This location wasn't overlooked by neighbours. Plus, it was pitch black. She re-entered the house via the rear kitchen door, left the door wide open, picked up Sally's Dad, and laid him down on the jeep's back passenger seat. Back in the house, she untied the ropes around Sally, put the ropes in a pocket, and carried Sally to the jeep. She dropped her on top of her father. She re-entered the house and moved the chair Sally had been sitting in, placing it back into the spot it had been when Fontonia had first entered the property. Using a separate key on the car key fob, she locked the back kitchen door once she was outside. She got into the Land Rover, started the engine and drove northwest out of Stanley.

Twenty minutes' later she was in an area that was completely uninhabited and rugged. The sea was to her right. Wind was buffeting the jeep; snow was falling fast; the sound of waves smacking the shore were just about audible. She slowed the vehicle in order to find a spot off the road that would suit her purposes. It only took her a couple of minutes to find that place – a flat strip of land that was fifty yards wide and led to a cliff, beyond which was a forty yard drop onto rocks and seawater. She reversed up the coastal road, stopped, engaged the gears in first, gunned the accelerator, lifted her foot off the clutch, and droves as fast as she could, going through the gears as she did so. She yanked the steering wheel right and went off the road. She stopped and turned off the engine. The vehicle was pointing at the deadly drop. She got out and hauled Sally into the front passenger seat and her father into the driver's seat. No seatbelts were applied. The jeep had no airbags.

She leaned into the driving area while keeping her feet outside. She placed the man's foot onto the clutch, his other foot onto the accelerator, and turned on the engine. She pressed Sally's Dad's leg to rev the accelerator. Then, she put the jeep into fourth gear. This was important for two reasons: fourth gear would indicate the Land Rover was travelling at speed; it would also mean an extremely slow start when the clutch was lifted. She pulled the dad's leg off the clutch, slammed the door, and watched the four wheel drive vehicle amble at slow speed toward the edge. It went over. Even within the din of the weather, Fontonia could hear the crash on the rocks below the precipice.

And that was everything that needed to be done.

If cops could be bothered to analyse the road, they'd see that the jeep was travelling at high speed before it careered off the road.

All injuries sustained by Sally and her father would be attributed to the crash.

Fontonia's footprints in the snow would be obliterated by more snow, in minutes.

Sally's home was secure and normal – no blood, no sign of violence whatsoever.

The accident would be due to a tragic driving miscalculation within treacherous weather.

The only question the cops would be asking themselves is why Sally and her father were out at this hour and where were they going. That didn't matter. The cops would never get answers to that question.

She walked ten miles back down the coastal road. It was hard going, but she'd done far worse in her training and subsequent deployments. She reached her car, near Sally's home, drove it to her cottage, and called Casero. "Terry Maloney. He lives near Goose Green. He's got a gun range and access to military weapons. That should be our next stop. But, we also have a problem. There are two blood hounds down here, trying to find our target. I think they're British. Their names are Ben Sign and Tom Knutsen. What are your instructions?"

CHAPTER 10

The following morning, Knutsen gathered up logs from the wood shed outside the cottage. He carried as much as he could into the house. Sign was cooking bacon for their breakfast. Knutsen placed some wood into the log burner and got a fire started. He felt low and knew that Sign felt the same way. They were getting nowhere with the investigation. No leads. No breakthroughs. Nothing. He sat next to the fire and held his head in his hands.

"Cheer up, old fella." Sign handed him a bacon bap. "A hearty breakfast will put a smile back on our faces."

Knutsen ate in silence while Sign did his best to lighten the mood.

As he ate, Sign said, "People say I was the most successful MI6 officer of my generation. It's certainly a flattering observation. And it's fair to say that I've had a number of significant successes. But, for every great success, there can be ten other operations that end in failure." He smiled. "My goodness me, I've had some stonking failures. We all have. I've been caught in rough places by rough men and had to escape or blag my way out of the situation. I've run agents that turned out to be double agents, working for the other side. I've targeted individuals who I thought had access to secrets I needed, paid them money, until I found out they were fraudsters." His smile faded. "And on more than one occasion I've had loyal foreign agents simply disappear. They were my friends. I tried to track them, day and night. But they were gone. Vanished in Russia, the Middle East, Asia, places like that. Of course, deep down I knew what had happened to them. Snatched; interrogated; executed; bodies dumped in the sea, or similar. But I didn't give up looking for them until I finally accepted the inevitable." His smile returned. "Ask any intelligence officer, cop, fireman, doctor, or soldier, and they'll all tell you the same thing – no matter how expert we are there will always be matters that fall through the cracks. A foreign spy successfully persuades an MI6 officer that he wants to defect to Britain, wherein the truth is he wants to steal our crown jewels. A specialist police unit spends months observing a drugs warehouse, based on information from a snitch; armed officers raid the warehouse; it's empty; the snitch had tipped off the drug gang. A highly experienced team of firefighters try to rescue a mother and daughter from a blaze in their home; but they're too late. A senior doctor gives CPR to a man who's collapsed on the street; the man vomits in her mouth and turns green; he was dead before she could get to him. A sergeant and his eight-man commando unit come under heavy fire in Afghanistan; they're trained to deal with this; they fight bravely; but ultimately they have to beat the retreat or die. Failure. It permeates the sharp end of life."

"Win some; lose some." Knutsen finished his bap. "You're saying we should chalk this up as an inevitable failure?"

Sign leaned forward, his expression earnest. "I never accept failure. Nor do you. I know all about your incredible police record as an undercover operative. Men like you and I never walk away until the job is done."

"That doesn't mean we succeed."

"Then, sir, we die trying."

Knutsen nodded. "We need a lucky break in the case. We've already agreed that we can't tear the islands apart, knocking on the door of every Tom, Dick, and Harry who lives here. We have to try to remain under the radar. Right now we have to be reactive, not proactive."

Sign leaned back. "We are being proactive. Remember, we believe there is a four person Argentinian assassination unit on the ground. Possibly it's comprised of two men and two women, based on our analysis of the flight rosters. I've ensured that all routine police and military patrols west of Stanley are temporarily suspended, save for emergency situations. That frees up the assassination unit to cause mischief. We're giving them enough rope to hang themselves. And in the process, they'll lead us to the fifth man. As far as I can see that's anything but being *reactive*."

"How will they lead us to our target?"

"They'll do so because they'll deploy brutish tactics. They'll give us a paper trail."

"What do you mean?" Knutsen went wide eyed. "You mean they'll torture or kill people and we wait to see where it leads?! Jesus Christ, Ben!"

"I don't want that to happen. I just want them to make a mistake."

There was a loud knock on the door. Knutsen answered.

Colonel Richards was there, accompanied by a police constable. Richards said, "I need you and Sign to come with me. Right now!"

"What's happened?"

"The barmaid in the pub the men drank in on the night of their... drowning." Richards had to choose his words carefully because a cop was present.

"Sally?"

"Yes. Sally. We can't be exact on timings, but sometime around midnight she and her father drove on the northern coastal road out of Stanley. They lost control of their vehicle and veered off a cliff. They're dead."

Sign was now standing alongside Knutsen and had heard everything Richards said. He placed his hand on Knutsen's shoulder. "We'd best get our boots and jackets on."

Forty five minutes later they were on the area of rough land where Sally's vehicle and come off the road. In front of them was the cliff. On the beach below was the mangled wreck of Sally's Land Rover. A police officer was down there, searching through the vehicle. The cop who'd attended Sign and Knutsen's cottage with Richards wandered off while saying he was going to find the path down to the beach so that he could assist his colleague.

Now that they were alone, Richards could speak freely to Sign and Knutsen. "This looks like an accident. In all probability it was. But, I hate coincidences. Four men who frequented Sally's pub died. Then Sally dies. What was she doing up here?"

"What's north of here?" asked Knutsen.

"Nothing to speak of. It's uninhabited. The only reason the coastal road extends beyond this point is to help farmers access their sheep and to help my men set up camp to do their foot patrols. There's no reason why Sally and her father would be up here at such a late hour."

Sign asked, "Who was driving?"

"Her father. He owns the pub in Stanley. He has no debilitating health conditions and, like all islanders, he knows how to drive in snow." Richards pointed at the road. "The constabulary has done an accident assessment. The jeep was driving normally on the road; speed in the region of fifty miles per hour. For some reason it lost control, came off the road, drove over the patch of land we're standing on, and went over the cliff. Seatbelts weren't on. There are no airbags in the vehicle. Sally and her father died on impact. Their bodies are at the hospital. Sally's father had a broken neck and broken limbs, as well as lacerations to his torso. Sally also had many lacerations, but she died from massive blows to the head. The lacerations would have come from the shattered windscreen and shards of metal from the doorframes. The blows to the head and neck would have come from the dashboard." Richards walked right up to Sign. "I know you interviewed Sally. Did you spook her? Maybe she didn't tell you the whole truth." He pointed north. "Maybe the fifth man is out there somewhere and she was going to see him. Possibly she was trying to warn him that you two were snooping."

Sign nodded. "You could be right. Were there provisions in the car? Food? Blankets? Clothes? Anything that might assist a man on the run?"

"There was the usual cold weather emergency provisions that islanders carry in their vehicles at this time of year – a tent, spare fuel, sleeping bags, water, tyre chains, torches, oil, tinned rations, a flare gun, et cetera."

"Most of which could be useful to a man who is in hiding. Were one or both of them carrying mobile phones?"

"No."

"That's odd. People driving in these conditions tend to carry phones in case of emergency." Sign peered over the edge of the cliff. "I presume you found the phones at their house."

"They didn't use mobile phones. We've checked. Sally's father had a radio transmitter that linked him to the police. But on the night of the crash he wasn't carrying it."

Sign nodded. "The accident investigation is in good hands. There's nothing we can do here."

Richards grabbed Sign by his collar. "What you can do is tread more carefully! This accident smacks of distraction. Sally and her father took their eye off the ball while driving. You made them scared. And desperate to help the fifth man."

Sign disagreed but didn't say so. "I'd take your hand off me if I were you."

Richards smiled. "Why?"

"Because Mr. Knutsen is pointing his gun at your head. And trust me – he'll have no qualms about pulling the trigger."

Richards slowly turned. Knutsen was behind him, the muzzle of his handgun inches from Richards' skull. Richards released Sign. "Maybe I should never have got you two involved in this!"

"Only you can decide. But, it's too late now. We've been commissioned by the British Ministry of Defence and we'll see this project through to fruition." Sign crossed his arms. "What gear was the jeep in when it crashed?"

"Fourth gear." Richards was impatient. "It shows they were driving at speed."

"Yes." Sign held out his hand. "I'd like the keys to Sally's home, and her address."

"It's already been searched! There's nothing in there that gives any clues as to the whereabouts of the fifth man."

"I'm sure you're right. But there's never any harm in having a fresh pair of eyes and all that. Colonel – the keys and address! And be quick about it! I'll return the keys to your base once we're done."

"I'll come with you."

"There'll be no need. Drop us back at our cottage. We'll drive to Sally's house ourselves."

Knutsen's gun was still pointing at Richards' head.

Sign nodded at his colleague.

Knutsen lowered his weapon.

Richards sighed. He gave Sign the keys and the address. "Look – there are accidents on the islands. It comes with the territory. But, right now it's a sensitive time. The islanders have lost four of their sons. Now they've lost one of their daughters. In the space of a week. I'm here to not only protect the islands from an Argentinian invasion; I'm also here to keep the peace. Tread lightly." He turned to Knutsen. "And if you ever pull a gun on me again I'll walk through you and make sure you disappear. Do you understand me, soldier?"

Knutsen held his ground and smiled. "Let's hope it doesn't come to that, *sir*."

"Good." Richards' anger receded. "There's someone you should talk to. His name's Terry Maloney. He lives near Goose Green. Call my secretary and she'll give you the exact address. He runs a gun range. Sometimes we let our soldiers do target practice on the range."

Knutsen asked, "Does he have military weapons? Specifically SLRs and Brownings?"

Richards shook his head. "Islanders are not permitted to have military weapons of any sort. Maloney's no exception. But, he is a gun enthusiast. If someone is illegally in possession of trophies from the war, maybe he knows who that person is."

"Maybe Maloney is the fifth man." Knutsen placed his gun under his belt.

"Impossible. Maloney has one hand after he had to have the other amputated a few years ago. He was firing one of my men's assault rifles on the range, under supervision. He got carried away and momentarily ignored instructions. The rifle discharged and mashed his hand. There's no way he could have rowed to shore from Wilson's boat. Plus, he's seventy years old. He doesn't strike me as someone willing or able to get on a boat at midnight with four drunken sailors."

Sign made no attempt to hide his irritation. "Why didn't you tell us about Maloney before?"

"Because I didn't know about him until 0400hrs this morning. Turns out my troop commanders knew about him and secretly used his range. They knew I'd never allowed that breach of protocol. But I overheard two of my sergeants talking about him and moaning that they couldn't wait to get back on patrol and fire off some rounds on Maloney's range. I spoke to the sergeants and they confessed that they'd been out to Goose Green regularly. I told them they could face disciplinary charges for not only using the range, but also for falsifying records of ammunition taken out on patrol and ammunition accounted for when they return. We're supposed to know the number of every single military bullet in our base. Any discrepancies have to be investigated. Alas, I'm a busy man. I defer that responsibility to my troop commanders."

Sign was deep in thought. "Don't discipline your sergeants. Just give them a stern telling off. We don't want Maloney to be at the forefront of their minds."

When they were back at the Bluff Cove cottage and Richards was gone, Sign said to Knutsen, "Don't worry about Richards. He's juggling balls. I don't blame him for being tense. Come on, let's go."

They drove to Sally's house. Once inside, Knutsen said, "I'll start searching the place."

"Not yet," said Sign. "Follow me." He went upstairs and looked at Sally's bedroom. He entered her father's room and looked around. The bed hadn't been slept in. He looked at the adjacent computer desk. The laptop looked like it was switched off. He moved the computers mouse. The screen lit up and required a password to activate the desktop. The laptop hadn't been shut down; it had gone into sleep mode due to hours of inactivity. He examined the chair in front of the desk, rocking it back and forth. The wood creaked with each movement; its legs were a fraction loose. He got prone on the floor and examined the carpet. He got to his feet and walked downstairs. Knutsen followed him into the lounge. The small smart TV was on standby mode. Sign picked up the controller and pressed the enter button. The TV activated and showed the YouTube home page, with subcategories. He spun around and looked at the chair where Sally had been murdered. He sat on it, intertwined his fingers and closed his eyes. Knutsen knew him well enough to leave him in peace when he became like this. Knutsen began an expert search of the house, opening drawers and cabinets in the kitchen, bathroom, and bedrooms, looking under beds and behind pictures, lifting furniture, examining paperwork in the father's desk, and doing many other things. He was looking for any clue as to why Sally and her father would have driven away from their home at such a late hour. He found nothing of interest. Ignoring Sign, he searched the lounge. Once again, he saw nothing unusual.

He said to Sign, "This has been a waste of time."

Sign opened his eyes. "Not exactly. We must leave. We need to visit Terry Maloney. But first we must drop Sally's house keys off at RAF Mount Pleasant. We don't want to infuriate Richards further by not adhering to our word to him."

Javier Rojo pulled his car up outside Terry Maloney's cottage. Surrounding the property was a rolling landscape. In spring and summer, heather, waterlogged gullies, and rocks would have been visible in the rugged countryside. Now, as far as the eye could see, a blanket of snow covered everything. Maloney's place was two miles west of Stanley. It was a location where a man could find peace and solitude.

Rojo was wearing winter gear and boots. He trudged through snow but didn't knock on the door. Instead, he walked around the property, and stopped. Facing away from the property, he placed his hands in his pockets and hunched to make it look as if he was cold. In truth, he didn't feel the chill. He'd operated in far worse climates and was adept at training his mind to zone out from any discomforts afflicting his body. He stared at the gun range. It was one hundred yards away from the house. He walked to the range. Like everything else around here, it was covered with snow. But, based on his knowledge of ranges, and the shapes and other indicators, he could visualise how it looked when clear of snow. There were sandbags at the end of the fifty yard range, low metal fences either side of the four-lane alley, more sandbags at firing stations, a waist-height metal box for spent cartridges, a separate unit for fire extinguishers and other emergency equipment, and two flags – halfway down the range, outside of the fences, that were operated by underground cables attached to switches on a post near the firing stations. A flick of one switch would activate a red flag – visible to shooters and telling them to lower their weapons, activate the safety catches on their guns, and under no circumstances shoot at anything on the range. The other switch would activate a black flag, meaning it was safe to commence target practice. On the range itself were posts that were grounded in troughs that allowed them to be moved to different sections and be fixed in place. Targets would be attached to them when Maloney or others used the range.

"Can I help you?" a man shouted. He was standing outside of the house, but made no attempt to walk over to Rojo.

Rojo turned, and walked over to the man. He smiled and said in a South African accent, "I was just admiring your shooting range. I bet you're looking forward to the snow melting so you can get the range active again."

The man looked suspicious. "How can I help you? Not many people come out here."

Rojo held out his hand. "Max Bosch. I've recently arrived on the islands."

The suspicion remained on the man's face as he shook Rojo's hand. "Terry Maloney. I own this place and pretty much everything you can see beyond it. How did you know about my range? It's barely visible in this weather."

Rojo shrugged nonchalantly. "Last night I had a drink with some locals in Stanley. They got talking and mentioned your range. I don't have any business today so I thought I'd take a drive out and do some sightseeing. I was intrigued by your range so thought I'd take a look." He smiled wider. "When I'm back home in Durban I like to spend a few hours on my nearest shooting range. It helps me destress after long flights."

"Are you police? Army?"

Rojo's smile remained. "Nothing as glamourous as that. I work for an insurance company. Can I come in? You'd be a lifesaver if you had coffee." He stamped his feet on the ground. "We don't get winters like this in SA."

Maloney laughed, his suspicious expression no longer evident. "Sure. But, if I were you I'd head straight back to Stanley after you've finished your drink. They've forecast more heavy snow in an hour or two. You don't want to get stuck on the Stanley road. Come in. I'll put the kettle on."

In the lounge was an open fire. Maloney placed two logs on the flames and used bellows to blow air into the fire. Once he was satisfied it was roaring nicely, he said, "Bloody heating in this place is faulty. Sometimes it works; other times it doesn't. If he can get here, I've got a man coming out this afternoon to take a look at the gas tank and heating unit. Keep your coat on and take a seat by the fire. How do you take your coffee?"

"No sugar. Milk if you've got it; no milk if you haven't." Rojo sat by the fire.

When he returned with two mugs of coffee in his one hand, Maloney also sat near the fire. His breath steamed as he spoke. "What guns do you use on your range in South Africa?"

Rojo beamed. "We get access to all sorts of crazy stuff. Assault rifles. Pistols. Machine guns. Crossbows. It's fun. I must admit I don't know the make and models of the weapons. The instructors just hand them to us, tell us how to use them, and we shoot at the targets."

Maloney smiled. "That does sound like fun."

"What do you use on your range?"

Maloney held up his left arm. "No hand, no shooting. Those days are behind me. Ah, it's mostly military patrols that use the range. When they're coming through here I let them camp on my land. They get bored. I let them fire off a few rounds. They like it, and it reminds me of the times when I could fire a weapon." He drank his coffee. "What's an insurance guy doing down here?"

Rojo pretended to look bored. "Just completing paperwork for a claim. I specialise in shipping. There was a vessel here that had an accident. The skipper's insurance with us. I guess he took out the insurance by shopping online for the best deal. He chose us. Doesn't matter that we're headquartered in South Africa. Most things are done on the Internet these days. But, there was an accident. When that happens we still need to do things the old fashioned way. My company flew me over to take photos of the boat, speak to the police and coastguard, get them to sign some forms, and then I fly back. It's all just a formality."

"Which boat?"

"A fishing vessel. Four islanders died while sailing it at night."

"Yeah, I know about that. Wilson, Taylor, Green, and Jackson. They drowned, I heard. Weather must have got 'em."

"That's my assessment. I have to visit their next of kin. I hate that part of my job – you know, meeting people when they're grieving. The only upside is I'll be there to get them to complete various documents so they get our insurance pay out. Then I get on the next plane out of here, whenever that will be."

"It'll be no more than a few days. The RAF bods at Mount Pleasant are good at keeping their runway clear of snow, even at this time of year. The only reason planes are grounded is because of high winds. The snow will last for another month or so. But, the winds will die soon." Maloney stood. "You'd better hit the road. This isn't a day for sightseeing."

Rojo swallowed the rest of his coffee. "You're right. But, before I go there is something you might be able to help me with."

Sign and Knutsen drove out of RAF Mount Pleasant, on route to Maloney's place, fifty eight miles west of Stanley. Knutsen was driving and had the windscreen wipers on full.

Knutsen said, "When I dropped Sally's keys off with Richards' secretary, I was told we shouldn't stray too far from Stanley today. Apparently the weather's going to take a turn for the worse."

Sign said nothing.

Knutsen carried on driving for another fifteen minutes, before saying, "You're very quiet."

Sign looked at him. "I'm thinking."

"Oh, I'm sorry I…"

"No, it's alright. I have been dwelling on matters pertaining to this morning." Sign rubbed his face and inhaled deeply. "I have a strong intellect. But, so do lots of people. What has always made me different from most other clever souls is my ability to read people and situations. It stood me in good stead within MI6 and it should stand me in good stead in this case. However, knowing *how* something happened is one thing. Knowing *why* something happened can often be a different challenge altogether. Colonel Richards lied to us this morning. I could tell. His story about overhearing his two sergeants talk about Maloney is, frankly, cock and bull. The question plaguing me is why he'd lie. Why did he know about Maloney and not say anything to us in London or when we first arrived here? The British guns on Wilson's trawler are integral to the case. They will lead us to the fifth man because he supplied the weapons. I'm convinced of that. Maloney has a shooting range that is laid out and equipped to accommodate military guns. It sounds highly improbable that Maloney is our man, but it's likely he may have an inkling as to who on the islands has access to weapons that were used in the Falklands War. It is also likely that the fifth man used his weapons on Maloney's range. So, why would Richards decide to withhold that information until this morning?"

Knutsen's mind raced. "There are a number of scenarios. He didn't think it was relevant, until this morning when the penny dropped that it could be a useful lead. Or, he didn't want it leaked to his bosses in London that he breaks rules by letting his men use Maloney's range. Similarly, he may be bunging Maloney a few quid for use of the range; in doing so he's misappropriating government funds. Or, maybe he doesn't want us to find the fifth man. This has all been a charade."

"Then why tell us about Maloney? And there's one thing I'm absolutely certain about – Richards wants to find the fifth man. He wants war. Nothing is going to take equal or higher priority over that imperative." Sign stared out of the window. "But your other points are salient. In my experience, ninety percent of the time people lie to cover their own backsides. Ten percent of the time they may lie for other reasons that are nothing to do with saving their skins; even then they may be lying to protect someone they care about." He nodded. "Roberts knew he was breaking operational procedures by letting his men use Maloney's range. And a stringent audit of his budget would show that a few hundred pounds here and there were taken out of petty cash and could not be accounted for. But that was okay until Wilson and his friends died. Richards was officially in the wrong, though one has to be sympathetic to the colonel. In a place like this it's hard for him to keep his men motivated, particularly when he's sending them on God-awful and boring treks across the islands. Keeping moral up is key. Richards had to use a stick to get his men off the base. But he also dangled a carrot – a chance for his boys to let rip with their guns on Maloney's range, in an environment that was wholly less sterile than the shooting range in Mount Pleasant. He didn't tell us about Maloney for two reasons: first, he hoped we'd have found the fifth man by now; second, he was embarrassed. The trigger point for him telling us about the rifle range was Sally's death. He suspects she was driving to see the fifth man. Richards doesn't want any more islanders to die on his watch. That's why he told us."

Knutsen smiled. "You have your answer. So, you think Sally was going to see the fifth man – either to warn him off, or supply him, or both?"

"No. I think she and her father were murdered."

Knutsen glanced at him. "Driven off the road?"

"I very much doubt that. You and I have both done offensive and defensive driving courses. The stretch of land between the road and cliff is approximately fifty yards long. And a Land Rover is a heavy vehicle. If someone driving another vehicle smashed into Sally's jeep, it may possibly have caused the Rover to go off road. But there was ample time for Sally's father to stop the vehicle before the plunge. I don't think the murders took place in the countryside where their bodies were found. I think they were killed in Sally's house."

Knutsen frowned. "There's no evidence of any struggle in the house. I've worked murder scenes when I was a cop. There are always signs that something bad had happened."

"Not when highly trained spies are involved. The father's computer was still on, though it had gone to sleep. It's not a weak assumption to make that he would have shut it down before driving. Sally's TV was on standby. She was watching music videos. And we know it was her because, given his age, it is far less likely that her father was watching young rock bands on the television. So, Sally was in the lounge; Sally's father was in his room. That, I believe, is the correct deduction. The father's chair was rickety. Maybe it had been that way for a while. Or maybe something put a strain on it on the night of his death."

"All of that makes sense, but there's no evidence of foul play."

"Correct, Mr. Knutsen. Therefore, now we must explore my imagination based on my experience of these types of matters. What would I have done if I was their killer? We must ascertain the *how* before addressing the *why*." Sign pictured himself approaching Sally's house. "Sally was facing the front of the house. If I force entry through the front door, Sally will see me in the hallway. She will scream. Her father will rush downstairs and realise why Sally is so perturbed. I then have two problems to deal with at once. Probably I could deal with that but it doesn't serve my purpose because I want quality time with Sally alone. If she's witnessed me seriously assaulting her father, she will be too traumatised to help me. So, I enter the house through the rear kitchen. Sally is oblivious to my presence. I'm silent as I take each step, though I'm assisted by two factors: the volume of Sally's music and the fact that if there's anyone upstairs and they hear a creak on the stairs they'll assume Sally's going to the bathroom. I glance in Sally's bedroom. It's in darkness. I move to the next bedroom. A man is sat at his desk, his back to me. He's on his laptop. The man's of no use to me. I grab his head and jaw, rock him back in his chair so that he's off balance, and twist his head as if I'm removing a corkscrew. I put the man's chair upright and leave the corpse there. I return downstairs, approach Sally from behind, and inflict significant injuries on her. But I don't use weapons and I'm careful not to draw blood. I tie her to a chair and talk to her. I will tell her that her father's unconscious but he'll be fine. I question her about Wilson, the fifth man, and the guns." Sign paused. "This is where we get into the realms of the unknown. We therefore need to further stretch our imaginations to conjure up what Sally might have said to her assailant."

"It's probable she said nothing of value to her interrogator. She told us she knew nothing."

"But, we weren't putting the thumb screws on her. That said, I don't think she knew who the fifth man is. She was genuinely upset by the deaths of Wilson, Taylor, Green, and Jackson. If there was anyone out there who could help us ascertain what really happened on the boat that night, I believe she'd want us to talk to that man. And if she didn't trust us, she'd call the police and give them the identity of the witness. She didn't know there was a fifth man on the boat until we told her. Or, so she says. But if she was lying to us, I believe she'd still call the authorities after we visited her and would have given them a name – most likely the call would have been anonymous. That call wasn't made. Sally carried on with her life, as normal. She wasn't withholding a secret. No. We can rule out the possibility that she supplied the name of the fifth man."

"I still think there's a strong probability she had nothing to say."

"You could be right." Sign frowned. "But pain's a funny old thing. It can jog memories, or bring to the fore matters that may now be significant. The assailant would have threatened her with further pain, maybe even death." He looked at Knutsen. "She'd have mentioned our names. Possibly she'd have asked her captor whether we were working with him or her. The assassin would have said yes. That means we're now targets. But, it's also possible that she remembered something else – maybe someone she'd met, or maybe the name of someone mentioned to her by her father or a friend." He breathed in deeply. "It is possible that name was Maloney. If so, we must tread carefully at Maloney's house."

"What happened next?"

"Sally was bludgeoned to death. Her injuries to her head would be consistent with a dramatic fall over a cliff, in a vehicle that had no air bags. The assassin carried the father downstairs and placed him on the back seat of the Land Rover. The assassin cut Sally free and also placed her in the back of the car. He re-entered the car and made sure the house looked normal. Then he left the house, locked the door, and drove the vehicle out of Stanley."

"Why didn't he turn off the TV and shutdown the father's computer? Surely, an assassin of this calibre would have better tradecraft?"

"He or she has perfect tradecraft. The Argentinians know about the fifth man. They're sure we know about the fifth man. The TV and laptop were left on in order to make it appear that Sally and her father left the house in a hurry. Any British official in the know about the fifth man would wrongly assume that the two publicans were urgently visiting him in the dead of night. But that lead is now dead to British investigators, because Sally and her father are dead. So, the assassin drove them a few miles up the coastal road, chose a spot to go off-road and send the vehicle over the cliff, accelerated hard on the road, swerved onto rough ground and stopped. He placed Sally in the front passenger seat, and her father into the driver's seat. The father's feet were placed on the clutch and accelerator. The assassin leaned in and engaged the gears into fourth. Land Rovers have sufficient grip and power to drive off in fourth. Fourth gear was important – it would indicate the father was driving at speed when the crash happened; it would also mean that – from a standstill - the vehicle would amble at one or two miles an hour until it was able to pick up speed. That meant the assassin could easily duck out of the vehicle after she removed the father's foot from the accelerator. The assassin watched the vehicle drop over the cliff, then walked to her car, most likely near Sally's house, called her colleagues to tell them what she knew, and vanished."

Knutsen nodded. "Do you think the assassin's left the islands?"

"No. I remain convinced that we're dealing with a team of four. They'll stay here until the job is done – executing the fifth man. Then they'll extract via covert means."

"If there's a possibility they're on to Maloney, I need to be prepared." He withdrew his handgun and gave it to Sign. "I cleaned it last night, but a lot's happened since then. Plus we've been out in this damn weather. Can you check it for me?"

Sign removed the magazine, expertly stripped down the gun, checked its working parts, reassembled the weapon, and placed the magazine back into its compartment. He handed the gun to Knutsen. "It's in perfect working order."

An hour later they were approaching Maloney's remote cottage.

Sign put his hand on Knutsen's arms. "Stop the car. Now!"

Knutsen could see why Sign had issued the instruction. Seventy yards away was Maloney's house. Parked outside the front was a pick-up truck. Next to it was a jeep.

Sign said, "On foot from here. We enter through the front door, with force if necessary."

They walked towards the house, their boots crunching in the snow and making depressions of up to six inches. It was hard going, and they had to keep their arms partially extended by their sides to maintain balance and avoid toppling over. The front door and its immediate surroundings were covered by a canopy. There was scant snow here. Any that had found its way onto the porch was regularly shovelled off the decking by Maloney. Knutsen stood on one side of the door, his back against the exterior wall. Sign did the same on the other side of the door. Sign nodded at Knutsen and held up three fingers, then two then one. Sign turned the door handle. It was unlocked. He pushed the door open. Knutsen swung into the entrance his gun at eye level. Sign put his hand on Knutsen's shoulder in order to guide him if the former cop got disorientated. It was the classic way that that small teams of special operatives worked when storming a building.

It all happened so fast.

Maloney was on the kitchen floor.

A man was standing over him, pointing a pistol at his head.

Maloney's face was bloody.

The man spun around to face Knutsen and Sign.

Knutsen shouted, "Drop your gun!"

The man looked startled.

Maloney kicked his stomach, causing the man to reel back by a foot, and lose his aim on Maloney's head.

While still off balance, the man shot Maloney in the chest, and turned to run out of the rear door.

Knutsen shot him in the leg.

But the man, kept moving, limping through the snow, a blood trail behind him.

Knutsen ran.

The man was heading towards the gun range. It was a futile escape. Beyond the range were mountains and nothing else. He'd either bleed or die from the weather conditions and terrain before he made much more than a mile on foot.

Sign rushed to Maloney and examined the wound. It was catastrophic. Maloney was still alive but would not be able to survive the injury.

Knutsen slowed to walking pace.

His quarry turned and raised his gun.

Knutsen threw himself to the ground, a fraction before two bullets were fired at the spot where he'd been standing. He kept his breathing calm, while maintain his pistol's aim on the man. He shouted over the noise of the wind, "Stop! It's no use."

The man staggered onto the range, turned, and fired more shots. The bullets were only just wide of their mark, penetrating the snow inches away from Knutsen's prone body.

Knutsen got to his feet.

Sign held the back of Maloney's head. "We're British army investigators. Who did this to you?"

Blood was pouring out of Maloney's mouth. His eyes were wide; his teeth gritted.

"Who did this to you?!" Sign repeated.

Maloney coughed and arched his back, his face screwed up from the pain. "He said...said..."

"Yes?!"

"Name... Max Bosch. Insurance. South African."

Urgently, Sign asked, "Did he ask you about someone on the islands who has access to old British Military guns? Did he ask you about a fifth man on Wilson's boat on the night Wilson and his friends died?"

Maloney nodded.

"What did you tell him?!

"Man comes here… my range…uses his guns."

"Name?!"

"Peter… Peter Hunt. Lives… lives on west island. That's all I told him." Maloney was struggling to breathe. "Then you arrived."

"Was Hunt on Wilson's boat on the night Wilson died?"

"Don't… don't know."

"Did he test his weapons on your range close to the date Wilson died?"

"Day… day before. Get me help. Please!"

Help was of no use. Maloney only had seconds to live. "Help is on its way. When did Hunt use the range before that day?"

"Two… maybe three months ago." Maloney went limp. He was dead.

Sign rested his head on the floor. In Latin, he muttered, "Mortui vivos docent."

The dead teach the living.

Sign ran out of the house.

The assassin was halfway down the shooting range, wildly shooting off rounds as he tried to make further distance from the cottage. Knutsen was at walking pace, following him, his gun at eye level.

The killer dragged his useless leg a few more yards, collapsed onto the snow, forced himself around to face Knutsen and aimed his gun in Knutsen's direction. He fired twice, but the bullets were nowhere near Knutsen.

Sign was running as fast as he could in the heavy snow. He had to get to Knutsen. His colleague's Glock 37 .45 calibre handgun would have punched a massive hole in the man's leg. Chances of survival were slim. But, like an injured and cornered tiger, the man was still capable of inflicting death on anyone who came near him.

Right now, the man wasn't going anywhere. He was three quarters of the way down the range. He knew there was no way out of this mess. There was splashes of blood all along the path he'd taken from the house.

But, he was ex-special forces.

He was Rojo.

He was a highly trained assassin.

He wasn't going down without a fight.

He had two more bullets left in his gun. It took all of his strength and willpower to raise his weapon. His hands were shaking due to adrenalin and shock. He tried to muster every semblance of control. He pointed the gun at Knutsen and fired.

Knutsen yelped and fell to the ground, just as Sign reached him. The bullet had grazed Knutsen's right arm. It was agonizing. Knutsen was breathing fast while lying on his back. He stared at Sign, who was crouched over him, a look of utter concern evident on Sign's face. Knutsen asked, "Do we need him alive or dead?"

Sign didn't answer.

"Alive or dead?! I can't use my right arm. And… and I'm shit at shooting with my left arm."

Sign looked down the range.

Rojo was trying to lift his gun. One bullet was left in the chamber.

"We can't allow him to make a mobile call to his colleagues. He has the information he needs. We must shut him down. He won't talk in prison. He'll never betray his associates."

"Then shut him down!" Knutsen thrust the gun into Sign's hand. "Shut him down!"

Sign moved away from Knutsen. He hadn't fired a weapon in years. He'd turned his back on delivering death by his hand. But, having Knutsen's pistol in his hand brought everything back. Maybe it was muscle memory. More likely it was training and decades of using a weapon in the most extreme circumstances.

Rojo fired his last shot. It grazed Sign's jacket but didn't touch flesh.

Sign walked fast down the range, firing two shots into Rojo's chest. He stood over the dead man and put another bullet into his brain. He sighed and crouched. He'd knew that later he'd feel emotion about how the day had unfolded, but now was not the time to dwell on such matters. He searched Rojo and found nothing – no ID, phone, wallet, receipts, maps, or anything else that might prove useful. He walked back to Knutsen. "How are you, dear chap?"

"Stings a lot, but that's about it. Pull me up." He extended his good arm.

Sign got him to his feet. "We'll get you sorted. Let's get in the house." When inside, Sign used Maloney's landline to call RAF Mount Pleasant. "My name is General Ben Sign. I need to speak to Colonel Richards urgently." When Richards was on the line, Sign said, "I need you to come to the house belonging to the man you mentioned to me this morning. Bring three trusted men who are privy to the knowledge about the fifth man. Also bring two body bags, bleach, a mop, bin bags, and shovels. Two of your men must not be squeamish and must understand how to leave a house pristine after a killing. The third needs to be medically trained to deal with a minor gunshot wound. He must bring supplies." The colonel tried to reply, but Sign snapped, "Just do it now!"

It took Richards and his three soldiers two hours to arrive at the scene. They'd made excellent time, given Richards would have had to assemble his men and their kit before making a drive that ordinarily would take at least an hour and a half, usually more in this weather.

Richards entered the house with his soldiers. "What are we looking at?"

Sign pulled him to one side, out of earshot of Richards' men. He had to partially tell the colonel the truth, and partially lie. "The man on the floor is Maloney. He needs to be disposed of. The site around the killing needs to be sanitised. I can tell you how to do that, if you like."

"I know how to do it!"

"There's another dead man on the shooting range. He killed Maloney. Knutsen and I had to shoot him. He also needs removing and disposing of somewhere. No one must know about this. The snow contains blood. It needs rotavating. That's what the shovels are for. More snow's coming, I know, but we need to cover the blood in case someone comes here in the next hour or so. No one must know what happened here."

"And what *did* happen here?"

Sign gave him a version of the truth, adding, "The man in the firing range was trying to kill us. He could be the fifth man, or a friend of his. He came here to shut Maloney up. But, I can't yet tell you for certain that I'm right. I need to continue my investigation to be sure."

Under no circumstances could he tell Richards that there was an Argentinian assassination squad on the ground. If he did so, Richards would be compelled to spring into action. Sign's under-the-radar investigation would have zero chance of progressing.

Richards nodded. "Okay. We'll dispose of the bodies and clean up the place. I'll make sure my three men don't talk. We'll patch up Knutsen. You're going to need to check the jeep outside."

"I'm not hopeful. Most likely it was bought with cash. It's untraceable. There'll be no car insurance, no road tax, nothing that links the car to its owner."

"DNA?"

Sign shrugged. "If you want to DNA test every islander, good luck with that. They might think something's a little off. It will set tongues wagging."

Richards stamped the ground. "Damn it." He composed himself. "You're right. This needs to be covered up." He glanced at Knutsen, who was being patched up by Richards' medic. "We'll sort this mess out. As soon as Knutsen's been attended to, I want you both to get out of here. Head back to your cottage. Lie low for the night. I'll try to find out the identity of the dead man on the range, though I'm not hopeful." He looked at the ground. "If he's the fifth man, you've killed the only hope we had of proving that Argentina committed an act of aggression on British nationals. There will be no UK retaliation. The Argentinian spy ship will have got off scot-free."

Sign said, "Come with me." Outside the cottage, Sign said, "There is a possibility that the dead man isn't the fifth man. In fact, I can't see why the fifth man would come here and kill Maloney. The fifth man is scared and in hiding. He might be worried that men like us might put two and two together and link him to Maloney. That's one thing. Shooting a man in cold blood is another matter altogether. Trust me on that."

Richards did. He'd seen a lot of death during his time in the SBS. "We'll sink the killer and Maloney in the sea. They'll never be found. That may be the end of the case. If so, you and Knutsen will be on the next flight out of here, once flights resume."

Sign couldn't let that happen. Quietly, he said, "This isn't dead in the water. There's still hope. Give me and Knutsen a few more days to find out if the fifth man's still alive. By the way, that's not a request. We'll do what we like. I'm just being polite to you."

Richards laughed. "You really are a piece of work. Okay, I'll grant you that window. But, if the killer isn't the fifth man then who is he?"

"My guess is he's a private investigator, contracted by Argentina to source the fifth man. He failed; we won. Argentina can't deploy another investigator to the islands while this weather holds and flights are cancelled. We bury this and we bury it fast."

Richards nodded.

Knutsen emerged from the house. His arm was strapped to his chest, but aside from that he looked well.

Sign said, "Mr. Knutsen. We need to examine the dead man's car. After that, it is time for us to make our excuses and leave. The colonel has this in hand. I will drive us home."

Casero called Sosa. "Our friend, Mr. R, has not called me. I've tried his mobile several times but there's no answer. Something doesn't feel right. I'll keep trying his phone over the next two hours. If he still doesn't answer, I will call you and Miss F and give you both fresh instructions."

Sign and Knutsen were back at their Bluff Cove cottage. Outside, it was getting dark. Sign insisted that Knutsen sit in front of the log burner. Sign lit the fire and went into the kitchen to prepare lamb cutlets seasoned with rosemary, mash potato, vegetables, and an onion and pepper gravy. When the dinner was cooking, he returned to the lounge, holding two glasses of brandy. He handed one out to Sign. "I know you're not a good shot with your left arm, but you can probably hold one of these." He smiled and sat opposite Knutsen.

Both men felt weary. Sign stretched out his legs. Knutsen was moving awkwardly in his seat, trying to get into a comfortable position. He said, "Sod this thing." He removed the sling, tossed it on the floor, and raised and lowered his injured arm. "Mobility's fine." He stood and walked to the dining table. On it was his Glock. He picked up the weapon with both hands, placed his left foot slightly in front of his other foot, slightly bent his knees, and aimed at a pot that was hanging from a meat hook in the kitchen. "Can you come here? I need your help."

Sign obliged.

Knutsen said, "Stand in front of the gun and place your palm against the muzzle. Give the gun two strong pushes. I want you to mimic the recoil of a .45 calibre weapon." Knutsen wanted to see if the action put his aim off. And he also wanted to know the effect it would have on his injury. Sign pressed twice. Knutsen nodded and lowered his weapon. "I'm good for head shots. My arm smarts a bit, but other than that I'm fully functioning." He placed the gun back on the table. Both men returned to their seats by the fire and sipped their drinks.

Sign asked, "How did the medic treat you?"

"He checked the wound to see if there were any bullet fragments or bits of cloth in the cut. There weren't. So, he disinfected the wound, put a local anaesthetic around it, and gave me three stitches. The stitches aren't going anywhere for a week. I asked the medic if I could exercise with my arm. He told me I could because the stitches are as strong as skin. I guess the sling was just for show – make me look like a wounded soldier." He smiled.

Sign rubbed his eyes. "I haven't killed anyone in years."

"I know." Knutsen watched his colleague. "How do you feel?"

"I feel like I had to do a job under extraordinary circumstances, but…"

"It still doesn't make it any easier. I'm sorry."

"For what?"

"For getting shot and leaving you to execute the assassin. I should have been more careful."

Sign shook his head. "You did everything right. We both know that things rarely pan out according to plan when guns are involved. That said, I truly regret that we didn't get to Maloney quicker. And I regret that I didn't advise Sally to stay somewhere safe until this matter was concluded. Their deaths are on my conscience."

Knutsen could see the anguish on Sign's face. "None of this was your fault. Sally and Maloney were murdered by Argentinian assassins."

"And I should have been one step ahead of them!" Sign slapped his hand against his thigh. "It was obvious that they'd speak to Sally, though I didn't anticipate they'd take such drastic measures. That's my fault. I didn't know that Sally was aware of Maloney and his gun range. That's also my fault." He downed his brandy in one gulp.

"You're being too hard on yourself. In any case, we can't look back. All that matters is what happens next."

Sign nodded slowly. His voice was distant as he said, "I must predict the future. And this time I must be accurate." His voice strengthened as he looked at Knutsen and said, "I don't think the remaining three assassins know about Peter Hunt. That information had only been imparted to the killer a second or two before we arrived at Maloney's house. The assassin had no phone on him. It would have been impossible to communicate Hunt's name to his colleagues. The protocol was simple and effective – the killer drives to Maloney's house; he carries no ID and mobile phone; the vehicle is either purchased or more likely rented for a week from a local farmer; it would have been a cash transaction; the assassin would call his colleagues when he was back in his accommodation. So, what happens next? His colleagues will be getting worried because they haven't heard from him. But, they'll not be overly worried for a few hours, just in case his silence is due to a misfortune – his car's broken down, something like that. But, we're dealing with professionals. There is the possibility that the killer placed his mobile into a waterproof bag and buried it a mile or so from Maloney's house, before arriving there. The assassin I shot is the man who entered this country using a fake passport in the name of Max Bosch. He's pretending to be a South African shipping insurance specialist. But wherever he was staying on the islands, he won't have used that name to secure a hotel room or holiday let. And when making the booking, he'll have switched accents to another nationality. He'll have also given the booking receptionist a different lie as to why he was here."

"We could make some enquiries. Knock on the doors of every hotel, B&B, and holiday cottage in and around Stanley. There can't be many of them."

"We could, but it will still take time. Moreover, we have three problems. First, I doubt Bosch has left anything compromising in his room, and even if he has what use will it be to us?"

"His mobile phone would be tremendously useful. It would give us access to the other three assassins. We could send them messages, pretending to be Bosch or whatever his real name is."

Sign shook his head. "I doubt they communicate via text messages. But if they do they'll have one-time codes that clarify the sender is legitimate."

"One-time codes?"

"They're unbreakable. If I send a message saying, *Let's meet at the usual RV in one hour*, I'll end that message with the word *Stradivarius* at the beginning or end of the message. The next message will have the word *Illinois*. Or random words like that. The code word can only be used once per message, and each code word is unique to the sender. The other assassins will have memorized Bosch's one-time code words before leaving Argentina. So long as he uses the correct code words, and uses them in the correct sequence, they know it's him sending the messages. And when they reply to him, he will know their respective code words. It's failsafe unless men like me can access the words. That is impossible. But, I suspect they're not using texts with one-time codes. I think they're calling each other, while being very careful about what they say on the phone. Reception on the islands is currently hit and miss. They won't risk a text message failing to be sent or received. Only a person-to-person call can guarantee that information has been relayed." Sign swirled his glass, even though there was nothing in it. "His phone is useless to us. The second problem we have is that Richards has added heavy weights to Bosch and Maloney and dumped them in the sea. We don't want to start making enquiries about a man fitting Bosch's description. It would undermine the whole point of making him vanish."

"And the third problem?"

"If we start making enquiries with multiple locals, we become visible to locals. And, if we become visible to islanders, it's only a matter of time before we become visible to the three assassins. That must be avoided at all costs."

"Because their next play is to find us and make us talk. We think Sally gave her killer our names."

"Yes."

Knutsen intertwined his fingers, ignoring the jolt of pain in his arm. "It would be *quite* hard to find us. Our cottage isn't registered in our names. Richards secured the booking. But…"

"There is Richards." Sign's eyes glistened. He liked seeing Knutsen work out what Sign had already worked out. It made him proud of his colleague. "Carry on."

"If the assassins are clever, they'll assume that Richards is somehow involved in our presence here. They might even deduce that he commissioned us to investigate the deaths of Wilson and his mates, and find the fifth man. They might think we're accommodated in Mount Pleasant. Or they might conclude that we're somewhere else, because we want to distance ourselves from the military base. Either way, the best way to get to us is through Richards."

"Correct."

"But, he's guarded by an army. The assassins know they can't get to the most senior British commander in the Falklands."

Sign wished that were true. "We must prepare for any possibility. The assassins are now desperate. And we know for a fact that they have no problem with torture. When they conclude," he looked at his watch, "any moment now that the assassin calling himself Max Bosch is missing, they will decide he's dead. They will check Maloney's house and decide that he too is missing, presumed dead. They will put two and two together and hope that Maloney told Bosch something of vital importance. But, Bosch took that information to his watery grave."

"Do you think that they'll assume you and I killed him?"

"Yes."

Knutsen was deep in thought. "Richards is an impossible target. Maybe they'll go for someone else who they think knows our whereabouts? Maybe the governor of the islands?"

"They know the governor won't be privy to this investigation. He'll be the last high ranking person to know about the fifth man and the possibility that his islands may be used as a launch pad for an assault against the Argentinian coastline. No, the assassins won't go after the governor."

"They'll go after Richards. You should warn him."

"I can't tell him about the assassins."

"Things have changed!"

Sign took Knutsen's glass, walked into the kitchen, and returned with more brandy for them both. "Change is in the eye of the beholder. It is up to Richards to deduce what we have deduced – that Sally and Maloney were murdered by an assassination squad."

"Oh come on! You can't leave Richards' fate to his own ability or otherwise to correctly deduce the threats around him. Tell him about the Argentinian operatives. Get him to summon the SBS unit in Antarctica. They'll hunt down the assassins and kill them."

"They'll be able to kill them, but they won't be able to hunt them down. They don't have our skills."

"Then, we track them down!"

Sign sipped his brandy. "You and I have a hunt on our hands, but it is not to chase assassins. Our focus is to get to Peter Hunt. We must stay rifle shot on that task. Richards can look after himself."

"But if he can't he'll lead them straight to us."

"We must take our chances."

Knutsen frowned. "There's something you're not telling me. It's not in your nature to be cavalier about someone's life. You wouldn't leave Richards hanging."

Sign placed his glass down and stared at the fire. "I've ensured that Richards is not at risk. He doesn't know this, but I've extended the lease on this cottage for a further week. And I've used my name to make the booking."

Knutsen was incredulous. "You're bringing the assassins to us!"

"Yes, and it will be all three of them. They won't take chances by just deploying one or two operatives."

"Jesus!"

Sign laughed. "Look on the bright side. The local agent I made the booking with only works nine to five. She's off work for the night. The assassins may canvas hotels and cottage lettings tonight. But if they strike lucky, it won't happen until tomorrow. We have a good night's sleep ahead of us." Sign drank the rest of his drink and stood. "Peter Hunt is our priority. I've Googled his name. Alas, there's no trace of such a man on the islands."

"That doesn't mean anything. Half of the islanders don't use Internet."

"Yes, and Hunt lives on the west island. Hardly anyone lives there. He likes to be away from the world and all its trappings. But, because he lives on such an uninhabited island, he won't be difficult to find." He looked around. "I need the car keys. Where did I put them?"

"Surely you're not thinking of driving somewhere tonight?"

"You're coming with me."

"What?"

"Don't worry. After today's events, you and I need to witness something pleasant. The journey won't take long."

Sign drove the car three hundred yards, pointed it at the sea, and stopped. Sign said, "Headlights remain on full beam. We disembark."

They got out of the car.

Sign pointed. "Can you see them?"

Knutsen could. Hundreds of penguins were huddled together on large rocks. "This is what you brought me to see?"

"Of course."

Knutsen smiled. "Before coming to the islands, I'd never seen penguins in the wild."

"And now you have. No matter how many bad things there are in the world, life goes on. Come on. Dinner's ready."

Casero called Sosa and Fontonia. He said the same thing to both operatives. "We must assume something unfortunate has happened to Mr. R. Whether Sign and Knutsen were involved cannot be determined. But we need to locate them and find out what they know about our target. Sign and Knutsen can then be disposed of. Sweep Stanley and any other place they might be staying in outside the capital. Get me their address. Report back to me. And then we'll pay them a visit."

CHAPTER 11

The following morning, Sign cooked omelettes with cheese and ham. He called upstairs. "Mr. Knutsen! Downstairs if you please. Breakfast is served." It was six AM.

Two minutes later, Knutsen emerged. He was fully dressed, though bleary eyed.

"You look like you slept in a hedge," joked Sign.

Knutsen wasn't in the mood for wise cracks. "Kept rolling in my sleep onto my injured arm. It's on the side I always sleep. For every thirty minutes I slept, I was awake for thirty minutes. I feel like shit."

Sign handed him his breakfast and made two mugs of strong coffee. As they ate in the lounge, Sign said, "Today we're going after Peter Hunt on the west island. Hopefully this will be the end of the case."

"It might be the end of our lives if the Argentinians get to us before flights are allowed to resume and Hunt can testify."

"True. So, let's enjoy our food while we can. We have a long journey ahead of us. I don't know when we'll next eat."

Thirty minutes later, Knutsen was sitting in the car, while Sign secured the cottage. He locked the back door from the inside, went into the lounge, pulled out a cabinet drawer by only two millimetres – the gap being barely perceptible to the human eye, stepped out of the cottage, and locked the front door. He got into the car's driver's seat and turned on the engine. "We must traverse the entire east island to get to the port at New Haven. That will take us several hours. The ferry crossing to Port Howard on the west island takes two hours. And when we get there we must meet a man who specialises in the conservation of elephant seals."

Knutsen shook his head and muttered, "Elephant seals? Why doesn't that surprise me?"

Sign drove the car away from Bluff Cove.

Sosa spent the morning visiting hotels and B&Bs in Stanley, plus booking agents who rented cottages in the capital or within a ten mile radius of Stanley. The seventh place she attended was a coastal house in the capital. She knocked on the door.

An elderly woman answered. "Yes?"

"Hello. I'm enquiring about your holiday let in Bluff Cove. I saw it advertised on your website."

The woman looked over her shoulder. "Lizzy. We have a customer." The woman returned her gaze on Sosa. "My daughter deals with bookings." She went inside.

Lizzy came to the door. "How can I help you?"

Sosa pretended to look distracted and emotional. "I'm looking for my uncle. His name's Ben Sign. I've been trying to call him, but his phone doesn't seem to be working. I need to reach him urgently. I have some sad family news. I wondered if he'd rented your cottage."

Lizzy frowned. "How do you know about our holiday let?"

"Your website. I…" Sosa wobbled on her feet and slammed a hand against the wall to maintain her balance.

"Are you okay?"

Sosa smiled. "I'm alright. It comes and goes. Pregnancy does weird things to the body."

Lizzy smiled sympathetically. "Is it your first?"

Sosa nodded.

"I've got two – boy and a girl. Trust me – pregnancy and childbirth is a walk in the park compared to what happens afterwards." She drummed her fingers on the hallway. "Are you a local?"

Sosa shook her head. "I arrived here a week ago. I need my uncle to go to England. We've got a funeral to arrange. It's…" Sosa started sobbing. "It's hard. I've got no husband or boyfriend. I've got to look after this," she patted her stomach, "myself. I shouldn't be down here, but we've got a very small family. No one else could make the trip. They're too old or ill. I just need to know where Ben is."

Lizzy said, "Wait here." She went further into the house and returned with a business card. "We normally don't give out the names of our guests to strangers, but under the circumstances I don't see any harm in letting you know that last night a Mr. Ben Sign secured our Bluff Cove cottage for a week." She handed the card to Sosa. "The address is on there. Please tell him that if he has to leave early, his holiday payment is non-refundable."

"I… I understand. And thank you. I've also tried emailing him, but have had no response."

Lizzy shrugged. "We get used to it at this time of year. Phones. Internet. During winter they're unreliable. When are you due?"

"Five months and two weeks."

Lizzy smiled. "Are you hoping for a boy or girl?"

"I don't mind. The bastard who got me up the duff has done a runner. Boy or girl doesn't matter, so long as they help me out when they're older." Sosa looked at the card. "Thank you. I'll drive to Bluff Cove now. Ben's always been good to my family. He'll make sure I get home safely."

Sosa turned and walked away. When she was out of sight of Lizzy she called Casero and gave him the location of Sign's holiday let.

Casero said, "We'll meet half a mile north east of the house, in one hour's time." He hung up.

Knutsen was getting bored because of the length of the journey across the east island and because Sign had to drive at less than forty miles an hour due to the weather conditions. The beads of snow striking the windscreen were playing havoc with Knutsen's eyes. God knows how Sign retained focus on the road. Knutsen said, "Let's play a game. We go through the alphabet. I choose a subject and start at A. You follow with B. Then it's my turn. You good with that?"

Sign sighed. "Yes, I'm *good with that*, to use your awkward strangulation of proper language."

"Okay. Subject is movie titles. A is Avatar."

"What's that?

"It's a sort of fantasy sci-fi blockbuster."

"Never heard of it."

Knutsen shrugged. "That shouldn't surprise me. B?"

"Buffet Froid."

"What?"

"It's a French film, made in 1979. What I like about is it's a Buñuelian depiction of the far-from-discreet crimes of the bourgeoisie."

Knutsen sighed. "This isn't going well. Look – can we just focus on films that might have shown at our local multiplex cinema?"

"I've never been to a multiplex cinema."

"Shut up! C – Captain America."

"That doesn't make sense."

Knutsen was exasperated. "Why?"

"Because grammatically it is illogical and from a technical standpoint it is false. What does *Captain America* mean? Moreover, you can have a captain who is American. But you can't have a captain of America. The rank of captain is too low. Only a president holds the entitlement to be referred to as *the president of America*. But even he or she isn't referred to as *President America*. Are you sure the film you refer to is real?"

Knutsen slammed his hand against the dashboard. "Forget this game. Let's play another. I spy with my little eye something beginning with *more fucking snow!*"

Casero stood by his car on the side of the road leading to Sign and Knutsen's cottage. He was wearing a fleece, woollen hat, gloves, waterproof trousers, and hiking boots. Fontonia and Sosa pulled up in their respective vehicles. They opened their windows. Casero called out, "Follow me." He got back into his jeep and turned off the road, driving down a farm track. After two hundred yards he stopped and turned off his engine. His colleagues did the same. He exited the car and waited for the two female assassins to join him. Like him, they were wearing Arctic gear. Casero said, "On foot from here. If you hear a vehicle, get off the road asap and take cover."

They walked back to the road and headed to the Bluff Cove cottage. Wind and snow battered their faces. They had to lean slightly forward to compensate for the gusts that were striking them. But this was easy. During their time in Special Projects they'd completed horrendously long winter treks in the Andes. And they'd had to survive in the mountains for weeks.

It took them fifteen minutes to reach the house. There were no vehicles outside and no internal lights visible. Casero silently gestured to Sosa, commanding her to cover the rear exit. She moved to the back of the cottage and waited, her sidearm held in both hands. He pointed at the front door. Fontonia tried the handle. The door was locked. It took her less than a minute to pick the lock and open the door. She stamped her feet to shake snow off of her boots and entered, her pistol held at eye level. Casero followed her. Both were silent as they swept through the house, checking every room for signs of life. When they were satisfied no one was here, Casero unlocked the rear kitchen door to allow Sosa to enter.

Casero said, "You two take the upstairs rooms. Leave no trace. I'm particularly interested in passports, other forms of ID, maps, phones, flight tickets, hire car purchase receipts, photos, and any hand-written notes. But keep an open mind. If you find anything of interest let me know. I'll search downstairs." The women were about to go upstairs. "Oh, and ladies – make sure this is an A+ search. Everything, repeat everything must be left exactly as you found it. Take photos if necessary, so you can reassemble items in the exact position you found them."

As the women set to work, Casero examined the kitchen. He searched cupboards, lifting up plates, bowls, pans, and the plastic cutlery tray to see if there was anything hidden beneath them. He looked in the bin, but didn't move anything. As far as he could tell, there was nothing unusual in there; only scraps of food, tins, and plastic disposable trays; certainly he couldn't see and pieces of paper that might contain information that was memorized before being screwed into a ball and discarded. He looked in the fridge. There was food in there, but nothing unusual. He went into the lounge. The log burner contained dying embers. But that told him nothing about when the occupants of the house were last here. Depending on the quality of the burner, the type of wood used to fuel it, the settings applied in air inflow and outflow, and the length and diameter of its chimney, a log burner could stay lit for twenty four hours or could extinguish in a fraction of that time. He opened drawers in a chest. Inside there were an instruction manual listing how to operate the house, emergency numbers for police, fire brigade, and the hospital, a few brochures on the Falklands and its attractions, and a guest book for visitors to write their feedback on their stay in the cottage. There was nothing in the cabinet that was personal to Sign or Knutsen. He closed the drawers, and searched the rest of the room, looking behind cushions on the armchairs, lifting up the chairs' padding, peering underneath the furniture, examining ornaments on the mantelpiece, and rifling through a DVD collection that was adjacent to a small TV. He found nothing.

Sosa and Fontonia came downstairs.

Fontonia said, "Upstairs has been sanitised. It's as if they were never here."

"It's the same downstairs." Casero sat in the armchair used by Sign and cursed. "We're dealing with highly trained professionals. They may be current or former special forces or specialist police. But, I think – given the tradecraft deployed here – that at least one of them has had significant intelligence experience. Shit!"

"We can handle special operatives," said Sosa.

Casero shook his head. "That's not what's bothering me. We'll have left a trace of our presence here."

Fontonia and Sosa glanced at each other, looking confused.

Fontonia said, "We searched the place exactly as you told us to. All items are inch-perfect in the same position we found them."

"Inch perfect isn't good enough!" Casero looked at the drawers. "Even a millimetre or two out of place can be enough to warn someone that an intruder has been in his house, if he knows we're coming and he's set us up for a fall." He breathed deeply. "Still – maybe it doesn't matter that they know we've been here. If anything, it might work to our advantage. They'll know they're dealing with experts. As such, they'll be under more pressure. Their ability to maintain their pristine standard of espionage etiquette will most likely falter."

"We don't have time to wait for that to happen."

Casero agreed. "We must assume that Rojo is dead and that Sign and Knutsen killed him."

Fontonia said, "Maybe the British military killed him."

Casero shook his head. "Let's work back from the problem. Sign and Knutsen were engaged by someone to investigate the murders of Wilson and his buddies. We must assume that the Brits are aware that there was a fifth man, so far unaccounted for, who was on the boat that night. They're as desperate to find him as we are. That's Sign and Knutsen's job – find the fifth man. But this is a *very* serious task that could lead to war. By extension, Sign and Knutsen are very important people. I find it implausible that Richards wouldn't know that Sign and Knutsen were on the islands. Most likely, he commissioned them to find the fifth man, or at least he was brought into the inner circle of military people who knew about the top secret deployment of the investigators. If I were Sign or Knutsen I wouldn't want Richards to interfere with my mission. I'd want to work off the radar and minimise the chances of locals finding out that their islands may soon be used as a battle launch pad. But now and again, I would need Richards' assistance. Sign and Knutsen killed Rojo; Richards cleaned up the mess. So, where does that lead us? And where have Sign and Knutsen driven to today?"

Sosa said, "It will be linked to Maloney."

"Yes." Casero looked at Fontonia. "Let's pluck out a possibility or two."

Fontonia thought it through. "Goose Green is a narrow strip of land on the east island. To its east are us and Stanley, plus a few farmers. To the west of the strip of land is not much apart from a chunk of the island, largely uninhabited. It's possible the fifth man lives there."

"Or?"

"He lives on the west island. There are no checks on the ferry between west and east islands. He could easily transport his guns."

Casero nodded. "Maloney is either dead or he's in protective custody. Either way he might have given Sign and Knutsen the identity of a man who used military grade weapons on his shooting range. If so, the investigators have gone looking for him." He stood. "We now have no leads, aside from Sign and Knutsen. Therefore, we must find them and see where they take us. But, we don't know what they look like, or what car they're driving. In this weather, only emergency services and farmers venture into the remote parts of the islands. Even farmers don't go out unless absolutely necessary; their cattle are brought into their ranches until the snow thaws. So, we have an advantage – Sign and Knutsen may stand out. I want you two to cover the western chunk of the east island, beyond Goose Green. One of you should sit tight in Goose Green – it's a bottle neck; every car passing through will be easily spotted. And one of you should take a drive west of there. I'm going to the ferry port in New Haven. I'll make enquiries there. Depending upon what emerges from those enquiries, I may travel across to Port Howard." He checked his watch. "Okay. Let's lock up the house and get moving."

Sign drove his vehicle onto the ferry. He and Knutsen were the only passengers on the boat. The ferry pilot was amazed when they'd turned up and requested tickets. He hadn't needed to ferry customers for days. But, he was a professional and had no qualms about making the crossing, even though the cost of doing so outweighed the price of the tickets.

For most of the journey Knutsen remained indoors, using his injured arm to lean against a wall and do a standing version of one-arm press-ups. The actions hurt, but were essential to get blood flowing and teach his arm to ignore pain.

Sign was on deck, the hood of his waterproof jacket covering his head, the collar of the fleece underneath rolled up so that it covered his chin. Only his mouth, eyes, and nose were exposed to the harsh elements. Snow and an icy wind lashed his face. His father had been a merchant sailor in his younger days. Until he passed away from old age, his father adored second hand book shops and antique dealers, searching for obscure books about naval history and exploits, old maps, ships' logs, souvenirs from early twentieth century explorations, and indeed anything that took his fancy because it reminded him of his own adventures at sea. Sign's father had been evacuated from London during the Second World War and had been relocated to the country. After his parents' death, he'd been placed into foster care, moving from one family to the next. That wasn't for him. He was an extremely intelligent boy, but didn't have the ability to stay on at school and go to university. He also had fire in his belly. Age fourteen, he joined the merchant navy. After six months of training, he boarded a train from Devon to Lowestoft in Suffolk. It was the longest journey he'd taken alone. All he had with him was a sack of clothes and his seafaring qualification certificate. The train journey, he'd often recount, was relentless. He was so scared that he'd fall asleep and miss the Lowestoft station. But he got there and reported to the port's merchant navy office that allocated work. In those days, one could choose which ship one wanted to be on, depending on which part of the world one wanted to go to. Sign's father had chosen to go on an old whaling boat that had been converted to carry food. It was bound for Bombay, as the capital was called back then. As he approached the boat, his sack on one shoulder, he looked at the rusty old vessel and wondered how it was possible for the boat to make the journey. But, he didn't hesitate. He approached the gangplank in order to get on board. It was then that a man emerged at the top of the gangplank – a six foot eight black man. He looked like a giant. Sign's father had never seen a black man before. The man walked past him without uttering a word. He smelled of fire. The sight of the man heightened his nerves and excitement. He was truly about to embark on an adventurous life that would take him to places and civilisations he'd only read about in books. The black man's job was to shovel coal in the ship's engine room. He, and other salty tough sailors – as foul mouthed as they were – looked out for Sign's father. They adopted him and gave him rules – he wasn't allowed to smoke, drink, or curse, until he was sixteen; when they got to shore, the older men would head to bars and chase women, but he wasn't allowed to come with them; when off-shift at sea, they could play cards and gamble with cigarettes, and he was allowed to watch but not take part; and he had to keep reading books so that he didn't become as illiterate as they were.

Sign's father travelled the world, on different ships, for the following twelve years. He went to places that, in some cases, were relatively unexplored. As a child, Sign would listen with awe to his father's accounts of giving a carton of cigarettes to natives in the Amazon so that he and a pal could borrow their dug-out canoes and paddle up piranha infested waters; doing a similar trip up the Congo; getting lost in Hong Kong and nearly missing the ship's departure time; sailing around the treacherous Cape Horn; and so many other adventures. But the one adventure that had captivated Sign the most was hearing about his father working on an icebreaker that was sent to carve a channel and free up a boat that had got stuck in the Antarctic. The icebreaker had also got temporarily stuck. His father and the rest of the crew spent three days on the ice, playing football and making snowmen to while away the time, before the ice shifted and they were able to get moving again and rescue the trapped boat.

As Sign looked south from the ferry, he felt like he was close to his father's adventure. He was holding a cardboard carton of black coffee. He raised it and said, "Dad – this is to you. Like father, like son. Without our adventures, there is no meaningful life." He drank from the carton and headed inside. "Mr. Knutsen. Port Howard is visible. We will be disembarking very shortly."

It took Casero four hours to drive to New Haven. The ferry was in port, having returned from Port Howard. Casero parked his car and entered the ticket office. He spoke with impeccable English to a bored-looking islander working behind the counter. "I wish to speak to the captain of the ferry. I'm on official business."

The islander looked nonplussed as she picked up a walkie-talkie and said, "Rob. There's someone here to see you. Don't know what it's about."

One minute later, Rob emerged from a room while eating a sandwich. His forearms were exposed and covered in black oil. He was wearing red all-in-one overalls and wellington boots. He looked at Casero. "You wanted to see me?"

Casero nodded. "Can we speak in private, in your office? I'm from London."

Rob shrugged. "Sure. Come his way." He led Casero into his office and shut the door. The room was tiny, with only a desk, two chairs, telephone, computer, overflowing ashtray, walkie-talkie, barometer, and maps of the strait between the east and west Falklands stuck to the wall. He gestured to the seat and took his own seat behind his desk, while finishing his sandwich. "How can I help you?"

Casero was composed as he sat down and replied, ""I'm on official business. *Military* business. Have you taken any passengers over to the west island today?"

Rob's eyes narrowed. "Do you have credentials?"

Casero waved his hand. "Call RAF Mount Pleasant and tell them that Ben Sign is making official enquiries. They'll vouch for me. Also, tell them that I've warned you that your shipping license will be suspended unless you cooperate with me."

Rob placed his hand on the phone.

"Make the call. I'm sure you have the number. But, if you don't I can recite it for you."

Rob lifted his hand. "What's a London military man doing down here?"

"Something that should be of no concern to you. All I want is a bit of information."

Rob dusted crumbs off his fingers. "I've only made one crossing today. Two men and their jeep. I got back twenty minutes ago."

"Who were the men?"

"Don't know." He picked up his walkie-talkie. "Sally – do you know the names of the blokes I took west earlier today?"

Sally replied, "No. They didn't use a bank card to buy the tickets. Only cash."

"Okay. Thanks." Rob placed the walkie-talkie on his desk and looked at Casero. "No names."

Casero nodded. "What did they look and sound like?"

"They sounded English. One of them had a posh accent. And I can tell you exactly what they looked like. Come around here." Rob was staring at his computer.

Casero peered over his shoulder.

Rob clicked on a file. "My boat has cameras. We have to for insurance reasons, in case there's an accident at sea." He spent a few seconds fast forwarding the video feed from the last crossing before hitting the pause icon. "There we go. That's them, getting out of their car."

Casero memorised the faces of the two men in the image, plus the number plate of their vehicle. "Did they say what business they had on the west island?"

"I didn't speak to them. I've no idea why they wanted to make the crossing on today of all days. The sea conditions were rough enough to make even me a bit queasy."

Casero sat back in the chair, opposite Rob. "Those men are of no interest to me. I know who they are. Like me, they're on official business. But, now I'm here I wouldn't mind visiting the west island. Would you take me?"

Rob looked at the wall clock. "Jesus! I thought I was done for the day."

"I will pay you double and put in a good word to the military base, saying you've been an enormous help."

Rob rubbed his beard. "I can do it, but I won't be able to bring you back today. You'll have to overnight it in Howard. I'll collect you 0900hrs tomorrow and bring you home. If you can't make that time, you're stuffed tomorrow. We're expecting a storm midday. No way am I taking my misses out there when that shit kicks off."

Casero smiled. "0900hrs return is perfect." He stood and held out his hand. "I'll get the tickets from Sally and see you on the boat in a few minutes."

It was one PM when Sign and Knutsen stopped outside a hut in the miniscule Port Howard. Sign pulled down on a rope attached to a bell, outside the front door. A man opened the door. He was in his forties, wiry, medium height, had tousled brown and grey hair, a chest length beard that was tucked into the neck of his blue hemp jumper, and was wearing corduroy brown trousers and boots that were strapped to waterproof calf protectors.

Sign said, "Mr. Oates. Ben Sign. We spoke on the phone. And this is my colleague Tom Knutsen."

Oates gestured for them to come in. The hut wasn't a residential property. It was purely one room and a toilet. The room was crammed with paraphernalia to do with conservation on the west island. There were books about fauna and flora on the island stacked on the floor, maps of the coastline with red pins pierced into various locations, post-it notes with writing stuck next to them, and photos of elephant seals and penguins, all of them with felt pen hand writing at the base of the shots, with the names of the creatures – Pink, Fat Boy, Gorbachev, Cleopatra, Grunt, Boss, and others. There was also a table that was strewn with papers and a bottle of rum. On the floor in the corner of the room was a tea urn. Oates picked up three dirty mugs, washed them in the bathroom sink and poured tea into them. He added a dash of rum to each mug and handed drinks to Sign and Knutsen. He sat on the edge of the table, took a swig of his stewed brew, and asked, "How can I help you."

There were no seats for Sign and Knutsen. So they stood and sipped their drinks. Sign said, "This is the first time we've visited the west island. We're seeking local knowledge and we thought you'd might be able to help."

Oates sniggered. "I'm not a tour guide." He pointed at the photos. "I monitor and sometimes help elephant seals. I also keep an eye on their habitat and feeding grounds."

Knutsen asked, "You work for the government?"

"Nah, mate. I work for a charity, though we do get funding from the Ministry of Agriculture, Fisheries and Food."

Sign said, "We're not looking for a tour guide. Mr. Knutsen and I work for the Ministry of Defence. We're based in London and are down here to do an independent survey of the west coast of the island."

"You mean you want to find out where the Argies would land if they assaulted this island."

"Correct."

"Those types of surveys have been done to death by your pals in Mount Pleasant."

"Yes. But Whitehall wants fresh eyes to analyse the island. So, they sent us. All we're hoping to gain from you is a little local knowledge. We were told that you know the island inside out."

Oates shrugged. "I guess I do. I've been here for eleven years." He placed his mug on the table and crossed his arms. "There's not much to tell you that you can't read in a book. The island's smaller than the east island, but not by much. We've got hills and small mountains on this side of the coast; further west it's flatter. Most people live in Port Howard, but there's not many of us. The last headcount of the island put the total at one hundred and forty one. The majority of adults here are sheep farmers. There's a handful of us who do different stuff."

"What kind of different stuff?"

Oates rolled a cigarette. "We've got a small school, petrol station, airstrips dotted around the island, a shop, one B&B in Howard, one doctor's surgery, and a few ports. They all need servicing and maintaining. We've also got two RAF remote radars – one in the north, one in the south. Sometimes we get RAF blokes out here to check they're working. They stay for days, sometimes weeks. Then they bugger off." He lit his cigarette. "Aside from that it's sheep, sheep, and more bloody sheep."

Sign asked, "What's the road network like here?"

"It's pretty good. It has to be because people rely on it to survive. But, there aren't many roads. All the farmers have quad bikes, or other off-road vehicles, so they can go cross-country when they need to. Think of this place as the Wild West; or more accurately some remote part of the Andes. There's no police or other emergency services here. If anything bad happens, we rely on people flying in from the east island. Trouble is, there are no flights at the moment. We're on our own."

Sign pulled out a piece of paper. It contained five names. Four of them he'd made up. "I have a list of people who may be able to assist Mr. Knutsen and I to analyse the west coast. That said, I concede the list may be wholly out of date or inaccurate. Would you mind taking a look at the list?"

Oates took the paper and looked at the names. "You're right. I've got no idea who four of these blokes are. I know everyone on the island. Either these four were before my time here, or your blokes in Whitehall got it wrong. Maybe they live on the east island." He prodded a finger against the paper. "But this guy, Peter Hunt. Yeah, I know him. He lives near Hill Cove. There's a direct road from Howard that will get you there. It's about a thirty mile drive. You can get there in under an hour."

Sign faked ignorance. "I must apologise. We were sent down here at short notice. We were given no briefing in London. They just told us to get on a plane and do the job. The only thing supplied to us was the list of names."

"And for the most part that was a crock of shite." Oates dragged on his cigarette. "How can Hunt be of interest to your Whitehall people? I know the coastline better than anyone. I can tell you what you want to know."

"But, you're not an islander, are you?"

"No. I'm from Devon. I did my undergraduate degree in Environmental Sciences at the University of Exeter and my PhD at the University of St. Andrews. Then I moved down here."

Though Sign had never been a smoker, he liked the aromatic smell of Oates' cigarette. It reminded him of his father's pipe tobacco. "Therein is the problem. We are required to obtain signed affidavits from a select number of islanders who know the west coast. Only islanders. We need to report back to London with statements about the locations islanders fear would be most vulnerable to an attack. For some strange legal reason, we're not permitted to obtain statements from non-islanders, no matter how expert their testimonies may be."

Oates extinguished his cigarette in his tea. "What kit are you carrying in your jeep? You need to be prepared for anything right now. I can lend you stuff if you need it. I'd drive you over to Hill Cove myself, but I've got a call with our North America office. I'm hoping to reintroduce wolves onto the island. I'd source them from the States. But, it's an uphill struggle because the farmers hate the idea. But, I'm still plugging away with the concept. We used to have wolves here. They became extinct in the nineteenth century. Sorry I can't be of more help today."

Sign smiled. "You've been more than helpful. Our car is carrying a tent, food, a gas stove, flashlights, flares, blankets, maps, knives, an axe, medical kit, spare clothes, tyre chains, tools, and spare fuel. We've come prepared."

"Sounds like you have." Oates rubbed his beard. "My dad was in the army. At one stage I thought about joining the military. But, you know how it is – boys tend to do the opposite of what their fathers want them to do. So, I chose this life."

"And you chose an eminently laudable vocation. If you do succeed in introducing wolves onto the island, I will come back. I've always been fascinated by wolves." Sign shook hands with Oates. "Good luck with your work, sir."

Sign and Knutsen left, got in their car, and drove towards Hill Cove.

It took five minutes for Casero to drive along Port Howard's coast road.. He estimated he had less than one percent chance of spotting their vehicle. Most likely they'd already driven away from the port. If that was the case, it didn't really matter. He knew where they lived. Whatever information they found on the west island could be easily plied out of them back at their cottage in Bluff Cove. But he was curious and persistent. He stopped his car, turned around, and drove back towards the port. That's when he spotted the car. Its headlights and windscreen wipers were on. Casero stopped his car, turned the engine off, and ducked down. He heard the car pass him in the opposite direction. He waited two minutes before sitting upright, engaging the engine, turning his car around, and following the route the vehicle had taken. It was the only route out of Port Howard. He drove close enough to the jeep in front of him, noted its number plate, and slowed down so that there was more distance between him and his quarry. The car belonged to Sign and Knutsen. Casero smiled, though was tense and alert. There was zero room for complacency. He tried calling Sosa and Fontonia but there was no mobile phone signal. He'd gotten used to that. He didn't need the female operatives for back-up. It would take them half a day, at least, to get here. Plus, he was armed with a handgun and an assault rifle with sniper scope. He could handle himself. But, it would have been nice to let the women know that they could stand down from the search of the western part of the east island. He drove onwards, following the road north west, before it bended to face south west. The road changed direction again, heading directly west to Hill Cove and beyond.

Knutsen said, "We've had a car behind us since leaving Howard. It's keeping its distance."

"I know." Sign was squinting to avoid his eyes getting disorientated from the snowfall. He knew it was unusual for two cars to be on the road in these conditions. "It could be innocent, but let's get the measure of the driver. Gun at the ready, if you please. It most likely is a farmer." He stopped the jeep on the side of the road. "Stay here. I don't want him spooked." Sign placed his hand on the jeep's roof and faced the oncoming car. He waved his hand.

The car slowed, flashed its lights, and stopped behind Sign's jeep.

Casero got out. His pistol was hidden in a pocket.

Sign called out, "We're trying to reach the coast. Do we take the left turn a mile ahead, or do we keep going west."

Casero walked up to him. "Which part of the coast are you going to?" His accent was pitch perfect Falkland Islands.

"Roy Cove. This damn snow is playing havoc with my bearings. We've got to get there before night fall. We're instructed to take samples of the seawater to test for levels of salinity."

"Scientist types?"

Sign smiled. "Yes. We're doing a survey. But we're not from here."

Casero pointed up the road. "You're going the right way, mate. Once you hit Hill Cove keep going for a few more miles. Then stop. You'll have to reach Roy Cove on foot. I'm heading that way myself, though not as far as Roy Cove. I'll stick behind you for part of the way. If you get in any trouble, whack your hazard lights on. I've got vehicle maintenance kit in the boot of my car."

Sign called out, "Much obliged. What brings you out here this afternoon?"

Casero rubbed his hands together. "I'm missing a sheep. Her son is pining for her like hell and won't eat. I've got to find mum, put her in my pick-up, and reunite the happy family. I can think of better things to be doing." He turned and headed back to his car. "Take it steady on the road."

Sign got back into his vehicle and drove. "We must be careful. It is possible that I've just met one of the Argentinian assassins."

Casero followed them. He knew they weren't heading to Roy Cove. No one lived there because there was no road access to the coastal location. That meant that instead of turning northwest off the road they were on, passing Roy Cove and heading to the uninhabited West Point Island, they'd stay on the road that led to Hill Cove. Only one person lived there. A mile north of the cove there was another dwelling. Beyond that, the coastal road continued for approximately six miles before stopping. Logically, that meant Sign and Knutsen were going to see one of the two men. He followed Sign's vehicle for fifteen minutes, flashed his lights, and overtook their jeep. He waved his hand while glancing in the rear view mirror and drove at speed. He wanted to be out of sight. He drove close to Hill Cove, but not too close. After driving his vehicle off the road for one hundred yards, he stopped and began covering his car with snow. Sign and Knutsen were at least a mile behind him. And given visibility was appalling, even when they drove past his disguised vehicle they wouldn't be able to see him or his car. He grabbed a holdall containing binoculars and a rifle, and set off on foot.

Peter Hunt was in his house, polishing boots and wiping down waterproof smocks with a wet cloth. He lived alone. He'd never married, and his parents had passed away a few years ago. Mostly, he farmed the adjacent remote land, though money was scant in the winter months. It was only when the lambing season was well and truly over that he was able to slaughter some of the lambs, sheer the older sheep and sell their wool, and have any meaningful income. Before then, running costs remained high. The sheep needed to be housed and fed, his stone cottage was leaky and cold and needed constant repairs, ditto his two barns, and his vehicles were in regular need of new parts due to the strain put on them. So, in the off-season he supplemented his income by doing other things – hunting for game and selling it in Port Howard, catching and smoking river and sea trout and gift wrapping them in string, straw, and wooden boxes, and posting them to delicatessens in England and France, cultivating herbs under LED grow-lamps and selling the crops to anyone that would take them, and getting cash-in-hand for helping other farmers on the island with repairs and supplies.

Hunt was forty one years old, five foot nine, had a weathered face that was tanned all year round, was bald, and had the strength of an ox. Like most farmers, he was a stickler for routine and hygiene. He bathed every day; his clothes were washed after every shift; his other kit and tools were cleaned regularly, and always after usage; and every morning and evening he always smothered Norwegian cream onto his hands and feet to prevent his skin cracking from prolonged exertions and exposure to wet conditions. And yet, there was no mistaking his aroma – he smelled like an animal.

He went into one of the barns. Inside were his beloved sheep. Separated from them, in a pen, was his ram. Perceived wisdom amongst farmers was that one should keep rams and sheep away from each other until breeding season. For the most part that was true. But Hunt had learnt that putting his ram in the same enclosure as the females helped bring a calming influence on the ladies. He didn't know why that was. But he knew it worked. He picked up a handful of nuts from a bowl and held them under the ram's nostrils. The ram had big horns, and was cantankerous, but he never attacked Hunt. His master gave him what he wanted – food, the opportunity to mate with the other sheep, a free reign of a stretch of land in the warmer months, and a cosy home when the weather was dire.

Most people wouldn't have been able to hear the car approaching – the wind was too noisy. But Hunt had an excellent sense of hearing. He had to have that; one survived out here by one's wits and capabilities. He walked back into the house and looked at the road. A jeep was approaching. That was very unusual. Even in the summer, not many people ventured out this far. The last time he'd seen another human being was a week ago, and that wasn't anywhere near here. He started feeling uneasy as he looked through a telescope that was positioned on a window ledge. The car was drawing nearer.

He didn't like this one bit.

He grabbed his daysack. It contained everything he needed if he had to bolt to rescue a sheep or attend to any other emergency. He placed it on his back and looked at his telephone.

Sign stopped his vehicle outside Hunt's cottage. "Let's tread carefully. Hunt will be suspicious of us, simply because he hasn't seen people out here for a long time. He will be exponentially on his guard when we start asking questions."

Sign and Knutsen approached the front door. Sign knocked.

There was no answer.

Sign knocked again and called out, "Mr. Hunt?"

The door opened a few inches. Hunt said, "Yes?"

Sign smiled. "My name is Ben Sign. And this is Tom Knutsen. We're from London. We're investigating an incident that took place near Stanley. We're talking to islanders to see if anyone witnessed the incident. May we come in?"

"What incident?"

"Four men fell off a trawler at sea, a mile out from Port Stanley. They drowned. Their names are Eddie Wilson, Rob Taylor, Billy Green, and Mike Jackson. We want to understand what happened that night."

"Who's *we*?"

"Mr. Knutsen and I are accident investigators. We work for a London law firm and represent the interests of Wilson and his friends. There may be an insurance pay out. But, we need further testimonials before we can close the case. Anyone who can help us do that will be financially rewarded."

Hunt tried to look perplexed.

Sign could tell from his expression that it was an act.

Hunt said, "I only go to Stanley about twice a year. I read about the drownings in the paper, but I wasn't anywhere near Stanley when it happened. You should be talking to people in the capital, not people on the west island."

Sign maintained his smile. "We're trying to cover all bases. So far we're not making progress. The men were carrying weapons on the ship when they died. We understand that you're a weapon enthusiast. We are speaking to people like yourself to see if there's anything you might know about the men's state of mind when they sailed out on the night of their deaths. *Please* may we come in? It's dreadfully cold out here."

Hunt didn't buy that Sign and Knutsen were who they said they were. His stomach was in knots. "Okay. Just give me a moment." He shut the door.

Signed snapped at Knutsen. "Cover the back!"

Sign tried to open the door, but it was locked. He kicked the door, near the handle, but it held fast. He heard an engine start up. The sound was coming from the back of the house. He raced as fast as he could to the rear of the property. One hundred yards away was Hunt, driving a red snowmobile. Knutsen was pursuing him on foot, but the vehicle was too fast and was making ground.

Sign shouted, ""Tom. Our jeep. Now!"

Sign ran their car, and drove it a few yards beyond the house. He stopped. Knutsen jumped in.

Knutsen was breathless. "He was on the snowmobile before I could get to him."

Sign drove the jeep as fast as he dared in the slippery conditions. The snowmobile was still visible, driving north along the road. "Where's he heading?"

"As far away from us. Is my guess." Knutsen rubbed his injured arm. "I could have shot him, but what would have been the point in that - shooting a witness?"

"You made the right decision. We need him alive." Sign tried to keep pace with Hunt. "He's scared. We just need him to come to his senses when he realises there's nowhere to go."

Sign was gaining on Hunt. He was one hundred yards behind him. Hunt looked over his shoulder, pulled down fully on the throttle, and drove his snowmobile off the road. He was now on undulating land, travelling at fifty miles per hour.

"No!" shouted Knutsen. "Our jeep won't make it out there. Let me out. I'll go after him on foot."

Sign stopped the car. Both men disembarked and ran along the tracks the snowmobile had carved in the snow. Hunt was at least three hundred yards away. Knutsen was holding his handgun, but the distance was too great to put a shot into the snowmobile to try to immobilise the vehicle.

Sign slowed to a walk and placed his hand on Knutsen's shoulder. "We stand no chance. We know where he lives. He can't escape the inevitable."

They turned to walk back to their jeep.

As they did so they heard a loud bang. It was unmistakably a rifle shot. They spun around. Hunt was motionless on the ground. His snowmobile was careering haphazardly in different directions before it hit a rock, and tumbled in the air before crashing to the ground. Sign and Knutsen ran as fast as the deep snow would allow them to. They were one hundred yards from Hunt when two more shots rang out, bullets hitting Hunt and causing his body to slightly move. Both men threw themselves to the ground.

Knutsen muttered, "The man you met on the road. He *was* an assassin. Somehow he got here before us. We're easy targets."

Sign looked at Knutsen. "You don't have to do this. I can check the body on my own."

"Not a chance." Knutsen got to his feet.

So did Sign.

They trudged through ever-thick snow. It felt like they were wading through waist-height water. When they reached Hunt, there was no doubt he was dead. He had two bullet holes in his chest and one in his head. His killer was an expert marksman. Sign and Knutsen looked around. There wasn't any sign of life, let alone a sniper. Sign checked the body while Knutsen stood guard, his gun in both hands while he scoured any place that might be a good location to lay prone and fire three kill-shots. Sign found nothing in Hunt's clothes. He rolled him over and pulled off Hunt's daysack, the contents of which he poured onto the ground. There was a small blanket, torch, tin of baked beans, flask of water, compass, flare gun, box of matches, and a knife.

"No mobile phone," said Sign.

"He had no idea what he was doing beyond getting away from us. When he lost us, he'd have waited up for a few hours, maybe even overnight, before heading home." Knutsen crouched next to the body. "We got our fifth man, but we got to him too late."

Sign looked at the horizon. "Why hasn't the assassin killed us?"

"What do we do?"

"We notify Richards. There's nothing more to be done here."

They walked back to their jeep, sat in the vehicle, and tried to stay warm while the engine idled and powered the heater.

Knutsen called Richards and notified about what had happened. "We found him. The fifth man. But he's dead. He didn't talk before he died. We've got no evidence." After Richards spoke, Knutsen hung up. "He's sending a helicopter to retrieve Hunt. After it's arrived, we're to drive to Port Howard. Richards is supplying us a boat and crew. They'll transport us and the jeep back to the east island."

Sign bowed his head. Quietly, he said, "So be it."

"Are you okay?"

Sign smiled, though his expression was bitter. "I've always hated failure."

"We could, at least, get the assassin. He's got to get off the west island. Odds are he's going to be on the ferry tomorrow."

"Odds? Yes, what odds are we dealing with?" He looked out of the window. "For the most part the assassins had exactly the same problem as we had – they were searching for a needle in a haystack. Like us they'd have searched Port Stanley. When that didn't throw up any results, they'd have searched a few miles further afield. Then they partially struck lucky – they got Maloney's name. But we came up trumps. We killed Maloney's assassin and we got a deathbed confession from him. We got Peter Hunt's name. Thus, we become the people to pursue because we can lead the assassins to the fifth man. The person I met on the road was not a local farmer. He had an air of command. I have a nose for these things. He's special operations and I would go further to say that he is probably his unit's team leader. He will have wondered where we went today. He has to use his instinct. Collectively, we've exhausted the eastern side of East Island. That leaves the western side of East Island and West Island itself. He'll have deployed his two other assassins – we think they're women – to ground beyond Goose Green. Meanwhile he'll have taken the ferry to Port Howard. Before doing so he'll have spoken to the ferry captain. The boat has cameras; I spotted them when we boarded. No doubt the team leader benignly persuaded the captain to show us images of our faces and our vehicle. That's how he got on to us."

"The case is closed! We tell Richards about the assassination unit. His men take down the sniper at Howard."

"But, then we don't get the whole unit. The women are on east island, I'm sure of that. They'll get off the island by boat, submarine, or light aircraft. The male assassin will never talk. We'll get him, but not the others." Sign looked at his watch. "What time does the helicopter arrive here?"

"Richards estimated about an hour to ninety minutes."

"Then we must move fast." Sign engaged gears and turned the jeep around. He drove to Hunt's cottage. "Stay here." Sign entered the property via the rear door. He knew exactly what he was looking for. In the lounge he found a shotgun. It was loaded with three cartridges. He held it in one hand as he searched the kitchen. He picked up a fish knife – one that had a thin and flexible blade – and tucked it underneath his belt. He went into the upstairs bathroom and opened a cabinet. Alongside many other items, a pair of tweezers were in there. He secreted the tweezers in his pocket, walked downstairs, left the cottage, and opened the passenger door. "We need to go back to the body. Time is of essence."

Knutsen had no idea what was going on as Sign led the way back to Hunt and his crashed snowmobile.

Sign stopped next to the body. "At least two of the assassination team will vanish forever if Richards learns the truth of what happened today. Thus, we must muddy the waters in order to enact absolute retribution. Richards must never know that Hunt was assassinated by Argentinians. I must warn you though – this is going to be messy and will only buy us a day or two. It won't take the coroner in King Edward VII Memorial Hospital long to realise something is amiss. Meanwhile, we must corrupt a crime scene." Sign used the knife and tweezers to dig out the three bullets. He had to cut deep into the head and torso to get them. The wounds looked even more savage as a result of his primitive butchery. He placed the bullets in his pocket. "Your pistol, sir," He held out his hand.

Knutsen gave him his gun. "What on Earth are you doing?"

Sign didn't reply. Instead he fired three shots into Hunt, each in the exact location Hunt had been shot by the sniper. Sign handed the pistol back to Knutsen. He placed the shotgun in Hunt's two hands, curled the dead man's finger around the trigger, and fired the gun into the air. He removed the gun and aimed it at a tree that was one hundred yards away. He walked to the tree. The pellets from the blast had caused no damage to the bark. He walked back to Knutsen and gave him the shotgun. "This thing's useless beyond fifty yards. I'm going to walk back to the tree, cover my face, and you're going to shoot me."

"What?!"

"Just do it." Sign walked to the tree, stood in front of it, and crossed his arms in front of his eyes.

Knutsen was breathing heavily, his arms were shaking. He blinked fast as he raised the gun. No doubt Sign knew exactly what he was doing, but this seemed preposterous.

"Get on with it, Mr. Knutsen," Sign called out.

Knutsen breathed in deeply. He knew Sign was cavalier. But this request was beyond the pale. But, he didn't want to let his friend down. He steadied his legs, leaned forward, and aimed at Sign's chest. One second. Two seconds. Three seconds. Every instinct was telling him not to take the shot.

He pulled the trigger, dropped the gun, and ran to Sign.

Sign was still standing. He withdrew his arms from his face and smiled. "That smarted a bit, But on the plus side I've got pellet holes in my jacket and a number of minor pellet holes in my flesh. It's nothing worse than getting stuck by thirty wasps on a hot summer's day in Hyde Park. Come." They walked back to the body. "Place the gun in his hands. Then we must retire to the warmth of our vehicle and await the arrival of Colonel Richards."

When they were in the car, Knutsen asked, "What the fuck was that all about?"

"Deflection; diversion; call it what you wish. Why is Hunt dead? Because he attacked us with his shotgun. I have damage to my clothes and wounds to prove it. You ran to my rescue. Hunt fired again, but his aim was off. He raised his rifle one last time to kill me. You fired twice into his upper body. He fell to the ground, but was still alive. Hunt pointed his gun at me again. You had no choice other than to take a head shot. In doing so, Hunt flipped onto his side and let off a shot that hit the tree. The forensic analysis of Hunt's hands and forearms will show cordite on his flesh. I am walking wounded, though to be honest I'll pluck pellets out of my chest with Hunt's tweezer. They've only penetrated a couple of millimetres. You killed Hunt to save me. Job done. No need to say anything about an assassin."

"You are mad!"

Sign laughed. "I'm pragmatic." He looked upwards. "Richards is ahead of schedule. Hunt's helicopter has arrived."

They exited the car. When the helicopter landed, Richards and four armed men got out.

Knutsen pointed to the place where Hunt was laying. "He's over there. About three hundred yards."

The men left their commander and went to retrieve the body.

Richards walked to Sign. "What happened?"

"We found your fifth man. Alas, he was somewhat skittish. He fled, we pursued, he opened fire on me," Sign tapped his jacket, "matters escalated, Mr. Knutsen had to shoot him, matters further escalated, Mr. Knutsen had to kill him."

"God damn it!" Richards ran his fingers through his hair. "We wanted him alive!"

"So did I." Sign looked at Richards' men. They were carrying Hunt to the helicopter. "We found the fifth man for you. I would hazard a guess that he was in a state of paranoia. He tried to kill me because he was no longer rational. Do you have an update on when flights will resume to London. Our job is complete."

Richards exhaled slowly. "Two to three days. The high winds will have abated by then."

"Excellent."

Richards looked at Sign's lacerated jacket. "I'll get you to the medical centre in Pleasant."

"No need, dear chap. I've had far worse. This is just a graze; it's not a deep cut."

Richards nodded. "My boat's waiting for you in Port Howard. Try to get there within the next forty minutes. The vessel's high speed and can make the crossing in forty minutes. That should give you enough time to get back to your cottage before nightfall."

"Thank you, colonel."

Richards was about to head to the helicopter, but hesitated. "Is there anything you're not telling me?"

Sign grinned. "Heaven forbid! There are however some loose ends, namely what Hunt's connection was to Wilson and the others."

Richards shrugged. "We won't be bothered to pursue that. Almost certainly he's a mate of a mate of a mate. That's how it works down here."

Sign nodded. "You didn't get your war."

"Not *my* war. An attack on the islands is an attack on Britain. Justice hasn't been obtained."

"We lost a battle. If there's a similar incident in the future, let's hope the outcome is in our favour." Sign walked to the jeep. "Time to go home," he said to Knutsen.

Using binoculars and while prone on the ground, Casero watched the helicopter take off. And he saw Sign and Knutsen drive away from the area where Hunt was shot. When helicopter and car were out of sight, he stood and called Fontonia. "The fifth man's dead. I'll be back on the east island tomorrow. We'll meet at 1400hrs hours at the farm track we parked on this morning. We have one more job to do. Then we'll exfiltrate the islands at 1700hrs. Call Miss S and relay these instructions. There's nothing more we can do today." He picked up his holdall and walked to his car.

Four hours' later Sign and Knutsen were back at Bluff Cove. Sign looked at the drawer he'd opened by a fraction. It was fully closed. "They've been here."

"The Argentinian assassins."

"Yes. But not to worry. Maybe they thawed out and made themselves a nice cuppa."

"Shall I check for bugs?"

Sign reached into the fridge and withdrew a joint of beef brisket. "Yes. I doubt they've planted any because they had to move too fast to search this place plus get on our heels. But one can never be too certain." He diced onions and braised them with the brisket and root vegetables within a casserole pot on the hob, before adding a bay leaf, thyme, pepper, mustard, and red wine into the pan. He placed the dish into the oven, peeled potatoes, and placed them into a pot for par-boiling and roasting nearer to dinner time. He entered the lounge. Knutsen was searching every piece of furniture. Sign said, "Supper will be served in around two hours. Once you've completed your task please get the fire lit. Meanwhile I'm going to have a long bath and extract the pellets some fool shot at me." He smiled and headed upstairs.

When Sign had finished bathing and attending to his wounds, he dressed, came downstairs, placed twenty three ball-bearings on the kitchen counter, turned on a hob to parboil the potatoes, poured two glasses of brandy, and entered the lounge. The fire was lit and Knutsen was sitting in his armchair. Sign handed him a drink and sat opposite him.

Knutsen said, "For an eavesdropping device to work and transmit in these weather conditions and landscape, it would have to be very sophisticated and no smaller than my fist. Certainly it wouldn't be a tiny bug placed under a table or in a lampshade. The logical place to install it would be the ceiling or walls. The walls are stone, and haven't been corrupted. The ceiling could have been corrupted, but it would take at least half a day to open it up, insert a device, and re-plaster and paint the ceiling in the exact colour of the rest of the ceiling. I've looked in and under furniture, in drawers, cupboards et cetera, et cetera. There's no listening device in the cottage."

"Excellent work. You've earned your supper." Sign sipped his drink. "They may come for us tomorrow."

"I know."

"If we tell them something of interest, be under no illusions – they'll kill us."

"Let's make sure that doesn't happen." Knutsen felt weary. "Have you done something like this before?"

"Meaning?"

"Acting as bait? Just waiting?"

Sign smiled. "Like a tethered goat? Yes, many times. But, the point of tethering the goat is to lure in the encroaching tiger or leopard. The predator doesn't know he's walking into a trap. Nearby is a hunter with a gun. It's a tried and tested ploy to kill desperately hungry beasts."

Knutsen rubbed his fatigued face. "If we get out of this alive and make it back to London, the first thing I'm going to do is put shorts and a T-shirt on and sit on a deckchair in a park. I hear southern England's having a heat wave at the moment. I'm sick of the weather down here."

Sign laughed. "By contrast, I shall catch a matinee classical concert at the Barbican or Cadogan Hall. It will take my mind off all matters pertaining to our pursuit of the fifth man."

"Do we have any new cases to work? Anything in our in-tray?"

"Yes. But they're all minor fare – fraud, cheating husbands, vetting of potential employees, and establishing why a woman threw herself onto a train track in Guildford. I could resolve the cases in my sleep and without leaving the comfort of our West Square flat. Still, they pay the bills."

"But, they don't fuel the fire."

Sign's eyes twinkled. "No they don't, Mr. Knutsen. We must hope for a case that is considerably more engaging." He entered the kitchen, drained off the spuds, added them to a metal tray, poured oil over the potatoes, and put the tray into the oven. He returned to the lounge. "As usual, before you sleep make sure you clean your gun We must be on our game tomorrow."

CHAPTER 12

Sign was up and dressed at six AM. He'd barely slept during the night because he'd felt uneasy. That sense was still with him as he placed breakfast food on a chopping board, ready to be cooked when Knutsen emerged, and brewed a pot of coffee. He wondered whether he was making the right decision by staying here until flights resumed. It would be so easy to get accommodation in RAF Mount Pleasant. No one would be able to get to him and Knutsen if they were housed there. But, he still felt a figurative bitter taste in his mouth because matters had not been concluded in the way he would have liked. The only way that could change is if they stayed away from the military base. He and Knutsen had to take their chances. Moreover, there was something that he hadn't told Knutsen. It was a thought that had been nagging him ever since Richards had first visited them in London. The thought wasn't based on any evidence. Rather, it was a question he had; a 'what if', as he liked to call such notions.

He put his fleece on and walked outside. For the first time since he'd been on the islands, the sky was blue. There was still thick snow covering every inch of land, and the temperature was bitterly cold, but a complete lack of wind and no cloud cover showed the islands in a very different light. The landscape around the cottage was stunning, one could see for miles, distant mountains looked like they were only a short walk away whereas they were in fact a long day's walk from Bluff Cove, and all around him was eerily silent.

He stood for a moment, taking in the vista. But, his thoughts weren't on the surrounding beauty. Instead, he tried to imagine where the assassins would come from. Most likely they'd be on foot and would approach from different directions. Was it the right thing to do to put Knutsen in this kind of peril? He didn't know. Knutsen would balk if he told him to leave while he could. Still, he felt a duty of care over his business partner. Plus, he needed him. Knutsen had been in many tight spots during his career as an undercover cop. He was a grownup. He could handle tough situations. That's what Sign kept telling himself. Over and over. But, it was one thing dealing with drug barons and their gangs in London, it was another thing altogether confronting highly trained nefarious types who operated in the secret world. But, there was no one else Sign would rather have by his side. For the most part in his MI6 career he'd worked alone. But, when he'd needed to work with others he'd always applied the same standard in his assessment of them: is this someone you want to stand shoulder-to-shoulder with in the trenches, before the whistle blows and you have to go over the top? Knutsen was that man, without a doubt. It was simple – Knutsen would take a bullet for Sign; Sign would take a bullet for Knutsen. There was no need to overthink that cast iron principal. And yet lesser men and women would never understand that fundamental of sacrifice.

He looked west. He was certain the man he'd met on the road yesterday would be taking the first available ferry out of the island this morning. No way could he have gotten off the island yesterday. And, because he was sure the man was the leader of the assassination team, Sign knew the man would want to be here in person to enact the coup de grâce – the final blow that would put Sign and Knutsen out of their misery. He was coming, Sign was sure of that.

He walked around the perimeter of the house, taking in everything he could see. He and Knutsen were so exposed here. And they only had one gun. They were like chickens in a coop, awaiting three savage foxes to enter. There was nowhere to go; no means of fleeing; no chance of fighting back. That had to change.

He re-entered the cottage.

Knutsen was downstairs, pouring coffee. He was also frying bacon, tomatoes, mushrooms, eggs, and toasting baps. He grinned as he saw Sign. "I thought I'd cook for a change. I'm sick of your shit food."

"Quite right, sir." Sign slumped in a chair. "Visibility is superb today. I wish it wasn't. We are sitting ducks."

Knutsen brought the food through to the lounge and handed Sign a plate of breakfast. "If we're sitting ducks, so are they. We'll spot them before they spot us. What time do you think they'll come here?"

"Early afternoon. I would imagine they want to get off the islands later today. The clock is ticking."

"Eat your food. Drink your coffee."

Sign forced the breakfast and beverage down his neck. He knew he needed the sustenance. But it was a chore to get nutrients and caffeine in to his stomach. "How many rounds do you have left for your Glock 37?"

"Three full magazines. Enough to take down a lot of people."

"Good." Sign put his plate and mug to one side. "Your breakfast has given me a second wind. We must think unconventionally."

"That's what you do."

"Indeed. But, 'amateur improvisation' is probably a more astute term of reference for situations like this. What will the assassins do?"

Knutsen placed his last portion of food into his mouth. "They'll want to overwhelm us, and they'll want to do so up close and personal. There's no advantage to one of them taking a sniper position. We're of no use to them dead. Not until the end, at least. So, they'll come in to the house. They'll shoot us, but not kill us, or they'll physically over power us. They'll tie us up. And that's when the good stuff starts. They'll want to know everything we know about the fifth man. They'll be merciless."

Sign nodded. "I won't tell them a thing." He stared at Knutsen.

Knutsen said, "Nor will I. And the beauty of it is we've genuinely got nothing to say. We got very close to Peter Hunt but not close enough to get him to talk. They can torture us all they like. We never got a confession out of Hunt. So, it's like trying to draw blood out of a stone. They'll get nothing."

"And then they kill us."

"Yep. There's no other outcome."

"I agree with your analysis." Sign stood. "You think I was wrong not to inform Richards about the Argentinian unit. Right now you're probably thinking that I should eat humble pie, call Richards, and get him to send soldiers here."

"The thought had occurred to me."

"Even if I wanted support, it's too late for that now. In all probability, one or both of the women are watching our house. If they see soldiers enter the cottage, the assassins will abort their operation. That would be unacceptable."

"What do you propose?"

Two hours later, Casero boarded the ferry in Port Howard. On this occasion he wasn't the only passenger on the boat. The break in the weather had prompted west islanders to travel to the east island to reconnect with friends and family based there, or to collect supplies in Port Stanley. Casero was glad. He'd been worried that he might be making the journey with Sign and Knutsen. But, Fontonia was watching, from distance, their house in the west island. She'd told Casero that they were both back in Bluff Cove.

From a vending machine, he poured himself a black coffee and strolled on deck. The air was still bitterly cold, but was calm. The sky was azure. For a while, seagulls followed the boat before turning back to land because they sensed they were straying too far from the shore of the west island. Casero sucked in the icy air. He liked the Falklands; they reminded him of the place where he'd grown up in southern Argentina. He had no opinion on whether the islands should belong to Argentina or not. He wasn't interested in politics and power-based land-grabs. His only motivation in life was to do the job in hand. That said, he didn't want to see Argentina and Britain to once again use the Falklands as a battleground. In his view, politicians never understood war. He'd seen too much death to readily embrace a situation where young Argentinian men were told to lay down their lives for a small plot of land. If Sign and Knutsen had learned something from the west islander who'd been shot, they'd take that information to Colonel Richards. They'd have to testify in a British court of law. Then, UK forces would unleash hell on Argentina. Casero's country would be outgunned. It was his duty to get to Sign and Knutsen, make them talk, and then dispatch them.

He walked around the deck for the duration of the journey. When the boat was a few hundred yards from New Haven, he entered his vehicle, checked his weapons, and waited to disembark.

Sign poured coffee in to a flask and handed it to Knutsen. "You're going to need this to stay alert and warm."

Knutsen took the flask and nodded. "Let's do this."

Sign walked out of the house, acutely aware that he was probably being watched by one or more assassins, and got into the jeep. He reversed the car a few yards, and drove it so that it was close to the open front door. The gap between the car and door was only two yards. It would be impossible for anyone with a long range scope to see what was happening in the gap. Knutsen crawled out of the house, entered the rear passenger area, and stayed low. Sign drove the car twenty yards forward, slowed, and said, "Now!"

Knutsen rolled out of the car and dashed into the disused sheep pen outhouse.

Sign leisurely turned the car and drove it close to the front door. He stopped the vehicle and got out. He hoped he was being watched as he leisurely walked around the jeep, pretending to check lights and tyres. He opened the bonnet and leaned forward, looking at the engine. After closing the bonnet, he entered the house, picked up an empty wine bottle, a rubber tube he'd cut off the washing machine, stuffed both in his jacket, exited the house, and crouched by the vehicle's petrol cap. Now, he couldn't be seen. He opened the cap, inserted the tube into the tank, sucked on the other end of the tube, and placed it in the bottle after petrol hit his mouth. While spitting petrol out of his mouth, he waited until the bottle was full. He raised the tube, withdrew it, and screwed the cap back into place. He entered the house, shut the door, placed the bottle on a table, tossed aside the tube, thrust a rag into the bottle so that it was dowsed in the flammable liquid, extracted half of it, and placed a lighter next to the bottle.

Now all he and Knutsen could do was wait.

Casero stopped his car on the farm track, close to the house at Bluff Cove. Sosa and Fontonia were there, standing next to their vehicles. It was two PM. Casero said nothing as he walked to the women. He looked in the direction of Sign and Knutsen's cottage. It wasn't visible, due to the fact that the track was in a hollow and the house was in a dip beyond an elevated stretch of land.

Fontonia said, "They're both in the house, though I haven't seen Knutsen for an hour. Sign, however, is in the lounge. He's pacing backwards and forwards. He's also checked his car. I guess the clear weather has given him an opportunity to ensure everything's in working order. But, he turned the car around to face the road. Presumably they're making a road trip later today."

Casero nodded. "We have no time to waste. Move quickly. Approach the target from the directions we discussed."

They set off on foot, all of them carrying handguns.

Knutsen tried to control his breathing. He was shivering, having been in the tiny sheep pen for two hours. Even the cold-weather attire he was wearing couldn't protect him from the cold. It was the inability to move that was causing him to shake. He had to get control of that physical symptom; had to focus on anything that took his mind of his circumstances. He arched his back to try to relive the muscular tension in his back, got on one knee, raised his pistol, and muttered to himself, "Get your shit together."

Sign walked back and forth in front of the lounge windows. Sometimes he held a phone to his ear, even though he wasn't speaking to anyone; other times he gesticulated with his arms while speaking aloud anything that came into his head. The key objective was for him to appear to a surveillance expert that he was doing stuff. As importantly, he had to be visible.

After all, he was the tethered goat.

Knutsen couldn't see him. And neither of them had mobile phone reception. They were both very alone, their only hope being that they'd stick to their drills and come out on top of the situation. Sign was the most vulnerable, and reliant on Knutsen. But, Knutsen could be shot dead before he got anywhere near his quarry.

Sign kept pacing, even when he got the tiniest glimpse of a person in the snow about eighty yards away. The person was no longer visible.

It was happening.

Sign breathed in deeply. He wasn't scared. That emotion had no purpose in moments like this. And he'd faced death so many times that it now just felt like part of life. But, he was worried about messing this up. He hadn't been able to save Sally, Maloney, and Hunt. If he lost another innocent life he really would be a failure.

He moved to the centre of the room, not caring if he was visible to the assassins. There was no point in playacting anymore. The killers knew he was here. They were coming in to finish the job.

Fontonia slowly approached the cottage from the north. The snow was hampering her progress – it was at least a foot deep. But, she kept her gun held at eye level and focused on the back door.

Sosa walked towards the property from the west. Her job was to incapacitate Sign or Knutsen if they fled the house. It would be a shot to the leg. Then she'd all the injured man into the house so that he could be interrogated. She passed the dilapidated tint sheep pen, got onto one knee, and pointed her gun at the cottage.

Casero reached Sign and Knutsen's jeep. He'd approached the house from the south. He crouched behind the vehicle. The front door of the cottage was only four yards away. He gripped his gun.

Knutsen saw a person walk past his location, stop, and kneel. The person was holding a pistol. It was difficult to tell if the assassin was male or female – a hat, bulky jacket, and other winter clothes hid all indicators of gender. The person had his or her back to Knutsen and was just waiting. Possibly he or she was intending to enter the house through one of the two windows on this side of the cottage. That would be the only way in from the west. More likely, Knutsen decided, she was tasked to shoot Sign if he tried to escape.

He recalled what Sign had said to him earlier in the day.

When they come, don't think like a policeman. Don't call out to them, give them a chance to surrender, attempt to arrest them, or do anything full stop that gives them a second of breathing space. If you give them that second, you're a dead man. They're cold-blooded executioners. The only protocol to be had is to kill them once they're close to the house. No mercy. No hesitation. We can examine our consciences at a later date.

Knutsen aimed his gun at the back of the person's head, pulled the trigger, and watched the head turn into pulp. The person fell forward, blood seeping into the snow.

Sign, Casero, and Sosa heard the shot. All of them reacted.

Sosa raced as fast as she could to the back door. It was unlocked. She pulled it open, ready to storm the building and put her gun in Sign's mouth. But, Sign was standing in the archway between the lounge and kitchen, facing her. He was holding a wine bottle with a flaming rag in its neck. Firebomb. Sosa tried to spin around but she was too late. Sign hurled the bomb at her feet. The bottle smashed. Flames encased her clothes. She dropped her gun, and ran screaming away from the house. She was a ball of orange fire, the colour vivid against the backdrop of the pure white landscape. Sign picked up her gun and shot her in the head. She collapsed to the ground. He put two more shots into her back, knowing that both would have penetrated her lungs. She was dead.

From behind, an arm wrapped itself around his throat. A gun was put against his face.

Casero held him firm. His mouth was close to Sign's ear. "If you wish to live I suggest you do exactly as I say." He dragged him back into the lounge.

Knutsen ran through the snow as quickly as he could. Sign's firebomb hadn't done any damage to the kitchen. He entered the property, breathing fast, his handgun made ready to kill anything that shouldn't be here.

Sign was there, upright. Casero was gripping him tight and using Sign's body as a shield. Aside from the assassins arm, there was barely anything visible of the man holding Knutsen's friend.

Casero said, "Your name is Knutsen. You're holding a Glock. Am I right in thinking it's a 37? That would make it a forty five calibre gun. If you shoot my arm, the bullet will make a mess of my limb. But it will also penetrate Sign's throat. He'll die; I may also die. If you deliberately shoot him in a part of his body where there are no vital organs, the bullet will travel through his body and into mine. But, odds are that both of us will die from shock and blood loss. The only good outcome from this is if you don't pull the trigger. All I want is information."

Despite the cold, Knutsen was sweating. He kept his gun pointing at both men. "You'll kill us when you're done!"

"Maybe I will; maybe I won't. The future is always so terribly uncertain."

Knutsen looked into Sign's eyes. Sign showed no fear.

Knutsen's finger was wrapped around the trigger.

What to do? What to fucking do?

Sign wrenched Casero's arm off his throat and dropped to the floor.

A split second later, Casero opened his mouth.

Knutsen shot him in the chest.

Casero fell back onto the floor.

Sign got to his feet and picked up Casero's discarded gun.

Casero was wheezing, his face screwed up in agony.

Sign crouched beside him and examined the wound. "You have no friends to help you. They're dead. Mr. Knutsen's bullet has made an awful mess of you. I suspect you've got one minute to live. I regret to inform you that I can't repatriate your body to your homeland. You were never here; we were never here; and no one can know why we weren't here. But, I will ensure your body is treated with respect."

Casero was struggling to breathe.

Sign leaned in closer. "You and I don't want war. We're professionals. I'm asking you to do one last thing – be a professional to the end. Will you do that for me? Will you do that for yourself?"

Casero's eyes were wide. Blood was coming out of his mouth.

"You killed a man. His name was Peter Hunt. He supplied military grade weapons. You saw us go to his house. You shot him."

"I... I... saw him die. I didn't do that."

"Oh come on! You were there. You wanted him dead. It was the sole reason you and your colleagues were on the islands."

"It... It was an incredible shot. Whoever killed the fifth man is an expert shooter. But I can't take credit for the kill. Nor can my colleagues – they were on the east island."

"Well, if you didn't pull the trigger, who did?"

"Don't... don't know. Didn't see a shooter." Casero's back arched. "Ask yourself – where was Hunt going when you tried to speak to him?"

"When he got onto his snow mobile and headed north? I've already asked myself that question." Sign stood. "Do you know the answer?"

"No... No." Casero's eyes were screwed tight. "I thought Hunt may have spoken to you. That's... that's why we came here. Information."

Sign glanced at Knutsen. His colleague was no longer pointing his weapon at Casero. Sign returned his attention to the assassin. "Men like you and me walk in the shadows. And we die in the shadows. We don't get medals; recognition; meaningful relationships; peace; or a hero's funeral. But we do get solitude. And that's not a bad thing. After all, how many people can move around the world amid billions of people who don't the slightest inkling of who we are?" He gripped Casero's hand. "It is a rare occasion where men like us bump into each other. We know in a shot that we are one and the same, even though we also know that we can never be kindred spirits. That is our nature – to be alone. You've served your country. This is your hero's funeral." He released Casero's hand.

Casero exhaled one last time. He died.

Sign said to Knutsen, "We need to hide the bodies in the sheep pen. They can be properly dealt with later. Tomorrow, we have a final job to do."

CHAPTER 13

At six AM, Sign and Knutsen left the Bluff Cove cottage. They'd never return. In the boot of the car were their bags containing all their belongings. Knutsen was driving. He'd reasoned that if he was strong enough to help Sign carry three bodies into the outhouse, he was strong enough to turn a steering wheel. In any case, his arm barely hurt now.

It was funny. When Knutsen had first arrived here he'd felt like a fish out of water. Most of his police career had been spent operating in urban environments. The Falklands was as far removed from that as possible. Even Port Stanley was nothing more than a large village. And yet, during his stay on the islands he'd become enamoured with the climate and harsh but spectacular terrain. And as brutal as conditions could be in winter, he found the islanders' way of life endearing and effective. They lived a simple life, were happy, always accommodating, helped each other out at the drop of a hat, were hardworking, and wouldn't swap their circumstances for any others in the world. And they were a peaceful bunch. The only people they hated were Argentinian politicians and generals. They just wanted to be left alone.

As Knutsen drove the jeep onto the road, he said, "I presume we're going to RAF Mount Pleasant?"

Sign answered, "We are but not just yet. I want to have another peek at the west island. After that, we go back to London."

Knutsen frowned. "We didn't achieve our task, but most certainly our business on the islands is concluded. Why go back to Hunt's house. We'll find nothing there that can change the fact that the fifth man is dead."

In a distant voice, Sign said, "I want to know how he died."

Knutsen slapped the steering wheel. "He was shot in the head! A bullet in the brain doesn't tend to help people live a longer life!"

Sign ignored Knutsen's sarcasm and frustration. "New Haven, if you please." He checked his watch. "If we make good speed we should be able to board the nine AM ferry."

At eleven AM they disembarked the ferry, in Port Howard. Knutsen had barely spoken to Sign during the journey. As far as he was concerned, this was a waste of time. Sign, he believed, was trying to salvage his reputation. No doubt he was hoping to find something in Hunt's house that explained why Sign and Knutsen had never stood a chance of speaking in depth to Hunt before the Argentinian assassin killed him. It was a folly. Sign and Knutsen had unwittingly led the assassin to Hunt. The fifth man had panicked and fled. The Argentinian took the incredible shot. Hunt was dead.

Sign said, "I called Oates yesterday evening. He's expecting us. Or rather, he's expecting me. Please take me to his hut."

Two minutes later Knutsen parked outside the conservationist's workplace.

Sign said, "The only reason I want to see him alone is because he's more likely to help if the meeting is one-to-one. But, if you want to come in you have my blessing. I don't want you to feel that I'm excluding you."

Knutsen huffed. "You *are* excluding me! I've no idea why we're here."

Sign touched him on the arm. "I have to protect your reputation. I'm here on a hunch. If I'm wrong, I might as well firebomb myself, just as I did to that poor woman yesterday. I'll go out in a ball of flames. You, however could get another job; your dignity intact."

Knutsen looked at Oates' hut. He breathed deeply. "Is there any danger in there?"

Sign smiled, his expression warm. "No, dear chap. I'll be safe."

Knutsen looked at the dashboard and nodded. "Okay. I'll wait here."

Sign got out of the car and knocked on the door.

Oates opened the entrance.

Sign said, "Mr. Oates. So good of you to see me at short notice."

Oates moved aside, let Sign in, and closed the door behind him. He rolled a cigarette, placed it in his mouth, poured two cups of tea, and sat on his desk. "How can I help? Did you get any joy out of Hunt?"

"He was most helpful. Alas, he's a busy man and could only give us thirty minutes of his time. Our survey of the west coast needs input from others." He walked to a map of the island on Oates' wall and placed a finger on Hill Cove, where Hunt lived. "The road from Hunt's place goes north for another few miles. That would suggest someone else lives at the end of the road. Unfortunately, when we were interviewing Hunt the weather was drawing in. We had to return to the east island. I wonder if you could shed any light on who might be worth talking to in this sector." He placed his finger on the end of the road.

Oates peered at the map. "Yeah, I know who lives there. Harry Monk. He'll be happy to help you out."

"What does Monk do?"

Oates shrugged. "Farmer, like most people here."

"He's a local?"

"Yes. I knew his parents better than I know Monk. They used to let me use some of their farming equipment to restore sea defences. They're dead now. Monk lives on his own. From what little I've seen of him, he's a nice enough bloke. But, I don't use the equipment he inherited from his parents. He had to sell a lot of it. Six months ago he lost a lot of money. I heard it was because he'd invested in a business venture in the east island. He had to pare his farm back to the bone."

"Does he live alone?"

Oates frowned. "What's with all the questions? Just go and see him. He should be useful."

Sign sipped his coffee. "I'm a busy man. Any statements I obtain from islanders who know the west coast of this island must be taken from credible witnesses. Such credibility doesn't just pertain to their knowledge of the island; it also pertains to their character. For example, I've been told not to speak to anyone whose property, or parents' property, was damaged in the Falklands War. They would hold a grudge against Argentina. Their statements would be biased, driven by anger."

Oates sucked on his cigarette. "Pope lives alone." He looked away. "I'm trying to remember; give me a minute." He looked at Sign. "Yeah, I remember. His dad once told me that they had a fishing business on the east island. It was back in the late seventies and early eighties. Dad would work there Monday to Friday, then come home to work the farm at weekends. But, it didn't work out. The farm was too high maintenance and needed him here fulltime. Plus, he said the fishing business wasn't doing so well. He moved back to the west island."

"How old is Pope junior?"

Oates shrugged. "I've never asked him. At a guess I'd say mid-forties."

"Thank you. From what you've said I don't see any reason not to speak to him. May I use your name by way of introduction?"

"Sure."

Sign was about to leave, but hesitated. "Do you happen to know who he was trying to do business with on the east island – the venture that lost him so much money?"

"I do actually." He walked to a filing cabinet, opened a drawer, and rifled through files. "Monk was investing in four trawlers. His idea was to create a fleet that could dominate fishing catches off of Port Stanley. He came to me because he wanted to pick my brains on sea beds, fish migration, and ultimately the best locations for his new trawlers to set up anchor and drop nets. Part of my job as a conservationist is to know shit like that. I was happy to help. Four trawlers ain't going to make much of a dent in sea life. If anything, it's useful. Too many fish in the waters means elephant seals start breeding like crazy. We need a balanced ecosystem here. If the seal population gets too big, I have to cull some of them. I'm the only person on the island authorized to do so. And I fucking hate that part of my job." He pulled out a file. "Here we go." He opened the file. "To give Monk the information he needed I had to go through formal channels. Technically, the charity I work for can't demand money for information. We're not a business. But we can request financial donations. That's what we did with Monk. I asked him to donate five thousand pounds. I drew up a contract. The money paid to us was signed by the investors in the trawler business. Alongside Monk, there were four others." He handed Sign the file. "At the bottom of the first page you'll see their names and signatures."

Sign looked at the paper and handed the file back to Oates.

Oates looked Sign in the eye. "Four of the men in that document recently drowned. I know that from the local rag. You knew it anyway. You're not here to analyse the west coast, looking for points of vulnerability to attack, are you? You're here to investigate the deaths of the four men."

Sign was silent for a few seconds. "On the night they drowned, there is evidence to suggest that there was a fifth man on board the trawler. The fifth man witnessed the deaths of Eddie Wilson, Rob Taylor, Billy Green, and Mike Jackson. He panicked, got into a dinghy, and paddled to shore. Since then, he's gone to ground. I'm working an angle. It is possible that an Argentinian vessel cut across the bow of Wilson's boat. It caused him to urgently change course. After that, I don't know. What I do know is that four men washed ashore, dead. The fifth man can help me fill in the gaps as to what happened that night."

"You think Pope is the fifth man?"

"No. I've already identified the fifth man. But, I haven't interviewed him yet. I need to tread very delicately. He's understandably scared and confused. He may clam up; he may run; he may blame himself for what happened; he may do any number of things. I must treat him with the utmost respect and kindness. Just knocking on his door and introducing myself won't do. I must speak to someone who knows him. I'd like that person to come with me to the fifth man's house and tell him that I'm not a threat and will do nothing to him. I am a stranger from London. I need a local by my side. Someone the fifth man trusts."

Oates looked at the wall-map. "I'm not stupid. You've not spoken to Hunt because you can't do so yet. Hunt is the fifth man. And you're hoping Pope, his nearest neighbour, is the man to calm Hunt down."

Sign didn't answer him fully. "Mr. Oates. I'm dealing with some very deep waters. A man of your intellect can probably estimate just how deep those waters are and why they are dangerous. Can I rely on you to keep our conversation private?"

Oates turned to face him. "I don't want to know how far this goes."

"And I'm not going to tell you. But I would ask that you don't call Hunt and Pope and tell them that I'm driving to see them this morning. To do otherwise would not be in their interest, your interest, or my interest. Between us, we have an island to protect."

Oates stubbed out his cigarette. "We're conservationists." He laughed for a few seconds. "Sure, I won't call them."

"Thank you. Does your charity have a website?"

"Of course."

"I get paid by results. If matters come to a successful conclusion I will transfer ten thousand pounds to your charity and I will express a desire that the funds are funnelled into the research and animal welfare work you're doing on the west island." He walked to the door. "Good day to you, sir."

When Sign was in the car, Knutsen asked, "Where to?"

"We drive west to Hunt's house, but we don't stop there. Instead we follow the road north for a few miles. There'll be a farmstead at the end of the route. Its owner is a man called Harry Pope. I want to talk to him."

Sixty four minutes later they stopped outside Pope's property. As well as a cottage, there were outhouses, a barn, and a paddock in the ranch. A Hilux pickup truck was parked outside the cottage. There was the sound of a chainsaw coming from the rear of the complex.

Sign said to Knutsen, "Whatever happens, don't take your eyes off Pope. And keep your gun close to you at all times."

Both men exited their jeep. Sign knocked on the door. There was no answer. He waved his hand to gesture to Knutsen that they should walk to the back of the house. They did so. A man was there. He was hunched over a tree trunk that was resting on a saw bench, using a chainsaw to slice chunks off the wood. He was wearing a face mask and goggles. Knutsen stopped in a spot where the man couldn't see him, ten yards from the saw bench. Sign walked ahead, sticking close to the cottage's wall, and stopped in a place where he was visible to the man.

Sign smiled and held up his hand. He called out, "Mr. Pope?"

The man turned off his saw and removed his face attire. "Who wants to know?"

Knutsen gripped his handgun, hidden underneath his jacket.

Sign said, "My name is Ben Sign. I work for the military. I wanted to speak to you about one of the islanders. It's a private matter. But, don't worry – this doesn't involve you. May we speak inside?"

The man rested his chainsaw on the bench and loaded the cut wood into a wheelbarrow. He looked annoyed. "What's this about? I'm busy."

"I assure you this won't take up much of your time. Are you Harry Pope?"

"Yep, that's me." The man wheeled the barrow to a nearby woodshed. In doing so he caught sight of Knutsen. "Who's he?"

"That's Tom Knutsen. He works with me."

Pope tipped out the logs into the shed and shut the door. "Why's he flanking me? Is he armed?"

Sign's smile broadened. "Heaven forbid, no. We just didn't want to surprise you. Are the logs for your cottage's fire?"

"Of course they damn well are," said Pope as he walked past Sign, removed his gloves, and opened the kitchen door. "Come in, but make it quick. I've got a shit ton of jobs to do before the sun goes down."

Sign and Knutsen followed him in to the house.

Pope put the kettle on, washed his hands, and turned to them. "So, tell me."

Sign replied, "You obviously know Peter Hunt, just down the road?"

"Yes." Pope's expression was suspicious.

"Tom and I work for the Royal Military Police. There's been an accident involving Mr. Hunt. We've been tasked to investigate the incident."

"Accident? What kind of accident? And why aren't the local old bill looking in to it?"

Sign took a step closer to him. "It's a delicate matter. Hunt was shot. We're exploring the possibility that he was attacked by an Argentinian reconnaissance unit. Possibly they were compromised by Hunt. They shot him and fled. Thus far, this is a military matter, not a civilian police investigation."

Pope frowned. "Is he alright?"

"Yes, yes. He'll need a week or so in hospital, but it's nothing serious. He's conscious and is recovering. We've interviewed him but unfortunately he didn't know who his assailants were. But, we know they were Argentinian. The bullet extracted from his chest was Argentinian. We wondered if you'd seen any unusual activity on your stretch of the coast? Perhaps four men; a boat?"

Pope relaxed. "Can't say I have, but then again would I spot them if they were nearby? I don't know anything about military stuff, but I'm guessing blokes rocking up here in the middle of the night, or whenever, must be Special Forces or something. Why would they be doing a reconnaissance of the coast?"

"To examine potential beach heads for a sea-born assault by thousands of troops. It's a tricky business. They'd have been taking samples of the sand on the beach, checking water levels in the coast, seeing whether armoured vehicles would become bogged down when they drove off landing craft, and many other things." Sign walked out of the kitchen. "Let's sit in the lounge. It will be far more comfortable."

"It's messy in there. Don't..."

"Nonsense." Sign stood in the centre of the lounge, looked around, and called out, "Mr. Knutsen!"

Knutsen put his pistol against Pope's head. "Get in there. Don't try anything. I'm good at this stuff." He pushed Pope into the room.

Sign said, "Sit in that chair and put your hands on your forehead. Don't do anything silly. My colleague is an excellent shot."

Pope did as he was told. "What the fuck's going on?!"

Sign remained standing. "That rifle leaning in the corner of this room is an FLFAL 50.61. The FAL was originally designed in Belgium, but it was subsequently manufactured in Argentina and used in the Falklands War. It is a highly effective assault rifle. It is illegal for a civilian to possess one."

Pope glanced at the gun. "It... it doesn't work. It's just an antique. My dad found it after the war."

Sign picked up the weapon and examined its workings. "It's been regularly cleaned; there are bullets in the magazine; a sight has been attached; modern shock absorbers have been fitted onto the stock. This gun is most certainly on active duty." He placed the gun down. "You used this weapon to kill Peter Hunt."

"What?!"

"It's okay. We don't need amateur dramatics." Sign sat down. Knutsen remained standing, his pistol pointing at Pope's head. Sign said, "Let me tell you what you already know. In the late seventies and early eighties, your father worked in the east island. The war happened in ninety eighty two. It was brief and chaotic. Guns, bullets, landmines, and other munitions were left on battlefields. Your father fancied himself as a trophy hunter. He picked up guns and bullets – British and Argentinian – and brought them back here. I don't know whether he did that during the war or after. Either way he'd collected himself an arsenal. It wasn't unusual. The war was brutally short. Most British forces buggered off after their victory. Largely, it was left to islanders to clean up the mess. I'm sure some of them kept trophies as well. From time to time we all bend rules. But your father's trophies must have been fascinating to you. You were only a young kid at the time of the war. When your parents recently passed away you wanted to use the weapons. You enrolled your friend Peter Hunt, because he had access to Terry Maloney's shooting range in Goose Green. You and Hunt would spend quality time there, firing at targets. It was illegal but it didn't warrant anything more than a slap on the wrist by police."

Pope's eyes were venomous. "Fuck you!"

Sign was unperturbed. "Using military-grade guns for target practice is one thing; using guns to kill people is another thing altogether. You entered into a business arrangement with Eddie Wilson, Rob Taylor, Billy Green, and Mike Jackson. You invested, with them, in the purchase of four trawlers, to be based in the east island. But, the business deal went sour. You lost money. That would have hurt. But you kept your mouth shut and did nothing. You were waiting for the right moment. That moment presented itself when Wilson and his pals decided to take on an Argentinian spy ship that had been lurking around the islands. Wilson knew you had British guns. He called you, asking to borrow them. You complied, with the stipulation that you had to be with them on that fateful voyage. Wilson thought nothing of that demand. He assumed that you just wanted to ensure that your guns were kept in good order. But, he didn't foresee the real reason you had to be on the boat that night. When Wilson and his friends got close to the Argentinian trawler, they opened fire on the vessel with the British guns you'd given them. Most likely it was amateur hour. Wilson and his men were drunk and probably didn't want to kill anyone. They just wanted the boat to go away. But, things then got serious. You shot Wilson, Taylor, Green, and Jackson, with one of your Argentinian war trophy guns. By this time, the spy ship was sailing fast away, fearing it had been compromised. And no doubt it was damaged by gunfire. You didn't care. You dumped the bodies in to the sea, left the British guns on board, and took your Argentinian weapon to the emergency dinghy and headed back to shore. It was all a set-up. Everyone in the know would assume that Wilson and his pals had been killed by Argentinians. You knew where that could lead, but you never knew it would lead back to you. And you did all of this because you wanted revenge. Wilson and his friends never paid you back after your silly investment. You wanted them dead. However, there is one thing I'm not entirely sure about – why did Hunt flee his house when Knutsen and I went to see him? And why did you kill him?"

Pope bowed his head. "He... he knew. I told him. He'd leant me the money to invest in Wilson's project. He hated Wilson and his friends as much as I did." He looked up and removed his hands from his head.

Knutsen stepped forward, tightly gripping his gun.

Pope smiled. "It's a tough life out here." He looked at Knutsen. "Take the shot. Go on. I confess to the murders. Your friend is right about everything. Take the shot."

Sign said in a firm voice, "That won't be necessary unless you do anything stupid." He used his mobile to call RAF Mount Pleasant. "I need to speak to Colonel Richards."

The switchboard operator told him that Richards had worked a night shift and was currently sleeping.

"Wake him up! Tell him I have the fifth man in custody and he needs to get to the west island right now! This is where he and his men need to land their helicopter." He gave the operator details of their location.

One hour later, Richards and four men were in Pope's house. Sign told the colonel what had happened. Pope was placed into hand and ankle cuffs and put on the chopper.

When Richards was alone with Sign in the lounge, he said, "So this was a local murder enquiry all along?"

Sign nodded. "When you first came to see me in London, I wondered if that might be the case. You thought it was the Argentinians who killed the men. But your insight that there was a fifth man on the boat rang alarm bells with me. I wondered if he'd cleverly staged their murders to look like a foreign power had killed them." He smiled. "When investigating matters like this, sometimes the obvious is not so obvious."

Richards nodded. "Pope will be kept in a secure wing in Pleasant. He'll be flown to London on one of my military jets. He'll stand trial and will get life imprisonment. He's killed five men. There'll be no chance of parole."

"Good." Sign smiled. "Oh, and talking of killing people, there is a somewhat delicate matter I need to impart to you. The man I shot at Maloney's place was an Argentinian assassin. He belonged to a four person unit who were here to kill the fifth man. The other three are dead. Their bodies are in the sheep pen at the Bluff Cove cottage. It would be terribly kind of you if you could arrange for the discrete disposal of the bodies."

Richards' eyes widened. "An Argentinian assassin unit?! You killed them?! Why didn't you tell me about them?"

"I didn't want to bother you with such matters." Sign checked his watch. "I believe you've lifted the ban on flights. Knutsen and I will be on the first flight out tomorrow. Meanwhile, tonight we're staying in Port Howard. There's a lovely B&B there. And the owner is a charming host. For dinner she's going to cook us lobster, fried seaweed, mash potato, and roasted lemons, served with a mustard pickle relish on the side. Hopefully she'll also throw in a nice bottle of dry white wine to accompany the dish." He held out his hand. "The case is closed. You owe me and Mr. Knutsen fifty thousand pounds. Goodbye Mr. Richards."

Richards shook his hand. "Thank you. Thank you both very much. Have a safe journey home."

As Sign walked out of the house he called out, "And I hope you have a lovely retirement. Avoid military reunions. They are so tiresome."

CHAPTER 14

Two days later, Sign and Knutsen were back in London. Despite having lived and worked in the capital for the majority of his adult life, it was the first time Knutsen noticed how frenetic and crowded the city was. As they sat in a cab, taking them from Paddington Station to West Square, he looked out of the window and thought his senses were going to overload. His eyes were wide as he looked at cars, people walking along streets, shops, buses, government buildings, high rise commercial properties, and boats as they drove over Lambeth Bridge to cross the Thames. His passenger window was open, because London was enduring a heatwave and the cab was stifling. The aperture enabled him to gain a variety of smells as they made their journey – petrol, diesel, food, overheated tarmac, coffee, perfume, and other scents. The noise was incredible – cars, horns, men using equipment on roadworks, helicopters, emergency vehicle sirens, music, voices, and shouting. It felt like the antithesis of the islands. He was relieved when they pulled up in the quiet retreat of the Edwardian and regal West Square. Sign paid the cabby. Both men entered the communal apartment block.

When inside their flat, Sign dumped his luggage on his bed and called out to Knutsen, "One hour for showering and changing. After that, I suggest we take a stroll."

An hour later, Knutsen emerged into the lounge. Sign was on his laptop, reading an email. He looked at Knutsen. "What on Earth are you wearing?"

Knutsen was in knee-length shorts, a T-shirt that had a picture of a surfboard emblazoned on its front, sandals, and had polarized wrap-around black sunglasses on his forehead. "It's hot out there."

By contrast, Sign was wearing immaculately pressed trousers, a striped shirt, and brogues. He'd shaved. Knutsen hadn't. He looked like a gentleman cricketer, about to partake of cucumber sandwiches and glass of Pimm's in the VIP stand at Lords. Knutsen looked like he was about to have a bottle of beer with some slacker dudes on a beach in Bali.

Sign said, "We need to adjust to the robust entanglement of our home's surroundings. We must mingle with the masses and recalibrate our bodies' tempo. I have the perfect solution. Chop chop. We have a walk to do."

It was late afternoon when they entered Borough Market. The venue was one of the largest and oldest markets in London, dating back to the twelfth century, and possibly even earlier. It sold fine speciality foods, was overlooked by Southwark Cathedral, and was nearby to the southern end of London Bridge. The sprawling venue was busy, in large part because discerning customers knew that at the end of the day they'd get discounted prices on produce.

Sign placed his hand on Knutsen's shoulder. "Follow me, Mr. Knutsen, and ignore the hustle and bustle. I know exactly where to go to fetch some delicious items for our supper." He stopped in front of a fruit and veg counter and addressed a thin man working the stall. "Good day to you Rick. What do you have for me today?"

Rick beamed and said in a London accent, "Mr. Sign. Good to see you sir. It's been a while. What are you cooking?"

"Most likely fish."

Rick patted some of the veg. "In that case, take a look at these beauties. Lemons from Spain. They're in season. Got some lovely parsley if you're hankering after a nice white sauce. Green beans are from a farmer in Berkshire. He knows his stuff. Spuds are the best I've seen in a couple of seasons – you can mash 'em, boil 'em, or roast 'em. And the carrots – blimey, sir. They hold their shape, ain't too sweet, and can be cooked whole or, as I prefer them, cut into slithers on one of them mandolin things. Just watch your fingers if you use that damn thing though."

Sign nodded approvingly. "Excellent, Rick. We'll take them all. Please bag up enough of each to satiate the appetite of two hungry men who've had to endure airplane food for the last fourteen hours." He looked at a basket of chillies. They were different shapes and sizes, some red, others green and yellow. He picked up a red chilli and held it to his nose. "Where did you source these?"

As Rick was placing Sign's order into brown paper bags, he replied, "There's a bloke I know. He's got a loft above his house in North London." He winked. "He grows all sorts of stuff up there, under lamps. These lovelies will be perfect for a few days. After that they'll dry out. But, you can still use them when they're dry."

"I'll take a small bag of them. A mix, if you please."

"Will you be looking to have a pudding? These strawberries are from East Kent. And these are from the Isle of Wight. I can't split them apart in terms of taste. They're the best in the world. Nice dollop of cream on them and you'll be job done."

"Why not."

After paying Rick, they walked to one of fifteen fishmonger stalls.

Sign spoke to a ruddy-faced proprietor. "Larry. How's your beautiful lady? Is she still working the flower stall?"

Larry grinned. "You bet she is. She keeps an eye on me. Stops me from chatting up the women-folk."

Sign laughed. "Quite right." He peered at the array of fresh fishing resting on ice. "I'm interested in this fella. Where was it caught and when?"

The fish was a two foot porbeagle shark. Wearing plastic gloves, Larry picked it up. "Caught off Dorset yesterday. Came in this morning with a load of other stuff. Fresh as a daisy."

"I'll take it. There's no need to clean the fish. I'll do that myself. Do you recommend steaming it in a foil parcel with butter, white wine, lemon, and herbs?"

"Bang on, sir. It should take about forty five minutes in the oven, but you can't go wrong with steaming it for an hour."

Sign and Knutsen walked back to West Square. Sign prepared the food, ready to be cooked an hour before they wanted to eat. He poured two glasses of Calvados and entered the lounge. He gave one of the glasses to Knutsen. Sign sat in his armchair. Knutsen was facing him, in his armchair. Sign raised his glass. "To the successful conclusion of the fifth man case."

Knutsen chinked his glass against Sign's glass. "How did you know that the fifth man was the murderer?"

Sign sipped his drink. "I didn't know for sure. It was a hypothesis. Throughout the investigation, I wanted to prove myself right or wrong. It transpired I was right, but it could have gone the other way. Regardless, we must be bold in our deductive processes. Poor Sally gave us no valuable information, simply because she didn't know what was valuable. It was only when she was under extreme duress by one of the assassins that she blurted out a nugget of valuable intelligence, from her memory vault. The name of Maloney. Thankfully for us, Richards gave us the heads up on Richards, though he imparted that data too late. Maloney was shot by an assassin; we killed the assassin; Maloney told us about Hunt; Hunt bolted when we tried to speak to him; and in doing so he inadvertently told us that he was running to a place of safety. Little did he know that the opposite was true. He called Pope when he saw us. Pope mobilised with a rifle. He shot Hunt before we could catch up with him. When I questioned Oates about whether someone lived near Hunt, I was wondering if someone could get to Hunt quick enough to kill him. Distance was key, as was the fact that the road north of Hunt abruptly ends after a few miles. Oates told me about Pope. I ascertained that Pope had motive to kill Wilson, Hunt, Taylor, Green, and Jackson. He became my prime suspect."

"But, we had to get rid of the assassins first."

Sign waved his hand dismissively. "They were nothing more than pit bulls, trying to latch their jaws onto our heels. Still, they wouldn't have stopped unless we stopped them first."

Knutsen smiled. "You followed an audit trail to Pope. But, when you were speaking to him, you said stuff that you couldn't possibly have known."

Sign looked out of the window. "I knew some things; other things I said were filling in gaps; and there is the most important component – imagination and bluff."

Knutsen laughed. "In my neck of the woods we'd call it the ability to *bullshit*."

Sign looked at Knutsen. "When a man is terrified, the correct use of bullshit will chill him to the bone." His expression softened. "I will cook dinner in a moment. But, I must warn you that while I'm doing so you must shave and change into a suit and tie. I too will adorn a suit. We have a guest who will be joining us for dinner. We must look the part. She's our next client."

Knutsen frowned. "What's the job?"

"She's head of MI6's Russia Department. That means she's very high ranking and tipped to be the next chief of service. But she's hit a roadblock. She wishes to know why her prize foreign agent no longer wishes to spy for her. She also has a personal matter that she wishes us to look into. She has a twin sister. But they were separated at birth. She wants us to find her sister." Sign stood. "Mr. Knutsen – up and at 'em; onwards! We must be on point. I fear this next case may be our toughest yet. Remember – nothing will be what it seems. The case won't be merely about a person who's lost their nerve, or a mundane missing person investigation. It will take us into the bowels of national security. And we journeymen will have to follow that path, no matter what the cost to our lives."

THE END

THE RUSSIAN DOLL

A *Ben Sign* Espionage Story

By

Matthew Dunn

FORMER *MI6 SPY* AND *BEST-SELLING*
AUTHOR

PROLOGUE

Moscow. Fifty years ago.

In exactly twelve minutes and thirty three seconds time, female twins would be born. They'd never see each other again. One of them would be named Jayne; the other Susan. Jayne would return to England with her English parents. Susan would vanish.

    Backtrack fourteen minutes. The pregnant mother was gripping her husband's hand in a grimy Russian medical centre. The pregnant woman was Elizabeth Archer. She was a professor of Russian Studies & Culture at Oxford University. Her husband, Michael, was also a professor at the same university. They were gifted and contrarian types who'd travelled to Russia despite Elizabeth's advanced stage of pregnancy. Before planning the trip, she'd had her last scan at St. Thomas's Hospital in London. The hospital had advised her not to travel. Elizabeth and Michael never did what anyone in authority told them to do. They ignored the advice, didn't tell the airline booking agent that Elizabeth was heavily pregnant, and boarded a nine AM Aeroflot flight to Moscow. They wanted the offspring to enter the world in unusual circumstances. They thought it would be cool if the delivery took place in Russia.

That decision was a dubious one. Elizabeth had gone into labour three weeks ahead of schedule. And she'd done so while undergoing a routine health check in the medical centre. There was no time to get her to hospital. The delivery had to take place in the underequipped and staffed centre. The Soviet Union medical centre was underfunded and overstretched. Paint was peeling off dank walls. The place was crowded with patients who were elderly, or young, malnourished, drunk, injured, or suffering internal symptoms they couldn't explain to the staff but were nevertheless agonizing. The noise in the small complex was deafening. Patients were shouting; trollies with metal containers were rushed back and forward, a loudspeaker system blurted out instructions every few seconds, doctors were barking orders at stressed nurses, fights periodically broke out, a receptionist was screaming at a man in crutches to wait his turn in the queue, and all the time tinny music was played at full volume from the centre's speakers in each corner of every room. The music was designed to calm the occupants of the building. It had the opposite effect.

It was a miracle that Elizabeth was given a private room to give birth. As well as her husband, a midwife, two other nurses, and a doctor were in the room. She was very lucky to get this amount of attention. Still, the whole situation was horrific. Elizabeth was in agony while lying on a bed that smelled of urine. One nurse dabbed a cold flannel against Elizabeth's brow. It didn't help. The midwife stood at the business end of the birth, callipers in her hand in case her baby twisted in the womb and needed to be wrenched out. The callipers looked like a medieval torture instrument. The doctor was leaning against the wall, a clipboard in his hand. For the most part he looked bored and exhausted, though now and again he'd mutter an instruction to the nurses, who in turn would look at him over their shoulders and exclaim obscenities at the useless man.

Michael was sweating nearly as much as Elizabeth. His hand felt like it had been squeezed of all blood, due to the strength of his wife's grip. Now, more than ever, he wondered whether the trip to Russia had been a good idea. But, it was too late for regrets. He stayed by his wife, telling her that everything would be alright, when in truth it seemed like the opposite was the case; saying anything that came into his head and, like all fathers in this situation, fundamentally failing to say anything meaningful. There's nothing meaningful to say to a woman who feels like her body is being torn apart.

Elizabeth – normally an elegantly dressed woman, with platinum blonde hair, high cheek bones, blue eyes, and a curvaceous yet trim figure, now looked a mess. Her hair was matted, some of it clinging to the soiled sheets underneath her. The radiant shine she'd obtained towards the latter stages of pregnancy was now replaced with an oily paste of moisture that made her skin look like the seal fat lather applied by long distance cold sea swimmers to their bodies. Her eyes were red. And her lips were bloody from her teeth clenching in to them.

She didn't care what she looked like. Nor did she care that her legs had been forced into the most un-ladylike position. She just wanted this to be over. Fast. What she did care about was the room. It stank. Not from her, but from previous patients. She had no medical training, but it didn't take a genius to work out that the room was totally unhygienic. The nurses weren't wearing gloves; bloody swabs were tossed into a metal bowl that already contained other crimson swabs that were not from her; the room smelled of cheese, decay, iron, body odour, shit, and piss. This wasn't a place to bring a child into the world. Still, she wasn't going anywhere now until the job was done.

She stared at the midwife. The woman placed her hands between Elizabeth's legs and helped her guide the baby out. The baby's umbilical cord was cut; the baby was washed, wrapped in sheets, and placed into a cot.

After that, everything changed.

Crimea. Four years ago.

Petrov Asina was a twenty seven year old Russian man who'd joined the army age eighteen to escape the humdrum of his impoverished upbringing and resultant boredom of having to survive every day in an apartment in the outskirts of St. Petersburg. The flat was in a tower block that was thirty stories high. There were twelve other apartment blocks nearby, each looking, he often reasoned, like an old person's decaying tooth. The buildings were grey, except when the rain came – then the exteriors turned black. He grew up in a one bedroom home that housed his parents, Petrov, and his sister Natalia. His parents were smart but poor. Father was a teacher; mother a poet who wrote all day but barely made more than a few roubles for her work. They were tired and had long ago run out of puff. There was no chance they'd get a second wind to carve a new life. But, they adored their children and wanted them to have a better life. The problem was they were conflicted. Petrov and Natalia excelled at school. However, their parents only had enough money to pay for one of them to go to university. And even that was a stretch. His father had to take a night job as a security guard, getting only a few hours' sleep here and there to accommodate his day job as a teacher. His mother gave up poetry and got a job as a shipping clerk. Still, they had to choose which child they would financially support and which child they would condemn to a life comparable to theirs. Petrov had lost track of the number of times he'd heard his parents arguing about this subject in the kitchen while he and his sister tried to sleep on their blow-up air beds on the floor. The siblings knew their parents were significantly stressed. And they knew how much they loved their children. They should never have been placed in this situation.

Petrov had the academic rigour to go to university. So did Natalia. Sometimes in life choices have to be made by others, because those mostly affected by the choices presented to them simply cannot decide on the right course of action.

Petrov did what he thought was the honourable thing to do. He took the choice away from his parents. On his eighteenth birthday he entered an army recruitment office in St. Petersburg. He had no idea about the army; had never expressed an interest in any matters pertaining to the military. But he had a clear vision. In the army he'd get fed, clothed, and would be able to sleep for free in barracks. He'd be paid but wouldn't need much of his monthly salary. The cash could help pay for a cottage, on the coast, a few miles west of the city. His parents and sister could live there. This was their only way out of the hellish existence they'd endured for so long. The army recruitment sergeant eyed him with a look of disdain. He told Petrov that his hair was too long and that his physique was scrawny. Petrov had replied that hair could be cut and muscles could be expanded. He looked at posters on the wall – sailors smiling on the decks on battle cruisers; marines storming beaches; pilots disembarking from fighter planes, weirdly, a big breasted blonde on his arm as they walked across the runway. It was all bullshit. But, one poster caught his eye. It looked more serious; more real. It was a photo of a man jumping out of a plane, high above the ground, his arms and legs outstretched, equipment and guns strapped to his back, no parachute deployed. The man looked like a diving bird of prey. More importantly, he looked free. Petrov pointed at the poster and said he wanted to be that man. The sergeant laughed, saying that to be that man Petrov would have to serve in one of the parachute regiments before surviving selection into Spetsnaz, Russia's Special Forces unit. Petrov was undeterred. He liked the idea of freefalling through air, no matter what it took to get that qualification. And when the sergeant told him that elite forces get a higher pay than regular units, he was rifle-shot focused on joining the paras. The sergeant wasn't convinced that Petrov would make it past day one of training. But, he had a job to do and that included meeting quotas of military applicants, regardless as to whether they were suitable for the job in hand. He signed Petrov up for a pre-selection assessment with the 106th Guards Airborne Division, headquartered south of Moscow.

A week later, Petrov attended the assessment course and passed. Two weeks later he began his training in earnest. It was brutal, exhausting, and lasted six months. He earned his parachute wings and was top of his intake. He was officially a paratrooper. And by now he was physically bigger and the fittest he'd ever been. He was a man. Life in the Airborne Division was relentless – constant training exercises, deployments to various parts of Russia, sniper schools, HALO and HAHO qualifications, unarmed combat drills, and excruciating physical training that involved running, mountain climbs, swimming in freezing waters, gym PT, and twenty mile marches with one hundred pounds on his back. He couldn't say it was boring. But – elite or not – back then, Russian military units never saw combat. And though Petrov wasn't a bloodthirsty type, he'd increasingly wanted to test his skills in war. It made no sense to do all this training and not put it to good use. Also, he was changing. Maybe it was because his testosterone levels had increased; possibly it was because he'd been carved into a warrior who had no fight to fight. For three years, that was okay. He carried on doing what he was doing and each month saved up his money for the coastal cottage he wanted to buy his parents. But, boredom is a killer, even if it's crammed with twenty hour days of non-stop activity. Petrov wanted more.

He was twenty two when he applied to Spetsnaz. In Russia, for the most part the concept of Special Forces is very different compared to SF in, for example, the UK and US. In fact, Spetsnaz doesn't translate to the western term *Special Forces*. More accurately it translates to *special soldier*. And there are tens of thousands of Spetsnaz soldiers spread across Russia. Most of them are embedded in regular units. They are not Special Forces. Instead they are soldiers who are tasked with doing things that the rest of their unit haven't been trained to do – parachute insertions at night, reconnaissance, intelligence gathering, and other things. They are highly trained but Petrov was aware that they were not as good as the elite British Royal Marine Commandos or Parachute Regiment soldiers. They were certainly nowhere near as good as SAS, SBS, SEALs, and Delta. Petrov wanted to better himself, rather than move into a unit that thought it was special but wouldn't survive contact with a superior Western unit. He did his research and discovered there were three Spetsnaz units that were completely autonomous from the regular military units. Instead, they worked for the SVR, GRU, and FSB, the foreign and domestic intelligence agencies. These units were small, spent years honing their skills, and only allowed the very best operators to apply to be in their ranks. The units were Directorate "A" (Spetsgruppa Alpha), Directorate "V" (Spetsgruppa Vympel), and Directorate "S" (Spetsgruppa Smerch). Alpha was a counterterrorism and assassination unit. Vympel was a counterterrorism and counter-sabotage unit. Unlike Alpha, it primarily operated on Russian soil. Smerch was a capture or kill unit that operated primarily in the North Caucasus, tracking down bandits, though they also operated elsewhere in Russia. Alpha, he'd heard, was the unit most comparable to Western SF, given it could work anywhere in the world.

He approached his commanding officer in the Airborne Division. While stood to attention in his CO's office, he said, "Sir, I wish to apply to Directorate Alpha."

From behind his desk, the CO looked at him with a cold stare. "That doesn't surprise me. You're one of my best men. Why wouldn't you wish to climb several rungs up the ladder? But, look at it from my perspective. If you succeed in Alpha selection, and that's a big *if*, I'd be losing a highly effective paratrooper from my regiment."

"Are you blocking my request to undergo Alpha selection, sir?"

The colonel drummed his fingers on his desk and looked away, deep in thought. "No." He looked back at Petrov. "I have a son your age. He's not in the military. That doesn't matter. What does matter is how I would respond to him if he approached me and told me that in his heart he wanted to take a huge risk in order to pursue his dreams. What would I say? Would I say he didn't have my permission? He'd hate me for life, and would ignore my stance." He clasped his hands. "Sometimes in life we parents must bite the bullet and let our children fly to their zenith or nadir. You have my permission, corporal. I will arrange matters. That will be all. Dismissed."

Two months later Petrov turned up at Alpha's training establishment. Out of an intake of forty applicants, only three passed the six month selection process; a process that would make other combat units in the Russian military drop their jaws. It wasn't like anything that Petrov had experience before. Airborne Division selection and training was a walk in the park compared to Alpha training. He was one of three people who passed. He felt proud. But then he had to receive continuation training by serving Alpha troops. They gave him no quarter. To them, he was a newbie who hadn't proven himself. In their minds it was simple – when they went into combat they had to have the right man by their side. Petrov had done Alpha selection; but now he was back to square one – he had to show his colleagues that he was up to the task. He was. He served with distinction for three years.

It all changed in 2014.

Russia's neighbour Ukraine was tearing itself apart. The new Ukrainian president was seen as a Western lackey; half the country liked the shift in politics, the other half yearned for a return to communism; war broke out in the eastern peninsula, particularly the Crimea; Russia couldn't tolerate the collapse of the Ukraine into Western democracy; more importantly, it needed to secure the Crimea to ensure that Russia had a land channel to its fleet in the Black Sea. Russia decided to take action. It had the support of the Ukrainian rebels, but they were for the most part amateurs. Russia needed to send specialist troops in to the Crimea.

It did so. They were nicknamed 'Green Men' due to the fact they wore green army uniforms with no insignia. There were rumours in the Ukraine and the West that they were elite Russian troops; but Vladimir Putin, the president of Russia, didn't admit that until months later. Some of the green men were airborne guards, tasked to protect airports and other installations, others were Spetsnaz tasked with arming and supporting rebels. Alpha was sent in with a very different remit. The political landscape of the Ukraine was on a knife edge. Russia needed popular opinion to side with the pro-Russia rebels. And the best way to do that was to make the Ukrainian government and its forces look like a travesty.

Petrov didn't know why he and eight other green men were monitoring a village on the Crimean border with Russia. He assumed it was because there was some kind of strategic value to the zone. He was prone on the ground, on a hilltop, watching villagers in the valley below go about their daily business. His rifle was pointing at them, even though he could perceive no threat. The villagers didn't know the green men were only a quarter of a mile away. The green men were camouflaged, hiding amid bushes and trees.

Petrov wasn't in charge of the eight-man unit. He was a sergeant and was outranked by the captain leading the platoon. So, he had to follow orders, even though he didn't know what those orders were. He waited for several hours, maintaining his surveillance of the village.

The captain gave his first and last order. "We move in to the village now and kill any human we see – men, women, kids, old, young, it doesn't matter. Kill them, and then we extract over the border. This is for Mother Russia, and this is for our ally the Ukraine. When we get back to base I'll tell you why this needed to be done. Meanwhile, don't blink. Do your job."

He led his men down the escarpment above the village. The green men were armed with assault rifles, grenades, and pistols.

Petrov knew this was all wrong. But, it's very hard to disobey orders when you've spent years getting in to the unit you've dreamed to be a part of. Alpha was his family. All that sweat and toil to get into the unit couldn't be wasted. Even though his stomach was in knots, he continued walking, telling himself that he was kidding himself if he thought organisations like Alpha never did black ops. The captain was right, he reasoned. There had to be a purpose behind this. It was part of the bigger picture. He could either follow what he'd been taught in training, or he could follow his conscience. He chose to grip his rifle and stand shoulder-to-shoulder with his comrades.

When they reached the village, the captain was the first to unleash hell. He tossed a grenade at a group of women who were clustered together around a well and were beating dust out of their homes' rugs. The grenade exploded. So did the women.

All of the Alpha men opened fire, except Pavlov.

Men, women, and children were running haphazardly while screaming. Some of them fell to the ground, injured or dead. Others sought cover in their houses or behind walls. Where they hid didn't matter to Alpha. They torched buildings, burning occupants alive, shot people in the head, despatched wounded villagers who were lying on the ground, killed their goats and sheep, and grabbed an elderly man who they assumed was the village elder and hanged him with a length of climbing rope.

It was a massacre. What Petrov was seeing was a set of images that would were being branded onto his brain and would stay with him for the rest of his life. He wanted no part of this slaughter. And he wanted it to stop. He ran to a house that hadn't been torched. Other Alpha men were oblivious to him. They were smiling, just focused on their quarry, shooting and killing like madmen. Petrov went to the top floor of the house. He was alone in there. He guessed the people who lived here were already dead on the street below. He raised his rifle and aimed it at his captain.

The captain was moving further down the central path in the village. Petrov was in no doubt that he was either a madman, a psychopath, a sociopath, or any other label one could apply to a sick fuck. The captain hurled another grenade, this time at a bunch of kids. Petrov counted. One, two, three, four. The grenade would go off in two more seconds. All of Alpha's grenades had been primed for a six second detonation. There was nothing Petrov could do to save the kids. But, he could try to make this end. He counted two more seconds, the grenade went off, obliterating the children, Petrov pulled his trigger, the captain's head was turned into mush.

Petrov ran out of the house, screaming, "Sniper! Sniper!"

The Alpha men stopped in their tracks then darted for cover.

Petrov grabbed the dead captain under his shoulders and dragged him back toward the escarpment. The other Alpha men scanned windows and other places with their rifles as Petrov stayed out in the open and continued hauling the captain's limp body. The Alpha team thought it was the bravest thing they'd ever seen.

One of them shouted, "Let's get out of here!"

The Special Forces men retreated, their job done. Most of the village was ablaze. At least forty people were dead.

They reached Petrov and the captain four hundred yards up the escarpment. The captain was on Petrov's shoulder. Petrov was breathing fast, struggling up the hill towards the Russian border.

One of the men put his hand on Petrov's arm. The man was a highly experienced operative. "We'll carry him from here. What you did was incredible. You should be dead. I'm going to recommend you for the Gold Star Medal." It was the highest award that could be bestowed upon a Russian, and was also known as *Hero of the Russian Federation*. "I can't guarantee you'll get it. We were never here. The captain's body will be disposed of by us. So, if it's impossible for you to get a medal, know that Alpha can picture that medal on your chest."

They took the body off Petrov's shoulder and hauled him up the hill. Petrov spent a moment catching his breath, bent over, his hands on his knees. He looked back at the village. It was a sight no man should have seen. He turned and followed his colleagues towards the border.

Before they got there the captain's body was burned until it was a crispy and molten carcass. It was then tossed into a pond, weighed down by rocks. It was the kind of burial they all expected. They left him there and escaped to Russia.

Three months' later Natalia Asina was in the kitchen as she watched her older brother take a walk along a remote footpath alongside the clifftop close to the cottage he'd bought for his parents. The cottage was ten miles west of St. Petersburg – far away from the hurly burly of city life; close enough to long distance city rail and airplane hubs. Natalia was twenty three, a brunette, fluent in English and French, had no boyfriend or any meaningful friends for that matter, was career-driven, had recently graduated from St. Petersburg State University with a degree in politics, and had passed the gruelling selection process to join the SVR, the successor to the KGB. In one week, she'd be moving to Moscow to start her training.

Her parents had paid for her education.

Petrov had paid for the cottage.

The timing of both events had been awful. Her parents had used up every last penny to give their daughter a better life. Petrov had hoped to give his parents a retirement home. But, their father keeled over a year ago with a heart attack. He was dead before he hit the ground. Their mother had contracted pneumonia. If she'd had any money left she could have paid for hospital care and drugs. She was broke, mentally and physically. She died on her bed, Petrov and Natalia by her side.

Natalia had made a pledge to herself that she would repay the debt to her family. Petrov was all she had now. He couldn't last forever in the army. She'd look after him when she could. And if he had any future money problems, she'd help him out.

Something was wrong with Petrov since he'd been granted a four week holiday before he was required to return to Moscow. He seemed distant, forced himself to smile but in doing so had a grin that looked like a cracked porcelain vase, would never talk about his work, and he drank vodka day and night. When he was sleeping in the two bedroom house, Natalia could hear him from her room. He'd shout out noises that had no meaning, with one exception: several times every night he'd yell, "This is wrong! Stop it! Stop!"

Natalia watched him from the kitchen window. After walking over a slight rise in the footpath, he disappeared from view. She was cooking beef stroganoff for dinner, with plenty of potatoes on the side. She hoped the carbohydrates would soak up the alcohol in Petrov's system. He'd never been a big drinker before. And since he'd joined the army he'd been a fitness fanatic. Now, there was something wrong with his state of mind. But, she had to tread gently with him. Petrov was her intellectual equal, they'd been extremely close as children, never judged each other, and always helped each other and their parents. Maybe that was because the family had grown up in poverty. Or maybe it was simply because they loved each other unconditionally. The last thing Natalia wanted was to cause an argument with her brother.

The only reason she knew he worked in Spetsnaz was because it was mentioned to her by her vetting officer, as part of her recruitment into the SVR. She never told Petrov that she knew which unit he worked in. It didn't seem relevant. He'd tell her himself, if he wanted to, she'd reasoned. She was proud of him before he joined the army; proud of him when he joined the army so she could go to university; proud of him now. But she was worried. Something was troubling him.

She went upstairs to use the bathroom. She was not the prying type, though that would have to change when she became a spy. Petrov's bedroom door was ajar. She didn't want to go in there, but something was telling her that she should. She entered. His bedroom was a mess – bed sheets and blanket twisted into a shape that resembled a coiled python; sweat stains on the bottom sheet; soiled clothes strewn on the floor; empty vodka bottles on a bedside cabinet; the rest of his clean clothes unpacked, within his open suitcase. This was so unlike him. He was always previously meticulous, even before he joined the army. Growing up with parents in a one bedroom flat typically induced almost OCD-like behaviour. It had to be that way – every inch of space had to be accounted for and kept functional and clean.

She closed the door, used the bathroom, and returned downstairs. He needed her, she decided. But how could she help him if she didn't know what was wrong? She knew that Spetsnaz Alpha was an extremely tough gig. They were the most elite special forces that Russia had to offer; always first in and last out. It didn't take a rocket scientist to work out that Petrov had been to the Crimea. But the Russian government was still denying any involvement in the Ukraine crisis. She wouldn't know what happened in the Crimean Peninsula until she joined the SVR. Even then, it might take months, even years, before she was granted clearance to know the truth.

The stroganoff was slowly simmering. The potatoes were boiling. There was nothing more she could do until she served dinner in thirty minutes. She decided to venture out and meet her brother. She put on her walking boots and a coat and leisurely followed the coastal footpath. Though it was cold, the air was still and the sky was clear. She glanced back at the cottage. Petrov had chosen well when he purchased the property. It would have been idyllic for their parents. Mum and dad loved the sound of sea, the smell of heathland, solitude, peace. It broke her heart that her parents didn't live long enough to enjoy their new home. She carried on walking, going over the rise where she'd last seen Petrov, and following the route down on the other side. That's when she stopped. Petrov was sitting on the edge of a cliff. The drop beyond was eighty yards. Ragged rocks were on the beach below.

She forced a smile and walked to him. "Brother, dear. Dinner's nearly ready."

He looked at her. His expression was odd. It seemed to Natalia that he didn't recognise her. He had crimson bags under his bloodshot eyes, his face was pasty, his hands were white as they gripped tufts of grass where he was sitting. His legs were dangling over the edge of the cliff.

"Why don't you come back to the house? It's getting cold out here and the sun will be going down soon." Natalia tried to sound jovial and matter-of-fact, though internally she was scared. "Come on Petrov. I know you're a tough guy, and all that, but even you can get ill if you're not on the move."

Petrov opened his mouth. No words came out.

Natalia frowned. "What is it? Are you drunk?"

Petrov shook his head. He spoke. "No amount of drink can make me drunk."

She crouched beside him and placed her hand on his hand. "I've heard that the downtime is always the worst for soldiers like you. Maybe you shouldn't have come here. It might have been better if you'd stayed in Moscow and gone out for a few beers with your army friends."

Petrov shook his head. "They're not my friends."

In a gentle voice, Natalia replied, "Oh come on. You love their company. You once told me that no one understands a soldier as well as another soldier."

He bowed his head. "I was wrong." He looked at the sea and inhaled deeply. "I wish you well in your new career. But know this: one day you'll realise you're working for a bunch of barbarians. They think they're clever. They're not. They're inhibited by a necessary bloodlust that's determined by a need to exert power on others, both domestically and overseas. That's Russia's Achilles heel. Elections are rigged. We don't care. All we want is the tough man in power. He gives us what we want, even if there's a trail of blood behind him."

"Petrov. You're not making sense. Maybe it's the vodka talking."

Petrov sniggered. "Vodka. It's my medicine. But it doesn't work. Nothing works. Not fucking walks up here, not the quiet, not noise, not company, not books, not TV, not bullshit newspapers, not food, not fucking life itself!"

Natalia's smile vanished. All attempts at trying to convey a calm persona evaporated. She took his arm and tried to pull him to his feet. "Back to the house; food; I don't mind if you drink; sleep; tomorrow's another day."

Petrov pushed her away, with sufficient force to cause her to fall onto her back a few yards away from him. He shouted, "Three months ago my unit was sent into the Crimea. It was a top secret mission. The Russian president was the brains behind our task. But, I didn't know what the task was, until it was too late. The Alpha men with me slaughtered a village. I wouldn't help them. So I killed my captain and pretended it was done by someone else. A fucking village of innocent people! The idea was to make it look like the Ukrainian forces had done the job. That way there's more support for the rebels. And Russia gets what it wants." His voice became quieter. "I watched kids... you know, kids, turned into a million pieces; old people trying to hobble to their homes, but getting sprayed with automatic gunfire in the back; men acting as human shields to protect their families, but all of them getting wasted; people burning to death. The fucking fire. Smell of burning flesh. Screaming. Gunfire all the time. Bangs. And all because of a fucking chess move by the Russian government." Anger was in his voice as he added, "Go and work for the Russians. Do their bidding. But know this: you'll be working for a bunch of psychopaths who don't care about you or anyone else. They sent me to slaughter people. Why? Why would they do that?"

He turned to face the sea.

Natalia screamed.

Petrov launched himself off the cliff.

His body smacked the rocks below.

He was broken and dead.

CHAPTER 1

Modern day.

It was late summer and early evening in London. Tourists remained in the capital, either staying overnight in hotels or intending to catch the last train out of the metropolis and head home or to cheaper accommodation. Their presence doubled the population of London to sixteen million. After a day of sightseeing, they were now seeking relaxation – going to west end theatres, dining in Soho or elsewhere, strolling along the River Thames embankment, riding the London Eye so they could see the city from on high as the sun went down, having a few pints of beer or glasses of wine in alfresco bars or pubs, sitting on pleasure cruisers, or taking their kids to Leicester Square so they could enjoy illuminated fun fare rides.

Londoners eschewed most of these activities in favour of heading to various parts of the city so they could be at home, though some of them had a couple of post-work drinks with their colleagues before jumping on a tube. All Londoners know that the city is actually a multitude of villages, glued together at the hip while retaining their autonomy. A north Londoner rarely knows much about south London, and vice versa. Ditto east versus west versus the centre. And even within those zones, the diversity is incredible – different cultures, classes, property prices, shops, restaurants, history, dialect, crime-levels, types of crime, and jobs. London is not a *melting pot*, as it's often described. It's a series of different identities that are held together by a spider web of interconnecting transportation links. And it's also one of the loneliest places in the world.

Tourists come and go and mean nothing to Londoners beyond the fact that visitors clog up streets and encourage tacky street vendors to set up their stalls. Residents might occasionally socialise together, but for the most part they scurry to their bolt holes at the first opportunity when they've completed their day job, like rats darting in every direction after they've fed on a tasty carcass. A person could live in a part of London all his or her life and not know anything about a residential street that was only four roads away. Everyone under the age of forty should live in London at least once; everyone over the age of forty should move out.

Not everyone complied with that mantra.

Ben Sign was forty nine years old and lived on the top floor flat of a converted Edwardian terraced house in south London's West Square, in Southwark. He was a former senior MI6 officer, tipped to be the next chief until he resigned because he refused to buy-in to the backstabbing power-hungry nature of those who wished to get to the top in Whitehall. A year ago, he'd set up a private detective consultancy.

His business partner was Tom Knutsen, fourteen years his junior, a former Metropolitan Police undercover operative. There were two bedrooms in the West Square flat. Sign slept in one of them; Knutsen the other. Sign was a widower. Knutsen was to be married, but his fiancée was murdered. They knew all about loss and grief. West Square was their base of operations. It was also the location where the two men, with wholly different in backgrounds and outlooks, could keep each other company, eat good food, put the world to rights while sipping a post-dinner Calvados, walk the streets of London, and challenge each other's way of thinking. They were two lonely men who'd been given a second chance at finding true friendship. And that's what they were: colleagues and friends. Nothing more; nothing less.

Sign was tall, slender, had clipped brown and grey hair that was singed at the ends by a barber in St. James's in order to produce a perfect cut, spoke with an aristocratic accent, and bought his suits and casual attire in Saville Row. And yet, he was from humble origins. His father was once a merchant navy officer, always travelling, before becoming an academic. His mother raised him with very little money. His brilliant mind was his way out of his modest but loving upbringing. He got sponsored to go to Oxford University, gained a double first class degree in politics, philosophy, and economics, and was tapped on the shoulder to join MI6. He was regarded as the most successful spy of his generation. Now, out of MI6, he still had a hotline to the prime minister, foreign secretary, defence secretary, home secretary, Met police chief, and heads of MI6 and MI5. They weren't going to ignore his talent. If they had a problem they and their officers couldn't solve, they'd call Sign.

For the most part, Knutsen was different, though, like Sign, he had a good intellect and had gained a first at Exeter University before joining the police. While he didn't possess Sign's brilliance, he complimented the former spy master very well. And that was why Sign had chosen him to be his business partner, over and above a number of other candidates from the intelligence agencies, police, and special forces. Knutsen had energy, could mingle with folks from all walks of life, had the advantage of not being as posh as Sign, could run a hundred metres in ten seconds flat, and was still young enough to not overthink the consequences of putting a bullet in a man's skull. He was an expert marksman and a dab hand at unarmed combat. So was Sign. But Sign had inflicted and seen too much death and destruction in his career. These days he preferred to think; not maim or kill.

Knutsen was nearly as tall as Sign. He had short blonde hair, an athletic physique, spoke with a working class London accent even though he grew up in the West Country, and owned one suit that he'd bought at a discount price in Marks & Spencer in Oxford Street. He knew London like the back of his hand – years of infiltrating ruthless gangs will grant a cop that knowledge – but didn't have Sign's grasp of the world, nor his ability to deduce the solution to seemingly intractable problems from the comfort of his chair. Sign was his mentor, there was no doubt. Knutsen didn't feel awkward about that. He was bright enough to realise that there was so much he could learn from the former spook. He also realised that a lifetime spent with Sign would barely scratch the surface of Sign's brain. That didn't matter. Knutsen was here for not only companionship; he was also here for the ride. It is rare for a man to be in the presence of brilliance. That said, Sign could be a cantankerous so and so at times. At home, Sign had his strengths. He was a superb cook, meticulous with his ablutions and keeping the flat clean and tidy, for the most part polite, and could regale Knutsen with mind-blowing tales about his past exploits. It was never boring living with Sign. But, Sign also had a propensity to irritability when their only cases were mundane – investigating potential infidelity, financial fraud, the vetting of potential employees, and the like. Sign hated work that didn't flex his intellect. He grew morose and snappy when he didn't have a job that made his head hurt.

Below them there were three other flats in the building. Sometimes they were temporarily occupied by students and city workers. Right now they were being refurbished by the landlord and were empty. Sign and Knutsen were glad of that. They liked being left alone. And their apartment was a treasure trove. The bedrooms, bathroom, and kitchen were modest in size, though Sign had transformed the kitchen into a chef's paradise. There were meat hooks attached to the ceiling, holding pans, ladles, clusters of garlic, vines of tomatoes, and, on occasion and when the season dictated, pheasants and other game - bought in nearby Borough Market - that needed hanging for up to a month before cooking. On the kitchen windowsill were pots of growing chillies, basil, tangerines, and lemons. A magnetic strip was attached to the wall and held knives that were old yet razor sharp, one of them having been used as a murder weapon in Jaipur in nineteen fifty six, another that had been used by an unfortunate adventurer to cut open a dead bear in Canada so that the man could sleep inside the animal rather than freeze to death, and the rest a collection of blades that had been used by a Chinese knife thrower within a circus in Hong Kong. Upon moving in to the flat, Sign had ripped out the useless electric cooker that the landlord had installed. He'd ordered a top-notch gas cooker. A reformed strangler who called himself Hip Hop had helped him fit the new cooker and dispose of the old one. Hip Hop owed Sign a few favours. It was the least he could do. But, it was the much larger lounge that was the centrepiece of the property. It was stunning; least ways for two bachelors. Women would probably say it needed a female touch. Sign and Knutsen didn't care. They currently had no women in their lives. They were blokes and they could live how they damn well liked. The room had antiquities sourced from Burma, Mongolia, France, Patagonia, and Japan. Three armchairs were in the centre of the room – two facing each other next to a fireplace; the third on the other side of the room. On the walls were paintings, framed military maps of various parts of the world, bookshelves containing academic journals, leather-bound out-of-print works of fiction, poetry, non-fiction, and a diary written by a British naval officer during his voyage to America in 1812. Persian rugs were on the floor. The curtains adjacent to the double window were heavy and crimson. The mantelpiece above the fireplace had candles, oil lamps, a revolver that had belonged to a Boer soldier, and an Arabian dagger that had its tip embedded in the mantelpiece's wood and was vertical. There was a tiny dining table, about the size of an average table in a Michelin Star restaurant, that was in one corner of the room.

It was six forty five PM. Sign and Knutsen were in suits, shirts, ties, their shoes polished. They were expecting a female guest for dinner and had to look the part. Sign was roasting and steaming shark, boiling potatoes and vegetables, and making a gravy consisting of sweated onions, fresh herbs, red wine, a homemade vegetable stock reduction, and a stick of aniseed. Satisfied that the meal was underway, he turned his attention to the dining table. With precision, he laid out a starched white table cloth, used a hot iron to flatten it, added pristine silver cutlery and two sets of polished wine glasses per person, set mats, and placed a bottle of white wine and a bottle of still mineral water in the centre – both in ice buckets. He went to the drinks cabinet – a Victorian piece of furniture he'd purchased in Kenya – and withdrew a bottle of French Cognac. He poured some of it into two brandy glasses.

He said, "Mr. Knutsen. Our guest arrives in less than ten minutes. Before she arrives we shall have a sharpener while sitting in our armchairs."

Knutsen took his drink and sat in his chair, facing Sign. "Why the VIP treatment?" He pointed at the third armchair in the room. "Normally you sit clients on that, and then tell them to bugger off after they've told us their sob story."

Sign sipped his drink. "I don't recall ever telling a client to *bugger off* or variants of that vulgar phrase."

"What about that bloke who thought his wife was possessed by the devil?"

"Oh, yes. He was wasting our time. I admit to being a tad curt with him." Sign swirled his drink in his brandy glass. "Why the VIP treatment on this occasion? Our guest is Jayne Archer. She's fifty years old, British, and single, no children."

Knutsen smiled. "So, the fancy meal and dining table placements are because you might just have the hots for her?"

"Hardly. I want to show her respect. She's a very senior MI6 officer who's just been promoted to head up the service's Russia Department. It's a plum posting. She knows me, and I know her, but not that well. Our paths rarely crossed due to the different nature of our work in MI6. And just to clarify – I do not have the *hots* for her and nor does she have the hots for me. Romance is not an emotion that features in her prevue, nor mine for that matter. All that matters to Archer is her work. Be careful of her. She's sharp."

"As sharp as you?"

Sign waved his hand dismissively. "I'm just a buffoon who gave up the opportunity to have the best job in Britain in favour of working a poorly paid business in partnership with an out-of-work cop."

Knutsen laughed. "We all make mistakes. But, I came out alright from your faux pas. I got a place to stay and a bit of cash in my pocket."

Sign smiled. "You've never made mistakes in your life?"

"Not really."

"You executed your fiancée's murderer in cold blood, could have been imprisoned for life, but instead got sacked from the police."

"Oh yes, there is that." Knutsen stated, "Any minute now a government servant is going to knock on our door, hoping to engage us on a case. I imagine she's on a good salary, but how's she going to be able to afford to pay us? With our running costs and personal draw-downs from our company, we're operating at a twenty K per month overhead."

"She has family money. She can afford our fees."

The downstairs intercom buzzed.

Sign said, "Mr. Knutsen. Would you be so kind to let Miss Archer into our humble abode?"

One minute later Jayne Archer was in the lounge. She was medium height, slightly plump, had blonde hair that was cut into a functional bob, was wearing the smart brown skirt and matching jacket that she'd worn to work in the day, and wore black shoes that had a centimetre high heel. From distance she looked plain. But up close there was no mistaking there was something special about the woman. Her eyes glistened and flickered as they took in everything around her. She radiated a weird aura – it felt like a kinetic energy. Her expression looked benign; but if one examined her with greater perception it was one of a person who knew she could outwit everything around her. Knutsen thought she reminded him of a crocodile, waiting partially submerged in water, its fake grin visible to prey, immobile, letting the quarry come to the reptile, and then striking with deadly speed. Sign was right. Be careful.

Sign sauntered up to her, his arms outstretched. "Hello gorgeous. I hope you like our digs. It's an oasis of calm amid a sea of madness." He embraced her and kissed her on both cheeks. "Will you have wine or something stronger? Dinner will be about ten minutes."

In a well-spoken voice she replied, "I'll have a whiskey with a dash of water."

"Quite right."

She looked at Knutsen. "Who is this handsome man?"

Sign placed his hand on Knutsen's shoulder. "Tom Knutsen; my business partner; former cop; undercover mostly; preferred conforming to criminal gang culture rather than the gang culture of the Met; left the police after a rather unfortunate lapse of judgement; joined the business a year ago; single; messed up in the head; loyal to me, and only me; university educated but can play the part of a bruiser; very useful with a gun; kills people for me." He looked at Knutsen. "Have I missed anything?"

With sarcasm, Knutsen replied, "Cheers. You've summed up my life in a nutshell."

"Excellent, dear chap. I'll let you two get acquainted while I serve up dinner. I do hope, Miss Archer, that you're not averse to fish. You haven't gone all mid-life crisis vegan or some such nonsense?"

"Fish is fine", she replied.

When Sign was in the kitchen, she sat opposite Knutsen, her drink in her hand. "I heard that you and Ben broke two very big cases within the last year."

Knutsen nodded. "I just did the donkey work. It was Ben who solved the problems."

"Does that rile you?"

"Nope. I know my strengths and weaknesses."

"Why did you join the police?"

"Would you like me to reel off a bunch of clichés? Stuff like, I wanted to protect and serve; get an adrenalin buzz; see parts of London that most people don't know; risk my life for others; that kind of shit. Truth is I wanted a job. And I wasn't dumb. When I joined there weren't many graduates entering the police. They thought I was a wonder-boy, even before I started my training. I thought it was a load of bullshit. But, I needed the cash."

Archer's eyes were locked on Knutsen. "And yet you eschewed more cash by gaining fast track promotion in favour of staying a lowly undercover cop. That says something about you."

Knutsen shrugged. "Undercover work gets extra pay and is all expenses paid. I don't need much beyond a room, bed, and a bit of grub in my belly. I had no need to become a superintendent or chief constable. Like Ben, I've never been power-hungry. We're not like you. "

"I don't seek power. I seek answers. You, however, seek solitude. You are like a monk. But one day you'll pine for more." She looked over her shoulder and called out, "Ben – would you like some assistance?"

Sign entered the room, two plates of food in his hands, the third nestled in the crook of his arm. "Nonsense! Since when do guests help their hosts?" He placed the plates on the dining table. "Dinner is served. I will pour the wine. It's a lovely 2016 Canapi Pinot Grigio. I selected it from my vintners in High Holborn. If one examines one's palate when sipping the wine one can detect tropical fruits and citrus. It is the perfect accompaniment to a solitary shark which has lost his way off the Dorset coast and yearns for warmer climes. Please be seated. We must have rules – no business talk while we eat. We can discuss why the three of us are in the same room when we have our post-dinner coffee and brandy."

After tasting the first mouthful of food, Jayne said, "This is delicious, Ben. You were always a good chef. Do you remember when you cooked us camel in a sand pit in the Yemeni desert? You, me and twenty eight other recruits. We were so naive back then. Well, all of us except you. I remember you unearthing the camel after it had been slow cooking for three days in charcoal. Goodness knows how you sourced the camel. I guess it was road kill. You carved it and served the meat alongside rosemary potatoes, juniper sorrel, chick peas infused with star anise, and dreadful wine you'd stolen from the nearby police station. You'd built a bonfire out of the trunks of sun-baked trees. And before we ate you sang us an old Yemeni song about a pauper's feast. You were always designed to be unusual."

Knutsen asked, "You both trained together?"

Sign tucked in to his food. "For six months, when we joined MI6. Then poof! We were sent our separate ways, like dandelions blown into a wind of multiple directions and agendas. We were carried across all parts of the world. Most of us never saw each other again."

Archer looked at Knutsen. "We were all superb. But Ben was different. He was top of our class. He saw the world and its possibilities in a light that even other brilliant MI6 officers couldn't fathom. Still, you had your flaws, didn't you Ben?"

Sign smiled as he ate. "The head of the training program felt he was an expert in all matters espionage. I told him that I'd pay for him to have a two week holiday in Hawaii if he could stop me sleeping with his wife. If he lost, he had to do me the honour of making me the top student of his batch. He accepted the bet. He said I didn't know where he and his wife lived. His wife had been faithful to him for nineteen years. He thought he was on to a winner. That was until he found me in his house, asleep alongside his wife on their double bed. Of course, I never touched his wife. But, I did sleep with her. He lost the bet." Sign sipped his wine and giggled. "Poor old William. I don't think he recovered from that. Part of me wishes I'd had the opportunity to apologise; part of me thinks he was a fool to take on the wager. Still, I regret that he passed away last year."

Archer addressed Knutsen. "In MI6 we are encouraged to take on the impossible and make it our mistress." She looked at Sign. "How have you been since you left the service?"

Sign munched on his potatoes. "It depends on what day of the week you wish to analyse me. Over the last year I've been broke, solvent, sad, lonely, happy, brimming with energy, slothful, intellectually stimulated, bored, charming, irascible, and happy. How have I been? I've lost a few strands of hair since I left the service. Apparently, in men, it's either due to too much testosterone or too little. My barber estimates I've lost two percent of my hair, compared to a year ago. I know for a fact I've lost nine thousand and eighty three hairs – not enough for anyone to notice. The average head has at least one hundred thousand hairs, more if you're blonde or a red head." He looked at Knutsen. "How have I been since I left the esteemed MI6?"

Knutsen looked at Archer. "I didn't know him when he was in your organisation. All I can say is that ninety percent of what Ben says is utter bollocks; ten percent is so precise it hits you like a sidewinder missile."

Jayne smiled. "The ninety percent is the chaff to deflect attention away from the ten percent." She looked at Sign. "Isn't that correct, Ben?"

Sign tucked into his shark. "I am like anyone else. I lie up until the moment I tell the truth. How have you been Jayne?" Sign didn't look at her.

Archer smiled. "You always were the brightest boy. I've been better, but I don't want your pity."

"You won't get any from us." Sign poured more wine for Archer and Knutsen. "We're candles, Jayne. We burn with ferocity, we shed wax, we extinguish. Are you extinguishing?"

I'm..." For the first time Archer looked unsettled. "I don't know." She composed herself, her poker face back on. She said to Knutsen, "Anything I say to Ben must be treated in the strictest confidence. Your police security clearance isn't high enough to be privy to matters pertaining to British Intelligence. Still, if Ben trusts you then I have no problem talking in front of you, providing you stick to the rules."

Knutsen shrugged. "When I had to pretend to be someone else while I spent quality time with a bunch of psychos who would have cut my head off if they found out who I really was, I got used to keeping my mouth shut. Security clearance or not, I wonder if you've spent chunks of your life living in fear."

"I have." Archer carried on eating. "As you both are aware, I've recently been promoted to head up the service's Russia Department. Even though I was born in Russia and speak the language fluently, I'd never served in the department before. I suspect the service wanted an outsider to run the show. MI6 has a long track record of being contrarian."

"Congratulations on the appointment." Sign slashed his knife into the shark's flesh. "Any fellas in your life?"

Archer laughed. "I have plenty of *fellas* in my life – male colleagues, my hairdresser, doctor, the chap who serves me wine at my local brasserie, my bodyguards when I'm overseas, and others. But, I certainly don't have a lover. What about you, Ben?"

Sign carried on eating. It seemed to Knutsen that he was deliberately being cavalier. "Two women dead. Two chaps left standing. Mr. Knutsen and I are not yet in the mood to start courting pretty ladies. That may or may not change." He finished his food and placed his cutlery on his plate. "So here we all are – loveless entities." He smiled. "I bought the camel off of a Bedouin. It was riddled with disease and parasites, and was dying. I purchased the unfortunate creature with a carton of cigarettes. Did you notice that I didn't eat the animal? I hoped I'd poison the rest of the recruits. I reasoned some of them would die; others would be hospitalised for a sufficient duration to render them unable to continue their training. I had everything to gain, because I'd be the last man standing."

Archer looked at Knutsen. "He may be lying; or he may be telling the truth. You and I will never know."

Knutsen nodded. "I'm getting used to it." He stood. "I'll clear the plates and put the coffee on."

"Excellent idea," exclaimed Sign. "Let's retire to our sumptuous armchairs. I have a smashing Lemorton 1972 Calvados. It won't conflict with the coffee. The calvados will be our *Le Trou Normand* – our means to obtain a hole in our stomachs after a hefty meal, though traditionally Le Trou Normand refers to a spirit that is served in France midway through a meal, not at the end. But we shall defy convention."

Two minutes later they were in their armchairs, coffee and calvados on small tables adjacent to each chair.

Sign said, "And now to business. You have a problem, Miss Archer – one that your peers, subordinates, and superiors cannot solve,"

Archer sipped her calvados. "I have two problems; both of them delicate."

Sign rubbed his hands. "Excellent. Juicy intrigue or salacious indiscretions. Or both."

"Ben – stop being flippant." Archer winked at Knutsen before looking back at Sign. "We can all playact and be chameleons. You don't need to put on a performance for me. I will see through it."

Sign nodded. "It's the layers beneath that you'll struggle to discover." He closed his eyes, clasped his hands, and leaned back in his chair. "Proceed."

Archer addressed Knutsen. "MI6 is a cell-like structure. Think of it as a honeycomb. I do things that my boss isn't cleared to know about. He does things I'm not cleared to know about. In headquarters there are people in the room next to me who have no idea about my work, and I've no idea about their work. There are different departments. None of us knows what another department does. Most importantly, none of us know about each other's foreign agents. It has to be that way. Secrecy is paramount. So, what I'm about to tell you is information that is only privy to a small number of security-cleared individuals. If you break my trust, Tom, I'll crucify you."

"Get on with it, Jayne. We have no time for melodramatics!" Sign remained deep in thought, with his eyes closed.

Archer kept her eyes on Knutsen. "I'm about to break the law by telling you something. If MI6 found out why I was here, they'd put me in prison and throw away the key. Breaching Section 1 of the Official Secrets Act is no trivial matter. It's one step away from treason."

Sign was getting impatient. "And yet here you are and here we are. And if we all have to spend quality time together in clink, you can look forward to the possibility of me telling you one day how I really sourced the camel. I'll give you a teaser – it involved me donning a chequered silk dish-dash and riding the beast across fifty miles of desert. It was very *Lawrence of Arabia*."

Archer sipped her coffee. "I run a female Russian agent. She's SVR, posted to Russia's London station. She's only twenty five years old."

"Her access?" Sign's tone was curt.

"She knows the names of every Russian spy in Britain."

"Her motivation to spy for you?"

"She hates Russia. Or more precisely, she hates the Russian regime." Archer placed her cup back onto its saucer. "Her brother was in Special Forces. He was deployed to the Crimea. He witnessed his colleagues commit a state-sanctioned massacre. He killed his captain, though his colleagues never found out it was him who pulled the trigger. He was riddled with guilt, took to drink, and committed suicide. My agent saw him take his life."

"And at that moment, his guilt transferred itself into her. She spies for you because it is her only was of slowly but surely bleeding the guilt out of her system." Sign opened his eyes. "But, something's gone wrong."

Archer nodded. "Without doubt, she is the best agent the Russia Department has. Only I am allowed to see her. She's single-handedly giving us the ammunition to dismantle not just the Russian spy network in Britain, but also its presence in France, Germany, and elsewhere in Europe. Plus, she has knowledge of Russia's footprint in the States. Some of this information is in her head. Other names she has to steal from files and by the use of interpersonal guile. It's a fraught task. She's walking a high wire tightrope. We all know what would happen to her if she got caught."

"Yes, we do. Why has she stopped spying for you?" Sign was looking straight at Archer.

"I didn't say she had."

"I'm accelerating proceedings. If she'd gone missing and you simply wanted us to find her you wouldn't have given us the information you've just supplied. Instead, you'd have spun a cock and bull story about why she's of value to you and why you need her back. No. You want us to get into her head. She's stopped spying for you and you want to know why."

"Correct." Archer was cautious. "I don't know if I'm doing the right thing, being here."

Sign huffed. "What's her name?"

Archer said nothing.

"What's her name?!"

Archer looked at Knutsen, then Sign. "Okay. So this is the bit where I break the law. Her name is Natalia Asina."

Sign took a swig of his calvados. "Given her age, she's of a low rank in the SVR. But, given her access to the names of Russian spies, she has a highly confidential, but desk-bound job. She's not yet been unleashed to be a front-line operative. She's an analyst. Correction – she's a human resources specialist. She has to monitor Russian spies in Europe and elsewhere. Her remit is welfare. If a Russian spy needs help, she directs support to that spy."

"Yes. But, not all spies. She's only cleared to know the identities of low to medium ranking agents in Britain. She has to manufacture access to the names of the top Russian spies in the West."

"Of course. But, at great risk to her wellbeing, until recently she was able to do that and pass that information to you. Now, she's got stage fright. You want us to work out why."

Archer looked cold as she replied, "The *why* is pertinent but not paramount. I just want her to continue to do her job."

"The *why* is most certainly pertinent if we are to tear apart her brain and ascertain the reason why she's no longer cooperating." Sign dipped his finger in his drink and placed it in his mouth. "How many MI6 officers are privy to the identity of Natalia?"

"Alongside me, the chief and four other high ranking officers."

"What are their views on this matter?"

"The chief is putting enormous pressure on me to get Natalia back on track. The others have offered to meet her. But, I've declined that offer. She'd clam up further. Probably she'd flee to Russia. She only trusts me."

"That must change." Sign said, "Tell me about her personal life and character."

It was clear that Archer didn't like being interrogated in this way. "She's single, though she had a boyfriend at university. She split up with him when she got the job offer with the SVR. Her parents are dead; she's pretty; no financial problems, though she's on a meagre salary; fluent English; intelligent; perceptive; lives in a one bedroom flat in Battersea; no pets; likes to go to nightclubs on a Friday night, but only to dance; drinks alcohol but not to excess; doesn't smoke; has never taken drugs; listens to music."

"What music?" asked Knutsen.

"Indie music. My Bloody Valentine, The Orb, Primal Scream, The God Machine. And other stuff that I'd never heard of until I met her."

Knutsen looked at Sign. "I like her."

Sign shook his head, a look of disdain on his face. He asked Archer, "What are her Achilles heels?"

"Hatred of Russia and vulnerability. Both can produce in her emotions and skewed decision-making. A woman bearing anger and fear can feel very frightened. She's terrified of herself and of others."

"As a result, we have the measure of her." Sign slowly exhaled. "Miss Asina is lost in the world. The only mentor she has is a manipulative MI6 officer. She's being raped by the system, on a daily basis. But, that's not why she's stopped spying for Miss Archer. No. There's another reason. We must determine the cause of her volte face."

Archer nodded. "I want a second opinion. Will you meet her? I would set up the meeting and say you are both serving MI6 officers."

"As you wish."

Archer's poker face was gone. "Ben – I'm asking you to do this because I respect your judgement. If anyone can get through to her, it's you."

"My dear, of course. Now, you have a second reason for being here."

Archer nodded. "I was born in Moscow in extremely insalubrious circumstances. At least, that's what my parents told me. My parents were professors at Oxford University. They specialised in Russian politics, language, and culture. After I was born, my parents returned with me to England. They raised me well, educating me, inspiring me, and teaching me many matters Russian. It's why I'm fluent in the language – both spoken and written. They taught me. They encouraged me to work in government, in some capacity. In particular they wanted me to one day get a job where I could combat the excesses of Russian regimes."

"Russian or Soviet Union?"

"In my parents' minds they were one and the same. By the time I was at university, they told me that it was my decision, and my decision alone, as to what career I chose."

"But, the ground work had been done." Sign placed his fingertips together. "They'd brainwashed you into hating Russia. No doubt they paid for your university education. And they'd been fabulous parents throughout your life. You felt you'd let them down if you didn't pursue a job in a government department."

"Yes."

"But, there would have been a trigger point for their hatred of Russia. And it would have been something that was personal to them."

Archer both loved and hated the fact that Sign was always so damn accurate. "My father died six years ago, of natural causes. My mother is in a care home in London. Her brain is completely lucid, but she suffers from a multitude of physical ailments that render her unable to look after herself. I visit her regularly, work allowing. The last time I saw her was a week ago. I'm hoping that she will soon be able to move into my house. But her medical tests need to be complete before she can be discharged; plus, I need to convert the interior of my house to accommodate her disabilities – a stair lift, walk-in bath, handrails throughout the property, panic alarms, et cetera. The reason I mention my last visit to see her is because that was when she told me something that shocked me. Before I tell you what it is, I must reiterate the my mother's brain is as sharp as it always was and her memory is rifle shot precise. She doesn't have dementia or false memories."

Knutsen asked, "What did she tell you?"

Archer breathed in deeply. "She told me that I wasn't the only one to come out of her womb. I have a twin sister. Her name's Susan. I came out first. My birth was straightforward. Susan's birth was complicated. My mother and I were sent to hospital. Susan was kept in the medical centre where we were born, allegedly to be monitored by doctors and nurses. Something happened. My mother and father never saw Susan again. She was snatched by the Soviet authorities. My parents and I were forced to get on a plane out of Moscow. They had no choice. Soldiers made them leave. Ever since, my parents had no idea if Susan was alive or dead."

"Which is why your parents hated Russia and why they indoctrinated you to think the same way." Knutsen asked, "Before a week ago did you have any inkling, any suspicion, that you had a sister?"

"None whatsoever. I was in shock when my mother told me. I'm still in shock."

Knutsen leaned forward. "Why didn't your parents tell you about Susan before?"

Archer raised her hands. "What good would it have done? Telling me that I have a twin who may be alive or dead in Russia is hardly information that a good parent would wish to impart to their daughter."

"So, why tell you now?"

It was Sign who answered. "Because Jayne's mother knows that her daughter has just been promoted to head up MI6's Russia Department. Jayne is an adult who's now in a position to potentially find Susan. Her mother felt the time was right to burden her daughter with her secret."

"Yes, that's right." Archer smoothed her hands over her skirt. There was no need to do so. Her skirt was immaculate. "My mother is security cleared by the service. I was allowed to tell her about my postings within MI6." She lowered her head. "I wondered if you could help me find out what happened to Susan. I realise that I'm presenting you with two wholly different cases – Natalia and Susan. What are your fees?"

"The cases may have some crossover."

Archer frowned.

Sign said, "If it's a government or corporation, we charge a fixed rate: half up front, half upon successful completion of the job. If it's a private client, we charge variable rates, depending on the circumstances of the client. What steps have you taken to find Susan?"

Archer looked frustrated. "I've tasked my analysts to do traces on the name Susan Archer, and to see if we have any details of the birth of British twins in Moscow in the month I was born. They've had zero results. I've spoken to the man who was third in command of our Moscow station at the time. He's retired and is in his eighties. He doesn't know anything about the incident. The second in command and the head of station died a few years ago. I've also spoken to two KGB defectors who were based in Moscow when Susan went missing. They couldn't help. I believe they don't know anything."

"Have you asked Interpol or the Metropolitan Police to submit a formal request for assistance to the Russian state police?"

"Yes. Russian police were helpful. They said that details of births in the Soviet era were notoriously inaccurate. Many were not even recorded. They couldn't find any records of Susan's birth."

"Could your mother be lying to you?"

Archer sighed. "I knew you'd ask me that. No, she's not lying. She has no reason to lie. She was crying when she told me about Susan. They were genuine tears. She was shaking. Her face was flushed. Plus, my mother has never been good at lying."

"She's kept this secret from you for fifty years. She clearly has some ability in deception."

Archer looked angry. "She withheld a secret that was deeply personal to her. That's very different from lying."

Sign smiled. "I agree." He crossed his legs, glanced at Knutsen, and looked back at Archer. "Our terms for both cases will be as follows. You'll pay us nothing up front. But you will pay us all expenses incurred during the investigation. And if, as we dearly hope, one or both cases are successfully resolved, you can then pay our company a success fee of your choosing, depending on what you can afford."

Archer was silent for a few seconds. "That's… that's very kind. I realise it's not your normal terms and conditions. Are you doing this because I'm an MI6 officer – helping a fellow pilgrim and all that?"

"No. I'm proposing this arrangement because I don't want us all to end up in a god-awful British prison. If we take a chunk of money from you upfront, and it's discovered why we received that money, we don't have a leg to stand on in the eyes of the law. Discretely pay us after the event, not before." Sign stood and walked to the mantelpiece. Next to the embedded knife was a small wooden chest encrusted with platinum patterns of cacti, won by him in a game of Texas hold 'em poker in a Moroccan souk. He opened the box. Inside were seven mobile phones. He withdrew one of them, and its charger lead, and handed it to Archer. "This is your hotline to us. It's deniable. There's only one number stored in the phone. That number reaches one of my phones, also deniable. Never use your name when calling. Never text or email."

"I know how to conduct tradecraft!"

"Yes, but you've never broken British law!" Sign towered over her. "Follow my instructions to the letter, pay any expenses we require, set up the meeting with Natalia, do so in a way that doesn't scare her off, and," he checked his watch, "get an early night tonight."

Archer tried to hide her anger. "As you wish. Good day to you gentlemen." She shook hands with Knutsen and Sign and left.

Sign slumped into his armchair and sipped his calvados. "What do you think?"

"I think you were very hard on her."

Sign shrugged. "People like Archer must not be given a millimetre of due deference. To do otherwise would mean they'd snatch a mile of our souls. She'd have the upper hand. We'd be slaves. I couldn't allow that to happen, and she knew that before she set foot in this room. She doesn't know me that well but she knows *of* me. She knew she'd be intellectually outgunned."

"God, you can be an arrogant bastard."

"Not arrogant. Arrogance is a propensity to look down on the weak and not help them. I don't look down on anyone; and I help people. And when I help them I do need them to surrender to their rescuer. When a person is drowning in a lake, and a lifeguard comes to that person's rescue, it is no one's interest for the drowning person to panic and try to fight off the chap who's trying to haul the person to shore. When a client engages us, they must submit to our ways of doing things."

"You mean you mentally break them?"

"I put them in their place. Then I start work. And at the end of a successful investigation, no one is more delighted than me when I see a client has a beaming smile on his or her face."

Knutsen asked, "How will Archer set up our meeting with Natalia? She's already told us that Natalia's skittish and will most likely do a runner if anyone else in MI6 tries to meet her."

"Jayne Archer is like me. She nudges the world into a direction of her choosing. That said, getting Natalia to meet us will not be easy. I suspect she won't say anything to Natalia. She'll bounce us into the meeting. Almost certainly the encounter will take place in a hotel room."

"God, you bloody spooks!" Knutsen laughed. "Mate – that was a nice dinner tonight. I'd score you at least five out of ten."

"Five?!" Sign had a twinkle in his eye. "The meal was perfect."

"I'd have preferred gravy rather than that sauce thing you made."

"Gravy with fish?! You heathen."

Knutsen asked, "Why is Natalia so important to Archer? I get the sister thing; but Natalia? That's just business."

Sign undid his tie. "Being an MI6 officer is a peculiar job. We know our agents better than we know our colleagues. Agents trust us with their lives. We communicate with them in English or their language, hold their hands, hug them when they're crying and scared, talk to them about their families, talk to them about anything that matters to them in their private lives, offer them hope, assistance, tell them they should only trust their handler, buy them nice dinners, cheer them up with a drink or two, talk about the latest Strictly Come Dancing results or any other mundane nonsense that comes into our heads, take them shopping, pheasant shooting, fly fishing, buy them perfume, or any other activity that flicks their switch, and all the time we do that because we want them to betray their countries and risk their lives. It's a contract between handler and agent. We look after them and make them feel special; they spy. The agent signs up to the contract, as does the MI6 handler. And the agent knows that the charming and considerate handler is sending them to their death. But, at the same time it's a marriage of sorts. Platonic love is a constant. Both handler and agent share one overwhelming fear: failure. Together, they try to make the relationship work." He arched his back. "Natalia is special to Jayne. She gives Jayne what she needs – information. But the marriage is on the rocks. Jayne doesn't like that. She's come to us because she thinks of us as mediators. Jayne's pride is at stake. She doesn't want the marriage to fail."

"Because it would damage her career?"

"No. Because she doesn't want Natalia to be sad."

Knutsen stood. "I need to get out of my suit. Once I'm in jeans and T-shirt, are you up for a couple of pints at our local boozer, and a game of darts?"

"One hundred percent, sir. But, I must warn you that I've been practising darts at the pub, without you knowing."

Knutsen laughed. "You really do talk bollocks."

CHAPTER 2

The next morning, Archer entered the care home that housed and treated her mother. It was located in Godalming, a forty five minute train journey south of Waterloo station. The place was on a hill, close to the prestigious Charterhouse School, and was once a sixteen bedroom private house, with six acres of beautiful grounds, that – during its two hundred and twenty three year existence – had been lived in by a high court judge, film star, opera singer, general who'd seen active service in World War Two's Operation Market Garden, American evangelist who'd turned the place into a venue for his religious cult, and a Turkish billionaire. The property had gone into receivership after it was discovered that the billionaire was avoiding UK tax and was making most of his money by illegally buying and selling blood diamonds, ivory, and vulnerable black girls and young women from Africa for use in European brothels. After five years in prison, the billionaire was thrown out of Britain. That's when the care home took possession of the property. The new owners, husband and wife, were Quakers, doctors, conscientious objectors who'd served in numerous battles in the Vietnam War as combat medical soldiers, subsequently worked for NGOs in Central and South America, set up their own malaria treatment hospice in Papua New Guinea, and could afford to buy the property after the wife's father, an investment bankers whose principles she loathed, had bequeathed his daughter five million dollars in his will. After he died, the husband and wife agreed that the money earnt via greed needed to be fed back into society. They bought the three million pound property on Charterhouse Road, spent a substantial sum on getting it converted, employed highly trained staff, and opened for business as a care home. It was their retirement of sorts. The husband and wife were now in their eighties. They were no longer up to the task of 24/7 looking after others – younger people did that for them – but every day they'd visit the fifteen occupants of the facility to check they were okay, were being cared for, and to see if they had any special needs. The home was one of the most expensive in southern England, but it had to be that way. The location was beautiful, the grounds were stunning, and the staff were highly paid because the Quakers only wanted the best for their residents. Their staff included two groundsmen who'd previously worked at Kew Gardens, a chef who'd trained in a Michelin Star restaurant, two on-call doctors who could have taken other highly lucrative jobs in the UK or overseas, nurses who were on twice the pay they'd have received if they'd stayed in the NHS, two Polish cleaners who were given free accommodation in a lovely cottage on the grounds, free food, and a healthy salary, and two mechanics who ensured that all medical machinery in the home were operating correctly. Thirty percent of all profits from the business were donated to the NHS, ten percent to the local church and state schools, and the rest was used to run the impeccable facility.

Some of the patients were here long-term; others were brief visitors who stayed until they were able to be safely cared for by their family. Jayne's mother was somewhere in between both camps. She wanted her mum to live with her in her house in south west London, but she also needed her to be fit. Jayne couldn't keep a constant eye on her; she was summoned overseas at short notice; and she wasn't medically trained.

Jayne approached the reception desk. She smiled. "Hello Ricky. They've got you working front of house today."

Ricky shrugged. "Gives me a chance to put my feet up. I've clocked seventy hours doing nursing duties this week." He held up his phone. "Since I've been here from six this morning, I've managed to get to level seventeen on Call of Duty. How are you Miss Archer?"

"I'm just checking in." She patted the carrier bag she was holding. "I've brought mum some Belgium chocolates and an academic thesis on how massive landmass, frightening winters, a depressed population that is spread out, alcohol and other substances, and an overwhelming sense within the population that life isn't worth living, will inevitably produce a collective sense of being inhuman. It doesn't refer specifically to Russia. It doesn't need to."

Ricky munched on an apple. "You sure know how to cheer your mum up." He nodded toward the corridor. "Usual place. She's had breakfast."

Jayne walked into the communal lounge. It was a very large and sumptuous yet eclectic room that had a mixture of old and modern fittings, with large bay windows overlooking the grounds' manicured lawn and array of bushes and trees that were trimmed into different shapes – Jayne always thought of the gardens as indicative of a set from Alice In Wonderland - , leather armchairs, oak side tables, gold rimmed paintings of city and county side scenes from 1920s England, widescreen wall-mounted television, Nintendo Wii which could be used by residents between the hours of ten to eleven AM so that patients could exercise their limbs by playing bowling, white-water rafting and other video games, a library containing books that ranged from the classics to popular modern-day fiction, a green-felt-clad table that was used for communal games of bridge and other card games, and The Heaven Telescope, as it was nicknamed by residents. The telescope was long, mounted on a tripod, was pointed out of a window at the sky, had once been owned by an eighteenth century astronomer who'd discovered previously unknown stars, and the more religious residents of the home liked to think it gave them a glimpse of the place they'd be going to when their presence on Earth was no longer needed.

Simon Doyle's face lit up when he saw Archer. He was the co-owner of the care home. Eighty three years old, holding a cane, the American was, as ever, immaculately dressed. Today he was wearing purple corduroy trousers, brogues, shirt and cravat, and a waistcoat with a time piece attached to a chain nestled in a breast pocket. "Jayne my dear. How's my sexy broad doing today?"

Archer laughed. "I keep telling you not to call me that. Your wife will be jealous. Anyway, you're too young to be referring to me as a *broad*. I think that term went out of fashion in America in the forties."

Doyle looked mischievous. "Some terms stand the test of time. I'm an old fashioned guy. Anyway, my wife's back in the kitchen, checking on the lunch menu with the chef. She doesn't know about our little affair."

Archer smiled wider and put on an American accent. "Do you think you've got enough left in your pants to keep up with this gal?"

Doyle shrugged. "We won't know until we find out." He hobbled over to her and put his arm on hers. He looked over his shoulder. "She's in her usual spot at this time of day – in one of the bay window sections, by the table, reading. Hey, we're serving tea and coffee in a few minutes. Do you fancy a hot one?"

"That would be lovely. How's she doing?"

"Pretty much the same as before. She gets tired after dinner, wakes early, can get in to a chair and bed but has to summon a lot of energy to get out, incontinence remains an issue but she and we are managing that, her blood pressure's a bit low, occasional dizzy spells persist, speech and cognitive faculties are good, muscle wastage is constant but slow, no signs of cancer or any other terminal disease, and she's in good spirits." He rubbed Archer's arm. "It's just old age." He patted his hip. "And I know all about that. This hip replacement of mine is a nuisance; it's on the side I always used to like to sleep on. I keep forgetting. Wake in the night feeling like I've been bitten by a rattlesnake down there. Mrs. Doyle never swears except when she's lying next to me in our bed and I wake her up at three in the morning because I'm yelping like a pig that's been shot in the arse." He looked at Elizabeth, who was on the far side of the room. Elizabeth was reading, oblivious to her daughter's presence and out of earshot of Doyle's conversation with her. "The only thing that's changed is she's getting dehydrated. We have to administer fluids via intravenous drips. She's on one now. At the moment it's not a twenty four hour thing. The doctors and nurses have judged that she needs a top up only twice a day. It's not your ma's fault – she drinks plenty. It's just the liver and kidneys aren't processing stuff as well as they should." He looked back at Archer. "We can't release her into your care just yet. But, I don't see why she has to be here for much longer. Once you've finished getting your house converted it will be fine, providing either you or a care worker can be with her when she's awake. Even when she's not awake, you'll need to think about night time routines. She'll want to pee fairly frequently. And other bodily functions."

"I know." She embraced Doyle and stood back. "How are you and your wife doing?"

Doyle laughed. "We're not spring chickens anymore. But we've got good people working this gig. All me and my gal do is potter – check on menus, chat to the residents, write quiz questions for Thursday night's residents competition, sit in front of our accountant and listen to him telling us how much this place costs to run, sign documents, have a nap in the afternoon, take a walk around the grounds before dinner, get one of the gardeners to drive us down to Waitrose once a week. Our days of heavy lifting are long gone. But, we like it here. Two crazy Yanks living the life in leafy Surrey. We only came here because my gal thinks she came from English stock. She isn't. I researched it. She's part Irish, French, Italian, Scandinavian, and Austrian. She knows that I know that. But, we don't talk about it. What's the point? Her heart's in England." He nodded at Elizabeth. "Go and sit with her. I'll make sure you get two cups of tea. Let's keep swapping notes. I'll let you know when your mother's ready to be released; you let me know when you're ready to have her." He was about to attend to his duties but hesitated. "Jayne. I know you've spoken about this before, but don't feel guilty about putting Elizabeth into a care home. You haven't got someone to help you out, you're busy, and your ma does need medical supervision. She likes it here. And she needs support. *Professional* medical support. Better this place than being in a hospital bed, trust me."

"I know. I just wish my damn job wasn't pulling me in all directions right now."

"Even if it wasn't we wouldn't recommend releasing her just yet from medical care. I'm not saying that because I want your money. We don't operate that way. If you didn't have the bucks to pay our fees we'd still keep het here for free if you wanted. Or we'd refer her to the NHS."

"Bless you Simon. The world's a better place with you and your wife in it." Archer walked to her mother. "Hello Mum. Mind if I join you?"

Elizabeth looked up. "Jayne, my dear. I wasn't expecting you for a couple of days. Is everything okay?"

Archer sat next to her mother. "I just thought I'd stop by for a cup of tea with you. Also I have news."

Elizabeth gripped her daughter's hand. "Susan?"

Archer chose her words carefully. "Finding out what happened to Susan will take time. But, I am on the case. I've engaged an expert to look into the matter. He's ex-MI6."

Elizabeth placed her book to one side. "Does he know Russia?"

"Yes. And he's the smartest person I know."

Two orderlies came to Elizabeth's chair. One of them removed her drip, while the other poured tea. When they left, Elizabeth sipped her tea. Her hand was shaking from nerve damage. "Being smart is one thing. But, does he have the capabilities required to find out what happened to Susan?"

Archer nodded. "He was on the fast track in MI6, tipped to be the next chief. He threw it all away to become a private consultant. He's significantly better than anyone if have at my disposal in my department. Plus, he has the advantage of being independent."

"He can break laws to get to the truth."

"Correct."

Elizabeth slowly placed her cup and saucer on the table, careful not to spill the drink. "Do you trust him?"

"He's very discreet."

"Do you like him?"

Archer pondered the question. "We joined the service at the same time and did our training together. After that, our paths rarely crossed. From what little I've seen of him, and what I've heard about him I'd say he's charming, ruthless, kind, rebellious, results-driven, hates boredom, feels dislocated from people, and carries sorrow in his heart. It's hard to answer your question. He's a chameleon who changes shades depending on the environment he finds himself in. I suspect it would take me a long time to find out who the real person is beneath his various disguises."

Elizabeth raised an eyebrow. "He's not the only one in your world who has multiple personalities."

"True."

"How will he go about establishing what happened to Susan?"

"He didn't tell me and I didn't ask him." Before her mother could interject, Archer held up her hand. "He'll have his methods and he'll want to keep them private, for two reasons: first, he won't want me interfering; second, if he does have to break rules, he'll want to do so without implicating me."

Elizabeth laughed, making no attempt to hide her sarcastic tone. "How very noble of him." Her expression changed. In a softer voice she said, "He does sound like the right person for the job. I shall think of him as a solitary falcon, watching everything from high altitude, and waiting to dive to Earth when he spots his quarry." She rubbed her arm and winced. "Be a darling and get me a new set of bones and muscles. All that prancing around like an idiot, with the other residents, in front of the Wii box while pretending to be skiing down a slope at Whistler, doesn't seem to be having the desired effect on my body. If anything, it just puts more aches and pains in my body."

Archer could feel herself getting emotional. She kept it in check, just. Elizabeth wouldn't have wanted to see her daughter cry. She had enough on her plate without having to comfort a distraught daughter. "Simon told me that you're making good progress. The only reason he'd like you to stay here for a bit longer is because the staff want to monitor your levels of hydration. But, if you still need the IV drips on a daily basis, that won't stop you from moving in to my home. I can administer the IV. The doctors and nurses will teach me, and teach me other things. They've very kindly said that I can do a week's medical course here before you're discharged."

Elizabeth smiled. "I do like it here. The staff and facilities are excellent. It's peaceful, but also stimulating." There were four other residents in the room. They were watching TV or chatting. They couldn't hear Elizabeth and Jayne. The rest of the patients were out in the grounds or receiving check-ups in the onsite medical centre. She pointed at each resident. "After Gordon graduated from Eton he was a batsman for the England cricket team, a fashion photographer in the sixties, a school caretaker, a failed polar explorer, and a ship's captain who used to smuggle marijuana from Morocco, Mexico, and Nigeria. Muriel helped design and build Apollo 11, the first craft to put men on the moon. Before then she was a folk singer, occasional prostitute, and a campaigner for black rights. She was a rebel with a Harvard-educated brain that excelled in rocket-science. Toby was unofficially the first man to swim the entire length of the River Thames. He did so after a drunken bet with his friends. He went to Cambridge University, and was kicked out for punching a don in the face because the academic had declared that sodomy had no place in a Christian society. He joined the French Foreign Legion and was court martialled and severely beaten after he skipped parade in the Legion's Djibouti base in favour of erecting a huge placard overlooking the military camp saying 'All Frenchmen Are Closet Homosexuals'. When he was released from military prison, he returned to Britain and ran a safe house for rent boys. He educated them and got them back on their feet. He was awarded an OBE for his sterling work. Yvonne owned two casinos in Bogota, moved to Ireland in the nineteen seventies, made bombs for the IRA, then became an special branch informant, moved to London, married a film director who cheated on her and died in mysterious circumstances, and hit the headlines when she walked down Oxford Street, topless, campaigning for the sale of untampered milk." She smiled. "Look at us now. We're old. All we have is the memory of the trails that we blazed in our past."

Archer looked at Gordon, Muriel, Toby, and Yvonne. "You might find it boring living with me."

Elizabeth shook her head. "Gordon's got cancer and wouldn't survive an operation. Muriel has dementia. Toby has Parkinson's Disease. Yvonne keeps trying to kill herself. People here come and go. Most of them go out in a box, so to speak. I will miss the people in this room. But, we're all resigned to the inevitable. Plus," she drummed her arthritic fingers over Archer's hand, "who'd want to miss out on spending time with Jayne Archer? One of the most brilliant students of her generation at Cambridge University, a knowledge of Russian history, language, and culture, that would make most academics extremely unsettled, a glittering career in government, travelling the world, informing and changing government and international organisations' policies, identifying that spy ring in Munich, so many other huge achievements, oh, and putting that KGB defector in the boot of your car and driving him across the border between Pakistan and Turkmenistan. You could have been killed then, and so many other times. But, you held your nerve." Elizabeth sighed. "I just want to have a hot bath without medical staff standing in the same room. I'll be happy and mentally stimulated in your home in Putney. I'm looking forward to driving my mobility scooter down the river promenade. When the sun's out, the Thames glistens like a huge excitable shoal of silver bass, chasing food just beneath the surface. And when it's dark, the river becomes moody yet alluring, it's black surface only visible from the Victorian lamps that straddle the Thames. I like to think the river is grumpy at night yet asleep. I adore that. It reminds me of your father when he was alive." She waved at one of the orderlies before looking back at Archer. "It's that time of day where I'm required to go for a stroll in the grounds. When will you come back?"

"Anytime you like. Same time tomorrow? I want to update you on progress with the new fittings in my house." She held up her carrier bag. "By the way – chocolates and a book. I'm not sure if sugar and a psychological analysis of the human condition is what the doctor ordered, but to hell with it." She placed the bag in front of Elizabeth.

Elizabeth smiled. "Same time tomorrow, but only if your work allows." Her smile vanished. "When I look at you I look at Jayne Archer, and I also look at Susan Archer. Every day, I've carried that burden for fifty years. I look at you, I look at her. It's been torture."

Archer kissed her mother on the cheek. "It's the bravest thing I've ever known."

That afternoon, Archer was back in London. For two hours she spent time in MI6's headquarters in Vauxhall Cross, checking in on her department, reading telegrams, and attending a meeting in a board room with other senior members of the service. After that, she left to attend an agent meeting in Mayfair.

She approached Duke's Hotel. The old building was tucked away in a short cul-de-sac within the heartland of one of London's wealthiest districts. It was hard to find unless one took a cab to the venue, was only a five minute walk from Buckingham Palace, was small yet luxurious, old, had a solitary and creaky lift, and a tiny bar that was world renowned for its martini cocktails. She took the elevator to the fifth floor. There was no one in the corridor. She walked past rooms until she got to where she wanted to be. She looked left and right. Satisfied she wasn't being watched, she knocked three times on the door, waited five seconds, and knocked twice.

Natalia Asina opened the door a few inches, though kept the chain lock in place.

Archer asked, "Would you like a coffee?"

The phrase was the pre-agreed code between Archer and Natalia that it was safe to meet. If Archer had asked, "Would you like to have a cocktail downstairs at six?" it would have meant that she suspected she was under surveillance. In that case, Natalia would have shut and locked the door, opened the room's sash window, walked twenty yards along the twelve inch wide exterior ledge, opened another window, and entered a room that was three rooms adjacent to hers. Then, she'd stay in the back up room that was paid for by Archer. Archer would meanwhile try to draw the surveillance team away from the hotel. And when the time was right, Natalia would leave the premises. But, it wasn't a failsafe routine. The drop from the ledge to the concrete ground was eighty yards; Natalia was scared of heights; and there was no guarantee that a surveillance team would leave the hotel when Archer aborted the meeting. Still, it was the only escape plan available to Natalia.

Natalia fully opened the door. Archer entered. Natalia closed the door and bolted the entrance.

The room was small, contained a double bed, chair and desk, wardrobe, chest of drawers, and a bathroom. Archer sat on the edge of the bed. Natalia sat in the chair.

Natalia puffed on a vaporiser electronic cigarette. Normally she smoked tobacco cigarettes, but smoking was not permitted in the hotel. "Why did you wish to see me?"

Archer thought that Natalia looked tired. Normally the pretty young Russian's face was taught and brimming with health. Now there were bags under her eyes, her face was pasty, and her posture was hunched, as if her body was fatigued and craved sleep. Archer replied, "I wanted to see that you're okay. Are you okay? You don't look like you're firing on all cylinders."

Natalia opened the tank of her vaporiser, squired in double menthol e-liquid, closed the tank, sucked on the device, and blew out a large plume of vapour. "The embassy's running on empty. There's so much damn work. Doesn't matter if you're SVR, GRU, or a mainstream diplomat. Lines between us are getting blurred."

She was referring to the Russian embassy in Kensington Palace Gardens, London, within which were twenty three undeclared SVR officers and GRU officers. GRU was the military wing of Russian Intelligence.

Archer nodded. "We're giving the Russians lots of headaches; the Russians are giving us lots of headaches. How will Brexit affect trade deals with Russia? Will the British ever be able to prove that the Novichok nerve agent poisonings in Salisbury were sanctioned by Vladimir Putin? What's our latest stance on Syria? What's Russia's next move in the Middle East? Are we going to maintain sanctions against Russia? Will billions in dirty Russian money laundered in our banks be unfrozen? The list goes on and on and on."

"It does." Natalia looked at the corner of the room. "Some of those issues are above my paygrade. But, I can tell you that our embassy's the busiest I've seen it since I moved here three years ago."

Archer felt like a mentor to Natalia. The Russian was young and relatively new to the secret world. By comparison, Archer had seen so much in her vocation. And if there was one thing she'd learned during her lifelong career as a spy it was never to be surprised by the surprising. In due course, Natalia would embrace that truism. But not yet. She was still learning. Archer asked, "Have you thought about what I said in our last meeting?"

Natalia was irritated. "I told you then and I'm telling you now – I can't do this anymore."

"But, you haven't told me why you won't work with me anymore."

Natalia threw up her arms in exasperation. "What is there to say apart from the obvious fact that if I'm caught, I'll be chopped up into little pieces, put in hundreds of parcels, and posted to all four corners of the world?!" She inhaled on her e-cigarette, in an effort to calm her emotions. "I've given you a lot so far."

"You have. You've given me the names of half of the undeclared Russian spies in the London embassy; ditto the embassies in Paris, Berlin, Vienna, Washington DC, and other places. There's still a lot more I need from you. I need to know the senior SVR and GRU intelligence officers in the embassies."

"I don't know their names! They use aliases. Most of them don't even tell low-ranking people like me that they work for the SVR or GRU. They pose as diplomats to you and me. They ring fence themselves because they're petrified that one of their own, in this case me, might talk to someone who'll cut their balls off."

"With a bit of effort and ingenuity, you could establish their true identities. Plus, it's imperative that we find out the identities of the sleeper cells in The Netherlands, New York, Manchester, Rennes, Madrid, and Zurich."

Natalia huffed. "The sleeper cells are ghosts."

"You're still responsible for every agent in each cell."

"Via cut outs, usually three or four people. I can't get direct access to the ghosts."

"Identify the last cut out in the chain who has that access. Give me that person's name. Then we can come up with a plan to take it to the final level and get each ghost's name."

Natalia bowed her head and rubbed her eyes. "I made a decision two weeks ago that I can't do this anymore. I'm tired, scared, trust no one except you, and don't want to fucking die."

Archer leaned forward and said in an earnest and calm tone, "You're not going to die."

"Really?! Can you promise me that?! Jesus!"

"Natalia. I know you're scared. And I know how that feels like. I was scared every second of every day when I served overseas. And for the most part," She waved her arm, "it wasn't in swanky places like this. I've served in warzones, famine-ridden countries, crumbling cities where secret police were hunting me while I hid in grimy apartments, deserts in Iraq where there were insurgents on my heels, and mountains in Afghanistan where my special forces protection detail got blown up by surface to surface missiles and were butchered by the Taliban. I know fear. Dukes Hotel in Mayfair is not a place to be scared."

Natalia shook her head. "Then you know nothing. My people can get to traitors wherever they are. You were lucky to escape the Taliban. There is no luck involved if Russia deploys an assassination unit. You and I would be dead before we knew what had killed us."

Archer breathed in deeply. She was getting nowhere and needed to change tack. "I hear what you say. You're exhausted. You need some time off. I'll give you that. But I also need you to do something for me in return."

Natalia was still but said nothing.

"I want you to take care of yourself. And I want you to allow me to see you tomorrow so that I can check on your wellbeing. It will be a different hotel." She wrote the hotel name on a piece of paper.

Natalia looked at the paper, withdrew a box of matches, and burnt the note.

"Is that okay?"

Natalia nodded.

"Good." Archer looked Natalia up and down. "What is your cover for being out of the embassy this afternoon?"

"I told my boss that I was researching an anti-surveillance route between Piccadilly Circus and Harrods. I said I may need to go shopping on foot between both locations, in order to define the reason for my route if a British surveillance team was watching me. It's the usual tradecraft – give the surveillance team some explanation as to why you're doing what you're doing."

"That's a perfectly plausible lie as to why you needed to walk the route. But, we have a problem. You have no shopping, two of your nails have cracked polish, your hair looks shit, you have no expensive sample perfume on your throat, and your face is desperately in need of a makeover. You need to return to the embassy with a huge smile on your face and the image of a woman who's shopped until she dropped."

"*Shopped until she dropped*?"

"Don't worry about it; it's just a phrase that refers to women who had a good time buying stuff."

Natalia looked at her phone's clock. "I only have four hours before my absence will be viewed as unusual."

"Then we must engage runners. I'd estimate you are a size six. Shoe size four. Is that correct?"

Natalia looked confused. "Yes on both counts."

Archer picked up the room's phone to the concierge. When he answered, she said to him, "I need you to do me an enormous favour. The guest in the room I'm calling from is a relative. We're in a bit of a pickle. She's just received a marriage proposal and has been invited out to dinner this evening to meet her fiancé's parents. She needs to look the part. We need a size six skirt and jacket from Harrods, Channel No. 4 perfume from Harvey Nichols, a hairdresser, manicurist, and beautician who can come right now to her hotel room, dresses and size four court shoes from Oxford Street, and do make sure that all clothes purchased are kept in the branded shopping bags. I will pay. This is an emergency. Do you have people up to the task?"

This was the most unusual request the concierge had ever heard during his twenty two years of service at the hotel. For a while, he was flustered. Then he said, "It is difficult, but I will see what I can do."

"Just get it done. I'll pay you extra if you achieve results. This is my daughter we're talking about. And she doesn't want to look like a bag of shit pulled up in the middle when she meets her prospective parents-in-laws." Archer slammed down the phone and smiled at Natalia. "So, now you can become a princess spy. I've just saved your ass and dignity."

Over the following three hours Natalia was pampered by the manicurist, hair dresser, and beautician. She was also fitted for the clothes purchased from Harrods. The garments needed tailoring in her room. Alongside Natalia and Archer, there were five people in her room. Archer sat on the bed, watching the workers buzz around Natalia like bees trying to make their queen the best she could be. At the end of the process, Natalia was transformed into a woman who resembled nothing short of elegant style and class. After the people left, Archer rang the concierge and gave him her credit card number. It wasn't in her name. It belonged to MI6.

Archer looked at the tasteful paper and twine shopping bags lined up in the room's corridor. "Go now. You paid for all of this out of your own cash. The receipts are in the bags. You can claim all money back from the Russian embassy. You'll get two thousand and sixty two pounds in compensation. That's what's come off my service's credit card; and that's what's going into your bank account when your accounts department pays up. Tomorrow your embassy closes at one PM. You'll meet me at three PM in the other hotel. There will be no need for all this rigmarole." She pointed at the bags. "Tomorrow it's your afternoon off. You can do what you like without being worried about explaining your absence from work."

The mobile phone that was Sign's lifeline to Archer rang at sixty forty five PM. Sign answered and listened to Archer.

She gave him details of the meeting with Natalia tomorrow. "Today I played a sleight of hand. Normally when we meet it's always one-to-one in hotel rooms. This afternoon I changed that. I told her that she hadn't covered her tracks correctly. That was true. She's naïve and has a lot to learn. But more important to me was that I wanted her to get used to the presence of others during our face to face meetings. It was a test. I got other people in the room. They were just hotel staff and beauticians. But it was a step in the right direction. Tomorrow we significantly up the ante." She told him what she had in mind.

"Good. We shall see you then." He ended the call and entered his flat's kitchen to make a cup of tea. Knutsen was out, collecting Indian takeaway for their supper. Sign was deep in thought as he stared at the kettle while it heated water.

Thirty minutes later, Knutsen arrived clutching a white carrier bag containing cartons of food. The aroma of Indian spices was unmistakable. Knutsen placed the bag on the kitchen counter and withdrew the cartons. "You told me to use my judgement and choose wisely. I've got us beef madras, tandoori chicken, Kerala prawn curry, lamb biriyani, turmeric potatoes, sag aloo, saffron basmati rice, chickpeas and lentils, mint sauce, and papadums. Oh, and I got four ice cold bottles of Henry Weston cider."

Sign looked at the mountain of food and smiled. "Are we expecting company this evening?"

"I was hungry. Help yourself to what you want." Knutsen grabbed a plate, heaped food on to it, opened one of the bottles, and carried his food and drink into the lounge.

Sign stared at the open cartons. "Which one is the joker in the pack?"

While sitting in his armchair and devouring his food, Knutsen called out, "Don't know what you're talking about, mate."

Sign wasn't buying that. "We do this once a month. Every time, and I mean *every* time, you smuggle in one dish, amid the others, that is so potent it is like eating molten lava. Last time we had curry, I lost the lottery and picked the joker. My body was perspiring more rapidly than it would have done if I'd been sitting fully clothed in a Swedish sauna."

"Just man-up and get on with it."

Sign served up a bit of everything. He reasoned that playing the numbers game would ensure he could push the lava to one side after a mouthful and at least have a near-full plate of less noxious food to fill his body. He grabbed a cider and sat opposite Knutsen. He sampled the meat and prawn curries. "Oh, you cad! There is no joker in the pack this time because you've tampered with them all."

Knutsen giggled. "Yep. I asked the restaurant to make sure they were hot enough to make putting your bollocks into a fire feel like a pleasurable experience." He couldn't stop laughing as he saw Sign breathing rapidly and sweating. "Work through the pain, mate. It gets easier. And think of the health benefits."

"There are no health benefits to being poisoned!"

"A fiver says you can't finish everything on your plate." Knutsen carried on eating, immune to the potency of the spices.

"A fiver is a fiver. Wager accepted." Sign carried on eating, his mouth on fire, his lungs feeling like they had locked up, and his shirt now a sodden mess. He gasped for air when he finished. He put his plate on the side table. "Next time I'm going to order from the restaurant. You can't be trusted."

Knutsen handed him a five pound note. "You better get showered and changed. I'll clear up while you're doing that."

Ten minutes later, Sign was back in his chair, slowly sipping his cider. He felt like his stomach lining had been attacked by bullet ants. But, at least he was no longer sweating and was in clean clothes.

Knutsen returned to his seat. "There's a bit left over. I might have it for breakfast."

"You really are beyond redemption."

Knutsen watched him. "Sometimes it takes an unexpected shock to the mind and body to kick start a train of thought."

"And you thought your curry trick would be just the tonic?! Foolish boy!"

Knutsen laughed again. "Look at it from my point of view. There's nothing on TV tonight apart from bloody dumb quiz shows and documentaries about farmers and their new born fluffy baby lambs. It was far more fun to watch you suffer."

Sign breathed in deeply. The internal attack on his body had abated. And Knutsen was right about one thing – the intensity of the meal was a cleansing process of sorts. That still didn't mean he'd trust him with food choices ever again. He finished his cider, walked to the drinks cabinet, and poured two glasses of brandy. As he returned to his seat, he told Knutsen about the call he'd received from Archer. "We must be in suits tomorrow."

All sense of hilarity was now gone from Knutsen. "I've never been to a foreign agent meeting before. It's above my paygrade."

Sign had a dismissive expression. "Your paygrade is the same as mine. But, I concede that it is a delicate and intricate process to win over an agent during a first meeting. Tomorrow, and in the presence of Natalia, I will ask you to do something. Don't, under any circumstances, be offended by my instruction. It will be directed for tactical reasons."

"Wouldn't it be better if I wasn't at the meeting?"

"No." Sign sipped his brandy. "Bring your handgun."

"What?!"

"Please."

Knutsen leaned forward, his brandy cupped in both hands, and sighed. "Look. I trust you. And I know you like to keep your cards close to your chest."

"Because often I don't know what the cards are until they reveal themselves to me."

"I realise that. But is a gun in a London hotel the right decision?"

"It shall be a prop. Do make sure it's loaded, though."

Knutsen leaned back and looked at the fireplace. It was now the beginning of autumn. The fire would need to be lit soon. It occurred to him that he'd have to call Dave, who supplied them with wood and coal. He didn't know why that thought had just entered his head. Maybe it was because it was a normal thing to think about. "Do you have a strategy for dealing with Natalia? Do you have a theory on what happened to Susan and if so how you can prove that theory to be fact?"

Sign looked at the fireplace. "You're thinking about calling Dave, aren't you?"

"Stop reading my mind and answer my questions."

Sign swirled brandy in his mouth. The spirit was a bad idea. It exacerbated the inferno atop his tongue. "I have an idea about Natalia and how to find out what happened to Susan. It may work, or it may fail. That isn't what's troubling me."

Knutsen was silent as he looked at Sign.

Sign placed his brandy down. "Call Dave. We need to stock up before every Tom, Dick, and Harry buys his logs." He looked serious as he addressed his business partner. "There's something that's worrying me about this case. It is based on the usual."

"One of your hypotheses."

"Yes. It is a nagging thought. When I get the nags, I don't ignore them. I do hope I'm wrong. I must prove myself wrong."

"What's the nag?"

Sign smiled. "Dear fellow: sometimes in life we must hold the upper hand until we are exposed as fools. You tried to trick me with your curry. I bettered you. But, I could have failed. The nag pertains to an issue that may go well beyond the current issues we're presented with. If so, we have a major situation. And if, as I hope, I'm wrong then I have my reputation to uphold. I don't want to tell you what's on my mind and make myself look stupid when it turns out to be a load of codswallop."

Knutsen nodded. "I understand. But I've yet to see you achieve anything other than the complete opposite of codswallop. Hold on to your nag. I'll stand by you."

Sign smiled. "You are indeed the finest friend. Now: let us drink our drinks. I'll put the coffee on in a moment. And I'll spray the lounge and kitchen with air freshener. This place smells like the back-end of a balmy Bombay."

CHAPTER 3

At two forty five PM the following day, Archer was sitting in an armchair in a room within the five star Langham Hotel, Portland Place, Regent Street. The room was far larger than the one she'd visited in Duke's Hotel,. Indeed, the whole hotel was huge by comparison to the bespoke but luxurious Mayfair hotel. She'd paid for the room using a credit card that was in the name of a non-existent French woman. Her attire was smart, but casual. The room contained four chairs, a stationary desk, a bed that was covered with expensive linen, a bathroom with complimentary designer soaps, and a minibar stocked with fine wines, mineral water, chocolates, and spirits.

Archer waited.

At precisely three PM there was a knock on her room's door. She answered. Natalia was there. Natalia gave the slightest of nods and entered. Archer shut the door, locked the entrance, opened the minibar cabinet, withdrew two bottles of water, and handed one to the Russian.

When both women were seated, Archer said, "I've been reflecting on your decision to put our work together on hold."

Natalia looked angry. "Not put on hold. I've made it clear – I'm not doing this anymore, full stop."

Archer calmly replied, "That's not acceptable. The job's not complete. You've come too far to quit now."

"Are you threatening me?! If I don't keep working for you then you'll throw me to the dogs?"

Archer shook her head. "Of course not. I don't work that way. You've done a brilliant job for my service thus far. That will always be remembered. But imagine the kudos you'll get if you hang in there a bit longer and give us the rest of the Russian spies. You will be rewarded – money, asylum in Britain, a new identity, a new life."

Natalia huffed. "There's no such thing as a new life where Russia's concerned. They'll find me and kill me. It may take weeks, months, or years. It doesn't matter. Their memories are long. My murder will be a message to others in the SVR, FSB, and GRU ranks that betraying the motherland only ever results in the death sentence. The SVR has a long reach. It can go anywhere. You could house me on the remotest Scottish island and they'd get to me. They wouldn't make it look like an accident or suicide. They'd want to hammer home to Russians that this was cold-blooded murder. Publicly they'd deny to Britain and other western countries that Russia had any involvement. But, Russians would know. My country is held together by fear of the state. My death would make many people think twice about working for the likes of you guys."

"That is true. But, you underestimate us. We can make Natalia Asina vanish and give birth to a new young woman. The Russian Intelligence agencies may be more brutal than us, but they are not as sophisticated. If MI6 helped you, the SVR would never find you."

"Mrs. Banks." Katy Banks was the alias Archer used with Natalia. The Russian spy didn't know her real name. "I believe that you believe in what you're saying. But you are not me. Should I gamble my life on the basis that you may be ninety nine percent right and one percent wrong?"

Archer sighed. "What your brother advise you, if he were still alive?"

"Don't try that one on me! He took his life because he was riddled with demons. I wanted his death to be revenged. I've done that."

"No you haven't. Not yet, anyway. Are you religious, Natalia?"

Natalia shrugged. "Not practicing. But I guess I have faith."

"Do you believe in the afterlife?"

The hostility was back in Natalia's expression. "I can see where this is leading!"

"I'm sure you can. So, to use the percentage ratio you used a moment ago, what if there was a ninety nine percent chance that the afterlife didn't exist, but a one percent chance it did? Would you risk shaming your brother's memory if the one percent turned out to be true? He'd be watching you. And he'd be sad that his little sister didn't have the courage to see matters through to their natural conclusion. He deeply admires you. I suspect that he believes that you have greater mental fortitude than he did at his end. He would be disappointed if his analysis of you turned out to be inaccurate."

"Stop it with the mind games!" Natalia stood.

"Sit down." Archer decided to change the subject. In a soothing voice she said, "I've ordered some tea and cake. It's your afternoon off and I know you like cake. Room service should be here any minute."

Natalia sat back down. "No more reference to Petrov."

"Agreed." Archer leaned forward. "I don't want you to be put in prison or killed. But, I do want you to work for me for a few more months. Russia is on a covert war-footing. We've had cyber attacks, meddling in the British and American leadership elections, assassinations, land grabs in the Crimea, indiscriminate bombings in Syria and Iraq, veto after veto in the United Nations Security Council, flagrant abuse of sovereign nations' air and sea space by Russian military craft, sleeper cells spread across the West, constant lies and misinformation, and ultimately the diplomatic relations between Russia and the West are the worst they've been since the height of the Cold War. If we're not careful, there'll be a flashpoint that will lead us to war. The flashpoint won't come from Russia. It will either happen somewhere that Russia, Britain, and its allies didn't expect; or, it will be the brainchild of Russia and in a place that Russia knows will matter to people like me. Either way, Russia is playing a very dangerous game. It thinks it knows how to play chess. But right now it has all the competency of an eight year old learning the game for the first time and going for broke. People like you and me must keep the child in check but resist going for checkmate. Containment is the right course of action in the current climate. We must protect Russia from itself. The alternative would be catastrophic. Western military action against Russia would result in the decimation of Russia as we know it. We don't want that. Instead, we want to play the long game. One day, we hope to see a Russia that has evolved into a democratic and less paranoid nation. You and I are taking steps to help that happen. Don't underestimate how important your work is to MI6. I know you love your country and hate the regime. So, let's get rid of the latter and focus on the former."

Natalia looked sarcastic as she smiled. "That's a pretty speech. But I might not be alive to see this new wonderful Russia you speak of."

"Maybe both of us will be long dead by then. But I like to think we'd have died of natural causes, with smiles on our faces because we knew that we'd influenced history." There was a knock on the door. "Thank goodness! Room service has arrived." Archer walked to the door and opened it.

Sign and Knutsen walked in.

Natalia stood, eyes wide, mouth open, shock evident across her face. "What the hell's going on?!

Archer went to her, but Natalia pushed her aside, grabbed her handbag, and tried to get past Sign and Knutsen.

Knutsen grabbed her and forced her back into her chair. "Stay there. You are not in danger."

Natalia was breathing fast. Her eyes were venomous as she glared at Archer. "I trusted you!"

Archer replied, "It's because you trust me that I've asked these men to be here. They're friends of mine. Do not be alarmed."

"Who are they?" Natalia looked at Sign. "He's MI6; senior; maybe your boss." She looked at Knutsen. "He's the hired gun; the man that protects people like you." She stared back at Archer. "You knew I wouldn't agree to meet anyone else from MI6, so you bounced me with this. You lied to me!"

"Natalia, we're just worried about you. And I don't think I can help you now." Archer pointed at Sign and Knutsen. "These men work for British Intelligence, but they they're employed in different circles to mine. They're independent. And they're untouchable. You can trust them as much as you trust me."

"Right now that trust is at a low point!"

Sign sat in one of the seats, crossed his legs, and clasped his hands. "My name is Ben. My colleague is Tom. They are our real first names. We will not be supplying you with real or fake surnames." He pointed at Knutsen. "Tom's job is to protect you. He won't hesitate to jump in the way of a bullet that's intended for your head. Tom – open your jacket and show Miss Asina what's attached to your waist."

Knutsen did so, revealing his pistol and holster, before closing his jacket.

Sign kept his eyes on Natalia. "Tom – be a good fellow and go into the corridor. Stay there until Natalia leaves. Shoot anyone who tries to disturb our meeting. Katy – leave now. I wish to speak to Miss Asina alone."

The instructions shocked Archer. She said, "Natalia's my agent. You have no authority to..."

"Yes, yes. Just get out and have a gin and tonic or latte downstairs, or go and see a movie, or do anything else other than being here."

"You arrogant..."

"Stop there, your tongue is equipped with a masterful command of English. Don't corrupt it by the use of expletives. Leave now. I'm in command now."

Jayne shook her head. "This wasn't the deal."

"Leave now!"

Archer's face was flushed red as she stormed out of the room. Knutsen winked at Sign and also exited.

When they were gone, Sign said to Natalia, "I do apologise for our unexpected arrival. Would you prefer to converse in Russian or English?"

She replied in English. "Who says I want to converse with you?"

"I did. You are in a pickle. I'm here to sort out matters."

"Against my will."

"You'll reconsider that stance." Sign scrutinised her, his gaze cold. "I've not read your file. I don't want to. I prefer to make my own judgements on people. MI6 and SVR files are usually filled with lies and guess work. I like to start afresh, because I never lie to myself." He picked a peanut out of an adjacent bowl and tossed it into his mouth. "You are refusing to continue working for MI6 because you are scared. That's understandable."

Natalia shouted, "And you think you can change my mind?"

"Actually, I don't want to change your mind. It's your brain. Why would I tinker with it?"

"Because it's what people like you do!"

"And people like you. But why don't we get off to a good start and agree not to do any tinkering. What say you?"

Natalia frowned. "What do you want?"

"Katy Banks has been hard on you, has she not?"

"She's just doing her job."

"Yes, but her job is a high wire balancing act. Have you heard of Phillippe Petit?"

"Should I have?"

Sign grabbed a handful of nuts and held them cupped in his palm. "He was an impeccably brave and crazy adventurer, specialising in tightrope walks. He decided to be the first man to do a tightrope walk between the Twin Towers. It was 1974. The towers had just been built, though were not quite completed and ready for occupancy. Petit enlisted the help of some friends. He and they devised a devious yet highly risky plan to infiltrate one of the towers, set up the tightrope, and allow Petit to do one of the most death-defying ventures of the last century. Of course, the whole thing was completely illegal. That didn't stop Petit. And absolutely nothing was going to stop him getting on the wire. His successful transition from one tower to the other is well documented, and was caught on video camera. It was breath taking and brought lower Manhattan to a standstill as people one thousand three hundred and sixty eight feet below him couldn't believe what their eyes were seeing above the streets. But here's the thing – what if it had gone wrong? What if halfway across the tightrope, Petit started losing his balance and knew he was going to fall? If that had happened, there would have only been one outcome: death. There could have been a way out. He could have used every muscle and instinct in his body and mind to correct his balance. He couldn't turn around, because the task would have been impossible. His only hope would have been to keep walking to the other side."

Natalia was quiet for a moment. "You think I'm on that tightrope?"

"Yes. Katy Banks is watching you. If you fall left, it's because you've given up on yourself. If you fall right it's because your treachery has been discovered. You're damned either way. So, Katy imagines herself on that tightrope with you. She can only make one decision. And it's the toughest decision."

"I must keep walking the tightrope if I'm to survive."

"Correct. You see, when you're walking a steel wire that is barely two inches thick, only you can finish the journey. Katy and I can shout instructions at you from our safe positions at your start point, but that's not going to help you. I don't want to change your mind or tinker with your brain. To do so would be catastrophic to your circumstance."

Natalia's demeanour mellowed; her tone of voice softened. "Keep spying or fall to the devil or the deep blue sea?"

"That's one way of looking at it."

"And the other?"

Sign rubbed his hands to get rid of peanut dust. "Petit couldn't resist high wire acts. It was in his DNA. And when the Twin Towers were constructed, he knew he was facing his Everest. Every neuron in his body was yearning to be up there. But, was he ready? That was the question. He practised for years; had successes in the incredible Notre Dame act; and failures on low slung wires. A wire is a wire, whether it is one foot above the ground or one thousand feet high. So, on the day he embarked on the Twin Towers escapade, the thought going through his mind was did he now possess all the skills to avoid death? He did. If he'd done the crossing a year or so before, he'd have probably died." Sign pointed at Natalia. "The problem you have is that you were put on the wire before you were ready. I'm here to safely take you off, dust you down, give you more training, and wait to see if you're ready to put one foot in front of the other on the tightrope."

Natalia was confused. "I thought Katy brought you in to bully me into doing my job for MI6."

Sign waved his hand while looking at the ceiling. "Well, there might have been an element of that in her thought process. The problem is that I never do what I'm told." He looked straight at her. "Slap whatever labels you wish to on me: guardian angel, mentor, manipulator, scoundrel, knight, barbarian, contrarian, doctor. It doesn't matter to me and it does matter to you. All that's relevant is I want you off the high wire."

Natalia rubbed her forehead. "Who are you really?"

Sign dabbed his handkerchief against his lips. "If you wish to choose one label, think of me as your consigliere – the person who advises you."

Natalia shook her head. "That's Sicilian mafia shit. And a consigliere isn't the boss. Are you saying I'm the boss who you're advising?"

"Let's work on that assumption, until it proves true or false."

Natalia's eyes narrowed. "You don't strike me as someone who has a boss." She sighed. "It doesn't matter who you really are. You obviously have power over Katy. Will I continue to meet her?"

"Yes. She will wish to check on your welfare. And she will continue to try to persuade you to spy for her. You will also separately meet me. Any attempts by Katy to force you to reveal more Russian spy names must be firmly but gently rebutted by you. Only I can judge when you are ready to recommence work, if indeed you will ever be ready."

"What is this? Some good cop, bad cop routine between you and Katy?"

Sign smiled. "No. Katy and I are not professional partners. And you'll find out that I'm nothing like a *good cop*." He reached into his pocket. "I've bought you a gift." He handed her a small box. "Katy said you were a fan of vaporisers, though normally prefer cigarettes. In the box are one hundred hand rolled cigarettes that I procured from the Balkans. You won't source finer tobacco anywhere else in the world."

Natalia opened the box.

"I'm not a smoker. But, I've been told that it's recommended to smoke one of them after partaking of a rich meal containing red meat. These are not fags to puff on while you're having a morning coffee. Savour them for special occasions. The box is hermetically sealed. The cigarettes should last several months."

Natalia placed the box in her handbag. "Thank you."

Sign checked his watch. "You are off duty tomorrow. I'd like to meet you for lunch. I've already taken the liberty of booking a table for two for one PM at Simpson's In The Strand. One PM, tomorrow. You'll be there."

Natalia looked horrified. "Meet you in a public place? You must be crazy!"

"You'll be there. This is all part of your training. Plus, Simpson's does a lovely roast on Sunday. It's extremely satiating. You won't need to worry about cooking your supper tomorrow evening. The table will be booked in the name of John Scott. Obviously, it's an alias name."

"Why do we need to meet? I may have plans tomorrow."

"You don't. I suspect you hide when you're not working, afraid of open spaces. And we need to meet because you may be able to help me." He stood and extended his hand. "Good day to you Miss Asina. I will leave now. Wait ten minutes before you depart. Katy has paid for the room. You just grab your bag and leave."

Natalia shook his hand. "Do my colleagues know who you are?"

Sign's only response was, "I don't exist." He left the room.

Before heading home, Sign went to a butcher's shop in east London. The place was established in eighteen seventy six, was close to a warehouse which once housed sheep which were slaughtered in the Victorian era by being pushed off ledges so that their front legs were broken and they could easily be dispatched, and was thirty yards from where Jack the Ripper killed one of his victims. Now the establishment was run by a burly cockney who'd spent time in Parkhurst Prison for dissecting a dead gangster who'd tried to extort money from him, had tripped on pigs' blood while holding a gun at the butcher's head, and had accidentally blown his own brains out. The butcher had tried to dispose of the body the best way he knew how. Unfortunately, forensics technology got the better of him. Police found cremated body parts in the furnaces of local hospitals. And they had CCTV footage of the gangster's last whereabouts before he went missing. The butcher went down for contamination of a crime scene and mutilation of a corpse. He was a simple fellow. But he knew his meat and was utterly loyal to those who stood by him. Sign had helped him get his business back when he was released from jail. He told the butcher that his motive for doing so was that he needed a wise and skilled artisan in the neighbourhood who understood fine cuts of flesh. It was a white lie. In truth, Sign knew the butcher was on his uppers and needed a helping hand. That's why he'd stepped in to help him.

"Hello Brian."

Brian smiled. "Mr. Sign, sir. What a pleasure." Brian was behind the counter in his shop, wearing a bloody apron, preparing his produce for the following morning. On the nearby work surface were a brace of hares, partridge, chicken, lamb cutlets, shanks of beef, and an array of offal. Once preparations had been completed, all of the meat would be refrigerated overnight, before being displayed the next day.

Sign asked, "Do you have my order?"

"Of course." He went into the rear room that was kept at two degrees Celsius, walked past carcases that were hanging from the ceiling, unhooked what he needed, and re-entered the shop. "Here we go, sir. She's a mighty fine specimen." He laid the muntjac deer on a slab, underneath which was a large sheet of brown oven-proof paper. "It took me a while to source her. This one came from the north. Do you want me to butcher her for you?"

"I'll do that." Sign walked behind the counter and examined the beast. Like all muntjacs, it was small; approximately two feet long. "I like to do my own butchering, because I want to respect the food I eat."

"Quite right, sir. I wish all of my customers were as discerning and skilled as you. But you won't stop me from packaging her up." Brian rolled the paper around the carcass and bound the parcel with hemp twine. "Job done." He handed the deer to Sign.

"How much do I owe you?"

"Twenty quid."

"The meat is worth at least five times that amount."

"Twenty quid and just promise me you'll come back here when you need some nice bangers, or a beautiful rib-eye steak. I'll be charging you full price then."

Sign smiled, paid him the money, and placed the deer on his shoulder. He walked back towards West Square. He must have looked odd, wearing a suit and lugging an unusual package on his shoulder. The sun was going down as he reached the Thames embankment. People were still out, though not as many as in the height of summer. Sign adored this part of London. And he loved the different light, smell, and temperature of autumn. Particularly in London, for him summer was two or three months of enduring life in a cauldron. Now, the air was crisp and had the first hints of a bite. It felt like he could breathe again. On the other side of the Thames were the Houses of Parliament; nearby to it, the headquarters of MI5. When he was in MI6 he'd visited both buildings many times – briefing ministers and high ranking counterparts in the Security Service. He was glad those days were behind him.

A woman was walking towards him – tall, pretty, late thirties, wearing jeans and a white blouse, and with long brunette hair that was entwined in layers so that it was raised over her shoulders. Her name was Ruth. She'd once worked with Sign in MI6. He'd heard she'd recently left the service and was now employed as lecturer at University College London. At first she didn't notice him; her eyes were fixed on the Thames and she had headphones on. But when she did see him, she smiled. Ruth was the only woman who Sign had wondered about having a relationship with after his wife was murdered. They'd gone out on a date of sorts to a cinema viewing of The English Patient. He'd held her hand. But back then he knew in his heart that he was still an emotional mess. It wouldn't have worked. They were different times. But, as he saw her now he felt different.

She walked up to him. "Ben! What a lovely surprise." She kissed him on the cheek. "How have you been?"

"Good. How about you? I haven't seen you for at least four years."

"I'm fine, thank you. You may have heard that I've quit the cloak and dagger stuff. Now, I'm earning peanuts teaching bored students." She laughed. "But it beats killing time at three AM in the departure lounge of an international airport, before boarding a plane to some hellhole. What have you got on your shoulder?"

"A dead deer."

Ruth leaned against the wall by the Thames, in fits of giggles. "Of course you have. I'd expect nothing less from you." She composed herself. "What are you doing these days?" A cloud shifted and exposed the sun to her face.

Sign was for the briefest of moments lost for words. "Private consultancy. I'm still in West Square. I've got a lodger who's also my business partner."

Ruth raised an eyebrow. "*Just* your business partner?"

Sign smiled. "It's a he, and he is not of that orientation and nor am I. We work cases."

"So, you're private detectives? Philip Marlowe, Sam Spade, Sherlock Holmes types?" She laughed again.

"More like Inspector Clouseau." Sign took a step closer to her. "You… you look good Ruth. Life outside of the madhouse must be the right tonic."

Ruth smiled. "And you look like you haven't aged since I last saw you. Is there a Mrs. Sign in your life, keeping you on the straight and narrow?"

"Alas, no. I work, I solve problems, I cook. Talking of which, I'm cooking up a storm tonight. Unless you're busy you're welcome to come over to dinner." He patted the deer. "I have to do something with this thing. It's enough to feed the five thousand."

Ruth averted his eyes. "I… sadly I can't."

"You have other plans. I understand."

Ruth pushed herself off the wall and went right up to him. She touched his cheek. "It's not that. I'm getting married. It would be appropriate for me to go to any man's house for dinner, providing I didn't fancy the pants off the man."

Sign nodded. In a quiet and tender tone of voice, he said, "I missed my chance."

"It wasn't your fault. The timing was awful for you." She kissed him on the lips. "Goodbye, Ben. I still remember when you held my hand. I can feel it now. It felt like you were transferring your enormous energy to me. It was the most romantic and extraordinary experience I've ever had." She walked away, her back to him, one hand rubbing her face.

Sign watched her until she was out of view. He sighed and continued his walk to his home.

Thirty minutes later he slammed the deer onto his kitchen chopping board, grabbed a meat cleaver, and expertly hacked at the carcass until it was in different joints.

Knutsen wandered into the kitchen, opened the fridge, and took out a can of beer. "What the fuck are you doing?"

Sign removed three knives from the wall mounted magnetic strip. The knives were of different weights. "I'm making dinner. And I'm going to freeze everything I don't use in separate bags. The deer must be respected and butchered now. It will feed us for many meals."

"Oh okay." Knutsen went into the lounge and put on the TV, while opening his beer can. He flicked through channels before exclaiming in a loud voice, "Cocking Christ. There's bugger all on TV!"

It took Sign thirty minutes to finish the job of boning and filleting the deer. He laid two immaculate fillets on the board and packaged the rest up for use on other days. He made a cranberry jus, infused with lemon, heather, pepper, and whiskey, peeled potatoes, made clapshot - boiled and mashed suede with added chives, and placed kale into a saucepan of cold water, ready to be boiled ten minutes before they wanted to eat. He walked into the lounge. "Tonight we are Scottish." He poured himself a single malt whiskey and sat in his armchair.

Knutsen asked, "Is everything alright? Looks like something's on your mind."

Sign wasn't going to tell his friend about his encounter with Ruth. "Sometimes we forget there are other things in life," was all he said.

Knutsen knew Sign was withholding something from him, but he wasn't going to press him further. It was obvious it was a personal matter. "How did you get on with Natalia?"

Sign made a conscious effort to change his mood. It was time for him to get his business head back on, he told himself. But the image of Ruth's face bathed in sunlight remained with him. What a fool he'd been for not wooing her when he had the chance, he concluded. He breathed in deeply. "Natalia is an egg shell that has cracked but has not yet bled yolk."

"Because if she cracks further, all the king's horses and all the king's men couldn't put Natalia together again."

"Correct, if a tad flippant." Sign sipped his whiskey. "There is a problem."

The downstairs doorbell rang.

Knutsen exclaimed, "Who's coming here at this hour?"

Sign sighed. "Stand by your beds. We're about to endure the company of a vitriolic woman."

"Archer? You invited her?"

"No. But I know it's her."

He was right. One minute later Archer was in the lounge. "What the hell were you thinking, ordering me to leave the hotel room?!"

Sign asked with resignation, "Would you like a drink?"

"No!"

"To take a seat?"

"I'll stand!"

"Would you like to dine with us? I've procured muntjac deer. The deer are native to Asia though have been introduced to Britain. The one I bought was raised in Northumbria. They're delicious to eat."

"I'm not hungry!"

Sign chuckled. Then his expression turned icy cold as he looked at Archer. "Then what are you and what do you want? My patience right now is cigarette paper thin."

Archer hesitated, uncertainty on her face. In a softer tone she said, "I want to know what you were playing at, kicking me out of the room."

Sign kept his eyes on Archer, unblinking, his clipped tone of voice like a precise hydraulic hammer. "There was no *play* to be had today. You needed to be out of the hotel room so that I could curve Natalia's way of thinking. If you'd have been present, Natalia would have been conflicted. The two of you have history. I was the unknown quantity in the mix of an established handler-agent relationship. She'd have been confused – looking at you, wondering what she should do; looking at me, wondering whether I'm right or you're right. You had to be away from her proximity in order for me to do my job. And I do not care one jot if that's put your nose out of joint." He placed his fingers together, and closed his eyes.

"I wanted you to give me a second opinion! Not... not push me out of my job!"

"I have my methods. They are sound."

"Not when they result in my agent thinking I've been demoted!"

"Boring."

Archer's anger was at its zenith. "This is anything but boring!"

"Still boring."

Archer's face was flushed as she looked at Knutsen, then back at Sign. "I need to get Natalia back on track. She trusts me. She doesn't know you."

Sign smiled. "She no longer trusts you. I made sure of that."

Archer's mouth opened wide. "What?!"

Sign drummed the tips of his fingers together. "Don't worry. It's all for a reason." He opened his eyes and looked at her. "I have also demoted myself to the role of advisor. It is deliberate. You and I need Natalia back in the saddle. I don't care if my ego is dented in the process. It seems, however, that you very much care about your status and prestige. We both know that is the road to hell. We must be dominant when we have matters under control; subservient when we don't. What's more important to you – Natalia or your pride?"

Archer sat in the spare armchair. She said to Knutsen, "Get me a drink."

Knutsen smiled. "Get it yourself. I'm sure you're capable of doing so."

Archer cursed, got a drink, and sat back down in her chair. She addressed Sign. "I want your assessment."

"I'm sure you do." Sign's tone of voice was deliberately patronising. He leaned forward, his demeanour serious. "Natalia respects you. There is no doubt in my mind that the information she's given you about Russian spies in the UK and elsewhere is one hundred percent accurate. Nor do I doubt her motivation to spy on Russia. But she is withholding a secret from me and you; of that I'm certain."

"What secret?"

"I have a theory, but no evidence. Nor do I want to coax the secret out of her. Not yet, anyway. Think of her as a virgin bride on her wedding night. Foreplay is required. Every move must be delicate and with her consent. Matters must not be rushed until she's ready."

Archer rubbed her face. "I don't have much time to placate the blushing bride! In three months, Natalia is going to be posted back to Moscow. When that happens she's of no use to the service because she will have lost her access to the names in Europe."

"Then I must move with the patience and tunnel vision of a fly fisherman stalking a trout on the River Itchen." Sign looked at Knutsen. "What do you think of Miss Archer's indignation about my approach?"

Archer threw her arms up in despair. "Knutsen's not a trained intelligence officer! His opinion is worthless. No offence intended, Mr. Knutsen."

"None taken," replied Knutsen.

Sign kept his eyes on Archer. "Mr. Knutsen is a highly experienced undercover operative who'd had years of experience navigating the nuances of different agendas within those around him. And he's highly intelligent. Last night he tried to poison me with tampered curry. It was an emboldened and mischievous thing to do. Mr. Knutsen – what do you think about my approach with Natalia versus Miss Archer's indignation?"

Knutsen looked at Archer. "I trust Ben. I don't know you. Sometimes when running sources, or agents as you call them, one needs to know when to ease off the gas. You brought Ben in to solve Natalia's stage fright. Going at her like a bull in a china shop will achieve the opposite of what you want. My opinion? Wind your neck in and let him do his job."

Archer had never been spoken to like that before. Thankfully, her intellect overpowered her anger at the comment. She smiled. "*Wind your neck in*? It's a bit of a robust comment but it hits the target." She addressed Sign. "Are you confident your methods will work?"

"You can take a horse to water but you can't make it drink. I'm confident I can get the horse to the water, but after that all of my confidence evaporates because only Natalia can decide whether to sup from the lake." Sign decided to drop his icy demeanour. "It must have been hard for you to bring me in on this case. I respect that. I will try my best to make this work for you, because I know that you are the best case officer for Natalia. I can't replace you. I'm just a sticking plaster. All I'm here for is to patch her up and hand her back to you. But, I know what I'm doing. Please, Jayne, let me help you and Natalia."

Archer stared at her drink. "Alright. I understand that you have your methods and I have mine." She looked at Sign. "What about Susan?"

"I have a strategy. It's in play, though only at stage one." Sign went silent.

Archer nodded. "Very well." She looked at Knutsen. "No more rudeness. Get this woman another damn drink."

Knutsen laughed, stood, and took her glass to the drinks cabinet.

CHAPTER 4

At nine AM the following morning, Knutsen was on foot in London. It was the first time in a while that he'd had to wear a coat. Rain was pounding the city and the umbrella he was holding, cars had their headlights on because the sky was filled with black clouds and there was reduced visibility, very few people were walking in the area he was in because it was too early on a Sunday and because of the weather. And those that were out were dashing to tube or mainline stations or bolting to then warm refuge of coffee shops. By comparison, Knutsen walked steadily along the embankment, crossed the Thames into Charing Cross, and stopped by the tube station there. He looked around. Here it was busier than on the south bank. There were newspaper vendors, miserable-looking groups of tourists who'd been dropped here by coach and told to have fun until they were collected at five PM, buses and cars, honking their horns, the occasional police car racing to the scenes of nearby vehicle accidents, and shops that were opening up for business despite it being a Sunday. Having worked in London all of his adult life, his current surroundings and activities with were so familiar to him. He could never work out whether he loved or loathed the capital. There was immense energy here, history, diversity, pride, manifold activities, big green spaces that were protected by Royal Charters, brilliant restaurants, pubs that looked the same way they did in the days of Shakespeare and latterly the Kray Twins, buildings constructed in the seventeen hundreds that were nestled alongside ugly 1950s properties that had been made a few years after the World War Two blitz, cathedrals, street performers, theatres where every self-respecting actor desired to work, and music halls. But, there was also crime, poverty, grime, tension, an urgency that raised the blood pressure of every commuter passing through the capital, and thanks to terrorism these days London was an armed police state. What glued the city together, in Knutsen's view, was the mighty Thames. But he never thought of the river as glue; rather it seemed to him to be a massive serpent, slithering through the metropolis, not caring that it's belly was gliding over the bones of murdered men, women, children and babies who'd been disposed of in the river over the centuries. The river carried so many secrets. It didn't care. It was older than humanity. And when humanity became extinct, the serpent would still be here.

Knutsen looked down the Strand. He walked, counting his steps. He passed theatres and shops. He also passed an alleyway where a drunken and unfaithful woman had been strangled to death by her lover, a shop where he'd spent a bitterly cold winter's day prone on its rooftop with a pair of binoculars while watching a transit van that was illegally parked up and contained enough plastic explosives to destroy half of the Strand, a café where a man had entered and slit a man's throat because the victim owed him a fiver, a pub which a woman had tried unsuccessfully to burn down and instead had accidentally set fire to herself, prompting her to run down the road engulfed in flames, and the location outside a tobacconist where Knutsen had rushed at an armed robber who was holding a sawn-off shotgun, had taken a blast of pellets to his body armour, had fallen to the ground, and fired two shots from his pistol into the criminal's head.

Knutsen stopped outside Simpson's In The Strand. He turned around. From Charing Cross tube station to here, he'd taken exactly four hundred and seventy two steps.

He looked up. The sky was still black; the weather showing no signs of abating. He walked back to West Square.

When he arrived home, he shook his umbrella free of rain water, removed his coat, and entered the lounge. Sign was in the kitchen, cooking bacon, eggs, and toast.

Knutsen said, "I did what you asked."

"Excellent, dear chap.!" He brought Knutsen a plate of food. "I'm not partaking, given I have a big lunch ahead of me. But you most certainly will need this after your excursion in the inclement weather this morning. It will be your last meal until supper."

Knutsen devoured the food. "It's busy on the Strand. The rain's helping, though. Natalia will minimize walking distances. She'll either take the tube to Embankment or Charing Cross and walk the rest, or she'll get a cab to the restaurant from her home."

"She'd be wise not to get a cab. They are notoriously unhelpful when it comes to trying to spot a trail. Natalia's smart and she's been trained. My bet is that she'll walk from Embankment tube station."

"I'll do my best to spot her but it's not going to be easy. I've no idea what time she's going to arrive, plus, every sane person out there has got an umbrella covering their faces."

Sign went back into the kitchen and returned with two mugs of black coffee, one of which he handed to his colleague. "You'll spot her. She'll walk slowly – slower than you. Last night or this morning, she'll have done what you've just done. The difference being she did so to research an anti-surveillance route. You, however, are on counter-surveillance duty."

Anti-surveillance was the technique deployed by intelligence officers to see if they were being followed. If they spotted a tail, the trick was not to let the hostile surveillance team know that you know they're there. By comparison, counter-surveillance was used when anti-surveillance was impossible or likely to be inconclusive. It usually required a team of intelligence officers stuck reasonably close to a colleague who was going to an agent meeting. Their job was to spot whether he or she was being followed , communicate that to the IO, and then disrupt, by any means, the hostile team following him or her. Today, Knutsen was going to be a counter-surveillance team of one.

He placed his plate in the kitchen sink, returned to his armchair, and drank his coffee. "Do you think she's in danger?"

"No. But I want you to get used to this procedure. Based on today's lunch, I dearly hope that you and I will shortly be going to a place of significant danger." Sign smiled. "Therefore it's best that you dust down your skills here, before we go there."

Knutsen looked resigned as he sarcastically said, "Fucking fantastic. It's always a rollercoaster with you." He swallowed the dregs of his coffee. And checked his watch. "I'm going to clean my pistol and then get back out there. Good luck. And given we haven't got military or police-grade comms, make sure you've got your mobile fully charged up. It's the only way I can get your attention short of running down the Strand firing shots in the air."

When Knutsen had left the flat, Sign brushed his teeth, shaved with a cutthroat razor, showered, applied eau de toilette, and got dressed into a tailored charcoal grey suit, immaculately pressed expensive double-cuff white shirt with a cutaway collar, gleaming black leather Church's shoes, blue silk tie which he bound in a schoolboy knot, and fitted gold cufflinks that had been given to him as a gift by an Indian tea plantation owner who was being hassled by rogues who wanted him to diversify and harvest vast quantities of drugs. He placed his mobile phone in one of the inner pockets of his jacket, and three hundred pounds cash in the other pocket. He examined himself in a full length mirror, straightened the knot on his tie, grabbed his house keys and an umbrella, and departed his home. Outside West Square he hailed a cab. "Simpson's In The Strand, if you please," he said to the driver. As he sat in the car as it took him towards his destination, he looked out of the window and wondered how Knutsen was faring in the god-awful weather. He'd be on or close to the Strand now; just waiting; trying to blend in, as opposed to looking like an armed killer.

Sign paid for the cab and entered the restaurant. He was ten minutes early and hoped that Natalia wasn't already here. After giving his false name to the reception desk, he was ushered to one of the oak-panelled booths that lined the right side of the restaurant. Thankfully, it was empty. The remainder of the large room contained open-plan tables that were not suitable for discreet conversations. So far, the restaurant was three quarters full. During the week the venue was a favourite for politicians, high-ranking military officers, Whitehall Mandarins, and famous Shakespearian actors who liked to fortify themselves with a hearty lunch before their matinee performances in the nearby theatres. Today, the mix of clientele was more eclectic. There were middle and old-aged, well-dressed, American, British, and Australian tourists, London residents who'd opted for the restaurant's refinement over getting a roast lunch in a pub, and a pair of respected food critics who were compiling a *100 Best Restaurants In London* feature for Time Out magazine. Customers were drawn to the venue because it was steeped in history and refused to move with the times. It was a throwback to an age of civility and manners, served thoroughly British food, and not one restaurant in the capital cooked better cuts of meat. Having been established in eighteen twenty eight as a smoking room, it was also once a coffee house and a national chess venue, until it was transformed into a fine dining establishment. During its history, it was a favourite of Sir Arthur Conan Doyle, Oscar Wilde, many other famous authors, playwrights, prime ministers, and royalty. P.G. Wodehouse called it *a restful temple of food.*

Sign had switched his mobile phone to silent and vibrate, before entering the restaurant. His phone vibrated It was a text message from Knutsen.

Spotted her. On foot from Embankment tube. Nothing to report. ETA 10 mins.

Sign waited, thinking through the conversation he was going to have, considering her possible responses, how he would reply to her answers, and ultimately how he could help her. Perhaps it was because he was in such an esteemed chess venue that his mind was thinking this way, establishing how the game of chess is going to proceed before the game has even started. But, like all great chess masters, Sign possessed the ability to rip up the rule book and change pre-determined tactics if the lay of the board required him to do so.

Natalia was shown to his table. She was wearing a box-cut lilac jacket, a silk scarf around her throat, black suede trousers, and ankle-length boots. The clothes looked expensive, but in all probability she'd bought them in one of the markets that specialised in selling cheap replicas. Still, she looked at home here as much as she would do having a glass of wine in a Chelsea bar, or perusing the boutique shops in Bond Street that sold designer brands, fine jewellery, and arts and antiquities. She sat opposite him, looked around, before returning her gaze to Sign. "So it seems you are a *dyed in the wool* Englishman who harks back to the good old days of Great Britain's empire."

Sign laughed as he placed his starched white napkin on his lap. "I've also eaten sheep's testicles in a Bedouin tent in the Yemen. I adapt, depending on my circumstances. Would you like a glass of wine?"

"Yes. White. You choose. My knowledge of wine isn't good."

Sign gestured to a waiter, who came to the table. "A bottle of Maximin Grunhaus, please. And would you send the carving trolley over."

The waiter replied, "Of course, sir."

When the waiter was gone, Sign said to Natalia, "I would like us to enjoy lunch and avoid business as much as possible. There is a small matter I'd like to discuss with you, but we can leave that for when we have our coffee. Are you hungry?"

Natalia nodded.

"Are you averse to large cuts of meat?"

"I'm Russian. What do you think?"

Sign smiled. "Then we are indeed sitting in exactly the place you and I should be."

Another waiter wheeled the craving trolley to their booth. On its surface was a razor sharp carving knife and two huge joints of meat.

Sign asked, "What do you have for us today?"

The waiter replied, "Twenty eight day dry-aged roast rib of Scottish beef and Daphne's Welsh lamb."

"Excellent. I'll have the beef." He glanced at Natalia.

"The same."

Sign rubbed his hands together, his expression enthusiastic. "And could we have a selection of sides – roast spuds, veg, the usual."

The waiter expertly carved the beef. From the middle section of the trolley she withdrew bowls containing vegetables and served them onto the plate. She asked, "Gravy?"

Sign grinned. "It would be a crime not to. And a healthy dollop of horseradish sauce for me."

"Me to," said Natalia.

After they were served their food the waiter wheeled the trolley to attend to other customers. Their wine was delivered and poured, Sign raised his glass, "I took the liberty of ordering German wine. So, here's to Germany. We have to mix things up in this place otherwise we Brits really will start thinking that we rule the world."

Natalia smiled and chinked her glass against his. "It's the same in my country."

"Empires come and go." He started eating his food. "Empires are like children in sweet shops – they overindulge, get sick, and have to go home." He sipped his wine. "Do you have other siblings?"

"No."

"Parents?"

"They died a few years ago." Natalia cut into her beef.

"I'm sorry to hear that. Which part of the motherland do you hark from?"

"Saint Petersburg."

Sign nodded. "A beautiful city. I've been there many times."

"As a tourist?"

"No. As a man who was being hunted by people you may know."

"I see." Natalia ate a mouthful of her food and washed it down with some wine. "I have an uncle and an aunt. They live in Moscow. They're poor. Good people. They're all that remains of my family." She delicately cut her vegetables. "Who are you really?"

"I've told you. I'm Ben."

"You know that's not what I'm asking."

Sign said nothing for a few seconds. "I understand that your brother was a ghost. I too am a ghost. But your brother and I are different. He had a chain of command. I only answer to my conscience."

"You don't have a boss?"

"No."

"How do you have this freedom?"

Sign was about to take another mouthful of food but stopped, staring at his plate. "I emancipated myself."

"Because you wanted to or because you needed to?"

"Both." Sign's tone of voice was subdued as he added, "I had a wife. She was all I needed. She was an NGO worker. She was murdered in South America. After that things changed for me. For a long time I thought life didn't make sense. I knew I was spiralling. Probably, I still am. But I have control mechanisms. One of the most important of them was for me to recognise what I could deal with while I was grieving and what I couldn't deal with. I made choices. I could no longer bear being in a hierarchy. I don't like being in large groups of people unless no one knows me. So, I try to restrict my professional and personal life to one-to-one encounters." He waved his hand toward the rest of the restaurant. "Like men used to do here. They found peace by sitting opposite each other with a chess table between them. They were loners; so too the brilliant scholars and artists who frequented this place. They were gregarious on the page, but when they weren't working they only needed the company of one person."

"So, you are shutting yourself off from the world."

"No. I'm creating a world of my choosing." Sign finished his food. "You know what that's like."

The observation struck home. She said, "It's not just grief that does that. It's a number of things. I like to think of it as dodging bullets. Love, hate, anger, awkwardness, regrets, hope, failure, sadness, happiness that's dashed – who wants any of that?"

Sign frowned. "You're a very young woman; old and young enough to be my daughter. You have your whole life ahead of you. Don't be like me until you have to be."

Natalia smiled, though looked sad. "Maybe."

Sign said, "There's something I need you to do for me. I'd like you to go back to Russia for a week. Tell your boss that it's a family emergency to do with your uncle and aunt. They have health issues. Something like that. Your boss won't be suspicious because it's a trip to your homeland. Say you'll only be gone a week and will check in every day at the SVR headquarters in Moscow."

"Why do you want me to do that?"

Sign handed her a slip of paper. "Memorise this and destroy it. A woman called Susan Archer was born in the medical centre in Moscow listed on the paper. She's English. She was born fifty years ago. The precise date is on the note. She has a twin. The twin returned to England with her parents. But Susan vanished in Moscow. Obviously this was back in the Soviet Union era. I wondered if you could do some research to see if you could find out what happened to her."

Natalia looked at the paper. "Is this important?"

"It has some importance, though not to our line of work. It is not a dangerous enquiry."

Natalia shrugged. "I don't see why not. In any case, I'm due some leave, given I haven't had a holiday for two years. But you'll have to pay for my flight."

"Of course. The sooner you can fly the better. Let Katy know when you have the dates. She'll arrange to get the money to you. But don't tell her about the Susan Archer enquiry. It's a matter that's personal to me." Sign paid cash for the bill. When they were alone, he said, "I must confess there is another reason I want you to go back to Russia. I want you to have a change of scenery. It will do you the world of good."

It was late afternoon when Sign returned to West Square. Despite the weather, he'd walked from Simpson's in order to aid his digestion and burn off calories. He called Archer. "I had lunch today with Natalia. I've asked her to go to Russia ASAP, for a week. She'll be flying economy class, for obvious reasons. I need you to pay for her ticket."

"Why did you ask her to do that?"

"It's based on a gut instinct. She's been living for too long in a pressure cooker – both at work and at home. I want to release the steam in a place she feels largely safe, but partly scared. And most importantly I want her to check in to her Moscow headquarters so that she's reminded why she hates the place and the politicians who run it."

"That makes sense. Yes, it's a good idea."

Sign said, "Knutsen and I will also travel to Moscow. We need to keep an eye on Natalia. But, the main purpose of our trip will be to investigate what happened to Susan. I have an alias passport with a Russian visa. Knutsen doesn't. Can you use the service's fast track system to get him the necessary documentation? I doubt Natalia will be able to travel until Tuesday at the earliest. But that's still a tight turnaround. Knutsen and I need to be flying on the same day as Natalia, though on a different flight."

"It's tight, but can be done. I'll need his passport photos. Get him to bring them to me this evening." She paused. "Actually, why don't you both come over to my house. I'll rustle up some food." She gave him her home address in Putney. "Let's say seven o'clock."

"We'd be delighted." Sign rubbed his belly. "Though don't cook anything elaborate or too filling. After the lunch I've had, s small plate of beans on toast would suffice." He ended the call and called out, "Knutsen! Are you having a nap?"

Knutsen emerged from his bedroom, looking bleary eyed. "Might have been."

"Nap time's over. Do you have any passport photos?"

"No."

Sign checked his watch. "We have an appointment at seven PM in Putney. That only gives us less than two hours to be where we need to be. There's a photo booth on Waterloo Station. Go there now, get the photos done – they must be passport standard – and while you're at it pick up a bottle of wine from the off license there. Do it as quickly as possible, get back here, shower, shave, and get changed into casual attire. We're going to see Jayne this evening. She's going to help us travel into the mouth of the beast."

Knutsen rubbed his face. "Okay. Do I need to bring my gun this evening?"

"No. Jayne's unarmed and is highly unlikely to kill us by other means." He smiled and pointed at his suit. "I need to get out of this work clobber. If we move quickly, we can get this done. We'll hail a cab at six thirty. That's our deadline."

When Knutsen was gone, Sign poured himself a small whiskey and drank it while having a bath. He tried to relax but his mind was racing. He thought about Natalia and Susan. Natalia was Russian; if Susan was still alive, in all probability she might as well have been Russian. But, his brain didn't just focus on the two women. He was thinking about moving parts, like a Swiss watchmaker who was trying to engineer a highly complex timepiece and get everything to sync together. Different variables raced through his brain. One stuck, and he didn't like that moving part one bit.

He got out of the bath, dried himself, dressed into smart but casual attire, and made himself a green tea. He placed a record onto his player and relaxed in his armchair as he listened to Bach's Toccata in d minor. He finished his tea and shivered. Shortly he'd have to put the flat's heating on, light the fire, or both. Summer was gone; autumn was upon Londoners. That was good. West Square was magical in the colder months. Residents draped tasteful white lights on the trees in the square. It transformed the place into a fairy tale setting. Sign's brain transcended most ascetically beautiful things in the world. But he was a sucker for the lead up to Christmas. Probably that's because he remembered his deceased father giving a five year old Sign a pen knife that was contained in a brown paper bag, while the two of them were sat by the Christmas tree in their modest home, while Sign's mother was cooking a lovely roast on Christmas Day. Sign's father – back then a merchant marine officer – had said to him, "Don't tell your mother I gave you this. I got it off the captain of my ship who'd tried to defend himself from a polar bear in the Arctic. The captain was dead by the time I and other sailors got to him. I followed the bear for hours, with the intention of killing him or her. I had a rifle. Finally, I had the bear in my sights. It was approaching its cubs. I couldn't take the shot. It just seemed wrong to do so. The cubs ran up to the bear. Before they reached it, the bear collapsed to the ground. You see, the captain had used the small knife you're holding to penetrate the bear's throat. The bear simply ran out of breath. It starved of oxygen. This knife is a bear killer." Sign still had the knife. It was in a drawer in his bedroom and was as sharp today as it was when the captain thrust its blade into the bear's gullet while the bear mauled him and subsequently tossed him onto ice like a rag doll.

Knutsen returned. "What are you listening to this shit for?"

"It's Bach. He was a genius. Do I need to educate you further?"

"No thanks. And by the way, people who describe other people as geniuses do so because their mental faculties are severely restricted."

"An astute observation." Sign got out of his chair, removed the record and placed another on.

Knutsen was wide eyed. "Where the hell did you get this from?"

Sign shrugged. "After lunch I perused a delightful record stall outside the Royal Festival Hall. The owner of the stall specialised in your kind of music. He educated me and recommended I buy this."

Knutsen was stunned "You bought this for me?"

"I bought it to prove a point." Sign smiled. "The point being is it's never too late to challenge one's senses. Actually, this band is rather good."

The record was an album by the band Groove Armada, a two-man English electronic act who collaborated with well-known rap, soul, rock, hip-hop, and jazz artists. The track playing was *Superstylin'*, a thumping upbeat house track, with influences from dub, speed garage, reggae, and dancehall.

Knutsen shook his head. "I went to see Groove Armada play live in Brixton Academy. I was with some mates of mine who were big-time drug dealers. They were nice blokes, though I'd infiltrated their gang to bust them when the time was right. The concert was amazing." He hesitated as he stood outside the bathroom. With an earnest tone, he said, "You never fail to surprise me." He entered the bathroom and turned on the shower.

Fifteen minutes later, Knutsen was shaved, refreshed, and wearing jeans and a T-shirt. He entered the lounge.

Sign said, "You're wearing that? Strong move."

Knutsen shrugged. "I don't have to get dressed up for Her Nibs."

"Quite right." Sign checked his watch. "We have ten minutes before we need to leave. That gives us just enough time for a sharpener." He poured two glasses of Calvados. Both men sat in their armchairs.

Knutsen took a gulp of his drink. "Why do I need passport photos?"

"Because I'm going to turn you into a spy. In the next few days you and I will travel to Moscow. Jayne is going to get you a passport and visa. The passport won't be in your name. We have to decide what to call you."

Knutsen blew on his lips, making them vibrate. "John Smith will do."

"Too obvious."

Knutsen giggled. "Something like Engelbert Humperdinck."

"In that vein. What about Ernst Stavro Blofeld?"

"You want to send me to Russia with the name of a Bond villain?!"

"It's just a thought."

Knutsen knew that Sign was being silly. He liked it when he was in this mood. "Harry Palmer?"

Sign smiled. "Though I loved Michael Caine's portrayal of the anti-hero spy in the Ipcress File, I fear the name may be a little bland. What about Red Adair?"

"Jon Bon Jovi?"

"What?"

"Never mind. Plácido Domingo?"

"You don't speak Spanish. What about Jack The Hat? In a parallel universe you'd have been a London east end criminal."

With sarcasm, Knutsen said, "Yeah, that would really work when I'm trying to get through immigration."

"I won't be standing next to you. I'll be okay."

Knutsen chuckled. "I like the theme though. How about Ronald Kray?"

"Spot on. Alas I already have an alias passport. It would have been perfect if I could have travelled as Reggie Kray." Sign checked his watch. "Time to move. Grab a coat, or umbrella. It doesn't look like the weather's giving in today."

Thirty minutes later they arrived at Archer's house in Putney. It was a town house, in a quiet cul-de-sac, overlooking the Thames.

Knutsen said, "Blimey. This area's a bit posh." There were six other detached properties in the immediate vicinity. "How much do you reckon it costs to buy one of these gaffs?"

"*Gaffs*? Are you getting into Kray Twins character?"

"Actually the term gaff originated in Ireland and was adopted by 1950s working class Londoners."

Sign looked at the Thames. There were rowing teams on there, despite the weather. "I would estimate that each house around us costs at least a million to buy. That's a lot of money for a three bedroom place. Come on. Let's get this over with." He rang the doorbell.

Archer let them in. "I can't move far from the kitchen because I've got a Chinese stir fry on the go. Can you do me a favour? I've got two heavy boxes at the base of the stairs. They need lifting up to the first floor. Dump them wherever you can. They contain equipment for a stair lift for my mother."

Sign and Knutsen obliged. It took both of them to carry each box. When the job was done, Knutsen looked around. The house was pristine, modern, and quite functional. Quietly, he said, "I'd say this place needs a woman's touch, but obviously that hasn't worked so far."

Sign replied, "She's a busy person and doesn't spend much time here."

"How did she afford this place?"

"Back in the eighties her parents were quite the academic celebrities. They wrote some non-fiction bestsellers about Russia, were also put on a lucrative lecture circuit and were engaged as after dinner speakers. It earned them a lot of money – enough for them to buy a house in Oxford and to put a sizeable deposit down on this place for Jayne. Jayne picked up the slack of mortgage payments. She must have paid for the house by now. And bear in mind, back in the eighties this place would have been at least half the price of its current value."

They went back downstairs. Knutsen put the bottle of red wine he'd bought on the kitchen counter. He asked Archer, "Would you like me to open this?"

Archer was busy frying strips of beef. "Absolutely. And be a darling and pour three glasses. Corkscrew's in the top drawer. Glasses are in the cupboard above." She was wearing jeans, socks, a jumper, and had no makeup on. Knutsen didn't blame her. It was Sunday; she could look however she damn well liked.

Knutsen said, "I've put my photos in the lounge. I'd like to be called Ronald Kray."

"Don't be ridiculous." Archer added spices into the wok, stirred the meat for a few seconds, and added soy sauce. "You'll be called Thomas Peterson." She briefly glanced at him. "Russia is no joke. Thomas is important because it is an elongation of your real forename. Peterson is sufficiently different from your real surname but it also has origins in Scandinavia. When constructing an alias, it's always important to bring an identity as close to your true identity, without the alias betraying who you really are. Least ways, that's important when you're an amateur. As you become more experienced, you can be more elaborate with your identities." She added finely chopped spring onions, tomatoes, zest of lime, and a splash of orange juice into the pan, before turning the mixture down to simmer.

Knutsen poured the wine, while looking at the vegetables on the chopping board. "Are these for dinner?"

"Yes, but they need to be added to the pan five minutes from serving."

"Would you like me to chop them for you? I'm not as good at cooking as Ben, but I'm a dab hand with a knife."

Archer smiled. "Be my guest. That's very gracious of you." She walked into the lounge, holding two glasses of wine. Sign was in there, sitting on the sofa with his feet up on a foot rest. She handed him one of the glasses. "I do think it's a clever idea to send Natalia to Moscow for a week. But, are you sure it's wise for you to go to Russia? Last time you were there you were tortured."

Sign smiled. "Torture's overrated."

"And Knutsen? He's not trained for this."

"If he can infiltrate the seedy side of London, he can work in Moscow. Same cities; different languages."

Archer sat in a chair. "You know it's not that simple."

"Do you remember the first time you were deployed after our training? I certainly remember the first time I was sent overseas. Was I ready? Not in a million years. But, I knew it was an extension of our training. It was the chance for me to go it alone and to achieve nothing, great success, or slip up and fail. Those first forays into the jungle are tests. And they're essential. Remember: on day one of training we were told we would never be wrapped in cotton wool. The service always knows that at some point it must deploy us and keep its fingers crossed. Knutsen will be fine, I'm sure of that. Correction, I will make sure of that."

"So long as he knows the risks."

"He knows risk as well as you and I. After all, he's lived most of his adult life fearing execution by thugs,"

Quietly, Archer asked, "Is everything alright? You don't look or sound like your normal self."

Sign shrugged. "It's nothing untoward aside from I bumped into someone today who meant something to me but is untouchable. The encounter reminded me that I keep the world at bay, but wish for slivers of hope, only for those slivers to be dashed. There is nothing worse than false hope."

With a sympathetic tone, Archer replied, "Hang on in there. One day you'll meet the right woman. You'd make a splendid husband." She smiled. "Women like challenges. You're brilliant, irascible, good looking, non-conformist, polite, a good cook, clean, and a pain in the arse. Were it not for the fact that I'm off the market, I'd shag you."

"Charming." Sign sipped his drink. "Are you mentally prepared for the strong possibility that Susan's dead?"

Archer hesitated before replying. "As you rightly say, sometimes it's better not to have hope. Part of me wishes my mother never told me about Susan. But, the cat's out of the bag. I grew up in a loving household. My parents were a bit eccentric and were certainly very demanding in terms of what they expected from me academically. They put me under a lot of pressure. I often wondered what it would have been like if I'd had a brother or sister. I doubt I'd have been under my parents' microscope as much. Now, decades on, that doesn't feature in my thinking. Instead, the two overwhelming drivers I have are fear and curiosity. If Susan's alive I worry about what kind of life she's having. If she's dead I will have to grieve for her. But how do you grieve for someone you've never met?"

"We will need to cross bridges when we get answers."

Archer asked, "How will you go about making enquiries on Susan?"

Sign replied, "I have contacts and resources and they must remain private, even from you. But, my findings will be handed to you on a plate. At that point, you alone will be entitled to judge my success or failure."

Archer nodded. Quietly, she said, "I won't blame you if you can't trace Susan. It was so long ago. In all probability, all traces of her have vanished. And if you discover she's dead, at least I can relay that to my mother and hopefully give her closure. You won't have wasted your or my time."

Knutsen entered the lounge, sat down, and sipped his wine. "Right. Chillies, peppers, ginger, and coriander are chopped. I also tasted the sauce. It was okay, but needed peppercorns, star anise, lemon juice, a teaspoon of sugar, bamboo shoots, and water chestnuts. I had a rummage through your cupboards and found most of what I wanted. The meat sauce is now much better." He smiled. "So, what are you two old spooks yarning about?"

Archer replied. "We were talking about the case, and we were also talking about you and whether you're ready to go to Russia."

Knutsen placed his glass onto a side table. His expression was serious though his tone of voice flippant as he quickly said, "See, here's the thing *love*. I had a mate of mine – his name was Phil - who was a complete scumbag. He was a geezer and would make your guts ache with laughter if you went out for a few pints with him. Popular guy. Always carried a gun or blade, or both. Would take a bullet for any of his pals. Phil thought I was a safecracker. He needed me because he was about to do a bank job. He'd done many in the past, until his previous safecracker got shot by SCO19. So, that's when I came in. The Met wanted to stop him in his tracks, not just because he was robbing banks but also 'cause he had no qualms about gunning down civilians when he was on a job. Trouble was, we had no evidence. So I was sent in by the Met as the *get the evidence man*. He was suspicious of me at first. Put a gun against my head. Asked me all sorts of questions. Punched me. Checked me out by getting his foot soldiers to make enquiries around my fake home address. Asked me which school I'd been to and the names of my teachers. Spoke to the teachers. And on and on and on it went. He was smart. For five weeks he raked over every detail of my false identity, and during that time he kept me locked in a room. No windows, Just a bed and a pan for me to shit and piss in. My alias identity held up. He let me out of the room, took me to his tailor in Battersea and bought me a suit, shirt, tie, pair of shoes, and then took me to a lovely brasserie in Covent Garden where we had lobster for lunch. After that, I was part of the family. Before that, it was a living hell – sleep deprivation; buckets of cold water thrown over me; beaten day and night; tested on cracking safes; constantly questioned about previous jobs I allegedly had done; asked if I was an undercover cop; fed little; and overall treated like a piece of trash. I knew it was an initiation test of sorts, to get into the gang. I didn't blink. No way was I going to let those cunts get to the real me. It paid off. They took me on the bank job. It was a place in Norwich. I wasn't just there to open safes. I had to disable cameras, blow up thick tempered glass screens, and I was a shooter. There were three of us in the bank. Outside there was a driver and further away from him were two spotters.

The job had been planned to the inch. The trouble was, my mate did his usual nut job thing and was going to execute the manager unless he let us in to the vault. It was a bit of a shit situation. Cops were on their way but couldn't enter until cash was nicked. We had to have that evidence. So, I had to make a decision on my own. Phil was holding his gun against the manager's head, while screaming at the other bank staff. He had that look in his eyes. I knew he didn't give a shit. He got off on killing more than he did on money. Split second decision. I shot him and his two colleagues. Clean shots. They were dead before they hit the ground. Then I ran out and shot the driver. The spotters were a fair distance away, but I managed to wing them. They didn't get far when they tried to escape. SWAT picked them off." He grinned as he picked up his wine and looked at the floor. He raised his head and stared at Archer. His voice was icy as he said, "I could give you a dozen or so other examples of what I've done, Miss Archer. You think you're special? Try seeing and doing what I've seen and done." He nodded at Sign while keeping his eyes locked on Archer. "I know he's done similar and has been put through the meat grinder. Like me, Ben kept to the script and never cracked. I don't know whether you've properly been tested. Maybe you have, maybe you haven't. But, when you discuss me out of earshot while I'm rescuing your pathetic excuse for a meal, always remember that you're talking about a fucking grown up who's spent his entire adult life expecting a bullet in the back of his brain." Knutsen smiled. "That reminds me. I need to turn the sauce down and put a pan of water on to boil. Enjoy your Jason Bourne conversations about how great you are and how naive I am." He went into the kitchen.

Archer looked at Sign. "I can see why you chose him to be your business partner."

Sign smiled. "Mr. Knutsen is a man of many hidden depths. And I never underestimate him." With sincerity he added, "He is also a gentleman who wishes to be respected. Go into the kitchen, talk to him, help him with the meal. You don't need to apologise – he'd feel awkward. Just ask him about his life."

CHAPTER 5

Two days later Sign got a call from Archer. She said, "The passport's ready for collection. Get Tom to meet me on Vauxhall Bridge at eleven o'clock this morning. I've seen Natalia and given her cash. She flies tomorrow on an 0845hrs British Airways flight. That means you're on. Book your flight now. Tomorrow it's time to visit Russia. Natalia's going to meet you at sixty thirty this evening in The Coal Hole pub on the Strand. You can discuss in-country logistics with her then. Do you need anything else from me?"

"No. I'll take over from here." When the call ended Sign stood in the centre of the lounge, deep in thought.

Knutsen was in the kitchen, brewing coffee. "All okay?"

"Yes. We fly tomorrow." He gave him details of what Archer had said.

Knutsen handed him a mug of steaming black coffee. "Are you sure about this?"

"Why wouldn't I be. Natalia is our only hope of discovering what happened to Natalia. And in doing so, we're putting Natalia back in the saddle."

"Killing two birds with one stone."

"Something like that."

Knutsen was earnest as he said, "When I asked if you were sure about this I wasn't talking about Natalia and Susan."

"I know, dear chap. You were talking about me. Don't worry. I've been tortured and threatened with death in other countries as well. That doesn't stop me going back to the places. We put one foot in front of the other."

Knutsen sighed. "Come on Ben. It's never as simple as that. When we go to Moscow you might get flashbacks or trauma or both."

Sign blew on his coffee. He was quiet for a moment before saying, "I do not for one moment underestimate the devastating consequences of trauma. I've seen men, stronger than me, who've achieved so much in their lives and have finally cracked. When it happens, it's often a fairly minor thing that breaks them down. A trigger, as I call them. There was one chap who'd served with me in Afghanistan, Iraq, Russia, China, and Colombia. We'd witnessed a lot of appalling behaviour – beheadings, massacres, the results of artillery strikes, mutilations of children, rape, hangings, and so on. We also dealt out our punishments – assassinations, drone strikes, tricks that persuaded war lords to get in a vulnerable position so we could put bullets into their head. It would take me a long time to tell you even ten percent of what went on. But, the chap I served with lost his mind when he saw a car accident in Swindon. He was just standing on the side of the road. The car hit a boy on a bike and smashed him. That was the trigger. A random event that dug up the worst recesses of my colleague's memories. But, despite everything I've gone through, not least in Russia, I don't have those trigger points. I know why. There is nothing that could be done to me, or I could see or do, that in any way comes close to the grief I have for my murdered wife. I carry the relentless burden of grief. Others carry the horror of trauma."

Knutsen nodded. "Grief makes you bullet proof."

"I would gladly relinquish that armour in a nanosecond if it would give me my wife back."

"I bet you would, mate." Knutsen didn't want to press Sign any further. His colleague had a thousand yard stare. His thoughts were not in the room. They were elsewhere. Knutsen said, "I've got to do the Cold War shit and meet Her Nibs on a bridge, we've got to book a flight, need to pack, and you've got to brief a girl who's lost her nerve. We've got our work cut out today."

Sign looked at him. "We have indeed, sir." He looked at his watch. "I'll make the flight bookings. From memory there's a 1040hrs Aeroflot flight out of Heathrow. Aside from the carrier Natalia's travelling on, there's another early morning British Airways flight, but we must avoid BA. I will also source accommodation close to Moscow."

"A hotel or B&B?"

"No. The place I have in mind will be free of charge."

"Do you have access to weapons in Russia?"

Sign nodded. "Yes. But bear this in mind – if you have to use a gun it will be because Natalia's in danger from her own people. Any assault on FSB or SVR personnel in close proximity to Natalia would mean that Natalia is fully compromised. We would have to grab her and use a covert exfiltration route out of Russia. As a backup, I will arrange for that exfiltration out of St. Petersburg. But the use of guns and my covert get-out-of-Dodge-card must be a last resort. We want Natalia to remain in the SVR and safely fly out of Russia without raising any suspicion from the authorities there." He gulped his coffee. "I don't want to offend your knowledge, but do I need to brief you on how to pack."

Knutsen wasn't offended. "Before I used to go on an undercover job, I'd strip naked, place my bag on my bed, alongside clothes, ID, and cash. I'd check my bag and wallet to make sure there was zero documentation – shopping receipts and stuff – that could be traced to Tom Knutsen. And I'd check every single pocket in my clothes. Only after that was done would I pack."

"Excellent. I do the same. Do you have any tattoos?"

"No."

"Have you ever been arrested?

"Loads of times, but only as a result of undercover work and always in a different name."

"Good. Our cover for flying to Moscow will be simple. We are high school teachers at the Cotswold School. You teach history; I teach languages. We are in Russia because we are, as per UK educational law, required to do a risk assessment analysis prior to a planned school trip to Moscow. We intend to take twenty students to the capital in January next year. But, we can't do so until we've checked the hotel they will be staying in, and looked at all the usual potential risks – fire hazards, transportation, crime, et cetera. We have a Skype call at four PM this afternoon with the head teacher of the Cotswold School. He and I went to university together. I've used him in the past. He will brief us and ensure that we're temporarily on the school list of staff, should anyone in Russia call the school to verify our credentials. Are you happy with that?"

"Makes sense. History was always my strong point. But we're going to have to dot the Is and cross the Ts. Which hotel are the students staying in? Are we staying in the same hotel on tomorrow's trip? What activities are we planning for the kids? And what's currently on the history and languages curriculum?"

"The head teacher will brief us on our role at his school. Regarding the hotel, I have that in hand. We won't step foot in the place. But, I know the concierge. He's Muslim. I saved his daughter after she stupidly went to Syria to join ISIS. As a result, he is utterly loyal to me. He will confirm to anyone who calls the hotel that we are booked in there, are staying there, and have been talking to him about hotel fire evacuation procedures and other mundane emergency protocols. He'll cover for us in every respect."

Knutsen smiled. "Sounds like you've got all angles squared away."

"Let's hope so. But always remember, things rarely go to plan. Now, you need to get ready and go and see Jayne. Please don't tell her that Sunday evening's Chinese meal was only edible because you stepped in to rescue the dish. Oh, and say please and thank you. In other words, don't be yourself."

Knutsen laughed. "I'll try my best." He went to his room to change.

Sign opened his laptop and placed three mobile phones on his desk. He needed to make calls to three people in Russia.

Ninety minutes' later, Knutsen was back in the flat, clutching his passport in the name of Thomas Peterson. Sign was still sitting at his desk. Knutsen asked, "How's it gone?"

Sign closed his laptop. "I've booked our flights, have arranged our accommodation, secured a trawler out of St. Petersburg should the need arise, and have spoken to a criminal who can get you a Makarov pistol and three spare magazines."

"Blimey! You've been a busy bee."

Sign stood and arched his back. "If you have to use the gun, get cornered, and have no way out, kill me and turn the gun on yourself."

Knutsen was stock still. After ten seconds he said in a quiet voice, "I'm sure it won't come to that, Ben."

"One must prepare for every possibility." Sign smiled. "Don't worry, old fella. I'll make sure that we minimize risk to Natalia and ourselves. Okay, you and I need to pack. Make sure you shut your bedroom door. Life is traumatic enough without me seeing you in your birthday suit."

At four PM they had the Skype call with the Cotswold School head teacher. He told them that they were now officially members of his staff, that his reception desk was instructed to forward any enquiries about them to his PA or to him in person, that Sign was teaching Year 11s Russian language and culture, and that Knutsen was teaching Year 10s the history of Russian Tsars. He gave them the names of other key members of staff, thumbnail sketches on their backgrounds and personalities, and details of the school's location in Bourton On The Water and its local amenities and foibles – including pubs, what beers were on draft, what the council was doing to deal with a petition to oust a high street fish and chip shop that had a particularly noisy extractor fan, flooding issues with the River Windrush that ran through the centre of the village, and the fact that the last remaining cash machine in the village had been excavated by criminals who'd nicked a digger lorry from the nearby industrial estate, had dug out the ATM, and driven off with it into the night. He also said that he'd issued a newsletter to parents, advising them that Simon Priest and Thomas Peterson, the false names being used for the Russia trip, were now formally on the staff-roll of the school and had previously worked in remote charity schools in respectively Africa and Nepal.

After the call, Knutsen said to Sign, "He's pulled out the stops for you."

Sign replied, "I have lots of people who pull out the stops for me, primarily because I've pulled out the stops for them. In the case of the head teacher, I saved him from a fall from grace when we were at university. He'd been accepted for teacher training, with the proviso that he had to undergo security vetting to assess his background and suitability to teach minors. The problem was that he was one of the biggest dealers of cannabis to university students. He had a barn in a nearby Oxfordshire village. It was on a farm, owned by his father. But father had dementia and hadn't a clue what his son was up to on his property. In the barn were a third of an acre of lamps and cannabis plants. It was an extremely lucrative cottage industry. I knew about this because the teacher-to-be was my friend. I didn't condone his extra curricula activity, but nor did I do anything about it. I've never taken drugs. People who had a few puffs of his weed seemed very harmless when intoxicated. And they were functioning – attending lectures, getting essays done, zero violence towards others. They weren't like the strung out heroin or meth addicts I'd read about. And my friend was a good chap. Most of the profits he made from dealing were put into his father's health care and upkeep of the farm. His mother didn't feature. Years before she'd run off with an Australian exporter of snakes and other deadly creatures. One day I got summoned to the dean's office. He grilled me on whether I had any evidence about my friend's illegal affairs. He said matters were getting serious, beyond my friend being potentially expelled from our college. Of course, the dean was tipping me off. I went straight to my friend and said that he was going to be busted by the cops. He panicked. I told him I'd help. We went to his farm, removed the lamps which I sold to a very friendly local gypsy called Frank, and we took all of the cannabis pot plants outside of the barn. My friend suggested we burn them. I told him not to be ridiculous – the smell would carry for at least a mile. I had a better plan. At 0500hrs the police drug squad hit our campus. They found nothing. They searched my friend's farm. Again, nothing. No doubt they were extremely frustrated. And I wonder how long it took them to realise that every member of the Thames Valley Police drug squad had one cannabis pot plant in their homes' gardens."

Knutsen was incredulous. "You planted one pot in every drug cop's house?! How the fuck did you do that? How did you even know who the cops were?"

Sign smiled. "There is a reason why I was later recruited into MI6. Anyway, my friend completed his degree, like me got a double first, and he successfully entered the teaching profession. And now he's helping us with our cover story to enter Russia."

"Jesus! You've led an odd life."

"I prefer the word *unusual*. A rich tapestry of life is never cluttered with swathes of dullness. You know me well enough to understand that I do not tolerate chapters of mundanity." Sign grabbed his wallet and keys. "So, now I'm off to see a Russian spy. Do me a favour while I'm out. I've ordered a hare from my butcher in east London. Would you mind collecting it, bringing it home, and skinning the hare?"

"Er, no problems. The only thing is I've never skinned an animal before."

"Use one of my sharp, thin blade, knives to make an incision in the fur from throat to anus. Then simply peel the skin off the flesh. It's easy. Oh, and you'd be a champion if you could get dinner on the go while I'm seeing Natalia. Chop the hare's head off, gut the animal, pan fry the head, liver and kidneys in butter, add white wine, mustard and mixed herbs, gently simmer the sauce, remove and discard the meat after about an hour, take the sauce off the heat, braise the whole hare on a high heat with equal measures of rapeseed oil and butter, in a separate pan gently sweat chopped shallots and garlic, place sauce, hare and onions into a casserole dish, add one tin of tomatoes, and place the casserole into the oven on seventy degrees heat. Do you think you could do that?"

Knutsen rubbed his face and said with resignation, "I thought I was your business partner, not your sous chef."

"We must all aspire to have more strings to our bow. By the way, when you walk to the butcher's shop, stop off at the independent record stall I mentioned, outside The Royal Festival Hall. I've pre-ordered a vinyl album for you and it's ready for collection. The stall doesn't close until five thirty. It's a very limited edition of early Jane's Addiction. I've paid for the record. Just give the proprietor my name. He's expecting you."

Knutsen screwed his eyes shut and shook his head. "How… how the hell do you know about Jane's Addiction? And, Jesus, the record must have cost you a packet."

Sign stood by the door. "The stall owner is a very knowledgeable chap. He was once a roadie for Nirvana, whoever they are. He's educating me. I like turning my tastes on their head. He also let slip to me that he spent five years in Wandsworth Prison for smashing an electric guitar over a rather rude audience member at a Faithless gig. He's quite a character. Alas, the audience member is now a quadriplegic as a result of his head trauma."

Knutsen opened his eyes. "You bought the record as a gift?"

Sign smiled. "No. I bought it as bribe to get you to cook tonight. When I'm gone and you've returned home in possession of the hare and the record, put the music on loud, cook while you have a couple of beers, put your feet up with a glass of calvados, and enjoy the fact that you've got a couple of hours of escape from my nonsense." He winked at him. "Adieu Monsieur Knutsen." He left the flat.

Fifty minutes later, Sign was in The Coal Hole pub. The establishment was a tasteful yet traditional London boozer, with a rich history. Once it was the place where coal was stored for use in the nearby Savoy Hotel; actors from Shakespeare's day frequented the place when it was converted into a hostelry; Gilbert and Sullivan performed there; and the late actor Richard Harris used it as his local pub after he'd made a mint from selling the rights of his West End play and had enough money to have a permanent room in the Savoy. Over the centuries, it hadn't changed much. It was medium sized, but not spacious; instead it had nooks and crannies where people could talk in private, as well as an upstairs and downstairs bar. The place was clean, but embedded within the old walls was the smell of long ago hops, tobacco smoke, smog, and fossil fuel.

Natalia was standing at the bar.

Sign stood next to her and ordered a pint of pale ale. After he was served and the barman moved away to attend to other customers, Sign spoke without looking at Natalia. Instead he stared at the bar. "In the bag by my feet is a mobile phone and charger. The only person who has the phone's number is me and Tom. Keep it with you at all times during your trip. I've stored my number in there. It is listed as *House Repair Man*. I've also enclosed five hundred dollars and the location of a dead letter box in Moscow. Memorise the location and destroy the note before you travel. If you have anything of interest to communicate but are worried about using the phone, use the DLB and text me saying you've just paid the invoice for the repair to your boiler."

Natalia took a sip of her wine and smiled. Like Sign she was staring forwards. "Did you put a suicide pill in the bag as well?"

"No, because there's no need for that." He drank some of his beer. "Tom and I will be on a different flight tomorrow. We'll be in country late afternoon. I truly hope we don't have to see you during your trip."

"So do I." Natalia finished her wine, picked up the bag, and left.

CHAPTER 6

The following morning Archer was summoned to the office belonging to the chief of MI6. She was feeling nervous, but not because she was seeing her boss. Natalia had flown out of London an hour ago. For one week the young woman was a free agent. Sign was right to send her to Russia. From what Sign had told Archer, Natalia had nothing to do when she was in the motherland, but just her presence there would reinforce in her mind why she spied against her country. And it would give her a much needed break. She was getting claustrophobic and paranoid in London. Hopefully, a break would get her judgement and courage back on track. Still, the fact that, for a few days, she couldn't be protected by Archer made the MI6 officer anxious.

She entered the room adjacent to the chief's office. It contained two secretaries and one mid-ranking intelligence officer. The IO beamed as he saw Archer, stood up behind his desk, and said, "Lovely to see you Jayne. How are you settling in to your new job?"

"Good thank you."

"Excellent." He nodded toward the door that led to the chief's room. "He's waiting for you."

She opened the door, without knocking, closed it behind her, and said, "Sir, you wanted to see me."

The chief was standing by his desk, flicking through a file that was marked Top Secret, Your Eyes Only. He closed the file and looked at Archer. "Take a seat."

The large room had no windows, walls were adorned with framed photos of every previous chief since the service's creation in 1909, artificial flowers were in pots on the floor, and the only furniture in the room were the chief's desk and chair and four armchairs. The chief sat in an armchair, opposite Archer. He was medium height, early fifties, had receding dark hair, a slight paunch, and was wearing a shirt, tie and pressed trousers. His suit jacket was on the back of his desk chair. Aside from his glistening eyes, that right now were peering at Archer over the top of his spectacles, he looked like an unremarkable middle aged civil servant who wouldn't stand out of place in the Department for Transport or the Department for Work & Pensions. And yet, he'd led a remarkable life. His father was a catholic priest and his mother was a Church of England vicar. While trying to feed and shelter Bosnian Muslims during the siege of Sarajevo, both died from Serbian sniper fire. He was in his early twenties at the time and was climbing Everest, while serving as a lieutenant in the Household Cavalry. When he got to the summit, he radioed base camp news of his successful ascent. The radio operator there said that a friend had been trying to get hold of him – a chap that the chief had gone to university with at Harvard and had momentarily been a lover before both young men decided they weren't gay. His friend was now a paratrooper and part of the peacekeeping force in the Former Yugoslavia. The operator patched his friend through to the chief's radio. He learned about his parents' deaths while sitting on the summit and overlooking the world. He descended the mountain in treacherous conditions. The siege of Sarajevo was still raging – it was the longest siege of any city in modern warfare. The chief passed selection for the SAS. Via Bosnian Serb propaganda video footage, facial recognition technology, and various contacts, he ascertained the identities of the four Serb snipers who were on duty the day his parents died. When he was granted a few days' leave, he paid them a visit in Serbia, armed with a handgun. Their dead bodies were never found. Three years later he joined MI6. Since then he'd served in nearly every continent and was regarded as one of the brightest spies of his generation. He was a tough man, but wise.

He said to Archer, "I wish to have an update on Natalia Asina."

Archer kept her eyes fixed on the chief's penetrating stare. "I am making progress, but I'm not there yet. Baby steps, nudge her thinking, get her back in the saddle when she's ready."

"We don't have time! We need a download of her brain before she's shipped back to Russia for good."

"I know. And that's why she's my number one priority."

The chief look bothered. "I'm getting pressure from the Americans, French, Germans, Austrians, and others. They all want to know two things: who is our source and when will our source give us the names of the high ranking SVR and GRU spies in their countries. I can deal with the pressure. But, there are other wheels in motion. *Political* wheels. The Yanks think our relationship with them is diabolical and at an all-time low."

"They're right. We can't trust them while they have a lunatic dictator as president."

The chief didn't respond to the comment. "The Europeans are in a chaotic frenzy as a result of Brexit. They're turning on each other. The only sane partners we have now are Canada, Australia, and New Zealand. The PM wants me to build bridges. I've told her that the best way we can do that is to give gold dust to our foreign intelligence counterparts." He was silent for a few moments. "Natalia's knowledge is the gold dust. You must get her to continue to spy for us."

"She spies for me, not you, sir."

"Yes, yes! I know how it works." He looked away, irritated. "What steps are you taking?"

"I've been meeting her regularly, counselling her, and today she's on a plane to Moscow so she can get a breath of fresh air outside of London. She'll be back in a week."

"Alright." The chief asked, "Are you up to this job?"

"Which job? Running the Russia Department or running Natalia?"

"Both."

"I am. You shouldn't need to ask me."

The chief sighed. "These are trying times. Sometimes I wonder whether I'm up to my job. I meant no malice when I posed the question to you. We're all floundering amid shifting sands."

"I know, sir. I don't envy you." Archer asked, "Would you like me to make you a cup of tea? I could murder a cuppa right now."

The chief smiled. "That would be extremely gracious of you, Jayne. Once it's poured, let's sit down and talk about anything other than Russian spies and politics. In fact, I'll tell you about the time, twenty years ago, when I was in a bare knuckle fight in a wasteland in Algeria and lost because one of the members of the gambling audience stabbed me in the back with a three inch blade."

Four hours' later Archer visited her mother in her retirement home in Godalming. The grounds were still wet from rain the day before, but now the sky was clear and there was no wind. She decided it would be nice to take Elizabeth out into the beautiful grounds. She pushed her mother in her wheelchair, along one of the many footpaths that ran between manicured grass, sensationally sculptured medium-sized trees and hedges, flower beds, and vegetable plots that were wired off to protect the crops from being eaten by hedgehogs. The air was rich with the scent of the moist grass, pine, rhododendron, bay, and burning logs of birch that had been cut, stored and dried since last winter, and were fuelling an exterior stone fireplace. She looked at the beautiful house that contained the residents. Smoke was billowing from three of its chimneys. Inside the house, lights were on, making the windows look amber, as yellow light mixed and reflected off the gorgeous heavy and currently parted crimson curtains. Patients were in there, some playing cards or board games, others reading or watching TV. Though Godalming was a small town, the care home was sufficiently far from the centre to be completely untroubled by the hurly burly of everyday life. It was, Archer always thought, a refined and magical oasis. She stopped by a small pond that contained frogs, carp, newts, and other aquatic life. Two ducks, a male and female, were on its surface. They'd lived here for two years. The residents called them Bonnie and Clyde, due to their proclivity to nick stuff out of people's hands or pockets.

From her handbag, Archer withdrew bread and a bag of raisons which she handed to her mother.

Elizabeth said, "Raisons?"

"I've researched it. Apparently ducks shouldn't eat bread. It swells up in their throat, plus is difficult to digest. The bread's for the greedy carp."

Elizabeth smiled and started tossing the food. "I'm hoping to see the old fella today." She kept her eyes on the pond as the ducks chased after the bread and ignored the raisons. "There he is! Do give me a hand."

Archer helped her mother out of her chair, fully supporting her weight, and assisted her to get on her knees. Elizabeth handed *the old fella* chunks of bread. He was a thirty pound carp who was often shy and other times brazen and greedy. Today he had no fear and sucked the bread from Elizabeth's fingers. Archer lifted her mother back into her wheel chair.

Elizabeth shivered, despite wearing a shawl. "Autumn's upon us."

"Are you cold, mum?"

"No. Shivering's a good reflex. It shakes off fear." She patted her daughter's hand. "The estate is beautiful at this time of year. I know I must leave soon, after all the tests are complete, but even this ancient been-around-the-block gal can get the collywobbles when change is afoot." She looked at Archer. "I'm looking forward to moving in to your house. It will be lovely to spend time with you and see the Thames again. But, I will miss the old fella, Bonnie and Clyde, and the bonkers residents." She laughed. "They are a crazy bunch." She pointed at the house. "But, all of them in there would make an obituary writer have a wet dream. They have so many stories to tell about their lives."

"You can visit them, mum."

"True. I have their mobile numbers in a black leather-clad notebook that your father gave me because he wanted to stop me forgetting stuff when I went to the shops. I never used it for shopping lists. Now, I've used it for listing who, one by one, will die."

Archer said in a curt tone, "Don't get maudlin. We've spoken about this before."

Elizabeth replied in a matter-of-fact tone, "I'm not being maudlin. It is what it is. Try being my age and thinking that you're going to live forever. Sorry to disappoint you." She tossed more bread. "We all get buried or incinerated. I don't worry about that. What worries me is, in a year's time, I'll be ringing up my friends in the estate, to see if they'd like to join me for a gin and tonic or a trip to the flicks, and I'll have forgotten they're dead. I'll have to cross their numbers out in my notebook. I have no bucket list. Instead I have an imminent dead list."

Archer pushed her mother onwards, passing sycamore, and a rabbit warren that drove the groundsmen crazy as much as the mole hills. "I'm trying to find out what happened to Susan."

Elizabeth smiled. "That's kind. You know that I don't mourn her. It happened so long ago. I was a wreck at the time. But I had to bring you up. I had to function. So, I kept telling myself that someone kind was raising Susan, even though I was conscious that I was telling myself a lie. I don't believe in mothers' instinct and all that nonsense. I believe in facts. But, sometimes we have to fib to trick our brains. Now that you're head of the Russia desk, do you think you've got the power to get to the bottom of what happened to Susan?"

"I don't think power's the right word. What I do now have is significant autonomy and access to expert resources. That said, I wish you'd told me about Susan before."

"Don't be angry with me. I was protecting you. And you weren't in the Russia Department. You wouldn't have been able to do anything." Elizabeth looked up. "Clouds are coming in. We'd better turn back before it rains."

"It might not rain."

"It will, according to my phone's weather app. It's predicting a downpour this afternoon." Elizabeth breathed in deeply. "Let's just wait here for a minute. If it does start raining I want to feel the droplets on my face. It'll make me feel alive. And anyway, my skin's waterproof." She ran a finger over Archer's hand. "It's a weird thing – you're all I have now, and yet you may not be all I have. Your father and I spent fifty years trying to find Susan. I know Russia, I speak Russian, I have contacts there, though all of them are now old and retired, or dead. I persisted, but got nowhere. Susan vanished on the day she was born." Tears ran down her face. "It's… well, it's…"

Archer wrapped her arm around her mother's back. "Mum – you've carried this burden for too long."

"So did your father. It broke him in the end, I'm sure of that." Elizabeth rubbed away her tears. "It's just I'm not a smart academic anymore, and I don't want to be. I want to be a soppy old lady who looks back on her life and takes pleasure from my memories. That's hard to do when one of the memories is a mystery; a very *painful* mystery." She looked at her daughter. "It's a fool's hope, I know, but I keep having this image of you me, and Susan together in your house. It's stupid of me, I guess. But, it is what it is."

Archer pushed her mum back to the care home. "When I was a teenager I used to fantasise about marrying the actor Jeremy Irons. I loved his voice and his elegant mannerisms. The fantasy put a smile on my face. It might have been a foolish thought but most certainly it wasn't a wasted dream."

Sign and Knutsen arrived in Sheremetyevo International Airport, one of Moscow's largest transportation hubs. It was the first time Knutsen had been to Russia. As he stood in the queue for passport control, he yawned – not because he was tired, instead because he wanted to look bored and unsuspicious. Sign was behind him, ten people back. He couldn't help Knutsen now. Knutsen was on his own.

The queue was moving at a snail's pace. Passengers on the Aeroflot flight in to Moscow had been warned by the plane's captain that there might be delays getting through immigration and security due to increased analysis of passengers by airport authorities. The captain didn't need to elaborate why that was the case. Passengers knew that everyone entering and leaving Russia were treated as potential terrorists or spies.

It took Knutsen thirty minutes to reach passport control. He handed over his false passport. The man behind the desk scrutinised the passport and repeatedly looked at Knutsen. He asked in English, "What is the purpose of your visit?"

Knutsen yawned again. "I'm a teacher. I'm bringing some of my school children to Moscow early next year. I'm travelling with a colleague. We have to make sure it's safe to bring them here."

The official frowned. "Why would it not be safe?"

Knutsen put on his strongest London drawl. "It's not that mate. It's a pain in the arse. We have to do the same thing if we take them on a day trip to Madame Tussauds or the London Eye." He screwed up his face and sucked in air, as if he was trying to stifle another yawn. "It's the bloody law. We have to check everything, down to is it safe to cross the road, can we get gluten-free food, are there minibars in their hotel room that they can raid? You know – that kind of stuff. So, the teachers have to come here in advance and check it out. Have you got kids?"

The man nodded.

"Then you know what it's like. Eyes in the back of your head all the time." Knutsen smiled. "There's only one advantage on these bloody risk assessment trips – we get to have a few bevvies."

"Bevvies?"

"Booze, drinks." Knutrsen winked at him. "I've heard you Russians have got some brilliant Polish vodka in Moscow."

For a moment the official looked stunned. Then he laughed. "British sense of humour. I get it. Only Russian vodka here. Polish vodka is rubbish." He handed the passport back to Knutsen. "Enjoy your stay. Before you travel with your school children check the website of The Ministry of Foreign Affairs of the Russian Federation. It's in English. It will tell you if there are any security threats in the area where you will be staying."

Knutsen put his passport in his coat pocket. "Nice one, mate." He grabbed the handle of his trolley bag. "By the way – do the bars stay open late here?"

"Da. Of course." The official waved his hand.

Knutsen walked onwards.

Twenty four minutes later Sign joined Knutsen outside the terminal they'd arrived in. They walked together to the taxi rank. Sign peered into the window of the taxi at the front of the rank and said in fluent Russian, "The Ritz-Carlton hotel, please."

When they were on the move, Knutsen asked Sign, "We're staying at the Carlton?"

"It's a smashing five star hotel, in the centre of the city."

This didn't make any sense to Knutsen. Sign had told him that their accommodation in Russia was free. However, it was highly likely that Sign knew the manager of the hotel and had cut a deal with him or her. Knutsen kept his mouth shut.

As usual, traffic into the city was horrendous. While Knutsen stared out of the window, Sign was jabbering to the driver about anything that came into his mind – questions about the Russian world cup; weather; restaurant recommendations; how long the driver had worked his cab; roadworks; and a raft of other local matters.

When the taxi dropped them off outside the hotel, Sign placed his hand on Knutsen's shoulder and quietly said, "This is not the end of our journey. Keep an eye on my case." He walked to the porter standing beneath the regal hotel's entrance and asked him to hail a cab, adding that they needed to work this evening before checking in. Five minutes' later they were on the road again. After travelling five hundred yards in the dark and almost gridlocked traffic, they were dropped off outside the beautiful St. Regis Moscow Nikolskaya hotel.

Sign said to his colleague, "Walk with me."

They pulled their trolley bags down the road and turned into a side street.

"Now we wait." Sign checked his watch. "Timings are never precise in Moscow." The street was only illuminated by lamps. Sign and Knutsen were in the shadows. Sign stared at his phone. It pinged. "ETA five minutes."

Knutsen was certain that they were being picked up by one of Sign's assets. However, he had no idea where they were headed. All Sign had told him before they'd departed London was that it was best if he didn't know where their accommodation was until they reached the place. That comment had really annoyed Knutsen. But he also was highly cognisant that Sign had his methods. And it had also occurred to Knutsen that this may well have been the first time that Sign had deployed overseas with a British colleague. During his MI6 career, Sign worked alone. Now, Sign was figuratively having to hand-hold Knutsen, letting him witness his spy tradecraft while at the same time not telling him what was happening until they were in a safe place.

Sign's phone pinged again. A car approached. Sign moved quickly to one of the street lamps. The car slowed, then stopped.

Sign grabbed his bag and said, "Quickly now!" He got into the back of the car. Knutsen followed. The car pulled away.

The driver was a male, in his late twenties, short haircut, but that was pretty much all that Knutsen could discern about the man from his angle in the back passenger seat. The driver was silent as he drove north. One hour later they were out of the city. They continued north on the A104. Either side of them was black, the only illumination coming from vehicles' headlights. The further they drove, the fewer cars they encountered. The driver turned off the main road, onto a gravel track. Now there were no cars or any signs of life whatsoever. Six miles later he stopped.

Ahead of them was an isolated and stunning large wooden house, on the banks of a lake. It had illuminated oil lamps hanging on the porch's canopy, strings of solar-powered white-light bulbs draped over fences that were either side of the property, two chimneys emitting smoke, and windows that were a golden glow due to interior lights.

The driver turned off the engine and got out.

Sign nodded at Knutsen. "So here we are dear fellow. Our journey has ended." He smiled and got out of the car.

When out of the vehicle, Knutsen arched his aching back. The travel to Moscow had cramped the tall man's muscles. He breathed in deeply, inhaling a multitude of smells including the fresh breeze that was gently wafting over rippling lake water, burning logs, and aromatic aromas from trees that were shedding their leaves in the cool autumn air.

Sign walked up to the driver. "Yuri – how the devil are you young sir?" He embraced him.

Yuri grinned and replied in Russian, "It's so good to see you my friend." He pointed at Knutsen. "Should we trust him or pretend we trust him?"

Sign laughed. "We trust him. Come on, let's get inside and say hello to your dad. I hope he's preparing a nice meal."

They entered the property. It was a four bedroom house. Downstairs was a big lounge that was open plan with a kitchen. The lounge had a fire blazing, four fishing roads resting on struts in the wall, other fishing equipment beneath the rods, a stuffed twenty pound trout in a glass cabinet on an antique mahogany cabinet, lit candles, mismatching armchairs and sofa, photos of Yuri's dad, Yuri, and his deceased mother, a battered balalaika that had once belonged to a White Cossack warrior and was leaning in the corner of the room, hermetically sealed copper jars of tobacco from Asia and America, bottles of wine and vodka stored in buckets, coils of rope and twine scattered on wooden furniture surfaces, books haphazardly piled on the floor, paintings of the rural landscape adjacent to the property, small TV that was manufactured in 1987 and only worked intermittently, oak bowl on a coffee table that contained six briar pipes, gun rack of rifles, and a rug in front of the fire. Lenin was lying on the rug. He was a two year old huge Eurasian wolf, and had been rescued by its owner from a farmer who'd tried to kill the animal when he was a cub.

The kitchen had a long, waist-height, work bench that acted as the only partial barrier to the lounge. Behind it was a stove, cupboards, microwave, refrigerator, chest freezer, mugs that were hanging on hooks under one of the units, pots and pans hanging from other hooks in the ceiling, sink, two wooden baskets containing an array of berries and vegetables, pots of herbs, string of garlic bulbs draped over a window ledge that overlooked the lake, vine of tomatoes that were attached to the door handle of one of the cupboards, and spot lamps in the ceiling that cast a golden glow over the room. On the stove was a large metal pot. Flames were underneath it, and whatever was in the pot was producing a delicious aroma.

Yuri's father, Gregor, was standing behind the workbench, holding a knife. On a chopping board in front of him was a fourteen inch chunk of meat. Gregor was in his early sixties, medium height, built like a wrestler, had a black beard, bald head, and a scar that ran from one eye to his jaw. He was wearing waterproof trousers, boots, and a jumper reminiscent of the type worn by submariners when on deck. The sleeves of the jumper were rolled up, displaying his massive muscular arms and tattoos. When he spotted Sign he put down the knife, smiled, and walked into the lounge, his arms outstretched. "Ben! My friend! Part of me was hoping you'd get arrested by the secret police in Moscow." He hugged Sign, then took a step back while keeping his hands on Sign's arms. "The other part of me didn't want my food to go to waste." He turned to Knutsen and switched to English. "And you are Thomas. It won't be your real name, or it might be close to your real name. I don't need to know your surname because it will be false." His smile remained. "I will think of you as Thomas The Tank Engine – full of steam; always up to mischief; strong as a herd of oxen." He laughed. "Yuri used to watch Thomas The Tank Engine when he was a boy."

"Shut up, dad." Yuri was pouring four large glasses of neat vodka.

Gregor laughed louder and shook Knutsen's hand. "Welcome Thomas."

Knutsen felt like he was in the presence of an unstoppable force of nature. He pointed at Lenin. "Erm, is that a wolf?"

Gregor nodded. "His bite is ten times stronger than a dog's bite."

Knutsen eyed the wolf. "I thought you'd say something like that. Is he dangerous?"

"Only if he wants to feed. Don't worry – I fed him before you arrived. You should be safe for a few hours."

Knutsen kept his eye on the animal. "It's just that I get uneasy around dogs and… things like that, ever since I was attacked by pit bull when I was a kid. Wolves are a step up."

Gregor put his arm around Knutsen and stroked Lenin. "But now you are a man. You and Lenin will become great friends. You're taking him for a walk now. He needs to do a shit and piss."

"What?! A walk?"

"Follow the shore for half a mile, then bring him back. Keep him on the lead. There are rumours that there's a female wolf nearby. Lenin will bite your head off and escape if he gets her scent. Be firm with him. Show him who's boss. And talk to him. He's calmer that way. Well, usually it keeps him calm."

Yuri handed Knutsen a lead and a torch. "Don't touch his tail, or his rear legs. In fact, don't touch him at all unless things go wrong. If he does get aggressive, pin him down by his neck and hold him for ten minutes. Be *very* strong. Don't let his jaws get anywhere near you. He should be fine after that."

Knutsen breathed in deeply. His heart was racing. To himself he said, "Okay, let's do this." To the wolf he said, "Lenin – if you pull any crap I'll cut your dick off. You got that mate?" He attached the lead and walked Lenin out of the house.

Gregor and Yuri were sniggering when Knutsen was gone.

Sign smiled. "You are naughty."

"Is there a better way to be?" Gregor patted his son on his shoulder. "Glasses on a tray, bottle next to them, put them on the rear balcony. I need a moment alone with my friend."

"Sure, dad."

When Gregor and Sign were alone, Gregor said in Russian, "Come with me into the kitchen." He pointed at the vat on the stove. "I've sweated down onions, ceps, garlic, and added water, tomatoes, herbs, a deseeded chilli, two cloves, beer, and broiled pig's snout. Once the reduction is complete I'll strain it off, discard all but the liquid, and use the sauce as a gravy." He spun around. Alongside the chopping board with the joint of meat were two other chopping boards. One of them had potatoes. The other had vegetables. "I'm thinking boiled cabbage that's then caramelised in butter and pickled in vinegar, shredded and fried potatoes, and cold cucumbers coated in a lovely vodka and lemon sauce. I brewed the vodka last winter. All of the vegetables are either grown by me or foraged by me and Yuri from the woods." He slapped the meat. "And here's the masterpiece. It's cut from the side of an Elk, meaning it will be tender. There's a friend of mine twenty miles up the lake. He rears a lot of animals, and has a wooded and enclosed thirty hectare plot containing elks. Occasionally he lets me take Lenin in there so that I can give him the freedom to remember how to hunt. It's important because I'm hoping to release my dear friend back into the wild when he's five. But he must know how to survive. Lenin killed this elk. Some of it I gave to him; the rest of it is in the freezer. I paid my friend for the meat. I will roast the joint. Yuri will take care of everything else while you, me, and Thomas have a drink by the lake." Gregor looked satisfied with everything around him. "What do you think of this evening's meal?"

Sign gently punched his fist against Gregor's arm. "Thomas and I have just arrived at the finest restaurant in Russia."

"You have." Gregor oiled a roasting pan, placed the meat into the dish, put the pan in the oven, dipped a finger into the vat's sauce and placed it in his mouth, nodded with approval, and rubbed his hands together. "Keep your fleece on. It will be cold outside." He walked out of the house and onto the long rear balcony facing the vast lake. He said to Yuri, "Thank you, son. Over to you. Grab yourself a vodka and get on point in the kitchen. It's my turn to cook tomorrow. Usual drill. Divide and conquer."

Gregor and Sign sat on wooden chairs. There were two other chairs on the balcony, but they were brought from the lounge this evening. Gregor and Yuri lived here alone; they didn't have many visitors since Gregor's wife died in her sleep on the balcony. When she passed away she was in a third chair that matched the two that Gregor and Sign were in. For a while, Gregor and Yuri kept the third chair until they could no longer look at it, due to their grief. They burned the chair on the lake shore and said a prayer for the woman they so dearly missed. That was ten years ago. Gregor and Yuri had muddled through ever since.

The balcony was twenty yards long and contained handmade flaming torches that were fixed in plant pots on the rail that separated the balcony from the lake. Water was beneath them, lapping the struts that supported the exterior seating area. The torches illuminated glimpses of the lake; aside from that it was impossible to see anything beyond the rear of the house.

Gregor handed Sign a glass, took one for himself, and raised his glass. "To that crazy escape we did in Belarus."

"Amen to that." Sign chinked his glass.

Both men swigged their vodka.

Gregor said, "Tell me about Thomas."

Sign looked at the lake. "He's an ex-cop; single; killed the man who murdered the woman he wanted to marry; is sometimes quiet, other times has a mouth like a sewer; highly intelligent, but not worldly wise; and is one of the finest fellows I've met."

Gregor nodded. "I like him. Except the cop bit."

Sign smiled. "Don't worry. He never liked being in the police."

"He's a rule-breaker?"

"Most certainly. But, his moral compass is pointing in the right direction."

Gregor poured them another drink. "So, why are you here? I don't need specifics."

Sign replied in a quiet voice, "It's a babysitting job. I have an asset in Moscow. The asset's lost her nerve. I've given her a task that shouldn't ruffle her fear. It's the first step to getting her back on to the road to recovery. Thomas and I are here in case she needs us. Then we fly home."

Gregor nodded, his expression sombre. "She's in the very best hands. But take care, my friend. The old guard in Russia is being replaced. Trust no one except Thomas, me, and Yuri." He laughed. "Remember that crazy guy Anatoly Shkuro?"

"How could I forget? He put a bullet in his head a day after I asked him to plant a bomb under an ambassador's car. I should have known that Shkuro had cracked."

"There was no way you could have known. It was bad luck. You gave your instruction to him a few hours before his nerves went into meltdown. Before that he was fearless and mental." Gregor shook his head. "You were with me when we watched him through the sights of our sniper rifles as he walked up that mountain in Afghanistan, entered a Taliban village, strangled the leader, and jogged out of the village. He *was* mental, or an adrenalin junkie, or both. I guess it takes its toll on the mind and body in the end." He gripped Sign's arm. "You did nothing wrong. You saved his crazy arse so many times. The point is that men like you can control people's minds ninety nine percent of the time. But, then there's always that damn one percent."

"Yes. I hate the one percent."

Gregor looked left. "Mr. Tank Engine! You have returned! And Lenin hasn't killed you! This is a good evening! Join us for drinks."

Knutsen sat next to them. Lenin was with him, attached to his leash. The wolf laid down at Knutsen's feet. Knutsen stroked him. "That was interesting - walking something that might want you for dinner."

Gregor roared with laughter. "But look at you now. No fear of silly little pit bulls. And you've made friends with a wolf. Lenin doesn't let anybody but me or Yuri walk him. You must have something special in you. I thought that might be the case. But, I wasn't sure. It was my test. If Lenin tried to kill you, it meant he was suspicious of you. Therefore I'd be suspicious of you. But, he has accepted you. Therefore I accept you."

Sign leaned over and held his fist in front of Lenin's mouth. Then he stroked him. "Gregor – you do talk nonsense."

"Always." Gregor poured Knutsen a glass of vodka. "I must check on dinner. I hope you're both hungry." He walked into the house.

Knutsen asked Sign, "Alright – what's the deal with Gregor?"

Sign watched bats swoop near the torches. "I met him in Butyrka prison, Moscow. He and I shared a cell together for three weeks. I was being held on suspicion of espionage. Gregor was in there pending trial for mass manslaughter. He was a highly decorated submarine captain. While sailing his vessel in the Bering Sea his submarine snagged on a fishing net, careered off course and walloped into a huge subterranean rock. It was a catastrophe. The vessel was very badly damaged and took on water. Its engines cut out and the submarine sunk to the sea bed. Sailors drowned. Gregor tried to save the rest but it was a hopeless cause. Nevertheless he worked tirelessly for over forty eight hours, in freezing water, swimming back and forth with no light, trying to resuscitate his men and drag them to the few remaining areas where there was air. It was a herculean task. But, the Russian navy did nothing. It knew where the submarine was, yet took the decision that its crew should die. They didn't want bad publicity. So, they kept the incident secret, with the intention of salvaging the vessel without the world's media knowing what had happened. Eventually, all of Gregor's crew were dead. It broke his heart to do so, but he had to leave them in their watery grave. He escaped the tomb via a torpedo tube and swam fifty yards to the surface. His lungs were bursting and he was suffering the bends. But, he was lucky. A Russian naval ship was static, over the scene of the incident. He was pulled on board and given medical care. And when he was brought back to shore he was arrested by military police for dereliction of duty. When we were in prison together we spoke. He couldn't forgive the Russian authorities for not coming to his crew's rescue. I told him that he might be of use to me and that we should stay in touch."

"How did you both get out of prison?"

Sign shrugged. "For me it was easy. Britain's Special Branch was holding a GRU spy. Our government said it would hand over the spy in exchange for me. The exchange was done and I was released. When I got back to England, I sent a note to the head of the FSB. The note contained the exact grid coordinates of the submarine accident and simply said *I shared a cell with the captain. If you lay a finger on him and keep him in jail for another day I will tell every Russian, American, British, French, German, Japanese, and Chinese media outlet that the Russian navy is run by a bunch of spineless fools*. I didn't need to say anything else. Gregor was released."

"isn't the FSB suspicious that he may be working for MI6?"

Sign shook his head. "That was the beauty of my demand. The Russian navy was severely embarrassed. In a private ceremony, Gregor was awarded Russia's highest medal. And quite rightly so, even though Gregor knew it was given to him to shut him up. What it did do, however, was grant him freedom and infinite respect. No one watches Gregor and no one in this country dares touch him. He's invincible. And he works for me on odd occasions. We've done a lot of jobs in various parts of the world. He's useful to me because he's very precise."

"Precise?"

Sign didn't elaborate.

Gregor walked on to the balcony, with a huge grin on his face. "Dinner's nearly ready. Are you two swapping war stories? What is it you Brits say? Something like *pull up a sandbag and swing the lantern*?" He rubbed his hands together and sat next to them. "Time for one more drink before we eat. Now, tell me Mr. Tank Engine – how did you kill your girlfriend's murderer?"

Natalia was sitting on her room's bed, within a cheap hotel in central Moscow. She'd checked in to the hotel two hours ago, had called Sign to say she'd arrived safely in Russia, and had done little else since aside from purchasing a burger from a nearby street vendor. The room was clean, small, and functional. She'd tried watching TV, but couldn't concentrate. The journey had been tiring and she felt uneasy being in her country's capital. Her stomach was cramping and her mind was giddy. She knew that had to stop. The temptation to get under her bed's duvet was almost overwhelming, but she told herself that to do so would be submitting to fear. She had to spend the next hour or two in a state of calm meditation. After that, she'd sleep. And tomorrow, she hoped, she'd be relaxed and confident. So, she sat on her bed, her hands placed together in front of her face, as if in prayer, her eyes closed, her breathing deliberately deep and slow. She silently repeated the line that Sign had said to her when he asked her to briefly visit Moscow.

It is not a dangerous enquiry.

Her cover for staying in the hotel was sound. Though she was ostensibly in Moscow to see her aunt and uncle, they lived in a one bedroom high rise apartment. They didn't have room to accommodate her. Also, they lived in the outskirts of Moscow. Natalia wanted to be near to the SVR headquarters in case she needed to work. Tomorrow evening she'd visit her family. Sign's suggestion that the purpose of her trip was due to a medical emergency was apt. Her uncle had been a chain smoker all his life. He now had emphysema. Her aunt needed MRI and CT scans after suffering from blackouts during the last few months. Natalia had previously spoken to them on the phone from London, suggesting that they move to the house that her brother had bought near St. Petersburg. But they'd rightly refused the kind offer, given it was too far away from medical facilities and they didn't drive. Natalia had a bit of savings, not much, but she hoped she could help them with their health care costs. It deeply saddened her. If they died she'd have no one left aside from the woman who called herself Katy. Ben and Tom wouldn't feature for much longer in her life. They were hired help, she could tell. Soon they'd move on to another project. And even Katy might vanish from her life if Natalia couldn't get her act together and prove her value to MI6.

She stopped meditating and walked to the only window in the room. She was four stories up from the road below Cars were bumper-to-bumper in the evening traffic, producing a river of neon headlights. Either side of the vehicles were low-rise shops and office buildings. In the distance were taller buildings. The city was buzzing and aglow with a multitude of illuminations. Tourists would have thought it looked cool. But Natalia didn't think of it that way. She knew that underneath the veneer of the cosmopolitan, post-Soviet, hip metropolis was the same old dogma of corruption, cruelty, and disregard for life. Russians understood that; most tourists didn't. Everyone who lived here were acutely aware that they were ants that could be squashed without a second thought by the government. They were disposable. To the governments and previous tsars, that mind set made sense. Who wants to run the biggest country in the world if it's getting overpopulated? And how can one stop the country fragmenting into smaller countries without holding the motherland together with the use of a rod of iron and brutal punishments on its populous? It's why Natalia and so many other Russians hated their homeland – they knew there was no feasible alternative to how rulers governed such a vast chunk of the world. It left Russians with two choices: leave or accept how matters have always been conducted for centuries. Natalia had chosen to leave, but she'd done so as a Russian spy. Her career choice now seemed utterly ridiculous..

She changed into her bedtime attire, drank some water, and got into bed. She thought she'd fall straight to sleep. She didn't. She thought about Petrov and how, at the end, he looked so utterly alone in the world; her parents and how exhausted they were with life, and her own lonely and unusual life. Sign had been right in his comment to her when they'd dined. She was young. Ordinarily she shouldn't be ready in life to resignedly accept her plight and the realities of her day-to-day existence. Most women her age were dating, going out in the evening with friends, communicating with pals on social media, going on holidays, dreaming about the future and joyous events, sometimes laughing, other times sad. She had none of those things, not even sadness. Her life was all about survival.

She turned off the bedside light. Her eyes remained open. After thirty minutes, she closed them. Before sleeping she decided she had two choices: die you as an emotional and physical wreck; or get a new life in Britain. But to get the latter she'd have to complete her work for Katy. And before that she'd have to do her best to find answers to Susan Archer's disappearance.

CHAPTER 7

Early the following morning Knutsen was woken by the sound of squealing. Bleary eyed, he put his clothes and boots on and went downstairs. He couldn't see anyone in the house, though lights were on and the kettle was boiling. But the squealing was louder and he could hear men shouting from outside. He opened the front door and walked outside. Gregor and Sign were chasing a mid-sized pig that was bolting along the lake's shoreline. Yuri was standing nearby, holding Lenin on a leash.

Gregor was apoplectic, shouting in Russian, "Stop, you little fucker!"

Sign ran ahead of the pig, stopped, turned to face the swine, and held out his arms. The action confused the pig. It slowed sufficient for Gregor to catch up with it and attach a lasso to its neck. He dragged the beast back towards the house and placed it in a nearby pen. As he walked past Yuri he muttered, "I told you to bolt the door! The others in there might be docile but this one's a lively bastard. If you hadn't grabbed Lenin he'd have ripped the pig apart." He smiled as he walked to Knutsen. In English he said, "Good morning Thomas. Unless absolutely necessary I would advise you never to keep animals and wayward sons. I'm going to make a pot of coffee for us all, but take your time. It will stay warm on the stove." He went into his house.

Knutsen wandered over to Sign. For the first time, he could properly take in the surroundings of the house. Aside from the small wooden barn containing the pigs, there was a chicken coop, small outhouse for smoking and drying fish, pond that was fed by a tributary from the lake and contained a fish trap at its entrance, two horses and one pony in a paddock with a large shelter, garages, large gas unit that supplied the house, tractor, and an assortment of other farm equipment – some of it in good condition, others rusting and cannibalised for spare parts. The land was also farmed for crops, though most of the plots were bare at this time of year. It was hard to tell how much land Gregor owned. Aside from the two hundred yard fence that stretched from the house and followed the lake's shore, there were no discernible man-made boundaries. The only natural boundaries were the lake and a forest that was either side of the track into the property and four hundred yards away. On the vast lake, a rowing boat was tethered to a post, fitted into the slim beach. On the far side of the lake was another forest that stretched for as far as the eye could see. Knutsen estimated it would take at least three hours to row to the other side. And goodness knows how long the lake was. It was impossible to see where it began and ended; at the very least it was a mile long, probably considerably longer. One thing was clear – there were no visible dwellings near Gregor's farmstead.

Sign was checking the rowing boat.

Knutsen asked him, "Sleep okay?"

"Like a hibernating bear." Sign walked towards the house. "Let's get a brew down our necks. Then you and I need to fetch some breakfast."

Knutsen followed him. "Breakfast? How far is the nearest shop?"

"Too far." Sign entered the house.

The fire was lit. Lenin was curled up in front of it, having become fatigued after his five mile walk with Yuri this morning. In the kitchen, Yuri was pouring freshly brewed coffee. Gregor was sitting in the lounge, smoking his pipe and reading a week-old newspaper.

Gregor flicked the paper, and tossed it onto the fire. "The world has gone mad." He gestured to the spare armchairs. "Sit and have a drink. Then you must work for your supper."

The comment didn't seem to faze Sign, who slumped into a chair. By comparison, Knutsen had no idea what was going on.

Yuri served them mugs of coffee and said, "I need to check the chicken wire. We've got a family of foxes nearby." He left.

Gregor put his hands around his mug. "Have you heard from your asset?"

Sign nodded. "Today she's going into SVR headquarters. It'll make or break her. All we can do is wait here, unless there's an emergency."

"Da, I know. Do you have a back-up plan if the wheel comes off?"

"Yes. But, I'm not going to tell you what it is." Sign winked at Gregor. "Officially you are a Hero of the Russian Federation. You're the last person I should be speaking to."

Gregor chuckled. "*Hero of the Russian Federation.* What a joke." His expression turned serious. "My men drowned in a steel coffin."

"You tried to save every one of them. Your efforts were nothing short of spectacular." Sign sipped his coffee. "You have survivor guilt. That's all. We discussed this a few years ago. And look at what you and I subsequently did to the identify and neutralise the butcher in Myanmar, our heist of dirty bank money in Bahrain, the trick we played on the CIA in Venezuela, that bloody long trek through the jungles of Borneo to catch the man who slit Jacob's throat, and that incredible two mile shot you took on the side of K2 to knock off the head of the man who wanted to set fire to the world. There are so many other examples." Sign smiled. "Not bad for a sailor."

Gregor waved his hand. "That was then and this is now." He stood and took two guns off the rack. "Mr. Thomas. I presume you can shoot." He handed Knutsen one of the guns. "You and I are going hunting in the forest now for this household's dinner. Meanwhile Ben is going on to the lake to catch our breakfast."

Natalia entered the headquarters of the Sluzhba Vneshney Razvedki, in the Yasenevo district in southwest Moscow. She approached the security desk, showed her passport, and was told by the guard behind the desk to wait. He made an internal telephone call and told her to wait. Five minutes later a man swiped his SVR on an electronic recognition pad on the inside of the rigid clear plastic barriers in the lobby, came through the gate, and smiled when he saw Natalia.

He approached and said, "Good to see you." He nodded at the security guard. "She is who she says she is. Give her a temporary pass." When Natalia was issued the pass, the man said to her, "Come with me."

She followed him through the gates and into the huge building.

As the man led her along corridors with offices either side, up lifts, and along more corridors, he jabbered. "It's the busiest here that I've known it for years. We've got all this terrorist shit to deal with, organising missions in Syria that look like we're targeting ISIS whereas instead we're wiping out the rebels who want to oust that psychopath president who our politicians support, cyber attacks against the West – and my goodness, you should see the size of the cyber team now, I bet it's four times the size since you were last here, bolstering the Crimea, monitoring North Korea and China, alongside the FSB dealing with the usual internal shit within Russia, and having fun and games with Brexit, Europe in general, Britain, and America." He stopped by an office. "And we're clearing out the rotten apples. What we did to the Skripals in Salisbury is a drop in the ocean. We're going after every single defector, no matter where they are, and we'll send them to Hell." He knocked on the door and entered.

A fifty three year old man was sitting behind his desk. He was slim, wore glasses, had silver hair, and was wearing a suit. He stood when he saw Natalia, and walked into the centre of the oak panelled room. "Natalia. Take a seat." To the man who'd escorted her to the room, he said, "Leave us now." When they were alone, he sat behind his desk. He was the head of the SVR's Britain Department and had served in the foreign intelligence service for thirty one years. During his career he'd been posted to Tokyo, Islamabad, Kabul, Kiev, Munich, Washington D.C., and three times in London. Some SVR officers thought he was destined to be the next director of the service; others thought not because he loathed politics and wanted to stick to what he did best. His name was Alexander Surikov.

Surikov asked, "How was your flight?"

Natalia replied, "We need a better national airline."

Surikov smiled. "Technically, Aeroflot is semi-privatised. Where are you staying?"

"You know the answer to that."

"I do. Does the hotel serve your needs?"

"I've slept in worse places."

Surikov nodded. "We do what we have to do. How are your aunt and uncle?"

"I'm seeing them this evening. Things are not looking good."

"Your aunt should get her scans as soon as possible. Regrettably your uncle may be beyond repair."

Natalia hadn't told anyone in the service about her relatives' medical condition. She said, "I just need to check on them and see what I can do to help. But, I can't stay long. We're really stretched in the London office."

"I'm sure you are. How are you finding it there?"

Natalia replied with part lies and part truths. "London looks like it's under martial law. There are cops everywhere, armed with Heckler & Koch submachine guns, and wearing body armour. Every inch of the city is monitored by CCTV. There's brilliant food to be had, and the cinemas and theatres are great. But I don't go out much. Actually, I don't go out at all when I'm not working. It's a scary place. We work really long hours in the London office. When I get home I just want to sleep. And I don't feel that I belong in London. It feels so alien to me."

"You are young and this is your first posting. You'll get used to operating in strange places. Are you planning to do any work while you're here?"

Natalia replied, "I'd like to decompress as much as possible, alongside my family duties."

"Quite right. I was going to suggest the same."

She added, "But I would like to do some research. Can I have access to our archives section?"

"For what purpose?"

"I'd like to look into an old case. It's to do with the disappearance of Sergey Peskov in nineteen sixty eight." Peskov was a KGB officer, based in London, who'd gone to meet a British asset in Manchester and had never been seen since. His disappearance was a mystery to the Soviet Union. "I have a contact who has told me that she knew Peskov. My contact thinks he was assassinated by British authorities. I don't know much about the Peskov case. My understanding is that it was assumed by us that he'd defected and his identity had been changed. If that's true, he'd be an old man by now, or dead. However, I imagine in the current climate it would be good if we could prove he was killed by the British. They might stop finger pointing at us about the Salisbury thing if we confront them with some home truths."

"Good thinking. Who's your contact?"

"It's delicate. She's not yet fully recruited by me. If I'm successful in getting her on board I'll happily tell you her name. For now I have to tread carefully."

Surikov pondered the statement. "I understand." He smiled. "You are putting your field training to use. Don't worry – one day soon I will give you the freedom to get away from your analyst desk job. Enjoy it while it lasts." He slapped his desk. "When you get to my age you soon find yourself back behind one of these damn things. Yes, you can have access to the archives and investigate the Peskov case. You are right – it would be good to have some dirt on the Brits. The UK, America, NATO, the whole bunch of them, are rattling their sabres at us." He stood and held out his hand. "Good work Natalia. But, make sure you have some time for yourself as well. You look tired. I don't want you to burn out."

Natalia shook his hand. "Thank you sir." She left his office.

While Gregor and Knutsen were stalking through the nearby woods, Sign was in the lake, sitting on Gregor's rowing boat, casting the line from a fly fishing rod. Due to the depth of the lake he'd opted to use a reel loaded with a sinking line. On the tippet was a gold head nymph and two droppers containing pheasant tail flies. After the line was extended he silently counted to fifteen before beginning the retrieve using a figure of eight hand technique. There were no strikes. He cast the line into a different spot and counted ten before retrieving. Still nothing. This didn't perturb Sign. He was used to the complexities of fly fishing and the odd temperament of the trout he was targeting. He looked at the lake. Five hundred yards away was a ripple on the surface. This was good. It meant that it was less likely the trout would see him and it gave them extra courage to chase after aquatic life. He rowed there, let his boat gently drift, and cast again. His line pulled tight. He'd had a strike. He raised the rod to twelve o'clock and played the fish, sometimes pulling it in, other times letting in run in case it snapped the tippet line. The process lasted ten minutes before he was able to net the trout and despatch the fish using a wooden priest. The trout was at least three pounds. He placed it in the hull of the boat and cast again. Forty minutes' later he rowed to shore, tethered the boat, and walked to Gregor's house, his rod and other kit in one hand, the two trout he'd caught dangling by their gills in the other. As he neared the property, Gregor and Knutsen emerged from the forest. Gregor had two ducks lashed on a piece of rope and slung over his back. Knutsen was carrying a goose that he'd shot while it was flying close to the lake. Both men had smiles on their faces. They'd caught dinner and like all respectful hunters they'd only killed what they needed for the cooking pot.

When the men were inside, Sign set about cleaning the fish, pan frying them, and cutting slices of bread. It was a simple yet hearty breakfast. He served up the plates of food on the dining table. Yuri came into the house, washed his hands, and sat with them at the table. For the most part, the four men ate in silence.

When they'd finished, Gregor rubbed his stomach and had an approving look on his face. "All days should start this way. Yuri and I have some jobs to do on the farm today. After that we'll prepare the birds. Do you have plans today? If the answer's yes you may borrow one of my cars. If the answer's no I have a tree that needs felling and turning into logs."

Sign gathered up the plates and placed them in the kitchen. "Thomas and I have to see someone today. Thank you for the offer – yes we'd be grateful to use your car. We'll be back before dinner."

Lenin walked up to Knutsen and nuzzled his ferocious jaw in his lap. Knutsen stroked him.

Gregor beamed. "Take the wolf with you if you like. He enjoys car travel. Just make sure you leave one of the car windows a few inches open so he can get the outside smells. Keep him on a lead. And if anyone asks about his pedigree, for the love of God don't say he's a wolf. Tell them he's a huskie or similar breed. And don't let him near dogs, or children, or women, or anyone for that matter that you think he will kill for pleasure or food."

Fifteen minutes later Sign drove out of the farmstead. Knutsen was in the rear passenger seat. Lenin was half-on-half-off his lap, panting as he had his nose stuck out of the window. The wolf's one hundred and seventy pound weight was crushing Knutsen's legs. And Knutsen had to keep pushing his fur away from his mouth.

Sign looked in the rear view mirror and smiled. "I hope you're both sitting comfortably back there."

Knutsen made no effort to hide the irritation in his voice when he said, "This is weird. I should have stayed in the police. When you asked me to come with you to Russia you didn't mention anything about looking after a wolf, staying at a mad submariner's house, and having to catch my dinner."

"Ah, but dear fellow we must always strive to enrichen our lives with periods of the unusual."

"I'd like to see how you'd get on with a monster sitting on your lap. I can hardly breathe!"

"The drive isn't long. I'd say about ninety minutes."

"Ninety minutes! Oh, that's just bloody fantastic!"

Sign headed north on a road that followed the lake for six miles before veering northwest. All around them was countryside. Very few cars were on the road. At one point a car overtook them. In the rear seat was a young girl. She waved at Lenin and Knutsen. Knutsen gritted his teeth, put on a fake smile, and waved back. When the car was gone he said, "When we get back to London you're going to take me to a pub and buy me as many beers as I want."

"I'll do better than that, old boy. I'll take you to my club in St. James's. They do a lovely beef and ale pie and have an excellent cellar of wines and port."

Thirty minutes later, Lenin started retching. Knutsen screamed, "Pull over!"

But it was too late. Lenin vomited on the window, door, and Knutsen.

Sign tried to suppress laughter as he stopped the car on the side of the deserted road. "The poor fella needs some air. Take him out for a few minutes."

"He needs some fucking air?! God, you're going to pay me back big time for this." He took Lenin onto a grass bank, walked him back and forth, stopped to allow the wolf to have a pee, and brought him back into the car. "Right – wherever we're going let's get there fucking quick!"

Sign drove on. Twenty minutes later he turned the car into a layby and stopped. "We walk from here." He got out of the car. "Bring Lenin."

Knutsen couldn't work out who was more relieved to exit the vehicle – him or the wolf. He tried to wipe vomit off his fleece with blades of grass, but it only resulted in smearing the bile and slime further into his coat. Cursing, he followed Sign while holding Lenin on his lead. They trudged over rough, uneven, open ground, through a copse, and down an escarpment.

Sign pointed at a house boat that was moored on a river. "We reach our destination."

"A boat?"

"Yes, a boat and the man who lives inside the vessel." Sign strode onwards, then stopped sixty yards from the river, spun around to face Knutsen, and said in a quiet voice, "Listen. The man in there is friendly enough, but don't let that fool you. He was a mercenary in Africa in the seventies and eighties. People who worked with him gave him the nickname Mad Dog. You can imagine some of the things he did. None of them were pleasant or pardonable. He's retired now, but still retains contacts in his old world and dabbles in arms smuggling. He thinks I run a private military contractor company. Can you put on a German accent?"

"What?"

"A German accent. You're ex-GSG9 – the elite German police counterterrorism unit. Now you live in London and work for my company, though you're freelance. Make up the rest, if he asks you questions."

"I can't..."

"You're learning to be a spy and that means you have to think on your feet. Don't worry, I'll step in and pick up the slack if I sense you're faltering. One other thing – don't tell Gregor that we've been here. He hates the man after a job Gregor and I did in Sierra Leone a few years ago. To my knowledge, Gregor doesn't know he lives here. Regardless, let's tread carefully." He walked to the boat.

Knutsen was stock still for a moment. He sighed and said, "Come on Lenin. This can't be any worse than you puking on me."

Sign called out, "Knock knock! I'm looking for a crazy Russian guy who owes me money after he crashed my jeep in the Congo."

A man in his mid-sixties looked through one of the boat's windows, grinned, and walked out onto the vessel's gangplank. He was medium height, had a handlebar black moustache, long silver hair that was tied in a ponytail, and the physique of a soldier – slim and athletic. He was wearing camouflage army trousers, desert boots, and a green jumper. Wrapped around his forehead was a thin green bandana that he told people he wore to prevent sweat getting into his eyes, wherein the truth was he used it to hide the results of being branded by a red hot iron after he'd pissed off a tribe of Hutus. "Ben! My friend!" He held up his palm as he swaggered to Sign.

Sign slapped his palm and embraced him. "Good to see you, Anton. It's been a while" He pointed at Knutsen. "This is Thomas. He's German and doesn't speak Russian. He's an associate. Like I said to you on the phone, we're in Russia to do a rather tricky business transaction."

Anton switched in to English. "Nice to meet you, Thomas. Come aboard. What is that?" He pointed at Lenin.

Knutsen replied in an accent that he borrowed from the movie The Great Escape. "It's a Siberian husky."

"He looks like a wolf. Doesn't matter. Bring him in." Anton walked inside his boat. Sign, Knutsen, and Lenin followed.

The interior was narrow, cramped, but not cluttered. There was a tiny kitchenette midway in the boat, a single bed that folded up into the starboard, cupboards, fireproof metal containers of fuel strapped to the floor, a steering wheel and controls at the helm, and a triangular seating area that was permanently fixed to the rear of the boat.

Anton gestured towards the only place to sit. "Make yourself comfortable. The dog-thing can sit on the floor. I'm making tea with a dash of rum." As he prepared the drinks, he asked, "Thomas – how did you come to work with Ben?"

Knutsen replied, "He wants me to test weapons, to see if they're combat ready."

"Small arms?"

"That is correct."

Anton poured boiling water into a pot. "The types needed by special forces and mercenaries in unusual circumstances?"

Knutsen glanced at Sign. Sign nodded.

"Yes."

Anton stirred the tea leaves in the pot. "You are ex-military?"

"No. Police. I served in GSG9. Then I went freelance."

"Did you see action in GSG9?"

"In Germany. I've seen action elsewhere since I left."

Anton poured the tea and added a glug of rum to each mug. "Where is GSG9 headquartered?"

Sign held up his hand. "We all know its garrison is in Sankt Augustin-Hangelar, near Bonn. This is Thomas's first trip with me to Russia. It's a delicate situation for him, and for me for that matter. I want Thomas to keep a low profile, for reasons I'd rather not go in to. It wouldn't serve me or him if he was grilled by trusted friends like you."

"Alright. Keep your hair on." Anton smiled, brought the mugs over, and sat with them after carefully avoiding the huge wolf.

Lenin looked at Anton and growled. Knutsen stroked his head to calm him.

Anton addressed Sign. "Last time I saw you we were hightailing it out of Zambia. That was hectic shit. You really screwed over that South African mine owner. Can't remember his name. Hendrik, or something. Doesn't matter. He put the hounds on us. We'd be dead if you hadn't evaded those ex-Legionnaires by heading into the jungle. Also, it helped enormously that you managed to get the herd of elephants to stampede toward the Legionnaires. I still don't know how you did that."

Sign waved his hand dismissively. "I speak elephant and told the beasts that the men were coming to kill them."

Anton laughed. "Always the storyteller." His expression turned serious. "How can I help you?"

Sign sipped his tea. The taste reminded him of the time his parents had taken him on holiday to France and they'd gone to a bar-tabac at seven AM to get breakfast. Farmers were propping up the bar, taking a break from their four AM start, before heading back to work an all-day shift. Sign had marvelled at the sight of them having a nip of rum in their tea, so early in the morning. His father explained that it fortified them. Much to his wife's consternation, the father bought tea and rum for Sign to taste. Sign looked at Anton. "Thomas and I are shortly due to meet rather unsavoury customers. We will be discussing terms of a trade. They will likely get agitated and unpredictable. Guns will be involved. Therefore we need a gun; specifically a highly reliable pistol. I wondered if you could help us."

Anton looked at Knutsen. "To my knowledge, Ben no longer uses guns. So, I presume the pistol is for you. Are you right or left handed?"

"Right."

"Are you scared of recoil?"

"No, but I prefer precision over power, though ideally I like to opt for a combination of the two."

Anton nodded. "Because you don't want a shot man to have a few moments to shoot back. Yes, I can help you. Come with me." He walked onto the exterior bow of his boat, lifted a hatch, and withdrew a silk bag from a storage area. "This should do the job." He walked off the boat and into the copse. "Whose dog or wolf is it?"

Knutsen replied, "It's on loan. Ben and I are taking it to the meeting in the rural outskirts of Moscow. There will be six men there. We have intelligence that three of them are petrified of wolves. So, we got a dog that looks like a wolf, just to have a bit of leverage."

"Clever." From the bag Anton withdrew a MP-443 Grach Yarygin Pistol. He handed it to Knutsen. "What is this?"

Knutsen weighed the pistol in his hand. "It's an MP-443. It's a very good gun = accurate, reliable, packs a punch, and easy to strip down and clean. It's been issued to some Spetsnaz units but is not yet in service in the police."

"Very good, Thomas. You can see I've inserted targets of men in the forest. Most of them are only partially visible. I'll pick a target and you shoot."

Knutsen handed Lenin's leash to Sign. "Take him close to the boat. I don't want him getting jumpy when he hears the shots."

Sign walked off with the wolf, calling out, "If the gun's any good you can deduct its price off what you owe me."

Anton inserted ear defenders and quietly said, "Target two o'clock."

Knutsen crouched and put two bullets into the target."

"Excellent. Fast and accurate. That person's dead. Eleven o'clock."

Knutsen pointed his gun left and fired two more rounds.

"Perfect. Six o'clock."

Knutsen spun around and shot.

"That GSG9 training has obviously paid off."

They continued until all of the targets were shot. Then they walked back to the river boat. Anton said to Sign, "He is highly proficient. The gun is his, plus I've thrown in three spare magazines and a cleaning kit. Will you stay for lunch?"

Sign shook his head. "That's an extremely kind offer but we must get on the road." He shook Anton's hand. "Until next time, my friend."

"Ah, there might not be a next time. My adventures are catching up on me." He tapped his head. "A bullet I took in the shoulder in Chad is heading up towards my brain. Doctors can't remove it. Still, at least I know what I'm going to die from." He laughed. "When we face the devil we are no longer scared of the devil."

Sign nodded. "What was that music you hated so much when we were in Mauritania? One of the mercs kept playing it on his CD player."

Anton scratched his head. "It came from your country. Four girl singers." He smiled. "The Spice Girls, that was it."

"You're right." Sign placed his hands on Anton's arms. "When you're dead and before they close your coffin and put you in the ground, I'm going to put a record of the Spice Girls on your chest. They'll be with you forever."

Anton laughed. "Outstanding. But if you die first I'll put a jar of mayonnaise on your chest. I know you hate that crap."

"I would expect nothing less. Adios Anton." Sign walked off and handed Knutsen Lenin's lead.

When they were in the car and heading back to Gregor's place, once again Lenin was on Knutsen's lap. Lenin was licking Knutsen's face. Knutsen said, "Why oh why does the wolf like me?"

"Because you're like him."

"I might weigh pretty much the same as him but that's where the similarities end." Knutsen continued to let Lenin lick him, even though it prompted the ex-cop to wince. "I don't bite people, only have two legs, buy my food from the supermarket – though that's changing since I've been out here, am not looking for a mate, and I certainly don't sit on people's laps and lick them."

"Small details." Sign turned on to the main highway south.

"You seem to get on well with Anton."

"He was fine after I stopped him killing me in Kenya. We did a few jobs together after that. But throughout I knew all about his history. He and his men once got into a firefight with a Congolese army. Anton and his men were significantly outnumbered for days and besieged in their camp. It was hopeless. One night Anton crept out at night and entered the enemy's village, grabbed the army commander's six year old son, and dragged him back to his tiny base. The next day more fighting ensued. Finally, Anton wandered out across the grasslands, holding a white flag. The Congolese leader met him half way, expecting Anton to surrender. Anton shook his hand, tossed a hemp sack on to the ground, and told the commander that he and his men were facing a small unit of unspeakable creatures. Anton returned to his base. The Congolese commander opened the sack. His son's severed head was inside. Anton's men then mortared the bejesus out of the commander's army and opened fire with everything they had. They slaughtered the Congolese army."

"How the fuck can you be friends with someone like that?"

"*Friends*? How can Lenin be friends with you? He likes you now but if he's starving he'll kill you without a second thought. I used Anton for my own benefit. In my world we work in the dark side of morality and pray our souls remain intact."

Natalia entered the basement archive section of the SVR headquarters. It was a vast room that stretched the length and width of the building. Files of current and former cases were housed in tall shelves that were fifty yards long and eight feet apart. There were forty shelves in the archive. The room was illuminated by strip lights in the ceiling, some of which needed replacing because they flickered when electricity oscillated over the poor contact between light fittings and energy source. The place resembled a museum's vault of historical documents. One man worked in the archive. His name was Osip Delvig. He'd worked here for eleven years and prior to that he'd conducted various administrative jobs in the SVR and KGB. He was a wizened man, in his early seventies, widower, had arthritis in his nicotine stained hands, and liked the archive job because it meant he could work from nine until five and then lock up his room for the night and go home for a few cigarettes and drinks. Natalia had met him many times and they'd formed a connection because they both liked reading works by the brilliant literary novelist Franz Kafka and the Philip Marlowe crime stories by American author Raymond Chandler.

She smiled with genuine warmth as she saw him behind his desk that contained an antiquated computer, ink pens, paper, a packet of cigarettes that he wasn't permitted to smoke in the room, gold lighter given to him by his wife, and a deck of cards that he used to play solitaire to while away the time in what had to be one of the SVR's most boring and inactive jobs.

Osip looked up and removed his reading glasses. "Natalia my dear. This is an unexpected surprise. What brings you to the realm of secrets?" He liked to think of himself as the gatekeeper to some of Russia's darkest, hidden memories. His eyes twinkled as he asked, "Have you come to see me?"

Natalia sat on the edge of his desk. "Of course. You're the only sane person in this building."

As ever, Osip was wearing his favourite cardigan – brown wool, leather elbow patches, stinking of tobacco. "Are you married yet? Have children?"

Natalia shook her head. "No one will have me."

"More fool them. A young woman such as yourself should have a queue of men wanting to take you dancing. I regret to say that I am too old to join that queue."

Natalia kissed him on the cheek. "But, you can still dream. Did you finish the Marlowe books I leant you?"

"Long ago. If you come back tomorrow I'll return them to you."

Natalia stood. "I'm only in Moscow for a few days and I'm travelling light. Keep them until I return to HQ fulltime."

"As you wish. I've kept them in pristine condition. How can I help you?"

"I'm doing some research into the Sergey Peskov case in 1968. I'd like to have access to the files. I have security clearance."

"I know you do. Your boss called me before you came down here." He placed a finger against the side of his nose. "But I'd have let you have a peak anyway. Old files don't change the world. They simply remind dinosaurs like me that once upon a time we had a ball." He typed on his computer keyboard. "Peskov, Peskov, Peskov. Where are you? There we go." He walked along the shelves and entered one of the corridors between them. Two minutes later he returned and handed her three files. "Use the reading room. It's the usual drill. I'm not cleared to know the content of," he swept his hand toward the library, "my babies. Just return the files when you're done."

The reading room was a small annex, behind clear glass and subdivided into cubicles containing chairs and desks. Natalia sat in one of the cubicles. She had zero interest in the Peskov case. She didn't bother unbinding the elastic clasp that held the file closed. She just sat there, waiting. Two hours' later she walked back to Osip's desk and handed him the files. "These are interesting. They may help us on a current matter. There is an intriguing reference in one of the files. It refers to a Susan Archer. Can you check to see if there's a file on her?"

"Why is she important?"

"Nice try, Osip. Just see if we've got anything on her."

He checked his computer logs. "Yes. She appears on the system. The reference dates to 1968 – same year as your Peskov case. But we don't have her file. Her file's buried in the FSB archive."

Though this was annoying, it did make sense. The FSB was responsible for national state security and was the successor to the KGB. It rarely operated overseas, deferring that responsibility to the SVR and GRU. If there was something suspicious about Susan Archer's disappearance after birth in Moscow, it would have been recorded in Russian police files. But, if there was anything about her disappearance that touched Soviet and Russian national security it would be a matter for the KGB and its successor. The problem was that FSB officers rarely liked working with their counterparts in other Russian agencies. Nevertheless, the fact that Archer's name was in the KGB archive inherited by the FSB made her an interesting subject.

Natalia asked, "How do I get to look at the file?"

Osip pulled out a cigarette from his pack, twirled it, and put it back in. "You don't. You know what those bastards in the Lubyanka are like."

The Lubyanka was a large neo-Baroque building designed by Alexander V. Ivanov in 1897 and situated in Lubyanka Square in Meshchansky District of Moscow. In its history it had been the headquarters of various secret police organisations and a prison for dissidents, many of whom were tortured and executed in the building. The mere name *Lubyanka* sent shivers down the spines of Russians. And nothing within the beautiful yellow brick building had changed. It housed the FSB, state police, and a prison. It was business as usual.

Natalia played it cool. "Not to worry. It was just a thought. Hey – can you recommend a good restaurant I can eat in tonight?"

"There are plenty of good places to eat. You know that."

"I do but here's the thing – I'm going to be on my own and I don't want jerks hitting on me. I'm not in the mood for that stuff. So, I'm thinking somewhere discreet."

Osip pondered the question. "There is nothing more pitiful than a lonely, transient woman, dining alone. Come over to my place at eight." He scribbled his address on a slip of paper. "I will cook beef stroganoff and rice. It won't be fancy. You're safe with me." He laughed. "I haven't been able to get it up for a very long time. Nor do I have the inclination on such matters."

Natalia patted his hand. "It will be good to have dinner with a true friend. I never worry about you. I worry about myself." She smiled. "See you at eight. I don't like my beef rare." She walked out of the room. When she was out of the building and sufficiently far away from the place she texted Sign.

Sign, Knutsen, and Lenin arrived back at Gregor's house. Knutsen's gun was under his belt, his spare bullets and equipment secreted in his jacket. Gregor and Yuri were in the kitchen. On the chopping boards were the two ducks and goose; all plucked and trussed. Gregor was wiping a brush dipped in a soy sauce and marmalade marinade over the ducks' skin. Yuri was jabbing a knife into the goose and inserting a peeled onion, lemon, and a handful of herbs into its cavity.

Gregor's face lit up when he saw Sign and Knutsen. "Tonight we have a banquet, yes? I have unearthed potatoes that have been growing since last autumn, picked four mushrooms the size of saucers, boiled beans and left them to rest in a jar of bacon powder and brine after which they will be drained and flash fried in butter, and I have this beauty." He held up a red cabbage. "Half of it will be used as a coleslaw, the other half as a stir fry with sliced radishes, gherkins, pepper, spices, and slithers of fresh orange. I have also made a red wine gravy. Not bad, eh?" He put down the brush. "We will have a drink now on the lake balcony." He picked up a bottle of vodka and three glasses. "Mr. Tank Engine – after our drink Lenin will need some further training. This will be your responsibility while you're my guest."

They sat on the balcony. As Gregor poured the drinks, Sign said, "My asset needs to get access to the Lubyanka. It won't be easy."

"But she's working on it?" Gregor handed them drinks.

"Yes." Sign stared at the lake. "Whether she'll be successful is another matter."

"Was it your instruction that she must infiltrate the godawful place?" Gregor sat and followed Sign's gaze of the lake.

"No. She's following her own leads."

"Then this is good! She is mustering her own courage without anyone telling her she must become stronger." He chuckled. "That said, it was your clever idea to put her on the battlefield to see if she would fight or flee."

"True, but I've always hated this part. You counsel someone to go over the trenches and when they've summoned the strength to do so your heart's in your mouth because you know you've persuaded the person to die."

"Come on, friend. You told me this is a routine job. She'll be fine. I presume she's a Russian intelligence officer."

Sign looked at him and made the slightest of nods.

"She's doing the right thing. I just wish I could be of service to you these days. But, I'm getting old. Still, it would be nice to have one last crack at this ridiculous regime."

"You are of service. You've been gracious enough to give Thomas and I a safe house. Plus your cooking is nearly as good as mine."

"Nearly as good?!" Gregor swigged his vodka. "Everything you eat here is fresh from the fields and lake. You cook produce from markets."

Sign smiled. A gentle rain was sprinkling over the lake. The sound of the droplets hitting the surface was like that of a drummer making the most delicate and rapid taps on a cymbal. It was a beautiful sound and soothing. He walked to the wooden rail that separated the covered balcony from the lake. "You have a beautiful place here, Gregor. You deserve it after everything you've done for your country and for me."

Gregor wasn't going to allow Sign to get deep and meaningful. In a mischievous tone he replied, "I only worked with you because I didn't know anyone else in MI6. For all I know I could have got a much better partner."

Sign turned to face him, Knutsen, and Lenin, while leaning against the fence. "Do you think we've made a difference, over the years? Have all the things we've done made an iota of change?"

Gregor pondered the question. "We are caretakers who clean our buildings. But we always know they will get dirty again. So, we clean them again, and we keep reliving the cycle of cleanliness versus dirt. And we do so knowing, all the time, that we can't change the structure of the building. Instead we tart it up." Gregor laughed. "That's what we are – a bunch of tarts."

"I hear you." Sign grabbed his drink and sat in his chair. "After dinner and when it's dark I will take your sturdiest rod and go fishing again. I suspect there are zander in the lake. They are strong and their teeth are fierce. The zander will be deep in the lake but they will be feeding. If I net one we will have a sublime plate of food tomorrow evening." He stood. "I'll check on your fishing equipment. I'll need some heavy weights, a wire tippet, and a hooked lure that will imitate something like a frog or a small fish. After that, I'll help Yuri with the rest of the cooking." He walked in to the house.

Gregor felt at peace as he absorbed the vista in front of him.

Knutsen said, "He wants to be alone tonight. Sometimes he gets like this. I don't know if it's him collecting his thoughts about ongoing projects or he wants solitude for solitude's sake."

Gregor drained his drink. In a serious and quiet voice he said, "It's neither. It is his prayer time. He wants to say sorry for his memories. Leave him be when he's like this."

"His memories?"

"He'll be working through the alphabet, or adopting a similar ritual. 'A' is for Anna who he failed to rescue in Budapest. 'B' is Becky who tried to shoot him in Trieste. And on it goes until he reaches 'Z'. Then he restarts the alphabet with new names. And when he's finished it, he restarts it again and again. I'm making this up. I don't know his ritual. And I know less than ten percent of his past. But I know for certain that he needs to process and catalogue his background." Gregor poured himself another drink. "It's not trauma. Not in the strictest sense. Rather it's recognition that one has been thrust into the most unusual situations one can imagine. It catches up with the best of us. And it confuses us. Ben is the most intelligent man I've ever met. No man on Earth is mentally stronger. He fights the confusion and won't give up until he's beaten it at its own game. He'll win... I think."

"That sounds like trauma to me."

Gregor shook his head. "There are matters to attend to that are beyond the human condition and most certainly are beyond trauma. Ben is the warden of a prison of his own demons. He has to be tough with himself and have systems in place. Otherwise, the demons take over the prison." He looked at Knutsen. "Ben and I did many jobs together. One in particular stuck in my mind. We were in Las Vegas, of all places. Ben had constructed the most brilliant plan to entice three Chinese intelligence officers to Nevada. It took him six months to do so and the way he baited them and reeled them in was truly incredible. His objective was to negotiate with them. A thirty year old Chinaman named Sun Xin was imprisoned in a tiny steel cage in Qincheng Prison in China. He was autistic, a brilliant mathematician, had a photographic memory, but had physical limitations due to other disabilities. He was a man-child who should never have been locked up. He was frightened and didn't know what was going on. He worked for the Chinese ministry of defence. In the department's headquarters, video recordings caught him reading blueprints of a new nuclear missile system. The Chinese thought he was memorising the prints with a view to selling the details to the West. In truth he was just curious about the designs. And he wouldn't have had the gumption, knowledge, or desire to contact the West. Nevertheless the Chinese took a different view. They incarcerated him and treated him as a spy. In prison the poor chap was in a dreadful state. Ben didn't want him to defect. He didn't want him to relay what was in his head. He just wanted Sun to be returned to his mum. I was with Ben in a Las Vegas hotel room, with the three Chinese officers. Ben told them what he wanted. The men laughed. Ben pulled out papers and showed them to the men. They were exact copies of the missile blueprints. Ben said that he'd got them six months prior to Sun's arrest. And he added that he got them from a real British spy in the Chinese intelligence service. I suspect he was bluffing and to this day I don't know how he got the blueprints. He said that Sun was innocent and that anything he'd done was of no interest to the West. All that mattered was that he should be released. The Chinese men seemed reasonable. They said they'd return back to their country and tell their bosses that there'd been a mistake. Sun Xin would be released, they promised. They also said they would be investigating the identity of the real spy in their unit. Three months later a letter was received in MI6, addressed to the alias Sign had used when meeting the Chinese men in Nevada. Sign opened the letter. Inside was a photo. Sun Xin's face was unblemished and easily recognisable. The rest of his body was hacked to pieces. He was dead. It was a message, a warning, to MI6 – the innocents don't matter; don't fuck with us. It devastated Ben. All he wanted to do was the right thing." Gregor looked at the lake. "And that's why Ben wants to fish alone tonight. He wants to hook and reel in a monster. And tomorrow night he wants to eat the thing." Gregor sighed. "Memories, God bless them."

"Why did Ben go out of his way to help Sun?"

"Because of a small, but pertinent matter. Seven months prior to Sun's imprisonment, Ben was on the run in Beijing. Chinese secret police were hunting him. It was a desperate situation. The net was closing in. Ben knocked on a random door in the city. The apartment belonged to Sun's mother. Ben knew nothing about her or her son. He just wanted refuge until the police moved on. He told her that he'd been mugged and was in shock. He asked if he could have a glass of water. I suppose most people would have closed the door in his face. But, she let him in and made him a bowl of chicken soup. It was a Saturday. Sun was at home. Ben speaks passable Mandarin. He spoke to the mother and to Sun. An hour later he told the mother he would repay her for her hospitality – not with cash, that would have been rude. He said that if ever they needed shelter he would ensure they'd get it. And that was all there was to the matter. A brief moment of kindness from Sun's mother meant that Ben had zero qualms about pulling out all the stops to help her son. That's Ben." His tone of voice changed as he said, "Now! You must do your duty and give Lenin some training." He tossed Knutsen a bag. "Take Lenin to the paddock. The horses are not there – they're in their stables for the night. In the bag is a shoulder of beef. I want you to put Lenin on one side of the paddock. Extend your hand in front of your chest. He will sit. Don't speak to him. Back away carefully to the other side of the paddock, keeping your eyes on the wolf at all times. Then pull out the beef and hold it at arm's length. He will charge towards you. Don't flinch. I'm hoping he will accurately grab the meat in his jaws. Don't be surprised if you're bowled over when this happens. The combination of his weight, speed, and aggression will make it feel like you're being hit by a truck."

Knutsen finished his drink and said sarcastically, "Excellent. When you say you're *hoping* he will get the meat and not my arm…"

Gregor laughed. "If he gets your arm it will mean he's not ready to be released into the wild. The loss of your arm will be a small sacrifice in the context of Lenin's rehabilitation. Go to it, Mr. Tank Engine! Dinner will be in one hour."

Natalia visited her aunt and uncle in the outskirts of Moscow. They lived in a high-rise block of flats. Conditions in the building were squalid. The lifts were notoriously temperamental and stank of urine, there was graffiti on the grey stone walls on the ground level, the stairs up the eighteen story building were a place where teenagers hanged out and dealt or took drugs, and the building was surrounded by other tenement blocks of the same height. Despite the champagne swilling and oyster swallowing affluence of other parts of the city, this part of Moscow resembled a throwback to the darkest days of communism. In fact, the buildings had been erected in the 1950s. Ever since, the zone hadn't moved on. It was a place that had been forgotten by the state. Despite the poverty in the area, there was little serious crime. It was a ghetto of sorts. People had to get on with each other to survive. And they were tired. They didn't have the energy to steal from one and other. Plus, there was nothing worth stealing. Wannabe criminals in their midst knew there were far better pickings to be had a few miles south of their location.

And yet, like many of the flats in the area, her aunt and uncle's miniscule one bedroom home was immaculate. Her aunt and uncle were proud people. Her aunt had laid the table; on it were small cakes on her best crockery. She was wearing the dress she wore when attending church. Her uncle had dressed into the only suit he owned and a bow tie before greeting his niece at the door. This evening was a formal occasion, one that the aunt and uncle had been looking forward to for days. Everything had to be right. There'd be no talk of medical problems. No talk of any signs of weakness. All had to be proper and a splendid occasion.

Natalia embraced her uncle and aunt and sat at the table. While her aunt spoke to her, Natalia's uncle disappeared into the kitchen and re-emerged with a smile on his face. In both hands he was cradling a bottle of wine. Natalia had bought it for them last Christmas. It had remained unopened ever since. The uncle said that tonight was as good a time as any to partake of a good drop. He uncorked the wine and sat with the women. As they ate and drank, they spoke about a range of matters – how Natalia was finding London, Russian politics, the nearby dog that kept barking at night, Natalia's love life, British and American politics, and whether Natalia couldn't be persuaded to stay for dinner. Natalia steadfastly refused to capitulate on the latter demand. She had to see Osip. Plus, she knew there'd be no dinner. Or, if there was it would be made from food that would have been allocated for her aunt and uncle's meal tomorrow. She couldn't deprive them of that. She told them that she'd be returning to Moscow fulltime in six months and that she'd visit them regularly. She forced herself to smile as she added that maybe she'd meet a wealthy husband who'd buy them a nice house near the hospital.

After she left she paused on the ground floor of the building and wiped away tears. She walked outside and continued onwards to the nearest underground train station.

Archer met the chief of MI6 in the tea room of Claridge's., in Mayfair. She was exhausted, having barely slept in the night due to her worry about Natalia, and because she'd had to spend all day firefighting a crisis in the Russia Department after one of its assets had been caught by the FSB and allegedly committed suicide in his cell. She sat opposite her boss.

"I've already taken the liberty of ordering," he said. "A pot of earl grey tea, raison scones, and a frangipane tarte."

Archer yawned. "Sounds lovely."

The chief smiled. "You've been burning the candle at both ends. That's why I invited you here. And afterwards I insist that you go home and put your feet up. Don't cook. Order yourself a takeaway pizza. Watch some nonsense on TV. Get an early night."

The food and drink were delivered to the table. When the waiter was gone, Archer said, "It's hard to relax at the moment."

"I know." The chief had to choose his words carefully because their table was too close to other tables and they could easily be overheard by guests. "She will be alright. Trust her. She'll come back safely."

"You can't guarantee that and nor can I." Archer took a bite from one of the scones. She had to force herself to swallow the mouthful, given food was the last thing on her mind these days.

The chief poured tea. "You know the rule. We must accept that we are like parents dropping our children off for their first day at university. We have to let them fly, even though it galls us to do so."

"And at the same time we expect them to get a first class degree."

"Yes. We're fearful for them, and yet we demand significant achievements from them. There is a contradiction within that duality."

"Always the bloody contradictions." Archer blew over film of her tea. "This is make or break for her. Is it make or break for me as well?"

The chief didn't answer her question. "After this posting you should become one of the five directors. You'll be the first woman to achieve that seniority. After that you should consider applying for my job. I'll be long gone by then and there'll be at least one person succeeding me before you reach that point in your career, but it's worth aiming for."

Archer huffed. "That's if I'm good enough, or the right political animal."

"Why shouldn't a woman take my job?"

Archer felt herself getting angry. She wasn't normally like that and she knew it was just down to fatigue. "Come on. It's nothing to do with being a woman. And there's no such thing as the old boys' club. It's down to the logics of the job. A woman can be a minister or prime minister. But those jobs are vastly different to ours. Fifty percent of new entrants to our organisation are women. It's fine for a while. But, some of us gals want to get married and have kids. That's not great if you're constantly being posted overseas. So a few years after joining, we lose a swathe of women. At the mid and senior level it's only spinsters like me who hang on in there. That's okay. We made life choices. But then one has to apply logic. Just because I'm a woman and have stuck the course doesn't make me as good as the ten plus male candidates I'll be up against for a director post and subsequently for the top job. The men have to compete against each other. The best rise to the top. I compete against them as well. But I'm also singled out as the most senior women in the service. That means shit. I become a token. We've always applied the principal that the best person should get the job, regardless of gender, race, creed, or any other bollocks." She rubbed her face. "I'm babbling and that's because I *am* tired."

He stirred his tea while keeping his eyes on her. "In my experience results are all that matters in our company. One can be the most brilliant political animal, super smart, diplomatic as fuck, backstabbing, and sociopathic in ambition, but that means jack. To get to the top one must have at least one major achievement under one's belt. In my case it was that incident with the bomb in Nicosia."

Archer smiled. "We still can't believe what you did when you discovered it adjacent to the embassy – walking down the street with it, depositing on a mountainside, walking back to your station in the British embassy, like it was business as usual. People wanted you dead. You did your stiff upper lip thing. You didn't stop work when you heard the bomb explode. It was as if nothing had happened. The explosion was massive and would have killed hundreds, at least, including you. And there are so many other stories about you."

The chief didn't move. "What did you and your colleagues think when you all heard I was taking the top job?"

Archer didn't have to consider the question. "We thought we had a general who'd proven he can lead from the front."

"Precisely. None of you respected me for how I conducted myself in service boardrooms, Whitehall, Washington, or Paris. That meant nothing to you. What mattered is my track record in the field. There are many that rise to senior management who don't have such a track record. But that's where their career stops." He drank his tea without taking his eyes off Archer. "What you're doing with Natalia is ground breaking. I don't need to tell you how significant her work is and how it will influence geopolitics. Get this one right and you will have walked your bomb onto the mountainside."

"And thus I no longer become the token woman."

"Precisely. It's always results that matter, not what's between your legs."

Archer relaxed and laughed. "Bless you. That's the first time I've laughed in a while." She sliced the frangipane. "I think tonight I will get a pizza, have a nice bath, and watch a movie. Any recommendations on the latter?"

The chief didn't blink. "Genre?"

Archer served him the tarte. "Because I'm not a stereotype, it's not going to be some godawful rom com. I'm thinking war movie. Something where I can see good prevail over evil."

"In which case you could watch a superhero movie."

Archer shook her head. "Too far-fetched. War movie."

"I see. A Bridge Too Far?"

"Seen it."

"We Were Soldiers?"

"Seen it."

"Platoon, Apocalypse Now, Full Metal Jacket, or any other Vietnam War movie?"

"I think I've seen them all."

"In that case you must watch The Siege of Jadotville. It's based on a true story. You will like it." The chief's eyes twinkled. "And for good measure the leading man may well be to your tastes." He touched her hand. "My wife sends her best wishes to you and has asked me to give you an open invitation for a Sunday roast, at your convenience and when work calms down. Have a think about it." He asked a waiter for the bill. "I have to dash. Wretched meeting with an Egyptian billionaire who thinks he can oust the American president."

Natalia arrived at Osip's house. It was a modest bungalow in northeast Moscow, detached, and had a small garden at the rear that had been transformed by Osip, after his wife died, into an allotment that grew root vegetables. Osip guided her in to his home. The air was thick with cigarette smoke and the aroma of beef bourguignon. The home was lovely. Natalia suspected little had changed inside since Osip's wife had passed away. This was not just a man's house. The woman's touch was everywhere – framed photos of Osip's family, artificial flowers, a painting of a female opera singer receiving a bouquet at Carnegie Hall, beautiful drapes, a wooden bowl of fruit on a table, doily clothes on the arm rests of the sofa, scented air humidifiers plugged in to sockets, delicate blue lights strung alongside one wall, and everything was in its place. Osip, Natalia decided, had kept the home as a mausoleum in honour of his dearly departed. The only indication of a man's presence were a baked bean can that was stuffed with fag ends and empty vodka bottles on the floor, awaiting bin recycling day next Tuesday.

Osip poured her a drink. Clearly he'd had a few before she'd arrived. "The beef's in the slow cooker. We can eat whenever we're hungry." He sat in an armchair and lit a cigarette.

Natalia sat in the other armchair. "Thanks for inviting me. I saw my aunt and uncle before coming here. It was tough. They're not well and have no money."

Osip chinked her glass. "We drink to better times."

"We do." She sipped her drink.

By comparison, Osip downed his vodka and poured himself another. "How is London treating you?"

Natalia had to move fast. Osip was already drunk and she doubted he'd be capable of serving up dinner or remembering it was cooking. "London is fine. It's odd being back. I suppose I've grown acclimatised to Britain."

Osip chuckled. "Don't get too comfortable." He blew out a stream of smoke. "When you're back here you'll settle in to the way of things. Once a Russian, always a Russian."

"How are you coping, since Maria died?"

"Routine, booze, cigarettes, routine." Osip smiled, showing off his crooked yellow teeth. "It's all I have left."

Natalia nodded. "I know about loss. My brother killed himself in front of me."

Osip looked serious. "Ah, my precious flower. You should never have seen that." He wiped his mouth. "I was by Maria's side when she passed away from cancer. Her eyes were screwed up due to the pain. All I could think about was how she looked when I first saw her in a ballroom in Vladivostok, forty years ago. She glanced at me but she was keeping options open and checking out other men. It was the most courageous thing I've ever done – going up to her and asking for a dance. We got married a year later. She, or me, couldn't have kids; we never bothered to find out why, because it didn't matter. I wonder if it was my smoking that killed her, or the pollution in Moscow, or the long hours she worked. Who knows? All I know is for some weird reason I'm still here, a cigarette in one hand and a glass in the other. God is cruel."

"Amen to that." Natalia pretended to drink. "You've been doing your current job for a long time."

Osip poured himself another drink. "Over a decade. I'm just filling in the hours, waiting for my pension."

"You must know a lot of secrets."

"I told you – I'm not permitted to read the files in the archives."

"For sure, but you pick up gossip here and there from people who come to your room."

Osip laughed. "Of course. Nothing goes unnoticed."

\#   "And I bet you swap notes with your counterpart in the FSB."

"Yeah. He's like me. Killing time in the archive. Just waiting for the day he can spend all day watching football on the TV."

"You should go out for a beer with him."

Osip shook his head. "We meet up at least once a week. We go to a lovely bar in eastern Moscow. He's like me – widower who drinks too much."

Natalia smiled. "Maybe he'd let us read the Susan Archer file in his archive."

"Now hold on…"

"It won't be a crime. I have clearance. The only problem is it would require an official request from the SVR to the FSB. I don't have time for that. So, shall we have fun and cut some corners?"

"Cut corners?"

Natalia leaned forward. "You and your FSB buddy are in dead end jobs. I'm chained to my desk in London. No one cares about us. But, the three of us might be able to break a big case. I'm not exaggerating when I say that unravelling the mystery of what happened to Sergey Peskov could prevent the West going to war with us. I don't know who Susan Archer is but she's a lead in the Peskov case. Come on – this will be cool and exciting."

Osip thought about what she said. "Technically I wouldn't be breaking rules. I'm permitted to visit the Lubyanka archive to swap notes on their techniques of storage and my techniques. And you have clearance to pursue to Peskov case, wherever it leads. I don't see why not."

"I bet you've got his mobile number. Call him now. He'll be at home."

Osip placed his glass down. "Are you sure this isn't illegal?"

"I wouldn't ask you to do anything illegal. And who knows? If we break the case the three of us might get a nice end of year bonus."

Osip walked to a sideboard, picked up his phone, and staggered back to his chair. He looked at Natalia, nodded, and scrolled through his phone's contacts list. He made the call. Two minutes later he pressed the end button. "He'll let you in to his archive the day after tomorrow. You are not permitted to read anything other than the Susan Archer file. He doesn't want your bosses or his bosses notified about your visit. To do otherwise would bog us down in bureaucracy. I must accompany you. He is satisfied that he's helping mother Russia." He poured himself another drink. "Ten AM on Thursday. Meet me outside the FSB headquarters." He downed his vodka. "I feel tired." He fell asleep.

Natalia placed a blanket over him, turned off the slow cooker, left, and called Sign.

CHAPTER 8

At four PM the following day, Sign walked along the lake adjacent to Gregor's house. He felt restless and hoped that fresh air and exercise would settle his mind. But, he couldn't help thinking about Archer, her sister, and Natalia. He had a theory about all three, and yet it was unfounded and absurd. But, the theory kept bouncing back into the front of his mind. If his theory was correct he would be placed in a dreadful situation. He forced himself to think about other matters. The sun was shining, trout were skimming the lake's surface to feed on flies, in the distance a woodpecker was drilling a hole into a tree, and Knutsen and Lenin were visible in the paddock adjacent to the house. Knutsen's swearing was loud and carried over the water, every time the wolf knocked him over during their training exercises. Sign walked for another three miles, then turned back. He wanted to be in the house before darkness consumed the surroundings, and to help Gregor and Yuri prepare the fifteen pound zander he'd caught in the lake the night before. He smiled as he walked towards the house and the golden glow of its exterior torches and interior lights. The location was idyllic. Gregor deserved nothing less after everything he'd done to help make the world a safer place. Sign was glad his Russian friend was of no use to him now beyond offering a safe refuge. Gregor was always the type of man who would die with his boots on, but he'd do so here, not on a mountainside facing down encroaching hostiles. As he neared the house he could hear music. Gregor was on the lake-facing balcony, strumming his balalaika and singing a song, a glass of vodka by his side. Yuri was carrying logs into the house. Knutsen was on his back in the paddock shouting, "That's the last fucking time, Lenin. Training's over for the day. I thought wolves had good eyesight. Or maybe you're deliberately trying to piss me off." For Sign, everything was perfect in this place this evening – Gregor having a sing song to himself and the lake, the ever energetic Yuri helping his Dad out by doing chores, and Knutsen going twelve rounds with a huge wolf. It was an odd set-up. Sign loved that it was so.

He entered the house. The fire was lit. Yuri was peeling carrots and spuds. A white wine-based sauce, infused with dill, was gently simmering on the stove. Sign asked him, "Do you want me to take over catering duties? You could go outside and have a drink with your father?"

Yuri beamed. "No need. My father and I spend enough time together. Anyway, he likes your company. He doesn't know when he's going to see you again." He lifted the zander by its gills. "I intend to bake this in brown paper, with a few dabs of butter and some cracked pepper. What do you think?"

"Perfect, though a squeeze of lemon wouldn't go amiss. Do you want me to get you a drink?"

Yuri pointed at a glass of wine. "I cook while I drink and I drink while I cook."

Sign smiled and went onto the large balcony. He sat next to Gregor. While Gregor played his balalaika, they sang an old Cossack song together. When finished, Gregor put the instrument down and poured his friend a drink. "War is boredom punctuated by moments of terror. I sense you are in the lull before battle."

Sign took the drink. "You and I rarely had time to be bored. In any case, being here has given me time to think and soak up the free air. It is anything but boring."

Gregor chinked his glass. "To all travellers and adventurers. When we return home we refuel. Then we go out again because we cannot resist doing so. It's in our genetic makeup."

"One hundred percent." The sun was going down. Sign watched swallows dart over the lake. They were grabbing their dinner before the bats came out. "What's retirement like?"

"For me it's like this." He gestured to their surroundings. "But it probably is different for most others. I'm not stupid. I constructed a working farm. So, for me it's not retirement. It's redirection. The thought of me spending all day on a golf course or watching daytime TV fills me with dread. I don't care if I exert myself too much. I get up at four to feed the pigs, horses, and chickens. I tend to the fish in the pond, and periodically clear the pond of weed and mud. In season I nurture and harvest the crops. Off season I work the soil so it's got the perfect balance of nutrients. I help Yuri with logging and house and other repairs. We mend our vehicles. I'm active in the local council to ensure the lake isn't corrupted by human intervention. And I help Yuri to read. He's dyslexic." He filled his pipe and placed a match against its bowl. "The thing is, I might die younger than someone else but I will do so knowing I've put the effort in to life. Say I die at seventy. I guarantee I'll have been awake more than most who die at eighty. What was it Poe said – sleep being slithers of death." He puffed on his pipe. "It's not how long we live. It's whether we've lived at all."

"Quite right." Sign tried to relax.

Gregor looked at him. "The weight of the world on your shoulders? You seem distant."

Sign smiled. "It's the curse of having an overactive imagination. I see things that sometimes aren't there."

"And many times you see things that are there but can't be seen by others until it's too late for them. It's not your fault. Your starting point has always been to consider the near impossible and see if it becomes reality. Most people just take things at face value. You don't." Gregor blew a smoke ring and watched it swirl as it drifted over the balcony fence towards the lake. "You foresee complications?"

"I do. I hope I'm wrong."

"But, if you're right?"

"Lives will be ruined." Sign breathed in deeply. "In our line of work it sometimes pays to be wrong."

Knutsen and Lenin came onto the porch. Lenin was off the lead.

Gregor exclaimed, "He should be on his leash!"

Knutsen sat in a chair. "It's okay. I've cut his dick and balls off. He's not interested in female wolves anymore."

Gregor roared with laughter. "He's been hard work in training? Don't take it personally. It just means he likes playing with you."

Lenin sat next to Knutsen and rested his head on his lap. Knutsen rubbed the wolf's head. "He's alright. But, I just wish he'd stop knocking the hell out of me." He grabbed the vodka bottle and poured himself a drink. From his pocket he withdrew a chunk of meat and let Lenin grab it with his teeth. Knutsen leaned forward and quietly said to the wolf, "Don't worry, fella. I'd never cut off yer crown jewels. But do me a favour pal – don't keep flipping me three sixty when you charge." He placed his face against Lenin's snout. "Mind you, blokes like us aren't designed to be subtle. You crack on. More training tomorrow, if I get a chance." He looked at Sign. "Has she made contact?"

Sign nodded. "Tomorrow morning you and I need to be in central Moscow. Bring your gun."

"Sure thing. Do I need to kill people?"

"I hope not." Sign stretched his legs out. "Gregor and I have been incarcerated in Russia and it's not the only time I've been imprisoned here. It is not a recommended culmination of a trip to the motherland."

Gregor laughed. "The good news is there will be no cops knocking on our door this evening. We must change the topic. Tell me Mr. Tank Engine – why did someone as contrarian as you join the Metropolitan Police?"

Knutsen shrugged. "Why did a rebel join the Russian navy?"

"Touché. I suppose we wanted the adventure but soon realised we didn't like the conformity. In a different life you and I would have been bandits or similar. Still, I don't regret being in the navy and I must have had some skills in order to make it to the rank of captain of a highly classified submarine." He had a look of utter contentment as he added, "History has always shown us that the most brilliant military commanders are those that don't belong in the military." He stood and said in a strident voice, "I want to show you something, Thomas."

"No, I'm fine sitting here, pal. I've got bruises in places you wouldn't want to look at."

Gregor smiled. "You are an excellent guest and an amazing friend to Lenin. The wolf trusts me and Yuri. Now he trusts you. He won't hurt Ben because Ben is kind and firm with him. But, the wolf is wary of Ben because he can sense his intelligence. That doesn't matter. You, me, Yuri, Ben, and Lenin are a pack. Please do come with me. It's only a short walk. After dinner you can have a nice bath to ease your aches and pains."

Knutsen looked at Sign.

Sign nodded.

Knutsen said, "Okay. Lead on."

Gregor and Knutsen, and Lenin walked into the nearby woods. Gregor stopped and pointed at a large hole. "This is a burrow. In there is a family of four badgers. They are sleeping now and won't come out of the burrow until Spring. If you put your head close to the hole you might be able to hear the father snoring. The mother and her two offspring tend to be quieter."

"Gregor – what's the point of this?"

Gregor ignored the question. "Look at Lenin. He knows the badgers are in there, but they don't bother him and he doesn't bother them. They coexist. The adult badgers can bite through your knee cap. Lenin can crush your skull and disembowel you. But none of the animals here will touch us and nor will we hurt them. We are family."

Knutsen leaned towards the hole. His muscles ached as he did so. "I can hear the male."

"He is resting. They gorge themselves on fruit and foliage during the warmer months. It builds fat reserves. Then they hibernate. Ben found the adults when they were kids, one mile from here. They were vulnerable and had got separated from their parents. Ben searched for the parents but couldn't find them. So he bought the children back to my house. We didn't know much about badgers. This was before the days of the Internet where you can Google everything. We gave the baby badgers milk and kept them in the chicken coup. The chickens liked them. I like to think they adopted them, or thought they were odd-shaped chickens. One month later Ben dug this hole – not the entire burrow, the badgers had to complete the task, but he gave them the opportunity. When they were big enough, Ben released them at the entrance of the hole. They made it their home. The next season they mated and made their family. They've stayed with us ever since. Sometimes they bash our front door in the evening. We give them food and they go home."

Knutsen was growing impatient. "What's the point of this story?"

"The point is, Ben did this while recovering from two bullet wounds. He'd fled here after getting into a gunfight in Voronezh. He walked one hundred and fifty miles to my home. Yuri was young then and couldn't help. I pulled the bullets out and cared for him as best as I could. It was touch and go. He was bedridden and feverish for weeks. Then he got out of bed, went for a walk, found the badgers, and carried them back to my house. He had to lay low here for a while before he could leave Russia. So, he kept himself busy – working on the farm, caring for the animals including the badgers, hunting for dinner, and home-schooling Yuri." He looked at Knutsen. "The reason I've shown you the burrow and told you all this is because I want you to know that you made the right decision by not conforming to lesser people's rules. My farm and its surroundings function at the highest level. The humans and animals that live here or visit are their own masters yet respect others with the same mind set as them. You didn't make a wrong decision by joining the police, just as I didn't make a wrong decision by joining the navy. And we both made the right decision to leave our organisations."

"As Ben did – leaving MI6."

"But that's not the end of matters." Gregor pointed at the burrow while stroking Lenin. "It's the beginning. We carve a better future." He turned to face the house and placed his hand on Knutsen's shoulder. "You are blessed. Ben has complete faith in you. That's why I gave you Lenin for the week. If Ben trusts you then I trust you. In turn Lenin views you as a pack leader, just as the hedgehogs believe Ben is their father. We live together and we die together. And we help each other out. No hierarchy. No bullshit. Just life. Come – let's eat."

They walked back to the house, Gregor leading the way while holding a torch. Lenin was ahead of him, his nose to the ground. When inside the house, Gregor laid a vinyl record onto his player, and activated the turntable and stylus. The house was filled with the sounds of the jazz musician Charlie Parker. Gregor stoked the fire and held his hands close to the flames. Lenin laid close to the heat and yawned. Thank Christ for that, thought Knutsen – the wolf's finally tired. Yuri was finishing off preparing dinner. Sign was standing on the porch, staring at the star-filled sky.

Knutsen stood next to him. "I didn't take you for a stargazer."

Sign didn't take his eyes off the sky. "I know nothing about astronomy, and nor do I wish to. But I am intrigued in whether there are patterns of distance and location between the stars. I'm interested in patterns."

"Because that's what you do down here – search for patterns."

"Yes, ones that are imperceptible to the human eye." He looked at Knutsen. "As much as it pains me to say this, I hope we leave Russia the day after tomorrow. It will all depend on whether Natalia gets what we need in the Lubyanka. If she's successful, we'll have business to attend to in England."

The comment made Knutsen sad. He was surprised by his emotional response. When he'd arrived here he'd felt like a fish out of water. But now he felt at home. "We have to follow the paper trail."

"Indeed we do." Sign smiled sympathetically. "Don't worry. We'll come back here another time. Gregor and I keep an eye on each other, just as you and I keep an eye on each other." He looked at the lake. It was glittering with the lights from the stars. In a solemn voice he said, "It's hard to make friends in the secret world. But, on the rare occasions when it happens, it can be heart breaking because friendships should never be born in extreme circumstances."

Natalia went to her hotel room. She withdrew a sandwich from her handbag, sat on her bed, and ate. When she'd finished, she called Osip to remind him about tomorrow's appointment. He sounded relatively lucid, though Natalia knew that would shortly change. She asked him whether he'd arranged cover for his absence from the SVR archive in the morning. He said he'd enrolled a temporary assistant for the morning shift. Natalia suggested he set his alarm for seven AM, giving him enough time to get ready and travel to central Moscow. After she ended the call she laid on the bed, looking at the ceiling. She felt calm, though a muscle in her left cheek was twitching. She told herself that it was as a result of all the previous stress she'd been suffering and was not to do with any current or future stress she was unwittingly hiding from herself. She tried to think about pleasant matters. Where would she live in Britain if she got out of the SVR? City, town, village, or the middle of nowhere? Was she ready for a relationship? Would a relationship happen naturally when she least expected it to occur? What job would she like to do? What hobbies would she take up? Her breathing became fast and she no longer felt calm. All of the dreams seemed so out of reach. She felt trapped. She should never have joined the SVR and she should never have become a traitor. She'd started her adult life in a downward spiral. The only chance she had of clawing her way out of the black pit was to wholly rely on the assistance of Ben and the woman who called herself Katy. But, could they really help? Both of them had agendas. And if she didn't give them what they wanted would they simply walk away and leave her to her fate? One thing she was sure of was that she was out of her depth. In many ways that was a good thing. Ben and Katy seemed so self-assured. And there was no doubting their experience was exponential compared to Natalia's brief stint in Russian intelligence. Maybe it was appropriate that her fate was in their hands. She ran herself a bath and switched on the TV. Her mood was now one of resignation. What would happen would happen. She had no control over her future. Partially, that brought inner peace.

Archer surveyed the interior of her house in Putney. All of the adjustments had been made. The stair lift to the second floor worked; the handrails on the stairs that were previously difficult to grip were now replaced with cylindrical metal rails; the bathroom had been transformed to accommodate a disabled person; there was a wheel chair in the hallway; the two exterior steps to the front door had been replaced with a ramp; a mobility scooter was in the garage; and the spare bedroom had a motorised bed which could be raised to assist getting out of the thing or simply to assist breathing at night. Everything was ready for her mother's arrival. And that could happen tomorrow. Today Elizabeth needed one more batch of medical tests and a nurse from the care home was required by law to visit Archer's London home to do health and safety checks. The nurse also needed to install various medical kit – including an intravenous drip for the administration of medicine and oxygen tank and face mask for use in the night. The nurse would check on her once a week and after six months, providing everything was fine, would reduce her visits to once a month.

Archer poured herself a glass of wine, sat on the sofa, and flicked through a recipe book. She wanted to cook Elizabeth something special and comforting for her first night here. Shepherd's pie, she decided, was the right choice. She placed a piece of paper on the page containing the recipe and shut the book.

Not for the first time, she wondered how she would cope with living with her mother. Consistently, she'd concluded it would work. Elizabeth was a free spirit and hated being needy. She'd spend her days studying, perambulating southwest London, getting to know the neighbours, shopping, and writing letters to The Times about a range of matters including the reasons that had led Russia to become a totalitarian state, politics in the Middle East, why Brexit might lead to the break-up of the United Kingdom, and the socioeconomic factors that had allowed Americans to vote for a sociopathic moron of a president. And she could feed herself. Elizabeth was a good cook. Alongside her standard waist-height cooker, Archer had installed a knee-height oven and a knee height gas hob, fridge-freezer, and work surface with utensils. Elizabeth would be self-sufficient when it came to providing herself sustenance. Once again, Archer decided everything would be fine. In any case, she worked long hours and sometimes had to travel for weeks at a time. She and her mother would be able to live separate lives.

She sipped her wine and thought about her twin sister. Was Susan alive? Dead? And even if she was alive would she have anything in common with Jayne? Maybe it would be better if she was dead. It would close the chapter and end the uncertainty. No, that wasn't right. Jayne Archer wanted her sister to be alive, no matter what the outcome. She'd been ruthless in her career ambition, to the detriment of fleeting relationships with boyfriends, but one thing she was not was callous. If Susan was alive, Archer would do anything to be reunited with her.

CHAPTER 9

The next morning Sign and Knutsen were in a café, drinking coffee. They were two minutes' walk from the Lubyanka. At a sprint, Knutsen estimated he could reach the building in twenty seconds. His handgun was concealed under his fleece jacket. The weapon was needed as a last resort. And even if things went badly wrong for Natalia, the probability of the men being able to help her were slim. Certainly, they couldn't enter the FSB headquarters to extract her. And if an attempt was made to snatch her as she left the building, Sign would have to grab her and run while Knutsen pointed his pistol at anyone who was coming for her. Then they'd have to escape the city and head on foot across country to the exfiltration point. The chances of success would be thousands to one against. It was in their interests that Natalia held her nerve and walked out of the building without having aroused a drop of suspicion.

For the most part, Sign and Knutsen were quiet, though now and again Sign would make a comment in Russian – just in case they were being observed. Knutsen didn't understand what he was saying, but that didn't matter. In Sign's pocket was his mobile phone, set to silent and vibrate. It was his hotline to Natalia.

It was ten AM. In thirty minutes they'd leave the café and watch the main entrance to the Lubyanka, hidden from view from everyone, including Natalia when she left the building. There was nothing they could do now apart from wait.

Natalia and Osip entered the Lubyanka. The interior of the imposing, fortress-like rectangular building, had barely changed since the darkest days of its history. There were some modern touches to the décor but they did nothing to diminish the sense that the walls were and always would be drenched in blood. Natalia thought of the building as a man who hadn't washed for a century and tried to cover up his stench with a bottle of deodorant. So many people had been imprisoned, tortured, and executed in the building. Whether their ghosts remained here or not was down to the eye of the beholder. But, there was no doubting there was a smell that felt wrong. The dead people's blood had been painted over. But the blood remained. It was ingrained in the stone fabric of the Lubyanka.

After they cleared security checks, Osip led her through corridors containing rooms that had once held captive the famous spy Sidney Reilly, the Swedish diplomat Raoul Gustaf Wallenberg who'd saved thousands of Jews in the holocaust, and the Polish-American Jesuit priest Walter Ciszek. There were so many other people who'd been tortured and executed here. A lot of them were innocent of their alleged crimes. All of them deserved a more civilised tenure in the building.

Osip and Natalia went into the archive section of the FSB. It was located in the building's basement and had a similar layout to the SVR's archives – row upon row of files, almost no IT equipment, ceiling fans that helped prevent dust settling on the room's precious papers, spot lights, and a sign at the entrance saying that it was strictly prohibited to remove files without written authorisation to do so. Some of the files in the huge room dated back to the Bolshevik Revolution in 1917. The room was a treasure trove of oppression, pain, insurrection, and misery.

Osip shook hands with the only person in the room. "Alexander. Good to see you, my friend."

The head of the archive looked at Natalia. "The SVR is recruiting youngsters these days."

Osip placed a hand on Natalia's arm. "I can vouch for her. She's not like most of the others in the SVR. She doesn't have a political bone in her body."

"Then she's welcome." Alexander asked Osip, "Are we still on for a few drinks and a game of cards on Friday?"

"Absolutely. But, don't cheat this time." Osip smiled.

Alexander said to Natalia, "You are investigating the Sergey Peskov case, I'm told. And you have a lead relating to a Susan Archer. Why are you interested in her?"

Natalia feigned nonchalance and shrugged. "I've been instructed to look in to Peskov. I don't know why. It's beyond my paygrade. But, I'm pursuing all names referenced in the Peskov SVR file."

"You must have pissed someone off to be tasked with such an old case." Alexander laughed. "Okay. Come with me." He led her to a desk, behind which was a chair. He prodded the file on the desk. "Susan Archer. You're cleared to read it, but you are not permitted to take notes or make copies."

"I understand." Natalia sat on the chair.

"I'll leave you to it. Osip and I have some boring business matters to discuss." He walked away.

Natalia looked at the file. On its cover were uppercase words in red. The words were in Cyrillic. The English translation was *CODENAME SWITCHBLADE*.

She opened the file.

At 1207 hrs Natalia left the FSB headquarters. She was alone and walking fast. Sign and Knutsen followed her – Sign staying close to the woman, Knutsen remaining fifty yards behind his colleague in case FSB people were tailing Natalia and he had to take action. The prearranged drill was for Natalia to call Sign ten minutes after she left the building to let him know she was safe, or to text message him if there was a problem. But thus far she'd made zero contact.

After twenty minutes, Sign knew something was wrong. He called Knutsen. "Join me. My hunch is she's not aroused suspicion. But something's amiss. We'll follow her together."

They stayed close to Natalia. She made no effort to take any form of public transport. Sign assumed she wanted to walk in order to have time to think.

She arrived at her small hotel.

Knutsen spun around. There were too many pedestrians in the area to spot a skilled surveillance team in their midst. He followed Sign into the hotel lobby.

Sign muttered to him, "Move with me now. Put a smile on your face."

Sign and Knutsen walked briskly into the hotel lobby.

Sign came alongside Natalia, a grin on his face, put his arm around her waist, and said in Russian, "My favourite niece. Your aunt can't wait to see you for dinner this evening. Come on – let's help you with your overnight bags and get on the road."

Natalia was too highly trained to show any indications of surprise or resistance. But, inwardly she was flapping.

She forced a smile on her face as they walked past the bored-looking receptionist and took the lift to her room.

When inside, Sign said to her, "Sit down wherever you feel comfortable."

She sat on the bed.

Knutsen stood by the door, his gun in his hand.

Sign sat opposite her on the only chair in the room. "Were you compromised?"

Natalia shook her head, her eyes wide, no attempts now to hide her fear.

"Did the job in the Lubyanka prompt a relapse of anxiety in you?"

Natalia was breathing fast. "Not... not for the reasons you might think."

"It was something you read in the Archer file. Isn't that correct?"

Natalia was trapped in the room. There were bars on the window and there was no possibility of getting past Knutsen, even though he was facing the door. It was clear he was here to stop hostiles entering the room, rather than prevent her from leaving. She asked, "Are you both Russians? SVR? FSB? GRU? Special Forces?"

"If we were, why would we tell you?" Sign was motionless. "The bigger question is why would you ask such a thing?"

"Because I want to know if you're part of this problem!" She placed her head in her hands and rocked back and forth. "I'm dead. Fucking dead!"

Sign sat next to her and held her hand. Quietly he asked, "Were there photos in the file?"

Natalia sucked air through her teeth. It produced a hissing sound. "Three photos. One was of two babies. The other two were of women."

"And the photos have unsettled you."

Natalia pulled her hand out of Sign's hand. "Not just the photos. Everything in the wretched file!"

Sign nodded. "Tom and I are not Russians. We are British. And right now we're working for the United Kingdom's government. But, in doing so we're not representing our state's interests. We're representing you. And first and foremost that means we prioritise your protection. Natalia – this is not a game."

She looked hostile. "People who play games often spout that shit!"

Sign nodded. "You must use your judgement. Rely on your instincts."

Natalia glanced at him, uncertainty in her expression. "If you were Russian, I'd already be dead."

"Yes."

"And it doesn't serve the motherland's interest for me to betray it, unless this is some convoluted chess game."

"Russian spies and politicians are not that adept."

She bowed her head and stopped rocking. Her voice was almost a whisper when she said, "I can't fly out of Russia. Wheels are in motion. I will be arrested at the airport. Then I'll be taken somewhere and made to vanish."

"What wheels?"

Her expression was imploring when she asked, "Do you not know?"

"I have a theory. It is based on facts and supposition. I agree with you – I think you will be dead unless Tom and I do something to prevent that from happening. Will you trust me?"

Natalia looked uncertain.

"Trust is all you have now."

Natalia was utterly exhausted. "You told me I was young enough to be your daughter."

Sign nodded. "My wife and I never had children. She died before that was possible, though she was pregnant when she was murdered. We knew she was carrying our unborn daughter. I often wonder what it would be like to sit and talk to my daughter when she was a young adult. In fact, my life is a series of segments. I imagine changing her nappy and bottle feeding her when she was a baby; laughing with joy when I see her walk for the first time; taking her to a beach in Sussex and a bowling alley in Surrey; seeing her dance in beautiful white dress in my garden; helping her when she hit puberty; talking to her about her studies at GCSE and A levels; being the proudest father when I see her get her graduation certificate from a good university; meeting a boyfriend she's serious about; laughing with her when we watch a silly comedy while eating jalapeno and pepperoni pizzas; and ultimately looking at her and thinking she is similar to me but is entirely her own person." He looked away. "My imagination – it's a curse. I've carved an entire life that never had the chance to exist." He huffed. "It makes me stupid and foolish."

"No it doesn't."

Sign smiled, though the grin was bittersweet. He made a call on his mobile and when the call ended he stood. "Tom – we're taking Natalia to the safe place. I'll pay her hotel bill. You stay here until I'm back. Yuri will collect us. Gun down anyone who comes through the door before I'm back." Before he left the room he held out his hand. "Natalia – I need your personal mobile phone."

She handed it to him.

Sign withdrew the SIM card, snapped it into pieces, took out the battery, and placed the parts and debris into a bag. The bag would be carefully disposed of once they were out of the hotel.

Two hours' later they arrived at Gregor's house. Yuri carried Natalia's luggage to Sign's room, stripped the bed, put fresh linen on, showed her around the property, and told her that he'd be making a round of sandwiches and a pot of coffee for those in the house who were hungry and thirsty. He tossed a blanket on the sofa. That's where Sign wanted to sleep tonight. Gregor was out in the grounds, chopping wood.

Sign walked up to him. "We have a guest. A woman."

"I know." Gregor slammed his axe into the thick tree trunk that served as his chopping board. "Does that mean that while she's here I mustn't swear or break wind?"

Sign looked at the house. "She's in shock. I need to speak to her at length. Change nothing in your behaviour and routine. She must see that your home is filled with normal people who do and say normal things. It will make her feel secure."

"What shit has she gotten herself into?"

"Her potential imprisonment or assassination."

"That sucks. Tell me about her."

Sign gave him her biography.

Gregor arched his back and winced. "Okay. Let me go and say hello." He walked in to the house. Natalia was standing by the fire, shivering. Gregor beamed and strode toward her, his arm outstretched. His voice boomed as he said, "You are most welcome to my humble home. As well as us four ugly men, on site we have pigs, chickens, horses, trout in the lake and pond, a pair of ducks, a family of badgers, and a wolf. The wolf sleeps in here." He patted Lenin. "When he sees you eat with us he will accept you. Be careful though – he's not used to women being around." He laughed. "And you are a Russian spy. Your presence adds to my mad menagerie of misfits and troublemakers."

Natalia shook his hand. "Ben told me about you. You are a Hero of the Russian Federation."

"Nonsense! I'm an old man who eats and drinks too much."

Yuri put a platter of sandwiches and a pot of coffee on the dining table

"Let's get some food down our necks!" Gregor pulled out a chair for Natalia. She sat at the table, alongside the four men.

Gregor spoke while he munched on his sandwich. "I knew a Natalia once. She had beautiful hair, much like yours. I met her at the military academy. She did my washing for me. She wasn't allowed to. The men and women were segregated in different blocks. Some other bitch made a complaint that I'd turned up in the women's quarters with a bag full of my dirty linen. I was hauled in front of the academy's navy commandant. He bollocked me but struggled to keep a smile off his face. He said I was top of my class for a reason – I was unconventional and clever. He told me to fuck off back to my cadet class. There was no written disciplinary action. Secretly I think he admired what I'd done. You see – getting people to help you is a significant part of a captain's job. When we finished our training, I asked Natalia to be my date for the graduation dinner. It was a formal affair. I met her outside of the women's block. She was in a gorgeous black dress. When she walked towards me, the slit in her dress parted to reveal a glimpse of her suspenders." He winked at Natalia. "I thought I was in for a good night. But, she wasn't that kind of girl. I guess she had feelings for me, as I did for her. Trouble is, we then got posted to different parts of Russia. I never saw her again. And these were the days before mobile phones. I often wonder about her." He rubbed crumbs off his fingers. "If only I could turn the clock back and stopped myself from getting into a bloody submarine." He slapped Sign on the back. "What was it Sinatra sang - Regrets, I've had a few. But then again, too few to mention. I did what I had to do. And saw it through without exemption."

Sign smiled. "I've lived a life that's full. I've travelled each and every highway. And more, much more than this, I did it my way."

Gregor held up his hand. "Bang on, brother."

Sign slapped his hand and addressed Natalia. "Gregor and I go way back. We know all about darkness and death. After lunch Gregor and I will take you for a boat ride on the lake."

Uncertainty hit Natalia. "On the lake?"

"There's nothing to fear. It is a place that's brimming with life. Anyway, if one of us has an accident," he gestured to Gregor, "we have a captain who somehow managed to swim in freezing conditions for forty eight hours before making a fifty yard underwater vertical ascent out of his submarine. No Olympian athlete could have done that. We're in the very best hands."

Gregor leaned forward and in a mock solemn tone said to her, "I have gills." He giggled. In an authoritative tone reminiscent of when he was a highly respected naval commander, he said, "Gentlemen, if you please! We now have a lady on deck. Rules must apply. She uses the bathroom before any of us. Understood? If she's in there and you need a piss, you piss outside. If you need a shit, do it on the dung heap – it will be good for the manure. If she doesn't mind us swearing, then we can swear. If she objects to our swearing, we stop." He looked at Natalia and spoke directly to her. "In relation to all other matters, it's business as usual on my submarine. Any questions?"

Natalia shook her head.

"Excellent. Then we sail onwards as per our drills." Gregor rubbed his stomach. "We must think about catching dinner for this evening. But first we will give this lovely lady an opportunity to have some tranquillity. Ben, Natalia, let us depart."

Yuri started clearing up the plates.

When Gregor, Ben, and Natalia were outside, Gregor said, "Just one second." He went back into the house. "Yuri – the dishes will wait until we're back." He looked at Knutsen. "I want both of you to arm yourselves and hide two hundred yards up the lane. Stay there until we get back. If Russians come for us, use maximum force. And work as a team. Watch your angles. Excel in your weapon tactics. If there are dead bodies, leave them where they fall. Take Lenin with you. Like you he must know he's in combat mode. Command him that way. He will understand. To it gentlemen! Do not let me down." His smile was back on his face as he exited the house.

Gregor, Natalia, and Ben walked to the rowing boat, moored on the lakeside. When the three of them were in the vessel, Gregor rowed them out to the centre of the lake. He handed Natalia a rug to keep warm.

Sign said to Natalia, "Tell me everything."

Natalia momentarily glanced at Gregor.

Sign said, "I've trusted Gregor many times with my life, just as he's trusted me with his life. The tranquillity Gregor spoke of is here. It is the epicentre of loyalty and openness."

Natalia bowed her head.

"Head up, Natalia! Now is not the time to be coy."

Natalia looked at Sign. She breathed in deeply. "The woman who calls herself Katy – my MI6 handler... I've always known that Katy wasn't her real name. I now know her real name's Jayne Archer."

Sign was silent while keeping his gaze on her.

"The photos in the file were of Jayne and Susan when they were babies and their current age. Aside from different hair styles, they look nearly identical. The photo of Susan was a professional studio shot. The one of Jayne was a long distance covert shot. I recognise the backdrop – Westminster Bridge."

Sign said, "You are correct. The woman who calls herself Katy is Jayne Archer. Her sister is Susan."

Natalia sighed. "That's just the beginning. It's not the end." She paused.

"Come on Natalia. You can do this."

Natalia summoned her strength. "If I trust you and I'm wrong to do so, you might as well ask Gregor to use a paddle to club me to death out here."

"There'll be no clubbing today, thank you. Proceed."

She responded, "But, it will happen to me, somewhere."

"No it won't. Gregor, Tom, Yuri, and I are soldiers. You are one of us now." He smiled. "And we have a huge wolf to help us."

For the first time since she'd arrived at the farmstead, Natalia smiled. "Soldiers? My brother was a soldier. We're not soldiers. We're more than that, for better or worse."

"But we know how to be the very best combatants."

"You may do. I'm too young to know that stuff." She looked him directly in the eyes. "Jayne Archer is in fact Anna Vichneva. Susan is her twin sister Dina Vichneva. The twins' parents were a brilliant KGB male officer and female physicist. They were murdered by the KGB immediately after the births, because the KGB had a very specific long game strategy to use the twins. Jayne's English parents - Elizabeth and Michael - were not her real parents. They are English KGB/SVR moles. Elizabeth was eight months pregnant with her own child when the twins were born. The KGB instructed Elizabeth to rush to Moscow. They cut the baby out and killed it, with Elizabeth's consent. Jayne was given to Elizabeth and Michael and they were told to pretend they were her real parents. The KGB faked the birth certificate and medical details about the birth. The KGB told Elizabeth and Michael to groom Jayne to reach high office in the UK public sector - preferably MI6, but alternatively some other high security cleared post. The KGB kept Susan. The KGB's hope was that Jayne would be malleable to Elizabeth and Michael's grooming on the basis that Jayne would want to be in a position where she could track Susan in later years. Plus, Jayne would be brainwashed into hating Russia and joining MI6 by her 'parents' throughout her childhood. There was no guarantee this would work, but the KGB was hopeful it would pay off. Meanwhile, Susan/Dina was kept by her fake KGB parents in Russia. Susan's unwitting role was to act as KGB leverage at some point in the future, when the KGB/SVR needed Jayne to betray a UK secret. Susan was and still is innocent throughout. She didn't know her 'parents' were KGB. Nor did she know she had a sister. She grew up and lived an ordinary life in Russia. She got married, but like Jayne she couldn't conceive children. She got divorced and lived alone. Jayne's fake parents Elizabeth and Michael were not tasked to obtain secrets from Jayne. Instead their role was to position Jayne into a powerful government job. Susan's fake parents were tasked to simply raise Susan safely and keep her alive."

Gregor was silent.

Sign asked, "Is Susan still alive?"

"Yes."

"Why are you at risk? I think I know the answer but I want to hear details from you."

Natalia looked around the lake. "It is beautiful here." She returned her attention to Sign. "At the back of the file is a trigger."

"A trigger?"

"A Russian spy file is either of mere historical interest or it's a weapon. The Archer file is a weapon. The trigger was a piece of paper, dated four days' ago. It's very specific. Tomorrow Jayne Archer will be sent a photo of her sister. Alongside the photo will be an instruction. The instruction is: tell us who in the SVR is betraying the names of our officers in Europe and the United States. That person's me. The instruction also says that if she doesn't comply her sister will suffer an agonising death. The SVR knows Jayne is now head of the MI6 Russia Department. They've therefore made their killer blow. Under SVR instruction, her fake mother recently told Jayne about the existence of her twin sister. Jayne will have to decide whether she sacrifices her sister's life or my life. I know she will betray me."

Sign nodded. "She will."

"And there's nothing you can do about it. We've been outplayed by an ingenious Russian long game. It was all about having leverage at some point. That point is now. Jayne's stars and my stars have now aligned. Jayne's promotion and my treachery made the trigger possible." She shook her head. "You suspected all of this might happen."

"It was one of seven possibilities. But, I confess this was the one that kept haunting me."

"What can be done? Can we warn Jayne? Stop her from giving the Russians my name?"

"It's too late. Your name is in Jayne's head. Even if she's arrested in Britain, she'll find a way to speak to the Russians. Plus, she can't be arrested yet because she hasn't done anything. As we speak, Jayne has no idea about her background. All we can do is protect you." Sign nodded at Gregor.

Gregor started rowing to shore.

Sign said to Natalia, "This is what will happen – you and I will have zero contact with Jayne Archer; tomorrow we'll get you out of Russia."

"Tomorrow?!"

"Tomorrow evening. I have to make preparations. Trusted allies of mine will be involved. Even tomorrow will be a tight turnaround but I'm confident it can be achieved. When we reach Britain you will be placed into temporary protective custody. Your identity will be changed. You will then be given a place to live. You will lead an independent life."

"Da. A new life." A tear rolled down her cheek. To herself and quietly she repeated, "A new life."

When they reached land they walked to the house. Gregor whistled three times. Knutsen, Yuri, and Lenin got out of their hiding places and went to the farm. Yuri had a rifle resting on his shoulder. Knutsen was holding his pistol in both hands.

When everyone was inside, Gregor said to Natalia, "Get some rest. You will need it. The rest of us have some jobs to do."

Natalia was grateful. She was mentally and physically exhausted. "I will be safe?"

"Yes."

"I don't mind helping out."

"I know. But, you've done your shift today. Like all good sailors, you work, rest, eat, sleep, and work. Now is the rest part of the day. I've set the boiler's thermostat to permanent. There will be plenty of hot water if you want a bath. But, I must warn you – all we have in the bathroom is an anti-dandruff shampoo and a bar of soap. We weren't expecting female company."

Natalia yawned. "I'm so tired."

"Stress will do that to you." Gregor put his arm on her shoulder and guided her to the stairs. "Make sure you shut your bedroom door. Lenin is a bastard. Given half a chance he'll sleep on our beds. When that happens the sheets smell like something out of the bowels of Hell."

When she was gone, Gregor asked Sign, "Is her exfiltration out of Russia going to be cold?"

"Yes."

Gregor frowned. "She's not equipped for that. All she has is city work clothes."

"You and I had less when we escaped that gang in Kurdistan. And we did so during winter."

"*Less*? We were naked." Gregor was deep in thought. "We must do what we can to clothe her. To a man, a cold sailor who's on watch will tell you that there is no gift on Earth more precious than being given a warm jumper. Yuri – I have a job for you."

Yuri stood before his father. "It's going to be a shit job, isn't it?"

"It's a job, so wind your neck in. I need you to buy Natalia some clothes. Windproof jacket, thermal vest, jumper, lined waterproof trousers, pair of hiking boots, thick socks, gloves, and a woollen hat. The outdoor shop in Yaroslavl will sell what we need."

"What's her shoe size?"

Gregor looked at Sign.

Sign said, "I've no idea. Do you have a measuring instrument?"

Gregor rummaged in one of the kitchen drawers and handed Sign a tape measure.

Sign gave it to Yuri. "The ground outside is wet. Look at our footprints from our route to the lake. Discount the big prints. Measure the length of Natalia's prints."

Ten minutes' later Yuri was back in the house. "Twenty two centimetres."

Gregor asked, "What's that in shoe size?"

No one knew.

Gregor threw up his arms. "You'll just have to tell the shop assistant that her current shoes are twenty two centimetres long, that they are heeled work shoes, and you require boots that are a centimetre longer to accommodate thick socks. What's her clothing size?"

Yuri frowned. "Size?"

"You know – three, four, five, twelve, sixteen, all that stuff."

"No man knows what any of that means."

Gregor leaned against the workbench. "True."

"Shouldn't we just go upstairs and ask her what her measurements are?"

"She's probably sleeping. And even if she's not, the point of us solving this riddle is to supply her with a highly considerate and surprising gesture." Gregor grabbed his phone and searched women's clothes sizes on the Internet. When the results came up he exclaimed, "For the love of God, this is more complicated than trying to navigate a submarine through a minefield." He put the phone down. "It appears women come in all shapes and sizes, and none of the sizes are an exact science. Right – how tall is she?"

Yuri put his hand to his throat. "About up to here."

"That'll do. Tell that to the shop assistant. What about," Gregor waved his hands around his waist and chest, "women's body things? Do we need to factor that in?"

Sign was trying not to laugh. "No we don't. Buy her elasticated trousers, stretch thermals, and a baggy jumper. She won't look like she's on the front cover of Hiking Weekly, or whatever, but at least she'll be warm. Yuri – also, get herself something nice in Yaroslavl. If you're unsure, speak to a woman in one of the shops. Ignore them if they suggest perfume or any bathroom toiletries. Listen to them if they suggest anything more neutral but personal. If pushed, tell them that you're going out on a first date and just want to give your girlfriend something nice. Got it?"

Yuri nodded. "Got it." He took cash out of the safe and left.

Gregor said to Knutsen, "You and Lenin need to stay here and keep guard over her."

Knutsen angled his head, "Aye aye captain."

Gregor smiled. "The very best of my men were insolent." He patted Knutsen on the shoulder. "It was like herding cats. But you wouldn't want anyone else by your side if the shit hit the fan. Natalia's in the good hands."

The comment took the wind out of Knutsen's sails. Without a drop of sarcasm, he replied, "I'll protect her."

Gregor held his gaze for a moment, his eyes twinkling. He said, "Excellent. To your post." He turned to Sign. "Pick a rifle from the rack. We must now kill our dinner."

Sign and Gregor moved through the wood, their rifle butts firm in their armpits.

Sign whispered, "What are we hunting for? Anything that moves?"

Gregor replied, "I'll show you." He moved on.

Sign followed him.

Close to the lake's shore, Gregor crouched while still hidden amid the trees. He raised his fist, thereby silently indicating to Sign to also stop. He was motionless, on one knee, watching. He was barely audible when he said, "They carry a disease that humans are immune to but pigs can die from. We're hunting boar. We only need one. I have to cull them once a year, to keep numbers manageable and sustainable. They forage at this time of the day and at night. If we see one, I'll make a clean head shot. If there are other boars in the vicinity, fire shots over their head to scare them off. They're nasty fellows when they're angry."

"Why are we so close to the lake? Shouldn't we be deeper in the forest?"

Gregor smiled. "The boars like paddling in the shallow water. It's their playtime." His smile vanished. "This isn't sport. For every boar I cull I spend days constructing shelters and putting down food so they can reproduce and survive the winter. Like everything here, we coexist and help each other."

Three hours' later, Natalia came downstairs. She'd had a shallow sleep and a bath. Yuri was back. His face lit up when he saw her. He said, "I've bought you some things." He patted shopping bags that were on the table. "Things that will keep you warm. Apparently your route out of Russia might be a cold one. I've also bought you this." He handed her a book of poetry by Alexander Pushkin. "I struggle to read. Maybe you could read me a poem after dinner. Try on the clothes. I hope they fit."

Natalia looked at the bags. "You bought me these?"

"Yes. It was a difficult job." Yuri was now standing in the kitchen, chopping vegetables.

Natalia went to her room and changed into her new outdoors clothes and boots. Everything fitted perfectly. She returned to the kitchen, wearing her new attire. "Thank you, Yuri."

Yuri grinned. "You look perfect. Hey – have you got a boyfriend?"

Natalia wagged her finger. "Steady on tiger. Boyfriends are the last thing on my mind right now." She smiled. "But I appreciate you asking. Where is everyone else?"

"Just outside the house." Yuri wiped his brow as he dashed between pans of boiling water. "Here. Take this to my Dad." He handed her a basket containing a paint brush, large jar of homemade garlic marmalade, fresh herbs, bag of crushed ice, four tumblers, and a bottle of vodka.

Natalia wandered outside. The sun was going down, though the stunning surroundings were still visible. The torches on the lake-facing balcony had been lit. Others were dotted around the grounds. Sign and Gregor were standing next to a pit of coals. Above the pit was a boar that was skewered on a rotisserie. Gregor was slowing turning the swine. Knutsen was in the paddock, doing training with Lenin. He was throwing the boar's entrails high into the sky while screaming a variety of obscenities, including, "Why the fuck do I have to do this revolting job?!" Lenin was leaping, catching the guts and devouring them. The air was cold, but the heat from the torches and the fire negated any discomfort. Natalia thought she was in a dream. This place was magical. She handed the basket to Gregor.

"Did you sleep, my dear?" He asked.

"A bit."

"Then you are ready to fight another day." He opened the jar, poured the sauce over the rotating boar, used the brush to wipe the marinade around the skinned carcass, threw the herbs onto the coals to infuse the smoke, cracked open the vodka, placed handfuls of ice into the tumblers, and poured everyone a drink. He shouted, "Mr. Tank Engine! Drink time!"

Knutsen was now running around the paddock with the boar hide on his head and back. Lenin was chasing him. The wolf bowled him over, ripped off the hide, then looked confused. "It's okay, motherfucker," said Knutsen gently as he ruffled his head. "Apparently this is something to do with learning about how to spot a wolf in sheep's clothing. Except you're the wolf and all I had was a bloody enormous pig skin to teach you the lesson." He staggered to his feet. "One thing's for sure – if you can take me down you can take down a buffalo. Come on. Let's join the others." His body was throbbing as he limped to the roasting boar.

Sign asked, "Any broken bones?"

Knutsen grabbed his drink from Gregor. "Not fucking yet." He looked at Natalia. "Excuse my language."

"I don't mind." Natalia asked Sign, "Where are you taking me tomorrow?"

Sign assisted Gregor with the basting of their meal. "St. Petersburg. As you know, it's at least an eight hour drive. Yuri will take us there. He will be working through most of the night to ensure his vehicle can make the trip. The slightest vehicle impediment must be eradicated. We will be carrying spare canisters of fuel, food, bottles of water, and empty bottles to urinate in. We will not be stopping anywhere on route."

Gregor stepped away from his chef duties and addressed Natalia. "You're new clothes look good. Ben has brought me in to his confidence and told me how he's going to get you out of Russia. From St. Petersburg, you, Ben, and Thomas will sail on a ship that's bound for Liverpool. Ben knows the skipper. The journey will take seven days. Pack accordingly. Leave everything else here. We will burn what you don't need." He raised his glass and shouted, "Onwards, my friends!"

"Onwards," they all replied in unison before sipping their drinks.

Sign asked Knutsen to help Gregor with the boar. To Natalia he said, "Let's take our drinks onto the balcony." When the two of them sere sat there, looking at the lake, the roasting swine, and the torches, he said, "You are no longer a member of the SVR. You are no longer a spy for MI6. Soon your name will no longer be Natalia Asina. And once you're safely in Britain you will no longer be Russian. You'll be Ukrainian, though will have a British passport. In consultation with you, I will arrange all matters in relation to your living arrangements and your job."

The enormity of the changes hit Natalia. "Maybe I could be a teacher?"

"No. You would be listed on the school's staff list. Even though your name will be different, you must be invisible. You have seven days on our boat trip to think about suitable jobs. Don't reach for the stars. Take something that pays the bills and leaves enough left over to treat yourself now and again. Don't go on holiday outside of Britain. Under no circumstances use social media. Don't do Internet shopping, use courier services, and browse Internet websites containing political news. Ideally, don't use the Internet at all. Be constantly suspicious of people until you really get to know them. You will be financially secure. I will help you get a job. And you will receive a pension when you're sixty. It will come out of a government slush fund that has no links to the government. You are free to date and marry, but once again be very cautious as to whether to trust a lover. You will be able to contact me and Tom while we're still alive. It might be prudent to run a potential lover's name by us before you engage in a relationship. We'll do background checks and let you know if he's safe. Never, ever, speak to anyone about Russia. You've never been here and know nothing about the country beyond what you've seen on the news. You came to Britain after your parents died. You have no other family." He gave her more details about her new identity before concluding, "For the rest of your life, you will be off the radar."

Her voice was distant when she stated, "I must be held captive in Britain."

With kindness in his voice, Sign replied, "Don't look at it that way. It takes at least four lifetimes to experience ten percent of what Britain has within its shores. You will not be bored. On the contrary, it will be an adventure."

She nodded. "Will I see you and Tom again?"

"Only if there's an emergency."

"What will you do if Jayne Archer betrays me? And what about her fake English parents?"

"Her father's dead. Her mother and Jayne are close. I will deal with both of them."

"How?"

"By delivering them the truth." Sign didn't elaborate. He pointed at the others. "I'm retired from MI6 but still hold powerful sway within the highest circles in government. Tom is a former cop. Gregor is a former naval officer and assassin. You are now a former SVR officer. But, look at what you see. All of us are happy and carving a new life. Do not be frightened of the unknown. It can very often bring sublime joy."

"If you're retired from MI6, who's paying you to help me?"

"The person who's about to betray you."

"Then, how will you get your money?"

"I won't." Sign sipped his drink. "Money is considerably less important than a human life. Let's go and join the others. The meat smells delicious. It won't be fully cooked for an hour or so. But we can have another drink while we wait. I might even persuade Gregor to play his balalaika and give us a sing-song."

Natalia grabbed his arm. Her grip was tight. "If you'd already considered the possibility that Susan was going to be used as leverage against Jayne in order to flush me out, why did you send me to Moscow?"

Sign stared at the lake. "It was only a possibility. I needed to know the truth." He looked at her. "If I hadn't gotten to the truth, this time tomorrow you'd be dead. And we can't have that happening, can we?"

She released her grip. With a slight smile on her face and a lighter tone of voice, she said, "I'm actually a pretty good singer. Maybe Gregor and I could do a duet."

Archer served her mother shepherd's pie in her home in Putney. Elizabeth was now with her fulltime. The nurse had visited, supplied medicine and medical kit, made checks of the house, and departed after saying that everything in the property was perfect. Archer had made a real effort to make the house welcoming. Candles were lit; classical music was softly playing in the lounge; a bouquet of roses was in a vase adjacent to her mother's bed; the curtains were parted, revealing on one side of the house a view of the adjacent Thames and the old fashioned embankment lamps straddling the mighty river; a bottle of Elizabeth's favourite Rioja was in the centre of the dining table. It was evening. The sun had gone down. Daytime tourists had been replaced by evening revellers. The double glazing in the house meant they could barely hear them as they walked along the promenade. But, it was still good to see life in action.

Elizabeth ate her food. "I loved the peace and quiet in Godalming. But, I missed the vibrancy of London."

Archer poured them wine. "I've taken tomorrow off to help you settle in. Is there anything you'd like to do?"

Elizabeth shook her head. "Nothing special. I just want to get orientated. Depending on the weather I might take myself out on the scooter. How's your new job?"

"It's going okay. It's high pressure though."

"Any news on Susan?"

"Not yet. My team are still digging."

Elizabeth drank her wine. "Maybe I shouldn't have told you about her."

"Maybe you shouldn't. But you did and I understand why. If she's alive, I'll find her and bring her here." She added a few drops of Worcester Sauce to her meal. "What do I need to do to help you in the house?"

"Nothing. I can use the bathroom on my own; the bed is perfect; you've got a tumble dryer, so I don't need to worry about hanging up wet clothes; I'll get the measure of the local shops and if they're not up to scratch I'll order online; and I'm not stupid – I know my capabilities and limitations. I won't do anything that puts me at risk." She smiled. "Actually, there is one thing you can do to help – you can teach me how to use your TV. From what I've seen you've got three remote controllers and beneath the TV are electrical boxes of this that and the other. I don't know where to start."

"I'll write you a list of instructions." Archer was proud of the meal she'd cooked. "You know, mum, there are times I'm required to work odd hours. I don't travel so much these days, but there will still be times when I'll need to go away for a bit."

"I have two sets of spare keys. I won't be housebound when you're away."

"I know. But what I wanted to say is that most of the time I work during the day and come home in the evening. When I get home I have a bit of a routine. I cook or order a takeaway, have a bath or shower, pour myself a glass of wine or make a cup of tea, and watch something on Netflix or Sky. I don't tend to read because I spend a chunk of my day reading intelligence reports. I like to decompress by doing relaxing things."

"And you like to do so alone." Elizabeth fully understood. "Don't worry, dear. I won't get in your way. I get tired between seven and eight in the evening. Either the medication does that or it's just an age thing. Or it's a combination. Regardless, when I'm tired I go to bed. I won't be in your way and you won't be in my way."

"Sorry, I didn't mean it like…"

"I know. It'll be fine." She placed her knife and fork down. "You know I don't have long in this world. This is just a temporary arrangement."

"Don't speak like that."

"Face facts, Jayne. Soon – maybe months or maybe a year or so – I'll die in this house or while driving my scooter alongside the river. I'm just happy to be here for my closing chapter. By the way – tomorrow I'm going to cook us a lovely lasagne with some French beans on the side."

Archer smiled. "That will be lovely. Do you want me to buy the ingredients?"

"Don't you dare." Elizabeth finished her wine and smiled. "It will be liberating to A-Z prepare and cook a meal. I don't need fussing over." She yawned. "I'll load the dishwasher and head to bed. It's been a long day."

Archer squeezed her mother's hand. "It's good to have you home."

CHAPTER 10

At six AM the following morning, Sign, Knutsen, Gregor, and Natalia were outside of the house. Yuri backed his car towards them, stopped, and loaded the travellers' luggage into the boot of the vehicle. The air was crisp; there was frost on the ground; the lake was calm.

Knutsen crouched, gently wrapped his arms around Lenin's head, and held him against his chest. "I've got to go now, fella. Remember the training. You'll do fine when it's time for you to leave." He stepped back.

Lenin looked at him.

Knutsen nodded.

Lenin arched his back and howled at the sky.

Gregor walked up to Knutsen. "He knows you're going. It makes him sad, but also stronger. Now, more than ever, he wants his mate. He's just called to her and he will continue doing so for days, weeks, and months until she comes. If she doesn't come, he will leave to find her. I will let him." He held out his hand. "Goodbye Mr. Tank Engine. The journey isn't over just because you have sight of a port. You understand?"

Knutsen understood. "I'll look after her until the job's done." He shook his hand. "Thank you for being such a good host."

Gregor walked to Natalia and placed his hands on her arms. "You are British now." He smiled. "Learn to say please and thank you. Avoid black pudding and haggis." He kissed her on both cheeks.

Natalia and Knutsen got into the car.

Gregor walked to Sign.

Both men stared at the lake.

Gregor said, "When it happens, show no mercy."

"There'll be no mercy."

Gregor breathed in deeply and slowly exhaled. "You'll come back one day?"

"Of course." Sign turned to him. "My brother." He hugged him.

The two men didn't need to say anything else.

Sign got into the car.

Yuri drove them out of the farmstead.

Gregor watched them until the car was no longer visible. Then he whistled to Lenin. "Come on boy. It's just you and me for the day, until Yuri gets back tonight. I'm thinking we should go for a long walk. Maybe we could bag ourselves a couple of rabbits." When Lenin was by his side, Gregor looked at the empty lane and quietly said, "Keep moving; steady as she goes."

Five hours later the letter arrived.

It was addressed to Archer.

Her name and address were handwritten on the white envelope. Archer didn't like that. This wasn't a utility bill and she never received personal letters. She held it for a moment at her front door before going into the kitchen, sitting at the table, swigging her coffee, and opening the letter. She stared at in disbelief. Aside from the letter, there was a photo. The letter said:

Dear Miss Jayne Archer

I am writing on behalf of interested parties who live east of you.

You may or may not know that you have a twin sister, Susan Archer. I am happy to report that she is alive and well. She has just been made aware of your existence. She is unmarried, has no children, and works as a clerical assistant. I'm sure you'd like to meet her and return with her to your family home – either for a visit or for a permanent reunion. This can happen on one condition. You will be required to help me and my colleagues with a major problem. Your task will not be arduous. All I require is for you to give me a name. If you do that, your sister will be placed in your care. If you don't, the consequences for Susan will be dire.

You and I will meet tomorrow at midnight in the centre of Quaibrücke Bridge, Zurich, Switzerland. Susan will be close by. If you bring police or covert operatives, Susan will be instantly shot in the back of the head.

We know who you work for and we know your position within your organisation.

If you give me the name we desire, you and Susan will never hear from us again. If you give me a false name, you and Susan will have the Sword of Damocles hanging over you. One day that sword will fall with unforgiving accuracy.

Take a look at the photo. She looks just like you.

Travel under your own passport. Susan will be carrying her passport. It has a valid visa to travel to the UK. She will also be carrying one thousand dollars for flight and associated costs to get to your home. I look forward to seeing you tomorrow.

Archer looked at the photo and ran in to the lounge. Her mother was in there, reading a newspaper. "Is this her, mum? Do you think this could be Susan?" Her hand trembled as she handed the photo to Elizabeth.

"Where did you get this?"

Archer lied. "My team."

Elizabeth was unblinking as she examined the shot. "It's Susan."

"I know she looks like me but how can you be sure?!"

Elizabeth placed a finger on the photo. "It's not just the resemblance. She has a half-moon birthmark on her chin. Susan was born with the exact same birthmark." She looked up at Archer. Her eyes were watering. "Jayne – this is your sister."

Archer's heart was pounding.

Elizabeth asked, "Where is she?"

"Overseas. I can't yet tell you where. I can't tell anyone about this. But, I'm going to try to bring her here."

"Will there be a price to pay for getting her here?"

Archer slumped into a chair and held her head in her hands. "Yes."

"Is the price reasonable?"

Archer didn't respond.

In a sterner voice, Elizabeth repeated, "Is the price reasonable?"

Archer looked at her. "I don't know what the price is. But, whatever it is, I'll pay it."

It was late evening when Sign, Knutsen, and Natalia were told by the ship's captain that it was safe to leave the on-board container that was one of eighty five on the boat. The vessel had left Russian waters and the three of them were now free to move around the ship. They'd been given a three-bed cabin, close to the engine room; had access to a tiny bathroom that was shared by eight other sailors; and would eat breakfast, lunch, and dinner in the galley canteen. Sign had told the skipper that they must work their passage. Sign would help out in the galley, Knutsen would work in the engine room, and Natalia would help with any required repairs and maintenance. They'd start their chores tomorrow. The other sailors were a mixed bunch of Russian, Chinese, Indians, and Albanians. They didn't care about the presence of three strangers on their boat. They were used to smuggling people, drugs, exotic animals, cash, and precious metals. It's why they were loyal to their skipper. He paid them four times more than the normal salary for a sailor.

Knutsen, and Natalia were on the starboard side of the deck. It was dark, the only lights coming from the ship's electric bulbs. Russia wasn't visible. They were in open waters.

But, Natalia looked in the direction of Russia and said, "The divorce has come through. Sad really, isn't it?"

Knutsen replied, "Not when one of the parties in the marriage is a cunt."

"That's sort of true. But there are always two people to blame. I'm not some idiot woman who repeatedly mentally abuses her husband and goads him in to slapping her, then raises her voice three octaves when the cops arrive and pretends to be the victim so that they can arrest him and take him away. I betrayed my country. I'm anything but a victim. But, then there's the cooling down period. Husband and wife might have a moment to work out what went wrong." She raised her eyebrows. "It's too late now. No cooling down period. No reconciliation."

Knutsen nodded as he looked out to sea and felt the salty air on his face. "Where do you think you'll live in Britain?"

"I don't know. I like the countryside but I may be too exposed there. Maybe a big town or city. You can be more anonymous there. Do you have any recommendations?"

"Maybe Bristol, Bath, or Exeter. I grew up around there. It's a nice part of the country."

"Maybe." Natalia looked at him. "What will you do when you get back to England?"

Knutsen leaned against the ship's rail. "I'll help Ben close this job. After that, we'll shift to the next thing." He looked over his shoulder at Natalia. "It's funny when I hear myself using the word *job*. It sounds so impersonal, doesn't it?"

Natalia walked to his side and placed her hands on the rail. "Do you have a wife?"

Knutsen smiled but not because he was happy. "In my head, yes. In reality no. The woman I loved died."

"Ben told me the same about his partner. My brother killed himself. My parents are dead." She breathed in deeply. "The hardest part about grief is when grief no longer features."

"Yeah. We move on. It sucks." Knutsen turned and rested against the rail. "How do you fall out of love with a dead woman? Self-preservation, I guess. The memories become too painful."

Natalia touched his hand.

Knutsen looked at her. He wrapped his fingers around hers.

"I'm cold." She placed her body against his. "You smell of Lenin."

Knutsen laughed, placed his arms around her, and held her firm. "At some point in the next year or so, I'll go back and see the wolf. If he's in the wild, I'll find him. He'll recognise me. I hope he has a mate and cubs. And I hope he'll introduce me to his family."

"He will. He loves and respects you. You're his father. Or his big brother. Or his mentor. Certainly you're his pack leader." Natalia rested her head against his chest. "Very few men can achieve that with a highly intelligent savage beast. Lenin's frame of reference is not dissimilar to that of humans. When we left, he howled because he missed you and wanted love from a female wolf."

Knutsen was stock still, just holding her. "He's persistent. He'll find love."

"And you, pack leader?"

"I was an undercover cop. I lived for months, and sometimes years at a time, in the most godawful environments. The movies portray men like me as living on their nerves. It's not like that in reality. We become other personalities. We'll do anything to prove ourselves to the scumbags we have to mix with. We become a scumbag. That's how we survive the darkness and the fucking blood. There were no nerves, nor any room for love."

She touched his face. "But you are not that now, da? You are Thomas."

He looked at her. "No one calls me Thomas. My name's Tom Knutsen."

"Tom. Yes, that's a good name. Knutsen? You are Scandinavian?"

"In DNA only. I don't know. In fact I don't know much shit about any of my family background. Fucking orphanages will do that to a kid."

She stared at him.

He held her gaze.

They both smiled.

Then they walked inside.

Archer called the deputy head of the Russia Department and told him that she was urgently needed in Europe tomorrow to meet one of her agents. She instructed him to hold the fort while she was away and that she'd most likely be back in the office mid-afternoon the day after. After she ended the call she poured herself a glass of wine. There was nothing more that could be done today. Earlier she'd booked a hotel in Zurich and a flight, and packed an overnight bag. She'd be arriving in Switzerland at 1500hrs tomorrow.

She took her wine into the lounge and sat on the sofa. Her mother was sleeping in her room. Archer was glad. She wanted solitude so that she could collect her thoughts. What secret did the sender of the letter want from her? It had to be significant, given they were willing to exchange Susan for the information. And the letter used the word *name*. That could refer to a building or facility. More likely it was the name of a person. She was in no doubt that the letter was sent from the Russians; more specifically, SVR, FSB, or GRU. Her value in the Zurich meeting was because she had access to MI6 secrets about Russia. But, what secret did they want? Something that was hurting them the most. The name of a Russian traitor who was working for the British, Europeans, or Americans and selling out Russian assets.

Archer sipped her wine. She'd not heard from Sign during his trip to Moscow; ditto Natalia. But that wasn't unusual. They were only supposed to contact her if there was an emergency. Even then, Sign would deal with the emergency, rather than involve MI6. She was certain Sign had made no progress in tracking her sister. Now, that was a good thing. Another chess move was in play and it was to her advantage. She had to make her move with her unknown opponent. All that mattered was getting her sister to London. She'd lie about how she found her. It would be easy. If asked by the chief of MI6, she'd say some of her Russian agents – who couldn't be named – found Susan and got her out of Russia. It would be hushed up. She'd get a pat on the back from the chief. Susan would be given the right to abode in the United Kingdom. The matter would be closed.

Sign and Knutsen had failed, she decided. They were no longer of use to her.

Natalia's value to MI6 was now irrelevant. .

After all, she was the traitor who the Russians wanted to identify.

Forget trying to help her regain her courage.

Archer now had a wholly different use for Natalia Asina.

Archer had only become her case officer when she'd been recently promoted to run the department. And that's when Natalia had stalled. MI6 peers had acted sympathetic to Archer. These things happen, they'd told her. Try your best to get her back on track. But if you can't, no one will think of you as a failure. It was that word – *failure*. Everyone who'd spoken to Archer, and was cleared to know about Natalia, had dropped that word into their conversations with her. It was not only embarrassing. Her colleagues were very deliberately giving her a subliminal message.

We're judging you on the Natalia case.

Archer had spent a lifetime getting to where she was in MI6. And she didn't want her career to peak now. She wanted much more.

Natalia could be disposed of in a way that made Archer happy and everyone else happy. Archer would get her sister back. And, because Natalia was caught out by the Russians, the headache Natalia had created would vanish and no one would bandy around the word failure anymore. On the contrary, Archer would be branded a hero within MI6 and Whitehall because she'd inherited a lost cause but had still tried her best to give Natalia courage.

She finished her wine and decided she'd have an early night. Tomorrow was going to be a big day.

Knutsen and Natalia entered their cabin. Sign was lying on his bed, reading Moby Dick, by Herman Melville. He had a mischievous look on his face when he saw them. He held up the book so they could see the cover. "Do you think we'll spot a whale during our passage to England?"

"No," replied Knutsen. "Why have you got the single bed and left Natalia and I to have the bunk beds?"

"Oh, you know, dear chap. Man of my age gets achy joints. It's easier for me to get in and out of this bed."

"You're only bloody forty nine and you have the stamina and strength of a twenty year old athlete!"

"Ah, but it's night time when the creaks and groans set in." He chuckled and looked at the book. "It must have been cold on deck."

"It was."

Sign kept his eyes on the book. "Sometimes it's best to get warmth from wherever you can when the chill hits you."

Knutsen and Natalia said nothing.

Sign tossed his book to one side and looked at them. "When we boarded the boat, Thomas had three of Lenin's hairs on his jacket. They were loosely embedded in the fibres. Now he has two. The other one is on your jacket, my dear."

Natalia's face flushed red.

Knutsen replied, "Whatever. Just read your book and turn your fucking brain off. Seven days of listening to you will do my head in."

Sign gestured to the bunk beds. "Who's going to be on top and who's got to be underneath the other person?"

"Shut up, Ben." Knutsen looked at Natalia. "You choose."

"I'll take the bottom bed." She patted the mattress. "Sometimes I get seasick. I don't want to vomit over you."

Knutsen smiled. "Right oh. Top bed it is for me." He clambered onto the bed. "Ben – be a darling and turn the light out. We've all got early starts tomorrow."

Sign asked, "What about getting changed into our pyjamas?"

"We haven't got any frickin' pyjamas, and you know it."

Sign turned the light off and got into bed. "For seven days we must be like astronauts. They coexist, regardless of gender, in tight spaces. There is no privacy. They get changed in front of each other; go for a wee and poo in front of each other; clean themselves in front of each other. They become hermaphrodites. For the duration of this voyage we too have to become…"

"Shut up, Ben!" said Knutsen and Natalia in unison.

Knutsen added, "Just get some sleep, please!"

The room was pitch dark.

Five minutes later, Sign was snoring.

Knutsen rubbed his eyes and in an exasperated tone yelled out, "Ben – you're snoring!"

Sign giggled. "I never snore. But it did make you laugh."

"You bastard!"

CHAPTER 11

At four thirty PM, Archer arrived at the five star Zurich Marriott hotel. She was tired, but not because the journey was arduous – it was only a short hop, skip, and a jump from Heathrow – but rather because she had a mentally exhausting case of the jitters. Was this all some elaborate bluff? Was Susan really alive? Was Archer doing the right thing?

After checking in, she went straight to her room. Though luxurious, it was like so many other hotel rooms that Archer had stayed in around the world during her career. Luxury meant nothing to her. Only the most junior front-line MI6 officers got a thrill from travelling first or business class and arriving at a swanky hotel. Once you'd trawled the Earth, many times at unholy hours, the novelty of luxury was completely worn out. A bed was a bed; a bathroom a bathroom. No amount of chocolates on a pillow or complimentary this and that made a jot of difference. Hotels were places to get one's head down or to meet secret agents. That was their only purpose. Archer had booked the Marriott because she was pretending to meet one of her assets. It wouldn't make sense for a woman of her seniority to be assessed as slumming it when she handed in her expenses claims.

She showered, blow dried her hair, and changed into fresh clothes. She knew she had to eat to keep up her strength, though she wasn't hungry. At six PM she wandered down to one of the hotel restaurants and ordered *De Wildi* – saddle fillet of venison with a cranberry jus, hazelnut knöpfli, and red cabbage. When the food arrived she had to force it down her throat. After she finished, she returned to her room, drank a glass of wine, regretted doing so, drank two bottles of mineral water, and turned on the TV. She sat in the armchair, flicking through channels, unable to concentrate. But, there was nothing else she could do. As with so many of her MI6 missions, her hotel was her base camp. It was a safe place before she had to venture out. She was poised. The waiting was a killer.

Sign was serving dinner to the sailors in the galley. As he heaped food onto their plates, he told them to enjoy their food. To some, he communicated in Russian and Chinese; to the rest he communicated in English. Instead of the usual unrecognisable slop the crew were served at dinner time, he'd transformed the cuisine. Tonight the sailors were eating pan-fried chicken legs, cabbage and bacon, herb encrusted sautéed potatoes, and gravy that he'd made from chicken carcasses, fried onions, salt and pepper, and a dash of rum. It wasn't up to his usual culinary standard, but he had to work with the produce at his fingertips and the tiny kitchen at his disposal. The sailors had smiles on their faces as they asked for extra helpings. When dinner was complete, he cleaned the galley, made himself a coffee and went on deck to get some air.

Knutsen was sweating in the engine room. He was paired with a Chinaman who didn't speak English. The Chinaman had a rag around his head, was wiry, stressed, and had quickly realised that barking orders at Knutsen in Mandarin was of no use. For the majority of today's shift, the communication between the two men was conducted in crude sign language. The Chinaman tapped dials that registered the heat of the vessel's engines. He pointed at the red zone of the thermometers and wiped his flat hand against his throat. Knutsen interpreted this to mean that he had to monitor the dials and alert his colleague if the needle went too high. They also cleaned pistons while they were operating - Knutsen thought he might lose his hand in the process – and did a variety of other jobs all of which had the singular purpose of keeping the ship moving. When the two men working the nightshift arrived, Knutsen went on deck and joined Sign.

Natalia spent the day doing two jobs. The first was checking that all of the containers were secure on deck. The second was hanging from a rope over the side of the boat and applying rust treatment to the metal hull. The latter job was terrifying. Waves and foam were only a few feet beneath her. An Albanian called Edi lowered her down and pulled her up, and this went on for hours around the circumference of the ship. He had a permanent grin on his face. Natalia knew he was testing her. In fairness, what she did today was what he did day in day out. Still, it was arduous and Natalia was exhausted when she'd completed her tasks. When back on deck, Edi handed her a hip flask containing vodka. She took a swig and handed the flask back to him. He told her that she was an excellent worker. Tomorrow and the next few days would be considerably easier. Unless something went wrong on deck or on the hull, it would simply be monitoring the cargo and sides of the ship. He bade her goodnight.

. When Sign, Knutsen, and Natalia were back in their cabin, Knutsen sat on his bed and said, "Natalia is either already blown today, or she'll be blown in the next hour or so."

Sign looked at him. "Yes." He handed them disposable foil cartons containing warm leftovers from the galley dinner. "You'll have to eat with your fingers. I wasn't permitted to borrow galley cutlery." He tucked into his food.

Natalia sat next to Knutsen and ate. "I'd kill for a nice bath right now. Every muscle in my body aches. Instead, I'll have to use the bathroom sink to wash."

Sign smiled. "It's an adventure. Be thankful you have access to a sink." He sucked sauce off his fingers. "How do you feel, Natalia?"

"Like I'm living in a surreal dream."

Sign nodded. "Do not let reality become a distant concept. If you do, madness awaits." His tone of voice was stern as he added, "You are on a boat that is bound for England. You are in a cabin with Thomas and Ben. You were a traitor. You are no longer a traitor. You don't have a job. Your brother killed himself near St, Petersburg. Thomas has taken a shine to you. The Russians will shortly want you dead. These are facts. This is not a dream."

Natalia put her food to one side. "I know. Except the bit about Thomas."

"Eat. I will do my best with tomorrow's breakfast but don't expect miracles. You need fuel where and when you can get it." Sign finished his food. "We must also have some respite." He smiled. "I may not have been allowed to take some knives and forks out of the galley, but I did manage to nick this without the head chef knowing." He held up a bottle of rum. "The three of us will have a few drinks this evening and talk about pleasant things – the future; our favourite novels and films; the best restaurants in London; and whether Ben will ask you out on a date."

Knutsen sighed. "Give it a rest, Ben."

Natalia placed her hand over Knutsen's hand. "It's okay. I like pleasant thoughts." She looked at Sign. "Pour me a drink and describe to me the most beautiful part of Britain. I want it to be magical. Maybe that's where I'll live."

It was midnight in Switzerland.

Archer stood in the centre of the Quaibrücke Bridge, on the pedestrian walkway. Traffic was non-existent. And though the German quarter of Switzerland had bars, clubs, and restaurants that stayed open longer than their counterparts in the French cantons, there were few lights on in the regal buildings on the other side of the river. The air was still and cool. Her breath was steaming as she exhaled. Noise from the city was barely audible. There were no other pedestrians on the bridge.

She waited.

A car drove onto the bridge and stopped. A man got out and walked towards her. He was wearing a woollen overcoat and suit. He stopped by Archer and lit a cigarette. In a polished Russian accent he said, "You are Jayne Archer. I would like to see your passport."

Archer handed him her ID.

He gave it back to her. "Susan is in the car. She has a gun against her head. Do you want to see her without me and my men present?"

Archer nodded.

He went right up to her and put his face an inch from her face. "I want the name of the Russian who has been betraying my colleagues. You know that person. I don't want a code word. I want a real name."

Archer's heart was pounding fast. Was this the right thing to do? If she gave the name she'd be committing treason. Then again, who would find out that she'd committed treachery by giving the Russians the name of a traitor? And was it unethical to do so? By giving them a name, she'd be saving Susan. A traitor's life for an innocent's life. That was the equation.

She said, "Natalia Asina. She works in the SVR's London station."

"Give me the names of the men and women she's sold out."

Archer told him who was on the list of blown Russian agents.

The man made a call on his mobile phone. He supplied the name of Natalia Asina, then waited while listening. He nodded and ended the call. To Archer he said, "You are telling the truth. Wait here." He walked to his car.

Archer watched him.

The man didn't get in the vehicle. He opened the rear passenger door.

A woman got out.

She walked to Archer.

Archer held her breath.

The woman stood in front of Archer.

There was no doubt it was Susan.

Susan spoke in Russian. "You are my sister. Until two days ago, I didn't know you existed."

Archer hugged her. "Susan, Susan."

The woman frowned. "My name's Dina Vichneva."

"It's not your real name." Archer smiled and stepped back. "Do you want to see my home in London? My mother's there."

Susan had tears running down her face. "They threatened to kill me. I don't know what's going on. This is… so confusing. Yes. Let's go home."

Archer took her hand. "It's not confusing anymore. Come with me. I need to check out of my hotel and then we can get a night flight to England. You're safe now."

CHAPTER 12

Five days later, Sign, Knutsen, and Natalia arrived in the Liverpool docks. They travelled by train to London. Under normal circumstances, Sign would have suggested to Natalia that she stay at his house until she secured her own home. But, these were anything but normal circumstances. Natalia was blown. Archer knew where Sign lived. And though there was no reason why Archer would have told the Russians about Sign and his engagement by her, there was the possibility the Russians would re-contact her when they realised Natalia had vanished. Then, she'd give them Sign's name and address. His house wasn't safe. So, instead he paid upfront in cash for Natalia to stay in a B&B in Pimlico. It was walking distance from West Square. Sign and Knutsen would liaise with her on a daily basis and make sure she was safe. She wasn't registered with her real name in the temporary accommodation. Sign had taken the proprietor to one side and quietly said that she'd been battered by her husband and needed a safe place. He'd added that if any men came here asking about a woman with an Eastern European accent, the proprietor was to call the police and demand that an armed response unit was deployed to his B&B.

Day two after they'd arrived back in England, Sign and Knutsen were in the lounge of their apartment. Earlier today they'd gone to Sign's barbers in St James's where they'd been given a cutthroat shave and haircut. Now, Sign was in immaculate slacks, a shirt, and brogues. Knutsen was in jeans, a creased T-shirt, and flip-flops. They were sitting in their armchairs, adjacent to a lit fire.

Sign said, "We must establish where Natalia can live."

"It's her choice."

"She and I don't want it to be her choice, and rightly so. She knows parts of London, but everywhere else is a jungle to her." Sign placed the tips of his fingers together. "We must square the circle. She must live somewhere where she can be anonymous. But she must also have vibrancy and happiness."

"A rural town or city? I suggested to her the west country."

"That didn't help those Russians in Salisbury. It's too obvious to relocate her to a place like that."

"Why keep her in Britain?"

"Three reasons. First, I've pulled strings to get her a new British identity. I have no strings to attempt gaining a foreign nationality. Second, you and I must keep a weather eye on her welfare. Third, there is a ninety two percent chance that you and Natalia may become an item."

Knutsen smiled. "Ninety two percent chance? How did you come to that calculation?"

"I made it up, though I'm a millimetre either way from being correct." Sign was weary and not in the mood for banter. "She can't live in London in case…"

"Of a chance encounter with one of her former SVR colleagues."

Sign nodded. "But she can live close to London. Hertford springs to mind."

Knutsen agreed. "That's a great idea. Lovely town. Lots going on. Quick and easy access to London at the weekends when most of the SVR station is closed shop. Good rail links. It's a bit pricey though."

"She only needs a one bedroom flat."

Knutsen used his phone to browse the Internet. "I'm looking at Rightmove." After a few minutes he said, "Discounting the silly prices, we're looking at between seven hundred and a thousand quid per month."

"Perfect."

"How will she afford that? She's got no savings."

"I will pay until she has a salary coming in."

Knutsen stared at him. "That's very generous."

"I prefer to think of it as pragmatic."

Knutsen didn't need to tell his friend that he was lying through his teeth. "I'll get on to the real estate agents today. What about a job?"

"I'll arrange that. She'll work from home. I have one or two contacts that'll help her get on her feet and earn a living."

Knutsen knew that Sign had hundreds of valuable contacts in Britain alone. "We must take her out this evening."

"We will. I've bought us tickets to the Royal Albert Hall. We're seeing Verdi's Requiem at eight o'clock.. After, we will dine at Goya tapas restaurant in Pimlico. Then we'll walk Natalia to her B&B. You will need to change before this evening. You currently look like a beach bum on Mykonos." He smiled. "We only have a few hours so let's divide and conquer. I've already secured her a British passport. But, there are other matters to attend to. I need to open a bank account in her new name, make a few phone calls and get her a job, obtain a UK mobile phone in her new identity, and plant some misinformation that Natalia was spotted yesterday in Tokyo. Meanwhile, your task is to find her somewhere nice to live. It must be walking distance to the town centre. Preferably go for unfurnished. I'll deposit five thousand pounds in her new bank account to pay for new furniture and other set-up costs. Are you up to the task?"

Knutsen nodded. "Let's get it done. Deadline is six PM. Then I'll get showered and dressed into my best bib and tucker. We'll have time for a sharpener before we leave for the concert."

"Good man."

Knutsen stood. In a more hesitant voice he asked, "What are you going to do about Archer and her mother?"

"I'm going to deal with them tomorrow," was Sign's only reply.

Archer made a pot of tea and placed muffins onto a plate. She took the food and drink into the lounge. Susan and Elizabeth were in the room, playing cards. Archer sat with them and after two minutes poured the tea. In Russian she said to Susan, "Your British passport should be through tomorrow. You will have a permanent right to abode in Britain."

Elizabeth placed her cards down. "She can live here, can't she?"

"Of course." Archer looked at Susan. "Would you like that?"

Susan nodded. "I can't go back to Russia. And I don't know England. Plus, I want to get to know my real mother and sister."

"That's settled then." She handed Susan and Elizabeth mugs of tea. "I was thinking we should get some takeaway pizzas tonight. What do you think?"

Both nodded.

Archer smiled. Everything was perfect, though she wished her father was still alive to be part of this reunion. Fleetingly, she thought about Natalia. No doubt she was stopped at the airport when trying to depart Russia. The FSB and SVR would be merciless. She'd be tortured to within an inch of her life and executed. Still, that was the price to pay if one got exposed as a double agent.

She drank her tea. "I think we should all go for a nice stroll on the promenade before dinner." She looked at Susan. "I've booked an appointment for you tomorrow. It's with a neighbour who teaches English to foreign students. She's happy to see you for an hour a day at her home, until you've got a working knowledge of the language. She's not going to charge me. I'll show you where she lives when we go for our walk this evening."

Susan replied, "Yes, that would be good." She looked away, a tear rolling down her face. "Who were the people who raised me? The people I thought were my parents? Do you know?"

Archer shook her head. "I don't."

"It doesn't matter. They died a few years ago." Susan wiped away her tear. "How did you get to me? How did you get me released from the thugs who kept me in a cell for two days and held guns against my head?"

"It was Elizabeth who answered. "Jayne is in a powerful position in government. She exerted her influence with the Russians. She pulled out the stops to find you and to bring you to England."

Susan replied, "But there must have been a trade. Jayne must have given them something in return."

Archer said, "The British and the Russians do trades all the time. It's complicated. On this occasion, and with my prime minister's permission, I conducted what's called back-channel diplomacy. I told the Russians how Britain would be voting at the next UN summit. Simple as that. Me doing that served Britain's interest and Russian interests."

Susan breathed in deeply. "I don't know anything about politics." Her mood lightened. "Yes. Let's go for a walk." She looked at Elizabeth. "If I get tired on the way back, can I sit on your scooter?"

Elizabeth laughed. "Absolutely not, my dear! My scooter; my rules."

CHAPTER 13

The following morning, Knutsen fried bacon and eggs in the flat's kitchen. He felt invigorated, in large part because his trip to Russia and voyage home had been such a mind-blowing adventure. He'd never experienced anything like it before – the dramatic scenery, new friendships, constant fear over Natalia's safety, Gregor's amazing house and grounds, hunting for dinner, working like an oil-smeared naval lackey in the engine room during his passage home, and the look Natalia had given him as she'd briefly touched his hand when they were alone on deck together. Now, he felt more alive than he'd ever been. But it was good to be back in West Square. It was the same feeling he imagined most people had when they returned from an amazing holiday – great time, but comforting to be home and surrounded by familiar and personal accoutrements.

Sign emerged from his room. He was wearing a suit and looked pitch perfect – hair immaculate, clean shaven, shoes polished to the standards of a guardsman, trouser creases like blades, not a single piece of fluff on his Gieves & Hawkes royal navy blue suit, silk tie bound in a Windsor knot over a heavy cotton white shirt with a cutaway collar, and the aroma of expensive shower gel he'd purchased from Harrods and a bespoke cologne he'd bought from a perfumery in Chelsea. He sat at the dining table. "I have an appointment with Jayne Archer at ten AM. That gives me one hour."

Knutsen served up the food. "What have you told her?"

"My message to her was cryptic. I simply said I had news and no news and that we should meet at her house, alone." He ate his food. "Archer's mother will be out. If Susan is living with Jayne, she too will be out. I will be clearing the decks."

Knutsen sat opposite him with his plate of food. "Meaning?"

"Meaning the innocents maintain a rite of passage towards a wondrous world and the guilty starve to death on a cold rock." He looked at Knutsen. "As Gregor advised me, I will show no mercy."

"That was already your stance. Gregor didn't need to advise you."

"Correct. But sometimes it pays to have affirmation from a man one wholly trusts."

"Do you want me to help you today?"

Sign sliced his egg into two, allowing the yolk to flow over his pork. "I would like you to attend to Natalia. Before I leave, I will give you a plastic A4 folder. Inside is her British passport, the contact details of a woman who wishes to employ her as a freelance political analyst, a bank card and bank details, and a mobile phone. You will also furnish her with the details of the lovely flat you have secured her in Hertford. Take her there for a viewing today. She will want to make decisions about furnishings. I regret to say that you may have to go with her to Ikea or somewhere similar. I believe she moves in on Monday?"

"Yep. How did you get her bank card so quickly?"

Sign shrugged. "A bank card is only a bit of plastic and an account can be opened with a few taps on a keyboard. I know someone who can do these things in a matter of hours."

Knutsen eyed him. Sign seemed cold, distant, and utterly focused. "You have that look. You're about to mess with minds."

"I often do that for good reasons. But, sometimes… yes, sometimes…"

"It's okay. It has to be what it is." Knutsen finished his food and cleared up the plates. "Fucking Ikea?! Why do I get the shit job?!"

Sign smiled. He knew Knutsen was making light of the day's tasks. He also knew that Knutsen was trying in his own way to transfer strength to Sign, fully cognisant that Sign had the worst job of all. "Be happy today. Act excited in front of Natalia. Hold her hand when you go shopping." He stood. "I will get you the folder. Then I must leave."

At ten AM, Sign rang Archer's doorbell.

She let him in to her house.

They sat in the lounge.

Archer said, "My mother's gone shopping."

Sign was motionless. "And Susan? Where is your sister?"

Archer feigned ignorance. "I thought you were going to give me the answer to that."

Sign's voice was cold when he replied, "Tom and I didn't find Susan. We didn't need to. You found her with the help of the Russians."

"I… I don't know what you're talking about."

"You got Susan in exchange for giving the FSB or SVR the name of the person who'd been giving British Intelligence the identities of Russian agents."

"This is nonsense!"

Sign showed no emotion. "I withheld from you the real reason why I wanted Natalia to go to Russia. I tasked her to investigate what had happened to Susan. She found out everything, including why the Russians snatched her at birth. They wanted to use her as leverage against you. That event happened just over a week ago. You have betrayed an MI6 agent. Natalia is safe and far away from Russia. I made that happen. You and the Russians can't touch her."

Archer stood. "Get out of my house!"

But Sign didn't move. "Decades ago, your treachery would have put you in front of a firing squad. These days, you will face life imprisonment."

Archer paced back and forth. "I've done nothing wrong!"

"Your sister is living with you in this house." He tossed a photo onto the coffee table. "Mr. Knutsen took that yesterday. There are you, Elizabeth, and Susan, having a walk alongside the Thames. You all look very happy. There wasn't really a need to take the camera shot. I'd already spoken to the chief of MI6. He informed that you'd told him you brought your sister to England and had asked for the service to facilitate her legal status here. He was happy for you. He also told me that he was aware that Natalia was off the radar. He had no idea why. He assumed she'd gone back to work in Moscow. He doesn't suspect foul play on your part. That remains the case, because I didn't enlighten him. Sit down. There are things you need to know."

Fury remained on Archer's face. She sat.

"Elizabeth and Michael are not your real parents. They were KGB and SVR moles whose sole job was to raise you to hate Russia. Your twin sister was raised by KGB caretakers in Russia. They pretended to be Susan's parents. Your real parents were murdered immediately after your births. Your name is Anna Vichneva. Susan is Dina Vichneva. You are Russian. Elizabeth gave birth close to the time when you were born. She willingly let the KGB murder her child. It was all part of the plan. And Elizabeth knew there'd come a day when you'd be of use to her and her Moscow controllers. Susan/Dina was innocent throughout. Like you, she had no reason to suspect her parents were fake. Susan was just a pawn to be used someday to prompt you to betray the United Kingdom. You, however, are not innocent. You took the Russian bait. Were it not for my help, Natalia would be dead by now."

Archer sat in stunned silence. "My mother is a lie?"

"Yes."

"She knew the Russians wanted to give me the name of my double agent?"

"She knew everything."

Archer was trying to process the information. "I didn't… didn't give them Natalia's name."

"Yes you did! It was the only way you could get Susan. Don't make matters worse for yourself by lying to me!"

Archer bowed her head. In a barely audible voice, she said, "Natalia had dried up." She looked at him. "What would you have done? What would anyone in my position have done? This is my flesh and blood we're talking about. The Russians were threatening to kill Susan if I didn't help them."

"There is no doubting that you were placed in an impossible situation. You have my sympathies. You were forced to attempt the murder of Natalia Asina. This is what's going to happen. In two hours, Special Branch will arrest you. In a closed court hearing, I will testify to your otherwise good character. It won't result in a lenient sentence, but it may help your life imprisonment be a little more comfortable. Don't attempt to flee the country on your real or alias passports. You would be arrested at any port.. He stood. "The reason I'm giving you two hours is to allow you a brief window of time to sort out your affairs." He stood. "Do you understand what I mean? Good day to you Miss Archer." He left the house.

Archer was shaking when he was gone. She called Elizabeth. "Mum – are you on your way home?" She listened to her reply. "Good. I need to travel at short notice, but we've got a problem with the heating. I need to give you the number of the repair man I use."

Ten minutes later Elizabeth was back home. Archer helped her sit in an armchair.

Elizabeth asked, "Is Susan at her English lesson?"

"Yes. She won't be back for another thirty or so minutes. I need to pack and then I'll tell you about the heating." She went upstairs, picked up a pillow from Elizabeth's bed, returned downstairs, and stopped at the entrance to the lounge. "You're not my mother. You lied to me for all of my life. You're a Russian agent. You made me betray my country and a woman who had barely started her adult life."

Elizabeth's mouth opened; her eyes were wide. "How did you know..?"

"Shut up!." Archer walked quickly to her and shoved the pillow against Elizabeth's mouth and nose. She pressed hard and held the pillow in place.

Elizabeth was twitching, but unable to do anything because her limbs were so weak.

Archer held the pillow there for three minutes. Her face was red from the exertion and from stress. She removed the pillow. Her mother was dead.

She returned upstairs and placed the pillow back on to Elizabeth's bed. No doubt the pillow had Elizabeth's saliva on it, but almost certainly a police forensics examination of the cushion would conclude that any secretions were simply as a result of night time sleep. And Archer's fingerprints on the pillow would be totally explainable. After all, Archer had to regularly change Elizabeth's bedding.

But, it was highly unlikely the police would be involved. Elizabeth was dying; she'd returned home, sat in her chair, had a nap, and stopped breathing.

Archer regretted that Susan would have to find Elizabeth dead. There was no alternative to that. She grabbed her handbag, left the house, and walked to East Putney tube station. She was in a daze. After buying a ticket, she stood on the platform. There were only a handful of other travellers on the platform. She walked to one end, away from the other commuters, and waited. The electronic information unit announced that the next train was due to arrive in one minute.

One minute.

That's all she had.

A rush of wind coursed through the tunnel. The train was going to arrive at speed in seconds.

She waited.

She saw the train's headlights.

Timing was everything.

When the train was two yards away, she leapt in front of it.

Her body and head were mangled into pieces.

CHAPTER 14

Three days' later, Sign lit the fire in his lounge and poured two glasses of calvados. He handed one of them to Knutsen and sat in his armchair. Both men were facing each other. They were quiet for a while. Knutsen had been busy during the last forty eight hours, helping Natalia move furniture in to her new home. The men had barely had a chance to spend time together, Knutsen having arrived home at close to midnight during the preceding two days, and departing at six AM the following mornings. Knutsen had done his job. Natalia was happily ensconced in her new place. He'd see her in a week's time, after she'd settled in. She'd invited him over for dinner. He was looking forward to that.

Sign sipped his drink and looked at his colleague. "All that could be done is now done. Natalia is safe. Susan has legal ownership of the Putney house, thanks to a few tweaks in the property deeds. It's always good to have a dodgy lawyer on my books. MI6 Welfare Department will check on her regularly. Susan won't know they're MI6. Probably they'll pose as Social Services or Home Office. She'll be fine."

"Will you see Susan?"

"No. There's no need. It would serve no purpose."

"Plus, just sight of her would remind you of Jayne."

"I could handle that. Jayne was a professional acquaintance. Nothing more, nothing less. Susan must lead her own life now. The less she comes into contact with our murky world, the better. Ergo I must stay away."

Knutsen eyed him. "Did you know Archer would kill her mother and take her own life?"

Sign hesitated. "I gave her a two hour window for a reason. What she did with that window was up to her."

"In other words, you knew." Knutsen frowned. "I can't quite work out if I'm glad Archer's dead."

"Jayne wouldn't have lasted in prison. She knew that. Every second of every day she'd have been tortured by the demons of circumstance – knowledge that her mother was not her mother, not seeing her sister, the arm lock that forced her into betraying Natalia."

"Susan could have visited Jayne."

Sign shook his head. "Jayne knew the drill. She'd have been placed in a top secret military facility. She wouldn't be allowed to see other prisoners, let alone visitors. All she'd have to keep her company would be the silent memories in her head." Sign sighed. "What a tragedy." He placed his glass down, clapped his hands, and said in an upbeat tone of voice, "Let's take a stroll to Borough Market. I'd like to check out what my favourite veg and meat stalls have to offer. Grouse is in season, so maybe we could pick up a brace. Plus, they'll be quick to cook for this evening's supper. After dinner we could grab a pint or two at our local."

Knutsen smiled. "You're on, mate." He finished his drink. "Are we having a few days off work?"

Sign's eyes twinkled as he replied, "Oh no, my dear chap. Tomorrow we are being visited by a new client." He was brimming with energy as he added, "We must catch a serial killer whose victims don't want to be found by anyone."

THE END

THE KILL HOUSE

A *Ben Sign* Espionage Story

By

Matthew Dunn

FORMER *MI6 SPY* AND *BEST-SELLING* AUTHOR

CHAPTER 1

Today was death day.

Edward had been looking forward to the day for over a month. He was a patient man and liked to pace himself before killing. His ability to wait before a murder was predicated on one simple fact: he had to get to know his victim before he dispatched the person. With that knowledge, he could honour their history and personality. Most importantly, he had to understand what they liked doing.

He lived in a six bedroom detached house on a twelve acre estate in Britain. The property was at the base of a one-mile long steep stone track that was prone to severe erosion every time rain water from the hills cascaded down the route like a river. At some point he'd need to have the lane tarmacked, though he was loathe to pay the thirty thousand pounds required to do so, even though the track was the only way in and out of the estate. Officially the track belonged to the National Trust, but he was in ongoing and thus far fruitless negotiations with the agency to cough up and make the track resistant to water. So, once a year he got his staff to brush out the pot holes, apply a glue treatment, and fill the holes with ready mix concrete. The temporary repairs barely lasted through winter. But that was okay. He had an SUV. And, if he got completely cut off – as he often did when there was heavy snow – he could walk three miles through the adjacent forest to the nearest village where there was a shop and a pub that served food. Due to the geographical contours of the estate's surroundings, and its position next to the sea, the immediate vicinity had a micro climate that was tropical in summer and broody for the rest of the year. Around the top of the lane, at the base of the hills which once contained a communications station for WW2 bombers, there was usually a blanket of dense mist. The woods that straddled the estate were filled with unusual and beguiling trees and plants the like of which were not found anywhere else in the country. The author J.R.R. Tolkien had once strolled through the magical forest and had gained his inspiration for segments of Lord of the Rings. The estate was built three hundred and twenty years ago on bedrock land, one hundred yards above the flat sandy beach. Edward owned the beach. To get to it, one had to scramble down a long and treacherous river valley that had wooden steps and handrails in some parts, a rope at a ten foot vertical point, and nothing for the rest of the descent. So many times, Edward had tried to have the entire route made suitable for pedestrians. But, as with the constant decimation of the lane, the rugged nature of the location always succeeded over man-made constructions. Wind, rain, cold sea air, humidity, and frost crippled the walkway. And unlike the estate itself, the valley and cliff were made of clay. Iron railings wouldn't hold fast in the ground. Erosion was a constant problem. Now and again, huge chunks of the cliff would drop onto the beach. When it happened the noise was akin to a canon. The estate itself was however untarnished and stunning. To enter the estate one had to drive through a double electric gate. To arrive at the house, one had to keep driving down a sweeping long driveway, past old fashioned lamps that emitted a white glow, other lights embedded in the grounds, trees that contained magnificent Japanese blossom and fruit in season, large grassy areas, swathes of heathland, and a keep that had once been the lookout post for eighteenth century armed Customs officers who were trying to catch smugglers struggling up the valley with barrels of rum on their shoulders after rowing to the beach from their ship. The driveway ended outside the front door of the house, where there was a turning circle that was intersected with a fish pond. A majestic heron would occasionally fly up from the valley, its wings slow, its purpose precise, and gather up some of the hundreds of fish in the pond. The heron only snatched them when there were baby herons to feed. For the rest of the year it fed elsewhere. To the right of the house was a raised garden. It was designed as a croquet lawn and occasional badminton court. Apple trees and blackberry bushes bordered the garden. At one end were three pens that had once contained peacocks, though hadn't been lived in since Edward's five year tenure in the property. In the grounds were three other properties – a one bedroom cottage where Edward's housekeeper lived, tiny gate house that accommodated his cook, and a wooden house that Edward had commissioned to be built for his groundsman, shortly after he'd bought the estate for a bargain two and a half million pounds. There were no other houses at the end of the lane. The nearest external property was a farm close to the top of the track, adjacent to the main toad that one had to drive along to get to the village and elsewhere. The farmer kept cows in the fields either side of the lane. He also maintained a water filtration unit that was in the middle of the field and supplied Edward's estate. Edward didn't have to pay for the water. It was from the hills. The farmer was nice but blunt, as many farmers are. Occasionally he'd put his huge bull in the field. When Edward had first seen this happen he'd assumed it was for breeding purposes, though he was confused – the dumb animal just stood at the top of the steep field while the females stuck to the lower part of the grazing ground. One day the farmer explained to Edward that every three months or so he put the bull in there to calm the ladies down. Apparently his mere presence did that. In the grounds of the estate were a family of badgers who ate fallen fruit, rabbits, magpies, a pair of woodpeckers, buzzards who rode the thermals high in the sky, naughty squirrels who chased each other around trees near the sundial, and three foxes. It was an ecosystem. There was food aplenty for all, and the space to roam. There was no place on Earth more idyllic than the estate. Aside from the kitchen and basement, every room in the high ceilinged main house had a fireplace. The upstairs bedrooms all had en suite bathrooms. Downstairs there was a long dining room, reading room, vast lounge that had sliding full-length glass doors, enabling magnificent views of the sea, and a huge stone-paved kitchen that contained an Aga. The basement was divided into three rooms, two of which contained electrical utilities. The third was a stone clad wine cellar. The two stairways to the second floor were covered in rich red carpet, as were all the areas upstairs. Outside, there were wooden balconies on both the first and second floors that ran the entire length of the house. The property was large enough to house an extended family. But, Edward lived here alone.

It was early evening. The housekeeper had finished work an hour ago and was in her cottage. The groundsman was either in his hut or more likely having a few pints in the village before returning home with a kebab. Only the cook and Edward were in the manor house.

Tonight, the fifty year old, was wearing hiking gear. That wasn't usual at dinner time. Normally at this time of day he'd be in expensive trousers, shirt, jacket, and brogues. But, tonight he had a job to do. Nevertheless, he always had standards. His silver hair was cut in the style of a high ranking army officer – not too short but carefully trimmed with scissors and each hair singed at the ends to ensure the cut was millimetre precise. His face was shaved and moisturised with lotions he'd purchased in Paris. Behind his ears and on his throat he'd dabbed a few drops of a bespoke aftershave he had made for him by two perfumery experts in Rome. And before coming downstairs he'd had a jasmine-infused bath.

He was six feet tall and wiry, with the strength and agility of a swordsman. He'd never married because he preferred his solitude, though he'd had his fair share of female acquaintances. Women liked him. He was a gentleman, charming, clever, funny, and could regale an audience with tales about his adventures around the world while plying them with Bollinger champagne. Nobody in his social circle knew how he'd made his money. Some speculated he was a retired investment banker or lawyer; others a property magnet, stockbroker, former CEO of a major corporation, IT entrepreneur, physician, inventor, artist, or he'd inherited his money from his deceased parents. Based on his imparted knowledge, he could be any one of these things. His intellect and wisdom were outstanding. In truth, he was an orphan from an impoverished background who'd gained a double first at Oxford University before joining the Royal Engineers, after which he became a mercenary in Africa. That's when he made some real money. He'd killed miners. And he stole the mine's precious metals and jewels.

No one suspected that such a genteel, well-spoken and erudite man had such a legacy.

He wandered into the kitchen. His cook was standing by the Aga. He said, "Whatever you're cooking, it smells wonderful."

She didn't turn around. "It will be ready in five minutes. Tonight we're having braised oxtail in an onion and red wine sauce, sweet potatoes, green beans, and bacon lardons."

"Perfect. Should I sit in the dining room?"

"Yes. Pour yourself a glass of sherry. Please pour me one too."

He went to the dining room.

The cook's name was Hala. She was twenty seven years old and had gained employment in the estate one month ago after fleeing war-torn Syria. She was single and had no family in Britain. Edward paid her well. Her accommodation was free. He treated her kindly and never raised his voice to her. Plus, he let her eat with him. In her mind, he was the epitome of a man who'd grown up in a civilised society.

She served their food and carried two plates into the adjacent dining room. He was at the head of the table. She took her usual seat next to him on one side of the table. "I learned how to cook this from one of your recipe books."

Edward smiled. "Your English is improving."

"I read English books. And I listen when you talk." She ate her food and looked at him. "Thank you."

"For talking my own language?"

"Not just that. Thank you for everything."

Edward waved his hand. "We've spoken about this before. You don't need to keep thanking me. I need to eat; you cook. And you love cooking. It works out well for everyone." He placed some of the meat into his mouth. "Tomorrow is your day off. Do you have any plans?"

"I might go into the village."

"That's a good idea. Maybe go to the café. Buy a coffee. Read a newspaper or magazine."

"I... I worry I might be questioned. You know. Because I'm here illegally."

"Nonsense. No one questions anyone around these parts. You work for me. That's all people need to know." He patted his mouth with a crisp white napkin. "This isn't a police state."

She didn't understand.

Edward saw that in her expression. "It's not like Syria."

"Yes. Yes, it's not."

She was silent while she finished her meal.

Edward talked about anything that came into his head. He knew she would barely understand five percent of what he was saying, but he wanted her to listen to the tone of his voice and subliminally absorb his words.

She took the plates and cutlery into the kitchen and washed up.

She was standing by the sink as Edward walked in. His footsteps were muted by the noise of running water and the clatter of plates and pans bashing against each other. She was oblivious to his presence, thinking about his suggestion to go to the café tomorrow. Maybe she'd also take a walk along the coast. Certainly, she decided, she'd buy the pretty dress she'd spotted in the window of a clothes shop that specialised in selling retro and cool garments.

Edward stood behind her, placed one hand on her head, the other on her jaw, and snapped her neck. He let her drop to the floor, limp. He smiled, took a razor sharp knife from a magnetic strip, picked up her dead body, and carried her to one of the utilities rooms in the basement. There was a tool rack in there. He stripped her of all clothes, removed a hacksaw from the rack and started sawing. It was hard work dismembering a body. But it was worth the effort. He placed each body part into clear bags and put the bags into his large chest freezer. She'd make a fine meal.

Hala would have wanted it this way. For her there was no greater pleasure than feeding people.

Edward placed the skeleton and useless tissue into a bin bag. Later, he'd dispose of the bones in his grounds, somewhere close to the foxes' lair. He cleaned the floor and the tools he'd used to butcher her body. When finished, he went upstairs, poured himself a single malt whiskey, and made an international call. "I need a new cook. Usual drill – woman, traumatised, no family, desperate. Get her here as soon as possible. Standard rates." He ended the call, played Rachmaninov's Symphony Number 1 on his vinyl record player, sat in a leather armchair in his lounge and drank his scotch while gazing at the blue hue above the sea as the sun disappeared over the horizon.

He was happy. The kill had been perfect.

CHAPTER 2

Ben Sign and Tom Knutsen were in their two-bedroom flat in West Square, Southwark, London. The apartment was on the top floor of a converted Edwardian house. There were three flats below them. They were identical in size. Currently they were occupied by two arts students from a local university, a member of parliament who used his flat as a place to sleep during the week before seeing his family for weekends in his home in Cumbria, and two gay men who weren't an item but shared in common employment at a prestigious marketing firm. Sign and Knutsen didn't really know them. There was no point. Occupancy of the other flats was a revolving door – tenants came and went so frequently. Only Sign and Knutsen were the constants in the house.

Sign had procured the tenancy of the flat before Knutsen had moved in. As such, most of the décor was to his tastes. The bedrooms were reasonable in size and had spiral staircases in to the attic where two bathrooms had been installed. Spot lights were in the ceilings. Between both bedrooms was a hallway bathroom. The kitchen was small and contained meat hooks in the ceiling, hanging on which were vines of garlic bulbs, cherry tomatoes, rump of venison, brace of pheasants, string of grapes, and pots and pans. Global knives were fixed against a strip on the wall. The rest of the kitchen was standard – washing machine, dishwasher, oven and gas hob, and tiny cupboards. It was the large lounge that was centrepiece in the flat. It was strewn with antiquities and other artefacts – a six seater oak dining table, a neo-classical era chaise longue, a sofa, gold-framed oil paintings on the walls, bookshelves crammed with out-of-print non-fiction historical and academic works, a wall-mounted Cossack sabre, Persian rugs, two nineteenth century brass miners' lamps within which were candles, a five foot high artificial Japanese tree with a string of blue lights around it, seventeen century Scottish dirks in a glass cabinet, a laptop on a green-leather covered nine drawer mahogany writing desk, lamps, seafaring charts, and so many other objects of interest it made the mind swirl. On one of the shelves was a silk map that had been mounted between glass. It was the type worn under the garments of operatives working behind enemy lines. On its back were eight short paragraphs – in English, Dari, Pashwari, Tajikistan, Urdu, Uzbekistan, Turkmenistan, and Persian, together with the contact numbers of six UK diplomatic missions. The paragraphs asked for food and water, promised the reader that the bearer of the map wouldn't hurt him, and requested safe passage to British forces or its allies. On the front of the map was the title AFGHANISTAN & ENVIRONS, ESCAPE MAP. At one end of the lounge it was uncluttered. All it had was three armchairs facing each other, next to a fireplace, and tiny adjacent wooden coffee tables.

Sign was a former high ranking MI6 officer who was tipped to be the next chief of MI6 before he threw the opportunity away and decided to become a private detective rather than playing politics at the highest level in Western Intelligence.

Knutsen was a former Metropolitan Police undercover cop who'd resigned from the force after executing a criminal in cold blood because the scumbag had killed the woman Knutsen was in love with.

Sign, too, carried the baggage of tragedy. His wife had been murdered in South America while working there for an NGO.

Though both tall, neither men were physically alike. Sign was fifty years old; Knutsen thirty five. Sign's hair was a mix of grey and black; Knutsen's cropped hair was blond. Sign had the physique of a long distance runner; Knutsen looked like a middle weight boxer. Sign spoke like an aristocrat; Knutsen had the drawl of a south London geezer. Sign preferred to wear immaculate clothes from Saville Row; Knutsen was happy in shorts, T-shirt, and flip flops.

Though Knutsen had gained a first at Exeter University and Sign's intellect was through the roof, on paper they should have had nothing in common. And yet, somehow they gelled. They'd worked as equal partners in the private detective firm for eighteen months. Sign had selected Knutsen to be his cohort, having rejected numerous CVs of former intelligence officers and special forces operatives. There was something about Knutsen that Sign liked. He'd spotted a rebel. Sign too was a rebel. And he wasn't as posh as some people thought. He'd come from a humble background and had achieved academic and career brilliance purely on merit. Sign liked Knutsen. The former cop had been an orphan and was raised in dreadful conditions, yet had obtained so much before throwing it all away. Knutsen was also totally loyal to Sign and was fearless. Sign – once the man who'd worn the silk escape and evasion map under his vest and had succeeded in so many daring feats in his dramatic life – was no longer a man of extreme action. Like all middle age men, he now preferred to use his brain. By contrast, Knutsen was still young enough to go into a fight and fire a pistol with pinpoint accuracy. The men complimented each other.

It was mid-afternoon. Sign said to Knutsen, "I've marinated a whole salmon in teriyaki sauce, chillies, pepper, garlic, and honey. It's been in the fridge overnight. It will need to be baked in foil for an hour on high heat or two hours on low heat. Does it sound tempting for dinner?"

Knutsen nodded. "I'd have been happy with a burger but yeah I'll run with your salmon thing."

"Excellent, dear chap. I believe the perfect accompaniments are lemon and basil noodles, deep fried broccoli, and a drizzle of saffron and peanut sauce that I've made by hand. I've also taken the liberty of buying a bottle of Gewürztraminer from my vintner. It will complement the dish."

"A cold beer would have done." Knutsen asked, " I presume I need to get changed into the suit this afternoon because we've got clients arriving?"

"We both need to get into suits. But don't expect the clients to be similarly attired. They're poor and desperate."

One hour later, they were in their smartest suits and sitting in their armchairs. The downstairs intercom buzzed. Knutsen spoke on the flat's intercom. A man introduced himself. Knutsen buzzed him in and waited by the flat's front door. After thirty seconds, Knutsen escorted a man and women into the lounge and told them to sit on the sofa. Knutsen sat in his armchair, opposite Sign. The clients had swarthy complexions. The woman was wearing a cleaner's uniform that had a London hotel name printed on it; the man was wearing jeans, T-shirt, and a puffer jacket that he'd bought in an east end market.

The man asked, "Which one of you is Ben Sign?"

"That will be me." Sign gestured to his colleague. "This is Tom Knutsen. He is my business colleague. You may speak openly in front of us."

The man nodded. "Mr. Sign, thank you for seeing us. When you and I spoke on the phone I gave you brief details of our problem. I'd like to give you the full picture." He glanced at the woman before returning his attention on Sign. "You are not police officers?"

"We are not, and nor do we work for any other government agency. Anything you tell us in this room will remain strictly confidential."

The man clasped his hands. "We are both from Syria. My name is Marwan Zoghbi. This my wife, Samar. We arrived In London thirty one days ago. I drive a taxi. My wife works in…"

"Yes, we can see." Sign placed the tips of his fingers together. "You are in Britain illegally." It wasn't a question.

The man hesitated. "We have paperwork that says we have a right to work in the UK. The paperwork is fake."

"Where was the false documentation made?"

"I don't know. It was given to us when we arrived in London." Marwan bowed his head. "My parents and our daughter were killed by a barrel bomb in Aleppo. Samar's family were slaughtered by Islamic State. We are English teachers. Except we're not teachers now. We have to be invisible. So, we take the lowest paid jobs that other people don't want. It's so bad in Syria. We tried to stay on as long as we could, but the chaos became too much. We used up our savings to get here. We weren't the only ones."

"Of course you weren't." Sign added, "You're safe now, so long as you avoid the authorities."

It was Samar who replied. "We've heard there might be leniency on people who've fled war zones and live in England. But we're not here to talk about us."

Sign was silent.

Samar continued. "We came to Europe on a boat. We crossed the Mediterranean with over a hundred other refugees. Then we were smuggled through countries. Marwan and I made it to Britain. Some others were less fortunate. Do you know what it's like to live illegally in a country?"

Sign nodded. "I do."

"But, do you know what it's like to live amongst other illegals?"

"No, I don't. I used to work for British Intelligence. I worked overseas alone."

Samar breathed in deeply. "Illegals are a kind of network. In London we know each other and we support each other. It has to be that way. Who else can help us? We buy pay-as-you-go mobile phones. We text each other because calls are too expensive. But it's still communication. When we were on the boat there was a young woman. Her name's Hala. We don't know her family name. She was nice. She got a job as a cook at a big house in the country. I don't know where. She wasn't allowed to have a phone."

Knutsen asked, "Why not?"

"When she arrived in England she was told that her employer was very... particular on these matters. He was apparently worried that phone calls could be traced and therefore his illegal employees could be located by the police. It was his rule. No phone. Not even calls from a phone box to the rest of us. I suppose it wasn't an unusual demand, except..."

Marwan leaned forward. "Something is wrong. Hala got the job at the big house, wherever it is, and ever since no one has heard from her. But that's not where it ends. I'll tell you how it works. The people smugglers get us to England. When you arrive you're told what job you'll have. But we're never told what part of the country we'll be working in. It's scary but also exciting. We swap notes with other illegals. Then we're," he was searching for the right word, "funnelled. The smugglers use cut outs to get us to the place we need to be. So, we're handed over from one smuggler to another. I suppose they do that minimise risk. In our case four cut outs in England got us to London. The last man who dropped us here would have known the man who handed us over to him, but he wouldn't have known the third and fourth smuggler in the chain, nor the captain who sailed us across the sea, nor the men in Syria who got us out of that Godforsaken hellhole." He rubbed his face. "We're not just here to represent Hala. There are other concerned illegals that've lived here longer than us. They work in London. Like us, they're very worried, because they know twelve people they travelled with to get to England. Those people have vanished. Over the duration of the last year, twelve illegals were told they'd be working in a big house. A remote place. My wife and I and our friends think they all work in the same house."

Sign said, "But, you have no proof of that?"

"No." Marwan looked shaken. "There are however consistent themes. All of our friends have told us the same thing that Hala told us when she arrived in England. The house was owned by a rich Englishman. The house was large, had a lot of land, and needed staff. That's all we know. It's odd though."

Sign nodded. "Odd because the job doesn't fit the usual profile. Thousands of refugees are, to use your word, funnelled into more mainstream jobs appropriate for illegals. Taxi work, hotel cleaning, crop picking, anything where you can stay under the radar by being one of many in a company. I would suggest that Hala and the twelve other people are single and have no friends or family in this country."

"That's right."

"Gender?"

"Seven women. Six men."

"Age?"

"All of them in their twenties."

Sign was deep in thought. "What is the relationship between the other illegals who asked you to come here today and the missing people? Friends?"

"Friends?" Marwan shook his head. "Fellow survivors would be more accurate. We're worried about the thirteen people. Or, maybe we shouldn't be worried. Perhaps they're fine. It could be the house needs thirteen members of staff. I'm just surprised that none of them have broken the rule and discretely called one of us."

Sign shook his head. "I suspect timing and logic is everything. Give me names, months of their employment, nationality, and job description."

Marwan and Samar took it in turn to reply.

"Ahmed was employed as a gardener last December. He's Iraqi."

"Beydaan was employed in the same month as a housekeeper. She's from Somalia."

"Lina was also employed in December as a cook. She's from Afghanistan."

"Ibrahim was employed last February as a gardener. He's Libyan."

"Chit is from Myanmar, or Burma, or whatever you call the place. He arrived last April. He's a groundsman."

"Oleksander was employed in April as a housekeeper. She's from the Crimea."

"Fatimah arrived in June. She's from the Yemen and is a cook."

"Gbenga started work in July, as a gardener. He's from Nigeria."

"Aland was employed as a gardener in August. He's Iraqi."

"Khadija is from Libya. She arrived in England in September. She's a housekeeper."

"A'isha started work as a cook in September. She's Syrian."

"Zelimxan is from Chechnya. He began working as a gardener in October."

"Hala is the thirteenth. She is Syrian and is employed in the big house as a cook."

Sign memorised the details. "And no one in your network has heard anything from them over the last year? No phone calls? Letters? Social media posts? Text messages? WhatsApp messages? Anything?"

Marwan replied, "Nothing, Mr. Sign."

Sign was quiet for ten seconds. "We'll take your case."

Knutsen looked at him. "There is no case. Maybe the thirteen illegal immigrants are working at different houses. Or, if they're working at the same house, maybe it needs thirteen staff."

Sign replied, "It is improbable that numerous property owners have contacts with people smugglers. So, let's assume it's one house that is employing the thirteen people." He looked at Marwan and Samar and repeated, "We'll take your case."

Marwan shifted in his seat and looked embarrassed. "Money is...well, we can all pay you ten percent of our weekly salaries for however long it takes. But, we don't have cash to pay you now."

"As an English teacher you may be aware of the legal phrase *pro bono publico*."

Marwan nodded. "Latin term *for the public good*." He frowned. "You'll work for free? Mr. Sign, the reason I came to you was because you are the best detective. You are highly respected. I've read about you. And I hear you are utterly discreet. Why would someone like you work for free?"

Sign turned to face him. "Do you want an honest answer? Or do you want a half-truth?"

"An honest answer, sir."

Sign replied in his precise tone. "I've been in so many war zones. For a period of time it can be exhilarating. But after a while fatigue and fear kick in. At that stage one just wants to go somewhere without guns, artillery, and airstrikes. There are only so many times you can witness death, or even worse try to resuscitate or patch up the injured who are blatantly dying and have no chance of recovery. You and your good wife came to England due to noble reasons. You wanted peace. And you wanted to contribute to our society. At the moment you are short of a bob or two, as us English say. It would be a travesty for me to take what little money you have. And it would be a travesty if I didn't establish whether the thirteen illegals are safe. I owe that to you and to your friends. You told me you both taught English. Be more specific with your areas of expertise."

Marwan replied, "English language."

Samar answered, "I taught English literature and poetry."

Sign nodded. "Leave all of your personal details with Mr. Knutsen. I need to know dates of birth, languages, professional accreditations, and anything else that matters."

Samar said, "We're worried that…"

Sign snapped, "You don't need to worry with us. Remember – this is a safe place. And this is what I'll do for you. I'll get you legal residency in this country. And I'll get both of you jobs in a school or university, depending on your preference. I regret to say that I cannot fully extend that courtesy to your friends. There is only so much I can do before questions are asked. But, if I solve this case, I will lobby hard to help your friends."

Marwan and Samar were in shock.

"You'd work for free and do that for us?" Samar was incredulous.

"Yes."

Marwan asked, "Do you think the thirteen people are safe? Are my wife and I, and our friends, crazy to have mentioned all of this to you? It feels mad when I hear myself speak about this, now that I think about it."

"You are a concerned person, and soon you and your wife will be concerned legal citizens of the United Kingdom of Great Britain and Northern Ireland." Sign's mind was racing. "Where did you arrive in England?"

Samar answered. "Lowestoft. In Europe we were given false passports that showed we were residents of Germany. We crossed the Channel in a ferry from Rotterdam."

"Do you know the names of any of the four smugglers in England who got you to London?"

Marwan and Samar shook their heads.

"Did you memorise their vehicle number plates?"

Marwan replied, "We travelled at night. Everything happened so quickly. We were put in the back of transit vans. The rear number plates were covered with black plastic. I suppose the plastic was removed before we were driven off."

"Description of the smugglers?"

"Which ones? The four in England? The five who got us across Europe? The Mediterranean ship crew? The ones in Syria?"

"I'm only interested in the ones in England. In particular I'm most interested in the one who met you in Lowestoft. He's the person who allocated you and others like you your jobs."

Samar said, "I'd say he was in his thirties. He was British, I'm sure of that. The three others spoke with Eastern European accents. I can't be sure where exactly they were from. They wore hats and scarves. Probably they were also in their thirties, but it was hard to tell."

"Do you suspect that the people who smuggled you to London are the same people who smuggled the thirteen to the big house?"

Marwan answered. "It's the same people. The man in Lowestoft was the England boss. He wasn't like the others in this country. He carried a clipboard. He had some kind of authority – you know, that air about him. He was quick with his orders. I didn't want to be a taxi driver. He told me to shut up. I was in his country, he told me. I'd do whatever he wanted, he said. Hala was different. She was by our side in the docks when she was told to be a chef at the house. She was happy. She likes cooking. All of the others I've mentioned – the twelve other illegals – came through the Lowestoft route. Our friends told us that. I guess it's not the only people-smuggling route into Britain, and things change. Maybe the smugglers swap routes before the cops wise up."

Sign drummed his fingers on his adjacent coffee table. "Smugglers are adept at improvising, but if it ain't broke don't fix it. The Rotterdam-Lowestoft route is clearly working and considerably less risky than trying to land people covertly on, say, a beach in Devon. Also, there is an issue of trust. Lowestoft boss man has at least three people, maybe more, who he can trust to get men and women like you to the places he wants you to work. The smugglers will individually live at various points in the supply chain. To change a UK entry point would be annoying. Lowestoft boss man's team wouldn't take kindly to having to drive across the country to pick up illegals."

Samar said, "My instinct is that the Lowestoft man runs the human trafficking operation in the UK. Some of our friends made it through the Calais-Dover route, but they did so without help. We've not heard of other smuggling operations in the UK. Lowestoft man runs a…"

"Cartel." Sign stood. "Mr. Knutsen – please get all of Marwan and Samar's personal details. Tomorrow we set to work. Good day to you, Mr. and Mrs. Zoghbi. The consultation's over. I must leave now, as I have an appointment with my barber." He walked out of the flat.

Two hours later he returned. He changed out of his suit and donned more casual attire. After placing the salmon in the oven he poured two glasses of calvados, lit the fire, and sat opposite Knutsen in his armchair. "What do you think?"

"About your haircut or about today's consultation?"

"The latter, of course."

Knutsen sipped his drink. "I think you're off your fucking rocker, mate. The whole thing's a waste of time. Plus, we're not getting paid."

Sign laughed. "*Off my fucking rocker.* You do have a bulletproof command of the English language and rapier ability to cause one to question one's sanity." He stared at the fire. In a quiet and more tempered tone he said, "I however am not insane. One must use one's imagination. The case could be nothing. Or it could be something that reveals a systematic plot." He looked at Knutsen. "When you were a police officer would you laugh in the face of a mother who came to you saying her son or daughter had been missing for forty eight hours?"

"I..." Knutsen lowered his head. "No. Of course not. I'd have treated the situation seriously, even if I wondered whether the son or daughter had simply run away."

"And what if both her son and daughter had vanished, alongside eleven other children in the mother's neighbourhood?"

"A police task force would be set up. They'd start with multiple assumptions – kidnap, abduction into a cult, slavery, murder."

Sign nodded. "You and I are now a task force. We are in the absent company of the rationale minds of vulnerable adults. We can only have one assumption – we're dealing with a serial killer who's murdered at least thirteen refugees."

"That's a bloody leap of logic."

"It's a hypothesis based on what little we already know. The thirteen who all came through the Rotterdam-Lowestoft smuggling route were sent to work at a big house. They were housekeepers, groundsmen, and cooks. They were not permitted to communicate with any other illegals that voyaged here with them. That in itself is unusual. More unusual is the fact that not one of them ignored their master's instruction about communicating with others outside of his estate. When I told Marwan and Samar that timing was crucial I was referring to the duration of each person's employment. When one gets a new job, for the first month or so one tends to play by the rule book. After that, one tends to bend the rules. There are two scenarios in our case. The first is that they stayed at the house for say a month, then moved on to other employment."

"In which case, after they got a new job why didn't they buy a phone or write letters to people they'd fled here with?"

"Precisely. The second option is they were murdered before they emerged out of the month-long honeymoon period." Sign's voice was distant as he added, "There are numerous drug smugglers who swamp our shores with narcotics. But people smuggling is a more precarious science for the simple reason that one has to deal with the foibles of the human brain. Put more bluntly, there are very few people smugglers in Britain because it's a very tricky business. I would hazard a guess that Lowestoft man and his crew are the only UK-based organised crime unit that traffics human beings. The owner of the big house has access to Lowestoft man. Other estate-owners don't. We're dealing with one man and one house. That's my hypothesis."

"They work for him for about a month. Then he kills them."

"It's a theory."

"But a plausible one." Knutsen finished his drink. "Serial killer orders his victims from Lowestoft man. The profile of each person must meet the serial killer's requirements. He takes his time with them after they've arrived. He kills them when he's ready and before they break ranks and ignore his communications rules."

Sign let his imagination run. "The communications angle is the pragmatic side of timings. Get rid of them before they make a call that can be triangulated to his house. But, I also wonder if there's something else. Why not kill them on the first day they arrive at his estate?" He placed his hands together in front of his mouth, as if he was praying. "He wants to get to know them. Yes, that's it. And the only reason why he wants that is because he wants to kill them in a way that honours them. He needs to know their hobbies, likes, dislikes, what makes them laugh, and cry. The pleasure gained from killing them derives from the knowledge he has about his victims. He's playing God. If I'm right, we're dealing with a highly intelligent psychopath. He's killing people who should never be here. If I'm wrong then I'm a fool who's off his rocker and will gladly take on the chin any abuse you give me."

Knutsen nodded. "That's my job. Trouble is, mate, you haven't been wrong in the past."

Edward was sitting next to the fire in the reading room. He'd eaten his dinner and was relaxing with a book and glass of Casillero Del Diablo Merlot red wine. Later, he'd put on some classical music, or maybe watch a movie on the lounge's widescreen flat TV. But, for now he wanted peace and quiet. His meal had been basic – chicken, chips, and mixed vegetables. He was looking forward to the imminent arrival of his new cook. Hopefully she'd be able to cook him something more wholesome and tasty; perhaps something spicy that derived from the cuisine of her home country. For now he had to cook for himself. He was a good cook, but when left to his own devices he typically couldn't be bothered to rustle up a five star plate of grub.

He heard a weird noise in the grounds. It sounded like a pig that was choking. He placed his book and wine down, went to the cellar, picked up a crowbar, and went outside. Tonight he was wearing a thick cotton shirt, thin jumper, jacket, corduroy trousers, and brogues. His appearance was every inch that of a country squire. He followed the noise. It was coming from somewhere close to the wooden hut where his groundsman Zelimxan lived. There was no doubt the Chechen was home, given his lights were on, music was playing inside the property, and as usual there was a strong odour of marijuana coming out of the house. The pig-like noise stopped as Edward approached the hut. He heard rustling through the nearby bushes. He knocked on Zelimxan's door.

Zelimxan opened the door. "Hello, sir." He was holding a can of beer in one hand. Behind him was a fog of weed smoke. "Did you hear the badgers? They come here every night because I feed them. The male butts the door to tell me his family wants feeding. I give them leftovers from dinner. Male feeds first and he'll kick the shit out of his wife and kids if they try to stop him. After he's eaten he lets the rest eat."

"And what happened tonight?"

"It was my fault. I didn't think. I grabbed a kebab on the way back from the village. Ate half of it. Threw the rest outside for the badgers. Thing is, I forgot I'd filled the kebab with chilli sauce. Male badger took a bite. And that's when you heard him. He doesn't like chilli one bit." He laughed.

"I heard them in the undergrowth. They ran back to their set when I approached your house."

"Do you fancy a beer, sir? I've got a four-pack in the fridge."

Edward contemplated the question. "Why not."

Zelimxan turned.

Edward slammed his crowbar into the back of the groundsman's head. When he was on the ground, he struck the nape of his neck three times, as if he was dispatching a fish. Zelimxan was dead.

Today wasn't supposed to be Zelimxan's dead day. This wasn't planned. Still, sometimes Edward liked to improvise. He returned to the manor house, placed the crowbar in the kitchen sink, put cloths and bleach into a bucket that was half full of sudsy water, obtained a spade from one of the utility rooms, and returned to the hut. He lifted Zelimxan onto his shoulder and fireman carried him to a spot of heath land, amid woods and near to the badger set. For the next two hours he dug a deep hole, tossed the dead Chechen in there, covered the hole with soil, and replaced the squares of surface turf that he'd cut out before digging. It would only take a few days before the heath bound and the grave would be invisible. In any case, no one came here. But the grave was on the badgers' route across the grounds. They were precise animals and always navigated the estate in the same channels of undergrowth. When the grave was invisible, he'd plant a fruit tree in there. Zelimxan's rotting corpse would feed the soil. The tree would flourish. And in less than a year's time it would ripen and produce a crop of apples that the badgers could feed on. The gardener would have wanted his death to be this way. He liked the badgers. Edward returned to the hut, removed all traces of blood, turned off the music and lights, locked the door and returned to the main house.

He cleaned and stowed away his equipment, washed his hands, changed clothes, put his soiled garments in the washing machine, poured himself another glass of red wine, and put a vinyl record of Niccolò Paganini's *A Minor Caprice* on his player. It was time for him to relax. There was nothing sexual in his killings; but the feeling after a murder was the same feeling as one felt after love making. It was pure relief, calmness, a sense of not being in this world, satisfied tiredness, and overall a conviction that one had got the job done. It was the greatest emotion.

He didn't think of himself as a serial killer. Such a label, he believed, was a gross misinterpretation of his actions. In his mind he was a trained huntsman; a ghillie; someone who fed the deers in winter and culled them in warmer months so they couldn't overpopulate the planet. It was all about necessity and maintaining a healthy food chain. And illegal immigrants, of all people, needed to be lured to his estate and culled.

There was only one employee left on the state – Khadija, from Libya. She needed culling.

He made a call to the people smuggler in Lowestoft. "What is the news on my cook replacement?"

The man replied, "You'll have her in a couple of days."

"Good. I also need a male groundsman and a female housekeeper. As quick as you can."

CHAPTER 3

At seven AM the following morning, Knutsen showered, shaved, and dressed in jeans, T-shirt, and jumper. He entered the West Square lounge. The flat was chilly, in part because weather experts had predicted the preceding night would see external temperatures plummet to freezing; but also because the flat's temperature dial had been playing up over the last few weeks. He made a mental note to call a repair man to get the dial fixed. The heating hadn't bothered him and Sign since it'd become temperamental. But now they were heading towards winter they needed to resolve the problem. He lit a fire and entered the kitchen. Sign was in there, making breakfast. Knutsen put the kettle on. "What are you doing?"

Sign unwrapped a brown parcel that had been bound in twine. "Look at these beauties. Arbroath Smokies. I ordered them from Scotland and they were couriered to me by train. It's a long standing tradition. Previous generations would also order them and wait until the Flying Scotsman would bring them south. All of them ate the Smokies at breakfast."

Knutsen poured himself a mug of coffee. "I can see they're fish, but I've never heard of Arbroath Smokies."

"Smoked haddock. They're cured a few miles north of Arbroath, hence their name. And take a peek at these smashers." He picked up two large eggs from a box containing a dozen. "Goose eggs. I ordered them from a farmer in Lincolnshire. I will be frying them and placing them on top of our fish. I'd recommend keeping the yolk runny, but of course tastes vary."

"Runny is fine."

"Excellent, dear chap." He picked up a loaf of bread. "I took the liberty of purchasing this from our local baker, while you were still sleeping this morning. It's as fresh as a daisy. A couple of slices, not toasted, will be all we'll need to compliment the excellent fish and eggs. There'll be no need for salt or pepper. The fish packs enough punch."

Knutsen smiled. "Can I have ketchup with mine?"

Sign wagged his finger and faked a school masterly stern expression. "Don't be naughty, Mr. Knutsen."

"I'd have been happy with a bowl of cereal for breakfast."

"I'm trying to educate your palate." Sign chuckled. "The task is however like trying to push water uphill." He pointed at the lounge. "On one of the coffee tables are today's copies of The Financial Times, Telegraph, and yesterday's copy of the New York Times. Why don't you take your brew to your armchair, scan the papers, and brief me on current global issues. It will take me five minutes to prepare breakfast. So, you have five minutes to establish the contemporary machinations of the world."

Knutsen walked into the lounge while calling out, "Didn't you get any tabloids?"

"Tut, tut, dear chap. Don't play the thick yob with me. It doesn't befit a man who gained a first class degree from Exeter."

"I cheated."

"No you didn't."

"How do you know?"

"I spoke to your professors. They said you were one of their brightest pupils."

"You spoke to my professors?!"

"I had to do my due diligence before going into business with you."

Knutsen sighed, picked up one of the papers, and flicked through the pages. "Loony tunes US president still wants to build Hadrian's Wall around Mexico. Meanwhile, France is building an electric fence on its border with Belgium to keep out wild boars – something to do with the boars infecting French pigs. Iran is still mental, but isn't hiding the fact. Russia and Saudi Arabia deny they're mental. Looks like Brexit will be complete when our generation's grandchildren are retired. Stuff about immigration, blah blah. It appears that terrorists are having a few weeks off because they've not been up to much recently. Some rap star's married a stripper. Our retiring prime minister says she's considering going on *I'm A Celebrity Get Me Out Of Here.* Oh, and our home secretary's got caught sniffing coke. Not much else to report."

Sign placed their breakfast on the dining table. "And how much of that did you just make up?"

Knutsen sat at the table and picked up his cutlery. "The sad truth is – none of it, mate." He tucked in to his food. "More important than all that shit is that we haven't got a starting point that will give us a trail to the kill house. I still have doubts as to whether we should have taken on the illegals case."

Sign popped a chunk of haddock into his mouth. "We will have to manufacture a starting point and create an audit trail that leads us to Lowestoft man. Once we reach the end of the trail, we can get to the serial killer."

"We go from one smuggler to another on the UK side of the Rotterdam-Lowestoft route, and we do so in reverse."

"Precisely."

Knutsen said, "This is going to require some nifty foot work. And it's going to be extremely dangerous."

Sign wiped his bread in his egg's yolk. "Were you ever blown when you were an undercover cop?"

"No."

"Splendid. Are your former criminal contacts still active, or are they all locked up?"

"Half and half. I deliberately let some of them get away so I could use them to get to bigger fish. It was a balancing act. Trouble is, sometimes I had to let some of the big fish get away to get to their psychotic foot soldiers." Knutsen was thoroughly enjoying his meal. "It always depended on the priorities of the day. Catch a man-eating shark? Or catch a shoal of piranhas?"

"I understand your analogies." Sign wiped his mouth with a napkin. "We need to meet a shark who may be able to give us access to the smuggling route. He may not be a human trafficker himself, but he may know a man who knows a man et cetera." He finished his food. "We'll need to go undercover."

Knutsen frowned. "You've never worked undercover law enforcement."

"I haven't. But I have posed as a Norwegian shipping magnet who wanted to buy a high speed naval frigate from a brutal South African arms dealer; acted as a freelance political consultant in order to lure an Iranian general to Brussels and get him to spill the beans on Iran's nuclear program; used false flag intelligence agency identities against a variety of very nasty targets; successfully resisted torture in Russia; fished for salmon in Canada, alongside a Japanese exporter of vast quantities of heroin; placed a gun against the head of an Islamic terrorist bomb maker who up until that point thought I was an architect who was willing to sell him the structural plans of a prominent high rise building in New York; and sat in a tent with Taliban commanders who believed I was a disgruntled American army officer who was willing to sell out the location of US black sites in Afghanistan, providing he got paid for doing so. I could give you numerous other examples. I don't belittle what you did in your undercover work in London. But if your real identity was discovered, you had the recourse to call in the cavalry. I was less fortunate. In the places I operated overseas, I had no safety net." He took the plates into the kitchen. "I've spent my entire adult life under cover, knowing that if I didn't hold my nerve and think on my feet then I'd be dead."

Knutsen was silent, before saying, "Yeah, it was a dumb thing for me to say. Particularly to someone with your track record."

Sign returned to the lounge, sat in his armchair, and smiled. "It wasn't a dumb thing. You made the comment because quite rightly you were being proud of your accomplishments. Like me, you metamorphosed into different characters to do the job in hand. The only differences between us are you used to be a cop and I was a spy; we worked different geographical zones; and you defended UK law, whereas I broke other countries' laws."

Knutsen sat in his armchair. "What kind of criminal do we need to get alongside?"

"Ideally someone who forges documentation for illegal immigrants."

"I don't know anyone like that."

Sign was deep in thought. "Think about any of your criminal contacts who might have need for a forger."

Knutsen racked his brain. "There's a guy I know who brings in human organs from Africa. I presume he needs falsified UK documents in order to sell the organs to hospitals and the like. He might know a forger."

"A good thought. Forgers are a rare commodity, particularly ones who can successful mimic British legal documentation. I doubt there's more than one person who fits that bill in London." Sign nodded. "We meet organ donor. He leads us to forger. Forger either leads us directly to the Lowestoft smuggling route, or he leads us to someone else who can. The priority is identifying Lowestoft man."

"Perhaps the fourth smuggler might be able to tell us where the kill house is?"

"He might, but I'm not hopeful. I think Lowestoft man uses different UK-based traffickers to get the illegals to the house. The serial killer's not in London, I'm sure of that. His property's somewhere rural and remote. So, we must get to Lowestoft man and to do that we must follow, upstream, the London-Lowestoft river. The key player in that river is Lowestoft man. He's smuggler number one. The others are smugglers two, three, and four. Our starting point is smuggler four. For the sake of convenience, we will give the four smugglers names. 'Lowestoft Man' is already in use, so must stick. Now, what should we name the other three people?"

Knutsen laughed. "How about Tom, Dick, and Harry. Like in…"

"The movie The Great Escape. No, that won't do. The names refer to three tunnels. We're dealing with one tunnel, or more accurately a single chain. The men are working together. Their codenames must represent a unified and collaborative purpose. I think The Three Tenors is more appropriate. Lowestoft Man is smuggler one and is the conductor. Smuggler two is Plácido Domingo. Smuggler three is José Carreras. Smuggler four is Luciano Pavarotti. We'll drop the forenames of the tenors."

Knutsen agreed. "We get to Organ Smuggler; then Forger; then Domingo; then Carreras; then Pavarotti. And one by one they lead us to Lowestoft Man…"

"…who leads us to the kill house and the serial killer who owns the property. It's a plan, though we may have some bumps along the way. We must at all times be prepared to improvise if our train becomes derailed. I suspect Pavarotti is the only link in the chain who knows the identity of Lowestoft Man. I hope I'm wrong, but I doubt I am. If I constructed a smuggling route I'd minimise knowledge of my true identity. Therefore I must conclude that a highly successful human trafficker has done the same."

Knutsen said, "We're going to knock down the line of dominos. But, any one of those dominos could kill us to prevent us getting to the next domino."

"Ah, the life we lead."

"Shouldn't we just take this case to the cops?"

Sign shook his head. "It is ever thus in our line of work that one must weigh up one life against the lives of others. If we open this up to law enforcement they will gain infinite knowledge about a large number of illegal immigrants in this country. They will be expelled. I can't have that on my conscience."

"They're illegals. Maybe they should be expelled."

"They're scared people who don't want any trouble. We must let them have the peace they deserve. No, this is not a job for the police. In any case, we're better equipped to deal with this problem because we have skills the police don't have, and we're off the radar. There is also the small matter that the police may laugh in our faces if we present the case to them. There's not a drop of evidence that a series of murders may have taken place. All we have to go on is circumstance, my gut instinct, and the guts instincts of our clients. I made a pledge to our clients that I'd get them legal status in Britain. That would be impossible if the police were involved."

"Why do you care about Marwan and Samar?"

"Didn't you notice what was wrong during our consultation with them?" Sign placed a log on the fire. "Samar's left hand was twitching. She was blinking at twice the normal rate of a calm person. Her breathing was too rapid. Marwan kept crossing and uncrossing his legs. His hands were agitated. He didn't know where to put them. He kept looking at the window, as if he was expecting uniformed men to burst through. Samar and Marwan are suffering anxiety. Animals shiver to shake off fear after they've escaped a predator. It's a brilliant strategy. It's why they don't suffer stress-related disease. And after they've shaken off the fear, they go about their business as if nothing's happened. The problem Marwan, Samar, and others like them have is they've been shaking for months, maybe longer. The predator is still hunting them. And in their case the predator is the British government. That is unacceptable. So I have to step in and tranquilise the predator and let its prey move to higher ground. Why do I care? Because I hate seeing Goliath beat David. And I have an instinctual need to help the vulnerable in our world."

Knutsen digested Sign's words. "You're a very good man, Ben."

"As are you, dear chap." Sign's voice was more authoritative when he said, "We must spend the day creating our cover and strategy for meeting Organ Smuggler. Once we've stress tested the route in to him, you must call the chap."

Edward strolled around his grounds. The air was crisp. Leaves had dropped from trees. Normally his groundsman would rake them up before cutting the grass with a ride-on mower. That would have to wait until Edward got his new gardener. He walked up the long, sweeping driveway. Low-lying mist was static by his ankles; there wasn't a breath of wind. Frost was on the ground. His brogues made the frost crunch with every footfall. There was enough fallen fruit deliberately left on the heath to feed the badgers and birds through winter. The squirrels, too, would be fine given Edward regularly topped up a six foot high wooden feeder with nuts. Ahead of him, a fox jogged across the driveway. It wasn't scared of Edward, though was cautious and kept its distance. It was doing its usual early morning foray for food. Most likely it was looking to kill a rabbit on the farmer's field, though the task was fraught given the rabbits were probably hiding from the cold in their burrows. The tree blossom had gone. Berries were withered. Soon, the mile long steep track to the estate's gates would start cracking up. As he walked, he memorised jobs he'd do in person until he had a new groundsman – creosote the empty peacock pens; clean and tidy the groundsman's hut; ditto the cook's gate house; break the thin ice on the fish pond outside his front door; order new oil for the external tank that fuelled the mansion; bring to the house a wheelbarrow of logs that were piled up outside the distant double garage; fit new bulbs into some of the ground's lamps; spray blast the wooden balconies that were prone to becoming slimy during the summer; and dead head the large flowers so they could flourish in Spring. These were holding-pattern jobs. Running an estate required staff. But, Edward was anything but lazy. He was always prepared to roll up his sleeves and get stuck in to jobs, when required. He returned to his home. Khadija, his housekeeper, was in there. She was cleaning the lounge. He made a pot of tea, poured the drink into two mugs, and walked into the lounge. "Tea break. I've made it how you like. Lots of sugar."

Khadija turned off the vacuum cleaner and smiled. "Thank you, sir." She took her mug from him.

The Libyan's English was still poor. Edward was sympathetic to that and tried to dumb down his sentences and keep them brief. "Cold outside."

"Yes, sir. Very cold."

"Is your cottage warm enough at night?"

"Warm, yes."

"No problems?"

"No problems. Lovely house."

Edward smiled. "Good." He pretended to look worried. "Hala and Zelimxan have gone. They've got jobs in the north of England or Scotland, I think."

"Why they go, sir?"

"I don't know. I thought I paid them well."

"You give us good money and houses." She sat by the dining table and sipped her tea. "Maybe they want to live in the cities."

"Maybe. They're young." He stood by the glass doors. The sea was calm; the tide was out, exposing the sandy beach. "I'm getting a new cook and gardener."

"You want me to help before they come?"

He turned and smiled sympathetically. "Khadija, that's very kind but you have enough jobs in the house. Anyway, I can cook and it's winter. There's less to do outside in winter."

"Still jobs."

"The new people will be here soon."

"Okay, sir."

He decided to change the subject. "I know you love swimming in the sea down there. Too cold now."

"Yes sir, but I save my money to buy a protection suit."

"A wet suit?"

"It's not wet, sir."

"It's just what we call them. You'll go swimming when you have one?"

"Yes, sir. I don't want to wait until sun gets warmer."

"Then that's settled. I'll buy you one. It will be my gift." He swigged his tea. "Please clean the upstairs kitchenette. In particular can you clean the oven?"

"Yes sir."

"Thankyou Khadija." He smiled and walked out of the room. He needed to get changed into more robust clothing and commence his chores in his estate. Today was not Khadija's death day.

Sign was sitting opposite Knutsen in their lounge. "So let's run through this one more time. Where were you born?"

Knutsen was exasperated. "I've met him before, you know?! And I maintained my cover without your help."

"You met Organ Smuggler over four years ago. His memory might be hazy. Yours can't be. Place of birth?"

Knutsen huffed. "Epping. I grew up in Loughton, Essex, until I was eighteen. Then I hit London."

"Which schools did you go to?"

"Staples Road Primary and Debden Park high school."

"Who was your favourite teacher?"

"You didn't ask me these questions earlier today."

Sign leaned forward. "Who knows what questions might pop up if a gangster's put his pistol against your eyeball."

Knutsen sighed. "My favourite teacher was Mr. Richards. He taught history at Debden. He was once a Gurkha officer. He told us stories about his time in the army. We all liked him. Then he retired and was replaced by an utter bitch. Can't remember the cunt's name."

"That's good. What was the nearest pub to your house in Loughton?"

"The Gardener's Arms."

"Did you go in there, underage?"

"Nah. Mum and Dad might have caught me. Sometimes me and my mates would bunk off school and take a bus up to Buckhurst Hill. There was a boozer there called The Duke of Wellington. Don't know if it's still around. We'd play a few games of pool."

"What beers were on draft?"

Knutsen shrugged. "We drank Heineken. Don't know what the other beers were."

"That's understandable. Age nineteen you were sent to prison for five years, for grievous bodily harm. The prison was Chelmsford. Who were your pals in there?"

"Jimmy, Pete, Spence, Abdul, Mikey, Reza, Ian, Paddy, Nick, Larry, Simon, Ed, Will. None of us knew our surnames. We were just numbers, as far as the screws were concerned."

"Good. Repeat the names for me."

Knutsen did so.

"Excellent. And what did you do when you got out of prison?"

"Bit of this and that to start with. Mainly car and bike maintenance in a few places in south London. But it wasn't earning me much dosh. Fucking rental prices in London are a joke. So I fell in with a crew. We did a few bank jobs. That's when I met Organ Smuggler. Some of the crew worked for him in the past."

"Organ Smuggler's name?"

"Dave Hitch."

"Your name?"

"John Maloney."

"And who am I?"

Knutsen felt exhausted from the day's grilling. "You call yourself Henry Redmayne. But, as far as Hitch is concerned, I don't know if that's your real name. You run an import-export business out of England. I'm not prepared to give the exact location of your enterprise. I know you because you used to launder cash I nicked on some of my solo jobs. You need some forged documents for a transaction you're about to set up. I don't yet know what the transaction is. But that's okay. I trust you. You're paying me an introductory fee to get what you need."

"Perfect. Together with the hundreds of other questions I've asked you for," Sign checked his watch, "the last eight hours, you've past the test."

Knutsen breathed in deeply. He dropped his working class Essex accent when he said, "I was given days of preparation before I went undercover as a Met officer, but none of it was as mentally intense as what you've put me through today."

Sign smiled. "Different strokes, and all that." He went to the drinks cabinet and poured two glasses of calvados. "There we go, old fella. This will help lubricate the neurons." He handed Knutsen his drink and sat back in his armchair. His expression was serious and distracted as he quietly said, "More illegals may die before we get to Lowestoft Man."

"Yeah, that had crossed my mind."

Sign looked at him. "Our plan is the only way to catch the serial killer. We must hold our nerve and see the case through."

Knutsen sipped his drink while stretching his legs out alongside the fire. "Maybe there's no serial killer. This may all be a load of nonsense."

"No one would be more delighted than me if that turned out to be true. If we find the illegals safe and sound, we can breathe a sigh of relief, wipe our brows, and return home. The case will be closed because we've proved there is no crime beyond employing illegal immigrants. And that's information I'd not be taking to PC Plod or a lawyer."

Knutsen said, "But your antennae are twitching. You don't think that's going to be the outcome of the case."

"I don't."

Knutsen's stomach rumbled. "God, I'm hungry for some reason."

"That's because your body went in to hibernation today in order to maximise the energy required by your brain. Your body has now woken up. It wants sustenance." He finished his drink. "It also needs exercise. Come with me."

They walked on the promenade alongside the River Thames. It was dark and the air was cold enough to make the men's breath steam. Fog swirled around the golden glow of the beautiful old fashioned lamps that straddled the mighty river. They entered Borough Market, near London Bridge. One of the oldest and largest markets in London, dating back to the twelfth century, the indoors market was renowned for its excellent meat, fish, vegetables, and speciality condiments.

Sign walked to his favourite meat stall. "Mr. Jones, we'd like a cut of your finest beef, if you please."

Jones beamed. "Mr. Sign. It's been a while," he said in his east London drawl. He patted the produce in the chiller cabinet in front of him. "Got some beautiful rib-eye, sirloin, rump, joints if you fancy a roast, but if I were you I'd be going for this chap." He held up a slab of meat. "Hanger beef. Needs trimming and the sinew has to be taken out. Griddle it on all sides first and then finish it off in a pan with butter and herbs. Maximum cooking time is only a few minutes if you want it medium rare, and I recommend that's how you have it. Make sure you rest it after cooking for at least five minutes to stop the blood coming out."

"Excellent. We'll take the hanger. How much?"

"For you, Mr. Sign, this is on the house after what you did to help my kid."

Sign smiled. "Nonsense. We all have to earn a living. And plus, all I did for Rosie was get her out of juvenile detention after that pesky misunderstanding about her knife and the fellow she stuck it in when she found out he was selling crystal meth to school kids."

Jones wrapped the beef. "Ten quid then sir."

"It's worth three times that."

"It's the end of the day. Everything's at discount for punters like you."

Sign paid him fifteen pounds, took the beef parcel, and said, "Sometime over the coming days I'm hoping to procure a whole goat. I don't want it skinned or gutted. Is that something you can help me with?"

Jones grinned. "Not a problem. You've got my number. Give me a call when you want it. But give me two days' notice."

"Perfect. Good day to you Mr. Jones. And send my regards to Rosie." He and Knutsen walked to a vegetable counter. Sign pointed at the stall owner. "This is Rick. He's the most discerning supplier of vegetables in southern England."

"Southern England?!" Rick pretended to look offended. "North and south, mate. You won't find anyone better than me. I learn stuff. And I watch the weather forecast. I know when my suppliers are producing good annual crops and ropey annual crops." He grinned. "How are you, Mr. Sign?"

"I'm very well, thank you." He lifted the parcel of meat. "Hanger beef. I would suggest that it will go extremely well with some rosemary and cardamom roasted potatoes, cauliflower boiled and pan fried with a sprinkle of paprika and turmeric, and a homemade relish of cold and blended radishes, garlic, mustard seeds, lemon juice, olive oil, and shallots." He looked at the stall. "I need the spuds, cauliflower, radishes, and shallots from you. The rest I have at home."

"Nice one sir." He started placing the veg in brown bags. "Potatoes are from Hampshire. They're right tasty. Cauliflower's the best of a crop from a bloke I know in Norfolk. Radishes and shallots both come from a farmer in Somerset. One time he tried to kill me."

Sign handed over cash. "Thank goodness he failed. Who else would I go to get my vegetables?"

As they walked away, Knutsen asked, "Is there anyone in this part of London you don't know?"

"Plenty. But I make it my business to get to know the people who matter to me. Rick's got an excellent eye for crops. He's a nice fellow. There is a side to him, though. He took his terminally ill wife for a walk along the white cliffs of Sussex and pushed her over. The police could never establish whether he'd murdered her or whether she'd committed suicide. I know for a fact that it was a mutually agreed act of mercy. But that was back then and this is now. She's dead; she's happy; he's happy that she's happy. He told me that she had a smile on her face as she fell to her death."

"Jesus Christ! You do mix with an odd crowd."

Sign said, "I'll return home and cook while you call Organ Smuggler. I suggest you use one of the payphones in Waterloo Station."

Fifty minutes later, Knutsen was back in the flat. The smell of roasting potatoes was evident in the lounge and kitchen. Sign was boiling vegetables, chopping others, and preheating a griddle pan. He'd already trimmed the hanger beef to perfection and had cut it into two portions.

Knutsen said, "I was lucky to get hold of him. He was about to get on a flight out of Cairo. He'll be back in London around midnight. I'm seeing him in the morning."

"How did he sound?"

"Surprised to hear from me. I told him I wanted to talk to him about a business matter. He seemed fine once I'd dropped that in."

"Good." Sign put the steaks and chunks of cauliflower on the griddle. "Dinner will be served in ten minutes."

After they'd eaten, Knutsen rubbed his tummy and said, "That was right tasty proper grub. Just what I needed."

"My pleasure." Sign cleared away the plates, steak knives, and forks, and poured two glasses of cognac. He sat in his armchair.

Knutsen sat opposite him. The fire was lit. "Oh shit. I forgot to call Andy to come over and repair the temperature dial."

"I called him while you were calling Organ Smuggler. Andy's coming over at ten o'clock tomorrow."

"Thank fuck for that. I'm freezing my tits off when I get out of the shower."

Sign smiled. "I rather prefer to think of the experience as jumpstarting the largest body organ, namely our skin." He sipped his brandy.

"You do realise this plan of yours may not work. I'm pretty confident Dave Hitch, Organ Smuggler to you and I, can get us to Forger. But will Forger put us on to Domingo or anyone else in the Lowestoft-London people smuggling route? Maybe he'll put us on to a smuggler who's not part of Lowestoft Man's gang. If that happens we're screwed."

"*If* that happens we are not run aground. People smuggling is a niche criminal profession in Britain. There will be very few people who specialise in the activity. If Forger directs us to someone who's not part of Lowestoft Man's network, that's okay because that man will certainly know the name of someone in the Lowestoft set-up. But I think we'll be fine. I think Lowestoft Man controls all people smuggling in Britain. He's Mr. Big. That's my hunch, at least. But, the hunch is based on logic. Lowestoft Man needs to maintain an extremely low profile. He can't have amateurs attempting to work on his patch and potentially draw police attention to his covert smuggling chain. He wouldn't hesitate to permanently get rid of anyone who might compromise his operation. As important, I believe he holds the monopoly on all illegals fleeing war zones who want to enter Britain. He will not allow anyone to infringe on his monopoly." He placed his fingertips together in front of his mouth. "For presentational reasons I must not attend the Organ Smuggler meeting. And when speaking to him you must stick to the agreed vague description of me. But I must be present at the meeting with Forger. I will tell him what I want from him. As a result, I'm confident he will have no choice other than to put us in contact with Domingo."

"And if we get to Domingo how do we work through him to get to Carreras, Pavarotti, and ultimately Lowestoft Man?"

"We improvise. We accurately set up out stall with Forger. That's something we can control. After that we're in unknown waters. When we sail across the ocean, we can't predict whether we'll have a safe passage, or whether we'll be fighting to survive." He smiled. "The unknown is exciting."

Knutsen replied with resignation, "Were it not for your intellect and track record, I'd have you down as bonkers for saying something like that. We might get our throats cut."

"In my experience, the threat of death heightens the experience of life. Our odyssey will be an adventure, comparable to those of many ancient mariners who'd set sail to find the edge of the world."

Knutsen stood and sighed. "Can't you just talk like normal people do? You're making my head hurt. Right – I'm going to have a nightcap and then hit the sack." He walked to the drinks cabinet and poured himself another drink. When he returned to his chair his tone of voice was more cautious when he asked, "Do you fear death?"

"Of course. I don't believe there is an afterlife. That said I'm fascinated by the electricity in our bodies. It must go somewhere. Also, when our bodies are in the ground we're eaten by worms and we enrich the ground, plus…"

Knutsen held up his hand. "Stop there. I'm tired. Your answer wasn't what I was looking for."

Sign leaned forward and said in a precise and earnest tone, "I fear the deaths of others I care about."

Knutsen nodded. "Your wife's murder must have changed everything for you."

"We don't need to talk about that." Sign smiled sympathetically. "Right now, I will not allow the soldier by my side to take a bullet. Do you understand?"

Knutsen hesitated, then nodded. "Yes. Thank you."

"Good man. Now, dear chap, finish your drink and get a good night's sleep. You're on parade tomorrow. And while you're meeting a man who might slit your throat, I'll hold the fort here and ensure we get the heating repaired."

CHAPTER 4

Knutsen had a bad night's sleep. When he got out of bed he felt tired and emotionally exhausted. His dreams had placed him into a sweaty state of agitation. Many of them were recollections of his past – driving through London at high speed in a stolen BMW, trying to flee three police cars that were pursuing him and two criminals who had guns by their sides; being handcuffed to a railing and beaten, while a Russian mobster questioned him to check he was who he said he was; shooting a man who thought Knutsen was his friend; getting a Nazi tattoo syringed onto his chest; pummelling a yob's skull, just to prove how tough and ruthless he was to the criminals he was with in a pub; spending three days in a police cell while lying to the cops who were holding him; executing a man who'd killed the woman he was in love with; shoving a sawn-off shotgun into the mouth of a female bank teller; seeing the look of absolute fear in her eyes; and seeing an expression on the faces of the gang members he ultimately arrested – it wasn't an expression that held hatred, rather it was a look of disappointment. He'd spent so long being an undercover cop. Normally officers in that role are pulled out after two years and told to decompress before being deployed on regular police duties. Knutsen, however, had done undercover work for the majority of his adult life. He'd spent more time being John Maloney than he had being himself. The reason he'd been kept in the field so long was that he was so good at what he did. But, someone should have realised he would inevitably crack. Maybe that's why he killed his lover's murderer. He wanted a way out. The execution got him sacked. He was a free man and could now be Tom Knutsen. The problem was that he was now going back into the darkest recesses of his old world. And that's why the dreams had come back. Once again, Knutsen had to be Maloney. He had to think like him, look like him, smell like him, talk like him, drink like him, eat like him, and ultimately be an utter bastard.

He showered, but used neutral soap rather than a perfumed gel to wash himself. He didn't shave, though did brush his teeth. After getting dressed into jeans, boots, T-shirt, and a green army surplus-style jacket, he cracked open a can of super-strength larger he'd purchased on Waterloo Station concourse yesterday. He swigged half the can down and dabbed drops from the rest onto his jacket. It was only eight AM. While holding the can in one hand, he looked in the mirror. John Maloney was back.

He finished the rest of the beer and walked in to the lounge. Sign was sitting at the dining table, reading a newspaper.

Sign placed the paper down when he saw him. "I've made you a bacon butty with ketchup. It's the breakfast of champions, as Maloney would say." He gestured to the sandwich. "Get that down your neck."

Knutsen remained standing as he woofed the meal down. He spoke in his normal accent. "I'll need to leave in a minute."

Sign stood and walked to him. "Only speak like Maloney. He placed his hands on Knutsen's arms and examined him. He adopted a south London accent. "Good. Breath smells right. You had a hair of the dog this morning. Eyes look tired because you pulled a bender last night. You're currently crashing at a mate's house in London because you're lying low from filth. You shag prostitutes because it's cheaper than getting hooked up with a bird and all the shit that comes with that cluster fuck. You got it?"

"Yeah I got it."

Sign stepped back and spoke in his normal posh accent. "Good. You've checked every pocket in your clothes?"

"Of course. I always do. I stood naked by my bed, even though it's fucking freezing in here, and went through every garment twice before getting dressed."

"No wallet, credit card, debit card?"

Knutsen patted his trouser pocket. "Cash only."

"No gun or knife?"

"Nope."

"Good man. Mobile phone?"

"Yeah. Pay-as-you-go. Don't want it in my name. Swap them every few weeks."

"Perfect. Who are you?"

"I'm John Maloney."

Sign repeated, "Who are you?"

"John Maloney."

Sign smiled. "You're ready."

Knutsen nodded and walked out of the flat.

Edward walked to the cottage on his estate containing his housekeeper Khadija. He was carrying a large parcel. He knocked on her door.

The Libyan opened the door and looked nervous. "Good morning, sir. I not late for duties am I sir?"

He smiled. "Not in the slightest. I don't need you in the house until midday. I brought you this." He handed her the parcel. "It's the wet suit I promised you, plus rubber shoes and a waterproof," He rubbed his head, "skull cap. They'll keep you warm if you want to swim at this time of year."

Khadija beamed. "I can swim in these, even when it's cold water?"

"Yes."

"How much I owe?"

"Nothing. I hope they fit. I guessed your height and shoe size. Now, why don't you try them out before work?"

She giggled. "Yes sir, yes sir. I go swim now."

Edward walked back towards the house, but he didn't go in to his home. Instead he entered the nearby keep, climbed the ladder to the roof, and waited there. The vantage point gave him an excellent view of the steep gorge that led to the sea. The tide was in, but there was still a slither of sandy beach visible. He waited. Thirty minutes later he saw Khadija walk through the grounds. She was wearing her new wet suit and other gear. She entered the path that began the descent into the valley, disappeared from view for a few minutes, reappeared as she gripped the rope to get down one part of the descent, and gripped on to anything she could hold as she tentatively further descended down the lower path that had no railings. Edward smiled as he saw her run across the beach and wade into the sea. She threw herself into the water and began swimming. From what she'd told him, she'd loved water since she was a girl, swimming off the coast of Libya in the Mediterranean, laughing, diving to the seabed, learning front crawl, breaststroke, and back crawl, memorising the names of different types of fish, and floating while feeling utterly content and free. She was, he liked to think, an explorer. The water by his estate was a new place to study. It was nothing like the Med but it still contained wonders – flat fish, bass, conger eels, crabs, lobsters, beautiful plant life, cod, bream, and pollock. It was a rich feeding ground. And Khadija could swim here without fear of being blown to smithereens by allied bombers or a grenade. It made him feel proud as he watched her vanish from view when she went underwater to see what she could find. After she emerged she continued swimming back and forth, Thirty minutes later she got out of the sea and began the ascent back to the estate. It was a tough climb. US Rangers and commandos had used this gorge and nearby valleys as training grounds before D-Day. He left the keep and greeted her as she clung on to the bird stand near his mansion. She was breathing fast and smiling.

"How was the swim and the clothes?" he asked.

"Very…" she sucked in air, "very good, sir. I see lots of things. Different creatures."

"Splendid. I'll put the kettle on for a cup of tea. But I won't make the drink until you've washed and changed."

"Thank you, sir, for this." She touched the wet suit. "I felt the cold but not bad like just swim suit." She walked to her cottage, thinking she was in heaven. Edward was such a good employer. Her cottage was bigger than anything she'd ever lived in. She had TV, which helped her with her English and made her relax when she finished work; more than one set of clothes; good food; hot water; external surroundings that weren't decimated by military shells; a kitchen; a lovely bed that had a duvet rather than a germ-infested rag to keep her warm; and she sent the majority of her generous income to her family in Libya. Life couldn't be better.

Edward smiled as he walked into his house. Just now he'd done a good thing. He liked that. It made him feel righteous and at peace. He boiled water and put loose tea into a dry pot. Today he'd spend time using his computer to speculate on stocks and shares. He was never reckless when he did so. He was like a gambler who had a few million quid under his belt but only ever entered a casino with a thousand pounds in his pocket. Some days he made gains; others he made a loss. On balance it all evened out. But the exercise kept his brain active. And that was the crucial thing – keeping his razor sharp intellect firing on all cylinders. He made a bacon butty and wondered whether he should take an hour out of today's schedule to go to the village and seek an appointment with his parish counsellor. He was unwilling to give up his ongoing battle to get the National Trust to tarmac the lane to his estate. The counsellor was key to winning the battle. But, maybe the trip could wait until tomorrow. He never liked going in to the village. There were too many people there. They gossiped. And they were antagonistic towards him because he employed foreigners, rather than British people who'd lived here all their lives. They thought he was doing them out of a few bob. Bloody small minded country folk, he often thought. Still, he loved the countryside. And the solitude away from busybodies. On his estate he could command all pertinent matters. The estate was his control ground. He respected the people who worked for him. The villagers were insignificant ants who could be crushed under his foot. He finished his brunch. It was time to have a cup of tea and get to work. Khadija would be commencing her duties in two minutes' time.

Knutsen entered an industrial park in Reading. To get here he'd walked to the Elephant & Castle tube station, taken the Northern Line to Embankment, switched to the Circle Line to travel to Paddington overland station, taken a train to Reading, rode in a taxi to get near the park but not too close, and had completed the journey on foot. Due to his lack of sleep in the night and travel he was exhausted. But, that was good. He wanted to appear wasted and drained. He didn't need to play act the part of someone who was driving on empty. There was nothing pretty in the park – just warehouses. The only colours in the zone were the placards on each unit branding company names. In the immediate vicinity where Knutsen stood there was a printing company, Christian DJ and recording studio, catering company that specialised in sausage rolls, accountancy firm, bathroom fitters, school uniform shop, and Organ Smuggler's small unit that had a banner above its entrance saying *Medical Supplies*. He knocked on the door belonging to Organ Smuggler aka Dave Hitch.

A man opened the door. It wasn't Hitch. He was medium height, wiry, wearing white overalls, and had a knife scar under his lip. He was one of Hitch's men and a ruthless killer, though in his life he'd managed to avoid spending any time in a police cell or prison. He said, "Come in, sunshine," and locked the door after Knutsen was in the small industrial unit. "Take your clothes off. All of them."

Knutsen pretended to look mortified. "Oh, fuck off mate."

"I'm not your mate. Clothes off. I need to check 'em. If you've got anything dodge in there you need to tell me now."

Knutsen sighed as he undressed. "I've come here to see Hitch. I don't carry guns or blades when I meet someone who I've worked with before."

"People can change." When Knutsen was naked the man rifled through every pocket in his garments, plus checked the lining and collar of his jacket, and the insoles of his boots.. "Stand still, sunshine. No needles in your hair, right?"

"Yeah, right."

The man checked Knutsen's hair, examined underneath his testicles, between his buttocks, got him to slowly turn three sixty degrees with his arms outstretched, and said, "All good in the hood. Get dressed." When Knutsen was fully clothed the man called out, "Dave – he's clean."

Dave Hitch emerged from his small office at the rear of the unit. Like his associate, he was medium height and wearing spotless white overalls. But there the similarities ended. His full name was David Richmond Elgar Hitch. He was in his mid-forties and had no distinguishing features that suggested he'd led a life of crime. To the contrary, he looked like a scientist. He was wearing spectacles, had brown and grey short hair that was covered with a net, was clean shaven, and had an accent that he'd adopted from his parents and had been honed during his schooling in Eton. Age eighteen he was destined to attend the prestigious Yale University, but he'd decided not to bother and instead make some illegal money. After all, the whole point of university was to gain a rite of passage into a lucrative job. Hitch didn't need to sweat for three years reading dull academic books to achieve what he wanted. He was too clever for that.

He was carrying two fold-up chairs. He opened both and positioned them opposite each other. "Sit, John."

Knutsen sat in one of the chairs.

Hitch sat on the other. "What do you want?"

Knutsen looked around. "You got a beer?"

"No."

"All these bleedin' refrigeration units and not one of them has got a frickin' beer?! That's bollocks, isn't it."

"Why would I want to chill a beer rather than maintain the health of an imported liver?" Hitch smiled, though the look was cold. His eyes were unblinking and locked on Knutsen. "We haven't seen each other for over four years. Please do explain why you have a resurgent interest in me."

Knutsen looked nonchalant. "I need a contact. Thought you might be able to help. I'll pay. I just need a name and address."

"Interesting. How have you been keeping?"

Hitch's enforcer stood behind Knutsen.

Knutsen was unfazed. "You know how it is. Been trying to cut back on the booze and coke and avoid shit from filth. Trouble is life's shit and it is what it is. So, I do a bit of this and that. But nothing hard core anymore. No more robberies. Booze is my friend."

"Indeed." Hitch crossed his legs. He looked at the man standing behind Knutsen. "Get Maloney a can or bottle of beer from the petrol station."

The man left the unit.

Hitch stared at Knutsen. "It would be facile for me to ask if you've been turned by the police."

"Fac...? What?"

"Facile. Never mind."

"Whatever. I ain't a snitch and I'll throat punch you and your lady boy if you accuse me of that again."

Hitch smiled. "Your response is either the truth or good acting. Which of the two options would you choose, Maloney?"

"Fuck off. I'm not here to mess with your freak show business, or you, you tossing weirdo. I just want an in." Knutsen rubbed his stubble. "I need a guy who can do paperwork. *Good* paperwork. I've got a punter who wants cheap labour. But he needs to appear legit. He wants docs for every person he employs. I don't know anyone who can forge docs. I reckoned you might do. I'll pay you ten G's if you put me in the right direction."

"Ten thousand pounds? Where did you get that money from if you're no longer holding up Post Offices?"

"It's the punter's dosh."

Hitch examined his finger nails. "Who is your *punter*?"

"None of your business."

"You want me to give you a name, but you won't give me a name?"

"I won't give you a name, but the trade is fair. You get cash." Knutsen looked over his shoulder as Hitch's henchman returned to the unit holding a can of beer. Knutsen grabbed it off him, opened it, and said, "Don't fucking stand behind me again, pal. This is just business talk, not bleedin' *Godfather* shit."

Hitch nodded at his employee.

The man moved to his employer's side.

Knutsen swigged the beer. "That's more like it. How's business, Dave?"

Hitch shrugged. "It ebbs and flows. Supply and demand. I'm at the mercy of when and where people get severely ill."

Knutsen laughed. "So you can flog an organ. You're a cunt."

"We all do what we have to do to get by." Hitch asked, "Do you have the cash on you now?"

"Yep. It's clean cash." He pulled the bound wad out of his pocket and tossed it to Hitch's employee. "Count it, Scarface. In my other pocket is enough dosh to get me back to the smoke. You ain't touching that."

The henchman counted the twenty pound notes and nodded at Hitch. "All good."

Hitch looked away. "Finish you beer, John. I hope you're not too inebriated to forget what I'm about to say because I'm not putting anything on paper. The man you need to see is Michael Time. He works in London. He's the only person who can forge the documents your paymaster needs." He gave Knutsen Time's address. "I will call him and tell him to expect you at eleven o'clock tomorrow morning. He'll be there. I will not give you his mobile telephone number. Any transaction you have with Time is your business and I will not be linked to it." Hitch stood. "I know you're not on the payroll of the police. You're too... unstable. Now get out of my warehouse."

Nearly three hours' later, Knutsen returned to the West Square flat. He was relieved when he felt the warmth from the radiators. The repair man, Andy, had obviously fixed the problem with the thermostat. Sign wasn't home. Most likely he was out buying produce for dinner, or talking high politics with powerful government ministers in his St. James's gentlemen's club. Knutsen welcomed the solitude. He drank a pint of water to wash away the taste of beer and rehydrate himself, put all of his clothes in the washing machine, brushed his teeth, shaved, and had a bath. Afterwards, he felt normal. This evening he didn't want to inhabit John Maloney's brain. He made himself a cup of tea and watched last night's episode of University Challenge on BBCi player. This was the kind of decompression he was so used to after a day of mingling with scum. It was time to relax and spend a chilled evening watching TV and turning his brain off.

Sign entered the flat. On his shoulder was a dead goat. "Hello, dear chap. How did you get on with Organ Smuggler?"

Knutsen looked at the large goat and sighed because he knew chill time was over. "I got what I needed. Looks like you have too."

"I've been productive. As you will have noticed, Andy's sorted out the heating. I've procured this magnificent beast from Mr. Jones in Borough Market, and this morning I also had a lovely cup of coffee with a Christian DJ in Reading."

Knutsen couldn't believe what he was hearing. "You were in the industrial unit opposite Organ Smuggler when I met him? You followed me?"

"I watched over you, Mr. Knutsen. We no longer need to work alone. The roles can alternate depending on circumstances. Today you put your head close to the lion's mouth while I had a reliable rifle to dispatch the lion if it attacked. On another day, you could be the sniper. It's an analogy, of course. I didn't have a gun when I chatted to the DJ. But, by God I'd have yanked you out of Organ Smuggler's den if I had the faintest whiff of foul play." He laughed. "Organ Smuggler thinks he's cleverer than he is."

"How do you know that?"

"I looked at him through binoculars. In particular I paid attention to his eyes and body movements. Both betrayed insecurities. I could elaborate."

"Please don't." Knutsen pointed at the goat. "What are you going to do with that bastard?"

"*We* are going to make him in to many meals. Tea break's over. I need your help. Get black bin bags out of the kitchen drawer. Open them out so their flat. Stick them to the whole kitchen floor with tape. Place our two wooden chopping boards in the centre of the floor. And also please be gracious enough to put our meat cleaver, the longest Global knife, a wooden spoon, and several bowls on the kitchen counter."

Knutsen turned off the TV, once again sighed, and set to work while thinking that life was never like this when he was a cop.

Ten minutes' later, Sign said, "Excellent job." He was standing in the kitchen entrance, the goat still on his shoulder. "If you can temporarily retreat, I'll place the beast onto the chopping boards."

For the next hour they skinned, gutted, and butchered the goat and placed each usable portion of meat in the freezer, bar one joint that Sign wanted to cook for their dinner. They cleared up the blood–covered bin bags and placed them in the downstairs wheelie bin. Sign lit the fire and washed his hands. He placed the joint of goat in a casserole pot, and added turmeric, diced chillies, onions, slices of lemon, tinned tomatoes, fresh mint, and a can of cider. When the casserole was in the oven he poured two glasses of calvados, gave one to Knutsen, and sat opposite him in his armchair.

Knutsen elaborated on his encounter with Dave Hitch. "We're meeting Forger tomorrow at eleven o'clock. His name's Michael Time. I've got his address. But, that's all I've got. No other details."

"We don't need any other details."

Knutsen's limbs were aching. He knew why. He was an extremely fit man, but today his whole body had been in a heightened state of tension. Butchering the goat hadn't helped. He didn't understand how Sign, who was fifteen years older than him, always remained so calm and agile. "I need to relax this evening. And to do that I want to talk about normal things."

"Of course, dear fellow." Sign sipped his drink. "The goat joint will take two hours to cook. I've prepared it in a Moroccan sauce. When the meat is ready I'll grill aubergines and red peppers. The casserole sauce will not go to waste. And I'll prepare couscous. It's all very easy and can be done at the last minute. You're off duty now. You can relax in whatever way you see fit over the next couple of hours. Maybe go for a pint and a game of billiards."

Knutsen smiled. "Stop messing with me. You know full well that billiards doesn't exist anymore."

"A game of darts then?"

"Nice idea, but I'm cream crackered. I just want to chill in front of the fire." A thought occurred to him. "Were you happy to send me back undercover today?"

Sign's eyes were locked on his business partner. "No. But it was a test. A nudge."

Knutsen frowned. "A test?"

Sign wondered whether he should elaborate. He decided it was in Knutsen's interest for him to do so. "I selected you to be my business partner. I rejected CVs from former special forces soldiers and intelligence officers. I was intrigued by your career. What makes a man who gained a first class degree adopt a fake London accent and become a Metropolitan police undercover cop? How has that man survived so long in the filthy edges of the city? What made him become another human being?"

"It was a job. I haven't got some traumatic backstory. Mum and Dad still live in the West Country. I wasn't abused by them. Never bullied at school. Kept my head down. Bit of a boring childhood. Hadn't thought about it before, to be honest."

Sign nodded. "So, what would a loved and bored eighteen year old dream of? If he's unambitious, he'd probably hang out with his dull pals in the local park, take drugs, get a menial job in the local village. But, if he was clever, he'd look over the horizon. He'd want danger and adventure. I know that feeling."

"What's this? Fucking psychoanalysis?"

"No. It's answering your question. I wasn't happy to send you back undercover. Like me, you spent too long living other lives. Sustained periods of deception and constant fear takes a savage toll on one's mental health, unless one has an armour-platted brain. I wanted to see if you were bulletproof. You past the test."

Knutsen asked, "You've been in the game far longer than me. How have you retained your sanity?"

Sign chuckled. "Ignorance is bliss."

Knutsen didn't smile. "You're the opposite of ignorant. And your brain whirs at the speed of a jet fighter's engine."

In a measured and quiet voice Sign replied, "I'm driven by problem solving. I'll do what it takes to answer the riddles that plague our world. Men like you and I put ourselves second to get the task in hand completed. And when the task is done we are happy. The mind-set is not unique to spies and detectives. A boxer will deliberately take blows to the body to fatigue his opponent, before delivering the killer blow. A gymnast will put her muscles and joints through years of agony before taking gold at an athletics ceremony. A surgeon will lose friends and family because of his alleged aloofness, but he'll smile every time he saves a life. A chef will sweat, burn and cut his fingers, work unholy number of hours, and all because he takes pleasure in feeding people. There are many other examples. The point is that some people have a psyche wherein they deliberately sacrifice themselves in order to succeed. If one embraces that reality about oneself, one can avoid mental burnout."

"That's a load of bollocks."

Sign laughed. "It sounded good though, didn't it."

"Nope." Knutsen also laughed. "You do talk shite sometimes." His laughter receded. "That said, you have cheered me up by spewing crap."

"That was my intention. Now – I must insist that we have a game of darts at our local. The pub has a new draft on tap. We should taste the ale and see if it pleases our palate."

Knutsen stood. "Yeah, alright mate. I'll get my boots on." He turned as he reached the lounge door. "I'm genuinely intrigued as to how you survived all the shit you've gone through in your life. You should be a broken bloke."

Sign was still. "Every day is a new day. One foot in front of the other. I believe it's best to forget what's behind me."

CHAPTER 5

Edward woke up at seven AM, bathed, and got dressed into what he liked to call his 'rambling clothes' – sturdy trousers, walking boots, and a fisherman's jumper. He walked downstairs and entered the kitchen. He had a lot of work to do this morning so he decided he needed a hearty breakfast of bacon, sausages, scrambled eggs, and baked beans. He ate his meal at the table in the lounge that overlooked the gorge. The sky was free of clouds and it looked like there was no wind. The sea was calm. He finished his meal and kept staring at the sea. He stood up in a state of excitement, ran across his estate, and banged on his housekeeper's door.

"Khadija! Khadija!"

The Libyan opened the door. "Yes sir?"

Edward was breathless. "There are dolphins in our bay. I saw them while having my breakfast."

"Dolphins?"

"Yes. I saw three. There may be more. You must swim."

Khadija beamed. "Yes sir. I'll wear new wet suit and greet them."

"Right. No time to waste. I'm going to get my camera. I'll see you on the beach." He ran back to the house and placed his equipment into a small rucksack.

Khadija was only twenty yards ahead of him as he exited the house and followed her down the gorge. She was wearing her wet suit, waterproof trousers, and skull cap. The Libyan was moving down the tricky descent as fast as she could. She didn't need Edward's help. She was fit and young. By comparison, Edward was more cautious. He'd twisted his ankle on one occasion when making the descent, and had tumbled head first onto a rock on another occasion. He watched her make the final steps to the beach, as he walked slowly alongside the riverbed at the base of the valley. She plunged into the sea, diving down, desperate to see the dolphins. Edward reached the beach and leaned against the cliff. It was lovely to see Khadija so happy and free. In Edward's mind she was like a seal, darting quickly in different directions, sometimes on the surface, other times out of sight while having her solitary adventures. He'd not probed her on the specific details of the terrors she'd left behind in North Africa. Sometimes it was best not to ask. People needed to move on. What mattered now was that she was swimming in a safe place.

She emerged from the water, shivering. "I saw lobsters. No dolphins. Maybe they go away."

"You look freezing." He reached in to his rucksack, withdrew a towel, and walked to her.

She smiled as she took the towel.

And she gasped as Edward plunged the knife that was hidden underneath it into her chest. She fell onto her back, like a tree that had been expertly felled.

She was still alive, just.

In a calm voice, Edward said, "This won't take long." He leaned over her prone body and slammed the knife into her chest, five inches above the previous incision. She was now dead. He removed a small hacksaw from his bag and began sawing through Khadija's breast plate. It was hard work. But Edward liked exerting himself. It's why he'd had a hearty breakfast. After all, today was death day.

Once he'd sawed through eight inches of bone he thrust his hands into the cavity and wrenched the remaining breast plate apart. He used his knife to cut away tissue and puncture her lungs. He tossed her heart into the sea. Crabs would eat it, so he wasn't worried about covering his tracks. He collected numerous stones from the beach and forced them into Khadija's chest cavity. It was time to take her to her resting place. He dragged his rowing boat out of the old smuggler's cave and positioned it on the sea's edge. After placing Khadija into the boat, he pushed the vessel out a few yards, got in, and rowed. He knew exactly where to go. He stopped rowing when he was two hundred yards out to sea. Below the boat was a prime spot for crabs, lobsters, and conger eels. He eased Khadija onto one side of the boat while leaning back on the other side to avoid capsizing. "There we go, dear Khadija. You've always loved the sea." He kicked her out of the boat. Khadija's body would feed the sea life.

When he was ashore he dragged the boat back into the cave, and climbed up to his estate. He was proud of himself. The only annoyance was that he'd have to vacuum and clean the manor house until the new housekeeper arrived. Still, that was a small sacrifice to pay for the facilitation of the pleasure he'd derived from giving Khadija a lovely death.

Sign and Knutsen entered a small book shop in Charing Cross. A man in his late sixties was standing behind the counter, using a magnifying glass to analyse a seventeenth century map of China. He looked up when he heard his shop doorbell ring. "Can I be of assistance to you, gentlemen?" The man was short, quietly spoken, wore glasses, and was wearing his favourite cardigan with leather patches on the sleeves.

Knutsen walked up to the counter and extended his hand. "You must be Michael Time. I'm John Maloney. I believe you're expecting me."

"Yes, I'm Michael Time." He looked at Sign. "Who are you?"

"Henry Redmayne." Sign shook the bookseller's hand. "I have a delicate matter to attend to. Mr. Maloney advised me that you might be able to help."

Time walked to the front door, swivelled the sign to show he was now closed for business, and locked the door. "Mr. Redmayne – you strike me as a learned man." He walked back to the counter and picked up his magnifying glass. "Is this map genuine?" He handed the glass to Sign.

Sign peered over the map. "What is the date of the document?"

"1723."

Sign analysed everything. "This is odd. The Kangxi Emperor of the Qing dynasty realised that Chinese maps were not accurate enough and required scientific methods for mapping, so he sponsored a national wide geodesy and mapping programme based on astronomical observation and triangulation measurements. The Huang Yu Quan Lan Tu map took over ten years to complete from 1708. It was also the first on-the-spot survey map. It had forty one framings based on provincial boundaries and used pseudo-cylindrical projection and latitude and longitude cartography methods. Boundaries were defined in Manchu, while inland contents were defined in Chinese." He placed the glass down. "There are other details I could go in to, but you probably know those details. Who gave you the map?"

Time replied, "A man who wants it valued before it's sold in auction."

"Tell him he's wasting your time. This map is inaccurate. If it was made in 1723 why is it cluttered with errors? The coastline is wrong; borders are incorrect."

Time angled his head. "Inaccurate Chinese maps were still in circulation in the early seventeenth century. Not everyone had access to the state of the art cartography of that time."

"So I'd need to look closer at the way the map was made. Paper fibres; weight of the paper; ink; aging of the document; circumstances it came into your customer's possession; reasons he wants to sell it; his character and background." Sign smiled. "Alas, I do not possess that information. But you do. You're a forger."

Time said, "Dave Hitch vouched for you, John Maloney. But he didn't vouch for you, Henry Redmayne, because he didn't know your identity. Still, I make my own judgements. Come with me." He led them into a room at the back of the shop. The room was his workplace. It had a desk, on top of which was a green lamp, scalpels, ink pens, digital camera, and a laptop. Elsewhere in the room was a photocopier, printing press, stack of passport covers on the floor alongside out of date credit cards, a 1970s projector facing a white blind on one wall, shredder, numerous parcels of different weight paper, laminating machine, and a bookshelf containing official government files. Time said, "Take a seat." He sat behind his desk. Sign and Knutsen faced him. "How can I help you?"

Knutsen answered. "This is how it works, alright. I got paid a retainer by Henry. He wanted a bloke to help him make certain employees legit. So, I spoke to Dave and he put us in touch with you."

Sign said, "I need someone with expertise who I can trust. Documents need to be made for illegal immigrants. I run a hotel in London. I'm not going to say where. I need illegal immigrants for a specific reason. They will be working split shifts. One shift will be standard hotel work. The other shift will be working in the loft of my hotel. They will be manufacturing cocaine and crystal meth."

Time was unfazed. "Why do you need illegal immigrants for that task?"

"Because they'll keep their mouths shut."

"That makes sense." Time asked, "How are you going to get illegal immigrants?"

Sign shrugged. "I don't yet know. I have the business plan. But I don't have the correct manpower."

"If you do get the manpower what do you intend to pay me to produce legitimate documents per individual?"

Sign pretended to look deep in thought. "I wondered if you could help me on two fronts. First – putting me in touch with someone who smuggles in illegals to London. I don't want to employ illegals who've got here by themselves, because it's possible they'll have flagged themselves to the authorities while they're in London. I need people who are invisible. Second – I want you to produce passports with visas. My terms are simple. One thousand pounds per passport."

Time laughed. "I charge ten times that amount."

"I appreciate that. If I get the staff, my business intends to make at least one hundred million pounds per year. If you get me my staff and make them legitimate, you'll get one percent of all my profits."

"One percent?"

"You'll be a very wealthy man."

"One thousand pounds per passport and one percent of profits?"

"No. Once you get the one percent you'll no longer get paid for producing passports. Instead, we'll be in business. You take your one percent every year. People come and go. Any new illegals coming in to the country that I need will be given forged documents by you. And you'll make those documents for free. But one percent is a hefty chunk of my profit. This is not just about producing expert documents. You need to help me find the invisibles. And you'll need to keep doing so for as long as we're in business."

Time drummed his fingers on his desk and looked away. "You're sure you'll be making that amount of money per year?"

Sign replied, "I'm being *very* conservative with my figures. It's prudent to do so."

"Yes." Time reengaged eye contact with Sign. "I've never had a business proposition like this before. It's too good to be true." He looked at Knutsen. "How do I know this is not a sting operation?"

Knutsen answered in his false London accent. "Don't be a cunt. I'm getting a wedge just for getting Henry in front of you. Dave Hitch knows me. We go back donkeys. So do me and Henry Redmayne. Henry's a player and a very clever bastard. He keeps himself to himself. You know that sapphire job in Thailand five years ago?"

Time frowned. "No."

"It was big time. Me and three mates got it done in Bangkok. Fuck me, pal, people were screaming. We didn't give a fuck. We were on the clock. Henry was boss. He wasn't there, but he worked out the job, worked out how to get us out of the country with the sapphires, worked out how to sell the sapphires, and paid us on time. Fucking sting operation, you twat. You're talking to the wrong blokes. Henry's one of us."

Time powered up his laptop and searched on Google. "They never found the robbers."

"Thanks to Henry. Thai cops and Interpol and other pigs were fucking shafted." Knutsen placed one ankle on his other leg. "It takes balls to come up with a job like that. But it worked."

Time closed his laptop and addressed Sign. "You've decided to diversify."

Sign replied, "I've decided to redirect. Robberies no longer hold my interest. The drugs trade is booming but is fraught. And the reason it's fraught is because there are always weak links in the chain. If I employed a known British criminal it would be a matter of time before the police were on to me. That's why I want properly imported illegals."

Time smiled. "It's a brilliant idea." He pulled out a small black leather-bound notebook from his desk drawer. He waved it in front of them. "This is encrypted. If you stole it from me you'd never understand the gobbledegook on the pages. It's my client list and their contact details. You, Mr. Redmayne, are not the first person who discretely wants illegals, and you won't be the last. I agree to your terms. One thousand pounds per passport until my one percent of profits kick in." He placed the notebook back in the drawer. "I am, however, a businessman, and will not relinquish my other business interests in favour of your proposition. I'll do what you want and will service my other clients. Understood?"

Sign nodded. "Spoken like a true entrepreneur." He leaned across the desk. "We have a deal." He extended his hand.

Time shook his hand. "I am not, however, a people smuggler. Illegals are delivered to me. I process them for my end users. It's clean."

It was tempting to ask the killer question but Sign was too experienced to do so at this moment. "The sun's over the yardarm. Do you have anything fortifying in your shop that could help us celebrate such a profitable venture?"

Time stood. "I have a bottle of Merlot. But, it will have to be in mugs."

"Mugs are fine."

Time walked out and returned two minutes later with a bottle and three cups. He poured the wine and handed two mugs to the men before him. He sat back down behind his desk, raised his mug, and said, "To business."

In unison, Sign and Knutsen said, "To business."

Time asked Sign, "Where did you go to university?"

He lied, "I didn't. I'm self-taught. It's given me a breadth of knowledge rather than a narrow field of expertise. And you? Where did you study?"

Time smiled. "Yes. Let's not probe into our backgrounds, forcing us to lie." He sipped his wine. His tone was serious when he said, "I only meet each illegal immigrant once, and that is to take passport quality photographs. Obviously, the photos are not taken here. Once the documents are ready, I hand them to the man who brought the illegals to me. He pays me. That's how it works."

Sign decided now was the time to probe. "So, your smuggler associate gets them here all by himself?"

Time shook his head. "I very much doubt that. Logistically it would be impossible. There must be several people involved. But I don't know others in the organisation. Nor do I want to. My only point of contact is the man who delivers the illegal immigrants to London."

"John and I need to meet him."

"Of course."

"Do you wish to be present at the meeting?"

"No. I will call him and say that I have some business to put his way. I'll tell him that it suits me because I'll be able to forge more documents. Beyond that, I believe it's best if I'm kept at arms-length."

"I concur." Sign asked, "What's his character?"

Time laughed. "You can imagine. If you shake his hand, afterwards check to see you have the same number of fingers. Don't take your eyes off him for one second. When he meets you he'll be armed. I doubt he'll bring anyone else. He works alone once he's in the city. But be very careful."

Knutsen said, "If he's going to be armed, I'll be armed."

Time picked up his mobile phone and made a call. He spoke for three minutes before hanging up. He addressed Sign and Knutsen. "You're on. He'll meet you the day after tomorrow." He gave them details. "His name's Bobby Potts. To be clear, I don't want to know anything about the business deal you strike with him. But, just so you know, he'll charge a lot of money. Only a fraction of it will go to him. The rest will be fed back down the chain, all the way to places like Syria and Iraq. Everyone takes their cut."

Sign asked, "Where do the illegals disembark in Britain?"

"I don't know. Somewhere in east England is my guess. But I do know there's only one man in Britain who controls the smuggling route. Before you ask, I've no idea who that person is, or where he's based. Potts has the job of covering London. He's a foot soldier, not a boss. And it's possible he doesn't know who his boss is. It's like I said earlier – everything is about cut outs. He'll know the man who hands illegals to him to make the final leg to London. But he probably doesn't know the identity of the third link in the chain, or the fourth, et cetera." He stood and handed Sign his business card. "I need to re-open my shop."

Sign and Knutsen followed him in to the book store.

Knutsen left the premises, but Sign lingered in the shop, staring at shelf containing old books. One peaked his interest. He placed a finger on the book. "A fine novel."

Time handed the book to Sign. "It's not a first edition. If it was I'd have it under lock and key. But it was published a year after it was written."

Sign leafed through the first few pages of The heart of Darkness, by Joseph Conrad. "Marlow journeyed under extraordinary circumstances on the Congo to find Kurtz." He carefully closed the book. The reason why the classical novel had peaked his interest was because it reminded him of two things: first, the journey illegal immigrants had to make to get to Britain; second, his odyssey to find Lowestoft Man. "How much do you want for the book?"

"Three hundred pounds."

Sign withdrew a wad of twenty pond notes, counted notes, and handed cash to Time. "Three hundred pounds."

Time took the money. "The book's yours." He was impressed that the man who called himself Henry Redmayne carried so much cash on his person.

And that was the real reason why Sign had bought the book. He wanted to show Time that he was a no nonsense wealthy criminal, and a discerning one at that. "I will be in touch once I've met Billy Potts. Money won't start rolling in overnight. I have to secure a deal with the people smugglers, get the number of illegals I need into my workplace, train them, manufacture my produce, and sell the produce."

Time nodded. "You're building your business. I'm a patient man. It comes with the territory. Forgers need to have a steady hand. Above all, we must never rush a job. I'll wait."

Sign smiled. "You and I are alike. Good day to you, Mr. Time." He shook the forger's hand and left.

Edward went into one of the basement utilities rooms in his house. He opened the chest freezer and looked at the freezer bags containing the multiple body parts of his former cook, Hala. He removed them all, placing each piece of frozen flesh into two sturdy refuse sacks. He put each sack over his shoulders and walked upstairs. In the kitchen he lined up eight large white plates on the work surface and put Hala's flesh on the plates. Given the ambient heat from the nearby Aga, the parts would be defrosted by tomorrow. That was very important. At one PM the next day he had guests arriving. They'd need feeding. Edward was going to prepare them a feast.

That evening, Sign and Knutsen were in their West Square flat, sitting in their armchairs. The fire was lit. Both men were holding glasses of calvados.

Knutsen was riffling through various takeaway menus. "I'm thinking Indian."

Sign sighed. "Last time we did that you tricked me by ordering a dish with volcanic chilli. I thought my throat was going to burst."

"Chinese then?"

"Possible."

"Pizza?"

"Maybe."

Knutsen looked at the last menu pamphlet. "The burgers might be an option."

"I can't decide."

Knutsen was irritated. "You're the one who said you couldn't be arsed to cook tonight."

"I didn't used the phrase *arsed* and nor did I say I couldn't be bothered. I simply said I needed to think. I need all of my faculties. As much as I adore cooking it can take one's mind off the ball."

"We need to eat."

"You choose." Sign looked at the fire.

"Chinese it is then. Crispy duck, egg fried rice, sweat and sour chicken."

"Not sweat and sour. I find it too sickly."

"Fuck's sake. Alright. Duck. Rice. Stir-fried vegetables. Chicken in satay sauce. Noodles. Prawn crackers. Will that please his majesty?"

"Yes."

Knutsen used his mobile phone to order the food. After the call he said to Sign, "It'll be ready for collection in one hour."

Sign's voice was distant when he replied, "Good. I'll walk with you. I need to stretch my legs."

Knutsen put his phone and the menus down. "What's bothering you?"

Sign looked at him. It took him ten seconds to answer Knutsen's question. "It's the calm before the storm. You of all people know what I mean. We're plunging down, not breaking the water's surface to get air. I'm worried about you. We may have to do some dark and highly illegal actions. But that may be the only choice we have. I don't want to get you in trouble or cause you trauma."

The answer tugged on Knutsen's heart strings. But, he wasn't going to show that emotion to Sign. "Listen mate. If I have to share a prison cell with you I'm deliberately going to spend every waking hour boring the fuck out of you about '90s indie music, premiership football, and street names in London." He smiled. "Dark shit? Who gives a fuck? And who gives a fuck about jail time?"

Sign laughed. "Well said, sir. You do playact the part of an east end bruiser very well."

"And it is just an act, when needed."

Sign nodded. "We've got to Organ Smuggler, met Forger, and now we're teed up to meet Domingo. He will lead us to Carreras, who will lead us to Pavarotti, who will lead us to Lowestoft Man, *if* we play our cards right. Lowestoft Man remains the key. The three tenors won't know the identity of the serial killer. Nor does Forger. Lowestoft Man uses different smugglers to deliver the prey to the man we need to stop. We can't get to those smugglers. So, we stick to the Lowestoft-London route. Then we squeeze."

"Squeeze?"

"We do whatever is necessary with Lowestoft Man. Make sure your sidearm is in perfect condition."

"I look after my handgun." Knutsen sighed. "Changing the subject, Natalia's moving to Canada. I don't know exactly where. I'm not allowed to know. She's told me our relationship can't continue. She's had to move because the Russians are sniffing for her in Britain. Shame really. I thought we had a good thing going."

Natalia was a former SVR agent, the SVR being Russia's foreign intelligence agency, equivalent in remit to MI6 and the CIA. She'd betrayed her country and gave secrets to MI6. In their previous case, Sign and Knutsen had worked with her on a highly complex task. After her cover was blown, Sign had ensured that she had legal status to live in Britain. Knutsen had taken a shine to her and had seen her frequently after the case was closed.

Sign said, "I'm so sorry to hear that, dear fellow. I thought that one day the two of you might get married."

"So did I. But that's not going to happen. I really liked her. Well, actually much more than that. She's a proper woman. Young and all that and learning her way, but she's got her head screwed on. We never had an argument. She's kind. Clever. And it helped that I fancied the pants off her." Knutsen smiled, though his expression was one of pure regret. "We cuddled when she told me she had to leave. She was in tears. I tried not to cry, but I was shaking. Weird shit."

Sign chose his words carefully. "It's called love. Both of you were very brave to agree to Natalia's relocation. Maybe one day you'll be reacquainted."

"Never going to happen, mate. You know how it rolls. She's twenty four. The body clock will start kicking in. She'll meet another bloke and have kids. That's understandable. It's nature. Is what it is." Knutsen bowed his head. "That's the second love I've lost."

"The first was murdered. The second would have been murdered had she not exited our country. Your selflessness has ensured you saved the life of your second love. You could easily have talked her round to stay in England. But you didn't."

Knutsen looked up. "I *had* to let her go, in every sense. I don't like myself for it, though." He pointed at nothing in particular in the lounge. "All I've got now is this place, our casework, and you as a friend."

"You're young. Things will change." Sign checked his watch. "Let's take that walk to the Chinese takeaway. The Thames embankment will be looking stunning at this hour. And as we perambulate I will tell you a funny story about how I tried to recruit a highly religious Iranian terrorist by pretending to be a prophet of Muhammad."

CHAPTER 6

Edward was having a busy morning. He placed a white cloth on the rectangular table in his dining room, ironed the cloth while it was in situ, polished silver cutlery and laid them on to the table with precision, put tiny pots of artificial roses down the centre, wine glasses adjacent to the cutlery, three decanters containing his finest Pinot Noir, flowers into vases next to unscented candles on sideboards, and placed a vinyl record of Edward Elgar's *Symphony No. 3* on to his record player, ready to be played when his guests started arriving. In the kitchen he placed champagne flutes into the fridge. Sancerre white wine and Veuve Clicquot champagne were in the tall chiller cabinet, cold enough to be drunk once the gathering was underway. The last task was to prepare the food.

Hala's body parts were defrosted. *Nose to tail* was the phrase used by poorly paid chef's employed by French royalty hundreds of years ago. Never waste anything. From a pig's snout to its tail – everything edible had to be used. It's why French cuisine is so inventive and delicious. Lesser chefs from other countries and with a bigger budget were too privileged to understand that one must respect every ounce of flesh on a slaughtered animal's body. Genius was born out of the French chefs' meagre budgets.

He set to work.

He made a broth with her head and feat. After disposing of the flesh, the liquid would be transformed into a gravy. The arms were boned and rolled into portion sided paupiettes. He placed the portions into roasting pans, glazed them with oil, butter, and French mustard, and roasted them in the oven. When he'd butchered Hala he'd sawed her legs. Now, he transformed each cut into osso bucco-style steaks. He placed the steaks into big casserole pots, added tomatoes, bay leaves, diced onion, celery, and a stick of cinnamon. He put the pots on to the stove to simmer. He diced the lungs and kidneys and pan fried them with olive oil, herbs, and butter, before adding brandy. Once the intestines were chopped, he grilled them. When they were cooked he added them to pre-cooked pasta. Two days ago he'd made a superb pâté out of the larynx, liver, and pancreas. The pâté would be served to his guests with toast, as an amuse-bouche, to prepare their palates for the feast. He made a soup out of bone marrow, herbs, salt and pepper, and vegetables. The stomach was cut into slithers and was fried as if it was tripe. The brain and heart were minced and slow cooked in the Aga, together with lardons and red wine. Once the sauce was put through a sieve it would make a superb jus. The sauce's meat would be discarded in his green recycling food bin. Now came the tricky part. He placed a cut of Hala's uncooked and deboned arm into her bladder, aerated the bladder using a bicycle pump, tied the end off when it resembled a balloon, and boiled the bladder in a vat of water. The bladder was not going to be served. But the meat inside would be extremely tender and moist. It would make a tremendous accompaniment to the other dishes.

That was the body done.

Now it was the more mundane cookery chores. He prepared potatoes and vegetables – to be cooked nearer the time before the guests arrived. He placed the pan fried meat into dishes and put the dishes into a warm hostess trolley, and stacked expensive white dinner and side plates, and soup bowls on the counter. He'd be plating the food in the kitchen, when his guests were seated in the adjacent dining room, and would serve them as if they were sitting at a restaurant table. The final job was to prepare dishes for himself - food that resembled every course that his guests would be eating. They wouldn't notice that he was drinking chicken soup that had been poured out of a can, or eating a sirloin steak. They'd be too engrossed in their conversations with each other, drinking, and eating Hala. And they'd have no clue they were eating human flesh. Everything, he'd tell them, was from a pig. Nose to tail.

Edward was many things, but he wasn't a cannibal. No way could he eat human flesh. But it did amuse him that he was disposing of her body by getting others to eat her.

He showered and changed into a three piece suit, came back downstairs, made himself a cup of tea, sat in his vast lounge, and stared at the sea. His mobile phone rang. "I hope you're calling with good news."

Lowestoft Man replied, "I have what you need. Fresh off the boat. Housemaid, gardener, and a cook. Are you sure you still don't want your staff processed?"

Edward's voice was cold when he answered, "I don't want my staff to have papers. Legal documents give them the confidence to stray from my estate."

"Understood. In that case they should be with you in a day or so."

Edward ended the call and relaxed. It would be good to have three new illegal immigrants. It meant he could kill again once he'd got to know them.

CHAPTER 7

It was mid-morning the following day. Sign and Knutsen took the Central Line tube to Loughton, Essex. Both men were wearing rugged outdoor clothes and hiking boots. Knutsen had his handgun secreted in his jacket. Neither of them had been to Loughton before. The town was London overspill territory, filled with working class people who commuted in to London and nouveau riche who lived in brassy big properties close to Epping Forest.

The two men exited the station and walked down the high street. The place wasn't salubrious. There was a shop selling items for a pound each, betting establishment, ironmonger, dowdy hairdresser salon, second-hand car dealership, business promising cash loans at extortionate rates, cheap toy shop, numerous charities, off license, amusement arcade, fish and chip takeaway, curry house, grim-looking pubs, convenience store that opened at six AM and closed at eleven PM, and many other retailers who reflected the realities of a poor community. But things changed as Sign and Knutsen walked up the residential York Hill road, towards the forest. At the base of the road was a human sized model of Mrs. Tiggy Winkle, Beatrix Potter's hedgehog character. The model portrayed her as a kindly mother-like figure. The placard at her feet explained that her presence here was temporary and was part of the local library and Staple Road Primary School's efforts to encourage children to read. It appeared that there was more to Loughton than initial impressions suggested.

Knutsen was looking at his mobile phone as they continued walking uphill. "This place has got a bloody good swimming pool with a high diving board. Schools are rated highly. Dead easy to get into London. So what was all that shit on the high street?"

"It reflects lack of money. Nothing more, nothing less. The rich folk here shop elsewhere. Things will change, rest assured. But, not necessarily for the better. High streets around Britain are dying, as we know. People shop on the Internet. How quickly can you pull out your gun?"

"It would take me one second."

"Good." When they reached the top of the hill Sign said, "We're close to the forest. Now's the time to activate that App thingy on your phone." The App he was referring to was a satellite navigational device that not only pinpointed where they were, it also supplied the eight digit grid reference of their exact location. Knutsen had already pre-programmed the App to tell them where they needed to be and the route to get there.

Knutsen looked at his phone. "It says seven hundred and sixty three yards until we arrive at the spot."

"We're going to be slightly early. That doesn't matter. I want to see the famous forest. Since 1966 eleven recorded murders have taken place in the woods. Over the centuries the numbers of unrecorded murders in the forest must be exponentially higher."

With sarcasm, Knutsen replied, "We're going to a historical forest and all you can think about are murders."

Sign smiled. "That's not all I know about the forest. Epping Forest is a 5,900 acre area of ancient woodland between Epping in the north, and Wanstead and Leytonstone in the south, straddling the border between Greater London and Essex. It is a former royal forest, and is managed by the City of London Corporation. An area of 4,270 acres is a Site of Special Scientific Interest and a Special Area of Conservation. It gives its name to the Epping Forest local government district, which covers part of it. The forest is approximately 12 miles long in the north-south direction, but no more than 2.5 miles from east to west at its widest point, and in most places considerably narrower. It lies on a ridge between the valleys of the rivers Lea and Roding and contains areas of woodland, grassland, heath, rivers, bogs and ponds, and its elevation and thin gravelly soil, the result of glaciation, historically made it unsuitable for agriculture."

"How do you know all that?"

"I researched it this morning, while I was treating myself to a bacon butty and a mug of tea. You were still in your bedroom, or your bathroom."

"What was the point of researching stuff about the forest? Curiosity?"

"No. I needed to know dimensions and topography, in case we have to escape on foot."

"That makes a lot of sense." Knutsen switched to his heavy London geezer accent. "Right, time to get in role. I'm John Maloney. I've worked with Dave Hitch, but not recently. And I've worked with you. Your Henry Redmayne. Hitch put us in contact with Michael Time. He put us in contact with the bloke we're about to meet."

"Bobby Potts."

"Yeah. Domingo." Knutsen was walking fast. "You're a posh cunt, or at least you think you are. I trust you because of everything you've done for me and my old crew. Today is purely business. We want something. Potts can deliver what we want, if his head's screwed on. Simple as that. I play the bruiser. You play the calculating businessman."

"You're providing me with information I already know." Sign chuckled. "I have done similar work before."

"You have mate. The information I just gave you was for my benefit, not yours. I needed to hear it coming out of my gob."

"Fair play, dear chap."

They walked in to the outskirts of the forest. At first they had to descend a long escarpment, before reaching the wooded area in the valley. The forest was covered with frost and a low-lying fog or mist – neither Sign or Knutsen knew the difference between fog and mist and nor did they care to have that knowledge.

Knutsen led the way while monitoring his phone. "We're here."

They stood by an oak tree. This was the meeting place. Around them were European beech, hornbeam, silver birch, holly, butcher's-broom, and drooping sedge. The men's breath steamed as they waited while stamping their feet and rubbing their hands to stay warm.

Knutsen said, "Bloody cold down here."

"Try surviving in Siberia for a month in minus fifty degrees while on the run." Sign was looking left and right. "But yes, there is a bite in the air."

"Nippy."

"Chilly willy."

Knutsen laughed. "Colder than an Eskimo's pussy."

"Good lord man. You do have some unusual vocabulary." Sign tensed. A deer was fifty yards in front of them. It ran. "The deer didn't see us. It saw something else."

"I know. Here we go." Knutsen placed his hand in his jacket and clutched his sidearm.

A man walked towards them. He was in his thirties, medium height, stocky, bald, and was wearing army surplus boots, a puffer jacket, and jeans. He stopped in front of them. "I'm looking for a bloke called John Maloney." His accent was working class Essex. "I'm guessing that's one of you."

"That'll be me." Knutsen stepped forward. "You're name?"

The man held his ground while staring at Knutsen. "You tell me, sunshine."

Knutsen had anticipated that the initial encounter would be what he would describe in his undercover persona as a pissing contest. "We're here to meet Bobby Potts. That might be you. Or you could be a cop pretending to be him."

"Fuck off. I'm no cop."

"An undercover cop would say that."

The man put his hand in his jacket pocket.

Knutsen whipped out his handgun and pointed it at the man's head.

"Easy, easy, sunshine." The man withdrew his mobile phone. "I'm going to call Michael Time. I'll put him on speaker phone. He'll vouch for me." He made the call. Time verified his credentials. Potts put his phone back in his pocket. "You want me to pull out my gun or are we going to talk turkey?"

Knutsen didn't move for two seconds, his gun still pointing at Potts' head. Then he placed his pistol in to his pocket. "No funny shit. I'm here to protect my client. If you muck around, no cunt will ever find your body. You got that?"

Potts smiled, though his eyes were cold. "I'm here to see if I can make some dosh. I didn't come here for some agro." His expression softened. "Time said you want people." He looked at Sign. "Who are you?"

Knutsen replied, "That's none of your fucking business."

Sign placed his hand on Knutsen's forearm. In a calm voice he said, "It's okay, John. I'm Henry Redmayne. It's not my real name. It's my work name. John Maloney is John Maloney. But, I have to be more cautious. I don't mix in the kind of circles that you and John mix in. I prefer to keep my distance."

Potts walked right up to him.

"Careful, matey boy!" said Knutsen.

Potts stared at Sign. Then he nodded and walked back two paces. "You ain't filth." He looked at Knutsen. "Alright then. You two work together."

"It's temporary," replied Knutsen. "Redmayne's giving me an introductory fee, as he calls it. I set up the meetings, make sure he doesn't get hurt, and when he gets what he wants I get back to other jobs."

"How do I know if I can trust Redmayne?"

Knutsen replied, "We go way back. He's never let me and my mates down."

Potts was quiet for a moment. "Why do you need the immigrants?"

Sign replied, "For illegal work. I'm not going to tell you what kind of work. But I can tell you the work will be in my establishment in London. For obvious reasons, I can't disclose the location of the establishment."

Potts said, "How many do you need?"

"Twenty in the first instance."

"Twenty?" Potts addressed Knutsen. "Have you told him my rates? Ten grand per person if they're shipped here to order."

Knutsen nodded. "He knows the rates."

Sign added, "The money isn't an issue. The quality of my staff is. But if you get this right there'll be repeat business. Within one year I'm anticipating that I'll need one hundred illegal immigrants. After that, who knows. Regardless, you'll be a wealthy man."

This caught Potts' attention. "Men? Women? Age? What are you looking for?"

Sign replied, "Gender doesn't matter. They need to be healthy. And most importantly they must have certain characteristics that make them suitable for my employment."

"What characteristics?"

"I have a checklist. I won't share that list with anyone. Even John doesn't know the profile of the people I'm looking for." Sign folded his arms. "How do you get the immigrants in to the country?"

The question didn't flummox Potts. "I don't know and I don't want to know. They arrive and then they're passed from one handler to another. I do London. That's my thing. There'll be others like me who do different bits of the country. But I know London."

"Good. Then I'm talking to the right person. But there is a problem." Sign remained stock still. "I'm not paying for anyone until I've interviewed them. This principal places you in a difficult position because you won't want to make the effort to get them to London, get them processed by Time, only for me to tell you that they're not suitable. I don't have the ability to travel to places like Libya, Syria, and Iraq to interview them before they leave their countries. But, I do have the ability to interview them when they arrive in Britain. When I assess a candidate to be suitable, I call you and tell you the candidate needs to be delivered to London for me and me alone. You get your money. I'm happy. You've not wasted your time."

Potts dwelled on this. "It's not unusual. We get clients who want a certain type of woman. Usually it's prostitution but sometimes it's marriage. They need to see what they look like before they commit. But, from what you've said, you ain't looking for prostitutes or wives."

"Indeed, I'm not."

"Ten grand per person. You're happy with that?" Potts was doing the arithmetic in his head. He wasn't a clever man. But when it came to cash and business, he was street smart.

Sign said, "I'm happy with that. Ten thousand pounds per person."

"Alright." Potts pulled out his mobile phone again. "What's your number?"

Sign gave him the number of one of his deniable phones. "Only calls. No text messages. I have to be very careful."

"Same here." Potts stored the number. "You need to meet the handler who supplies me with merchandise for London. He's not the person who brings people into the country. But he might know the person who does. I'll give him a call later today and see if he's up for this. Then I'll call you. By the way, ten grand a pop sounds a lot of dosh, but it has to be spread around. I get my cut but so does everyone else involved. We're a business."

"Let's hope this is a fruitful business arrangement." Sign extended his hand. "I look forward to speaking to you on the phone."

Potts shook his hand. "Wait here for fifteen minutes before leaving. That'll give me time to get out of Loughton." He turned and walked out of the forest.

Edward's new housemaid, cook, and gardener had arrived. Two females, one male. The housemaid was Farzaneh, Iranian, age twenty eight. She'd fled Iran after writing a blog criticising the religious supreme leader of her country. The blog had not gone unnoticed. A friend of hers who served in the regular army had tipped her off that the Iranian Revolutionary Guard Corps was trying to track her down and put her in prison. He'd told her that her punishment would be getting stoned to death. She was pretty, had a petite physique, and spoke perfect English. The cook was a Saudi called Bayan. She was thirty five, a former teacher, and had suffered the wrath of Saudi authorities when she'd taught the girls in her class how to read. She'd suffered twenty whip lashes as a result and was told she could never teach again. The fanatical religious police, most of them ex-convicts who'd been forced to amend their ways, told her that she must never work again. If she contravened that instruction, she'd have her head chopped off. Like Farzaneh, Bayan also spoke English. She was attractive and a rebel. Saudi Arabia was not the place for her. Here she could be free to think and speak her mind. The gardener was Azzat. He was twenty years old, Afghan, spoke passable Arabic but no English, liked football, had never been with a girl, was tall and skinny, and knew nothing about the Western world. He was to all intents and purposes a boy. That needed to change.

Edward looked at them as they stood next to each other in his vast lounge. He addressed them as if he was a commanding officer inspecting his troops on a parade ground. Bayan translated his words so that Azzat could understand Edward's words. Edward said, "I run a tight ship. Your new homes must be kept clean and tidy. If one of you gets sick, the rest of you must pick up that person's duties until the sick person is recovered. No romantic liaisons are permitted on to the estate. In fact, no guests whatsoever. The hours you'll work are fair but rigid – I don't tolerate my staff turning up for work a minute late. You'll have weekends off work. There are enjoyable things to do around here. You can go to the beach, walk in the woods, play sports on the lawn that I showed you earlier, and go to the village. But never ever stray further than the village. England is not a safe place for illegal immigrants. Only my estate protects you. You're safe here. You'll find that I'm a good employer. I've prepared your homes. You have beds, televisions, furniture, bathroom toiletries, pots and pans in your kitchens, towels, washing machines, and all other basic needs. The only thing I couldn't buy you in advance of your arrival is spare clothes. Now that I've seen you I have the gauge of your size. Today I'll get you several sets of spare clothes. But, you'll need to let me know your shoe size. You'll be paid well. You can buy your food in the village. Or Bayan can give you the same food that she cooks me. Never call anyone, even from a payphone. Your calls could be traced. And if that happened you would be put in prison and sent back to your countries. You may call me 'sir' or 'Edward'; I don't mind either. I don't have a wife or children. Your homes are your homes. You are permitted to smoke and drink whatever you like in there. I've left instructions in your properties about refuse collection dates and recycling. Tomorrow you won't work but I will speak to you individually about the use of various equipment for your duties. Any questions?"

They shook their heads.

Edward smiled. "Good. Bayan – in the kitchen are three Tupperware boxes containing Hungarian goulash and rice. It's your meals for tonight. I cooked the food." The meat was taken from Hala's thighs. "I've also put milk, eggs, bread, and cereal in your kitchens for your breakfast tomorrow. If you have any problems understanding how to use your homes' appliances, let me know. I will see you all in this room at nine AM tomorrow. I bid you good night."

It was evening. Sign poured two glasses of calvados, handed one to Knutsen, and sat opposite him next to the fire. "I've made a casserole of diced braised mutton, shallots, tomatoes, fried bacon, fresh sage, French mustard, red wine, a dash of balsamic vinegar, roasted potatoes, and peas, It'll take another thirty minutes to cook. It's hardly Michelin Star cuisine, but It'll fuel us, much like farmers' fodder of old."

Knutsen sipped his drink. "Sounds good to me. After dinner can we take a stroll? I need to get some air."

"Of course, dear chap."

Knutsen wondered why Sign was so composed. "Do you not worry that we might not get seriously hurt, or worse? We've got to get through Carreras, Pavarotti, and Lowestoft Man, before we find our target. And our target could be infinitely worse."

Sign shrugged. "Worry doesn't help. We have a war chest – logic, deductive reasoning, honed skills and experience, and the ability to improvise. Admiral Lord Nelson had the same attributes. He'd go in to battle with meticulous plans but was willing to tear up those plans and change tactics if his enemy did something he hadn't predicted. Nelson is often described as an inspirational leader. I prefer to think of him as an extremely fast and accurate thinker. You have a first class degree and I…"

"Yeah, you're a freak." Knutsen laughed. "Bloody MI6 should never have grabbed a brain like yours and given it skills." He became serious. "We haven't got a huge amount of cash left in our business bank account. Our next case can't be pro bono."

"It won't be." Sign threw a log on to the fire. "We're doing this case because we're dealing with people who have no money and are being systematically exploited. Illegal immigrants are invisible. They work in hotels, car washes, restaurants, building sites, and other places. No one notices them. Some of the women are forced in to prostitution. The common theme is twofold: their employers don't want them to be caught out; the illegals' clients are getting bang for their buck and won't dob them in to the authorities. It's a sad dynamic because at the heart of it all is greed. The illegals are whipped like mules so they work harder. And when they fall to their knees and take their last breath, they're tossed aside and new blood is brought in. They're expendable." He added, "But, we're dealing with something much more calculated than selfish employers. We're dealing with a highly intelligent serial killer who's done something no one else has done – importing invisibles so that he can execute them. It's clever. No British serial killer in history has done that."

Knutsen sipped his drink "He's buying in livestock and slaughters them when he's ready to do so. *Invisibles*. I like that phrase. Jack The Ripper went after invisibles. Prostitutes in Whitechapel."

"But he didn't order them in, knowing they didn't want to be found. The prostitutes the Ripper killed were visible on the streets. They weren't invisible. People knew them. As an aside, there is debate as to whether the Ripper existed. There is strong evidence the alleged Ripper murders were the work of several murderers." Sign placed his glass down. "Every serial killer in history has been a predator. They've either gone away from their homes to select and kill their victims, or they've brought them to their home and killed them there. What we're dealing with is different. We have a spider sitting patiently in the centre of its web. The prey comes to him and is trapped in the web. The spider only has to move a few inches to devour them."

Knutsen shook his head. "Your analogy is good but not perfect. Bad luck or wind blows the insects in to a web. In our case the insects are being forced in to the web. The killer has Lowestoft Man to do that for him."

Sign clapped his hands. "Bravo and accurate! It is highly likely that Lowestoft Man knows the fate of the people he delivers to the killer. He is an enabler." He checked his watch. "I need your assistance in the kitchen. It would be kind of you to peel four carrots, thinly slice them, and place them in a pan of simmering salted water. I will prepare asparagus, fricassee some cabbage with cracked black pepper and a diced chilli, and uncork a lovely bottle of Merlot. The wine will be the perfect accompaniment to our meal."

After they'd eaten and washed the dishes they walked alongside the Thames. It was nine PM. The air was crisp and still. No other pedestrians were to be seen on the embankment. Even the sound of traffic was distant and only occasional. For ten minutes the men were silent, wrapped up in their own thoughts. Knutsen was internalizing the merits or otherwise of police involvement in the serial killer case. Sign was wondering how long it would take for Knutsen to snap and say that the case should be fully declared to the police. They walked on to the London Millennium Footbridge. Halfway across, Sign placed a hand on Knutsen's shoulder and stopped. He leaned against the railing, staring at the mighty river. Knutsen leaned next to him. Again, they were silent for a few minutes, both men enjoying what they perceived to be a city that was getting sleepy and ready for bed. At the same time they had thoughts cascading through their brains.

Sign sighed and wanted to think about anything other than people smugglers and a serial killer. In a slow, deliberate tone, he said, "I believe I may be ready to meet a woman."

Knutsen frowned. "Where the fuck did that come from?"

"It's been on my mind for some time. I don't believe that I want to get married again. But it would be nice to have a relationship."

"Got anyone in mind?"

"No. And I wouldn't know where to start."

Knutsen smiled. "You've got to put yourself out there mate."

"*Put myself out there?*"

"Yeah. It's unlikely you're going to meet the bird of your dreams during our investigation. This is hardly CSI shit – detective gets it on with hot forensics officer."

"I've no idea what CSI is, though I presume it's a television programme or movie." He held his hand up. "You don't need to tell me. So, how do I meet a woman? The right woman."

Knutsen considered the question. "Aren't there any birds at your St. James's club?"

"Their average age is one hundred and seventy six and their either married or devoted to charitable causes."

"Fair point." Knutsen rubbed his stubble. "Propping up a bar in a random pub isn't your style. Plus you won't meet the right woman by doing that. You're too old and posh to got to nightclubs. And, the image of you strutting your stuff on the dancefloor makes me want to throw myself in to the Thames. Have you got any mates who've got wives who know single friends? Trusted platonic women are a great way to get introduced to a nice lady. The wife has already vetted her. You get a stamp of approval before the get-go."

Sign smiled while continuing to look at the river. "Don't be overly flattered by what I'm going to say next. You're my only friend. The few other friends I had are dead. And it was only a few friends that I had. It's very hard to make lasting friendships in MI6. We're posted here there and everywhere, loose contact with each other, and most importantly we're bred to be loners. No, I don't have a friend with a wife who can introduce me to lovely divorced Cassandra during a manufactured dinner party."

Knutsen nodded. "Right. I know what to do. Back to the flat. Let's go."

With resignation Sign said, "I know what you're thinking of doing." He followed Knutsen back to West Square.

Once inside the flat's lounge, Knutsen said, "Power up your laptop."

Sign sat at his desk and did so.

Knutsen stood next to him. "You're going to need to register with an Internet dating site." He gave him details of the site he had in mind.

"Internet dating is ridiculous!"

"Why?"

"Because the starting point of getting to know someone is predicated with an air of desperation. Real life is somewhat more genteel."

"Yeah but you haven't got a real life. Just get on with it. Register on the site, I'll take your photo so you can upload it, and then you just wait to see if anyone likes you."

Ten minutes later Sign said, "I'm registered. Now it needs my personal details. Education – Oxford University. Age – fifty. Star sign – Sagittarius. Non-smoker. She must be... What the hell do I put in this section? It's asking if she should be brunette, blonde, curvy, slim, athletic, and it wants an age range."

"Just put in age range between forty and fifty. And click the button that says you have no preference on body type or looks."

Sign did so.

Knutsen watched the laptop screen. "One thing I'm not sure about is whether she should be university educated or not. Maybe click on the 'don't mind' button."

Sign wasn't enjoying this process one bit. Without typing he said, "Personal details. Former special operative who's served in many war ravaged parts of the globe. Commendations by the prime minister for bravery and influencing foreign policy. I saved thousands of lives to protect democracy. Now a consulting detective on extremely delicate cases."

Knutsen placed his hand on Sign's shoulder. "Don't put any of that. Women will think you're a fantasist. You might as well put you were the last man to set foot on the moon. Just say you were a diplomat and now work for a political think tank."

"Fair point." Sign entered his credentials. "My body type? Slim."

"Athletic."

"Alright! Athletic. No facial hair. Tall. Oh God! It's asking how I would describe my looks. Handsome or plain. What on Earth do I put for that?"

"Just click the 'rather not say' button. There's no button asking you if you look like an early twentieth century English king." Knutsen sniggered. "Put in your interests. You love cooking, reading, walking, all of that kind of stuff. Keep it real in this bit. You need someone who likes some of the things you like. Don't say anything about your passion for catching spies and serial killers."

Sign typed in his hobbies. He stared at the screen.

"You're not going to do this, are you?"

"No." Sign deleted the account, stood, and looked at Knutsen. "I'm too old fashioned."

Knutsen smiled sympathetically. "I know mate. But at least the process of going through that shit has got you thinking about what you'd say to a lady if ever you found one you liked."

Sign sat in his armchair. "Do you think it's too late for me.?"

Knutsen sat in his armchair. "Not at all. You're young."

"I'm fifty years old, have put a lot of effort in to life, and do not feel young. At least in my head. I've seen and done too much."

"You're a great catch. You're loyal, kind, and you cook. Plus you're weirdly intelligent and a woman will love that."

"*Weirdly?*" Sign smiled. "Weirdly." His expression and tone of voice turned reflective. "It's an odd thing though, isn't it, that despite one's intelligence one cannot find a foot hold in the normal world. I feel that I'm condemned to be dislocated. Most spies suffer the same shift of thinking. Former special forces soldiers get agonised by lack of camaraderie and purpose. Former MI6 officers are skewed by knowledge and an outlook that imprisons them in the secret world. A woman..." His voice trailed. "Could a woman cure that?"

"Yes. Only a woman who loves you could cure that."

Sign nodded. "Perhaps one day." He doubted he'd ever meet such a woman. His phone rang. It was Bobby Potts. He listened carefully for five minutes, thanked him, and hung up. He said to Knutsen, "We are to meet Carreras at two PM tomorrow in the outskirts of Colchester. I have the precise location. Carreras's name is Rob Green."

Knutsen stood. "I'll check my pistol."

CHAPTER 8

At nine AM the following morning Edward's new staff stood before him in his lounge. Farzaneh the housemaid, Bayan the cook, and Azzat the gardener, looked tired. No doubt they hadn't slept well, were disorientated, and anxious that they were capable of doing their duties.

Edward smiled sympathetically. "Don't worry. I will only need you today for an hour or so. After that you can rest, take a walk around the grounds, and perhaps go to the beach. Tomorrow you'll be working a full day."

Bayan translated his words for Azzat.

Edward addressed the women. "I would like one or both of you to help Azzat learn basic English. But, keep it specific. He needs to understand me when I give him instructions on matters such as cutting the grass, using the lawnmower, checking the level of oil in the outside fuel tank, and other gardening requirements. Listen to what I tell him in a moment and remember what I say to him. That's what he needs to understand for his job. He will also need to understand what to say when he buys food in the village. Protect him. He is alone and scared. Treat him as if he is your younger brother. Do you understand?"

Farzaneh and Bayan nodded.

Edward gave them instructions and told them to have a lovely day.

Sign and Knutsen were on a train out of London Liverpool Street. Their destination was Colchester. Sign was wearing a suit. Knutsen was wearing jeans, boots, and a hiking jacket, underneath which was his handgun. After thirty minutes of travel they were out of the metropolis.

Knutsen was looking out of the window. He said, "Nice to get out of the city. It's peaceful in the countryside."

Sign followed his gaze as the train passed a thatched house. Sign said, "I tend to disagree. In the house we just passed could be a man who murdered his wife and children. Who would know? The countryside can cloak a multitude of undiscovered crimes. Cities are less forgiving to felons."

A female passenger, who'd overheard Sign's comments, looked shocked.

Sign smiled at her. "Don't worry, madam. There is much to rejoice about within the empty spaces of our lands." He looked at Knutsen, leaned forward, and said in a quiet voice, "Be prepared. The man we're meeting will certainly have preparations in place."

Knutsen whispered, "Damn right."

Sign leaned back and wondered what he would do if Knutsen took a bullet from Carreras, Pavarotti, or Lowestoft Man. Though much younger than Sign, Knutsen had so many similarities to him. They were both lost in life, struggled to form relationships with others, intelligent, gentleman except when they were faced with adversity, could mix with all walks of life, and were unflinching in their duties. Knutsen was as brave as Sign. But that came with the territory. What mattered to Sign was that Knutsen was his friend. Odd how these things happen. Two years ago Sign would never have imagined that he'd strike up a bond with an ex-Met copper. But he was glad that by chance and design things had turned out this way. The design was Sign's selection of Knutsen as a business partner. The chance was that they became friends. Sign liked to think of them as 'club men' – males who had business interests in common but would also happily sit together in refined surroundings and talk about other matters. The analogy wasn't exactly correct, he decided, though the spirit of the analogy was spot on. Sign and Knutsen could share each other's company in many different surroundings – the cosy environment of their lounge in West Square, a fine dining restaurant, or a pub where they could play darts and pool. In upbringing, Knutsen was so different from Sign. That didn't matter to Sign. He'd seen too much of the world and had too much leftfield thinking to be bogged down by a stereotypical sense of class. What always mattered to him was a person's character, regardless of where they were from or what background they had. Knutsen was a younger version of him, albeit from a different life path. They both had a certain look in their eyes, though the looks were different but allied. Knutsen had a thousand yard stare; a gaze that was soldered by the countless witness of brutality by criminals who had no idea who he really was. Sign's eyes glistened as they pierced people's souls. But both sets of eyes were testament to the odd people they were. Sign breathed in deeply. There was no doubt about it; if Knutsen took a bullet Sign would pick up Knutsen's gun and kill everyone nearby. Sign had seen and enacted so much violence in his MI6 career. He'd semi-retired from that life. But, with Knutsen he'd make an exception and become the man he once was.

No. He still was that man. He just hid it from others.

Sign said, "I'm pondering on tonight's dinner. Possibly quail eggs served on a risotto of basil, cracked pepper, lobster, parmesan, saffron, a hint of garlic, and accompanied by a salad with lettuce, vine tomatoes, celery, olive oil, balsamic vinegar, and slithers of loganberries."

"Loganberries?" Knutsen chuckled. "You're crazy. I'd settle for fish and chips."

"Of course you would, dear chap." Sign looked at the woman near to them, knowing she'd once again overheard their conversation. "Madam, forgive me for intruding. My recipe? Or fish and chips?"

The woman smiled. "The quail eggs and risotto sounds lovely. Have you got an extra seat for me? All I eat are takeaways."

"Thank you ma'am." Sign looked and Knutsen and whispered, "Get her number. She's your age."

Knutsen shook his head, looked uncomfortable, and whispered back, "No."

"Why not. She's pretty and single?"

"How do you know she's single?"

"Takeaway meals plus other indicators. Get her number."

"No."

"You're not attracted to her?"

"Are we really having this conversation?"

Sign laughed. "With us, every day is an adventure." He looked at the nearby woman. She was pretty, possibly late twenties, had brown hair that touched her shoulders, and was wearing clothes that suggested she was a rebel of some sort. Sign was out of his depth on the latter point. Punk? Indie chic? Slacker? Student vibe? Anti-establishment? Happy in her own skin? Non-conformist? Labels didn't matter. What did matter was that Sign knew she was a free spirit. He said to her, "Please forgive us for our intrusion. My colleague is scared to ask if you are single and whether you could exchange telephone numbers."

Knutsen muttered, "For fuck's sake!"

The woman looked at Knutsen. She hesitated for a few seconds before saying, "I'm single." She smiled. "But men are not my vibe, if you get my drift."

Knutsen nodded and looked at Sign. He whispered, "You have one of the finest brains on the planet but you know fuck all about dating."

"I was married."

"Yeah and your wife was murdered." The blood drained from Knutsen's face. "Sorry mate. That was a fucked up comment. I've no idea why I said that."

"You were stating the truth." Sign looked out of the window. "I do concede I'm out of practise when it comes to affairs of the heart." He didn't elaborate; just kept staring out of the window.

Knutsen watched him and felt a pang of utter sorrow for his comrade. Sign had done so much for his country; had seen the very best and worst of humankind; and had embraced situations that were nigh on suicidal for him. Throughout his life he'd put himself second, with one exception – he'd briefly gained love. That was swiftly taken away from him. All he now had was his friendship with Knutsen. And yet Sign was never maudlin or prone to reflect on his loss. At least not in front of others. Knutsen did however wonder what went through Sign's head when he retired to bed. He breathed deeply and said, "We're going to be in Colchester in about thirty minutes. Do you fancy a coffee before we get there?"

Sign looked at him and half-smiled. "No, dear chap. At my age coffee and other diuretics tend to make me need the lavatory far too frequently." He checked his watch. "And shortly we have business to attend to. It would be severely inconvenient if I needed a pee in the midst of proceedings."

Edward walked through his grounds, sucking in the salty sea air and admiring the mist that clung to the hills. He was wearing clothes befitting of a country gentleman – tweed jacket, thick shirt, brown jumper, corduroy trousers, and horse riding boots. He felt at peace. Farzaneh, Bayan, and Azzat were living on his grounds. He was no longer alone. Soon that would temporarily change. But not yet. First he had to understand them. Once that was achieved he would give them a death of their pleasing.

Sign and Knutsen arrived in Colchester. The historic market town, situated in the county of Essex, was once the capital of Roman Britain. Now it was much like any pretty English town. Aside from a handful of tourist information centres explaining its heritage as Roman and the fact that it was the oldest recorded town in Britain, there was little else to suggest that it had once been a place where high ranking officers had plotted their next plans of attacks and legions of Roman warriors had camped before embarking on treks across Britain. Sign and Knutsen exited the train station and walked through the town. The weather was sunny and crisp. The town was busy with shoppers and people taking advantage of the opportunity to sit outside a café and admire their surroundings. The vibe was one of happiness. But Sign and Knutsen could not absorb that emotion. They were only focused on one thing – Rob Green, aka Carreras. They reached the eastern side of the town and entered a hire car shop. Sign had pre-booked a BMW 1 Series for their eight mile journey out of Colchester. The selection of car and model had been deliberate. The vehicle wasn't flash, but nor was it cheap. And it was the perfect model for an alleged successful hotelier to drive in congested London. It was small, practical, yet fast. Sign completed paperwork and took possession of the vehicle. The men drove out of town.

They arrived at a remote farmstead. Knutsen stopped the car thirty yards away from the complex that contained a house, barn, sheds, outside of which were a tractor, four ton lorry, and an SUV. They got out of the car, waited for a moment, and approached the house.

A man exited one of the sheds. He was wearing a fleece, waterproof trousers, and Wellington boots. He looked athletic and tough. He called out, "Can I help you?"

Sign replied, "We have an appointment with Mr. Green."

"Names?"

"Henry Redmayne and John Maloney."

The man eyed them for five seconds, withdrew his mobile phone, and made a call. "Boss – those two guys you told me about are here." He listened to the response, nodded, and ended the call. Addressing Sign and Knutsen he said, "Wait here a minute." He re-entered the shed and re-emerged with a shotgun slung over his back. He walked up to the men and patted the part of the barrel that was protruding over his right shoulder. "Pest control." He stood with them. His phone rang. He listened and ended the call. "Alright. Rob will meet you in the barn. You've caught us at a busy time. We're preparing for the next season. Come with me."

Sign and Knutsen followed him for seventy yards across the front of the farmstead.

The man opened the barn door and said, "After you."

They entered the barn.

The large building was empty of equipment, cattle, crops, or anything else that would suggest it was a container to keep an active farm's vital assets dry. Instead there was a man standing in the centre of the barn, facing Sign and Knutsen, his arms folded. Four men flanked him. Two of them were holding shotguns. The other two had their hands in their jackets. No doubt they had pistols secreted underneath their outer garments. The man in the middle walked closer to them. He was short, had a powerful stocky physique, cropped brown hair, and when he spoke it was with a London accent.

He said, ""I'm Rob Green. Confirm who sent you here."

Sign replied, "Bobby Potts. We were led to believe that you were expecting us."

Green spun around, looked at his men, and returned his attention to Sign and Knutsen. "You're here for business?"

"Correct."

"What kind of business."

"Lucrative business of a delicate nature."

Green walked up to Sign and put his face inches from Sign's face. "Delicate?" He smiled, though his expression was cold. He turned around and walked back ten paces. "Check 'em out. Thoroughly."

The man who'd led them into the barn placed his shotgun against Knutsen's head. Two of Green's men walked up to them, checked their pockets, and patted them down. Knutsen's handgun was removed and tossed to one side. Ditto both men's mobile phones.

One of the men said, "Can't be sure."

Green said to Sign and Knutsen, "Strip."

The men nearest to them stepped back. All of them were now pointing their weapons at the detectives.

Sign and Knutsen complied.

When they were naked, Green said to his men, "Check their arses and bollocks."

Two of the men grabbed Sign and Knutsen and bent them over. A third pulled their buttocks open and placed his hand on their undercarriages. The third man looked at Green and shook his head.

Green said, "Alright. They can get dressed. Give me the handgun and the phones."

Two minutes later Sign and Knutsen were fully clothed.

Sign feigned anger. "Do you treat all of your potential customers in this way?"

Green shrugged. "I don't know you. You've come to my home. If I'd come to your home I'd expect you to check me out in the same way I've just checked you out. What do you want?"

Sign was composed as he replied. "People. A large number of people. I have business interests in London that require staff who are not registered in the UK. I'm told you might be of help."

Green was silent for a moment before nodding at the man who'd led Sign and Knutsen into the barn.

The blow from the shotgun stock to the back of Knutsen's head was sufficiently powerful to force Knutsen on to his knees.

Green knelt in front of Knutsen and asked quietly, "Are you a cop?" He pointed at Sign. "And is this man your boss?"

Knutsen shook his head while wincing in pain. "No. I'm a bodyguard. Mr. Redmayne is a businessman."

"Bodyguard?" Green sniggered. "If that's true you've done a lousy job of protecting your employer." He looked at Sign. "Are you a couple of cops, come here to check me out?"

Sign held his gaze. "It appears this has been a waste of time."

"You got armed police outside my farm, waiting to come in after a set period of time?"

"No."

Green looked at their mobile phone. "They're burners." The term burner referred to phones that were untraceable and typically were only used for calls between two people.

Sign pretended to look angry. "Of course they're burners! We're not amateurs!"

"You're not amateurs? And yet you had to use Bobby Potts to get to me. Sounds like you're new to this lark. You've got no idea what you're doing."

Sign spoke in an icy tone. "I need people from outside this country. That *is* a new challenge for me. But, if you want to ask me about the nuances of sophisticated drug trafficking, arms shipments, counter fitting, money laundering, the sex trade, and a few other strings I have to my bow then you will find that there are many things that I know that you probably don't know. Don't fuck with me Green."

The comment gave Green pause for thought. "If that's true, how come I've never heard of you?"

"Because until now I've not given you a reason to hear of me. Let my bodyguard stand."

Green eyed Sign but said nothing.

"Let him stand!"

Green inhaled deeply, then nodded at the man behind Knutsen.

Knutsen was hauled to his feet.

Knutsen rubbed the back of his head, still smarting with pain.

Sign sounded every part the powerful and erudite criminal mastermind when he said, "I will forgive you, Rob Green, for what's just happened. You didn't know who I was. But that forgiveness will immediately expire if you lay one more finger on my colleague or me. If you choose to ignore that instruction, my men will come and kill all of you. They have their instructions." He looked around before returning his attention on Green. "And I can assure you that your bunch of amateurs would not like to meet my men."

Green was deep in thought. "How many bodies do you need?"

Sign held out his hand. "Our phones and our gun."

"Fuck that."

"Our phones and our gun! Then we can talk."

Green hesitated before handing back the weapon and the mobiles. Sign placed all into his inside jacket pockets. There was no point giving Knutsen his gun. It was obvious to Sign that Knutsen was still disorientated after the blow to his head and would stand no chance of accurately using his weapon if needed. Instead, Sign would use the gun if things didn't go to plan.

Sign said, "I need at least thirty illegals in the first instance, maybe more. There will be significant repeat business. But – and this is crucial – I need to vet the illegals upon arrival in the UK. Can you meet that volume of business?"

For the first time, Green looked like he'd lost control of the situation. "I can get you that number. But I can't guarantee you quality control. I'm part of a chain. Bodies are handed to me. I hand them to Potts. Potts gets them in to London."

"I thought so. But you get a very healthy cut for being part of the chain. Who do I need to speak to further upstream?"

"Upstream?"

"I need to speak to the person who brings the illegals in to the UK. Only he can help me with quality control."

Green looked at his men. "All of you leave, except Bill. Bill stay with me."

Bill was the man who'd hit Knutsen.

Green said to Sign and Knutsen, "Come with me."

He walked out of the barn and towards one of the sheds. He opened the door. Inside were two women and a child, both Middle Eastern. They were lying on mattresses and looked frightened. A large porcelain bowl was next to the makeshift beds and was full of urine and faeces. Green shut the door. "I was given them yesterday. They're from Iraq or Afghanistan or some shit like that. I don't know and I don't care. I'll get them to Potts tomorrow. He can do what he likes with them." He walked to Sign's car. "I can only process what I'm given. You've just seen what I've been given."

Sign nodded. "Which is why I need to ensure you're given the quality I need. You get that high quality product to Potts. He gives the illegals to me. We all make a lot of money."

Green rubbed his face. "I don't know man. The guy who delivers me cargo is like me. He's given illegals. But he's not the one who meets them off the boat."

"Who is?"

"Don't know. How are you going to get the people you want?"

Sign smiled. "Are you familiar with the history surrounding the creation of the State of Israel?"

"What the fuck?"

"The point is, after the war Jews were brought into Palestine from all parts of Europe. They were vetted at the entry point of what would become Israel. People were selected for jobs, much like the selection process when they entered concentration camps. The Brits and their Jewish senior allies handpicked individuals who they believed could become the Israeli leaders in their fields. It was a filtering process. I want to be at the dock where the illegals arrive. I get to choose who I want and who I don't want. But only I can make the decisions."

Green smiled. "This isn't just about staffing some of your hotels. You've got something else going on."

"Of course. And if you help me you'll be rewarded handsomely for your troubles."

Green paced back and forth for a few seconds. "Alright." He pulled out a notepad and pen, scribbled down a number, tore the sheet out of the pad, and handed the sheet to Sign. "This is the man you need to call. His name's Eric West. Don't call him until I've texted you that I've that I've spoken to him and he's happy to meet. And for God's sake call him from a different phone."

"Good." Sign held out his hand. "Pleasure doing business with you."

Green took his hand. "And you. Sorry about the precautions we had to take."

Sign gripped his hand tight and pulled him close, his strength too much for Green to resist. "I expect better treatment from Mr. West." He let go of Green's hand and said to Knutsen, "Do you want to return the favour to shotgun man by hitting him over the head with your gun?"

Knutsen looked at Green's right hand man. With an cold expression he said in a quiet tone, "Not this time."

Sign and Knutsen got in their car and drove off.

At five PM Edward took a stroll through his grounds. For him the weather was perfect – crisp, sunlight that was descending and producing long shadows, and no wind. His staff had finished their work for the day. Edward presumed they were in their cottages, resting or cooking. He wasn't concerned about them and didn't feel the need to check on them. They needed privacy and had to learn to fend for themselves. Tough love was how he thought of his approach to being an employer. He paid his employees a good wage; treated them fairly; never exploited them; gave them accommodation and free reign in his grounds; and spoke to them with curtesy.

The urge to kill them was strong but premature. He knew from experience how to counteract the urge. Meditation helped. So too exercise and any other activity that distracted him. He didn't think of himself as a sociopath or psychopath. Those labels were too crass. Sociopaths, he believed, had to learn right from wrong in order to survive in society. But it was a trick. Sociopaths don't truly understand why society deems certain acts to be wrong. They just play along in order not to get sent to prison. Edward was different. He had a strong moral compass and compassion towards others. If someone was in trouble he instinctively wanted to help. It wasn't an act. It came from the heart. So, why did he kill? He'd asked himself that question so many times. To his knowledge he had none of the usual characteristics of serial killers. He didn't have a traumatic childhood, no trauma full stop, didn't kill due to sexual reasons or hatred, had no specific agenda, wasn't selective about the age or gender of his victims, and murdered when he was in a state of calm. There were, he frequently concluded, only two things that made him kill. The acts gave him power over others. As importantly, he was insane.

He reasoned that insanity had its benefits. After all, he was wealthy, lived a happy life, had a plethora of knowledge, was charming when needed, took daily care of himself, and was a connoisseur of classical music and robust and hearty cuisine. He was highly functioning. It was just that his brain worked very differently from other people's brains.

He sat on the partially exposed roots of a tree and looked at the sky. Three buzzards were gliding high in the thermals, searching for mice or rabbits. Even though they were some of the most dim-witted birds of prey, he liked the buzzards. They were patient and only swooped when they were sure of a kill.

He closed his eyes and breathed in deeply. Like the buzzards, death kept him alive. It was as simple as that. That equation brought him utter contentment.

Sign and Knutsen were back in West Square. Sign was in a bad mood, sitting at the dining room table, spinning the phone that was his connection to Rob Green.

Sign said, "When is he going to text?!"

Knutsen was rifling through takeaway menus. "When he's got some news. Hold your nerve."

"I am holding my nerve!" Sign stopped spinning the phone and smiled. "Well, maybe not. I hate waiting because…"

"You can't control the ground around you when things are in limbo." Knutsen poured a beer and handed it to his colleague. "Get this down your neck and chill."

Sign sipped the real ale. "We should eat."

Knutsen continued rifling through takeaway menus. "Indian?"

"No! Not after last time."

"Chinese?"

"No."

"Pizza?"

"It's just posh cheese on toast."

"Thai?"

"Under normal circumstances yes. But these aren't normal circumstances. I need something more substantial."

"Thar rules out sushi then." Knutsen tossed aside the menus. "We'll have to go to the pub and see what they've got to eat."

"Good idea. But I can't leave here until I get the SMS."

Ten minutes later the phone pinged.

CHAPTER 9

Rain lashed the windows of the train as Sign and Knutsen travelled to Norwich. Both men were silent for the most part of the journey, their thoughts preoccupying any urge to pass the time by casual banter. Time on the long journey to East Anglia dragged, but it didn't bother the men. All that mattered to them was that they were one step closer to Lowestoft Man. But they had to get through Eric West, aka Pavarotti, to get to him.

Knutsen was tense and focused. His back was tingling – this always happened when he was about to do something risky – and his mind was racing. Sign was on another planet, his thoughts anywhere other than the carriage and exterior flat countryside surroundings.

It was as they neared the cathedral city of Norwich that Sign broke the silence. "I have been wondering whether we should procure a pet for our apartment."

Knutsen shook his head. "The lease on the apartment says we're not allowed pets."

"No one will know. The landlord never inspects the property."

"Never?"

"No. The landlord is a former Russian spy who I helped get out of Switzerland when his cover was blown. He and I have an understanding. We could get a dog."

"Too messy. And we'd have to walk the thing twice day. That would be incompatible with our work commitments."

"Alright. A snake?"

"What for? We don't suffer from an infestation of mice or rats."

"Maybe a parrot?"

Knutsen sighed. "We conduct the majority of our initial consultations with new clients in our flat. They're highly confidential. Parrots copy human language. We can't have a parrot that's blurting out secrets."

"I suspect not all parrots can mimic human language."

"Are you willing to take a risk? What do you know about parrots?"

Sign drummed his fingers on his leg. "Admittedly nothing. We could get a cat."

"It would be confined to the top floor of West Square. Do you want a pet or a prisoner?"

"Fair point. I was once in prison in…"

"Yes, we don't need to go there." Knutsen knew that Sign had no aspirations to have a pet. Instead he was using a banal topic of conversation to allow his brain to focus on more pressing matters. He'd seen this happen many times. Sign used banal conversation as a distraction. One percent of his brain would engage with his interlocutor on mundane matters, while ninety nine percent would be free to roam his serious thought process. Knutsen thought of it has chaff – the stuff warships ejected to throw incoming missiles off track. While the missile was confused, the warship went about its real business. "What do we know about Norwich?"

Sign entwined his fingers. "It is on the road to nowhere. It's the last city before the coastline of the drab North Sea. As a result, it has an almost self-sufficient culture. I believe it has the largest covered market in Britain. an excellent music scene, different pubs for every day of the year, good restaurants, excellent butchers who source locally, a thriving student population, superb library, lots of shops, and a sprawling residential district on the outskirts of the city." He nodded. "It's a city, but unusual."

Knutsen chuckled. "An oasis in East Anglia."

"That may be an accurate assessment." Sign looked out of the window. "As you full well know, a pet is of course superfluous to our requirements. It's bad enough that I have to remind you that Monday is bin collection day. Having another organic entity in the flat would be an unnecessary and unwanted burden. We should keep things as they are. That way we can remain focused."

"I'm not a burden."

"You forget the bins and can't cook."

"That's okay because you put out the rubbish and are a wizard with food. I however have something you don't have."

"What?"

"I can get down with the kids."

Sign laughed. "I doubt that phrase is contemporary."

"Probably not." Knutsen rubbed a knot in his shoulder. "Put it this way – I can play act the part of a man of lower standards."

"As can I."

"I know. But I'm younger than you. I come across more convincing to…"

"The folk you have to mix with." Sign noted that they were no longer travelling through countryside, rather suburbia. "We're in the outskirts of Norwich."

Five minutes later the train terminated at the city's station. They walked for thirty three minutes before arriving at a small restaurant that was tucked away near to the centre of the city, within a small conurbation of luxury flats, and adjacent to the River Wensum. The restaurant specialised in bistro French cuisine and had won a Rosette Star for the quality of its food. Sign and Knutsen were here to meet the owner of the establishment. Lunch service had finished, though the door to the restaurant was still open. The men entered. A waitress was front of house, stripping tables of starched white cloths and cleaning surfaces.

Sign said to her, "We have an appointment with Mr. Eric West. My name is Henry Redmayne. My colleague is John Maloney."

The waitress nodded and entered the out-of-sight kitchen. When she returned she ushered them to the only table that retained a cloth.

She asked, "Would you like tea? Coffee? Water?"

"No thanks."

"No thanks."

The men sat at the table.

A man entered the dining area. He was skinny, shaven headed, medium height, and was wearing chefs' whites. He said to the waitress, "I'll finish up. You knock off early. Don't worry – it won't be deducted from your pay."

The waitress beamed as she left the premises.

The man shook Sign and Knutsen's hands. "Eric West. Which one of you is Henry Redmayne?"

Sign replied, "Me."

West sat down opposite them. "Rob told me you're a man with fingers in many pies."

"Indeed I am."

West nodded slowly. "Got to in this day and age. Can't put all your eggs in one basket." He pulled out a vaporizer from his trouser pocket and inhaled vapour. "My restaurant barely covers running costs. It can be a good little earner in peak season. It's the slow months that fuck it." He placed his vaporizer on the table. "You want people." It was a statement, not a question.

Knutsen replied, "People with particular skills and backgrounds. They must be invisible to the authorities."

"Tricky business." West pointed at his kitchen. "In case you're wondering, we're alone. My next crew won't turn up until five PM."

"We appreciate your discretion." Sign interlocked his hands. "Mr. West. I am an entrepreneur. I've made the bulk of my earnings by not only identifying business opportunities but crucially selecting with great care the people I need to execute my transactions. I'm told you can help."

West nodded. "And Rob told me there will be a lot of money in it for him and me."

"Correct. And for others who assist you."

"Flat fees?"

"No. A share of my profits. And that will be an ongoing and evolving process. If my business grows I will need more staff. More staff, more profits. You get me my staff, I sell my produce."

"Which is what?"

Sign smiled. "Do you really want me to answer your question?"

"Not really." West looked at Knutsen. "What's your part in this, pal?"

Knutsen was unflinching as he replied, "I'm here to put bullets in to people who might take a dislike to Mr. Redmayne."

The comment didn't faze West. "Fair enough." He returned his attention to Sign. "How can I be sure you're legit?"

"I'm not *legit*." Sign's eyes twinkled. "That said, like you, I have legitimate businesses that keep the busy bodies off my back, plus I pay my taxes."

"What businesses?"

"For the most part, hotels. Can I see your menu please?"

The question surprised West. "Sure. Why not?" He went to the bar, returned to the table, sat down, and handed Sign his restaurant's menu."

It took Sign ten seconds to absorb the detail of the lunch menu. "I'm not a qualified chef but I do know a thing or two about the catering trade. This is a good menu. But I wonder if you might consider adding a poached quail egg to your line-caught sea bass?"

West rubbed stubble on his face. "Too expensive. I'd have to increase the price of the meal by three quid."

Sign was motionless and in command of everything around him as he said, "You know your business. I know mine. The bedrooms in my hotels would benefit from Egyptian cotton. The problem is I'd have to replenish the bedding on a regular basis. Room rates would be higher. I estimate I'd lose thirty percent of my customers. The cost benefit analysis is obvious. A quail's egg would enhance your dish and diminish your profit. We're businessmen, not artists." He leaned forward. "But what if you could source a quail's egg for ten pence and I could source Egyptian cotton for a fiver? We might be tempted."

West frowned.

"The point of the analogy is that luxury at knock off prices is worth the chase. I need luxury at knock off prices in order to take my ideas to a new level."

"Luxury meaning blokes who don't exist?"

"Blokes and women. I'm an equal opportunities employer."

West laughed. "Yeah right."

Sign told him about his stipulation to vet potential candidates for employment at their point of entry in to the United Kingdom.

West picked up his vaporizer, inhaled deeply, and blew out a large plume of vapour. "That's unusual."

"Would you hire someone without interviewing them first?"

West considered the question. "What are you looking for in your employees?"

"Nimble hands, discretion, a work ethic, a lack of desire to integrate in to British culture, some knowledge of science, cleanliness, at worst a basic understanding of English, single, no police record or any other record with the British authorities, and most importantly I want them to be scared."

West shrugged. "I can get you that type."

"There are other attributes that are important to me. Only I can select my staff. I wouldn't presume to staff your kitchen based on a tiny verbal checklist of your requirements."

"Yeah. I wouldn't let you." West was deep in thought. "You're not cops?"

"Do we look or sound like cops?"

"Customs and Excise?"

"No."

"MI5?"

"No."

"Any other government agency?"

Sign faked exasperation. "Would we tell you if we were? We're not here to play games." He looked at Knutsen. "Are we."

Knutsen stared at West. "No we're fucking not. Wind your neck in Mr. Norwich. You'll find out soon enough who you're dealing with. And it ain't undercover plod or any other cunts. We want people. You deliver, you get rich. Fuck everything else."

West shifted in his seat, clearly unsettled by Knutsen's intimidating presence and comments. "I just have to be careful."

Knutsen place his large hand on the table. "Not as careful as us. We've only got Rob Green's word that you're alright. But, my boss and I have seen it before. Someone who's alright can easily become not alright. We're judging you. So far we're giving you the benefit of the doubt. But a word to the wise – don't fucking judge us."

A bead of sweat ran down West's face. "I... I didn't mean any offence. I'm a businessman. This is a transaction."

Sign smiled sympathetically. "We fully understand. Things happen in London that don't happen here. You don't know what I'm capable of. There are people elsewhere who do. Now, back to business. When is your next shipment due in?"

West used a bandana to wipe his face. "Dunno. I get given the bodies after they've arrived. I give them to Rob. God knows what happens to them after that. I get a cut and walk away."

"So you don't meet them off the boat?"

"No. The guy that gives me the immigrants does. He gets them in to Lowestoft. Don't know how he does that. All I have to do is bring them here, feed and water them, get them new clothes, then courier them to Rob. He takes over from there."

"I see." Sign was calm as a cucumber as he said, "I would like to meet the man who facilitates the immigrants' entry in to Lowestoft."

West shook his head. "I... I don't know."

"I'm sure he's a lovely chap. I want to tell him what I've told you. And I must be in Lowestoft when the next shipment arrives."

West bowed his head.

"Call him and tell him I want to meet."

West looked up. "He's a hard man."

"Do we look like we're concerned in the slightest about that?"

"No." West was breathing fast. "Are you staying in East Anglia tonight?"

"Yes. A hotel."

"I'll need your number."

On a napkin, Sign wrote the telephone number of one of his deniable phones and handed the napkin to West. "Tell him I want to speak to him tonight."

That evening Sign and Knutsen dined in their five star Norwich hotel. They ate pan-fried duck that had been shot the day before on the fens, cabbage and bacon, sautéed potatoes, a medley of carrots, asparagus, beetroot, and a jus made from Madeira wine. They shared a bottle of Châteauneuf du Pape Ogier Bois and finished their meal with coffee.

When they finished their meal Sign dabbed his mouth with his napkin, looked away, and said in a distant precise tone, "Do you think we'd have been better men had we not made the choices we did?"

Knutsen looked at him and tried to keep his emotion in check. He'd lived a life on a knife edge. It had at times been horrendous. But it was nothing compared to what Sign had been through. Somehow Sign had maintained his dignity and love of humanity. Self-respect was the problem. He said, "I can count the number of men who've done what you've done on no fingers."

In a quiet voice Sign replied, "We do what we have to. And there other men like me. Admittedly there are few of us left."

"Do you remain in contact with them?"

"No. We wander alone."

Knutsen smiled. "You do talk shit sometimes."

"Were it thus." Sign's mobile phone rang. He listened to the caller and said, "Fully understood. There will be two of us. You may bring an associate. But no more than one. If you err from that you will gain no business from me." He hung up and looked at Knutsen. "That was Lowestoft Man. His name is Oscar Barnes. Are you fully prepared for what happens next?"

Knutsen nodded.

CHAPTER 10

Edward had made a decision. Tomorrow he would kill Azzat the gardener. The young man liked football. It would be befitting if he died in a way that paid homage to his love of the sport. Edward would render him temporarily unconscious before forcing a deflated football down his throat and in to his stomach. The football would be attached to a tube. The end of the tube would be two inches out of Azzat's mouth. Edward would use a pump to push air in to the tube and inflate the football to full capacity. Azzat's organs would be crushed and his stomach lining torn. He would die in agony. And the death wouldn't be quick.

The event would take place while Farzaneh and Bayan were off the estate. Before the kill he'd send the women on a pointless errand to the village. When they returned he'd tell them that Azzat was nowhere to be seen. He'd speculate that maybe the twenty year old Afghan had run away. Perhaps he had family in the UK he wanted to be with. Maybe he wanted to see more of Britain. He was young and youth breeds impetuosity. Or maybe he'd secured a higher paid job. If so, Edward would fake annoyance. He paid his staff well, he'd tell Farzaneh and Bayan. And he was loyal to his staff. Why would Azzat throw away a long term job in favour of a short term job that paid one pound per hour more than Edward was paying? It made no sense, Edward would conclude.

It was early morning. As usual at this time of day, Edward was showered, shaved, and dressed as a country gentleman. He walked around his grounds, building up an appetite before breakfast. The family of badgers were sleeping in their set. The sky was clear, giving easy visibility of the buzzards who rode the thermals, waiting for sight of a rabbit so they could feed. The foxes were nowhere to be seen but that was for the most part normal, the playful squirrels were chasing each other around the trunk of the oak tree, magpies were looking for scraps of food on the heathland, and the heron was poised over the fishpond, waiting for a chance to grab a bite to eat.

Edward shooed away the heron and continued his walk. He felt calm. It was the emotion he felt every time he was close to a kill. He smiled and went into the house. After making himself a cup of tea he prepared toast and marmalade and sat on the downstairs balcony that overlooked the chine leading to the sea. It was a glorious day. The sea was glittering and had ripples on its surface. Later, he'd take his boat out and use a spinning rod to catch some bass for supper.

Today would be a good day.

Tomorrow would be even better.

Sign and Knutsen entered the Port of Lowestoft. The sprawling harbour had seen better days as an importer of fish and engineering parts, though now it was having a resurgence as a supplier of renewable energy equipment. The men were on foot, sporting robust attire and hiking boots. Knutsen was armed.

The port was a hive of activity. Cranes were offloading freight from ships. Repairs were being made to vessels. Ocean-going boats were being refuelled. Workers in hardhats were tireless in their efforts to execute their duties. Orders were barked over loud speakers. A ship was leaving the harbour and sounding its horn. The sea was calm while being splattered by rain. There was nothing pretty about the docks. It was functional. But it was industrious.

Sign knew exactly where to go.

Block 5B. A warehouse used for the temporary storage of wind turbines. Normally the building would be locked. Not today. And the block was empty on this occasion. Sign and Knutsen entered the building.

Inside were two men, standing in the centre of the warehouse. Both men were short and wiry. One had cropped hair and a tanned, leathery face. The other had long hair that was tied in a ponytail.

The man with the ponytail had his arms crossed and looked stern. When he spoke it was difficult to discern his origin. Possibly East Anglian. Maybe West Country. More likely someone who'd diluted his English origin by spending large chunks of his life at sea. "I'm Oscar Barnes. Introduce yourselves."

Sign replied, "Henry Redmayne. We spoke on the phone."

Barnes looked at Knutsen.

Knutsen said, "John Maloney. I work for Mr. Redmayne."

"Obviously." Barnes walked up to them. There were small scars on his chin and forehead. His eyes were blue and appeared cold. "We have business to attend to." He gestured to his associate. "My colleague. You don't need to know his name. You're going to be cool with that."

Sign nodded.

"He's got a blade on him. He guts fish and other things."

"I'm sure he does." Sign looked at Knutsen.

Knutsen pulled out his gun and shot the unnamed man in the head.

Sign grabbed Barnes on the chin. "He was irrelevant. We never needed to know his name."

Barnes tried to back off, his eyes wide with confusion.

But Sign held him in a vice-like grip. "Tis a shame."

"What…" Barnes continued to try to break free. "What is this about?!"

"You know what this is about." Sign threw him onto the floor. "You traffic illegal immigrants. Some of them you feed to a serial killer. You get paid handsomely for that service. We would like to know the identity of the killer and his or her whereabouts."

Knutsen had his gun trained on Barnes, his hand steady. When he spoke his voice was calm and menacing. "I've got thirty bullets on me. I can use them to chip away at you. I don't want you to die until the last round goes in to your head. Before then I'll just slash at your extremities. You'll never before have experienced such agony." He fired his gun and grazed Barnes' left arm. "Bullet number one. Only twenty eight to go before I put you down."

Barnes gripped his arm, his face screwed up in pain. "Fuck... fuck you."

"Thought you'd say that." Knutsen shot half an inch of flesh off Barnes' leg.

Sign leaned over Barnes as he writhed on the floor. "Forgive my friend. He has a temper. But he won't stop until you give us a name and an address."

Barnes' eyes were venomous as he looked at the former MI6 officer. "You... you're in so much shit."

"I doubt that." Sign smiled. "There is a reason no one can hear what's going on in this building. Workers wear ear defenders. The dock is a noisy old place, dear fellow. We have time on our hands." He looked at Knutsen. "I suggest a shoulder."

Knutsen fired.

Barnes screamed.

Sign patted his hand against Barnes' face. "You're scum. But we can live with that. We don't want you. We want the man who you feed. Talk. If you don't my friend will keep this up."

Barnes was hyperventilating. "His name's... name is Edward McLachlan." He gave them the address. "Estate near Ventnor on the Isle of Wight. Remote."

"How many immigrants does he have?"

"Three. Farzaneh, Bayan, and Azzat. I don't know their surnames. Two women; one man. They live on his estate. Just like the others did."

"Before Edward killed them."

Barnes was rolling on the floor. "He doesn't kill them straight away. I'd know. He only contacts me after a kill. I think Farzaneh, Bayan, and Azzat are still alive."

"How many immigrants have you delivered to Edward?"

Barnes laid on his back, sucking in air. His voice was barely audible when he answered, "Twenty four. I reckon that's the tip of the iceberg. I knew before I got involved that he'd already got a taste for it."

Knutsen asked Sign, "Is he telling the truth?"

"Yes." Sign turned his back on the men and started walking towards the exit. "Dispatch him."

Knutsen shot Barnes in the head.

CHAPTER 11

At seven PM Sign and Knutsen walked down the mile long track that led to the kill house. It was dusk, though a full moon gave them sufficient light to navigate their way over the uneven route. All around them was silent. The air was still and cool. The abundance of animals that lived in the micro-climate were sleeping. The men felt like they were completely removed from humanity.

The entrance to the house driveway had closed electronic gates. Adjacent to the gates was a tiny house, within which lights were turned on and music was playing. Sign and Knutsen clambered over the ten foot high wrought iron entrance and continued walking down the long tarmac driveway. Either side of them were grass, heathland, trees, bushes, and ahead of them was the glistening sea. They passed the keep that had once been a look out post for armed Customs officers, in the eighteenth and nineteenth century. who were trying to apprehend smugglers hauling barrels of rum up the torturous chine. Sign and Knutsen followed the driveway left, passing the fish pond.

Now they were at the front door of the house.

Nearby were two other houses – a wooden property and a cottage.

The mansion dwarfed the other buildings. Classical music could be heard inside. Sign knew the composer but wasn't interested in the music right now. He tapped the metal door knocker several times.

Ten seconds later Edward opened the door. "Yes?"

Sign said, "Edward McLachlan?"

"Who wants to know?"

"We're from the National Trust. You may know that we own the lane to your property. It's been suffering water damage from flooding off the hills. We wish to know if you'd like to submit a complaint about our upkeep of the route. It's come to our attention that we are in breach of regulations if an emergency vehicle can't access someone due to potholes. We are taking signatures. This would only take a minute of your time."

Edward frowned. "Bit late for this now, don't you think?"

"We were hoping to catch residents after work. Are you Edward McLachlan?"

"Of course. I own this estate."

"Excellent. May we come in? We'll take your resident statement and then leave. By the way, we do apologise if we're interrupting your dinner."

"No, it's okay. Come in."

The men entered the house.

Knutsen said, "Please tell Mrs. McLachlan we're sorry to intrude."

As Edward led them in to the vast lounge he replied, "I live alone."

"That makes sense."

Edward turned.

Knutsen's gun was pointing at his head.

Sign said, "Edward McLachlan, you are a murderer. You prey on innocent foreigners who are in a vulnerable position. Your punishment is death."

Knutsen shot him in the head, stood over him, and shot him in the head two more times.

Sign exhaled slowly. "The end of the road. We have one more matter to attend to."

They went to the residences of Farzaneh, Bayan, and Azzat. Sign paid them ten thousand pounds each, told them that Edward was dead, that they'd been in severe danger, and that they should flee to anywhere in Britain that wasn't a city. Of course they were extremely confused and frightened. So much so that Sign had to be stern with them.

He summoned them together and said, "Walk to Shanklin village. Pick any pub. Ask the landlord to book you a taxi to Ryde. Take the ferry to Portsmouth. Get a train to London. Then head north. Do it now." Bayan translated what he'd said, for the benefit of Azzat.

The three ran to their houses.

Sign and Knutsen waited until the immigrants exited with their bags and went on their way.

Knutsen turned to Sign. "What about the body?"

Sign was calm as he replied, "I'll put it in a place on the estate that only animals frequent. They'll feast on him. His remains will be gone in a day."

The men were home in West Square at eleven PM. They were tired yet their thoughts were keeping them awake. Knutsen made a fire while Sign poured two glasses of calvados and prepared some roast beef and horseradish sandwiches. After they dined they say in their armchairs by the fire and sipped their drinks. For a while, both were quiet.

Sign broke the silence. "Are you bearing up, my friend?"

"Yeah, I'll be alright."

Sign nodded. "I believe you will. But always remember there's no other man on Earth I'd rather have by my side. Now, on different matters I've just checked my emails. We have a new case. Are you up for the challenge?"

"Damn right." Knutsen stared at the fire while deep in thought. Sign, he believed, was relentless. He was like a dog with a bone; superbly bright; courageous; ruthless; and at times unfathomable. And yet there was a side to him that only Knutsen saw these days – compassion, loyalty, and a way of looking at the world that made the world a better place. He looked at Sign.

Sign was looking at him, his eyes twinkling. "Were it so easy to analyse a lifetime of mischief." He clapped his hands and said in a strident voice, "For breakfast tomorrow I shall prepare sirloin steaks sourced from Borough Market, sautéed potatoes, poached goose eggs, toasted whole grain bread, and a pickle containing boiled cabbage, tomatoes, and a lovely vinegar I've sourced from Fortnum & Masons. What say you, sir?"

Knutsen smiled. "Sounds perfect, though a bowl of cereal would have been fine."

"Nonsense! We must have a breakfast of champions. Tomorrow we are back to work. And I do hope our case is a particularly tricky one."

THE END